New York Times bestselling author **Elizabeth Chadwick** has written over 20 historical novels sold in 18 languages. She lives in Nottingham with her husband and two sons. Much of her research is carried out as a member of Regia Anglorum, an early medieval re-enactment society with the emphasis on accurately recreating the past. She also tutors in the skill of writing historical and romantic fiction. Her first novel, *The Wild Hunt*, won a Betty Trask Award. She was shortlisted for the Romantic Novelists' Award in 1998 for *The Champion*, in 2001 for *Lords of the White Castle*, in 2002 for *The Winter Mantle* and in 2003 for *The Falcons of Montabard*. Her sixteenth novel, *The Scarlet Lion*, was nominated by Richard Lee, founder of the Historical Novel Society, as one of the top ten historical novels of the last decade. Her nineteenth novel, *To Defy a King*, won the RNA's 2011 Historical Novel Prize.

For more details on Elizabeth Chadwick and her books, visit www.elizabethchadwick.com, follow her on Twitter @Chadwickauthor, or chat to her on Facebook.

THE CHAMPION

Elizabeth Chadwick

sphere

SPHERE

First published in Great Britain in 1997 by Little, Brown and Company
Published in paperback in 1998 by Warner Books
This edition published in May 2006 by Time Warner Books
Reprinted by Sphere in 2006
Reprinted 2007, 2009, 2010, 2012, 2013

A CIP catalogue record for this book
is available from the British Library.

ISBN 978-0-7515-3869-4

Printed and bound in Great Britain by
Clays Ltd, St Ives plc

Papers used by Sphere are from well-managed forests
and other responsible sources.

MIX
Paper from
responsible sources
FSC
www.fsc.org   FSC® C104740

Sphere
An imprint of
Little, Brown Book Group
100 Victoria Embankment
London EC4Y 0DY

An Hachette UK Company
www.hachette.co.uk

www.littlebrown.co.uk

ACKNOWLEDGEMENTS

Writing a book is never a solitary affair, and on this page I would like to thank the people who have contributed to its creation in one way or another. As always, my appreciation goes to Carole Blake and everyone at Blake Friedmann for working so hard on my behalf and being good friends too, and to Barbara Boote at Little, Brown for the same. My husband Roger deserves a medal for his patience in listening to me read aloud the several rough drafts that it takes before my books are carved in stone – or laid in black ink!

Thanks are due also to my many good friends in Regia Anglorum re-enactment society. To Jon Preston for explaining to me the advantages and dangers of using a morning star and letting me try on his 'cheese-grater' helm; to Ivor Lawton for the beautiful medieval artifacts he makes and his detailed knowledge about them which he willingly shares; and to members of Deoraby, the Conroi du Burm and the Poor Cnichts of St Chad for patiently posing for my research camera.

The excerpt from 'Roundelay' on p. 84 appears by kind permission of Leslie Williamson.

The excerpt form 'Foreign Fields' on p. 244 appears by kind permission of Vivien Steels.

The excerpt from 'When Winter Comes' on p. 396–7 appears by kind permission of Ken Swallow.

CHAPTER 1

THE BRETON BORDERS,
SPRING 1193

Hervi de Montroi was in his tent with an obliging whore and a pitcher of the strongest cider he could lay hands upon, when he received the news that his half-brother Alexander had ridden into the camp.

It had been raining since dawn, a damp grey mizzle that concealed the tourney field in the mist and chilled the grumbling knights through their cloaks and quilted gambesons to the bone. It was springtide in the world at large, but these Breton borderlands seemed to be suspended in a time of their own. Hervi would not have been surprised to see Arthur, Guinevere and the entire court of Camelot emerge on shadowy horses through the rain haze veiling the trees. Certainly less surprised than to be informed that the youth he had last seen as a child of eleven years old at their father's funeral, and whom he thought pursuing a career in the church, was awaiting him at the communal camp fire.

The soldier who had delivered the news, and almost had his head bitten off for his trouble, dropped the tent flap and returned to his dice game.

'Bones of Christ!' Hervi swore, and sat up on his straw pallet. His head swam, and he had to concentrate to focus. Raising the stone cider jug to his lips, he took several hard gulps.

The young woman at his side rolled on to her stomach and regarded him through a tangle of greasy blonde hair. Hervi wiped his mouth on his wrist and gave her the jug.

'You have to go?' She looked at him over the rim.

Alys was one of the many draggle-tailed women who followed the knights and soldiers from tourney to tourney, war to war, washing, cooking, pleasuring and tending. Some became wives, others belonged to any man with the money to pay for their services. Alys was one of the latter, but ambitious to change her status, and Hervi frequently took advantage of her striving. No more striving today, however.

'Unfortunately, sweetheart, I do,' he replied with a mingling of regret and irritation. Mindful of his buzzing head, he leaned over to draw on his hose and attach them to the leather straps on his braies.

'Let me do that.' Returning the jug, Alys knelt before him to secure the trousers to his undergarment. Her fingers brushed against his naked thighs and her full breasts undulated within her chemise.

Hervi closed his eyes and swallowed. 'Stop that, you minx,' he groaned. 'I can't present myself to the lad with this tent pole in my breeches!'

Alys giggled. Her hand closed playfully over the bulge at his crotch before he pulled away.

Hervi took another swig of cider, belched, then grimaced at the sour taste that filled his mouth. 'Alexander.' He tested the name on his tongue and tried to interest his wits, but they had been bludgeoned from existence by a combination of drink and thwarted lust. Scowling, Hervi struggled into a shirt of stained yellow linen and laced the frayed drawstring. His mind held the image of a skinny, knock-kneed brat with thin features and huge hazel eyes beneath a mop of inky curls – a changeling, all the other de Montrois being broad and brash and fair. But that memory was at least seven years old, and probably as stale as the garments he had just donned.

'A bold name,' said Alys huskily.

'You think so?' Hervi fished around for his boots. 'Actually he was christened Alexandros to please his mother, but she was the only one who ever called him that.'

Alys raised her brows. 'Alexandros?' Her tongue fumbled the ending. She had drunk as much cider as Hervi.

'It's Greek,' Hervi said with a shake of his head. 'After he was widowed, my father went on a pilgrimage to the Holy Land, but only got as far as the Bosphorus. He came home with some hairs from St Peter's beard, and Alexander's mother. We never thought he would remarry – he already had five sons – but he was an unpredictable old bastard, and I suppose that Anna was too exotic for him to resist. He always said that she was the greatest treasure in Constantinople.' Hervi wriggled his toes down into the boots. In one place the leather sole was almost worn through, and in another the stitches gaped to show flesh. 'Ah, Christ,' he growled with a spurt of exasperation. 'Never mind the treasures of Constantinople, what in the name of Christ's ten toes is the little fool doing here?'

'Perhaps he brings you family news?' Alys suggested, covering her short chemise with her patched linen gown.

'Hah, the only news to interest me would be that I had come into an inheritance, and since there is only Alexander behind me in the line, I doubt that.'

'Then let him wait.'

Hervi glanced at her with irritation. He preferred Alys when her mouth was not occupied in speech. 'See if you can make some order of this chaos,' he said with a terse gesture around the small tent where scarcely an inch of floor was visible beneath the various items and debris of his nomadic existence.

She smiled and held out her palm. 'Other services cost more,' she said sweetly.

Hervi scowled, fumbled down inside his shirt for the purse he wore against his skin and found her a small silver coin. 'You're a leech, woman'.

'But it's not just blood I suck, is it?' she retorted provocatively as he stamped out of the tent into the soft noonday drizzle.

From the field beyond the tents came the muted thud of hooves bogged down in the soggy turf and the familiar crack of lance on shield as two knights practised their craft in preparation for the opening of the tourney in two days' time. Other eager beavers were about their swordplay, rusting their equipment so that they would have to spend all evening scouring and burnishing. Hervi had long since outlived such enthusiasm.

The first thing he saw as he approached the communal camp fire was the horse, its rib bones staring through the dull, mud-encrusted hide. Hervi's mouth tightened. A beast in that condition was an indictment of any owner. The knight holding the bridle gave him an eloquent glance. Hervi met it with an arched brow and thrusting past him to the warmth of the flames was brought face to face with Alexander.

The young man was as tall and slender as a willow sapling, and shivering so hard that he had little control over his muscles. A cloak of once good blue wool, now dirty and threadbare, hung on his shoulders and was covered by a filthy shawl of coarse homespun for added warmth. A cheap bone pin, bereft of all detail, secured the shawl to the mantle. Tunic and chausses were thin and frayed, and the shoes were ten times worse than Hervi's own.

All this the older man assessed with one rapid glance. Nor did he miss the long knife at the lad's belt. The black hair was a dense tangle of eldritch curls, and beneath its heaviness, Hervi perceived the longboat bones of the de Montrois, sleek and bold, but malleable still with youth. The straight black brows, the caramel-honey eyes were the legacy of Alexander's Byzantine mother, as were the slender, monkish hands. But there was nothing remotely monkish about the rest of Alexander's appearance at the moment.

'Well,' Hervi's flippant tone shielded a host of conflicting emotions, 'this is a surprise. To what do I owe this pleasure, assuming that I am indeed addressing my brother?'

The youth's pupils contracted. His throat bobbed convulsively. 'I can prove it,' he answered hoarsely. Fumbling beneath the shawl and the cloak, he tugged out a leather cord on which hung a small Greek cross of gold set with cabochon amethysts. 'It was my mother's. She brought it from Constantinople, and she always wore it on her breast, you know she did.'

Their fingers touched as the keepsake was passed across, and Hervi glimpsed angry red abrasions encircling the youth's wrists. The cross was warm from its bed against the boy's skin, its cord slightly damp. The gold gleamed in Hervi's palm, its richness speaking to him of wealth beyond his grasp. Beyond Alexander's too. Their father's Byzantine wife had been dowered with little more than this jewel and her exotic beauty.

'You need prove nothing, I know you are kin,' Hervi said brusquely, and returned the treasure. 'Stow it back where it belongs and do not be too swift to show it about. Men are robbed and murdered for less.'

Alexander struggled and fumbled, his hands shaking almost beyond his control. An unwanted pang of tenderness and rage cut through Hervi's irritation. 'What are you doing here, lad?' he asked on a gentler note. 'This is no place for an aspiring monk.'

The eyes flashed wide and the mobile lips curled in a snarl. 'I've never aspired to be a monk! I was pushed into the cloister against my will. I've left it and I'm never going back.' He sucked a rapid breath between his teeth. 'I've come to join you instead.'

'You've what?' Hervi was aghast.

'I want to learn soldiering; I want to become a knight.'

Someone laughed, hastily turning the sound into a cough. Hervi's face grew grim, and his lips were so stiff that it was difficult to speak. 'You won't learn at my fire,' he said brutally. 'I'm a mercenary. I earn my bread by the strength of my arm and the skin of my teeth. I cannot afford to be hampered by an untutored weakling on the run from the cloister. Go to our brothers and seek your refuge there.'

'They'll only send me back to the church to be beaten again . . . if they don't beat me first,' Alexander retorted, his eyes blazing with glints of amber and topaz. 'I'd rather starve!'

'You might have to,' Hervi growled, but his mind had settled on the disturbing words 'beaten again' and linked them to the marks on Alexander's narrow wrists. He knew that he could not turn the lad away in this condition. He'd be dead within the week.

The drizzle increased, the cobweb veils turning to harder, individual drops, plump and cold. On the field the knights abandoned their practice. Banners dripped, impotent and limp, from the tops of tents, their brave colours water-stained and dark. Hervi cleared his throat.

'Best come and shelter inside the tent until the rain passes over,' he said testily. 'But you need not think I am going to keep you.'

The young man inhaled to speak, but no words came. Instead, his eyes rolled upwards and his knees buckled. A lifetime of living on his wits catapulted Hervi forward to catch Alexander's falling weight before it struck the cauldron tripod. He was shocked at the lightness of the youth, the feel of bones uncushioned by flesh.

'Hey, Hervi, you make a good nursemaid!' crowed a balding knight with a heavy paunch.

'Shut your mouth, Osgar,' Hervi snarled.

The man holding Alexander's emaciated mount raised the bridle in his right hand to gain Hervi's attention. 'I'll tether him with your others, shall I?'

'Do what you want with him, Arnaud,' Hervi said through his teeth. 'Ride him in your next joust if you want!' A string of guffaws and good-natured insults ringing in his ears, Hervi threw Alexander over his shoulder and repaired to his tent.

Alys had found a besom from somewhere and was sweeping the debris into a corner with desultory strokes.

'Go to old Mildred and ask her for a flask of ginevra,' Hervi commanded brusquely.

The whore rolled her eyes heavenwards, leaned the besom against the tent pole and went out.

Hervi laid Alexander on the pallet and frowned down at him. What in God's name was he going to do with the lad? He had enough ado keeping his own body and soul together without the added burden of a green boy.

Alys returned with the ginevra and watched Hervi tug the blankets up to the youth's chin. 'How is he going to swallow this?' she asked, doubtfully eyeing the wide rim of Hervi's horn into which she had just poured a generous measure of the colourless juniper brew.

'Jesu, wench, it's not for him!' snapped Hervi. 'Can't you see he's out of his senses!' He snatched the horn from her hands and gulped at it, then choked on its burning strength.

Alys advanced to the pallet where, less than a quarter-candle since, she and Hervi had sported. Now the youth's long body occupied that space. He was as still and pale as death, his eye sockets bruised, his bones jutting at his flesh. 'Is he truly your brother?'

'Of course he is. Would I give up my bed to a strange whelp not of my blood?' Hervi rested the horn on his thigh and pushed his free hand again and again through his hair. 'Last I heard he was a novice monk at Cranwell Priory, but it doesn't look likely he'll wear a tonsure now, does it?'

Alys bit her lip. 'What are you going to do?'

'Christ, how should I know!'

She considered him through narrowed lids. 'You owe me for the ginevra.'

'And you owe me an afternoon's bed sport,' he retorted. 'Count it even.'

She glared at him, but he ignored her, all his attention for the still form on the pallet. With a toss of her head, Alys flounced from the tent, leaving it half tidied.

The rain pattered down, enhancing the scents of new grass, of budding forest greenery, of fungus, damp and mould. Outside, cut off from him, Hervi could hear the rise and fall of conversation at the fire, a sudden shout of laughter, the dull thud of an axe splitting a log. He finished the ginevra in his horn, and with his belly full of fire, sought the flask.

Alexander moaned softly, and his eyelids flickered. Hervi thrust a muscular arm beneath his brother's shoulders and raised him up. 'Drink,' he commanded.

Alexander choked and retched on the pungent strength of the liquor. Dusky colour flushed across his cheekbones, and his eyes brimmed.

'Steady, lad, steady,' Hervi gentled. 'I know it's got a kick like an earl's boot, but you'll feel better for it in a moment.'

A grimace twisted Alexander's lips. 'They used to brew this at Cranwell,' he croaked. 'The infirmarian kept it locked up, but I stole an entire flask for a dare.' His gaze met Hervi's. 'Then I drank the lot and was dog sick for three days.'

Hervi grunted. 'Those monks must think themselves well rid of you.'

The grimace remained. 'Not half as much as I think myself well rid of them.'

'You can't stay here, you know that.'

Alexander said nothing. An obdurate expression entered his

eyes and his lips tightened. Hervi stared at the youth in perplexity. He had only known Alexander the child – an engaging
imp towards whom it had cost nothing to be casually affectionate. Alexander on the verge of manhood was a different
prospect entirely. The little that Hervi had gleaned thus far suggested that he was dealing with someone who would push his
body until it dropped. Strong-willed, stubborn, and reckless to
the point of self-destruction; traits that could draw a man to the
heights of achievement and then kick him over the edge of the
abyss.

The tent flap opened on a draught of moist air. Hervi looked
round, half expecting to see Alys returning for another assault on
his purse, but instead found himself facing the far more daunting
prospect of the wife and daughter of Arnaud de Cerizay, the
knight who had taken charge of Alexander's horse.

'Lady Clemence?' he said with slight trepidation.

'Arnaud told us that your brother has come seeking succour
and that he is sick,' said Clemence de Cerizay. 'I have brought
some hot pottage from our cauldron, and I thought you might
want me to look at him.' Her voice was firm and clear, accustomed to being the authority of her family. She stood no taller
than Hervi's pungent armpit, and her build was delicate, but the
lady Clemence was another who possessed a will to beat down all
others beneath it, no matter her bodily strength.

At fourteen, her daughter, Monday, was half a head taller than
her mother and with unmistakable womanly curves. A shining
plait of bronze-brown hair, thick as a bell rope, hung down her
back, and her eyes were a clear, warm grey set beneath strongly
marked brows. In her hands, protected by a swathe of quilted
linen, was a wooden eating bowl filled with soup.

Hervi's stomach growled at the savoury aroma of the rising
steam. 'By all means,' he said with a wave of his hand, knowing
that refusal was not an option.

Monday knelt gracefully beside the pallet with the soup while
Clemence fetched Hervi's spare shield and used it as a support to
prop up the invalid. Hervi hovered, feeling like an outcast in his
own tent.

'You might as well know that Alys has gone off with Osgar,'

Clemence said over her shoulder. 'But I suppose you expected nothing less.'

Hervi shrugged and affected not to care. 'I haven't got a bed now, anyway,' he said.

Clemence gave a reproving cluck. Her daughter set about feeding pottage to the invalid, whose hands were too shaky to manage a spoon for himself.

As Alexander consumed the hot food, his colour improved and the chills started to subside. 'Thank you,' he said weakly to the girl. 'The last food I ate was three days ago, and that was no more than mouldy bread and burned gruel.'

'What makes you think you'll eat any differently here?' Hervi snorted, and was immediately castigated by the mother, her blue eyes fierce.

'God save us, Hervi de Montroi, I hope that neither of us is ever thrown on your charity. He is your own brother. Don't you care?'

'Of course I care!' cried Hervi, and commenced tearing at his hair once more. 'That's why I don't want him. He's run away from taking the tonsure. What earthly use is he going to be following the tourneys? How in God's name am I going to support him?'

Clemence de Cerizay rounded on Hervi with a tongue as sharp as a war sword. 'If you had silver to waste on a gallon of cider and a slut like that Alys, then you have enough to keep the lad at least until he is well enough to send on to something better,' she said forcefully.

'I didn't ask for him to come seeking me like a stray pup.'

'No, but he is here, and he is your responsibility.'

On the pallet, the invalid closed his eyes. The girl pressed her palm to his forehead. 'Mama, he's fallen asleep,' she said, leaning over him.

Her words filtered to Alexander through a haze thicker than the mizzle outside. The scents of dried lavender and woodsmoke drifted wraithlike through his awareness.

Another hand, rougher-skinned than the first, touched his brow and then the side of his neck. 'A mite feverish,' Clemence said. 'Keep him covered.'

The shield was removed from behind his back and he was eased down on to the straw pallet. Blankets were piled over him and their greasy, woollen smell filled his nostrils. Alexander kept his lids shut and they talked over him, as if he were not there. He learned nothing from their discussion that he did not already know – he had lice and he stank. The sores on his wrists were caused by the abrasion of cords; he had run away from the ordered life of Cranwell Priory, and in its place had chosen the dangers of the open road.

Heat prickled behind his lids and leaked through his lashes. He prayed for oblivion, but not as the monks had taught him to pray.

He dreamed that he was back at Cranwell, descending the dark dorter stairs to matins in the chapel. Cold stone beneath his feet, his breath a white mist in the midnight deep. Another cowled figure brushed against him. Fingers groped at his genitals and whispered an obscenity in his ear. In blind panic he struck out, landing a solid blow in the concealed softness of the other's eye socket.

There was a cry, the scuffle of feet struggling for balance, and then the bump, bump of a body tumbling down the stairs. His assailant's descent into what would have been serious injury or death was intercepted by two other novices further down the dark stairway.

In the flickering glimmer from a wax taper, Alexander found himself looking into the battered, vindictive features of Brother Alkmund, the sub-prior, and knew that his doom was sealed. He tried to run, but he was trapped on the stairs and seized. They twisted his arms behind his back and bound his wrists with rawhide cords. Then they cast him into the dank cells beneath the priory latrines, there to await his punishment.

He stood accused of the attempted murder of the sub-prior, and he knew that no one would believe that he had struck out in self-defence. He possessed a reputation that would preclude all mercy. Past crimes included stealing and drinking the infirmarian's store of medicinal ginevra, writing secular love poems in the scriptorium and singing them in the cloisters. Then there had been two attempts to escape, and gross insubordination to the rule when captured, resulting in a severe scourging. The list damned him out of hand. They had shown him lenience before. The raised pink and white welts on his back were a testament to how lenient they could be.

The fetid, musty smell of damp stone invaded his nostrils. He felt as if he had been buried alive. Faces leered at him – skulls clothed in cowls. Skeletons clattered out of the walls and performed the dance of death before his eyes, urging him to caper with them. In blind terror he ran towards the door, but his escape was barred by Brother Alkmund, a hoop of keys taunting on his forefinger.

Alexander felt bony arms close around him from behind and draw him towards the oozing prison wall. He screamed and resisted, striving to free his wrists of the cords while they bit deeper and deeper.

'Ah, Christ,' swore one of the skeletons irritably. 'How am I supposed to sleep with you making so much noise?' It shook him by the shoulder, and its foul breath filled his face, making him gag.

'Alex, you purblind fool, it's a dream, only a dream!' The shaking grew more agitated. One by one the skeletons rattled into the wall and vanished, dragging Brother Alkmund in their wake. On a huge gulp of air, Alexander surfaced from the nightmare like a swimmer too long underwater.

In the light from a tallow cresset lamp, Hervi's face loomed anxiously over his. Alexander felt the fierce pain of fully fleshed fingers digging into his shoulder.

'God's eyes!' Hervi swore. 'You were screaming fit to rouse the dead!' There was fear in his voice and his eye whites gleamed.

Alexander laughed weakly at his brother's choice of words, but there was little humour in the sound. Sweat-drenched, he lay back against the lumpy bracken pillow. 'You're hurting me,' he protested.

The fingers relaxed their pressure. A moment later the rim of a goblet was rested on his lips. Remembering the ginevra he hesitated, but when he realised that the liquid was nothing more threatening than cool, watered wine, he took a long, grateful drink.

'Do you want me to leave the light?' Hervi asked awkwardly.

'It doesn't matter . . . won't make any difference.'

'Then I'll leave it.'

Alexander turned his head and saw that his brother had assembled a makeshift pallet beside the one that should rightfully be his. 'I didn't mean to wake you,' he apologised.

'You could have fooled me.' Hervi lay down again, thumped the rolled-up tunic that was serving as his pillow, and hunched his cloak around his shoulders.

For a while Alexander stared at the canvas roof of the tent, watching the flicker of lamp shadows. Beside him, Hervi snored. The sound, the surroundings, despite their squalor, were oddly comforting. Alexander's eyelids drooped, and before long, he was deep in an exhausted slumber.

CHAPTER 2

It was well beyond noon of the following day when Alexander woke up. At first he did not know where he was and it took him a while to gather his sleep-scattered wits. His head felt muzzy and his limbs were weak. He held one hand up in front of his face. The fingers trembled, but he could control them, and although his bones felt hollow, the chills were gone.

Tentatively he sat up and gazed around his brother's tent. It was compact enough to be borne by a sturdy pack horse when dismantled, and its size was made even smaller by Hervi's untidiness. Of Hervi himself there was no sign. The crumbs of a finished meal were strewn on a crude trestle near the tent flap, and Hervi's jousting helm sat among the debris together with a sheathed long dagger. On the floor beside the pallet was a stone jug of wine, a beaker of milk, and a shallow wooden bowl containing a chunk of bread and two slightly wizened apples.

His appetite surged fiercely, but there was an underlying sensation of nausea that warned Alexander to be moderate. He drank the milk, ate half the bread and one apple, and leaving the rest for later, gingerly tested the ability of his legs to support him. He wobbled like a newborn lamb, but at least remained upright. His bladder twinged and he glanced around without success. Amongst all the flotsam of Hervi's life, there did not appear to be a piss-flask.

Alexander went to the tent flap and pulled aside the mildew-stained canvas. It had ceased raining and a smoky-white sun was poking through the bank of clouds somewhere west of noon. He had been in no condition to take notice of the camp last night, but he was sure that it had increased in size. There seemed to be more tents now, larger and finer, some with coloured stripes. There were carts and wains, there was noise and bustle, and he did not think it was due to the drier weather enticing people from their shelters.

The hucksters were out in force, the pie-sellers, women with trinkets and lucky sprigs, a man with two trained apes on slender chains. Whores, beggars, a chirurgeon barber with his tooth-puller's pincers on a cord around his neck. A monk walked into view and Alexander took an involuntary back-step, a cold fist squeezing his entrails. The cleric's tonsure needed shaving and his habit was old and filthy. The walk was in fact more of a lurch. Disquieted, but not surprised, Alexander realised that the man was drunk.

Once the monk had blundered from sight, Alexander felt safe to move, but not out into the swarm of activity; his balance was not steady enough for that. Instead he made his way slowly around to the back of the tent which faced open grass-land.

Two bay pack ponies were tethered beside a nondescript geld-ing. Alexander reasoned that they must belong to Hervi, for grazing with them was his own emaciated black horse. He waded further into the meadow, glanced round and relieved his bladder. Then he approached his mount. The stallion was too busy devouring the lush spring grass to pay him much attention. Alexander ran his hand over the prominent ridges of the ribs beneath the harsh, dull hide, and grimaced to himself.

Behind him, hooves thudded on the soft ground and he turned to see Hervi draw rein and dismount in one fluid move-ment from a handsome golden-dun destrier. In contrast to yesterday's image of a degenerate sot, Hervi was groomed to perfection, his mail shirt glittering beneath a shin-length split surcoat of blue linen, embossed in yellow thread with the de Montroi family device of three spearheads. He wore a richly tooled sword belt from which hung his scabbard, and the hand not controlling the destrier rested confidently on the braided leather sword hilt. Hazel eyes narrowed, fair hair wind-blown and bright, this was Hervi the warrior knight, and Alexander could only gape in astonishment and not a little disbelief at the transformation.

'Awake at last,' Hervi said curtly. 'You've missed most of the day.' Removing his hand from his sword, he tethered the stallion to a wooden stake knocked in the ground and commenced unsaddling him.

'You should have woken me.'

'I tried.' Hervi flashed him a wry glance: 'I broke my fast; Arnaud de Cerizay helped me to don my armour and we had a detailed conversation within three feet of your bed, and you did not so much as stir . . . Easy, lad, steady.' He smoothed the dun's sulky golden hide for a moment before unbuckling the cinches on the double girth. 'I even touched the beat in your throat before I left to make sure you were still alive.'

Alexander approached the horse. It threw up its head and its hooves danced a drumbeat on the soft meadow soil. Hervi grabbed the bridle and frowned a warning at his brother. 'He's trained to fight. Unless he's familiar with your scent, he'll savage you.' A grim smile curved Hervi's lips. 'Needless to say, he's never been taken as a prize in any tourney. No one wants him. Once you are well, I'll give you the grooming detail so you can become accustomed to each other.'

'Then you're letting me stay?'

'Do I have a choice?' Hervi said irritably. Relaxing his grip on the bridle, he returned to unsaddling the horse and cast a ferocious look from beneath his brows. 'But you will work for your bread, or there won't be any.'

Alexander swallowed the sudden lump of emotion in his throat. 'Thank you, Hervi,' he said huskily. 'I promise I won't be a burden to you.'

'Did they not teach you at the priory never to make vows you could not keep?'

Alexander's face twisted with revulsion. 'They taught me nothing but fear and hatred.'

Hervi deposited the saddle on the ground. His expression was thoughtful as he unhitched his sword belt and removed the gorgeous surcoat. 'Have you strength enough to help me take this thing off?' He gestured at the mail shirt.

Giving the dun a wide berth, Alexander came to his brother. Hervi crouched over, arms extended, and like a snake shedding its skin, began to wriggle out of the heavy garment. Alexander laid hold of the sleeves, then the body, and helped pull it over his head.

Consisting of thousand upon thousand of individually riveted iron links, the mail shirt was an item of great value, coveted by every fighting man. Only the rich and the fortunate could afford one. Alexander knew that this particular hauberk had once belonged to their father before being presented to Hervi as the means by which, as the fifth son, he was to make his way in the world. Alexander wondered what it would feel like to bear such weight, to fight in it.

Red-faced, panting slightly, Hervi straightened and took the precious garment before Alexander dropped it. As he rolled it into a cylindrical bundle, he glanced at the young man. 'Who is Brother Alkmund?'

Alexander went cold. 'No one, a monk.' His belly churned. 'Why do you ask?'

Hervi shrugged. 'You were talking in your sleep.'

'What did I say?'

'God knows, half of it was in Latin. You were reciting the Credo, but more as if you were defying someone than in duty to God. And you kept gibbering about skeletons coming out of the walls.' Hervi's eyebrows rose and three creases pleated his forehead. 'You yelled at this Brother Alkmund that you wished you had killed him when you knocked him down the stairs.'

Alexander shuddered. 'He's the sub-prior at Cranwell.'

'And?' Hervi prompted.

'And he lusts after novice monks,' Alexander said woodenly.

There was a telling silence. Hervi fetched a ragged square of linen torn from an old shirt and began to rub the horse down. 'Could you not have reported him to the prior?' he asked at length.

'He covered his tracks too well, picked his moments. He was high in authority, second only to Prior Guiscard, and I was a known troublemaker. Whose word do you think would carry the most weight?'

Hervi worked with purposeful strokes and a grim mouth. 'Did he touch you?' he demanded after another long pause, his voice quiet and hard.

'On the dorter stairs, going down to matins. But before that there had been beatings. He derived pleasure . . . carnal pleasure from the use of the birch.' Alexander shuddered. He could still feel the sting of the strokes on his naked back, could still see Brother Alkmund's lust-congested face as the scourge rose and fell, rose and fell. 'I punched him in the eye and he fell down the stairs into two other novices. If they had not been there to stop his fall, he would have tumbled all the way to the foot and broken his neck.' He spoke without expression; it was the only way he could maintain control of his raw emotions. 'My wrists were tied; I was beaten and thrown into the cells. They held me there for three days without food or water. It is not difficult to see skeletons dancing out of the walls when you think you are going to die.'

Hervi ceased work on the stallion, the rag clenched in his fist, his hazel eyes filled with disgust and fury. 'The sons of whores,' he said through his teeth.

'Not all of them were like Brother Alkmund. Many of them feared him, but they dared not speak out against his rule because he was so senior a monk. To have defended me would have brought trouble down upon their own heads.'

'I'd not have stood by and let a grown man abuse innocents with his perversions,' Hervi growled, and turned his head aside to spit. 'Did you escape, or did they let you go?'

'The preceptor, Brother Willelm, came to me on the third morning with bread and water. He freed my wrists so that I could eat, and he "forgot" to lock the cell door behind him. Brother Willelm disliked me because I would not obey the rules, but he liked Brother Alkmund even less. He thought that if I disappeared it would be better for all concerned, particularly the health of the priory. I begged and stole my way from Cranwell to London, then worked my passage across the narrow sea on a Rouen-bound wine galley.'

'Christ, I'd like to have an hour alone with those monks and a honed gelding knife,' Hervi muttered.

Alexander plucked a stalk of grass and shredded off the seedhead. 'I couldn't go to our brothers at Wooton Montroi. The monks would have concocted some tale more believable than mine, and I'd have been beaten senseless; you know what Reginald's like. Even if he agreed to keep me for the sake of the blood tie, he'd be constantly rubbing my nose in the fact that I'm the youngest son, born to a near-heathen and of small consequence. I could never live the life of a retainer at his hearth.'

'So you came to me instead,' Hervi said wryly.

'You didn't opt for Reginald's hearth either.' Alexander wandered over to the black horse again, and stroked its dull hide.

Hervi raised a pained brow, indicating agreement without making a comment that would draw him into deep water, and untied the dun. 'I'll graze this one a distance away,' he said. 'Two stallions in proximity will only lead to conflict, and your nag would likely be killed if they were to fight.' He shook his head in censure. 'I know you had a difficult time, Alex, but whatever my straits, I would never let a horse of mine descend to that condition.'

Alexander reddened at the rebuke. 'He isn't mine. I've only had him for three days.'

'Then where did you get him?'

'I found him.'

'You found him?' Hervi's tone registered disbelief.

Alexander twisted a handful of the coarse dark mane around his fist. The horse butted him affectionately in the back. 'I was walking through a forest near Domfront when I came across a traveller sleeping beside his fire.' He shivered at the memory. 'But the fire was cold and the man was dead. He was old; I think that God must have taken him as he slept, for there was not a mark upon his body. His horse was tied tightly nearby and frantic with thirst. I watered him at a nearby stream, then I said a prayer over his master and took that which he no longer needed – his cloak and shawl for warmth, the cold gruel in his cooking pot, the knife from his belt, and the horse.' Alexander released the hank of hair and smoothed out the kink that his grip had made. 'He's only young, I looked at his teeth. No more than four or five years old. He'll prove useful once he fills out.'

'Remains to be seen,' Hervi said without attaching any real meaning to the words, for his thoughts were upon all that Alexander had endured to reach him.

'I know he will.' Alexander's voice quivered with the force of his determination. 'And so will I. Hervi, I want you to teach me. I need . . .' The voice tore. 'I need to armour myself.'

A lump of pity and rage filled Hervi's throat and he had to swallow before he could speak. 'We'll start as soon as there's more meat on your bones,' he said huskily. 'You're not up to swinging a sword yet.'

Alexander nodded agreement, but when he looked at Hervi, his brown-gold eyes were ablaze. 'But I will be soon.'

Hervi returned the nod. 'Yes, soon,' he said gruffly. Certainly the lad possessed the grit it took to become a jouster, probably the aggression and recklessness too, but the price of such moulding came high. He crossed the space between them and slapped Alexander across the shoulders to dispel the dangerous burden of emotion. 'I've never had a squire before.'

Alexander smiled wanly. At least he had been accepted. Hervi might just as easily have substituted the word 'millstone' for 'squire'. He had never possessed an attendant before because he could not afford one. 'I'll pay my way,' Alexander promised. 'I can sing and play the harp. I also read and write, if anyone should need the services of a scribe.'

'Oh, there's always need for a song and a scribe,' Hervi declared, his tone still over-jovial. He squeezed Alexander's shoulder again, then returned to his horse and led it further into the field.

Alexander followed at a safe distance. 'Do you always wear your surcoat and mail when you go to practise?' he queried.

'I wasn't practising. I was seeking an employer.' Hervi had uprooted the tethering stake. Now he knocked it into the ground at the new place and secured the stallion. 'Most of us have patrons – greater lords for whom we fight. There are very few knights who take to the field alone. Individuals are more open to attack, always the first to be picked off. It is best to fight with someone to watch your back.'

Alexander tried to look knowledgeable. 'Did you find a patron?'

'Indeed I did.' Hervi's eyes gleamed. 'Although I should say "we", since I went a-wooing with Arnaud de Cerizay. We've been accepted into the retinue of Geoffrey Duredent of Avranches for the duration of the tourney. Twenty per cent of any prizes from captures go to him in person, and another twenty into the chests for the ransom of Richard Coeur de Lion from the hands of the German emperor. The rest is ours. Geoffrey has promised to feed us at his board on Monday, Tuesday and Wednesday. We have fought for him before; he's an open-handed patron.'

Alexander absorbed this, together with Hervi's enthusiasm, and felt a glimmer of anticipation spark through his veins. 'Aren't there any individual contests?'

'On the Thursday.' A warning note entered Hervi's voice. 'Only the best knights run head to head, some would say the most foolish. It takes great skill, long hours of training for both man and horse, and you have to be able to afford to lose. You only have one attempt at success. If you fail, you cannot recoup your loss unless you have another horse and the balls to go back and try again. Most don't.' He smiled sourly at his brother. 'Minstrels paint bold and glorious word pictures of tourneys, but they do not sing the truth.' He wiped his hands down his chausses as if disposing of the subject. 'Are you hungry?'

Alexander nodded. His stomach had digested the milk, bread and apple in short order, and was now ready to be refilled.

'Good,' Hervi said briskly. 'There's a stream at the foot of this field. I'll lend you my spare clothes and you can go and scrub the filth of the road from your body. We're eating at Arnaud de Cerizay's family fire, and that's a privilege worth using soap for. It was Arnaud's wife and daughter who came to care for you yesterday, Clemence and Monday. Arnaud took care of your horse.'

Alexander had vague recollections of a small, competent

woman with lines of laughter and of care at her mouth corners, and of a girl with a clear grey stare, and a shining plait of golden-brown hair.

'Arnaud and me usually fight together as a team,' Hervi said as he led Alexander back to the tent to find the replacement clothes. 'He has no great stature on the field, but few men ever get past his guard. His wife is the daughter of Thomas FitzParnell of Stafford,' he added with a little shake of his head, as if at some misfortune.

Alexander's ears pricked with interest. 'Stafford and his son are patrons of Cranwell Priory.'

Hervi stared at him. 'Thomas of Stafford a patron of monks?' he said in disbelief. 'Pigs might fly!'

'Oh, it's all kindling and no fire,' Alexander replied as they entered the tent. 'He's like Reginald. Pays lip service because it is essential for every man of standing to be thought of as generous and godly even when the opposite is true. He didn't take a crusader's vow, he paid silver to Cranwell instead – and half of the coins were clipped.'

'I can believe that. I doubt FitzParnell has a single generous bone in his body.'

Alexander looked curiously at Hervi. 'What is his daughter doing on the tourney circuits?'

Hervi rummaged among the debris scattered around the tent and found a linen bag fastened with a braid drawstring. 'She fell in love with Arnaud de Cerizay, who was a penniless knight recently employed by her father, and ran away with him rather than marry the man chosen for her. There was a huge scandal at the time, but you wouldn't remember, you were little more than a babe in arms when it happened.'

'No, I don't.'

'Arnaud took me under his wing when I first joined the tourney route as an aspiring champion with more dreams than good sense. We've watched each other's back ever since, shared the triumphs and the failures – of which there have been many. There's a clean shirt and some linens in here.' Hervi thrust the bag into Alexander's hand, delved again, and came up with a crumpled but reasonable tunic of sage-green wool. 'First town we come to, we'll find you some fabric for new clothes.' He bundled the tunic on top of the bag, together with a leather jar of liquid soap. 'Go on, get you down to the stream.'

Alexander made his way slowly down the field. His legs were aching and there was a gentle throb of renewed weariness behind his temples, but at least he was free. There was fresh air on his skin and the grey clouds had thinned to show streaks of blue between. He had a place in the world of his own choosing, and the wherewithal to climb fortune's ladder.

The stream was lined with sedges and stood about ten yards wide at its broadest point. A moorhen paddled frantically away from him in a race of silver droplets. Reeds long as jousting lances clacked and swayed together at the water's edge. Alexander dropped the clean garments on a patch of lush grass on the bank and sat down. For a moment he rested, a glint of afternoon sunshine warming his spine. In the distance he could hear the shouts of men practising their art and the thud of a lance against a quintain target. He imagined himself astride a warhorse, a lance couched beneath his arm, a shield braced across the left side of his body. The smooth power beneath him, carrying him towards the moment of impact. The shock of steel upon wood, pressuring him back against the high saddle cantle. Cries of adulation for his prowess. As he set about disrobing, a faraway smile played at his mouth corners.

The water came up to his midriff and it was cold. Alexander drew a shocked breath, his stomach clamping until it almost touched his spine. Shivers arrowed through him and his teeth chattered violently. Even had he been in the rudest of health with a surplus of meat on his bones, it was not the kind of day to linger over outdoor ablutions. He took the soap jar, tipped the contents over his head and body and set to with a will, scrubbing away several weeks of accumulated sweat and grime.

Beneath the pummelling his skin reddened. His eyes stung from the strength of the soap, and he squeezed them shut. He ducked his head in the stream to swill the soap away, then stood up, thrusting the water from his face and hair. Then, gasping with exertion and cold, he opened his eyes.

A young woman was approaching the stream, a stone water jar

swinging from her hand. She appeared to be lost in her own thoughts, her eyes upon her feet, which performed intricate little skipping movements in time to the tune she was humming. Her head was bare, proclaiming her unbetrothed, still a child, although her figure bore womanly curves. A heavy plait of rich brown hair secured with a blue ribbon hung to her waist, and as she came closer, Alexander recognised her as the girl who had fed him soup yesterday. This was Monday de Cerizay, the daughter of Hervi's partner, at whose fire they were going to dine.

She crouched upstream of Alexander and sank the stone jar in the water to fill it. Still singing, she raised her head, and her grey eyes widened as she saw him standing there, naked, his modesty and hers protected only by the transparent distortions of the water. Droplets trickled down the fine dark line of his chest hair and disappeared into the stripe of fuzz below his navel. Her cheeks reddened and she turned quickly to the jar.

Alexander wondered whether to speak or remain silent. It was not a situation for which he had any precedent. He decided that he would have to say something since he and Hervi were to be guests at her father's fire. 'Demoiselle.' He gave her the formal greeting, and thought how foolish it sounded,

She nodded shyly in return, and although her cheeks remained pink, she darted him another glance. 'Are you feeling better today?' Her eyes travelled to the discoloured bracelets on his wrists, then over the gaunt protrusion of his ribcage.

'A little.' He cleared his throat. 'It was kind of you and your mother to concern yourselves with me yesterday.'

'On the tourney circuit, we look after our own.' She stood up, the water jar overflowing. 'Hervi and my father have long been friends.'

'Yes, he told me. Tonight we are to eat at your fire.' In his own ears, his voice sounded stilted and awkward.

She hefted the jug and splashes of water darkened her gown. 'I have to go, my mother needs this,' she said.

Alexander nodded. He was shuddering with cold and could think of nothing else to say. But their eyes held for a long moment, each examining with curiosity something that was new and strange.

Abruptly the girl swung on her heel, water slopping over the neck of the jar, and made her way back to the meadow, her gait one-sided from the weight of the pot.

Alexander waded to the bank. Shivering violently, he dried himself on the old strip of linen Hervi had given him for a towel, his belly churning with a mixture of anticipation, fear and hunger at the thought of the meal to come.

CHAPTER 3

Monday sat at the small portable trestle table, chopping onion and cabbage to add to the meat, barley and spices already simmering in the iron cauldron. Her mother was putting the finishing touches to a surcoat she had promised to have ready for one of the competing knights by dusk. The brass needle flashed in and out of the fabric with a speed and accuracy almost too fast to follow, but Clemence was beginning to squint as the light faded and her eyes grew tired.

'Shall I light the lantern, Mama?'

'No, I've almost finished. Just this length here to do.' Clemence shook out the garment and turned it round. One half was blood red, the other a light orangey yellow.

'Who is it for?' Monday asked.

Her mother's lips tightened. 'Eudo le Boucher,' she said in a voice cold with distaste.

Monday swept the chopped vegetables into a wooden bowl and carefully tipped them into the cauldron. Eudo le Boucher was a man who not only fought to live, but lived to fight. He was her father's age, perhaps slightly younger, with a shock of prematurely iron-grey hair, disfiguring battle scars and eyes like black ice. Men avoided him if possible, but no one was foolish enough to make him their enemy.

'We have to eat,' Clemence justified, as much to herself as to her silent daughter. 'In the good times we have to save our silver so that we can weather the bad.' She bit off the thread on a broken tooth and held up the garment for inspection. 'I would lief as not sew for the man, but I cannot afford to refuse him.'

Monday stirred the stew with a large carved spoon and glanced at her mother. Clemence had been out of sorts for a couple of weeks now, tense and snappish, swift to find fault, slow to be pacified. Her father had been quietly avoiding his wife, a rueful look in his grey eyes. For Monday it was not so easy. Unless sent on a specific errand, she had no excuse to make herself scarce. It was not safe for a girl of her age to venture too far from her own fire. Even fetching water from the stream had its hazards.

She thought of her encounter with Hervi's half-brother and the motion of her stirring increased. Alexander de Montroi bore small resemblance to Hervi, who was huge and blond and hearty. There was a brooding quality about the younger man, a hunger of the spirit as much as of the body.

'Careful!' Clemence scolded. 'Watch what you're doing!'

A cloud of hissing steam billowed from the fire beneath the cauldron and bubbles of stew bounced on the iron sides before vanishing in wafts of burned vapour.

'Sorry, Mama.' Monday gave her mother a flushed, apologetic look.

'Daydreaming again,' Clemence chided with exasperation. 'Monday, you must learn to keep your wits about you.'

'Mama, I didn't mean to . . .' Monday broke off as a powerfully built man wearing a green quilted gambeson arrived at their hearth and commanded their attention. Eudo le Boucher was even taller than Hervi. Once he had been handsome, but the tourney circuit and the battlefield had taken their toll. His nose zigzagged down his face, following the line of successive breaks, and the flesh of his jaw was puckered from mouth corner to missing ear lobe where a sword had sliced him open to the bone.

'Is it ready?' he demanded.

'Of course,' Clemence said disdainfully, as if she had finished her sewing hours ago. Rising from her stool, she gave him the completed surcoat. Both her spine and her expression were as stiff as wood. Eudo's black eyes crinkled with amusement.

'I know that you like me not, Lady Clemence,' he observed,

'but you do like my money, and that makes us equals.'

'You flatter yourself,' she said coldly.

'Then that makes us equals too, since you do the same.' He delved in the money pouch at his belt. Monday watched her mother's mouth make small chewing motions and stepped up beside her, offering moral support.

Le Boucher assimilated the gesture and his amusement increased. 'Tell your daughter that she will spoil her face and her fortune scowling like that,' he said to Clemence.

Clemence drew herself up, her lips parted for a retort, but it went unuttered as her husband arrived at the fire. Le Boucher withdrew from any further confrontation by placing two small silver coins in Clemence's palm, and turned away, the surcoat draped over his arm.

She closed her fist over the money, her expression one of barely controlled revulsion.

'Your wife sews a fine seam,' the knight remarked pleasantly.

Arnaud de Cerizay murmured polite agreement and held out his hands to the warmth of the cooking fire as if at ease, but Monday could sense his tension. Eudo le Boucher never made conversation just to be sociable.

'I hear that you and Hervi are fighting for Geoffrey Duredent tomorrow?'

Her father gave a guarded nod. 'What of it?'

'It is your good fortune. So am I. And I have a new flail to try out. I warrant I can dent a few helms with it, and beggar some high-born striplings into the bargain.'

Arnaud made a noncommittal sound.

Monday wondered why le Boucher was lingering. Surely he could sense that he was unwelcome?

The knight caught her resentful gaze on him and stared her out with a smile. 'Have you thought about betrothing your girl yet, Cerizay?' he asked provocatively. 'She is almost a woman grown.'

Monday went cold and folded her arms across her breasts in a protective gesture.

'There is time enough,' Arnaud said repressively. 'And I shall consider long and hard before I settle her on anyone.'

'There speaks a wise father.' Smiling, le Boucher inclined his head and sauntered off in the direction of his own tent.

'The arrogance of that man,' Clemence hissed. 'I wish I had never consented to sew for him. Did you see the way he looked at Monday?'

Arnaud sighed heavily. 'Yes, I did, but I have to admit he was right. She is indeed almost a woman grown, and he will only be the first of many to look at her thus.'

'I don't want a husband!' Monday burst out, her arms still folded across her breasts, and fear surging at her core.

'I have no intention of betrothing you anywhere for the nonce.' Lines of care marred her father's face. 'I have encountered no man I consider worthy, and until I do, your honour is mine to the last breath in my body.'

Hearing the bleak note in his voice, Monday felt guilty. Her development into womanhood was the root cause of the problem. Nor was there a remedy unless she became a nun.

Her mother said nothing, but there was a look of utter weariness on her face as she stooped into the tent to put her sewing box away.

Their guests arrived shortly after that, Hervi as hearty and bold as ever and bearing a gift of six fresh duck eggs, their shells a delicate speckled blue. Clemence accepted them with pleasure, a smile returning to her face. Hervi seated himself at their trestle with the ease of familiarity. Alexander was more hesitant, torn between being polite and following his brother's casual example.

Monday murmured a greeting and busied herself setting out the eating bowls and a basket of small loaves in the centre of the trestle. She flickered a circumspect glance at Alexander and met his eyes on her in similar scrutiny. Both of them immediately looked away, but not before Monday had noticed that Hervi's rumpled spare clothes swamped the youth's gaunt frame. Her head was filled with questions, but none that she could ask without appearing rude or forward.

Indeed, the conversation during the meal that followed was carried almost entirely by Hervi and her father as they discussed their tactics for the morrow's tourney. Alexander ate in silence, but was obviously listening hard, absorbing every word like a young plant putting out roots in search of nourishment. Monday eyed his slender fingers gripping the handle of his spoon, contrasted them with the ham-like ugliness of Hervi's and her father's and found it difficult to imagine Alexander joining the two older men on the battlefield. It was much easier to see him as a monk. And he spoke so little that she half wondered if he had taken a vow of silence.

The repast was completed by a dish of raisins and slivers of dried apple. Alexander took only a small handful of the fruits and ate them slowly, declaring ruefully that he had lived so long without proper food that he had yet to adjust to eating a full meal again.

'You are young,' Arnaud said comfortably. 'You'll mend fast.'

'Yes, sir.' Alexander slowly chewed another sliver of apple, the taste sharp on his palate, and raised his eyes to Cerizay's shrewd grey ones. 'I want to earn my way in the world, not be a burden.'

'Oh, you'll earn your way all right,' Hervi declared, 'every penny of it.' He spoke brusquely, his words a shield against revealing tender emotions.

Arnaud considered the younger man thoughtfully. 'Can you fight?'

'A little. I learned to use a spear and shield before I was sent away to Cranwell, and before he died, my father had begun to teach me the rudiments of swordplay, and how to ride like a knight.'

'Aye, you weren't a bad little horseman for a ten-year-old,' Hervi acknowledged. 'Of course, it depends how much you have remembered, and if you have any talent for the other skills.'

Arnaud finished his dried fruit and continued to study Alexander with slightly narrowed eyes. 'Show me your hands,' he said suddenly.

Obedient but mystified, Alexander held them out to him, palms upwards. There was scarcely a tremor now. A line of tough, blistered skin marked the labour of gripping a hoe and rake in the priory's fields. His fingers too bore the rough texture of hard toil, but nothing could detract from their elegant symmetry. Arnaud took them in his, turned them over, pushed back the oversleeves and examined the long, scarred wrist-bones.

'Takes after his mother,' Hervi said. 'There'll never be any meat on him.'

'He's got time, and he is not as dainty as he looks,' Arnaud answered judiciously. 'See the strength of the bones here?' He raised Alexander's right wrist and presented it to Hervi like a horse-coper selling the points of a thoroughbred colt. 'See the span here? Add some weight and experience, and here sits a competent soldier.' He released the wrist. 'How old are you, lad?'

'He'll be eighteen at the feast of St John,' Hervi said.

'So he will likely not grow any taller.' Arnaud nodded.

'He stands need to. His head's already in the clouds!'

A faint smile crossed the older man's face and he turned to his daughter. 'Where are your knucklebones, child?'

As mystified as Alexander, Monday opened the small draw-string pouch at her waist, drew out the polished pig's-foot knuckles with which she sometimes gamed of an evening, and handed them to her father.

'Do you know how to play?'

Alexander nodded, his puzzlement deepening. Knucklebones was a game of speed, skill and manual dexterity. The bones were held loosely in the fist and then tossed in the air. The object was to catch them again on the back of the hand without dropping any.

'Show me.'

Alexander glanced at Hervi, then back at Arnaud de Cerizay. With a shrug he took the bow-shaped pieces of bone and closed his fingers over them. If this was some strange form of initiation ceremony, then it was a simple enough test to pass.

Drawing a steady breath, he tossed the knucklebones lightly in the air and shot out his hand to catch. The sequence of move-ments was almost too swift for the eye to follow. Two knucklebones landed squarely. A third rocked on the edge of his hand but did not fall. Alexander tossed them again, this time centring them precisely, and then once more with the same result.

'Go on.' Arnaud gestured when he hesitated. 'I will tell you when to stop.'

Time and again Alexander tossed and caught the bones, only dropping them once when Hervi moved on his stool and cast a sudden shadow over the play. At last Arnaud declared he had seen enough, and there was approval in his eyes as Alexander cupped the bones in his palm and returned them to Monday.

'You have good coordination, lad,' he commented, and smiled at Hervi. 'Perhaps even better than your brother's.'

'Anyone can play knucklebones,' Hervi growled. 'Lance and sword and mace are different matters entirely.'

'Oh, indeed they are, which is why he will have to practise until he weeps tears of blood,' Arnaud replied. 'What I am saying is that he has the potential to become skilled.'

Alexander flushed with pleasure. His mind's eye was filled with the image of himself dressed as Hervi had been that afternoon, a sword at his hip and a mail coat meshing his body. 'It is what I want to do,' he said fervently.

Hervi bestowed him a brooding look but made no more adverse remarks. Clemence de Cerizay rose abruptly and began clearing away the empty bowls and bread basket. Glancing at her, Alexander saw that her lips were pursed and her eyelids tense. He could sense her irritation, but did not know what was wrong. There was a rueful expression on Arnaud's face. Hervi examined his fingernails.

'Some of us are here by necessity,' Arnaud said. 'God grant you peace of soul, the gift of wise choice and the wherewithal not to squander your life. You will need more than prowess in battle to survive.'

'Yes, sir,' Alexander said on a more subdued note.

Arnaud considered him. 'Hervi tells me that you read and write Latin.'

Alexander moved his shoulders. 'Enough to get by. I was not the most apt pupil.'

'He wasted his time writing secular love poems,' Hervi said drily.

Arnaud shook his head. 'It matters not, it is another string to his bow when it comes to finding an employer. If he can prove entertaining company in the great hall of a snowbound winter's evening, as well as fight, then he will always have a hearth at which to warm his hands.'

'And a snug bed too, I'll warrant!' Hervi laughed, then bit his lip beneath Clemence's severe look. 'Speaking of which, it is time we made our farewells if I'm to be bright-eyed for the morrow!' He slapped Alexander's bony shoulder. 'Come, lad, the moon's half waxed already.'

Alexander rose from his stool and thanked the de Cerizays for their hospitality. The girl smiled at him, her loose plait of brown-bronze hair outlined by the lanternlight, her eyes wide and sparkling. He had wondered earlier whether to mention their encounter by the stream, but had decided against it lest it cause trouble for them both. He needed this niche in the world. The mother smiled too, but she seemed preoccupied, and although she warmly wished them good night, Alexander could tell that she was glad to see them leave.

He did not brood on the reason, for too many other thoughts were churning in his mind. Arnaud de Cerizay had said that he had the potential to become a knight, that with his background and the training to come, he was almost assured of a high career. Nervous excitement surged through his body. He thought of the girl's grey eyes upon him and embroidered on her look until his imagination was filled with the vision of hundreds of young women tossing flowers at him in admiration as he sat astride a champing Spanish war horse. Not even the mildewed smell of Hervi's tent and the scratchy texture of the coarse woollen bed blanket could dampen his enthusiasm. He had set his feet on his chosen road as a penniless beggar, but he knew that his destination would make him wealthy beyond compare.

And when that happened, the skeletons in the walls would be unable to touch him.

Arnaud de Cerizay lay upon his pallet and gazed up into the darkness. Beside him Clemence was silent, but he knew that she was not asleep. Her hair tickled his chest; the warmth of her thigh lay along his own. They had a modicum of privacy, their bed separated from Monday's by a gaily coloured hanging of woven homespun. On the other side of the screen he could hear his daughter's regular, soft breathing.

Arnaud wished that it was a midsummer evening so that he could see the pale glimmer of his wife's hair and the slender shape of her body. The thought stirred his loins to sleepy arousal. He had been twenty years old and she sixteen when they had eloped together and married against her powerful father's will. The lord of Stafford's blonde virgin daughter and a common household knight.

Another sixteen years had passed since that time, and through all the trials and hardships, the pain, heartache and drudgery, their love had endured. It had to. There was nothing else to armour them against the cold. The story of their elopement had passed into troubadour legend, was sung at every camp fire by young men no older than himself when he had burned his bridges.

Thinking of young men brought to mind Alexander de Montroi and he ran a gentle forefinger down his wife's bare arm. 'What did you make of Hervi's brother?' he asked.

'I thought him quiet,' she said, 'but not because there is nothing happening within. When he finds his feet, then we shall see.'

'I like the lad.'

'He seems pleasant enough,' she agreed, 'but he did not reveal enough of himself for me to make a judgement. Has Hervi discovered why he ran away from the monastery?'

'All he said was that the boy had good reason. He would not give me the details.' His hand drifted from her arm to the swell of her breast and gently stroked. 'Of course, he has only heard one side of the tale, and there are always two, and often more.' He was silent for a while, pondering, enjoying the silken feel of his wife's skin. She did not add to the conversation, which was unusual for her. Talking in the closeness of their bed at night, wrapped in each other's arms with the world at bay, was one of her favourite moments. She always had things to tell him, subjects to broach, matters to discuss. When she did not speak, he mooted another concern of his own.

'It might be for the best if Monday were to wear a wimple when she goes about the camp from now on,' he suggested. 'She has not ceased to be a child in my eyes, but in the eyes of other men, it is obviously different.' The memory of le Boucher's predatory gaze tightened his lips.

Clemence captured his stroking hand in hers and held it still. 'She has been a woman for almost a year now. You are right, it is time that she concealed her hair.' A tremor entered her voice. 'I was not much older than her when I first saw you across my father's bailey.'

Her words sent a pang through Arnaud's vitals. 'Your hair was loose then too,' he murmured. 'I had never seen anything so beautiful.' There was pain mingled with the remembered spark of the moment. Had they resisted temptation, he would still be doing guard duty at Stafford's hearth, and she would be some rich baron's wife. 'Do you have regrets?' he asked.

'Of course I do,' she said immediately, her breath soft against his bicep. He tightened it, preparing himself to hear what he would rather shut out. Her teeth nipped his skin. 'Fool,' she said with amused contempt, 'I would follow you to the ends of the earth and over the edge of the world, you know that – or you should by now.'

He was slightly mollified, but remained wary. 'Then what do you regret?'

Clemence sighed and curled in close to his body. 'Sometimes I yearn for the protection of the bars of my former gilded cage and the days when even my thinking was done for me. Flying high and free has its price. I fear for our daughter. She is so young and fresh. And there is no man on the tourney circuit I would entrust with her honour or her happiness.'

Not for the first time Arnaud was visited by guilt and a sense of inadequacy. He was an ordinary knight, competent, a better teacher of the skills than he was a fighter. His one act of folly in an otherwise responsible life had been to steal the exotic bird from its cage, and he had been paying for the sin ever since. There had never been a time when they had gone hungry, he had always managed to provide, and Clemence's skill with a needle enabled them to dwell in relative comfort for his trade, but he could not give her the security of the massive stone walls from whose shadow he had snatched her away.

'Come the autumn, I will try to find a permanent position in a lord's retinue,' he replied. 'There is bound to be someone in need of hearth knights with Richard in prison and Philip of France free to wreak his worst.'

'You will have to do more than try this year,' she said quietly.

Her tone sent a ripple of apprehension down his spine. 'Clemence?'

She guided his hand down over her body, to the gentle curve of her belly. 'I am with child again; for three months I have not bled.'

He felt the soft flesh beneath his palm, but could not discern if it was any more abundant than usual. The early nights of winter, the dark mornings, meant that he had seldom seen Clemence naked over the past few months. All conversation, all lovemaking had been conducted in the dark. 'But that's imposs—' he started to say, then closed his mouth, remembering the time he had left it to the last moment to withdraw, the seed spurting from his body as he jerked out of the passage to her womb.

'Are you sure?' It was a stupid question. Of course she was sure. The worry, the keeping it to herself was the reason for her sharp tongue. 'Ah, God, Clemence.' He freed his hand from hers and slipped it around her body, offering comfort, seeking it himself while he made a swift calculation. It was late April now, almost the feast of St Mark. By Martinmas, in November, he would be responsible for another mouth to feed. Fear assaulted him in a sweeping, physical wave. Clemence had almost died bearing Monday, her hips too narrow to comfortably accommodate the baby's head. Old Mildred sold potions to the camp whores whose fluxes came late, but their efficacy was as dubious as their contents, and he knew that Clemence would utterly refuse to dose herself. He could not bear the thought of losing her – she was all that he had – and cold sweat broke out on his brow.

'I will seek early for winter quarters,' he agreed huskily.

Clemence nodded against his chest. 'I wish I had told you

sooner, but I did not want to burden you until I was sure.' Her voice was small and muffled against the bulk of his body.

'You should have done.' He squeezed her against him, kissed her in reassurance, and thanked God for the darkness that concealed his expression, even as earlier he had been longing for the light.

CHAPTER 4

The tournament was to be held over an agreed area of three large fields, its boundaries set by the stream that supplied the camp on the northern and western edges, by a small wood to the south and by an abandoned hermitage to the east. No fighting was to take place beyond these markers. Anyone invading the nearby village to fight was to be disqualified immediately.

An enclosure of withy screens had been erected close to the centre of the first field where the fighters could claim sanctuary if they were in difficulty or needed to take a respite. It was here that Hervi brought Alexander as the morning sun climbed in the sky and the knights on the two sides began to warm up with practice charges and turns. Weapons glittered; banter was exchanged, both the pleasant and the aggressive.

'You should be able to see the combat from here,' Hervi said as Alexander entered the enclosure. 'Remember to be ready with my spare lance and shield if I signal to you.'

Alexander nodded, squinting up at Hervi astride the dun stallion. The older man held Soleil on a tight rein, the tawny head tucked into the deep chest. A solid jousting helm hung from a thong on the saddle and the blue and gold shield was slung out of the way across Hervi's broad back. The spare shield weighed down Alexander's left arm, and his right hand curved around the haft of a blunted spear. A water bottle was slung across his shoulder and in his pouch there were two honey cakes. Other attendants, similarly equipped, were arriving at the enclosure.

'How will you know friend from foe?'

'Easy,' Hervi replied. 'Each man shouts the name of his patron lord. And if he does not own one, then he is fighting for himself.

I am Geoffrey Duredent's man today. His opponent is Saer de Quinci. So, any man who cries "De Quinci!" on the field is fodder for the taking!' He reined the horse about. 'Keep sharp – and don't move from this enclosure. If you do, you become prey, and I don't want to afford a ransom for you!'

Alexander gave a rueful shrug. 'Small chance of that,' he said. 'I can scarcely lift this shield, let alone use it. Take care yourself.'

Hervi smiled. 'My watchdog will do that.' He jerked his head in the direction of the scarlet-and-black-clad figure of Arnaud de Cerizay, who was encouraging a rangy bay stallion to perform circles and back-kicks. With a final salute to Alexander, Hervi set off across the field.

Alexander unslung the shield from his aching left arm, deposited it on the ground, and leaning his spear against the withy barrier, looked over the top at the tourney field. The knights were beginning to collect in two ragged lines. Men riding out to join their prospective team occasionally clashed lances with an opponent, testing strength and bravado. Horses whinnied, clods of soil were flung from pounding hooves, and the smell of excitement filled the air. Alexander's throat grew dry and his heart began to hammer as if he too were physically involved in the proceedings.

'De Quinci!' yelled the youth next to him in the enclosure, and thumped the withy fencing. 'Quinci, Quinci!'

Alexander considered retorting with his own cry of 'Duredent!' but seeing the size of the youth, the bulging muscles beneath the leather jerkin, he kept his voice in his throat. Tonight, when the day's activity was over, he would compose a song to encapsulate all that he was feeling.

Above the shouts, the thud of hooves and rattle of weapons, a hunting horn blared a single, sustained note. There was a moment when the sound absorbed all other noise and movement, suspending them in its resonance, and then the two lines tore free and charged towards one another in a roar of motion.

The ground shook to the thunder of destrier hooves and the air glittered with the colours of linen and silk, the bright flash of spears like fish writhing in a net. The shock of individual impacts felt all as one to Alexander. With fists clenched on the withy barrier, he watched the blend and swirl of men, horses and weapons, and tried to follow the progress of Hervi's blue and gold, and the scarlet and black of de Cerizay. The thump and thud of weapons meeting shields lodged in his gut and tendrils of excitement unfurled through his veins.

A riderless horse thundered past the enclosure, a mounted knight in hot pursuit, his own mount straining under the burden.

'De Quinci!' screamed Alexander's neighbour, beside himself with excitement as the knight closed on the loose horse, a fine animal, richly caparisoned and well worth capturing.

Another competitor galloped up fast from the opposite side, his surcoat parti-coloured red and yellow to match the quartering on his shield. His right arm was raised, churning a flail in the air, and he brought the weapon round and down on the other man's helm with devastating effect. The knight had no time to defend himself. Although his helm saved him from serious hurt, the force of the blow and the clang of the flail against the iron stunned him and he was easy prey for his attacker to unseat. He struck the ground with bone-jarring force, and suddenly there were two loose horses.

The knight in the red and yellow caught the bridle of the nearest destrier and rode away to deposit his prize. At Alexander's side, the youth had ceased to shout, his eyes dark with shock. The unhorsed man slowly rolled over and started to crawl toward the enclosure. Biting his lip, the youth sped out to help him. Alexander's hesitation was brief. He did not have the ability to passively observe, half the reason his monastic career had foundered. Ignoring Hervi's strictures concerning remaining in safety, he grasped the spare spear for protection and darted out to do what he could.

Together he and the youth took the knight's arms and dragged him towards the enclosure. They were paid scant attention, for the fighting was concentrated down at the far end of the field, and they had almost reached safety when the competitor in the red and yellow returned to claim the ransom price from his victim.

'Duredent!' he bellowed, the sound a muffled boom emerging through the vent holes in his jousting helm. He swung the flail around his head, threatening the boys, his stallion plunging close.

Without pause for thought, Alexander grasped the spear in both hands and thrust it at the whirling flail. The shaft caught in the chain, and with a violent jerk, the momentum was suspended. The spear tore out of Alexander's grip almost dislocating his arms, but that same force and the sudden clumsiness of the trapped spear unbalanced the man in the saddle. His horse reared, and he was thrown, thudding down heavily at the horrified Alexander's feet.

Appalled, feeling sick, Alexander retrieved Hervi's spear, the flail still wound around the head socket, and retreated behind the barrier where the knight he had run out to rescue was now removing his helm.

The warrior in the parti-coloured surcoat sat up and stared around, his breathing stertorous through the slits in his helm. Then he lumbered to his feet, and drawing his sword, advanced upon the withy enclosure. Alexander backed, the spear braced. The knight ducked beneath it, closed his fist around the trapped flail and yanked it free. Then he seized a fistful of Alexander's tunic, lifted him bodily off his feet and slammed him down on his back.

'You want to fight, boy?' he snarled. 'I'll teach you a lesson you'll not forget.'

'This is sanctuary!' Alexander yelled through the pain. 'You can't touch me in here!'

'That's right, le Boucher, you can't!' declared one of the spectators, a stocky man wearing a stained apron, one eye hidden behind a large leather patch. 'You know the rule.'

The knight stared round the compound at the gathered, uneasy crowd of onlookers. He returned his sword to its sheath and nodded. 'Very well,' he said. Stooping, he grabbed Alexander by the scruff and hauled him back out on to the field. 'Now he's not in sanctuary; I can do as I choose with him.'

Alexander struggled against the bunched fist holding him captive. He was aware of the stunned faces watching from the enclosure, but no one was prepared to go beyond words to help him. Once more he was flung to the ground, and the huge knight stood over him.

'I doubt you're even worth the bother, vermin, but I'm going to lesson you anyway.' Eudo le Boucher drew the flail through his hand in a gesture that was almost sensual.

Across the battlefield, Hervi disengaged from his opponent to gain his breath, and glanced around. The eye slits in his tourney helm did not yield a good view of the field, but at least it was not dusty, as it would be later on in the season when visibility was frequently nil. To his right, Arnaud had just defeated one knight and beaten off another in a rare display of pure aggression. Usually Arnaud's performance was laconic, but today there seemed to be a burr beneath his buttocks.

There would be a ransom to share now, a good omen since the tourney was less than an hour old and there was still plenty of opportunity to reap the field. Hervi signalled to his companion, indicating that they should retire to the enclosure and take a brief respite before the next assault. His throat was parched and he needed a drink.

The two men started back up the field at a modest canter, their senses alert for a sudden attack. Then Arnaud swore, shook Hervi's sleeve and pointed towards the sanctuary. What Hervi saw made his blood run cold. He slapped the reins down on Soleil's neck, drove in his spurs and thundered up the field like a fury.

Alexander rolled away from the thud of the flail against his ribs a scream ripping from his throat, his knees doubling up. He heard the jink of the chain, the whistle of the iron end swinging through the air, and he squeezed his eyes tightly shut, tears wringing on to his lashes. The blow never descended. In its place he heard the snarl of his brother's voice.

'Strike again, le Boucher, and it will be your last act on God's earth!'

'Why should it concern you, de Montroi? Keep your face out of this!'

'He is my brother, my youngest brother, and I will know why you are beating him!'

'He attacked me first, with a spear. Was I supposed to smile and pat his head? God's eyes, I won't tolerate whelps like him darting in and out of the sanctuary, making a mockery of true knights!'

'I wasn't,' Alexander croaked from the ground. 'I was trying to help a fallen man.' He stared up at the mask of Hervi's helm. Below it, the broad shoulders rose and fell rapidly. 'He was going to strike him with that flail, so I stepped in.' He sat up, his arms folded around his ribs which felt as though they were on fire. It was impossible to draw breath except in short stabs.

'Let him go, le Boucher,' said Arnaud, manoeuvring his bay between Hervi and the standing man. 'Alexander does not know the rules; he's a green boy. It won't happen again. Is your pride worth so much to you?'

'He denied me a man's ransom!' Le Boucher jabbed a fore-finger at Hervi. 'I'll have the payment out of your own purse!'

'You will have no such thing!' Hervi's voice was raw with fury.

Alexander hung his head, feeling sick, knowing that this was all his fault. And yet he could not have just stood by and watched.

The knight whom he had rescued limped out of the enclosure, clutching his side. He had removed his helm and there were streaks of rust on his brow and cheeks where sweat and iron had met. He was in his early twenties, with light-brown hair, and a sparse ginger beard hugging the point of his chin. 'Call it even,' he panted. 'The lad unhorsed you, le Boucher, and if he had known the rules, he'd have put that spear to your throat and demanded a ransom of you.'

Hervi's helm swivelled in Alexander's direction. 'You unhorsed him?' He pointed at le Boucher.

Alexander nodded. 'I put the haft of your spear through the flail's chain and pulled him off his destrier.'

Hervi turned to le Boucher. 'I would forget the incident if I were you,' he said. 'Any claim you press can be met with a counter claim.'

'You would not dare!'

'Can you afford to try me?'

There was a taut silence. Le Boucher's mail mitten tightened around the handle of the flail. Hervi's dun stallion sidled.

From the far side of the field, but galloping up fast, came a group of three riders, their lances couched, signalling a challenge.

The tension broke. Eudo le Boucher ran to catch his mount's

bridle and swung into the saddle. 'Bold words, de Montroi,' he sneered. 'Yes, I can afford to try you to the end of your luck, but I doubt that you can pay my price!' Yanking the horse around, he rode away across the field.

Hervi cursed and turned Soleil. 'Get back inside that sanctuary!' he snarled at Alexander. 'And even if you see me dragged off my horse and killed, do not so much as lift your buttocks off the turf, understand?'

'Yes, I didn't intend to . . .'

'Go, curse you, I haven't the time to listen to your paltry excuses!' Without waiting to see if Alexander obeyed, Hervi couched his lance and spurred forward to meet the rapidly approaching challenge. Arnaud circled round and spurred with him, one man going hard left, the other to the right.

Alexander remained where he was long enough to see Hervi batter aside his opponent's shield, knock him off his horse and turn to deal with the man in the centre, then retreated to the enclosure.

'That was a brave act, lad,' said the competitor whom he had saved. 'I am grateful to you, even if no one else is.' He extended his arm. 'My name is John Marshal. If ever I can be of service to you, do not hesitate to seek me out.'

Alexander shook the proffered hand. He was tongue-tied by embarrassment and still too shaken to give a coherent reply.

John Marshal smiled. 'And you are called?'

'Montroi, sir. Alexander de Montroi.'

'I won't forget you, I promise.' The knight withdrew his hand, nodded pleasantly and with his squire in tow, walked off across the enclosure.

Alexander stared after him and clutched his aching ribs.

That evening, Alexander and Hervi dined a second time at the de Cerizays' fire, and there was much to talk about. Hervi and Arnaud had had an excellent day upon the field and taken several ransoms. Their enthusiasm was full-blown and every move and tactic, strike and counterstroke had to be discussed in detail. Also talked to death was Alexander's encounter with the scourge of the tourney field, Eudo le Boucher.

'I still cannot believe that you unhorsed him!' Hervi declared, his earlier fury at Alexander's insubordination mellowed by the day's triumphs and the excellent wine he was drinking. 'Jesu, he'll never live it down. Pulled off his horse by a green youth straight out of the monastery – David and Goliath!'

'He'll never live the grudge down either,' warned Arnaud, who had drunk more than Hervi, enough to become a trifle morose. 'He's a known killer.'

'God's life, the lad isn't likely to tangle with him again!'

'No, but we are.'

'Oh, close your mouth on your cup!' Hervi grinned indulgently and tilted the wine flagon towards his friend. 'Last one. We'll need to be sober for the morrow.' He glanced sidelong. 'How are your ribs now, Alex?'

'Sore,' said Alexander ruefully, and rubbed his hand over the tight linen bandaging in which he had been wrapped for support. The pain had been mitigated by John Marshal's presentation to him earlier that evening of a very fine gilded sword belt in token of his gratitude. 'For when you win your spurs,' the knight had said with a smile.

John Marshal, Hervi had discovered by asking around, was the nephew of the great William Marshal, lord of vast estates scattered throughout England, Wales, Ireland and Normandy, and a baron in high favour with the ruling Angevin dynasty. In his youth he had been the greatest jouster ever to level a lance on the tourney field. In his mid forties now, he was still a formidable warrior. That Alexander had brought himself to the attention of a member of the Marshal clan was another reason why Hervi had gone lightly on his younger brother.

'You can stay in camp tomorrow,' he told Alexander. 'There's harness and armour to be cleaned. For all your prowess on the field, I shall feel safer knowing you're nowhere near the conflict.'

Alexander gave a careful shrug. His ribs hurt too much for him to protest, and after today's adventure, he was not averse to spending a day by the fire.

Monday stooped to remove the empty flagon from between the men. The scent of woodsmoke and lavender drifted across Alexander's nostrils. Hervi's eyes narrowed on the girl and then filled with indignation. 'You've put her in a wimple!' he said accusingly to Arnaud. 'And she has such lovely hair!'

'It was time, and past time.' Clemence emerged from the tent where she had been fetching some sewing. 'You are not the only man to notice her hair, Hervi. She is a young woman, not a child any more, and this is a decent household.'

Hervi was startled by the prim note in Clemence's voice. 'Of course it is.' He recovered swiftly. 'I was just taken by surprise . . . and regret, if the truth were known.' He smiled at Monday. 'I remember her when she was a tiny maid no higher than my kneecap. Time passes too quickly.'

'Indeed it does,' Arnoud agreed with a maudlin nod.

Monday tugged at the edge of her wimple. 'It makes my head itch and it's hot,' she complained. 'I hate it.'

'You'll soon grow accustomed,' said Clemence. 'After a few weeks you will feel strange without a head covering.'

'Other girls don't have to wear one.'

'That has no bearing on what is fit for you.' Her mother's tone was sharp with warning.

'Yes, it does, I . . .'

'Monday, enough,' Arnaud interrupted. 'You are embarrassing our guests and shaming yourself. You wear a wimple because we have judged that it is time you did so. I will hear no more on the matter.'

The girl's chin quivered. She compressed her lips and took the empty jug into the tent, leaving an awkward silence in her wake.

With a rueful smile, Hervi rose to his feet, pulling Alexander with him. 'Your own fault,' he commented to lighten the moment. 'Now you have two women on your hands when this morning you had only one.'

Arnaud snorted with reluctant humour. 'She will come round in a while,' he said. 'Always stalks off in a temper, and then returns full of remorse.'

As Hervi and Alexander took their leave, Arnaud followed them to the perimeter of his fire. 'Two women on my hands, and one of them with child,' he announced. 'Before Martinmas I am to be a father again.'

Hervi's eyes widened. 'Small wonder that you fought like a

demon on the tourney field today!' he exclaimed. 'My heartiest congratulations to both of you.' He belted Arnaud between the shoulder blades. 'I will pray that the babe resembles its mother!'

Arnaud forced a smile. 'As long as both are strong and healthy I care not.' He gazed back at his wife with troubled eyes, and added, as if reassuring himself, 'She has Monday to help her, and we are going to seek winter quarters early. It is not as though she has been worn out bearing a child every year. We have tried to be careful.'

Hervi's expression sobered in the face of Arnaud's obvious anxiety. He had no comfort to offer; he knew nothing of childbirth except that it was messy and fraught with danger. Those thoughts would be uppermost in Arnaud's mind too. 'If you need anything, you know where to seek,' he said, and thumped him again, but more gently by way of support.

Hervi and Alexander were halfway across the camp when they encountered a man crawling through the grass in a drunken stupor. He wore the tattered habit of a Benedictine monk and the bald ring of his tonsure was fuzzy with stubble.

Hervi gave a snort of amused disgust and stooped to haul the sodden cleric to his feet. 'Lost your way again, Brother Rousseau? Alex, help me hold him up.'

Grimacing with revulsion, Alexander grasped the man's sleeve. Even to be near a monk made him shudder. The stench of wine and ginevra warred with the pungency of the man's unwashed body. Red-rimmed eyes surveyed him owlishly, then lost their focus. '*Carpe diem, quam minimum credula poster,*' he slurred, then belched. Alexander averted his head and fought the urge to gag.

'Do you know what he said?' Hervi enquired. 'He always speaks Latin when he's in his cups.'

'Enjoy the day, trust little in tomorrow,' Alexander replied in a constricted voice, as he fought not to inhale the priest's foul breath. The man was like one of the cadavers out of his nightmares.

'That sounds like Brother Rousseau's philosophy. Come on, his tent's just over here.'

They half dragged, half carried Brother Rousseau beyond

another ring of firelight occupied by a group of ragged-clad women and children, and brought him to a dilapidated canvas awning, one of its poles surmounted by a crude wooden cross.

Brother Rousseau collapsed from their arms on to his pallet. His eyes rolled in their direction. '*Dominus vobiscum,*' he said, making the sign of the cross with a wavering hand before unconsciousness claimed him.

'Go with God,' Alexander translated.

'I know that one. Come, he'll be all right. It isn't the first time I've seen him to his bed.'

Alexander gazed at the fire nearby. One of the women thrust out her bosom and pursed her lips at him in blatant invitation. Another, a straggle-haired blonde, rose from her place and approached the brothers.

'Hervi,' she purred, rubbing against the discomfited older man like a cat. 'I hear you took some fine ransoms today.' She wrapped her arm around his.

Hervi shook her off. 'Let be, Alys, I'm not here on business.'

She pouted at him. Her eyes slid to Alexander.

'Neither is he. Go and find Osgar if you're short of coin.'

'Oh, Hervi!' she said in an impatient voice. 'You know I prefer you!'

'You do at the moment because I've got silver in my pouch.' Lowering his head, Hervi took Alexander by the arm and set off at a determined pace. Hands on hips, Alys tossed her head and swayed back to the fire.

'I have seen her before,' Alexander said with a frown.

Hervi cleared his throat. 'She was in my tent when I brought you there out of your senses.'

Alexander looked at his brother with interest. 'Do you know her well?'

'Hah, only too well! She's a camp whore, good at her trade, but as fickle as a west wind and given to emptying a man's purse in short order. Don't you go getting any ideas,' he warned sharply.

'I wasn't; I was just curious.'

'Well, keep your curiosity above your belt.'

Alexander thought of several retorts, but was sufficiently prudent not to utter them. Hervi had a powerful right arm. Instead, he asked about the priest they had just helped to his bed.

'Brother Rousseau?' Hervi pinched the end of his nose. 'He's French, a former chaplain to some noble family in the Seine valley. He was thrown out for embezzlement and drunken debauchery, among other things. He acts as our confessor and comforter – when he's sober, which is not very often. Earns his money by baptising and shriving.' They arrived at their own tent and Hervi unlaced the opening. 'He is not a proper priest, but no ordained cleric will touch those who live off the tourneys unless they are very high nobility with the necessary bribe-silver. Any man who dies jousting is considered to have committed suicide and is therefore beyond the Church's grace.'

'I know. More than once at Cranwell the prior condemned such gatherings as this.'

'And I suppose that only made you all the more determined to sample the life for yourself,' Hervi said drily.

Alexander shrugged as he followed his brother into the musty darkness. 'Nothing could ever be more damning than the life I lived at Cranwell,' he replied bleakly, and knew that tonight his dreams would haunt him.

CHAPTER 5

'Again,' Hervi said relentlessly, and beckoned with his forefinger. 'Come at me again.'

The noonday sun sizzled overhead, and the air was motionless, saturated with the heat of late July. Alexander blotted sweat from his brow with his forearm and tightened his grip on the damp leather hilt of the sword. His left arm was encumbered by the weight of a shield, and a quilted gambeson hampered his body. Hervi was similarly attired, the high dome of his brow glistening and his breath rasping in his throat. Dust rose from the grassy Norman meadow on the western edge of Rouen. A three-day tourney was to begin on the morrow, and the competitors were out, honing the skills which Alexander was only just learning.

He tried to remember what he had been told. Don't go for the beckoning bright target of the shield, go for the man behind it, disable him. How to do that when your limbs felt like lead weights had not been explained.

Drawing a deep breath, he launched himself at Hervi, aiming high above the rim of the shield. Hervi ducked out of the way and directed a sweeping backhand slash at Alexander's right knee. The young man leaped over the blow and his sword flickered up inside Hervi's shield edge and touched his torso. Triumphant, Alexander withdrew, a half-smile on his lips. It was quickly wiped away as Hervi's leg shot out, swiping his feet from under him, and Alexander found himself looking along the length of a blade, a steel point in the hollow of his throat.

'Never assume that you have made a kill until your enemy is down,' Hervi panted. 'If that had been a real battle, the force of your strike would have done no more than nick me, probably not even that if I had been wearing mail. One good hit does not constitute a victory.' He removed the sword, leaving a crestfallen Alexander free to rise.

'Still,' he added judiciously, 'you're coming along. A month ago you would have got nowhere near me, and I'd have downed you with that first leg blow.'

'It seems to take forever.' Alexander puffed out his cheeks and remained on the ground for a moment, taking what respite he could.

'You are trying to squash what takes five years to learn into as many months,' Hervi said. 'Indeed, you are making far better progress than I anticipated. Rush your training and it will let you down when you need it the most.' Squinting in the sun's glare, he sheathed his sword. 'Enough for now. It's too hot to be wearing all this padding. This evening, when it's cooler, we'll work on your horseback skills.'

Alexander nodded with relief and rose to his feet. Within seconds he had removed the stewing weight of the gambeson, followed by his tunic. His shirt clung to his body, and perspiration gleamed in the hollow of his throat. 'If you want me, I'll be down by the river with my scribing tools.'

Hervi grinned. 'If you want *me*,' he replied, 'I'll be at Edmund One-eye's with a jug of wine.'

Alexander gave a knowing roll of his eyes and departed to collect his small portable lectern and writing materials from their tent. Then he mounted his horse and rode off in the direction of the river.

In the ten weeks that had passed since Alexander's arrival on the tourney circuit, Samson, as he had been named, had filled out with good grazing and a conditioning of oats and barley. His hide was like a black mirror, and beneath it, his muscles were long and fluid. He was intelligent, strong, but not too large, the perfect kind of animal to train up for the mêlée and individual joust. Even Hervi, who was seldom fulsome with his praise, had nothing critical to say about the stallion.

Alexander's mind turned to the comments meted out just now as he lay defeated in the dust. *Better progress than I anticipated; coming along.* 'But I want it now,' he said aloud, his tone full of frustration. Skill lay an unspecified time away and could only be attained through the sweat of learning and experience.

Samson's ears flickered and he gave a playful buck. Alexander tightened his thighs as Hervi had taught him. He no longer required a saddle to remain mounted these days, could ride at a canter bareback without falling off, and could vault astride without recourse to stirrup or mounting block. Hervi said that the true test of skill was vaulting to the saddle in full armour, and then controlling the horse with the thighs whilst manipulating a shield and lance in the hands.

Alexander had tried on Hervi's mail shirt while cleaning it. The weight had not seemed too bad, although it was mostly carried on the shoulders and upper torso. Once leggings, coif and helm were added, however, Alexander doubted that he would be able to leap into a saddle with any degree of agility. That too, apparently, came with the sweat of practice.

Man and horse approached the sleepy flow of the river. Here, on the edge of the Fôret de Roumare, the waters of the Seine were sluggish, turbid with tench, bream and pike, the blue reflection of the sky woven with green ribbons of water weed. Alexander dismounted, tethered Samson loosely to a low-growing red hawthorn and leaving him to graze, sat down on the river bank with his lectern.

He had made it out of a rescued piece of firewood, had patiently carved and polished it into shape at evening camp fires. Now it was a smooth wedge that rested comfortably in his lap, but could as easily be used at a trestle. The vellum was secured in place by two adjustable brass straps at the edges of the lectern. Hervi, so sure of himself on the tourney field, had watched with eyes full of awe as Alexander assembled the lectern, ground up the ingredients to make ink and commenced writing the first of the many letters with which he was to make his contribution to their daily bread.

The tourney folk quickly learned that Alexander wrote as neat a scribe's hand as was to be found in any castle or town, and that the finished missives, whether they be to impress a prospective lover or a future patron, were professionally executed. He charged a fair price, was willing to negotiate fees and most

important of all, he kept his mouth shut. Not a word of his
clients' business ever passed from his lips to another's, not even
Hervi's. Alexander's reputation grew, and with it the amount of
his custom.

Today's undertaking was a will, requested by a prudent but
pessimistic mercenary who wanted to divide his belongings fairly
between his offspring and yet leave his widow sufficiently provided for. Alexander selected a quill from the soft pouch at his
waist, trimmed it with a small sharp knife and unstoppered his
ink horn.

In the heat of the day, Monday felt as if she was frying. Her head
itched to distraction beneath the hated wimple. It was worse than
having lice. The tent was stifling, the lack of air filling the
enclosed space with a musty, earthy smell that made it difficult to
breathe. How she envied the men who could walk around bare-
chested in the heat, clad in nought but their braies, or the
children who splashed and played in the river shallows, naked as
God created them.

Monday folded the garment that she and her mother had been
stitching that morning – a winter cloak of double-lined grey
wool for Alexander de Montroi, to replace the threadbare blue
one that he still wore about the camp. Strange to think of winter
on a day like this. She envisaged the chill in an attempt to cool
herself, but although a shiver ran up her spine, the heat remained
as relentless as ever.

Her mother was resting on her pallet, her hands folded pro-
tectively over the visible swell of her pregnancy. Monday had still
not decided whether to be pleased or resentful about the coming
baby. More work and responsibility had devolved upon her
shoulders; her childhood had been curtailed, but she was looking
forward to helping care for an infant brother or sister. She found
herself constantly peering at babies and small infants, a maternal
pang stirring in the pit of her belly.

Clemence had enjoyed good health thus far, her complexion
radiant and her hair as lustrous as golden silk. She was in her
sixth month now, not yet so large that she was unwieldy, but
enough to show the world that she was round with child.

Monday had sensed her parents' conflict of embarrassment and pride; and beneath it the worry. The tourney route was a difficult place for a pregnant woman – difficult for any woman come to that, Monday thought with a grimace, and scratched her head through the thick fabric of the wimple.

Her father stooped into the tent, his brown hair curling in wet tendrils on his brow and neck. There was a gleam in his grey eyes and a smile on his lips.

'Is your mother awake, lass?' he demanded, and not waiting for a reply, pushed past her and drew aside the curtain that screened off the sleeping quarters.

Clemence sat up on her pallet, her face flushed, her fair hair a tousled thick braid. 'Arnaud?' She spoke his name, the muzziness of sleep still in her voice.

'Love, beloved, I have it, I have it!' he cried, his face alight as he took her hands in his and raised them to his lips.

'Have what?' Clemence asked.

'Our winter quarters!'

'You do?'

'A place in the retinue of Bertran de Lavoux, a permanent place.' Arnaud grinned from ear to ear. 'As one of his household knights with a daily wage and lodging for yourself and Monday. I'm to be hired as from Lammastide!' He glanced at Monday, sharing the news with her too.

Clemence stared at him, her eyes slowly clearing. 'A permanent place,' she repeated, as if to give the fact more texture.

Monday flung herself upon her father, squeezing her arms around his neck in a ferocious hug. She knew how important this offer was to them. The security of a place in the world, a chance to settle down.

His body shaking with laughter, Arnaud strove to prise her off. 'Give me room to breathe, child!' he declared. 'Else I'll not be fit to take up the position!'

Monday released her stranglehold and hugged herself instead.

'Hervi's to be hired too if he so wishes,' Arnaud added. 'I'll talk to him as soon as I see him.'

'Never mind Hervi, what about this position of yours?' Clemence demanded. 'Who is Bertran of Lavoux?' She was less ecstatic than her husband and daughter. In the past, Arnaud had been known to purchase a pig in a poke.

'Scold,' he said, his eyes dancing, then kissed her on the lips. 'He's a Norman border baron who has recently come into his inheritance. Apparently the former lord died of old age, and the household knights are mostly his contemporaries. Bertran is hiring new blood – experienced knights, but not in their dotage.'

'And he is to pay you a wage?' Clemence repeated, wariness and wonderment competing for a place in her expression.

'Twenty marks a year, plus board and lodging for all of us and my horses. I told him that both of you were skilled sempstresses and that pleased him greatly. We won't want for anything and there will be a secure roof over our heads – a castle roof. I know how much you miss that kind of security.'

Clemence shook her head, utterly bemused. 'It is too good to be true,' she said, and then suddenly she laughed, and her mood changed. Rising to her feet, she pirouetted around the tent, graceful despite her burgeoning body. Enchanted, Monday watched her mother, seeing a side of her that was very rarely exposed. Her father's expression was one of pure adoration, all the harsh lines of his face melted and tender. Monday felt a warm rush of love for both of them.

'Bertran also said that he was looking for a scribe, and I told him I knew of one,' Arnaud continued as he caught his swirling wife in his arms, kissed her and set her down on a stool. 'I'll have a word with Alexander when I see Hervi.'

Her eyes sparkling, Clemence clung to her husband. 'I haven't felt this giddy since the day we eloped!'

Arnaud chuckled, the sound pleasant and deep. 'Neither have I.'

'Can I be the one to tell Alex?' Monday asked. 'I've got to give him his cloak anyway.' She folded the garment over her arm. Her parents would probably relish a moment alone, and besides, the tent was not big enough to contain her own delight. She needed to let the fields and sky absorb the emotion fizzing through her veins, and she was bursting to share her news, as her father had shared his.

'Yes, go.' Her father's eyes never left his wife's.

'Do not take too long,' Clemence added for good measure, but the smile remained on her face.

'No, Mama, I won't.' The cloak draped over her arm, Monday left their tent and walked through the sprawl of the camp. The air was filled with dust, with the smell of singed horn and hot iron from the farrier's booth where the destriers were being shod. The more tantalising aroma of meat and onions from a cook stall flooded her nostrils. Sounds of the tourney life filled her ears, the cries from the stalls, the banter of the knights; the clang of smithy tools on weapon steel, and the duller thud of that weapon steel upon wooden shields. It was a life she would soon be leaving behind, and despite its hardships and uncertainties, she knew that she was going to miss it.

She stopped as an entourage of riders blocked her path – a nobleman and his lady escorted by two squires, two serjeants and a maid. The nobleman was in his middle thirties with a paunch bulging his ruby silk tunic and the porcine features of good living. The woman was a slender vision in a gown of the palest blue-green silk, embroidered all over with tiny golden flowers. Her head was covered with a gauzy veil, held in place by a thin gold-coloured circlet, and her braids hung free beneath it, pale blonde as new butter. She was perched upon a pretty white mare and the harness was of expensive red leather decorated with a row of tinkling little bells.

> And ilka tet of her horse's mane,
> Hung fifty silver bells and nine.

Thus had Alexander entertained them with a ballad about a man who encountered the queen of faeryland on a grassy knoll one day and was held in thrall by her for seven long years.

The company rode on, and Monday followed their progress with wistful eyes. Her work-roughened hands tightened on the cloak, and she vowed to herself that one day she would ride upon a milk-white horse and wear embroidered silk against her perfumed skin.

Enquiries among the booths and stalls sent her down to the river bank in search of Alexander. Women scrubbing their laundry and keeping a watchful eye on their splashing children directed her upstream, and at last she found him, seated in the shade cast by a willow tree. His shirt sleeves were rolled above his elbows, the laces at his throat dangling open as he bent over his lectern. Now and then he paused to consult a wax tablet at his side.

As if sensing her scrutiny, he ceased writing and glanced over his shoulder. Then he smiled. 'Mistress Monday?' he said, in both question and greeting.

'Your new cloak, it's finished.' Seating herself beside him, she put the garment down on the grass. 'I know it's not the time to be thinking of winter,' she added with a rueful glance at the burning blue sky.

He set aside the lectern to examine and admire the cloak. 'When I do need it, I will remember the day on which it was given and it will make a cold day seem warmer,' he said gallantly, and inclined his head like a courtier.

Monday blushed with pleasure. 'We both sewed the seams, but the embroidery is mine.'

'And very fine it is too. Even a great lord would be proud to own such a cloak.'

Her face reddened further at his compliment. She lowered her eyes and plucked at the grass stems around her skirt. 'The cloak wasn't the only reason I came to find you.'

'No?' He stoppered his ink horn to prevent the contents from drying out, and cleaned the tip of his quill on a scrap of linen. Then he leaned back on his elbows and gave her his attention.

She told him about the position her father had been offered and how it extended to him and Hervi too. 'At Lammastide, we are to enter the service of Bertran de Lavoux.'

'Does your father know him?'

'I do not think I have ever heard Papa mention his name. Why do you ask?'

Alexander shrugged. 'Normally patrons recruit men with whom they have ties, either of blood-bond or obligation. After that, they take on recommendation.'

Monday gave him a disapproving scowl. 'Have you not heard the saying "Never look a gift horse in the mouth"?'

'A man who does that is quite likely to find himself holding a nag,' Alexander retorted, then with a sidelong glance said more gently, 'Still, if it is a genuine offer, then it is excellent news. A roof and food throughout the winter, wages too.'

Monday was silent for a moment, deliberating whether to remain with him or take umbrage at the clouds he had put in her sky and stalk away. The former won. It was pleasant by the river in the dappled shade, and she had no desire to return to the stultifying heat of the tent.

'What are you writing?' she asked, to change the subject, and scratched her head.

'Oh, nothing, a will for one of the knights.' He nodded at her action. 'You can take it off if you want. I promise not to tell anyone.'

Monday deliberated. She longed to tear the hated wimple off, to be free of its itching constriction. From a view of common sense and reason, it was stupid that she should have to wear one at all in this heat, but the moral viewpoint was different.

'There is no one to see,' Alexander persuaded with a smile, 'and your face is as pink as a boiled salmon.'

Monday bit her lip, and hesitated, but his words tipped the balance. She didn't want to look like a boiled salmon. Raising her hand, she plucked the detested garment from her head. Her long golden-brown hair tumbled down, unwinding from its plait, damp tendrils framing her brow.

Alexander nodded approval. 'Much better.'

Monday looked at the wimple in her hands, and then stared out over the turbid glimmer of the water. 'On my way to find you, I saw a fine company riding to inspect the tourney field,' she murmured. 'There was a woman who wore a gown of silk so fine that I could almost see through it, and her veil seemed to be made of butterfly wings. And then I gazed down at myself, and felt as rough and drab as a sparrow.'

'You don't look it,' Alexander said gallantly.

She lifted her hair from her neck and puffed out her cheeks. 'My mother was born to great wealth and privilege. Once, the silk gowns, the fine horses were hers, but she gave them up to follow my father. I do not think that I would have done such a thing.'

Alexander eyed her thoughtfully. 'Is that what you want now? The silk gowns, the fine horses?'

'Of course I do,' she said, in a tone that suggested he was foolish even for asking. Her focus grew distant. 'Sometimes at night, when I cannot sleep, I lie and dream of all that might be mine. My clothes are made of the rarest fabrics, and someone else has the toil of putting in all those tiny stitches. Servants fetch and carry the water, launder the linen, cook the food. My skin is perfumed, smooth and soft. I have a lapdog, and I sit on my feather bed eating sugared plums and almond suckets. And when I ride abroad on my Spanish palfrey, people strew flowers in my path and exclaim at my grace and beauty.' Leaning over, she unfastened her shoes and discarded them. Having taken off her wimple, she reasoned that she might as well be hung for a sheep as a lamb.

The sun twinkled invitingly on the water. Monday inched down the bank until she could dip her toes in the river's cool, slow current. When she looked over her shoulder, she saw that Alexander was smiling. 'You think it funny?' she said defensively.

'No, no,' he said quickly. 'Or if I do it is only because I could not imagine the lady of your description dabbling her toes in the water on a hot summer afternoon.'

'That is the whole point,' Monday said fiercely. 'If I was wealthy, I could do as I pleased.' She swished her ankles and splashed the hem of her gown.

'Your wealth would all belong to your father or your husband.'

She tossed her head. 'Not if I was a widow,' she said firmly, refusing to tolerate a worm in the bud. 'My wealth would be mine to do with as I saw fit.'

He made a dubious sound. 'But you'd never smile. Your teeth would be rotten from eating all those sugared plums and almond suckets.'

'Well, what about you?' she said, somewhat impatiently. 'Don't you have dreams?'

'Yes,' Alexander said, 'but some are nightmares.'

She saw him flex his arms, as if against a restraint, and thought of the marks on his wrists, which, even after ten weeks, had not fully faded. 'About the monastery?'

He made a shrugging motion, but did not speak.

'Why didn't you want to become a monk?' It was a question Monday had often wanted to ask, but until now there had not been a suitable opportunity.

He dug a stone out of the grass and threw it into the water with a fierce thrust of his arm. 'My father died when I was eleven years old, and my oldest brother, Reginald, inherited his estate. It was his idea to fit me for the church, and I had no say in the matter since he was my official guardian. We were only half-brothers, and he had no fondness for me. There were twenty years between us.'

'Twenty?' Monday said with surprise, and then realised that there would be fifteen between herself and the infant her mother was carrying.

'My father was a widower with five sons when he went on crusade and brought home a Byzantine wife. I was the result of their union. She died of spotted fever when I was eight years old. Reginald never liked her; he thought her an infidel with strange ways. She was dark and pretty and not much older than him.' Alexander found another stone and hurled it after the first one. 'Reginald promised my father on his deathbed that he would make good provision for me, and so he did – Cranwell Priory. I was to be washed in the blood of the lamb until my fleece was whiter than mountain snow.'

Unconsciously he touched the leather cord around his neck. Monday knew that he wore a cross on it, had even seen it on rare occasions, a beautiful thing of real gold, set with precious stones. But obviously its value to him lay in more than material worth.

He saw her looking and tugged the jewel out of his shirt. 'My mother's,' he said. 'Reginald would have dearly loved to get his grasping hands on it, but my father made him acknowledge my rights before witnesses – Hervi being one of them.'

Monday nodded, although she could not begin to imagine what it must be like. To lose both parents and be put in the charge of a guardian who begrudged your existence and wanted to be rid of you as quickly as possible. 'So you did not settle at the priory?'

The cross sparkled in the sunlight. 'At first it was all right,' he admitted. 'For three years they tried with me and I tried to fit in. Devotion was not in my vocabulary, but I had a roof over my head in exchange for prayers and labour. Then our sub-prior died and a new one came to our community – Brother Alkmund.' His mouth curled around the word with revulsion. 'Everything changed. Within a month of his arrival I ran away, only to be brought back and scourged. He liked scourging, did Alkmund.' He looked at her sidelong. 'That is the stuff of my nightmares, the beating, the humiliation, the need to strike back.'

Monday made a small sound in her throat because she felt that she had to respond, but she knew that she was out of her depth. What did she know of such things? A life on the tourney circuit was difficult and dangerous, but throughout she had been cushioned by the security of parental presence and love.

He looked at her a moment longer, and when she said nothing, he turned his attention to the cross shining over the palm of his hand. 'As to my dream,' he murmured to the gold, 'I want my name to be known throughout England, the Angevin empire and beyond. I want Reginald to know that I can make my way in the world better than he can, and without the advantage of all his inherited privileges.' Then he shook his head and gave a short laugh. When he spoke again, his voice was hard and determined. 'I call it a dream, but it is more than that. It is my goal, my ambition, and every day that I live is a step more towards it.'

Monday swallowed and felt a little daunted. Her own dreams, despite their vividness, could not live up to the bitter determination she heard in his voice.

A shadow fell across the grass. Monday and Alexander turned simultaneously and saw Eudo le Boucher astride his destrier, with another horse on a leading rein. His chest was bare, the sweat trapped and gleaming in the mat of hair across his heavy pectorals. Rust streaked his brow and nose where he had been wearing his helm.

Alexander rapidly ducked the cross back down inside his shirt. Le Boucher's eyes followed the motion, making it quite obvious that he had seen the treasure.

'A little exposed for a tryst,' he mocked as he dismounted in a

pungent aroma of horse and perspiration. There were wet
patches on his inner thighs, and a narrow band of hairy skin
between hose and loin cloth.

Monday's cheeks burned. She withdrew her feet from the
water and grabbed at her wimple.

'Oh, Christ,' le Boucher snorted, 'grant me a little self-
restraint. I have seen women with more than just their braids
exposed. Mind you, I suppose they might have an effect on a callow boy.' He gave Alexander a disparaging look and led his horses
down to the water's edge to dip their muzzles.

'So you were unhorsed by a callow boy?' Alexander said softly.

Monday darted him a frightened look. His tawny eyes were
narrow and his breathing swift. She could see the rapid bump of
his heartbeat against the throat of his shirt. Her own started to
pound.

'That's right,' le Boucher said, without looking round. 'If you
had been a man you would have been dead by now for what you
did. Thank your God, renegade monk, that you are still in tail
clouts with Hervi to clean up your mess.'

Alexander quivered. Monday put a restraining grip on his
sleeve. Beneath her hand, the flesh was as rigid as a lance shaft,
muscle clenched against bone. She shook her head at him, her
eyes pleading.

Alexander swallowed and struggled, his eyes wolf-bright with
fury. He knew what he wanted to do to le Boucher. He also knew
that the consequences would far outweigh the satisfaction of
retaliation. In grim silence he acknowledged Monday's concern
and began gathering up his scribe's effects.

On the river bank, le Boucher pushed down his loincloth, and
with scant regard for decency, took his penis in his hand and uri-
nated into the water.

'Don't let me drive you away,' he grinned over his shoulder.

In the cool of the evening, Alexander couched the jousting lance
beneath his right arm and angled it across Samson's withers. His
left arm was occupied by one of Hervi's shields and he wore a
quilted gambeson over his tunic and hose. Samson snorted and
danced on the spot, as eager to begin as his rider.

Hervi was busy setting up a quintain so that Alexander could practise striking his target. The quintain consisted of a post and rotating crossbar. On the left hand of the crossbar was a sack of sand, on the right a shield. The object of the exercise was for the novice to attack the quintain, strike the shield dead centre, and make his escape before the sandbag swung around and struck him in the spine. It was intended to develop speed, accuracy and coordination. Tonight Hervi had decided upon a variation aimed at improving Alexander's precision. He had locked the crossbar so that it would not rotate, and had suspended a lady's garter from the empty shield hook – a dainty frippery of pale-blue silk embroidered with pink flowers.

'Right,' said Hervi, stepping away from the quintain, 'I want to see you lift that garter on to the point of your lance without checking your speed. Smooth and straight, one thrust.' He raised and lowered his brows, adding a note of innuendo to the command.

'Whose garter is it?'

Hervi shrugged. 'I found it,' he said innocently. 'Don't look at me like that, it is the honest truth.'

Alexander grinned. 'On some woman's leg no doubt,' he retorted, and controlling the reins and shield in his left hand, turned Samson, eased him into a short, bouncing canter, and approached the quintain.

'Steady,' Hervi shouted, 'steady.'

Alexander bit his lip and put all his concentration into the manoeuvre. There were so many things to remember, and he knew that he should not have to consciously think about them at all. The speed of the horse, the angle of the lance, his position in the saddle. The garter fluttered in the evening breeze, insubstantial as a butterfly, and the point of his lance missed the target completely.

'Don't think about yourself, focus on the lance!' Hervi bellowed as Alexander thundered past.

Alexander turned Samson and tried again, with the same result. Hervi pointed to the centre of his own forehead. 'You've got the brains, you've got the ability. Now use your instinct!'

Alexander gritted his teeth. A third attempt ended in failure, and as he turned Samson, tears of frustration glittered in his eyes. He knew himself capable of the feat, could not understand his inability to succeed. Through a sparkling blur, he saw Eudo le Boucher ride past, fully dressed this time and in the company of two other knights. Le Boucher smiled in his direction.

'You're wasting your time, de Montroi!' he shouted across to Hervi. 'Alys can sink a lance better than he does!'

Hervi made a rude finger gesture in reply. Alexander spun Samson and dug in his heels. Fury burned within him, banishing all other emotion. There was no space for doubt, only the motion of the stallion beneath him and the steel tip of the blunted spear. This time he lifted the garter from the hook as cleanly as a hawk striking its prey. The garment slipped down the socket on to the shaft as he brought Samson to a circling halt. Then he threw le Boucher a triumphant glare.

'We shall see,' said le Boucher, and with a mocking salute, rode on.

'One day I am going to throw le Boucher in the dust again, but from the back of a war horse this time,' Alexander vowed, his eyes narrow with passion.

Hervi grunted. 'Let be, Alex. He's a bad enemy to make. You talk of dust – best to let it settle, not dream of stirring it up.' Removing the garter from the lance, he rehung it on the quintain. 'Now, do that again, show me it was not just fortune.'

And Alexander did so, his mouth compressed to contain the heat of imprudent words. Instead, his anger went into his performance, and he lifted the garter from the ring time after time.

CHAPTER 6

The day had started gloriously, but now the hot August afternoon was changing. Monday glanced skywards. The sun had vanished behind a ragged patchwork of cloud, suffused with sulky pinks and darkening purples. She quickened her pace towards the cookshop on her errand to buy a roast fowl and a loaf for their evening meal. The family's iron cauldron and all the cooking utensils had been scoured and wrapped in sacking ready for the morrow's journey to Lavoux.

Edmund One-eye, the cookshop's proprietor, was a corpulent individual whose unprepossessing features were made even uglier by the puckered scar which twisted from upper lip to orbit on the left side of his face and disappeared beneath the leather eye patch. He had been a serjeant-at-arms until the injury had robbed him of employment. These days he prepared and sold food to the comrades beside whom he had once fought.

When Monday arrived at his stall, he was battening down in preparation for the imminent storm. The wind was beginning to snap at the banners on top of the tents and lightning flickered on the horizon.

'Mistress Monday!' His single eye lit up, the corresponding mouth corner curving towards it. 'What can I do for you?'

She told him, handing over the coins that her mother had given her, and an oval earthenware dish. 'We've packed the cauldron,' she added.

'You're for an early start then.'

'Tomorrow dawn.'

Edmund slid one of three cooked birds off an iron skewer. Its skin was charred by the fire, but Monday knew from experience that its flesh would be white and succulent. 'Then I wish you well. Your father deserves the chance to make a settled life.' He transferred the bird to her dish and gave her a bright glance from his single eye. 'Will you miss us, lass, when you're living like a great lady in your castle?'

'Of course I will!' Her tone was indignant.

'Ah, you're young. You'll forget us soon enough.' Edmund handed her a loaf and she put it in the woven bag hanging from her shoulder.

'I won't,' she said stoutly, and thrust her chin at him. 'Not ever.'

'I'll hold you to that.' He stooped to the shelf beneath his counter and produced a round, sticky cinnamon loaf, its surface smothered in nuts, dried fruit and honey. 'Here, give your mother this as a parting gift and tell her to look after herself.'

Monday's eyes widened in delight. She adored cinnamon bread, but it seldom came her way, being too expensive to buy except on feast days.

'For your mother, I said!' Edmund warned, but he was laughing. 'Best get it home to her before temptation or the rain do their worst!' He pointed at the purple-black sky.

Monday thanked him with a kiss on his scarred cheek, and hurried away. Mingled with her pleasure was a sting of tears. Whatever her new life held, she would indeed miss the kindness and humour of people like Edmund One-eye.

The wind gathered strength, bowling swirls of dust along the paths between the tents. It tugged at her gown and threatened to snatch the hated wimple from her head, and because she needed two hands for the dish, she could not hold the headscarf firm. Lightning blinked across the sky and the thunder cracked close. The first drops of rain thumped down as if scattered from an enormous hand. As Monday ran for cover, her wimple blew off and danced in the dust with a wanton life of its own. She swore roundly, then with a spurt of angry triumph, left it to blow where it would.

She reached their tent just as the heavens opened in earnest. Darting within, she set the purchases to one side and laced up the flap with nimble fingers to protect the interior from the deluge.

'Edmund One-eye sent you a cinnamon loaf and his best wishes, Mama,' she announced over her shoulder.

Clemence was sitting on her pallet, taking a desultory inventory of her sewing equipment. She neither acknowledged Monday's remark nor seemed to notice her lack of wimple. There was a tiny frown between her brows. 'I hate thunderstorms,' she said querulously.

Monday felt a twinge of apprehension. She knew of her mother's aversion to thunder and lightning, but Clemence had been in such high spirits recently that Monday was surprised to see her so affected. 'Papa says that the land needs the rain.'

'I hate the noise. It rolls round in my head until I cannot think.' Clemence wrapped up her leather sewing pouch and stowed it in a small coffer. Her fingers were trembling and there was a sticky sheen of sweat upon her delicate features, as if she had been painted with baker's glaze.

'Are you not well, shall I make you a tisane?' Monday said anxiously.

Clemence swallowed and nodded. 'The child has been restless today,' she said, and set her hands upon either side of her swollen belly. 'But now it is quiet. I have felt nothing for the last candle notch. Ah, Jesu, but my back aches.' She lay down on the bed and stared at the canvas tent roof. It bowed and billowed in the storm wind, and the sound of rain hitting its surface filled the spaces between the rumble and growl of the thunder.

Monday took her cloak, threw it around her head and shoulders and unlaced the flaps again to duck outside and borrow a jug of hot water from a neighbour's cauldron. When she returned, Clemence had fallen into a restless doze. Monday cast off the drenched cloak and set about making a tisane from dried elderberry and chamomile leaves. She wished her father were here, but he was saying his farewells around the camp. Men would ply him with drink as well as goodwill and she knew that he would be useful for nothing when he returned.

Gently she woke her mother and together they sipped the hot, fragrant brew. Monday begged a morsel of the cinnamon bread, her young stomach impatient with hunger and anticipation. Clemence gestured her assent, then lowered her hand to rub at her belly, the frown deepening between her eyes. When her daughter offered her a piece of the loaf, she declined.

Monday cut a generous wedge from the end with her eating knife, and with slow ritual took the first, heavenly bite. The sweet taste of honey and spice was utterly glorious, and she closed her eyes to savour the moment.

Beside her, Clemence uttered a small, clenched cry of pain, and the hand upon her belly gripped and tightened.

'Mama?' Monday's eyes flew open. 'Mama, what's the matter? Is it the baby?' The longed-for treat was hastily swallowed.

'I . . . I don't know,' Clemence gasped. 'It doesn't feel like the last time, and it is too soon by more than a month.'

'Perhaps it is something you ate.'

Clemence shook her head. 'This morning . . . when I changed my linens, there were spots of blood. My loins feel heavy now, as if I am about to burst asunder.'

'What shall I do?'

The terrified note in her daughter's voice drew Clemence back from the brink of her own terror. She tried to think beyond the heaviness in her mind, the ache in her womb, dull and sharp by turns. 'Fetch Dame Aude, the midwife,' she said, 'and then find your father before his cronies render him drunk on their goodwill.'

'But I cannot leave you here alone!'

'There is nothing you can do. I need a woman skilled in midwifery to tell me what is wrong. Go!'

Feeling sick when a moment ago she had been starving, Monday grabbed her cloak again, and with a last, anxious glance over her shoulder at her mother, hastened out into the downpour.

Alexander took the short-handled axe into his lap, dipped his rag in the bowl of oil at his side and proceeded to slick the iron blade all over. It was not a task that he particularly enjoyed, but it had to be done, especially in damp weather.

Outside, dusk had fallen and the thunderstorm had rumbled away in the direction of Evreux. The rain persisted, steady and solid, soaking into the thirsty ground. The morrow's journey to Lavoux seemed set to be a wet one. If they started out at all, he thought as he smoothed the oil over the hardened blue cutting edge of the steel. Clemence de Cerizay had been taken sick a few hours ago and the midwife had been sent for. So much Hervi had told him before going to lend Arnaud his company and support.

The lady Clemence was at least a month before her time. Alexander knew that children born early were capable of surviving – he had been one such himself, according to Hervi – but the odds were never in the infant's favour, And whatever happened, Clemence would be unfit to face a hard day's travelling. He and Hervi would have to decide whether to remain with the de Cerizays, or press on to Lavoux without them.

Alexander finished oiling the axe and wrapped it in a strip of waxed linen. Then he set it beside the rest of the weapons, ready for loading on one of the pack ponies come the dawn. Now that he had a moment to himself, he brought out his waxed tablet and a stylus, and sat down to continue composing the song that had been running round in his head all day.

> The summer is high, the woods are green,
> The skylark takes my heart on her wings,
> And I am free above the meadow bright . . .

He shook his head and crossed out the second line, aware that he was aping the words of other troubadours rather than exploring his own voice. *The skylark flies where my heart cannot reach?* He considered the idea doubtfully, and chewed the end of the stylus. He had no trouble writing scurrilous rhymes and ditties for the camp fire. *My lady's garter caresses my lance* was a communal favourite, but exposing gentleness was harder because it was more open to ridicule.

Why have a skylark at all? *I am a sparrow who wouldst be a hawk?*

Hervi burst in upon his ruminations, his blond hair plastered to his skull and water darkening the shoulders of his cloak. A bundle of fabric was tucked beneath his arm. 'Do you know how to shrive the dying?' he demanded peremptorily.

Alexander stared at him with wide eyes. 'What do you mean?'

'Christ, it's a simple question; do you or don't you?'

'I . . . well, yes, I know the Latin, but I'm not ordained.'

'You're all there is, so you'll have to do. Come on, get up.' Hervi seized Alexander's arm and dragged him to his feet. 'Here, put this on.' He shook out the bundle and presented his brother with a somewhat stained and tatty Benedictine habit. 'It's foul, I know, but it was the best I could do.'

'Have you run mad?' Alexander demanded, a blaze of anger and revulsion in his eyes. 'If there is shriving to be done, then fetch Brother Rousseau.'

'I tried,' Hervi snapped, his own eyes full of fire. 'But the toss-pot was stone drunk on his pallet and I couldn't rouse him. So I took his spare habit and brought it to you because beggars cannot be choosers. You're clean, you're sober, you've got a conscience and you're damned well half trained for the Church. Clemence de Cerizay is *in extremis*, otherwise I would not ask you.'

The fury left Alexander's eyes. 'Lady Clemence?' he said, and wondered why he had not realised it immediately. Perhaps because he didn't want to. He swallowed and groped for the dirty robe. 'What is wrong with her?'

'How should I know, it is a woman's thing,' Hervi said irritably, his face puckered in lines of worry. 'Something to do with bleeding from her womb and the child lying in a difficult position. She desires a priest. I said I would find one.'

The robe stank of wine and sour sweat. Alexander tugged it on over his own clothes and struggled not to retch. It was not just the stench of the habit that filled him with nausea, but the thought of what it represented and the burden being laid across his own shoulders. At his core there was a cold sensation of pure dread. He fumbled down inside his shirt, withdrew the gold and amethyst cross, and laid it openly on his breast. It winked dully in the light, looking totally incongruous against its shabby backcloth. But at least it made him feel more like a priest. He picked up the small flask of weapon oil, checked the stopper, and with an expression full of misgiving crouched out of the tent into the rainswept night.

The de Cerizay tent was pitched about fifty yards away on a slight rise. Despite Hervi and Arnaud's partnership on the tourney field, the two men preferred to keep their homes apart. It was less awkward, since one man was committed to a wife and family and the other was still sowing wild oats. Alexander squelched through the mud and paused outside the family's dwelling. A horn candle-lantern flickered, illuminating the laces on the flaps. Inside he could hear an anxious female voice and a man's broken murmur.

He thought about running away, and his muscles tightened, preparing him for flight. At his back, Hervi gave him a push. 'Go on,' he hissed.

Alexander closed his eyes, swallowed, and plucking open the tent laces, stepped inside. Arnaud de Cerizay was sitting on a camp stool, his head in his hands, and Monday was clinging to him and murmuring words of comfort. From the makeshift hangings beyond there issued a drawn-out moan, followed by a bitten-off cry. He saw Monday's fingers tighten against her father's shoulder. 'She will be all right, Papa, I know she will,' she murmured over and over again, as if trying to convince herself, and laid her cheek against the top of his head.

In response to the draught from the unlaced flaps she glanced round, and saw Alexander. Her body began to quiver.

'Hervi said . . . Hervi said that Lady Clemence had need of a priest,' he stumbled out.

'No, she doesn't . . . except to baptise the baby when it's born.' There was a note of panic in Monday's voice.

Her father slowly raised his head from his cupped hands, and looked at Alexander with dull eyes. The lines on his face were as deep as ravines. 'What are you doing here, son? Where's Father Rousseau?' His words were slurred, and there was a jug of mead close to his right boot.

'Hervi couldn't rouse him, so he fetched me instead. I know . . . I know the rituals.'

Arnaud gave him a long stare, then his eyes wavered out of focus and he flopped his hand towards the hangings. 'Go in,' he said. 'It is what she wants.'

'Yes, sir.' Steeling himself, Alexander went to the hanging and drew it tentatively aside. The midwife drew breath to challenge him, saw the robe he wore and the cross glinting on his breast, and instead beckoned him forward. There was blood on her apron and her hands were shiny with oil.

'See, Mistress Clemence,' she said. 'The priest is here.'

The woman on the pallet opened her eyes. 'It is too dark,' she whispered. 'I cannot see him.'

Alexander squeezed past the midwife and her assistant and knelt down at Clemence's side. The candle-lantern cast a false golden glow over her features. Her fair hair was dark with sweat and her fingers gripped the coverlet in spasm as she fought not to cry out.

'I am here,' Alexander said. He felt inadequate and frightened, but knew that he must not show it. He might not be ordained, but as far as this moment was concerned, he was God's representative.

Clemence seemed not to recognise him. The cords in her throat were taut with pain, with the struggle to remain lucid in the face of her mortality.

'I have much to confess,' she said weakly, 'and very little time.'

Alexander gestured to the midwives, and the two women made themselves scarce.

'Save your strength,' he said to Clemence, knowing that he had no right to be party to her confession. He was no more a priest than the people waiting outside the curtain. And yet, in all mercy, he could not withdraw. Her suffering blue eyes fastened upon the cross at his breast, demanding salvation. 'There is no need to make a full confession. God sees and knows all.' His voice choked on the words. 'Do you repent of your sins?'

She almost smiled, but her pain and need were too great. 'Not all of them,' she said.

'Do you have any mortal ones on your conscience?'

'No.'

Alexander removed the cross from around his neck and gave it to her to kiss and then hold in her hand. He removed the rag stopper from the flask of weapon oil, and anointing his finger, made the sign of the cross upon her clammy brow, and murmured the appropriate Latin words.

Clemence gave a sigh of relief. Her fingers tightened around the jewel as another spasm racked her body.

'Shall I summon the midwives again?' he asked.

She looked at him, and suddenly her eyes focused beyond the habit and absorbed his features. 'Alexander,' she whispered.

'Father Rousseau was . . . was not able to come.'

'It makes no matter,' she said. 'At least you are sober, and you know the words.' Clemence swallowed, her lower eyelids glittering with tears. 'I thought it was too good to be true, the promise of a second chance.' She bit down on her lower lip, fighting pain, the tendons taut in her throat. 'The child is lying across my womb with the afterbirth beneath him. There is nothing more that the midwives can do. Summon my husband and my daughter. I have so little time left . . .'

In the darkness before the hour of dawn, the rain ceased to fall and there was silence. In the glow of the candle-lantern, Monday knelt at her mother's bedside and stared numbly at the body which she and the midwives had washed and composed. The women had gone now, back to their own beds to snatch what sleep they could before the camp came to life. Monday was alone, and never more aware of it than now. Her father was sprawled on the floor outside the bedchamber in a stupor of drink and grief. Hervi was supposed to be watching over him, but Hervi too was snoring like a bear.

Even now, when she had been so intimately touching the body, she could not believe that her mother was dead. Only a few hours ago they had been packing their belongings in preparation for their new life. There had been no indication that it was to be Clemence's last day on earth. The midwives said that it happened sometimes; a bloody flux from the womb would carry off the mother-to-be in the month before she was due to give birth. They were compassionate but casual, for death was something they witnessed frequently in their trade.

Monday touched her mother's lifeless hand. It was smaller than her own, with tiny, almost child-like fingers. Fine bones and translucent skin in cruel contrast to the gross mound of her belly, still filled with the baby that had killed her. The midwives had said there was no point in attempting Caesar's cut, for the child in such circumstances was always dead. Tears brimmed in

Monday's eyes, as much of rage as of grief.

The hanging lifted and Alexander slipped quietly into the makeshift bedchamber. He had made himself scarce while the women stripped and washed the body. Now he crouched at Monday's side, his tawny eyes smudged with weariness. His breath in the enclosed space was clean of drink fumes, and he no longer wore the Benedictine robe, but was clothed in shirt, chausses and a green linen tunic that Clemence had made for him in the spring.

Monday swallowed the lump in her throat, and reaching to the top of the travelling chest beside the pallet, picked up the gold and amethyst cross. 'Yesterday morn we broke fast together and we talked about sleeping beneath a solid roof,' she murmured desolately as she returned the jewel to him. 'She was laughing and full of hope.'

Alexander hung the cord around his neck and tucked the cross down inside his shirt. Then he reached out, and taking Monday's hand from where it lay upon her mother's, squeezed it in his warm, living one.

'Why couldn't she have had what she wanted? Why did she have to be taken? Is God so jealous?' Her eyes flashed upon him, demanding an answer.

He shook his head, not having one. He wanted to say that he was not a priest, but after what had befallen earlier, that would have been cruel. Nothing would ease her pain just now. And so he just sat with her while the night passed away into dawn and the first liquid notes of the morning chorus broke over the tourney camp and ushered in a new day.

Dry-eyed, Monday removed her hand from Alexander's. 'This life kills and maims all who live it,' she said bitterly, and her expression hardened into one of grim determination. 'But it's not going to kill me.'

Bertran de Lavoux was florid and corpulent, with thinning sandy hair and a pointed chin-end beard. His lands, recently inherited from an elderly uncle who had died without issue, lay on the river Epte, midway between Gournai and Gisors, and Bertran, with the hunger of a man long denied, was set upon expanding his boundaries. His overlord, Richard Coeur de Lion, was a captive at the German court, awaiting a ransom payment that might never arrive. Bertran had taken this heaven-sent opportunity to change his allegiance and pay homage instead to King Philip of France. This gave him the sanction and opportunity to make war on his neighbour, Hamon de Rougon, whose fertile estates and water mills Bertran coveted. Thus the need for soldiers – men of his own choosing, men in their prime who were as hungry for reward as he was for land.

'We are stirring up trouble for ourselves,' Alexander said, and removed his hands from the bridle to chaff them with his breath. A raw January dusk was settling around the raiding party. Dull light glimmered on chainmail and helmets, on harness and spear tips. The protesting bellow of driven cattle filled the air, joining the moist steam of their breath. There were twenty cows, most of them heavy with calf, and a magnificent white bull with a heavy dewlap and short, stocky legs. Earlier that day the animals had belonged to Hamon de Rougon; now they were the property of Lavoux.

Hervi gave him a sharp glance. 'I didn't notice you having any qualms earlier.'

Alexander flexed his frozen fingers and replaced them on the reins. 'I was caught up in the heat of the moment,' he said uncomfortably. He could still feel the exhilaration of the raid fizzing in his veins – the sensation of danger creeping deliciously along his spine and tightening his scrotum. Crossing a forbidden boundary, outwitting the de Rougon patrols and stealing this prize herd from under their noses. It had been pure adventure until he had stopped to think upon the implications of robbing from a former crusader – one of Richard Coeur de Lion's battle commanders in the Holy Land. What had seemed brave now appeared foolhardy and tainted with dishonour.

Hervi glowered at him. 'That is no excuse. You're like a man who sleeps with a whore, and as soon as his urgency is satisfied, he despises her.'

Alexander's face burned at his brother's more than accurate sally. 'Well, do you think we should be doing this?'

'I do as lord Bertran commands. That way I receive my wages and keep a roof over my head. If you don't have the stomach to digest what you eat, then stick to your scribing.' Hervi's voice developed a snarl, and he kicked his horse on ahead, making it clear that the conversation was at an end.

Alexander was left to ride with Arnaud de Cerizay. The other man wore a blank expression beneath his open-face helm. Since his wife's traumatic death five months ago, he seemed not to care if he lived or died. Dull-eyed, grim-featured, he went through the motions of living without being alive. If food was set before him, he ate it; when spoken to, he replied, but it was an instinctive response to stimulus. If left to his own devices, he would drink away most of his wages, and no one could reach him. Not Hervi, not even his own daughter, although they shared a common grief.

'What will happen when Richard Coeur de Lion is released?' Alexander asked his taciturn companion. 'They cannot keep him a prisoner for ever.'

The mailed shoulders twitched as if at some minor irritation. 'I suppose that he will try and bring all his rebellious vassals to heel,' Arnaud said indifferently.

'Surely Lord Bertran is taking a great risk by swearing his allegiance to the King of France?'

'Perhaps.' Arnaud turned, revealing to Alexander an unshaven

jaw, the bones sharp beneath the flesh. 'But no greater than holding loyal to an overlord who may well have had his day. He is not
the only baron to turn away from Richard. Hervi is right. Bertran
de Lavoux pays our wages. It is best not to question.' And he too
drew his horse away, leaving Alexander frustrated and edgy.

When they arrived at Lavoux with their prize, Lord Bertran
announced with triumph that he would slaughter one of the
cattle and hold a victory feast that night. The declaration was
greeted with cheers by the soldiers milling in the great hall, their
tension still strung high with battle nerves.

'A song, Alexander, I want a song to celebrate!' Bertran
crowed, slapping the young man on his back as he tried to make
his unobtrusive way out of the press. 'Something to honour our
daring and valour!'

Alexander clenched his fists. 'Yes, my lord,' he said woodenly.
From the corner of his eye, he caught Hervi's warning glare.
The lord of Lavoux delved in his pouch and presented
Alexander with three silver coins.

'Earn them well, lad,' he said, dismissing him with another
hefty slap.

Alexander headed for the door to the forebuilding, brushing
past Hervi as he did so. 'A man who sleeps with a whore, eh?' he
said viciously.

Hervi winced. 'It's only a song.'

Alexander gave him a narrow look. 'You're right,' he said. 'It's
only a song.'

Hervi rolled his eyes heavenwards. Alexander strode from the
hall, his blood simmering with guilt and resentment. He was
tempted to hurl the silver down the nearest well, but the need to
have coin between himself and poverty kept his fist clenched at
his side. He trod across the bailey, past the gleam of the penned
white cattle, and gave them a swift glance. What made him feel
smirched and ashamed was knowing that Bertran de Lavoux had
given his loyalty to the King of France in order to have an excuse
for making war on his neighbour, who was holding firm for
Richard. Greed was the key. In the five months since arriving at
Lavoux, Alexander had discovered that Bertran was affable, generous and totally unprincipled, his word not worth the stale air

expended in giving it. Alexander did not want to serve such a man, but was constrained to do so by his own loyalty to Hervi.

He was so immersed in his fulmination that he did not see Monday until she touched his arm. He jumped, then apologised with a distracted air.

She smiled, but the expression did not reach her eyes, which were worried. 'Have you seen my father? Is he safe?'

'He was in the hall not long since.' Alexander gestured over his shoulder. 'And we all came home unscathed.' His mouth tightened.

Monday sighed. 'I worry about him. It is as though he has fallen into a deep pit from which no one can reach him. Every time he rides out, I fear he will do something foolish, that he will not come back.'

The pain in her voice jolted Alexander out of his self-centred irritation. 'It is not long since your mother's death,' he said awkwardly. 'The winter season always darkens the soul. Perhaps in the spring . . .'

She cut across his words brusquely. 'I lost her too, he doesn't seem to understand that.'

'I am sure he does . . .'

'He knows nothing but his own pain. Sometimes I think he even forgets that I exist.' She swallowed and forced her chin up. 'I did not stop you to complain,' she said, a quaver in her voice. 'Lady Aline asks that you attend her in her chamber. She desires you to write a letter to her sister.'

'I'll come as soon as I've tended the horses.' He squeezed her arm, trying to impart comfort.

She nodded and forced a smile, returned his squeeze, and hurried away across the bailey.

Watching the retreat of her slender form, he was filled with pity and made a resolution to find more time to seek her out and talk. Then he went on his own way, his mind occupied with the problem of a song he had no enthusiasm to compose.

Monday found her father in the crowded guard room with Hervi, a flagon of wine between them, and also a flask of ginevra. Her heart sank, for she could see that her father was drinking with the cold efficiency of a man determined to find oblivion in the bottom of his cup. Hervi, at least, was not matching him measure for measure, but neither was he doing anything to prevent his companion from sinking into a drunken stupor.

'Papa?' Monday sat down beside her father on the bench. She kissed his cheek and felt the scratch of unshaven stubble against her lips. His face was sunken and gaunt, broken veins spidering the skin.

He set his empty cup down on the trestle with deliberation and looked at his daughter. His gaze was steady, but already his focus was clouded. 'You should not be here in a room full of rough men,' he said.

'I came to see you, to make sure you are all right.'

A wintery smile creased his cheeks but failed to reach his eyes. 'Yes, I'm all right,' he said gruffly, and clasped her hand, his grip cold and dry. 'We weren't challenged even once, were we, Hervi?'

'Except by that bull,' Hervi said, with a cheerful shake of his head. 'Acelin fisted it between the eyes and it behaved after that.' He gave Monday a wink, and then launched himself in pursuit of a basket of hot bread that a servant was bringing through the door.

Monday watched her father reach for the flagon and tip more wine into his cup. 'I don't like it when you drink,' she said in a small, forlorn voice.

He shrugged and tilted the rim to his lips. 'I will do as I choose. It brings me ease.' Almost in defiance, he swallowed deeply, draining the contents.

'Papa, don't!' Monday beseeched, a lump of panic and misery swelling in her throat. 'You will ruin yourself!'

'Christ, do you think I care?' he snarled. 'I was ruined the day that I first set eyes on your mother. The devil's eel-trap. Once you've entered, you can never escape, and if you try, your soul is ripped out on the spines!' He reached a shaking hand towards the flagon, his face flushed with the bitter fury imbued by the wine.

Monday snatched the flagon from his hand and dashed it to the floor. The glazed pottery smashed into a dozen shards and the wine drenched the hem of her gown and splattered her father's boots and chausses. Heads turned. A momentary silence descended.

'The only mercy is that my mother cannot hear you!' Monday sobbed at him, and turning on her heel, stumbled from the crowded guard room, pushing past an astonished Hervi, his mouth full of hot bread. Behind her a babble of voices rose like froth in a brewer's vat. Arnaud de Cerizay put his head in his hands, and then, with a fluent curse, grabbed the flask of ginevra and upended its contents down his throat until he choked.

Weeping, Monday fled, and did not stop even when she heard Hervi bellowing after her to come back. Even if it had been her father, she would not have turned around, for the wound he had inflicted was too deep. He was killing himself before her eyes, and worse than that, he was killing her love for him too.

Monday sat at a trestle bench in the bower, a mound of sewing in front of her. A thick white candle burned on an iron pricket, shedding light on the fabric as she selected a needle from her wooden case. Now and then she gave a little sniff, and reached in her sleeve for a square of linen to dab at her eyes. She had done with crying she told herself, but it made no difference. She could not put her troubles from her mind, and at each surge of thought, a new film of moisture would blur her vision, making needle-work impossible.

In a rustle of silk and a waft of spicy perfume, Bertran's young wife Aline sat down beside her on the trestle. 'Something has upset you,' she said gently.

'It is nothing, my lady.' Monday compressed her lips and strove without success to thread her needle.

'Ah, nothing you want to talk about.' Aline took Monday's needle case and selected one for herself.

Monday shook her head. She could not imagine the lady of Lavoux being interested in her woes. Aline had masses of silky flaxen hair and eyes of moss-agate green, given emphasis by the subtle use of cosmetics. She was four and twenty, and Bertran was her second husband, her first having died on crusade. She was elegant, sophisticated and alluring. Monday admired her and felt dull and inadequate by comparison.

Aline deftly poked a length of green thread through the eye of her own needle. Monday looked at her companion's hands. She wore two rings, a simple one of twisted gold on her left, and a heavy, ruby-set signet ring on the middle finger of her right.

'It belonged to my first husband,' she said as she noticed Monday's scrutiny and spread her fingers to display the heavier jewel. 'He went on crusade with Duke Richard and succumbed to the bloody flux. He was too old to go on such a venture, the fool.'

There was a brief silence, but Monday's curiosity won out over her reserve. 'How old was he?' she asked as she finally managed to thread her needle.

'Nigh on fifty years, with more scars than an old bear,' Aline said neutrally. 'He stank like one too. Soldiering had been the main part of his life. He only took a wife because he decided it was time he begot an heir for his lands. I was fifteen years old when I married him, a terrified virgin.' She glanced up at Monday. 'I never quickened. For all he wanted to breed an heir, his manly equipment was not up to the deed. And then he left me to take the Cross. I was almost a virgin when Bertran contracted to wed me, and very little has changed!' she added with a bitter, rueful laugh and a shake of her head. She laid a smooth white hand on Monday's sleeve. 'A word of advice. When the time comes, you make sure you choose your own mate. Don't let your family have any say whatsoever.'

Monday was surprised, even a little bemused by the revelations. But Aline's openness encouraged her to speak. 'My own mother fled from an arranged marriage,' she murmured. 'She was the daughter of a powerful English baron, contracted to wed with a man full thirty years older than herself. But before the nuptials could be arranged, she eloped with my father, a household knight.'

Aline's carefully plucked brows arched towards her wimple. 'Truly . . . you are not spinning me some troubadour's tale?'

'Truly.' Monday stabbed the needle into the fabric as if she were plunging a dagger into flesh. 'And now my mother is dead, and my father is killing himself with bitterness and grief.' Those were not the words she had intended to say, but they emerged of their own accord like blood from an open wound. Her chin trembled, and the tears that she had been fighting threatened to overwhelm her. It became impossible to sew, and she had to put her needle down and reach for the kerchief in her sleeve.

Aline set aside her own sewing and curved a consoling arm around Monday's shoulders. 'How long ago did she die?'

'At Lammastide, in childbirth, on the eve of coming to Lavoux. It was all too late, all for nothing.' And the tears poured out in a scalding flood while Aline soothed and rocked her. The smell of attar of roses filled Monday's nostrils, heavy and sweet, so unlike the woodsmoke pungence of her mother's embrace, but comforting nevertheless because no one had held her thus for a long, long time.

At last she was able to sit up and dry her eyes. They felt heavy and hot, and she was still shaken by small, convulsive tremors.

Aline fetched her a cup of sweet spiced wine and made her take several swallows. 'I never knew my own mother,' she said softly. 'She died whilst I was still in the cradle. I was reared by an assortment of nurses and attendants until my father sold me in marriage to my first husband, and then again to Bertran. I am sorry for your grief, I would ease it if I could.'

'You are very kind, my lady.' Monday sniffed and wiped her nose. She continued to sip the aromatic wine and felt it warm its way to her belly and then into her veins.

Aline resumed her sewing. 'I do not know about that,' she said. 'If I am, it is because I feel sympathy for you, and it costs me nothing.'

Monday gave her a startled look, and Aline smiled wryly. 'God helps those who help themselves,' she said, 'and most of the time it is men who help themselves to whatever they desire, women included. So, I play them at their own game.' She tilted her head to examine her line of stitches. Then she looked from the sewing to Monday, her green eyes shrewd and hard. 'They see an attractive young woman, sweet and pliant of nature. Flirtatious but never beyond propriety, a gracious hostess who will hang on their every word, treat them like kings. But it is only what I want them to see, and not necessarily the truth. Do you understand?'

'I . . .' Monday frowned. 'You let them believe that they are having their own way, when all the time you are having yours.'

'Not all the time.' Aline raised a lecturing forefinger. 'You have to let them win on occasion, on the small things that do not matter. And sometimes a man will set his will in a particular direction and nothing you do or say will change him. You have to acknowledge that too and live around it if you can.'

'But what about honesty?' Monday asked, feeling decidedly out of her depth. To lie was to be lied to in return.

Aline gave a snort of amusement. 'Find me an honest, steadfast man who has any brains above his belt, and I will deal as honourably with him as he deals with me.' She waggled her index finger at Monday. 'I might as well ask you to find me a needle in a haystack.' Then her eyes softened. 'Well, no, that's not entirely true,' she murmured. 'There is one that I know, but he only goes to prove the rule.'

There was a brisk tap on the door, and one of Aline's other women opened it to admit Alexander, his lectern tucked beneath his arm and his pouch of writing tools suspended from his shoulder.

'Ah,' said Aline, 'my scribe,' and beckoned to him with a radiant smile. 'Come and be seated.'

Monday noticed that Alexander had taken time to have a wash and rake a comb through his black curls. The soldier's gambeson had been replaced by his best tunic of dark-green wool, and around his waist was the gilded belt which John Marshal had presented to him. His colour was high, the caramel eyes luminous and eager. Like a moth to a candle flame he advanced to the trestle and bowed over the smooth white hand Aline extended to him. Monday concealed her own rough ones beneath a swathe of material, and watched Aline with a mixture of resentment and admiration as she put her earlier words of wisdom into practice. Her flirting was gentle, nothing overt. Her voice took on a melting pitch as she admired the dexterity with which he mixed his ink and trimmed his quill.

Alexander cleared his throat and murmured a disclaimer, but his pleasure was obvious. Aline glanced at Monday to see if she was absorbing the lesson, then asked a question about how the vellum for the document was made. Flattered, Alexander explained, and Aline gave him her undivided attention, nodding seriously in the right places, her arms folded on the trestle and her head tilted towards his.

Monday wanted to kick Alexander, but she refrained. What good would it do? It was being proved to her that a man was easily manipulated if a woman had the skills, that a woman need not be defenceless in a hard, masculine world.

She lowered her eyes to her sewing and held her peace. But her mind was busy assimilating the new knowledge. Observing Aline and her effect upon Alexander, Monday realised that the arts she practised were not only a defence, they were also a deadly weapon.

But what about honesty?

> Tonight I drink of triumph's wine
> For Rougon's cattle are now mine,
> And soon he will have cause to weep
> For I will take his very keep.

Enthusiastic applause greeted the final verse of Alexander's song describing the raid on Rougon's cattle. War-scarred fists hammered the trestles and shouts of approbation rang around the hall. Alexander acknowledged the praise with a flourish which made them all laugh. He wondered what they would do if they knew he was being sarcastic and that the words he had truly wanted to sing were burning on the tip of his tongue. *The Ballad of Honourless Bertran.*

The lord of Lavoux presented him with an enamelled goblet in token of his delight in the composition. Alexander accepted the gift with a fixed smile and a dangerous glitter in his eyes. He sat down in his place and ran his fingers lightly over the strings of his small Celtic harp, drawing a shiver of notes. That at least was honestly bought with the coin from his scribing. A pity that he was using it to glorify the name of a man for whom he had little respect.

'See,' said Hervi, 'that wasn't so difficult.' He took the cup to examine it and whistled softly. 'Silver-gilt by the looks – worth something, this. You'll soon be able to afford a sword to go with that fancy belt of yours.'

'It's probably stolen too.'

'Ah, Christ, you really should have been a priest!' Hervi said in utter disgust, and gave him a push. 'Go on, they want you to sing again.'

Alexander fought his revulsion. He knew that even if his life depended on it, he would be unable to render them the ballad of the ignominious cattle raid. He racked his brain and came up with an old favourite by Bernard de Ventadour about the glories of warfare. The diversion worked well, the song was accepted with alacrity, but when it was over, there was a unanimous demand for him to perform the new song of praise again.

Prevaricating, Alexander looked around, caught the eye of the lady Aline, seated demurely beside her lord, and cleared his throat. 'I thought I would sing for the ladies first,' he said. 'It is not often they are entertained by gentler music.'

Bertran scowled. 'They can have all the gentle music they want in the bower,' he said curtly. 'This is not the occasion for sentimental drivel.'

Alexander's complexion became dusky. Aline leaned against her husband and whispered in his ear, her hand sliding along his sleeve until her fingers touched the back of his hand. Bertran narrowed his eyes but did not pull away. As she continued to murmur, he laughed and relaxed in his chair.

'Very well, a song for the pleasure of the ladies, if you must,' he said with a wave of his hand. 'But make haste about it.'

Aline smiled at Bertran as if she thought he was wonderful, and pressed her slim shoulder against his bulk. Then she turned her melting, feline eyes upon Alexander.

His colour still high, Alexander bowed to Aline and plucked the first bittersweet notes from the harp.

> When the spray begins to spring
> Where larks sing
> From a height where they cast no shadow
> My heart bursts into song.

Aline listened, her gaze upon him while she leaned against her husband and continued to stroke his hand. Alexander glanced away for a moment, and at one of the side trestles caught Monday's stare fixed upon him too, her grey eyes full of speculation and almost, he thought, reproach. There had been little opportunity to talk to her in the bower earlier. Besides, Lady Aline had been commanding all of his attention, and Monday had seemed so withdrawn and quiet that he had been discouraged from making an approach.

> Oh graceful lady, hearken to my plea,
> My love is pure as the birdsong . . .

Alexander ceased in mid-note as there was a commotion at the end of the hall near the forebuilding door. Heads turned and hands instinctively groped for swords, then relaxed as the diners realised it was only a soldier who had tripped over the hem of his cloak in his haste and overturned a trestle piled with flat trenchers of stale bread. The man righted himself, twitched his cloak straight, and limped up the hall at speed towards Lord Bertran on the dais.

Alexander had lost the thread of the song, and there was no point in striking up the tune again because he could see that something more urgent was afoot.

The soldier bent his knee to his lord, wincing as he did so. His hose were torn where he had stumbled, and a bruise was swelling on his jaw.

'My lord,' he announced without preamble, 'Coeur de Lion has been released from prison.'

'What?' Bertran's florid complexion blanched. He raised his right hand to tug at the sparse beard on the point of his chin, always a sign of agitation.

'He travels home even now and has sworn he will put all rebels to flight.' The man looked up, revealing a flush of wine and exertion across his prominent cheekbones.

'Swearing is one thing,' Bertran said harshly, recovering himself, 'doing is another. Besides, how do I know what you say is true? Only last week we heard that the King of France and Prince John had arranged with the German emperor that Richard was to be held captive indefinitely.'

'I tell no lie or mere gossip, my lord,' the man protested. 'I was told this in the town by a messenger from the French court who had stopped to water his horse en route to Prince John. He is warning all who support King Philip to be on their guard.'

Bertran put a sneer on his face. 'The lord Richard has been a long time absent; the landscape has changed, and Coeur de Lion is not God.'

'Yes, my lord. I am only repeating what I heard.'

'You should have saved your breath.' Bertran dismissed him brusquely and reached for his cup. 'I have no time for such foolishness.' But to those who sat close, Bertran was noticeably shaken.

A sheepish expression on his face, the soldier melted away, deciding that next time he would say nothing.

Alexander too made an unobtrusive exit before he was called upon to sing again in order to bolster Bertran's courage. The lord of Lavoux was quite right to say that Richard Coeur de Lion was not God. Any claim he had to be a deity came from a different quarter entirely. According to a legend, the counts of Anjou were the progeny of a sorceress named Melusine who had sprouted wings and flown out of a chapel window rather than be compelled to partake of the mass. The Devil's Brood, so the Angevins were known, and not without good cause.

Passing the raided cattle in their pen, Alexander thought gloomily that they had all just eaten the most expensive beef dinner of their lives.

CHAPTER 8

Lavoux's armoury was a place set aside in the keep's subterranean store room beneath the great hall. Here were kept bundles of spare arrows, spears, shields and the necessary raw materials to make such weapons. Most soldiers were expected to provide their own equipment, but items could usually be purchased from the seneschal, or the resident armourer.

Hervi had set up a drinking friendship with both men, and for a modest outlay of his wages had obtained permission to sort through the armoury for any likely pieces that might suit himself or Alexander.

Having made their way past barrels of wine and stockfish, brined meat, sacks of flour, crocks of honey and jars of tallow, the brothers arrived at the alcoves between the supporting roof pillars that housed the weapons.

Hervi knocked his fist against a barrel of pitch and drummed out a thoughtful rhythm as he surveyed the equipment. 'Reasonable,' he said. 'Could do with more spears. If they get lost over the wall during a siege, you never get them back, not like arrows. The pitch is a bit on the low side too, for putting the fear of hellfire into any attackers.'

Alexander lifted and balanced a spear. The point was as sharp as a sempstress's awl. During weapons practice, Hervi had made him attack a mail-clad straw dummy with one of these, and he had seen for himself the armour-piercing qualities of the honed point. He examined the ash haft for signs of weakness, and found none.

'Take it,' Hervi said. 'It's better than your own, and a man can never be too well equipped.'

Alexander gave him a wry smile. 'You think me a man, then?'

Hervi sucked his teeth. 'You will have to fight like one if Bertran keeps his gates shut against Duke Richard.'

'Do you think he will?'

'I suppose it depends on how much support he receives from Philip of France, and how well Richard fares once he takes to the field,' Hervi said with a grimace. Richard's reputation as a battle commander was unparalleled throughout Christendom.

'Even if Bertran does yield, Hamon de Rougon will have a large axe to grind.' Alexander's voice emerged muffled as he poked among a pile of fallen spear shafts on the floor. 'And he has held firm for Richard through thick and thin.'

Hervi eyed the curve of his brother's spine. 'We needed somewhere to spend the winter,' he said. 'Our coin would not have lasted until the growth of the spring grass, and once a knight begins to sell his equipment to live, he is on the downward path.'

'And what of his direction when he sells himself to a master he cannot respect?'

'What are you saying?'

'That the grass is green and the tourney season well underway.'

Hervi was silent. He rumpled his hand through his hair. 'We gave our oath,' he said at last.

'Then perhaps we should resign it and ride out.'

Hervi pursed his lips. 'I will have to talk to Arnaud.'

'If you can find a time when he's sober to do so,' Alexander said tartly.

'He grieves hard for his wife,' Hervi excused. 'I don't know how to . . .' He paused and pointed. 'What's that?'

Alexander tugged at a dusty object beneath the pile of shafts, and after a brief struggle drew forth a split and hardened leather scabbard, its shrivelled flesh still encasing the sword which it had been designed to hold. His palms suddenly damp, Alexander slid the weapon free. The two bone halves of the grip were slack around the tang where age had loosened the rivets. The pommel was of an old-fashioned three-lobed design, and the slightly damaged hilt had an interlaced pattern that on closer examination proved to be the coils of a serpent. There were two shallow depressions in the reptile's head where jewelled eyes should have shone. The blade was pitted and nicked, but repairable, and although the sword was light, the balance was perfect.

Alexander's own eyes glowed. A sword was an expensive accoutrement, not easily come by, and this had once been a magnificent weapon. 'It can be mended,' he said to Hervi, his voice quivering with enthusiasm.

Hervi bit back a smile. 'I should imagine so,' he said. 'Swords often need their grips refurbishing, and that piece on the cross-guard could easily be repaired by a smith who knows his trade.' He took the sword from Alexander and gave it a thorough scrutiny. 'It's too light for me, but it should suit your strength admirably.' His eyelids crinkled and the smile broke across his face. 'If you rummage further, who knows, you might come across a mail hauberk and helm in there too!'

For the rest of the day, Alexander wandered around in a daze of pleasure. He spoke to one of the other soldiers who fashioned scabbards in his spare time and commissioned his services. Then he visited Lavoux's smith and arranged to have the damaged hilt repaired. While waiting for the dinner horn to sound, he sat down in the bailey with Hervi's grindstone, and lovingly set about smoothing out the pits and nicks in the otherwise fine blade.

He was so preoccupied with his new possession that he did not notice Monday's approach, and it was only when she moved and her shadow entered his light that he raised his head. Immediately his eyes kindled and he made room for her on the small rectangular bench.

'What do you think?' He held up the sword for her inspection, his words drenched in love.

Monday sat down, tucking her skirts beneath her. She appraised both him and the weapon with solemn eyes. 'It is very fine,' she said. 'Or it will be when you have finished.'

'It was in the armoury under a pile of spear shafts. Hervi says it is old, but that doesn't matter. It was wrought by a craftsman. I can feel it in the steel.'

She watched him work, his jaw moving in unconscious rhythm

with his smoothing strokes. He had clever, graceful hands, quite unlike Hervi's huge spades. 'Will you remember me when you are a great knight?' she teased.

He grinned, but without looking up from his task, his teeth fine and white, as yet without the chips and gaps of the soldier's trade. 'Of course I will, but by then you will be a great lady in your own right with a horde of admirers queuing up to kiss the train of your silk gown.'

She laughed, but more as a defence than out of genuine amusement. 'So I will be like Lady Aline?' she said waspishly.

He paused for a moment and blotted his brow on his forearm. The late-afternoon sunshine glinted on the blade and the bare skeleton of the unbound grip. 'It is a game to her,' he said, 'one she plays very well but a game nevertheless.'

'I thought you were in thrall to her?'

He shook his head. 'I enjoy being summoned to her presence; I like her manner, the scent she uses, the wiles of her body.' He shrugged. 'Why should I not? Such things please the senses, but I know the difference between the game and the reality. I look at her, and I look at you, and I know which one is the truth and which the distorted mirror.'

Monday blushed, albeit that the compliment implied she did not have the alluring gifts of the lady Aline.

He resumed work upon the sword. 'You and I, we have much in common – we are friends.'

Monday nodded. 'Friends,' she repeated. The word was safe and comfortable, speaking of a bond beyond mere physical attraction. But it might be pleasant to have him look upon her as he had looked upon Aline de Lavoux. Dangerous too, even if it was nothing more than a game. The thought made her stomach leap, and her breath shorten.

The dinner horn sounded and Alexander carefully set his work aside. Then, on a sudden impulse, he held out his arm to Monday with an elaborate flourish. 'Demoiselle,' he said, with a mocking smile.

Monday laughed a trifle shakily at this parody of her wish. Performing an exaggerated curtsey in response, she tucked her hand in the bend of his elbow and let him lead her into the hall, her head carried high as if her old linen gown was made of the finest samite.

They had scarcely sat down to bowls of rich pork stew with onion dumplings and buttered field beans when the alarm was raised by Hervi, currently on duty and in charge of the watch guards. Spear in hand, he strode into the hall and straight up to the dais.

'My lord, there are troops approaching Lavoux,' he said curtly, with only the smallest bow of deference. 'They bear the banner of Rougon, and they have siege machinery.'

Bertran ceased chewing. 'Rougon would not dare!' he said hoarsely.

'Even so, it is true, my lord. They're approaching the south wall. What orders shall I give?'

Bertran wiped his eating knife on a clean trencher and thrust it back into its sheath. He spat the meat he had been chewing on to the floor and jerked to his feet. 'If Hamon de Rougon has come to lay siege to my walls, then he has come to die!' he snarled, and abandoning his meal, stalked from the hall to see for himself.

Alexander picked up his gravy-soaked trencher, and together with everyone else, crowded in Bertran's wake.

Hamon de Rougon's force was not particularly large, but it was armed to the teeth and well disciplined. Rougon himself rode at the head of his troop – a slender chestnut-haired man in his mid-twenties. A squire sat at his left shoulder, a spear in his grip from which flew the black and yellow de Rougon colours. At the rear of his troop, various baggage wains of supplies were rolling into view. An open-sided cart contained the components of a battering ram and a stone-thrower.

Bertran's eyes bulged at the sight.

Hervi leaned against a merlon and peered down at their visitors. 'Shall we send out a herald to discover what he wants, my lord?'

'I can see what he wants without recourse to a herald!' Bertran retorted acidly. 'All he will receive from me is his death!' He began biting out commands concerning the arming of the walls. Stony-faced, Hervi acknowledged them.

Alexander knew that grim look by now. Hervi thought Bertran a fool, but was not fool enough himself to say so. A man who did not observe the courtesies of warfare was not deserving of them himself if forced to yield. And frequently it was his troops who paid the price of that arrogance.

Monday grasped Alexander's sleeve and stared down at the force preparing to assault their walls. 'What will happen if Rougon succeeds?'

Alexander pulled a wry face. He could not tell her that at worst Hamon de Rougon would hang the garrison for cattle thieves as an example to anyone else thinking to trifle with him. 'That depends on his honour and compassion,' he said woodenly.

'Lady Aline thinks highly of him. She says that . . .' Glancing round, she lowered her voice. 'She says that he is worth two of her husband.'

Alexander snorted. 'That would not be difficult except in an eating contest.' Hervi was beckoning to him. Making his excuses, he hastened along the wall walk to join his brother.

'I want a tally of every stick and stitch of equipment we possess,' Hervi said tersely. 'Report back to me as soon as you have the information.'

Alexander nodded. His mouth was dry, his heart pounding. 'Where will you be?'

'Here, or on one of the other walls.' Hervi's brows knitted in a deep frown. 'Either de Rougon is a fool,' he muttered, 'or he knows something we do not.'

Alexander eyed the force now deploying beneath their walls, then gave Hervi a questioning look.

'With Coeur de Lion back in the saddle, Lord Bertran is now the one at a disadvantage. He has thrown in his lot with Philip of France, and that makes him a rebel. Those men below might only be the first kites to arrive at the corpse. Hamon de Rougon has claim to pick the largest bone. I think he desires to take ownership while there is still meat on the limb.'

'So you believe that more will come?'

Hervi shrugged. 'I hardly think that this is an empty gesture on Rougon's part. He may be young but he's a seasoned crusader.' He gave Alexander the mirthless parody of a grin. 'You were right to balk at raiding those cattle.'

'I was right about leaving too,' Alexander said, returning the grimace. 'Small comfort now.'

'Oh, no comfort at all, but at least you are going to learn to fight for your life. Stop standing there like a stuffed dummy. Go and do those tallies for me.'

CHAPTER 9

A foot probed viciously at Alexander's ribs.

'I'm awake,' he said indignantly, and pushed at his brother's insistent boot.

'Get up then, sluggard,' Hervi rumbled. 'It's time.' He was already dressed in his mail, a hunk of bread clutched in his fist. Moving on, he kicked the supine form next to Alexander and repeated the command, before taking a large bite of the food.

A cockerel crowed. Alexander threw off his cloak and sat up, his belly churning and his eyes hot from lack of sleep. Around him, other men were groaning and stirring. He wondered if they too had lain awake half the night, their minds dark with bloody imaginings.

Light blossomed as a flambeau was kindled and thrust into a wall socket. The air was the grainy charcoal colour of very early morning. Alexander lurched to his feet and made his way outside to splash his face in a water butt. He was reminded of the times he had been plucked from slumber to sing and pray in Cranwell's chapel. The stumble down dark stairways only half awake, comprehension still in the world of dreams. Skeletons grinning from the walls. He had seen them all too clearly last night, and it had been like looking in a mirror.

He dashed the water from his eyes and raised his head. The storage sheds and buildings in the bailey were still dark, their details indeterminate. Behind the curtain wall, the eastern sky was slowly paling. The cockerel crowed again and was answered by a rival from a different part of the ward.

The siege was entering its fourth day, and thus far Lavoux had held the would-be intruders at bay. There had been two assaults on the keep, and the black streaks of pitch staining the outer walls were testimony to Rougon's failure. But Lavoux had not emerged unscathed. The stone facings wore acne pits where the siege machines had hurled boulders against the walls. Several of the storage sheds in the part of the bailey closest to the assaulted wall had suffered hits. At the height of Rougon's fortune yesterday, the besieging troops had run a battering ram up to the gates and raised ladders on the wall either side.

The sortie had been unsuccessful, but it had also probed hard at Lavoux's defences, and Hamon de Rougon appeared in no way demoralised by his failure. The fact that he remained camped outside their walls led Hervi and the other experienced knights of the garrison to believe that de Rougon was expecting reinforcements, and that something had to be done about the existing troops before suspicion became reality.

Feeling more lively for the splash of cold water on his face, Alexander returned to the guard room to break his fast on a chunk of bread smeared with pork jelly, and a cup of wine. He chewed and swallowed without pleasure or appetite, but he knew that he had to eat something if he was to be capable of doing his duty. The next meal was at least six hours hence, on the other side of a battle.

Next he checked his weapons – a lance and shield, a long knife, and the old sword, now refurbished to a killing brightness. He had yet to use it in battle. The first assaults on the walls had been repulsed with sticks and stones, spears and molten pitch, without hand-to-hand contact. That would come within the next hour.

The light had paled to ash grey. Alexander made sure that his scabbard was firmly laced to his belt, and departed the guard room for the stables.

'Don't look so worried,' Aline said to Monday. 'When Hamon takes Lavoux, he will spare the lives of the garrison. His anger is for Bertran, not his soldiers.' She glanced towards the shuttered window. The sounds of men and horses came muffled through the thickness of the wood.

The two young women were cutting up a linen sheet to make strips of bandage. Needles lay to hand, strong thread and jars of powdered knitbone and lady's bedstraw. Monday knew that before the day was out, she would be called upon to sew flesh as well as fabric. She glanced sidelong at Aline. There was a glow of suppressed excitement about her companion. The name of Hamon de Rougon had been frequently on her tongue, as if she relished the taste of the words. She kept saying 'when', not 'if'.

'What makes you so sure that Hamon will take Lavoux?' Monday asked curiously. 'Hervi says that his force is too small to pose a real threat.'

Aline cut an arrow-straight line with the shears, then looked at Monday, a feline gleam in her eyes. 'Hamon will have a trick or two up his sleeve,' she murmured.

'How do you know?' Despite the other woman's reassurances, Monday was anxious. Aline had been behaving very strangely ever since the Rougon force had appeared beneath Lavoux's walls. Expectant, undaunted by danger. Last night she had danced around the room, humming to herself.

Aline was silent for such a long time that Monday thought she was not going to answer, but at last she sighed and laid her shears aside. 'I knew Hamon when I was a child and he was a squire in my father's household. I wanted to marry him, but my father had his own ideas of family advancement, and they had nothing to do with a squire of modest inheritance. The most we had were a few snatched trysts in secret corners during the summer before my wedding.' She gestured as she spoke, and Monday saw that the gold and ruby ring no longer adorned her hand. 'Even though no more than words and the gentlest of kisses were exchanged, my father would have killed us if he had found out, and neither Hamon nor I had the courage or foolhardiness of your parents to elope. Since that time I have been twice a wife and once a widow. He never married, but pursued his career on the battlefield with Coeur de Lion. Bertran grubs in the mud and steals cattle. Hamon is a companion of kings.'

Aline rose from the trestle, wandered to the hearth and poked the fire to life beneath the cauldron. 'Hamon has not only come for Lavoux,' she said softly, to the sudden burst of flame from beneath the logs, 'he has come for me.'

As the sun spread an orange glow across the eastern sky, Lavoux's force waited for the portcullis to be winched up. Depending on their nature and the state of their nerves, men either fretted their horses or soothed them with pats and murmurs of reassurance.

Hervi sat at Bertran's left shoulder, acting as his bodyguard, the bearer of his standard. It was not an enviable position, since the capture of the enemy's banner in battle was viewed as a necessary part of any victory, and its guardian was always a target. But of all the knights of Lavoux's company, Hervi was the most accomplished in feats of arms, and possessed the most brawn.

Alexander fixed his gaze on Hervi's familiar figure, and wished that he had the same air of confident arrogance in the saddle. His bowels and belly were threatening mutiny and his limbs were weak with fear. He knew that he would never be able to control his shield and lance, that he was easy prey and he was going to die. Some men were muttering prayers, but they were of small comfort to Alexander, whose past experiences of prayer all had grim associations.

Bracing his spear, he listened to the grinding squeal of the rusty portcullis chains and watched the solid grid begin to rise from the stone floor. Hervi's round-topped helm with its ventilated face guard turned. The mail mitten lifted in a salute to Alexander. The younger man saluted in return and gave his brother the wan parody of a grin. His own helm was of the old-fashioned variety with a nasal bar but no protection for the mouth and lower jaw. Nor did he possess any mail, but had to rely on a quilted gambeson, heavily padded with fleece. At least he would have the edge of speed over any man wearing mail.

Beside him, Arnaud de Cerizay gave him a nudge. 'Stay close to me,' he said, 'and tackle no one better armed than yourself. If you think you are out of your depth, disengage.'

Alexander nodded sensibly, although for the moment there was no room for anything in his mind but blind terror. 'Aren't you afraid?' he gulped out.

'Of what?' Arnaud demanded harshly. 'It's facing life that's the hardship.'

The portcullis was higher now, almost passable. Alexander fumbled to collect the reins and shield in his left hand, and hold the lance in his right. Samson pranced and sidled, sweat creaming his hide. 'I don't want to die,' he said huskily.

'You won't.' Arnaud's voice was hard, almost contemptuous. 'It's not that easy. If it was, do you think I would still be suffering?' He gave Alexander an accusing glare. 'Do you know why Hervi set me to protect you, boy?'

Numbly, Alexander shook his head.

'Because he knows the task will make it impossible for me to go charging into the thick of the fray in search of my maker.'

Alexander was lost for a reply. An apology would seem incongruous. Sympathy and platitudes would only earn him further scorn. 'I want to crawl under a stone,' he muttered at last.

'Too late for that, son. Brace yourself.'

The portcullis jaws widened above horse height and the soldiers surged beneath its fangs and out of the great gates. Samson strained at the bit, eager to gallop but held by Alexander to a rapid trot. The pace jarred his teeth, but he could not increase speed without barging the horse in front, nor slow down because of the ranks behind.

Then they hit the flat ground below the castle slope and Bertran's voice bellowed out the challenge. '*Lavoux! Lavoux!*'

The hard trot rolled into a gallop, the momentum increasing. Stirrup to stirrup, the men of Lavoux rode down upon the camp of the besiegers, and discovered too late that it was twice the size they had believed, and well prepared.

Realising the jeopardy, Bertran gesticulated wildly. A horn sounded three frantic bursts, the signal to turn back, then was silenced as the hornsman was cut down. The Lavoux knights tried to retreat, but discovered themselves surrounded, the jaws of the trap well and truly sprung.

A foot soldier hurtled at Alexander, his spear raised, the wicked point gleaming. For a moment Alexander was frozen with terror, but even as the barbed head flashed towards him, he reined Samson to one side, then reined him back fast. The man bounced off the stallion's shoulder and fell in the dust. A comrade darted forward to cover him, menacing Alexander with a battle axe.

Declining the challenge, Alexander whipped Samson around and spurred away. It was not a sound move, for he discovered that he had escaped the frying pan only to fall into the fire. Two knights now confronted him, their lances levelled, and there was nowhere to run and no sign of Arnaud. Time slowed down as Alexander faced the inevitable, and suddenly, miraculously, he was no longer afraid. Brought to the brink, he was forced to jump. The sick churning in his belly turned to fire and a sensation of cold rage flickered through his veins. If he was going to die, he would not do so alone. He brought his lance across, clasped his shield to his left side, and ducking his head, slammed his heels into Samson's flanks.

At the last moment possible, he yanked on the reins and commanded with his thighs. The stallion swerved, and as they passed offside the leading knight, Alexander rose in the stirrups and struck overarm with the lance like a foot soldier.

The head pierced through the mail and gambeson to lodge in flesh. Although there was not enough force behind the blow to kill, it was nevertheless disabling. The knight cried out in pain and surprise, and lost his grip on his own weapon. Alexander twisted his lance, tore it free, and put his opponent's horse between himself and the second knight.

They cursed him and he cursed back, his voice raw with fighting rage. And yet, through the frantic, furious clamour of his blood, he was perfectly rational. His mind was clear, he was able to think fast and react with whiplash speed. The two warriors backed off warily to consider how they should take him, one of them clutching at the bloody tear in his mail.

The uninjured man reached for the morning star flail looped around the pommel of his saddle. It was a deadly weapon, but it took skill to use. The backswing was capable of breaking the user's arm, or wrapping around the back of his head if he was not careful, but in the hands of an expert the spiked ball could punch holes in a shield and smash an unarmoured man to pulp.

The knight began to rotate the flail. Alexander braced his

spear, knowing that the only defence was to thrust it into the
impetus of ball and chain and jam it to a stop, as he had once
done to Eudo le Boucher. He kicked Samson and took the attack
to his opponent. Caught off guard by Alexander's assault, the
knight launched a premature blow. Alexander changed tactics
and rammed the point of his spear at the exposed right side.
Samson plunged forward and the lance pierced through mail,
through flesh and bone. The knight howled. His wounded companion tried to come to his aid, but was unable to lift his
damaged sword arm. Alexander wrenched the lance away just as
Arnaud arrived, breathless, cursing, his horse streaked with sweat
and blood.

'You young fool!' he roared, beside himself. 'Hervi might as
well have saved his breath!'

More Rougon soldiers were coming to aid their wounded companions. Swords and spears menaced the sky. '*Le Roi Richard!*'
came the battle cry. '*Le Roi Richard!*' and left of the field,
'*Marshal! Marshal!*'

Alexander spun Samson around and scanned the mêlée for
Hervi's banner. If the men had been ordinary reinforcements,
they would have used '*Rougon!*' as their rallying cry. The ones
they were using suggested that Coeur de Lion himself had
arrived to direct operations.

Across the trampled encampment, Alexander caught sight of
Lavoux's banner fluttering from its pike, and surrounding it, a
crowd of hacking fighting men. Then the lance wavered and the
banner dipped from sight.

'*Montroi!*' Alexander roared, and clapped his heels to Samson's
flanks. This was personal now. '*Montroi!*'

Grimly Arnaud ploughed after him. Although he would welcome death for himself, the lad was acting from the depths of
green inexperience and had to be stopped.

Alexander fought like a demon, forcing his way by pure frenzy
towards the place where he had seen the banner fall. In its place,
new colours had risen – three golden lions blazing upon a crimson silk background. Sweat stung his eyes with salt, his sword
arm was as hot as molten lead. The only thought existing in his
brain was to find Hervi and rescue him, nor did the futility of

such an ambition occur to him. It was what he had to do, and therefore it had to be.

'*Montroi!*' he bellowed again, at the full pitch of his lungs. A knight riding a muscular grey destrier blocked his path. Alexander's blow was parried easily on a parti-coloured green and yellow shield bearing the device of a snarling red lion. The surcoat was similarly emblazoned, and the raised fist was wrapped around the hilt of a magnificent war sword that made Alexander's look as small as a toy.

'*Marshal!*' the knight retorted, his voice ringing almost joyously through his helm, and his returning blow made a huge split in Alexander's shield and numbed his left arm all the way up to the armpit.

The grey stallion reared, forehooves striking. Samson plunged and kicked. Alexander rose in his stirrups to counterstrike, but the grey thrust against the black and Alexander lost first his balance, then his seat, and was thrown. He hit the ground with a jarring thud and the world turned to darkness.

'No, my lord!' he heard Arnaud shriek. 'For God's mercy do not strike, he is nought but a boy! I cry quarter. I yield!'

Shod hooves danced close to Alexander's prone body; too close. His helmet was struck a ringing blow and a kick thudded against his shoulder. His hearing faded in and out. He was aware of curses, of sharp questions and an earnest voice raised in argument. Another kick caught him in the ribs and he curled up, jerking his knees defensively towards his chin. The darkness intensified and engulfed him. His last thought was how easy it was to die. No glory, just the choking dirt beneath his cheek and a plunging warhorse above his body.

CHAPTER 10

The skeletons surrounded his bed, watching him from blank eye sockets. Brother Alkmund stood among them, his face cadaver-sharp, his fingers caressing a plaited scourge. Alexander closed his eyes, but he could still see his visitors through his lids, waiting for him to weaken.

'You're not real,' he snarled defiantly. 'You have no hold over me!'

Brother Alkmund smiled and caressed Alexander's cheek with the scourge. It was a feather touch, soft and wet with the blood of its last victim. Alexander's body jerked with revulsion. 'Begone!' he sobbed at the top of his lungs. His eyes flew open and were dazzled by the brilliance of sunlight slanting through the bower window on to the straw mattress on which he was lying.

Clutching a linen pad, Monday was recoiling from him. Overturned on the floor was a small brass bowl surrounded by a spreading puddle of water. Panting, he stared at her, then covered his face with his hand. Beneath his fingers his skin was moist, and a scent of lavender hung in the air. Hot pain throbbed through his shoulder and danced across his ribs. Glancing down at his naked chest, he saw the angry red marks of developing bruises on his body.

He was totally disoriented. A moment ago he had been in the crypt at Cranwell, about to join its other occupants in a state of living death. Now he appeared to be in the women's quarters at Lavoux, lying on a mattress in the space usually occupied by the sewing trestle.

'What am I doing here?' he croaked.

'You were knocked senseless in the battle. They allowed you to be brought here instead of throwing you in the cells with the others.' She eyed him sidelong.

'The battle?' He stared at her numbly while the images began to fill his mind. The clash of weapons, the cries of men, the neighing of horses. A morning star whirling on its chain, a spear reaming flesh. Suddenly he felt sick.

'Don't you remember?'

'Christ, nothing that makes sense.' His belly churned and hot prickles ran up and down his spine. Nothing made any sense. He had been on the ground, about to die beneath the hooves of a warhorse. It was impossible that he should be here now in the bower, with nothing worse than bad bruises. 'You mean everyone else is in the cells?'

Monday righted the bowl and began to mop up the spilled water with the pad in her hand. 'Duke Richard has confined all the garrison there until he decides what to do with them.'

Alexander shook his head in bafflement. 'You go too fast for me. By Duke Richard, I know you mean Coeur de Lion; I saw his banner on the field. But I do not understand why I am still alive, nor why I should be here in the women's quarters.'

Monday wrung out the cloth in the bowl, and wiping her hands on a dry square of linen, fetched a flagon. 'I do not know. Papa carried you in here out of your senses. There was a knight from the Rougon force with him, but nothing much was said. I was just told to care for you.' She poured out two measures of wine, the colour dark as blood, and handed him a cup. 'And after that, Papa was taken away under guard.'

Alexander took a tentative sip, not knowing if the drink would settle or aggravate his reeling stomach. Other images of the battle were intruding on his consciousness now, crowding together at the side of his mind and jostling for their place in the main arena of his awareness. The roared battle cries came back to him, and suddenly he went rigid.

'Hervi,' he said with sudden urgency. 'I saw the Lavoux banner go down. What has happened to my brother?'

Monday shook her head. 'I haven't moved from the bower since Lavoux surrendered to Duke Richard. Papa said nothing about Hervi before they took him away. Surely he would have done so if he had been wounded or . . . where are you going?' She started towards Alexander as he put the cup aside and began easing from the bed.

'I have to know about Hervi. Where's my shirt?' He swayed where he stood and had to plant his feet wide to balance himself.

She looked at him aghast. 'You can't go down to the hall, it's full of their soldiers!'

'If it is, then I am bound to receive a reply,' he said grimly, and walked towards the door.

'Without your shirt?' Monday followed him, the garment outstretched in her hand. 'I'm coming with you; you're not fit to be out of your bed, let alone roaming the keep.'

He halted, an impatient, slightly feverish glitter in his eyes. 'Don't fuss,' he snapped.

'If I am fussing, then you are being pig-headed,' she retorted as she helped him don the shirt, tugging it gently down over his injured shoulder and bruised ribs. 'Look,' she reasoned, 'perhaps Lady Aline could find out for you. She and Hamon de Rougon used to be sweethearts. He will listen to whatever she says.'

'Hervi's my brother, it's my duty,' he said through clenched teeth. 'I'll not hide behind a woman.' He jerked out of her grip and opened the chamber door. The smell of musty stone wafted from the twisting stairway, its darkness alleviated by the occasional wrist-thin arrowslit.

'Give me strength,' Monday muttered to herself behind him, and followed him out on to the stairway. He pretended not to hear. The steps curled around the newel post like the inside of a whelk shell, and brought them to the open gallery above the hall, the walkway protected by a series of decorated stone arches. The hall itself, spread out to their view, was packed with the retinues of Rougon, Marshal and Coeur de Lion. There was scarcely an inch of floor space to be glimpsed between the press of knights and soldiers. Harassed retainers moved amongst them, trying to serve food.

The leaders were seated at the great table on the dais, and Lord Bertran's chair was occupied by a warrior with a mane of red-blond hair and clean, powerful features. A tunic of vibrant violet-blue wool graced his body, gold braid twinkling at throat and cuff. At his side was a man of similar stature with neatly brushed black hair, beginning to grey at the temples. He wore a green and yellow surcoat with a red lion appliquéd on the breast, and his manner was more relaxed than that of his handsome companion. Alexander knew that this had to be the great William Marshal, a man who had risen from obscurity by military excellence and political diplomacy, and who was now a powerful baron, high in the counsel and esteem of kings.

Seated with these two great men was a slender, chestnut-haired man, handsome and vulpine. He was much younger than his companions, but did not seem discomposed in their presence, his manner both relaxed and watchful at the same time. Next to him, her eyes downcast, her manner modest and effacing, was Aline. Her own garments were sombre – a gown of dark-brown wool and a plain linen wimple, something of a contrast to her usual mode of dress.

Alexander drew a deep, steadying breath, and started along the gallery to the stairs that would bring him down closest to the dais. He had to know what had happened to Hervi; nothing else mattered. He was barely aware of Monday pattering anxiously at his side, nor of the pain of his bruises, except to be annoyed that his body would not serve him as he commanded. Instead of walking in a straight line, he moved as if he were drunk, and although he knew his purpose, his thoughts were disconnected and jumbled. A separate, rational Alexander watched the progress of the foolish one from the stone vault of the gallery and was powerless to intervene.

At the foot of the stairs, a thick-set guard blocked their path. The man's paunch was the size of a billowed sail, and he had a wickedly sharpened spear which he threatened to ram down Alexander's throat.

'I have to have audience with the lord Richard,' Alexander said, and swayed where he stood.

'Aye, you and every other man,' the guard sneered. 'You shouldn't be so eager to put your neck in a noose.' His gaze flickered to Monday, who was clutching Alexander's sleeve, partly to support him, partly to give herself courage. 'What's your business with him?'

'My brother, I need to find out if he is still alive.'

'One of the garrison, is he?' The guard continued to look at Monday as if he found her far more interesting than Alexander.

'Yes, a tall man, well built, with fair hair and beard. He was bearing Lavoux's standard. Do you know anything of him?'

The guard took his eyes from Monday. 'I know nothing,' he growled, 'except that Bertran de Lavoux was a traitor and a cattle thief, and that he couldn't carry out his mischief without men of a like mind to help him.' The spear point jabbed again, dangerously close to Alexander's face. 'You'll get your turn to plead your case on the morrow, before we hang them.'

Rage coursed through Alexander, lending him a surge of strength to match that of earlier. He grasped the spear two-handed by the base of the socket and the shaft, and used one of the ruses that Hervi had taught him in hand-to-hand fighting to wrench the weapon out of the astonished guard's hands and reverse the advantage. 'Now!' he snarled. 'I want to know about my brother now!'

Other soldiers rushed to help their unfortunate companion. Monday clung to Alexander like a limpet and screamed at the top of her lungs. She reasoned that the soldiers would not strike a woman to death, and to get at Alexander they would have to get at her first.

'Enough!' a voice roared above the fracas, with sufficient power to deafen those unfortunate enough to be immediately adjacent. 'Put up your weapons; stand aside!'

Silence fell, disturbed only by the rattle of swords and knives being returned to sheaths, and the shuffle of feet as men withdrew.

Breathing hard, Alexander removed the spear tip from the hollow of the guard's throat. Weakness flooded his limbs, and it was only will power and pride that kept him on his feet as the tall, red-blond man confronted and pierced him with a stare of blue ice.

Close to, Richard Coeur de Lion defied magnificence. Even

without the striking height and looks, the charisma of the man was all-encompassing. He shone as brightly as the sun – and at the moment, the famous Angevin temper was scorching.

'You dare to come armed into my hall and break the peace?' he roared at Alexander. 'On your knees, knave, for your life!' A hard hand clamped Alexander's shoulder and forced him down. In truth it was not difficult to do, for Alexander was on the point of collapse anyway. Without being told, Monday knelt too, her head bowed.

Alexander struggled against a fluctuating darkness at the edge of his vision. 'Sire,' he swallowed, 'it was not my intention to cause harm. Your guard threatened me when I was no threat to him. I did but defend myself.'

The brilliant blue eyes narrowed. 'No threat to him,' Richard said silkily, 'and yet you put a spear to his throat.'

'After he had put one to mine. I was only seeking news of my brother. I do not know if he is dead or alive. I know it matters not to any of you . . . but it matters dearly to me.'

There was a long silence when it seemed that every man present in the hall held his breath. A time of waiting for the royal rage to break over the young man's foolish head and utterly destroy him.

The tension swelled like a storm, and then, miraculously, passed over as the fury departed Richard's expression as swiftly as it had arrived. 'Get up,' he said brusquely, including Monday in his gesture.

'Sire, I do not know if I can,' Alexander confessed.

The hand that had forced him to his knees now took him beneath the elbow and raised him to his feet. Alexander staggered, then steadied, pride locking his knees.

Richard scrutinised Alexander from head to toe, a thorough assessment that seemed to take in every mark and flaw. Alexander became intensely aware of the shabby condition of his hose and shirt, that he was standing before his liege lord as a beggar and that he had nothing with which to bargain.

'Your name?' Richard demanded.

'Alexander de Montroi, sire. My eldest brother Reginald holds lands for you between Stafford and Wigmore.'

'And this is the brother about whom you wish to know?'

'No, sire. He would have an apoplexy if he could see me now.'

Richard's thin lips twitched. 'I take your word for it, since I do not know him personally. Then tell me what you are doing here, apart from seeking your news.'

Alexander met the blue eyes. They were filled with mocking humour now. Richard, it seemed, wanted to be entertained, and was prepared to be indulgent while it suited him. Beyond his magnificent figure, Alexander could see the courtiers gathered like spectators at a bear-baiting.

'Sire, he is my scribe,' said the lady Aline, pushing forward and dipping a curtsey to Richard. Her voice was devoid of the smoky, honeyed tones it usually possessed in her dealings with men.

'Your scribe?' Richard glanced at her coldly. 'And yet he has recently fought a battle. He bears the marks of a helm and coif about his face, and he did not end up in this condition from wielding a pen.'

Snorts of amusement greeted the sally. 'Indeed, sire,' spoke out William Marshal, 'I myself struck him down during the assault on our camp. He would not be alive now were it not for the intervention of another knight, and my nephew here.' He gestured over his shoulder.

His colour high, John Marshal stepped out from the gathering. 'He saved me during a tourney last spring season – took on a knight twice his size and ten times his experience and pulled him off his horse. It is a debt I openly acknowledge. Do not blame him for the company he has kept. He has good blood.'

Richard's eyebrows by now had almost climbed into his hair. He stared hard at Marshal and his nephew, then transferred his gaze to Aline. 'And you say he is your scribe?'

'Yes, sire,' Aline replied with candour. 'He writes as neat a hand as any clerk, and he has Latin at his fingertips. It is true that he took part in the battle and that he is learning the military arts, but his value to me is in the skill of his letters.' She pointed at Monday. 'Indeed, I know from my sempstress that he was unhappy in my former husband's service, but having taken his coin, was honour-bound to serve him.'

'A veritable paragon,' Richard said drily.

Alexander chewed the inside of his mouth and stared straight ahead. 'My brother, Hervi, was charged with bearing the Lavoux banner during the attack on your camp. I would know if he still lives, or if I have to bury him.'

'Assuming, of course, that I pardon your own life,' Richard said sharply.

'Then I would know so that he can bury me, or that by your mercy you will allow us to share a grave.'

Richard eyed Alexander thoughtfully. 'For all that you are near dead on your feet, you have a swift enough tongue. I wonder if you are bold to bandy words with me, or just plain foolish.'

Alexander held himself very still, nearer to collapse than even Richard could have guessed. 'I came to find out if my brother is alive or dead,' he said, enunciating each word with great care like a drunkard. 'I meant no offence.'

Richard continued to stare at him, and now his brows were level and brooding. 'You will count yourself fortunate if none has been taken,' he said, his voice softer now, with a rumble in it almost like a purr. Without turning, he addressed John Marshal. 'Go and seek among the prisoners for this boy's brother, and if he still lives, bring him here. Not for one minute would I contemplate sharing a grave with any of my brothers. I want to see what manner of man inspires such lunatic devotion.'

John Marshal bowed and departed. Richard took Alexander by the arm. 'Come,' he said, 'you have disrupted my meal far enough, you might as well join us.'

Somehow, Alexander managed to set one foot in front of the other, forcing his will beyond the boundaries of what had earlier seemed impossible. In a moment he would be able to sit down. For Hervi. He had to hold fast for Hervi.

Monday hesitated as Coeur de Lion drew a stumbling Alexander towards the dais. She did not think that the invitation included her as well, but Aline beckoned. 'Join us,' she commanded, with a slightly narrow look at Richard's back, her humility much less in evidence now. 'I am yet mistress in my own hall.'

Lavoux's dungeon lay beneath the store rooms, and in comparison to some that Hervi had experienced, was relatively civilised. It reminded him of a stable, for the floor was thick with straw and the torch sockets in the wall were reminiscent of hay mangers. Only one of these sockets was occupied by a burning brand. For the most part, the men of Lavoux's defeated garrison lay in darkness.

Hervi moved in the straw, testing the bruises on his body to discover which part of him ached the most. His mail had saved him from serious hurt, that and his swift reactions coupled with his solid bone structure. The closest he had come to severe injury was when the Lavoux banner had been torn from his grasp and someone had used its barbed point to run Lord Bertran through. Hervi had seen no reason to fight on and had surrendered, but not before his adversary had landed several solid blows. At least Hervi knew that Alexander was safe. Arnaud had told him that the Marshals had taken him prisoner, and although the lad had received a severe buffeting, he had sustained no mortal injuries.

'Although more by luck than judgement,' Arnaud had added wryly. 'He fights like one possessed, as much a danger to himself as to the enemy. I was sore pressed to stay with him. He just took off like a demon hot from hell.'

Well, that would have to be honed out of him if they got out of this broil alive, Hervi thought. Alex had to learn to fight with a clear head whatever the provocation. He eased his position again and wondered how best to lie to sleep, since no position was comfortable. Closing his eyes, he thought of the green fields above and beyond the dungeon, the bursting spring and a warm wind blowing over the tourney field. Rippling banners, the clack of a lance upon a quintain; the greasy smell of the cookshops and the camaraderie around the camp fire.

Inexplicably the scene changed, and suddenly he found himself standing in a chapel, clothed in the dark robes of a monk, while exultant plainchant soared around him in praise of God.

A key grating in the lock of the prison door jerked Hervi out of his dream, and he opened his eyes in time to see it swinging open to admit a knight bearing a flaming torch, and two men-at-arms with swords drawn. The knight stooped under the arch, then stood straight, the torch held on high, and Hervi recognised the earnest features of John Marshal.

'I seek Hervi de Montroi,' the young man announced in carrying tones, and gazed around.

Slowly, carefully, Hervi rolled over and stood up, every muscle in his body protesting. 'I am here, Sir John,' he said, and shuffled forward into the pool of light cast by the torch.

John Marshal gave him an assessing look. 'The lord Richard has summoned you to his presence in the hall – if you're capable of walking that far,' he added.

Hervi limped towards the cell door. 'I'm not a weakling,' he said proudly. The soldiers accompanying Marshal parted to let him pass, their swords held at the ready, their eyes flickering between him and the other prisoners. The air bristled with tension and fear.

'Why me?' Hervi asked Marshal as the door slammed shut between him and his companions, and the key turned.

'I was sent to discover if you still lived, and to bring you forth if it was so. Your brother was concerned for your welfare, and made the fact known to the lord Richard in no uncertain terms.'

Hervi groaned. Alexander's skill for troublemaking appeared to be unrivalled.

Marshal shook his head. 'There is small harm done, I think. Lord Richard was diverted by his boldness and open manner.' The knight gave Hervi the shadow of a smile. 'I was grateful myself for your brother's courage on the day that he intervened between myself and Eudo le Boucher. Such passion is rare.'

'I cannot share the sentiment.'

'You should, since I saved your brother's life in recompense on the field today.'

That silenced Hervi. Besides, by the time he had mounted the stairs to the hall, he was too sore and winded to be capable of a coherent sentence.

Marshal led him up the length of the hall, weaving between the crowded trestles. Hervi glanced at the mass of soldiers. More had arrived since that morning, swelling what had been modest forces into a full-blown army. He was led to the dais, there to kneel before Coeur de Lion and his assembled captains. A swift upward glance showed him Alexander seated amongst them. The boy looked ghastly, his eyes glassy and his complexion a yellowish-grey.

'So,' said Coeur de Lion neutrally, 'you are Hervi de Montroi, Lavoux's standard-bearer.'

'Sire,' Hervi acknowledged, his eyes lowered now in deference, his thoughts churning in futile rings of panic. Damn Alexander, what had he done?

'On your feet,' Richard commanded. 'I cannot judge a man by the top of his head.'

Painfully, Hervi did as he was bidden, unfolding to his full height, which was close to Richard's own. They were men of a similar physical type, fair of complexion, broad-shouldered and narrow in the hip.

Richard studied Hervi, his hands steepled beneath his chin, and it appeared that what he saw did not displease him. 'Your brother was afraid that he might have to bury you, what do you say to that?'

Again, Hervi looked at Alexander, a hint of a scowl contracting his brows. 'From what I know of Alexander, sire, it is far more likely that I will have to bury him, and not before too long.'

Richard's face creased. 'I see that you understand the concepts of brotherly love,' said the man who had spent most of his life feuding with his own siblings.

'Yes, sire, being one of six.'

Richard nodded to himself, as if confirming an unspoken thought. 'So you are forced to hire your sword for a living?'

'I have to take what comes my way, sire.'

'Even if it be a hangman's noose?'

'A man of my trade lives every day of his life under threat of death,' Hervi replied with a pragmatic shrug. 'If I let myself think about it too much, I would lose my courage. I say my prayers, I keep a sharp sword.' Once more his glance flickered to Alexander, who had sat silent throughout the exchange.

Richard gently rubbed a forefinger over the ruddy gold moustache on his upper lip. He too regarded Alexander. 'Are you satisfied now that you have seen your brother?' he enquired.

'Yes, sire,' Alexander said in a voice as grey as his complexion. 'But I would know what you intend doing with him . . . with us.'

Richard gave a slow, sleepy smile. 'Let us just say that I'm disposed to be lenient,' he said softly.

CHAPTER 11

Alexander was young, hardy, and above all, stubborn. Following
the trials and traumas of the battle and the feast, he slept for a
full night and day and night again, awaking on the second morning with a raging thirst and a craving, hollow stomach.

Coeur de Lion and his army had ridden away to bring another
rebellious vassal to heel, leaving Lavoux in the capable hands of
Hamon de Rougon. The garrison had been released and sent on
their way with their mounts, but not their weapons, and the only
members remaining were Arnaud, Hervi and Alexander.

'Although Lord Richard did not say why he so favoured us
above the others,' Monday said in a puzzled voice as she regaled
Alexander with the tale whilst he devoured a thick slice of ham
and strips of griddled egg between two slabs of bread.

'Perhaps because of the way I faced him in the hall.'
Alexander drank deeply from the cup of watered wine she had
brought him. 'He is a man who likes boldness in others, I think.'

'You were beyond bold,' Monday said with a hint of censure.
'You were downright foolhardy.'

Alexander continued devouring his breakfast. 'I needed to
know what had happened to Hervi. Nothing else mattered.'

Monday plucked at his coverlet where a loop of thread stood
proud of the weave, and frowned. 'Lady Aline acted very
strangely when she heard that Lord Richard had allowed us to
remain here instead of putting us out with the rest of the garrison.'

'In what way?'

'She came and looked at you where you were sleeping and
she said that Hamon de Rougon had told her something in

confidence about Coeur de Lion that made her uneasy for your well-being. She said that you should leave as soon as you were able.'

Alexander dusted crumbs from his palms and raised his cup to finish his wine. He echoed her frown, but then laughed and shook his head dismissively. 'If he had meant me harm, I would not be here now, breaking my fast so lavishly in the comfort of Lady Aline's chambers,' he said. 'Probably she misunderstood de Rougon, or you misunderstood her.'

'I do not think so. She kept gnawing her lip as if intending to say more, but it was something she had been told in confidence. In the end she said that you had a Byzantine mother, and that Lord Richard had knowledge of Greek ways, whatever that means.'

Alexander choked and almost spilled his wine. Monday's eyes widened with concern. 'What is it? Do you know what she meant?'

He set his cup down and grimaced. It was ironic, he thought, that she had lived her life among the sinners of the tourney circuit, and he had lived the latter years of his in the 'pure air' of a monastery, and yet he was the one whose innocence had been corrupted.

'Do not look at me like that, just tell me!' she cried.

Without answering, he rose and moved stiffly to the coffer where lay the Saracen gazing-glass that Lady Aline used to view her reflection whilst tidying her hair and arranging her wimple. Picking it up, he gazed at himself and wondered what lay therein to tempt other men. His features were clear and fine, but certainly not effeminate, unless it be in the symmetry of the long-lashed eyes. If he lined them with kohl as his mother had been wont to do, and concealed the rest beneath a veil, he might be mistaken for an eastern houri. But then, the men who were attracted to him had no love for the female form. They were not seeking a surrogate wife or mother, but their own flesh idealised. *There's a boy across the river with a bottom like a peach.* So had some Greek poet written thousands of years ago. Alexander recalled seeing a translation of the text in Cranwell's library.

He turned the mirror over and gently set it back down on the coffer. There had been nothing overt in Richard's behaviour at the feast, but thinking back, Alexander could pick out small nuances and inflections. The slight narrowing of the eyes as they perused him from head to foot, and then the occasional sidelong glances at the high table. The shiver down his spine, responding to an unspecified danger. And Richard had asked to see Hervi in the flesh, and had not been displeased that they were of a similar physical type.

'Tell me,' Monday repeated impatiently. 'Or I will go down to the hall and ask Hervi or my father.'

He swung to face her. 'Is Duke Richard returning to Lavoux on his travels?'

Monday wrinkled her brow. 'Something was mentioned about keeping supplies here.' She nodded. 'Yes, I believe so.'

'Then it is best that I am not here when he returns.' He looked at her puzzled, frustrated expression and raked his hand through his hair. 'In Constantinople,' he said, 'there are bathing houses where men go to meet other men in the same way that they would go to meet a woman. That is what Lady Aline meant by knowledge of Greek ways. Love between two men.'

Monday stared at him, her grey eyes puzzled. 'You mean like Hervi and my father?'

Alexander's complexion darkened. 'No, nothing like that,' he said with exasperation. 'That is just friendship. I mean a . . . a carnal bond.'

'But how can that be?'

There was no way on God's earth that Alexander was going to tell her. 'Just believe me that it happens,' he said. 'One of the reasons I ran away from Cranwell was because of that. A monk desired me to become his lover, a position I had no wish to fulfil.'

'And Duke Richard . . .?' Monday's eyes were huge by now as she tried to absorb what seemed preposterous. 'But he has a wife . . .'

'From political expedience. He is a soldier, he dwells in the company of men, while she resides in a nunnery at Beaufort en Valée. There is no place in his life for a woman, save perhaps his mother, and no one will ever match up to Eleanor of Aquitaine.' He moved awkwardly towards the bower door. 'I must speak to

Hervi and your father.'

'I'll come with you.'

Alexander drew a deep breath to refuse, but one look at the mulish set of her jaw banished the words and the notion. 'As you wish,' he sighed, and opened the door.

The great hall seemed empty in contrast to the sardine-barrel horde that had occupied it two nights ago. Now there were only a dozen or so off-duty soldiers and squires, two clerks, and a priest busy with tallies at a trestle. Neither Hervi nor Arnaud was to be seen.

Alexander and Monday left the hall and went out into the ward. The sun was shining and dust motes hung in the air. An old hound slept in a shady corner and hens pecked around his paws with a complete lack of concern. A mason was taking measurements with pieces of string and squinting through cupped hands at the stonework damaged during the siege, and the castle carpenter was sitting out in the fine weather, mending a long bench. Alexander asked him if he had seen Hervi and Arnaud.

'Hunting,' the man said, laying down his hammer. 'A whole party of them rode out not an hour since. The mistress desired fresh meat for the table. They'll be back afore dusk,' he added cheerfully, and whistled to himself as he manipulated a piece of wood in his hands.

Alexander cursed softly between his teeth. He needed to see Hervi now, not in half a day's time. 'Do you know where they went?'

'Couldn't say, my young master, but they took the hawks, so they'll be headed for open ground.'

Alexander nodded his thanks and turned in the direction of the stables.

Monday turned with him, almost running to keep pace. 'What are you doing?'

'Going to find them.'

'But they could be anywhere. Why can't you wait until they return. Surely a few hours will not make any difference?'

Hers was the voice of reason, but Alexander found it difficult to listen. 'If you had dwelt at Cranwell Priory, you would understand. There is no point you riding out with me. Go back to the bower.' His tone was brusque because he was agitated.

Monday jutted her chin at the rejection. 'Where you think I belong, minding my distaff and my needle,' she said coldly.

'Christ, Monday, don't be so awkward.'

'I am awkward!' Her voice rose indignantly. 'How can you say that when . . .' She stopped in mid-utterance as they heard a shout from the guards on watch and the creak of chains as the portcullis was raised. Then came the hollow ring of shod hooves clopping through the gate arch – far more horses than would constitute a hunting party.

Several riders rounded the corner of the stable block. Clad in armour, laughing together, they drew rein, Coeur de Lion among them. There was not the slightest chance of Monday and Alexander escaping unseen.

'Quickly,' Alexander muttered, 'don't fight me.'

Monday parted her lips to ask what he meant and was shocked when he covered them with his own, sweeping her into a clumsy but passionate embrace against the stable wall. Her spine was jarred by the difference in their heights. The grip of his hands was bruising, the pressure of his lips flattened hers against her teeth. She struggled in protest.

'Put your arms around my neck,' he muttered against her lips, as if breathing love words. 'Let Richard believe that we are sweethearts, that there is no room for anyone or anything to come between us.'

She hesitated, then did as he wanted, belatedly understanding his reason. As she raised her arms and drew him closer still, she thought to herself that despite kissing's evil reputation as a pleasure that could lead the weak into the graver sin of fornication, there was nothing here to tempt her.

A silence had fallen. Alexander slowly raised his mouth from hers and looked round as if with startled surprise to discover that they had an audience. Monday did not need to feign her blush and only hoped that the story would not go the rounds and end up in her father's lap. Alexander kept tight hold of her hand and squeezed it. His skin was clammy, and against her fingertips she could feel the rapid beat of his pulse. He truly was afraid.

Richard eyed the pair of them narrowly. At his side, his mer-

cenary captain, Mercadier, was grinning from ear to ear. William
Marshal's look was thoughtful. 'I see you are much improved,'
Richard said neutrally.

'Yes, sire.' Alexander glanced at Richard, then studied the
ground.

'And is this your usual behaviour?'

Grooms had emerged from the stables to attend to the horses,
and other knights were riding into the stable yard.

'No, sire, but Monday and I . . .' He made a gesture serve for
the rest, and drew her closer to his side. His fingers gripped hers
so tightly now that it was all she could do not to wince with pain.

'And an empty stable is a fine place for a tryst?'

Alexander said nothing, continuing to look at the ground. The
colour in his face was unfeigned.

'Get out of my sight,' Richard said with cold contempt. 'If
you are strong enough to swive a wench, then you're strong
enough to weather the open road.'

'Sire.' Alexander bowed, and still without raising his eyes,
dragged Monday away around the corner of the stables, to the
sound of guffaws from some of Richard's knights. He collapsed
against the wooden gable-end wall, his body quivering with nausea.

'I'm sorry.' He gave her a shame-filled look. 'It was the only
thing I could think to do on the spur of the moment. Otherwise
he would have invited me to keep company with him, and I
would have had to refuse in a more direct manner.'

'You hurt me,' she said. Her own legs were shaky, and she sat
down beside him, touching her crushed lips with her equally
crushed fingers.

'I know, I'm sorry, I'm sorry.'

They leaned against each other in silence to recover, he with
his lids closed, she with her eyes wide open. She watched the
cloud patterns change and form across the wide canvas of the sky
and tried to think of nothing. At length he took her hand again,
and squeezed it, but gently this time. 'I can sing songs about the
courtly arts, but I know nothing of them in practice,' he said ruefully. 'I would deserve it if you never spoke to me again.'

The core of her anger melted at his words, and with great

daring she kissed his cheek, as she would have done a brother. 'I forgive you,' she said, 'providing that you tell my father the truth before anyone else tells him a lie about my reputation.'

'I swear so.' He kissed her cheek in return, and then her lips, gently, chastely.

To her chagrin, Monday wondered what a proper kiss between man and woman was like.

Alexander escorted Monday back to the hall, but he could not bear to return to the inactivity of the bower, and made his excuses to Monday's troubled enquiry.

'I need some time alone to find my balance,' he said. 'I don't know if you understand, but it is as necessary to me as the breath of life.'

Monday pursed her lips, then slowly nodded. 'Yes,' she murmured. 'I do understand, but I confess myself jealous. I have to seek my own solitude inside my head. A woman's desire to go off on her own is viewed with suspicion. Why should she wander away except to sin? She is inviting trouble, she makes herself into prey, and if anything happens, the fault is all hers.'

'Monday, I . . .'

She shook her head and gave him a gentle push. 'Go on. Ignore my carping.' Turning from him, she walked swiftly across the hall to the tower stairs.

Alexander watched her, feelings of tenderness, bewilderment and exasperation joining the mêlée of other emotions churning within him. Then he too shook his head, but like a beast at the irritation of flies, and returned to the stables to saddle up Samson.

The stallion was delighted to see him and made a thorough fuss as Alexander harnessed him up. He bucked with high spirits when Alexander rode him out of the castle and down to the river meadow beyond the looming grey walls. Slackening the reins, he let the horse have his head and they burned along the river bank at a hard gallop. When the first exuberance had flown like sparks from Samson's hooves, Alexander steadied him to a canter, then eased him down to a swinging walk. Patches of yellow grass and bald cinder stains were the only indication that a camp had stood in the meadow. The river glittered, and three fishermen sat on the bridge, lines trailing in the current. On the opposite bank, a goat and two kids stood shoulder-deep in a clump of thistles, munching blissfully. The clash of battle seemed as distant as a dream.

Alexander drew Samson to a halt and began to go through the exercises which he and the horse had been painstakingly learning together. The rear, the back-kick, the change and turn of leading forehooves. Absorbed in his work, the rough edges were smoothed from Alexander's mind. A sense of control returned, and the feelings of panic and anger diminished.

He was nothing to Richard Coeur de Lion, a passing fancy along the way and quickly to be forgotten. Alexander had no great affection or loyalty to Lavoux and would harbour no regrets about leaving. Lord Bertran had been a brigand, and Lady Aline, although intelligent and beautiful, was something of a *belle dame sans merci*, a manipulator of men. He would lose nothing by riding out tomorrow.

That much decided, he relaxed and thought with anticipation of the open road and the opportunities awaiting on the tourney field. He cast his eye over the fields in search of the returning hunt, but there was nothing to see except lush meadows . . . and in the distance a single horseman watching him. For a moment he thought it was Coeur de Lion and his heart began to hammer. Samson threw up his head and uttered a stallion neigh of challenge.

Alexander reined him in short and turned to face the rider, head on, realising as he did so that it was not Duke Richard, but William Marshal. The baron had exchanged his armour for a plain tunic and chausses, although both were of excellent quality and spoke of the status he had carved for himself by a mixture of intelligence, astuteness and sheer athletic ability. The weakness of relief surged through Alexander's muscles.

'You ride well, lad,' Marshal complimented as he rode forward. A half-smile curved beneath his moustache. His face was powerfully boned, brow and cheek and jaw thrusting like rocks against the sun-browned skin.

Alexander reddened at the compliment. 'Thank you, my lord.

I practise when I can.'

'A fine horse, too. Is he yours?'

Alexander hesitated, and saw the Marshal's flint-coloured eyes sharpen. 'Yes, he's mine,' he said, and smoothed the glossy black neck.

'And yet you seemed uncertain for a moment?'

'Because I was not sure how to reply,' Alexander said, deciding that candour would serve him best with William Marshal. 'He is a gift of God really, since I came across him tied to a tree in a forest beside his dead master.' He told Marshal the tale, the stark details, bare of elaboration. 'I never sought to discover whose he might have been. I had burdens of my own, and the tourney life is a nomad one. By the time I had space to think, we were far away in Normandy, and besides, we had grown attached to each other.' He tugged affectionately on one of Samson's sharp, pricked ears.

'Then if he was not yours before, you have made him so now,' the older man said with a smile in his voice. 'I would like to see what else you and he can do.'

A glorious, golden hour passed in which Alexander became a willing pupil to William Marshal's tuition, and Marshal shed the burdens of his higher responsibility and became a young knight himself, back in the fresh meadow grass of his youth. His squires, hovering on the periphery of the encounter, were sent back to the keep to fetch lances, helms, shields and a quintain. Alexander was given a lesson in the art of jousting by the greatest jouster alive.

'The weight of the lance must be supported by the palm of your hand, not your fingers,' Marshal said, eyeing Alexander critically and riding around him to judge his posture. 'Yes, just so, but I think you need a lighter lance.' He snapped his fingers, and a squire came running with the required article.

'As your strength increases, so you will be able to use heavier weapons. You do not have the power to unhorse a man by brute force alone, so you will need cunning and skill and technique to win through. Therefore you must practise harder than any of your opponents. You have a talent; what you make of it is up to you.'

'As you made use of yours?' Alexander ventured.

The Marshal smiled and shook his head. 'You may take my career either as a warning or a spur. That too is your own decision.'

Alexander and his tutor tilted at the quintain, and then gently with each other, the more experienced and powerful man drawing his blows, Alexander learning with each run.

The sun had trailed towards the west and lay over the fields in a flood of late gold when finally they drew to a close in consideration of the horses, which were tiring, and repaired at a slow, companionable walk to the castle.

'Keep a clear head and you will go far, young man,' said Marshal with a benevolent glance at Alexander.

'Thank you, my lord.' Not unnaturally, Alexander was filled with a glow of pleasure and pride.

The Marshal rubbed his forefinger down his bony nose where the jousting helm had left a streak of rust. 'It was not so much a compliment as a warning,' he said. 'You live too close to the edge. This afternoon, with me, you have been using your mind as well as your gut, and the results have been promising. But I saw you take wild risks in the battle for Lavoux, and I have heard the tale from my nephew, John, about how you rescued him from a vindictive opponent on the tourney field by rushing out unarmed except for a spear. One day your rashness will be your undoing, unless you can curb it.'

The glow Alexander had been feeling turned to chagrin. He fiddled with a hank of Samson's mane. 'It is a reaction to fear,' he muttered. 'One moment I am almost emptying my bowels with terror; I want to run away and never stop; the next I am angry at my own weakness, and I charge into the fray without thought.'

'You cannot abdicate that responsibility,' Marshal said sternly. 'You will be nothing, a man used by other men, and that would be an utter waste of your life. I have seen today how swift your wits are when you have them about you – and I do not mean here in the meadow.'

Alexander's head jerked up, and beneath him Samson gave a spine-jarring leap. He grabbed for the reins and tightened them. 'My lord?'

'That girl, the young sempstress. Are you and she lovers? I judge not, although it was a handsome performance.'

'How could you tell?'

The Marshal's lips twitched. 'Unless you were trying to break the poor lass's spine your embrace was a shade too vigorous, and with the stables so close, you would not have engulfed her like that unless you intended to be seen.' He laid a reassuring hand on Alexander's shoulder. 'Don't worry, I believe you attained your goal. As a statement of rejection, it was crude but effective.'

Alexander risked a glance at his companion, but the stern features gave nothing away. William Marshal was known to be a man of high honour and discretion, loyal to the last drop of blood, and Richard Coeur de Lion was his liege lord.

'I will not be sorry to leave this place,' Alexander muttered as they rode into the shadow of the looming walls. 'It was supposed to be a sanctuary, but it has been nothing but a prison.'

'All experience is grist to the mill,' said the Marshal. 'Live and learn.'

Behind them, the notes of a hunting horn sounded on the sweet evening air, and riders appeared on the horizon, hounds loping beside the horses. Alexander glanced at them, then faced the keep. No, he would not be sorry to leave Lavoux, but if not for his sojourn here, he would never have encountered William Marshal and been given an afternoon's tuition in not only the art of jousting, but the art of life.

And when later, in the great hall, Monday asked him if he had found his balance, he smiled. 'Perhaps not,' he said, 'but the scales weigh more evenly than they did before.'

CHAPTER 12

NORMANDY,
SPRING 1195

'Hah!' yelled Alexander and dug in his spurs. The black destrier leaped from its hocks and plunged into a ground-eating gallop, the summer dust exploding in small puffs from beneath the reaching hooves. Hervi to one side of him, Arnaud to the other, Alexander levelled his lance and concentrated on the man he had chosen to take. He pinned his vision to the four nail heads slightly to the left of centre. Time slowed down. There was only himself, the fluid motion of the black, and the oncoming crimson and green shield.

The impact was sweet and clean, and his adversary's lance scarcely had time to rattle Alexander's shield before the man was propelled backwards over his saddle cantle and crashed on the dry ground. Alexander turned Samson on the space of a penny, and lowered his lance to the throat of his sprawled victim.

'I yield!' the knight cried, and gave Alexander his name and his oath of recompense. Alexander withdrew the lance, saw that Hervi and Arnaud were in no difficulty, and set off in pursuit of the loose horse.

Around the perimeter of the field and within the safety of the withy sanctuaries, onlookers cheered and shouted encouragement at the fighters. They wanted to see courage and wild bravado, to be entertained. Some of them even wanted blood. Alexander grasped the bridle of the loose destrier, a handsome although rather flat-footed bay. Useful for wet ground, he thought, as he led it over to the sanctuary where Monday was waiting.

'First ransom of the day,' he said cheerfully as he handed her the bridle. Then he removed his helm and glanced around.

A young woman captured his eye. She did not belong with the regular inhabitants of the tourney field but was, he guessed, one of the townswomen, out to view the spectacle. She wore a fetching gown of dark-blue linen, the colour and weave proclaiming her a person of some wealth. A veil of the finest gossamer silk covered her head, but her braid of corn-blonde hair had been allowed to remain free and was woven with scarlet ribbons. She cast a look through her lashes at Alexander, her eyes so deep a blue that they were almost violet. Fire sparked through his body and centred in his loins. His hands were suddenly damp on the reins. He noticed that there was an elderly maid by her side and a serving man, but no sign of a husband.

In the months since Lavoux, Alexander had discovered that his dedication to training had benefited his education in more ways than one. He had become capable of taking to the field as a competitor, could hold his own, and frequently enjoyed success. And with that success came advantages and pleasures, not least because of his freshness, his youth, and the dark good looks which the tourney circuit had yet to ruin.

There was a glamour about him, and he was discovering with some surprise and a great deal of gratification that women not only sought his company, they also sought his bed, or offered him theirs. It was still a novelty, and there were skills to be learned every whit as complex as those of warfare. The women used him, and he, in his turn, used them.

Monday had been speaking to him, and guiltily, he realised that he did not know what she had said.

'I asked if you are returning to the field,' she said impatiently, her slim hand competently clutching the bay's bridle close to the cheek strap.

'Yes, I was just taking a quick respite.' It was a weak excuse since the mêlée had only just begun and men were still warming up. He set the helm back on his head, looked through the eye slits at the townswoman, who was watching him with amusement, and saluting her, spurred back on to the field.

Monday scowled at the elegant young woman and led the bay

destrier away to Hervi's horse picket, where she tied him securely beside the pack beasts. Alexander was certainly proving himself this season, she thought, but she hated the changes his increasing skills had wrought on his nature. His confidence had grown with each success, until on occasion he rode very close to being conceited. He drank measure for measure with the older knights and he talked more than he listened these days, frequently about himself. The women who simpered at his passing, who threw ribbons and flowers . . . and themselves in his path, had led him to believe that he was God's gift to the female sex.

She had thought about reminding him of his arrival at their camp, half starved and in beggar's rags, of the tending he had received from herself and her mother, the kindness and consideration. Yes, her eyes flashed. *Consideration*, that was the word. She doubted that Alexander had ever paused to think about others in his headlong rush towards glory. She could still taste that kiss at Lavoux, inept, clumsy and desperate. He had needed her then. He needed her now in the guise of servant.

Her lips tight with annoyance, Monday gave the stallion a clump of hay to keep him quiet and went to her tent to fetch her cloak. Although the ground was dry, the sky was heavy, and it seemed likely to rain before the contest was over.

A woman was lying on her father's pallet, her naked body half covered by the blanket. A slack white arm was thrust beneath the pillow, and a mountainous blue-veined breast flopped over the side like a cow's udder, the nipple fat and brown. The woman's face was concealed, and all Monday could see was a mass of frowsy hair, the colour a brassy, alchemist's yellow with darker roots.

Her father sometimes took women to his bed for comfort. Monday was not happy when he did, but she bit her tongue and bore with it, hoping that it would ease his bitter longing and make him more amenable. At least he did not drink so hard when he had a bedmate, but it was a sordid price to pay. This was not the first time that he had lain with this particular whore, whose name was Grisel, but it was the first occasion that she had still been here beyond the dawn.

Tears filled Monday's eyes. She felt a stranger in her own

domain. The woman was lying where her mother had once lain, defiling what had been a warm and tender place. Monday felt unclean even for breathing the same air. Her stomach queasy with revulsion, she tiptoed to her own pallet, took her cloak, and beat a hasty retreat.

'Who was that girl you were talking to?'

Alexander forced open his eyes. A warm, scented bath, followed by a joust between the sheets almost as vigorous as that on the tourney field, had filled him with a pleasurable languor. The feather mattress beneath him was as soft as heaven, and the bedchamber of the town house prosperously appointed and airy. He could have stayed there forever.

'What girl?' he said, and yawned between clenched teeth.

His violet-eyed companion leaned over him and traced the contour of his lips with her forefinger. The tips of her unbound blonde tresses trailed on his naked chest and her thigh curved across his, her knee gently nudging his testicles. 'The one at the enclosure in the grey dress, the one you gave the captured destrier to at the beginning.'

'Oh, her.' He pillowed his arms behind his head and looked at his partner. Her name was Sara and she was the widow of a wine merchant forty years her senior and four months in his grave. She was spirited, self-assured and as voracious as a lioness – a contributory factor to her husband's demise. Given a choice after the tourney, between drinking around the fire with the other knights, or returning to the town with Sara to bathe in a hot tub and accept her hospitality, there had been no contest.

'Yes, her.' She nibbled at his chest and her thigh curved in a higher arc. He felt the wiry brush of her lower hair and the damp kiss of her sex. Arousal coursed through his body, winding around the languor.

'She is the daughter of a knight who fights with us,' he said with a shrug.

'But you know her well?'

'Yes – like a sister.'

'She has a pretty face.' The golden hair trailed over his stomach, following the touch of her lips. Gentle, fluttering kisses, the tickle of her tongue. Alexander closed his eyes and softly groaned.

'I have never noticed,' he said in a somewhat strangled voice, and arched his hips.

'Then you are either blind or a liar,' she said with amusement, and replaced the busy motion of her mouth with the moist heat of her sheath. 'And what of me, do I have a pretty face?' She sat upon him, barely moving, teasing him with the gentle squeeze of internal muscles. Had she done that the first time, he would have exploded, but he had more control now, and set himself to endure.

'Lady, you are as beautiful as the sun!' he panted.

She cocked her head and considered him, a mischievous smile in her eyes and on her lips. Then she ceased moving upon him, and taking his hands, cupped them over her breasts. 'Show me,' she said. 'Touch me where I am beautiful; worship me.'

The ensuing exploration was both the most erotic encounter that Alexander had ever experienced, and also the most enlightening. Instead of taking his pleasure as a God-given right, he learned how to give it, and discovered that the giving greatly enhanced his own body's responses.

Once more she began to move, rolling her hips in a slow but relentless rhythm. Through a haze of ecstatic sensations, Alexander wondered who had taught her the skills of this delicious torment. She had spoken of her deceased husband in dismissive tones as an old man – 'with no steel in his scabbard'. She must have had other lovers, and she was perhaps ten years older than himself, a world more experienced; but he had the steel, and at the moment he was admirably filling her scabbard. There was a song in it somewhere, but he could not think of the lyrics. The only words that came to mind as her pace increased and his hands clamped upon her round white buttocks were as primeval as the thrust and pull of their bodies.

Sara left the bed and padded gracefully to the flagon set on the coffer, her blonde locks curling to meet the delectable curve of her bottom. Alexander watched her movements with lazy appreciation. His lids would do no more than half raise, he felt so tired and contented. She returned to the bed, a cup in each hand, and sipping from one, gave him the other.

'I hope you like this,' she said, arching a delicately plucked eyebrow. 'It's a great restorative following exertion.'

Grinning, Alexander propped himself up on the pillow. 'To an oiled sword,' he toasted, making her giggle and playfully slap him. The taste of wine flowed over his palate, and then the raw tang of ginevra. He struggled not to gag, forced himself to swallow, and put the cup aside.

'You don't like it?' she queried with a moue of disappointment.

'It's the ginevra,' he said. The taste was in his throat, making him want to heave. 'I'm sorry. Even the smell of it makes me sick.'

She eyed him over the rim of her own cup. 'Then you won't want to kiss me again,' she said playfully.

He looked down at the embroidered coverlet, his mood of contentment seeping away to leave only weariness. 'Lady, I wish I knew what to say without seeming churlish. Truly I have an aversion to this drink.'

'Will you tell me why?'

He glanced briefly at her, then back down at the bedclothes. 'I once stole an entire flask of ginevra, drank the lot, and was as sick as a dog for three days. I was also whipped for the theft.'

'Ah,' she said, with a glint of comprehension. 'Are those the marks of a lash I felt on your back earlier?'

He resisted the urge to look over his shoulder or contort his arm to feel the slender white ridges raised on his spine by the thongs of Brother Alkmund's scourge. 'It was a long time ago,' he said, hoping to dissuade her.

Sara was not to be put off. A gleam in her eyes, she set down her cup and knelt beside him, her breasts peeking between the strands of her silky blonde hair. 'What is it like to be whipped?' Her hands reached for him, smoothing over his shoulders to touch the highest of the scars in a whisper-soft caress.

Alexander was both attracted and repelled by the honeyed tone of her voice, the lurking purr of excitement. 'Lady, you would not want to know,' he said, and withdrew from her questing fingertips.

'I might.'

Alexander reached for his shirt. The game had gone far enough, and in a moment it would cease to be a game.

Outside the house, clear in the evening still, came the sound of shod hooves ringing upon the beaten earth of the courtyard. Someone whistled jauntily, and seconds later a small stone struck the closed shutters with intentional force.

'Sara, Sara, open up!' cried a deep, masculine voice.

'God's bollocks!' Sara cursed, and flung off the bed and to her feet, her gaze on the shutters.

A second stone struck the wood and clattered to the ground. 'Sara, lass, open up!'

'Who is it?' Alexander dragged on his shirt, his lethargy replaced by a quivering tension.

'Huon, the captain of the watch,' she said. 'He stops by sometimes to make sure I'm safe.' She swore again.

'Then tell him you are.'

She gave him a glittering look over her shoulder. 'Don't be a fool.' She gestured brusquely. 'Hurry, get dressed.' Throwing on her chemise, she ran to the shutters, freed the catch, and threw them wide.

'Huon, it's late, I wasn't expecting you!' Her tone was full of reproach, but it bore a smoky intimacy too.

Dazed, Alexander flung on his garments. He could scarcely grasp that this was happening to him, although he had sung about it often enough in bawdy camp fire ballads.

The man shouted up some reply that Alexander did not hear, but Sara gave a throaty laugh in response. Then she closed the shutters and turned back to the room. By now Alexander was hopping into his shoes. 'Your lover?' he queried.

'One of them.' With efficient swiftness she smoothed out the twisted bedclothes and drew the coverlet straight.

'One of them?' His voice squeaked as it had not done for more than five years.

'Sauce for the gander is sauce for the goose,' she said pertly. 'My husband would not have denied himself a casual tumble in the hay along his road – neither does Huon . . . or you for that matter. Why should I deprive myself of what pleases me?' She took his barely touched goblet, tipped the mixture back into the flagon and wiped the dampness from the inside of the cup with the edge of his cloak. 'There,' she said with satisfaction, and gave him a push towards the door, 'nothing amiss. Go on, go down. He will begin to wonder why I have not come to open up for him.'

She took the bemused Alexander downstairs, through the darkened main chamber and into a screened-off store room beyond. There was a large trap door in the middle of the floor. Sara raised it by an iron ring in the centre to reveal wooden stairs descending into a dark undercroft. 'Wait here until it's safe,' she said, and gave him another push. 'Hurry.'

Such was the urgency of the moment that Alexander followed her insistence, and it was only as she dropped the trap over his head, consigning him to a musty-smelling darkness, that he had the opportunity to inhale the atmosphere and begin panicking.

He could not stand upright, for the ceiling was a good foot less than his height. There were things hanging from the beams, things he could not see, only discover by the accident of touch in the pitch blackness – dried salted sausages, bacon flitches, bunches of herbs. Two small furry bodies – probably conies. A plucked chicken for the morrow's table, its skin crepey and cold. He recoiled from that with a bitten cry of revulsion, his heart pounding and his palms icy.

The cellar terminated in a row of dusty casks. He blundered against them; the strength went from his legs, and he buckled to his knees on the gritty floor. Except for the lack of leather cords slicing into his wrists, he might have been back in the prison cell at Cranwell. It was a nightmare made into reality, and all the more potent for the pleasure that had preceded it. Punishment for a sin he had barely had time to commit, let alone confess. *What is it like to be whipped?*

At first he was unable to think beyond his fear. It filled his head, made him mad, until he was almost prepared to believe that Brother Alkmund was standing before him, whip in hand. 'No!' he bellowed. The denial rang around the space of the undercroft and echoed back to his lips. The air fell around the cry and settled in claustrophobic heaviness. He wondered which would be worse: to stay here in the dark alone with his terror, or risk being accosted by the captain of the watch as he made his escape. The roar of his own breath filled his ears, shallow and swift. Think, he told himself. In Christ's name, use your brain, not your gut. He scooped his fingers through his hair and swore. The curses bolstered his courage, made him bold enough to regain his feet. Making a conscious effort to breathe more slowly, he felt his way back down the undercroft. The cellar was a store room, not a prison, and the trap was not bolted. Beyond waiting for Sara and her guest to reach her chamber, he had no need to remain here.

He found the lowest step and set his foot upon it, his every sense alert. No sound came from the world above, no voice or footfall. He moved up to the trap and set the palm of his hand to its surface. There was no movement, and for a second the panic returned. He could imagine Brother Alkmund creeping up behind him in the darkness and seizing him by the legs. Gritting his teeth, Alexander bent his arm and set his full force against the trap. It yielded to his push and slammed back on the upper room floor with a thump loud enough to rouse the household. Alexander hastened out of the cellar, the shirt on his back saturated in cold sweat.

He darted from the store room into the main chamber. A night candle burned on a tall iron pricket, and by its light and shadow, he could see Sara's elderly maid sitting up on her straw pallet and staring at him as he crossed the room towards the barred iron door. She shook her head slowly in obvious disapproval but made no effort to raise a hue and cry. It was with more than a touch of shame and relief that he reached the door and raised the bar. Above him, he heard a man's voice raised in question, and Sara's throaty laugh cajoling him to come back to bed.

Outside, a fine drizzle had begun to fall, soft as cobwebs, and the air tasted of spring. Alexander inhaled with the relief of being free of the poky cellar, and if the truth were known, Sara's bedchamber. Several lessons had been learned in the course of the last two hours – about pleasure and lust, about arousal and control. He raised his head to the damp kiss of the rain and stepped out into the darkened streets of the town. The gates were barred until morning, but he knew that the payment of a coin would secure him a passage through the postern gate to the camp fires of the tourney field beyond.

Monday huddled in her cloak and took the bowl of steaming meat broth that Edmund One-eye ladled out to her. 'No charge, take it.' He waved aside her attempt to pay. 'You and your father are good customers, you're entitled to the occasional free dish.'

Monday gave him a wan smile over the wooden rim of the bowl. 'Do you mind if I drink it here?'

'Don't ask foolish questions. Here, come to the fire.' He drew up a low stool and dusted it off with a large hand. Monday sat down gratefully and cradled the hot broth, letting the warmth seep into her hands, for the evening was cool and the fine rain clammy.

Edmund One-eye gave the broth a stir to keep the chopped meat and barley swirling through the simmering water, and returned to cutting up scraps of meat for the pies he was going to bake on the morrow. He said nothing, but Monday was glad of his solid, comforting presence in a world that seemed increasingly hostile.

She sipped her broth and wondered where to go when she had finished. Her father and Grisel were drinking themselves senseless in the tent that should have been her home and haven. Hervi was similarly occupied with one of the camp sluts, and Alexander was in the town with that shameless woman, whose invitation had been so blatant as to be indecent. Monday's anger rose as she thought about it. Alexander's response had been blatant too, and the other men had cheered him on, the way they might cheer a dog going after a bitch. Her face burned at the memory of some of the comments.

Edmund scraped the chopped pork meat and fat into a bowl and wiped his hands on a scrap of clean linen rag. 'I daresay I'll have some cinnamon bread for you tomorrow,' he commented gruffly.

A lump tightened her throat at his kindness and the way he had time for her even when there were so many other concerns to pluck at his attention. Not all men were wastrels and idiots, she told herself, and thanked him with a quiver in her voice. For an instant she was tempted to confide in him, but pride bridled her tongue. He would have to be completely blind not to know about her father's drinking and whoring, the black bitterness that no one could pierce. Cinnamon bread and unspoken sympathy would have to be enough.

Monday finished the broth, and then there was no reason to remain. She would have been welcome, but pride again would not let her stay beyond her excuse to do so.

Edmund squeezed her shoulder as she rose to leave. 'I know most of what goes on in these camps,' he said compassionately. 'There is always a place for you at my fire if you have no hearth to call your own.'

This time she had no voice with which to thank him, and fled before she broke down in tears.

Hervi's tent as she passed it was dark, but from within came the sound of muffled giggles and the soft rumble of Hervi's voice. Monday bit her lip and hurried on. There was a treacherous undercurrent in his tone that set up a yearning in her own vitals, a curiosity about bodily pleasure. Lust might be a mortal sin, but it was evidently enjoyable too, or men . . . and women would not return to it time and again. It could not all be mere desperation to procreate in the face of death.

As Monday approached her own tent, her pace slowed and her feet dragged out each step. The churning in her belly turned to nausea and for a moment she almost turned away. She could not bear to think of her father and Grisel engaged in bed sport. But the sounds that came muffled through the canvas were thankfully of slumber. Compressing her lips, she laid her hand to the flap and entered the tent.

Her father was snoring on the floor where drink had felled him, his clothes marred by wine stains and the grease of pastry crumbs. Silverish beard stubble blurred the line of his jaw and his once taut, tanned skin was slack and yellow. 'Oh, Papa,' she whispered in a heartbroken voice, and knelt beside him. Grisel was not in the main part of the tent, but Monday's relief at small mercies was short-lived. Almost immediately she realised that the curtain to her father's pallet was drawn across, and from behind it came soft, stealthy sounds.

Rising, Monday tiptoed to the hanging. Now she heard the clink of metal, and shallow, rapid breathing, punctuated by indistinct, gloating whispers. The hair at Monday's nape stood on end. Seizing the curtain in her fist, she dragged it rapidly aside.

Grisel stared up in shock from the open coffer she had been plundering. Clemence's best silk gown lay in a crumpled heap, dried rose petals falling from the folds. It was Monday's comfort to take the gown out of the chest, to bury her hands and her face in the cool, shimmering fabric and draw in her mother's essence. Now her sacred relic had been violated and it was obvious that Grisel had been avariciously investigating the other items in the coffer – the combs and hair fillets, the delicate silk wimple that Clemence had brought from her other life as an earl's daughter, the silver strap ends for sewing on to a belt. On Grisel's wrist was a bracelet of Irish-worked silver that had been one of Clemence's favourite pieces, and around her neck was a string of amber and garnet beads that Arnaud had bought only three years ago as a twelfth-night gift for his beloved wife. Monday saw all of this, and then she saw red. Grisel's startled face dissolved before her eyes, and nothing was left but a blinding rage.

'You whore!' Monday screamed in rage and grief. 'Take your filthy hands away from my mother's things!'

'They're mine now!' the woman retorted, her eyes glittering and feral. 'Your father gave them to me. Your sainted mother has no need of them now she's in the ground, does she?'

'You lying bitch!' Monday howled. 'My father would never do that! Those things belong to me. Get out of here, you slut, get out!' She hurled herself upon the woman, fastening her fingers in the frizzy hair and pulling with all her strength. A great clump tore away in her hand, for Grisel's locks had been severely damaged by all the alchemist's preparations she smothered on them to render herself a fashionable blonde.

Grisel shrieked in agony but responded with nails and teeth, raking a nasty gash down Monday's throat and biting the side of her hand so that Monday was forced to let go of the frowsy hair. The girl kicked out and landed a blow in the whore's soft abdomen, but it was a momentary success. Grisel recovered far too swiftly, punched Monday on the chin, knocked her flat, and straddled her.

Monday saw stars. The blow to her jaw had snapped her teeth on her tongue and her mouth was full of blood. Grisel squeezed her throat and forced her head down against the floor. 'I am your father's woman now!' the whore spat. 'Your sainted mama is dead, and he hates her for being dead. I can have whatever I want from him, because I'm alive, and he needs me.'

'You slut, you whore!' Monday sobbed through a mask of blood and tears. She tried to kick Grisel, but her legs were hampered by her gown.

'Not any more,' Grisel taunted, with a flash of yellow teeth. 'You are going to learn to call me mother.'

'Never, I'll never do that!'

Grisel raised a clawed hand. 'You'll do as you're told!'

The hand never descended, for it was seized and Grisel was wrenched backwards off her victim. 'Stop!' Alexander roared. 'In God's name, what goes forth here?'

Monday struggled to her feet. Her gown was torn at the throat, and she could feel the heat of blood trickling down her neck. Her wimple was trampled on the floor and her hair tumbled in wild straggles to her hips. In her fist, she held a clump of Grisel's frizzy hair like a trophy. 'I caught her stealing my things,' she wept furiously. 'Plundering my coffer like a vulture.' Blood dribbled down her chin from her bitten tongue and her eyes were aglitter with rage and tears.

'The girl's mashed in her wits,' Grisel retorted, rubbing her wrist where Alexander had dragged her away. 'I have her father's permission to use whatever I want, since he's going to marry me. She's naught but a jealous child!'

'Jealous!' Monday was so choked with emotion that she could utter no more than the single word.

Alexander flickered her a look, then returned his gaze to the whore. 'You may indeed have Arnaud's permission,' he said, 'but in what frame of mind it was given is less clear. Nor is he capable of telling us at the moment. Since Mistress Monday is his daughter and his heir, I suggest you strip that jewellery, take your cloak and go to another fire for the nonce.'

Her small eyes narrowed. 'Who are you to meddle in my affairs?' she sneered. 'Keep your long nose out.'

'You would not want to fight with me,' Alexander said quietly, and tapped his fingers on his sword belt. Grisel tried to stare him out and failed.

He took a step forwards, invading her space. 'Which is it to be – on your own two feet, or arse over ears into the mud?' His voice was still quiet, but to a woman like Grisel, who was accustomed to men who bellowed, there was more threat in his soft tone than in an outright roar.

She drew herself up, but it was obvious that her battle was lost. 'I will tell Arnaud the moment he awakes, and he will make you pay for this moment,' she hissed.

Alexander said nothing, just took another step towards her, his hand going to the latch of his belt. She snatched the bracelet from her wrist, the beads from around her neck, and threw them on the floor at his feet. Then she spat, just missing the toe of his boot, and stalked from the tent.

'Sweet Jesu, what a viper,' Alexander muttered, and turned to Monday, then, with another muffled oath, strode over to her and engulfed her in his arms.

At first she resisted his offer of comfort, standing rigid within the circle of his embrace, hating him almost as much as she hated Grisel, but as he started to withdraw, she clutched his sleeves in a grip so tight that her knuckles blanched and the fabric of his tunic was imprinted with creases that would not drop out until the following day. She beat her head against his breast, and dry sobs racked her body.

'He does not see!' she wept. 'And I cannot make him open his eyes. All he does is hate my mother for dying, and me for being a part of her!'

'Hush, it's all right,' he murmured awkwardly, and stroked her hair with his open palm.

'No, it's not all right!' She pushed herself furiously out of his arms. 'What do you know? She gestured at the despoiled coffer. 'You have your jewelled cross and your memories intact. You come from bedding that slut in the town, the smell of her perfume on your skin and you tell me that it's all right! You are as ignorant as the rest of them!' Whirling from him, she knelt by the coffer and began to replace the keepsakes. It gave her shaking hands a focus.

She could feel him standing behind her, could feel his eyes boring into her spine. She wanted to scream at him to go away, leave her in peace, but more than the want was the need not to be alone.

'I know that I cannot understand your pain,' he said awkwardly, 'but I can see it, and irrespective of where I have been, I am here now. Rail at me if it will give you ease.'

She shook her head and sniffed. 'Railing will only make me feel worse.'

He cleared his throat. 'That scratch is nasty. Do you have some salve for it?'

She laid the silk gown in the coffer and smoothed it gently. 'In the smaller chest,' she said without looking round. 'Unless she has plundered that too. A stonework jar with a wooden stopper.'

He threw back the coffer lid and delved among spare drop spindles, hanks of wool, twists of powdered herbs, until he found the jar. Removing the top, he sniffed at the yellowish unguent, and recoiled.

'Goose-grease and herbs,' she said. 'It smells dreadful, but it works.' She was quieter now, the rage and grief dampened down to a smoulder.

'Sit still.' He turned her to face the light from the candle-lantern, and dipping his forefinger, very gently applied a smearing of ointment to the long gouge on her throat.

She made a tiny movement as he hurt her, then held herself still. 'If I had somewhere to run away, I would do so,' she said bleakly.

Alexander's fingers ceased their work. 'That would be very foolish.'

'You did,' she challenged. 'You ventured across the Narrow Sea on your own without so much as a bundle to your name.'

He shook his head. 'I had a destination,' he retorted. 'And still I almost starved to death. I slept rough in the woods like an outlaw; for a time I even was one, if you count the henhouses I raided for eggs, and the eels out of someone's trap.' He resumed the delicate work of his fingertips. 'Besides, I am male. It would be twice as hard for a woman to make her own way in the world. Belike you would be pounced upon and raped before you had travelled more than five miles, unless you had the money to hire the protection of servants. For all your misery, you are safer here.'

'I had thought about going to my grandfather,' she said shakily, 'but he disowned my mother when she ran away with Papa, and I do not know if he would give me shelter beneath his roof.'

Alexander finished anointing her injuries and wiped his hands on a scrap of linen. 'I know of your grandfather,' he said slowly. 'My family's lands are not far from his, and he was also a patron of Cranwell Priory. He might indeed give you shelter, but it would not be out of kindness or duty. You would be his pawn, a useful prize to sell in marriage to the highest bidder. I do not believe that your life would be any easier than it is now, although for different reasons.'

Monday swallowed and wiped her eyes on the back of her hand. 'Even if not easier, it could be no harder to bear.' Rising to her feet, she took a blanket from the pallet and went to her father, who had not stirred throughout the fracas. With tender care and not a little weariness, she laid it over him. Then, with a sigh, she went to the tent flaps and looked out on the smoky, damp night. 'I'm sorry for what I said earlier,' she murmured. 'I am grateful for your support.'

Alexander shrugged. 'Why should you be sorry for what is truth?' he responded. 'I had indeed come straight from a woman's bed, and I am ignorant . . . although not as ignorant as I was,' he added wryly, as he came to stand at her side.

CHAPTER 13

It was long after dawn when Arnaud de Cerizay stirred from a sodden slumber and forced open his eyes upon another day. He was lying on the floor of his tent and someone had covered him with the blanket off the pallet he had been unable to reach. There was a relentless, hot pounding in his skull and the sunlight glittering through the tent flaps was impossible to look upon.

'Monday?' he croaked, and made himself sit up. The tent was as neat and orderly as she always kept it, but there was no other sign of her presence. 'Grisel?' There was no response from that quarter either. Arnaud tottered to his feet, and shading his eyes, went to the tent flap.

Last night's drizzle had cleared the air, and the sun was noonhigh. He swore at the lateness of the hour, and at the women for not rousing him sooner. His stomach curdled and churned. Unable to face the thought of food, he sought around for the wine flask and discovered it empty. The only thing to drink was the water in the storage jar. He dipped the ladle beside it and swallowed several mouthfuls, wishing that he had died in his sleep.

Light blared into the tent as Hervi threw back the flap and ducked inside, his presence as blond and vital as the morning – and about as welcome.

'Have you seen my daughter?' Arnaud greeted him irritably.

'She and Alexander went into the town this morning to purchase supplies.'

'Good, there's no more wine.'

Frowning, Hervi stepped further into the tent. 'You drink too much for your own good.'

'Hah, that's rich coming from you!' Arnaud retorted belligerently, and went to rinse his hands and face in the bowl of washing water that Monday had left on the coffer.

'You will never find me malingering senseless in my bed at noon, my horses untended and my weapons uncleaned.'

The anger in Arnaud's belly churned upwards to scald his mouth. 'It is none of your business how I spend my time off the field,' he snapped. 'Do I ever moralise at you? What were you doing yester eve, if not drinking and swiving, eh?'

'But I rose at dawn. I have tended my horse, cleaned my weapons, practised my swordplay and prepared for the afternoon's tourney.' Hervi's frown deepened, and he pushed his hair off his brow in agitation. 'You say it is none of my business. I would agree, except that it is affecting your performance on the field. Alexander and I had to sweat like Trojans yesterday to cover for you. It's not fair to give the lad so much responsibility. Yes, he's good, but he has neither the strength nor the experience to be put in the situations he was. Three times you should have been there, and three times you weren't.'

'Are you saying that I am a liability?' Arnaud narrowed his lids. Hot pain pulsed and ricocheted around his skull. Hervi's words were all the more infuriating because they were spoken with concern rather than anger. They might even have been true, but Arnaud couldn't remember.

'You will be if you continue on this downward road. Yesterday we won because myself and the lad fought out of our skins. But it will not always be so. Your stamina lasted for no more than half the bout.' His voice softened. 'I am worried for you, Arnaud.'

'Are you? Or is it concern for yourself that brings you here this morning?'

'It is no longer morning,' Hervi pointed out. 'And yes, I am too fond of my own hide to lose it just yet – even if you have no love for your own. You are my friend, and I am offering you sound advice. If not for your own sake, then for Monday's. Pull yourself out of the quicksand while you still can. The girl needs a father's love, not a drunkard's indifference.'

'You know what you can do with your advice,' Arnaud snarled.

Colour flooded beneath Hervi's tan. 'Look,' he made a visible effort, opening his hand in a conciliatory gesture, 'come out to Edmund One-eye's, and I'll buy you bread to break your fast.'

Arnaud stared at Hervi's strong, blunt fingers, then beyond them into the earnest, raw-boned face. A part of him was desperate to accept the lifeline, to smile and walk out in the sun, but it was not strong enough to fight off the darker side, which asked what was the point.

'Find another partner,' he said, and turned his back. 'I dissolve ours.'

'Oh, in the name of our Saviour's suffering, Arnaud, don't be so pig-headed!'

'What did Christ know of suffering compared with mine?' Arnaud blasphemed, aghast at his own words, but unable to prevent them from spilling forth. 'Go on, get out, you're no longer welcome here!'

'Arnaud . . .'

The older man reached for his sword and slid it from the scabbard. 'Go, or do I have to use this?'

Hervi stared, his gaze widening in astonishment and affront. 'God's eyes,' he said hoarsely, 'You truly have lost your wits.'

'Get out!' Arnaud said raggedly, and took a pace forward, the weapon raised.

A muscle bunched in Hervi's jaw. 'You know where I am if you should think better and decide to apologise,' he said huskily, and strode from the tent.

Grisel was hovering outside, waiting her moment to air her grievances. She had a swollen lip and a livid bruise beneath one eye. Hervi grabbed her arm and drew her away. 'If you value your life, woman, go back to your own fire,' he told her. 'Arnaud's gone sword-wild. He'd lief kill you as talk.'

'But I need to see him,' she protested, trying to wriggle free.

'Not as he is now you don't,' Hervi said grimly, and hung on to her. He had no liking for Grisel, but he did have a conscience. 'I tell you, he is fit to kill someone. Let him be. Whatever it is will wait.'

Within the tent, Arnaud heard Hervi arguing with Grisel, their voices fading into the distance, hers still protesting. His wrist quivered with the weight of the sword and the need for a drink. He threw the weapon down on the floor and retreated to his pallet, where he collapsed, his knees tucked up to his chest and the low keening of a trapped animal vibrating in his throat.

Monday spent the morning in the town with Alexander, buying provisions, and by mutual consent neither of them spoke about the night before. Monday knew that her problems would not go away just for the ignoring, but she was in need of a respite, and as if sensing her mood, Alexander gave her just that. He took her around the booths and stalls, with a thoroughness and enjoyment rarely present in a masculine nature. Her father would have been yawning irritably by the end of ten minutes, but it was a full hour and a half before Alexander paused at a cook stall to buy them both honey cakes, and cups of wine from the booth next door. Following their brief respite, he drew her back into the fray.

'It's the thrill of the chase,' he said with a grin as he argued over the price of a belt buckle. 'That and being shut up in a monastery for nearly six years.' The buckle finally purchased for what he said was a bargain, he had bought her a new drawstring purse with tablet woven silk cords, and to put inside it, a pewter token of St Christopher, patron of travellers. Touched, she kissed his cheek, and he smiled and pressed her hand.

By the time they returned to the camp, Monday's feet were aching, but her spirits were refreshed. Alexander departed to prepare for the afternoon's tourney, and she made her way to her own tent. Her stomach began to churn nervously, for she was unsure of her reception. These days her father's moods were so unpredictable. When she had left that morning, he had still been dead to the world, snoring with his mouth wide open, the smell of stale wine surrounding him in a fetid miasma.

Now he was awake and aware. He had donned his mail and his surcoat; his hair was wet and sleeked back from his brow, and his jaw was smooth, but marred by a couple of nicks where his unsteady hand had not wielded the knife with sufficient care. He was buckling on his sword belt, his fingers clumsy, and there was a grim set to his mouth.

Entering the tent, she removed her cloak. Her father glanced at her from beneath his brows, and said nothing, but his lips tightened all the more. He slotted the tongue of the belt home and hitched it at his hips.

'Papa, where are you going?' she enquired.

'To find employment, where do you think?' he growled.

Monday bit her lip. 'I . . . I wanted to talk to you.'

'Then you should have been here sooner. I don't have the time now. Did you buy wine this morning?'

'Yes, Papa, I . . .'

'Good.' He cut her off with a brusque nod, and when she drew breath to speak, he denied her the words. 'Later,' he snapped. 'I've no time for your chatter now. God knows I've had a crawful today. Enough to make me sick.' He thrust past her and out into the bright springtide air. She saw him wince as the force of the sun dazzled his eyes and cruelly exposed all the new lines and hollows marring his once taut skin. Then he was gone, trying to stride out with purpose but lacking the coordination to make it convincing.

'Oh, Papa,' Monday said softly, and turned away with smarting eyes.

Dust shrouded Alexander's vision as he turned Samson to face the oncoming knight. The surcoat was quartered in brilliant orange and dark, rich blue, the latter proclaiming its wearer's wealth. The battle helm was decorated with a plume of feathers dyed the same blue and orange as the surcoat, and the roan warhorse looked to Alexander's discerning eye like a Lombard-bred stallion, the best in Christendom – although in this instance not entirely the best trained.

The horse's stride was choppy and uneven, and it was fighting the cruel, hinged bit every inch of the way. The rider was making a very poor show of handling the beast, and despite his magnificent equipment might as well have been unarmed. Controlling a surge of excitement at the thought of such an easy kill, Alexander spurred to meet his adversary. He held his shield close to his body, allowing no gap that might permit the other man to prise it from him, and guided Samson with his thighs and heels. Their opponent appeared to possess a complete lack of coordination. He tried to swing the roan side-on to Alexander and strike at the same time, but the manoeuvre almost unhorsed him. It was the work of a moment for Alexander to swipe aside the sword and send it end over end into the dust. A twist of the wrist, a flex of the bicep, and Alexander beat in under the guard of the blue and orange shield to lay his sword point against his opponent's mailed breast.

'Yield,' he demanded.

'Not to scum like you,' wheezed a breathless young voice from within the helm. 'Do you know who I am?'

'Someone who is about to lose his horse and some very fine armour,' Alexander replied, and prepared to take him captive.

'I am Henry FitzHamelin, and my cousin is Coeur de Lion himself!'

Alexander was singularly unimpressed by the revelation. The voice beneath the helm was no older than his own. If its possessor expected to be shown favour because he had royal connections – undoubtedly of the bastard variety – then he was sorely mistaken. And the mention of Coeur de Lion did nothing for his reputation in Alexander's eyes. 'Your cousin could be the king of the world as far as I care,' he said harshly. 'The shield of his name will not protect you today. You owe me a ransom.'

'Go swive yourself up the arse!'

Annoyed, Alexander prepared to jerk the young boor out of the saddle. Then, from the corner of his eye, he saw Osgar and Eudo le Boucher bearing down on him at a purposeful canter, their swords drawn.

'*FitzHamelin!*' bellowed Osgar, waving his sword about his helm. Alexander's gut plummeted. He was not afraid of Osgar – the man was all belly and no bite – but Eudo le Boucher was a different prospect entirely, and the knight had never forgiven Alexander for that unhorsing two years ago.

Alexander glanced round, but Hervi was over at the sanctuary, his back turned as he checked one of Soleil's forelegs, and Arnaud had not seen fit to take to the field at all. Cursing, he abandoned FitzHamelin and spurred Samson's flanks, the hunter suddenly becoming the hunted.

Osgar and le Boucher rode to intercept him. Their gaudy young employer brought up the rear, bellowing his family name in a cracked adolescent voice.

Alexander drew a deep breath. '*Montroi!*' he roared in Hervi's direction, and aimed the black destrier at the safety of the withy screens.

Alerted as much by the close thunder of hooves as by Alexander's frantic cry, Hervi raised his head, and a look of horror appeared on his rust-streaked features. Around him, spectators screamed and dived for cover. At the last moment, Alexander turned Samson. The horse swerved in mid-stride and avoided collision with the screens by no more than a scraped inch. Osgar's larger, more unwieldy horse ran out of space and rammed into the withies. Osgar flew over the pommel and landed in the enclosure, where he lay like a stranded crab, his hands still clutching the reins. 'Bastard!' he wheezed through his helm. 'You bastard!'

Hervi yanked the reins out of Osgar's grip, vaulted into the riderless destrier's saddle, and spurred in pursuit of his beleaguered brother.

Alexander wove and ducked like a Saracen bowman, using all his skill and agility to evade le Boucher and his inept young employer, for he knew that if it came to a straight fight he was finished; he could not match le Boucher blow for blow. Veering to the right, he began to work his way back towards the sanctuary, but two knights engaged in heavy combat crossed and blocked his path. He had to rein Samson sharply, and before he could spur on, le Boucher reached him.

There were no words. Eudo le Boucher was too experienced a warrior to waste his breath. He let his sword speak for him.

Alexander warded the first blow on his shield, and felt the impact vibrate all the way up his arm. He clenched his teeth, and out of sheer bravado made a vicious counterstrike. Le Boucher recoiled, as if he had not expected to find quite so much force behind the younger man's response. Alexander pressed with his thighs and Samson rose on his hind legs to strike at le Boucher's horse. The animal shied, and the blow that le Boucher had aimed at Alexander went wide. Henry FitzHamelin tried to make a crafty attack from the side, but Hervi's late arrival put a swift stop to that and forced the youth into a fight he would never have picked on the battlefield.

Alexander dodged another vicious swing of le Boucher's sword, and drawing hard on the right rein, commanded Samson to gallop for sanctuary. Le Boucher tore after him, curving around Hervi and FitzHamelin, and almost riding into the crimson and black colours of Arnaud de Cerizay.

'Out of my way!' le Boucher bellowed, by now as furious as a fly-goaded bull.

De Cerizay shook his head and lifted his sword. 'You'll have to come through me,' he challenged through his helm, and without further warning than that, launched a flurry of vicious, deliberate blows at the other man.

Somewhat taken aback, le Boucher defended the first onslaught clumsily, but rage at having his prize snatched from beneath his nose soon overtook his surprise, and he returned de Cerizay's assault twofold.

It was so swift that there was nothing anyone could do but bear witness. Alexander's relief at reaching the safety of the withy screens was replaced by the nausea of horror as he watched Arnaud de Cerizay cease defending himself and open his arms like a martyr embracing heaven.

'No!' the young man bellowed, in appalled denial. 'Arnaud, in God's name, no!' He dug in his heels and urged Samson back towards the brawl, but already it was too late. Le Boucher's blow struck home, and Arnaud took its full force across his open breast. Slowly, almost as if time itself was drawing back from the event, the knight toppled from his saddle and hit the ground, bounced once and lay still. His horse broke away then circled back, its ears flickering nervously.

Alexander drew rein in a flurry of churned soil and threw himself down at Arnaud's side. Beneath the slashed surcoat, some of the iron hauberk rivets had burst under the impact, but there was no blood, no gaping wound, and Arnaud's chest still rose and fell with the breath of life. Swiftly, but gently, Alexander worked to remove de Cerizay's helm.

Hervi, having allowed young FitzHamelin to run away down the field, dismounted and knelt at Arnaud's other side. 'Christ, you stupid, stupid lackwit,' he groaned at his friend, and tearing off his own helm, glowered up at Eudo le Boucher, who still sat his horse, the sword frozen in his hand. 'You murdering whoreson!' he said through his teeth.

Le Boucher's enormous fist clenched on the reins. 'I did nothing outside the rules,' he retorted harshly. 'Any man worth his salt would have defended that blow on his shield, but he just opened himself to it. The fool wanted to die.'

'You could have pulled back!' Hervi's eyes glittered.

'There wasn't time. Besides, how was I to know it wasn't a ruse on his part?'

'You can see it wasn't!'

'Now I can,' le Boucher said with a sarcastic flourish. He wrenched his horse around brutally, and it rolled its eyes, fighting the bit. 'De Cerizay should never have taken to the field. He's a toss-pot. Everyone knows that he is finished. Stop whining, Montroi. You know the risks we take as well as any man here.' He rode away, pausing only to collect the bridle of Arnaud's bay stallion, now his property by the law of the tourney field.

Hervi dug one hand through his sweat-drenched hair and cursed roundly.

Arnaud's face was grey, his breathing rapid and shallow. Alexander leaned over him. 'There is no open wound,' he said on a note of question and hope.

'No,' Hervi agreed, tight-lipped. 'But there will be much damage inside where we cannot see. He took the full force of le Boucher's sword across his breast, and then a heavy fall. I fear that . . .' He broke off and shook his head, unable to voice the fact that they were looking at a dying man.

'I'll organise a stretcher to bear him back to his tent,' Alexander said. 'And I'll find Monday.'

Hervi nodded wordlessly, and the young man departed in haste.

Arnaud's eyes flickered open, and he tried without success to raise himself up. Hervi laid a soothing hand on his shoulder.

'Lie still,' he commanded. 'You have broken your body enough.' He watched in concern as Arnaud's lids tightened and squeezed. Tears leaked and made spikes of the thick, dark lashes.

'I cannot even kill myself cleanly,' Arnaud groaned. 'I thought that le Boucher was bound to make a swift end.'

'Never look to le Boucher for mercy,' Hervi said, and then struck the ground with his fist. 'In God's name, were you so desperate that you had to seek your own death?'

'You know I was. After I threatened you with my blade, I knew that I was finished. I would have run myself through, but that would have been undeniable suicide. This way . . .' Arnaud choked and a trickle of blood appeared at his mouth corner. '. . . this way there is a chance of purgatory and after that to be with Clemence again.'

Despite his great grief and pity for his friend, Hervi found a moment to be glad that no woman had ever instilled such overpowering emotions in his own breast. He did not think he would ever seek his own death in the hope of being reunited with a loved one in the afterlife. 'Of course there is,' he muttered.

'You think I'm out of my wits,' Arnaud said with a bloodstained smile. 'It has been a long sickness, for I lost them on the day I set eyes on Clemence in her father's bailey and the rest of the world went away . . . It's going away now.' He choked and his eyes grew glassy.

Hervi gripped and shook the dying man's shoulder. 'Arnaud, stay, wait a moment, curse you. Clemence might be everything to you and the rest of us nothing, but what about your daughter? What about Monday? She cannot live this kind of life without a protector!'

'I appoint you her guardian,' said Arnaud with the certainty that came of long thought on the subject. 'You're decent and honest, and I know you will do your best for her – find her a good husband.'

'What, from amongst this rabble?' Hervi's voice rose incredulously.

'I trust you . . . You cannot refuse the wish of a dying man.'

'I will kill you myself!' Hervi declared, and Arnaud gave him a weary smile. The shadows beneath his eyes were darker than wine and his breathing had grown laboured. Drawn by the horror and fascination of impending death, a crowd had gathered. Brother Rousseau pushed his way through the throng. For once he was sober, but his breath could have stripped the bark from an entire forest. Kneeling down, he muttered a string of Latin phrases and made the sign of the cross in wine upon Arnaud's clammy forehead.

'*Vade in pace,*' he intoned. '*In nomini patris, et filius, et spiritus sancti.*'

'Papa Papa!' Monday screamed, forcing her way through the crowd and on to the field, Alexander at her heels.

A final breath rattled in Arnaud's throat. Even as Monday flung herself down at his side, his body twitched and was still.

At first she did not realise that he had died, for he was warm and pliable to her touch, and aside from the small dribble of blood at the corner of his mouth there was not a mark upon him.

'Papa . . .' She leaned across him, laying her head to his silent breast. "Papa, I'm here, wake up!'

His muscles were lax and unresponsive to her plea. His head lolled, the blood drying on his grey skin. Monday shook him, and he followed the tug of her hand, unresisting. But when she stopped, his flesh stopped too. She shook her head vigorously. It was a mistake, he could not be dead. But she had seen death often enough in her young life to know in her heart of hearts that she was railing at a corpse and that she was alone.

Hervi gently touched her arm. 'Let him be borne back to his tent,' he said, his deep voice cracked with tears.

'Why, because he is disturbing the sport?' she flashed, desiring only to wound as she herself had been wounded.

Hervi's great bovine body flinched. 'So that you may have peace in your grief,' he said reproachfully.

'Peace!' There was a world of sarcasm in the word.

'Listen, lass . . .' Hervi stretched out his hand, but she shrugged away from it, not wanting him to touch her. He withdrew, looking baffled and hurt.

It was Alexander who quietly beckoned to the two men he had hired as stretcher-bearers, and who saw to the practical details.

Monday watched them ease her father's body on to the woven

ropes, and compose his hands upon his breast. Father Rousseau hovered like a vulture. From the depths of his habit he produced a flask, took a swig from it, and having poured some of the contents into his hands, proceeded to flick drops over Arnaud's body whilst intoning a prayer. Monday thought that she was going to be sick.

Alexander gave the man a silver coin, thanked him for his prompt services and dismissed him with a shudder.

Monday walked beside the stretcher as her father was borne away from the tourney field. The clash and clamour of weapons rang in her ears. Death on the field was so commonplace that the sport had not even stopped to mark the passing of another victim.

'He won't even be allowed to rest in hallowed ground, he will be deemed a suicide,' Monday said later, as she knelt beside her father's pallet and looked upon his waxen corpse. Death had not taken the ravages of recent years from his face, rather it had brought them to prominence, a ruined landscape over stark bones. Once, Arnaud de Cerizay had been a handsome, strong young man. But not even an echo remained to the eyes of those who sat in vigil around him.

Monday looked bleakly at Alexander. They both knew that crossroads were the traditional burial places for those whom the church had cast out – a symbolic place of meeting and departure from pagan times. They were places where the corpses of felons, outlaws and murderers rotted to the bone beneath the soil, or swung from gibbets above the ground. Sometimes a priest would permit such an outcast to be buried within the precincts of his churchyard – usually for a vast fine in silver for prayers to bring the departed soul into a state of grace. She knew that there was not enough silver in her father's coffer to pay for such a privilege.

Alexander frowned thoughtfully. 'A priest might not allow him to lie in a hallowed grave,' he murmured, 'but there is nothing to stop us from burying him in hallowed ground of our own accord.'

'You mean without a priest's permission?'

'Yes.'

Monday stared at him with widening eyes. Several protests hovered on the tip of her tongue but were silenced by the sheer audacity of his suggestion. It was blasphemy, but no more so than having to pay a huge amount of silver into some churchman's coffer.

As if reading her mind, Alexander added, 'It used to happen at Cranwell sometimes – a villager's child would be stillborn and they would come at night and bury the body within our cemetery grounds. The prior used to turn a blind eye because it was too powerful a custom to be stamped out without a deal of ill-will and opposition.'

Monday bit her lip. In her mind's eye she saw them stumbling through a graveyard in the dark, her father's body sewn in a shroud. The images made her shudder and recoil, but the alternative was the haunted, unhallowed crossroads where unquiet spirits roamed the night, and she could not bear to think of leaving him in such a place. Surely God would understand.

'Then let us do it,' she said with sudden decision, and clenched her fingers in her gown. 'Let him lie within the hearing of prayers.'

Alexander was grooming Samson, a task in which he took great pride. In the early days he had been meticulous in this labour because he had wanted to prove to Hervi that he knew how to look after the horse, but the diligence had swiftly mellowed into a genuine pleasure. It gave him great satisfaction to see how other knights admired the stallion. Samson was proving a destrier of the highest calibre. He stood a little over fifteen hands at the withers, short-backed, powerful in the haunch, sturdy in the leg. For a stallion, he was also very biddable beneath Alexander's hand. Some men said that a good warhorse should be headstrong and vicious, but Alexander had never seen the sense in that belief. When your life depended upon the beast beneath you, God help you if you could not control it.

Alexander whistled softly between his teeth as he worked. He always found that grooming his horse made for good thinking time. He could air his thoughts, examine them and make decisions without being disturbed. The prospect of tonight's expedition to the priory graveyard in the town had set him on edge. He disliked entering holy precincts even in the full light of day. In the dead of night, it would be all too easy for his imagination to run riot. At least he would have the comfort of Hervi's presence. Following his initial disapproval, his older brother had been brought to see that burying Arnaud within the priory grounds was the lesser of the two evils.

'Do you want to lie at a crossroads when your time comes?' Alexander had retorted to Hervi's protest that they would be trespassing on God's ground.

As he had known, Hervi had shaken his head and grudgingly agreed to help them, all the while insisting that Alexander's tendency to flout church discipline would get him branded a heretic. And yet what else could they decently do? Arnaud de Cerizay deserved better than six feet of earth beneath a crossroads gibbet on the way to Verneuil.

Samson lipped at the back of Alexander's neck, leaving a kiss of grass-stained spittle. The young man pulled a face and wiped at the slobber.

'Where is Hervi?'

Lowering his arm, Alexander turned to face Eudo le Boucher. The knight was not wearing his armour, just a tunic of tan-coloured linen, although his sword still hung at his hip. His beard was neatly trimmed, his hair combed, and despite the war-ravaged face, he looked almost respectable.

'Away in the town buying a tanned hide,' Alexander responded with forced civility.

'Do you know how soon he will be back?'

'No, I don't.'

Le Boucher stroked his clipped beard and frowned. Alexander returned to grooming Samson, going over parts that were already burnished to a mirror brightness. He hoped that the knight would go away, but le Boucher displayed no inclination to do so.

'I understand that Hervi has been named guardian of the girl's welfare,' le Boucher said in a tone so deliberately casual that Alexander immediately knew he was after something.

'What of it?' he answered coldly, and wondered how le

Boucher had the gall to stand here and converse after what had happened yesterday.

'Why, nothing. I came to let Hervi know that I waive the ransom claim. Let the girl have her father's horse and armour for her dowry.'

Alexander said nothing because he did not trust himself to speak. He began teasing out Samson's tail until it rippled like a black waterfall. Le Boucher's way was to take, not to give. If he was forfeiting Arnaud's ransom, it was not for reasons of decency or compassion.

'Tell your brother why I came,' le Boucher said, and turned on his heel, almost colliding with Monday.

She gasped and sidestepped. He sidestepped with her. 'My condolences,' he said. 'Had I known the state of your father's mind, I would have drawn my blow.'

Monday faced him, her chin up and her eyes dry. 'You know what you may do with your condolences,' she said.

Alexander ceased grooming the horse and looked round, his hand closing around the haft of the hoof-cleaning knife and his heart thumping against his ribs. Few men would have dared to address le Boucher thus. The knight's fists tightened at his sides and his beard bristled. Monday trembled but held her ground. Alexander took a pace towards them, but before he could intervene, the tension broke as le Boucher shrugged, and once more stepped aside to go on his way.

'Tell Hervi,' he repeated over his shoulder. Saluting Monday with an ironic arch of his brow, he disappeared among the sprawl of tents.

'Tell Hervi what?' she said, breathing rapidly.

Alexander let the air escape his lungs on an explosive sigh of relief, and dropped the hoof knife from his clammy palm. 'He came to waive his claim to your father's horse and armour.' He glanced at her sidelong. 'Eudo le Boucher never, ever yields his gains.'

'So I am supposed to thank him, my father's murderer?'

Alexander shook his head. 'No,' he said. 'I do not know what he wants, but I am certain his gesture does not stem from compassion.' He wiped his hand down his tunic. 'You are fortunate that he did not flatten you with his fist.'

'Fortunate?' She approached Samson and stroked his strong, satiny neck. 'I have sewn my father in his shroud,' she said bitterly, 'as before that I sewed my mother. God forbid that if I ever bear a daughter, she should be as fortunate as I.'

CHAPTER 14

A warm spring night lay over the land. On the horizon, the faintest tinge of green showed where the sun had set. The town settled to sleep, the only sounds the occasional wail of a fractious infant, the squall of fighting cats, or the weaving footsteps of a drunk.

Above the houses, its pale stone softly gleaming, the Benedictine nunnery of the Blessed Virgin Mary stood like an icon on a pedestal, drawing the eye to admire, and the hand to piously sign the breast. It had been dedicated more than a hundred years ago, and wore its established place with high pride.

Within the hallowed precincts of its cemetery the soft clink of an iron spade tip cutting soil was interspersed by the distant, ghostly plainchant of the nuns offering devotion in their chapel. The sound of their singing sent a chill down Alexander's spine. In his mind he sang with them, knowing each word and nuance by heart.

He was surrounded by the graves of dead nuns. Come judgement day, there was going to be outrage when they arose from their dust and discovered a tourney knight in their midst. Given another occasion, he would have been amused at the thought, but now it filled him with unease. He was the instigator, the responsibility his, and here in the dark, with the chanting of the sisters filling the night, he felt its weight.

Hervi had taken the task of digging Arnaud's grave, for he possessed the sheer muscular strength required. His breath was ragged in his throat now, and in the dim glow of the horn lantern they had brought to shed light on their endeavours, his brow shone with sweat. He paused for a moment, leaning on the handle of the spade, and the singing washed over them in poignant eerie waves.

'How much longer?' Alexander asked with a glance at the dark hole, and then at Monday where she sat on the grass beside her father's shrouded corpse, her face composed and blank.

'Another half candle notch,' Hervi panted. 'Here, take a turn.' He handed the spade across, stepped out of the trench and went to sit with Monday, curving an avuncular arm across her shoulders. 'Are you all right, lass?'

She nodded and gave him a wan half-smile.

'Alex is right. It is better here than at a crossroads. Once the turf is stamped back over, no one will know but us. Listen, he even has a choir to sing for him, as you wished.'

Once more she nodded, without words, and reached out to stroke the cold bleached linen of the shroud.

Hervi frowned, and shifted position as if uncomfortable. 'I promise I will do my very best for you,' he said gruffly and squeezed her shoulder. 'Treat you as if you were my own daughter.'

Monday bit her lip and looked away. With a heavy sigh, Hervi released her and went to take the spade from Alexander. The soil had literally flown from the young man's exertions, and he was almost sobbing with the effort he was putting into each thrust and pull.

'Steady, steady,' Hervi rumbled. 'You would not last two minutes on the tourney field if you paced yourself like that.'

Alexander stepped out of the hole and rubbed his hands down his tunic. 'For Christ's sake, Hervi, let's just get finished and leave.' He glanced around nervously.

'It was your idea,' Hervi said as he jammed the spade into the soil.

'I know it was, and a good one, the best we could do for him, but these places turn me cold. If you had been whipped for some monk's lust and thrown into a pitch-black cell with your wrists tied, you would feel the same.'

'That was more than two years ago,' Hervi grunted.

'It seems like yesterday.' Alexander pushed his wet hair off his forehead and stood watching his brother for a moment. He both envied and resented Hervi's pragmatic outlook on life. Hervi had dreams, never nightmares, and those dreams were of nothing more ambitious than a good fire, an accommodating woman, and a flagon of the best wine. People might despair of his brother, but the despair was all theirs, never Hervi's.

The chanting had ceased. A scented quietness settled over the night and the laying to rest of Arnaud de Cerizay. They had brought him into the town at compline, before the closing of the gates, the shroud wrapped in a dark blanket and borne across Hervi's packhorse. Now they used that blanket as a sling to lower him into the grave they had dug.

Alexander produced his gold and amethyst cross and murmured prayers, first in Latin, then in French. 'Do you want a moment alone with him?' he asked Monday, and tried not to sound as if he was in haste to be away from the place.

Monday shook her head. 'I have had my time to say farewell while you have been preparing his grave, and before that whilst I was sewing him in his shroud.' She stooped to take a fistful of the moist earth from beside the hole, and scattered it over the swathed body. 'Sleep in God's peace, Papa,' she said, her eyes dry and burning. Then she turned and walked a little distance away, so that she could have a moment alone with herself.

The night was completely black by the time Hervi and Alexander had finished replacing the turf and tamping it down. The horn lantern was beginning to sizzle and gutter. Hervi wrapped the spade in the blanket and tied it to the packhorse, and Alexander went ahead to check that the way was clear. They had to find a place to lie up until the town gates opened at dawn. Two nights since, Alexander had bribed a member of the watch to let him out, but on that occasion he had been a young man alone, obviously returning from an *assignation d'amour*. The guard would be unlikely to let three individuals and a packhorse go through unsearched.

There was an orchard running along the convent's boundary wall – a sizeable sprawl of apple, pear and cherry trees interspersed with bee skeps, and it was towards this that Alexander moved on cat-light feet. Monday walked silently beside him. He could hear her quiet breathing, the gentle pressure of her footfalls. Behind them, Hervi led the packhorse, its hooves muffled in cloth overshoes.

All would have been well had it not been such a mild night at the end of spring, for it meant that they were not the only folk abroad. The nun's orchard was a favourite trysting place for young couples. It was also somewhere that the town whores brought their clients for a little privacy. The abbess had recently complained, and two members of the watch had been dispatched to patrol the area.

Alexander stopped short and touched Monday's arm, warning her to silence as they heard the approach of masculine voices in easy conversation and saw the horn watch-lantern swinging on its pole. Gesturing Monday to go back, Alexander extinguished their own lantern so that it would not give them away. A soldier's instinct kept Hervi from speaking out to ask what was wrong. He turned the horse and started back the way he had come. But if Hervi had the sense not to make a sound, the pack animal was not so burdened, and snorted loudly.

Hervi cursed beneath his breath and belatedly cupped his hand over the beast's nostrils. Alexander and Monday froze in mid-step.

The easy conversation ceased abruptly. 'Who's there?' came the wary challenge, accompanied by the scrape of a drawn weapon. 'Come forth, let yourself be seen!'

'Not a chance,' Alexander muttered through his teeth, and broke into a run, dragging Monday with him. Hervi vaulted on to the packhorse and rode after them, uncaring how much noise he made, the element of silence now a farce.

Down the hill from the convent they pelted and into the dark alleyways of the streets beyond. Although their eyes had adjusted to the night and gave them a certain amount of vision, they still splashed through noisome gutters and tripped and stumbled over lumps and ruts in the narrow thoroughfares. Alexander's wits raced with the speed of his feet. The town gates would be closed until dawn, and the guards from whom they were fleeing would quickly raise the hue and cry. It was only a matter of time before they were caught, and he knew that if they flung him into a cell, he would go utterly mad.

Dogs barked, lights flared in dwellings; doors and shutters were opened. It was as if a stick had been poked vigorously into a nest of sleeping ants.

'We can't keep on running!' Monday wasted breath to pant. 'For God's love, stop, before we make it ten times worse for ourselves!'

But Alexander refused to be beaten. He cut down a side alley that was so narrow there was barely room for the packhorse to pass.

'You go on with Monday, get her away!' Hervi cried. 'There's no need for us all to be captured!'

'There is no need for anyone to be captured,' Alexander replied between hard gasps for breath. 'I know another hiding place.'

'Where?'

'Just a little further.'

Hervi shook his head and looked over his shoulder. There were voices in the distance, urgent and excited, and the bobbing of several lanterns. 'Then be quick about finding it,' he snapped.

They hurried on through the dark, evil-smelling alley which grew even narrower yet. Just when it seemed it would trap them in a dead end, it flared like a fashionable hanging sleeve, and brought them out into the town's merchant quarter.

Alexander sprinted past the first three houses to the right of the alley and skidded to a halt at the fourth, a handsome whitewashed dwelling with its gable facing on to the street. Stooping, he picked up several small pebbles and threw them at the closed shutters of the gable window.

'Have you lost your wits?' Hervi whispered, his eyes almost starting from his head.

'You had best hope I have not!' Alexander retorted, and threw another stone. 'Sara, Sara, open up!'

After a moment in which Hervi came closer to the verge of hysteria, and Alexander wondered if he had disastrously misjudged the character of his inamorata of two nights ago, the shutters opened and a young woman looked out, her long blonde hair hanging over the sill like a bell rope.

'Sara, thank Christ; there's no time to explain,' Alexander

called up. 'We're being chased, we need a place to hide. Let us in.'

The head disappeared and the shutters snapped together.

Hervi cursed beneath his breath. 'This is the wealthy part of the town,' he said. 'They will hang us higher than the man in the moon. You truly are mad!' His gaze darted round the as yet empty street, knowing that it was only moments away from being full of zealous pursuers.

There came the sound of a stout bar being raised, and then the grating of a key in the lock. The door swung open and the blonde young woman studied her visitors, a cresset lamp in one hand, her eyes bright with excitement. 'Come in,' she beckoned. 'Hurry, yes, the horse as well.'

As soon as Hervi had led the pack animal over the threshold, Sara closed the door, locked and barred it. The key was one of several on an iron hoop in her hand. She wore a loose robe over her chemise in a style that returning crusaders had begun to make fashionable, the fabric a silky, delicate blue woven with a floral pattern in the same shade, and there were soft kidskin slippers on her feet. Alexander wondered for whom she was waiting this time – or perhaps she always slept like that.

'Bring the horse through to the back and tie him up in the yard,' she said to Hervi. 'If they knock on my door, I'll put them off the scent.'

Once more, Alexander encountered the dour maidservant and was given a look. Her rheumy eyes widened at the sight of a woman, another man and finally a bay horse tramping past her pallet in the dead of night. She made the sign of the cross, and stared after them in disbelief.

'You can stay in here,' Sara said as they reached the store room. She smiled at Alexander. 'You know where the trap door is, should you need to hide in the cellar.'

'Yes, my lady.' He could not help the small shudder that ran through him.

'My lady?' She sucked her cheeks. 'I have risen in the world, haven't I?' Mischief danced in the violet eyes.

Alexander reddened. Hervi said, 'Just now, I would even kneel to you as queen for what you have done for us.'

She bit her lower lip engagingly and batted her lashes at Hervi. 'Oh, it is nothing,' she cooed. Her glance flickered to Alexander and she gave a mischievous giggle. 'Myself and the captain of the watch are old friends. He will believe anything I tell him.'

In the months that followed, Monday often thought back to the night of her father's burial. The memory possessed a dream-like quality, the kind induced by eating too much cinnamon bread close to retiring. The more she tried to unravel the various strands, the more tangled they became, leaving her with an impossible knot at the centre.

The only thread that she had managed to loosen was the one that kept drawing her back into the heart of the tangle – that of controlling her own destiny in a world dominated by the egos and suspicions of men. She had seen that, despite all the barriers, a woman could do so. The lady Aline de Lavoux had risen above the vagaries of siege warfare and the machinations of her small-minded, big-headed husband, while Sara, the merchant's widow, lived her own life and made her own decisions with remarkable daring and aplomb. The most important thing, Monday had concluded, was to keep the spark of will alive despite all attempts to trample it from existence.

Not that Hervi or Alexander deliberately trampled, she thought, as she spread out the bolt of yellow linen purchased yesterday and prepared to cut it. It was just that they took her for granted. She was their wife, their sister, their servant. She cooked and cleaned, mended and tended. In return they protected her, gave her a secure place to sleep, their honour hers, but sometimes she found herself wearying of the bargain.

As she knelt over the fabric and made the first decisive cut with the shears, Alexander returned to the tent for a fresh lance. He walked with an assured, athletic stride, and the quilted gambeson he wore was of the highest quality. They had enough silver these days to afford the best equipment. Alexander and Hervi were an effective partnership on the field, one steady as a rock, the other as fast and mercurial as a shooting star. Sometimes Monday imagined her father riding with them, a ghostly third companion, and she was sure that Hervi and Alexander felt his presence too. Little enough was said, but the first cup they raised after any success they always drank in silence to honour him.

Employment for the winter season was assured. Their skill and the continuing warfare between Richard and Philip of France made it a certainty. Monday had forgotten the number of castles they had helped to besiege between, or even during, tourneys. Several times, Hervi and Alexander had fought beneath the banner of the lord John, Count of Mortain, Richard's youngest brother. He had been something of a black sheep during Richard's absence on crusade, when he had seized more than his due and plotted to take his brother's empty throne, but since begging Richard's forgiveness on bended knees he was now a staunch ally. He had to be, for there was no guarantee that the childless Richard would name him his successor.

'How goes it?' Alexander enquired with a half-smile, and tilted his head to watch her cut through the fabric with unerring strokes.

'Ask me that in a couple of days,' she answered with a smile of her own and a little shake of her head. She was embarking upon a new set of barding for the two destriers in the de Montroi colours of blue and yellow. 'Of course, they will be ready the sooner if you want to help me lay the seams.'

'I could think of no greater purgatory,' Alexander said with a grimace of mock-horror.

'You could always stir the cooking pot then, and leave me more time to sew,' she said mischievously.

He gave her a look sidelong to see if she was jesting. With an effort, Monday kept her face straight, and when her mouth threatened to betray her, bent conscientiously over her task.

'If I have time when I've finished my practice and written a letter for one of the men, I'll come,' he said with a martyred air.

Monday nodded as if she believed him. He made himself

scarce with alacrity, leaving her with a laugh on her lips and exasperation knitting her brows.

Hervi was sitting on the ground eating a chunk of bread and dry salt sausage when Eudo le Boucher joined him with a flask of wine and his own meal of half a fowl and a handful of dried fruit. Before the two men, the tourney field of Gournai was the dusty brown of summer's end, and beyond it lay other fields heavy with wheat and populated by harvesting villagers. Thus far their crops had been spared the burning of war.

'So,' said le Boucher between rotations of his jaw. 'Where are you bound next, Montroi?'

Hervi wondered why le Boucher wanted to know. The man was a thorn in his side, and he bore no love for his company, and yet, ever since Arnaud's death, le Boucher persisted in seeking him out. In another man, Hervi would have suspected the emotion of guilt, but he knew le Boucher incapable of such finer feeling.

'I have heard that the Count of Mortain has need of troops,' he said cautiously. 'I might seek his recruiting officer.'

'You would take John above Richard?' There was a note of genuine surprise in le Boucher's voice.

Hervi attended to his meal and did not reply, except to shrug. He was not about to tell le Boucher why he and Alexander preferred to avoid Coeur de Lion.

'Richard's the better soldier,' le Boucher said.

'Is that where you intend to go then, to Richard?'

'Haven't decided yet.' Le Boucher cleaned his teeth with his tongue and tugged crumbs from his beard. 'Depends what offers I get.'

They finished their meal in silence. Hervi was just about to rise and make his escape when le Boucher spoke again, his tone casual, his dark eyes narrow and calculating. 'Have you thought about seeking a husband for the de Cerizay girl?'

The hair at Hervi's nape stood on end. 'No,' he said more sharply than he had intended. 'Why do you ask?'

'I'm curious. She is not a child any more. Most girls of her age have been well wedded and bedded by now.'

'Arnaud left her in my care. I won't give her into another's unless I'm very sure of him.'

Le Boucher nodded thoughtfully. 'You don't want her for yourself then?'

Hervi choked. Le Boucher solicitously thumped his back and offered him a swig of his own wine. Red-eyed, Hervi glared at him. 'I ought to knock that notion from your skull with a war hammer,' he snarled, before being taken with another fit of coughing.

'I'd like to see you try,' le Boucher retorted scornfully. 'Your own skull is full of strange notions. Why should you object to my question?'

Hervi drew a strangled breath over his larynx. 'Monday de Cerizay is like a daughter to me, or a niece. I have known her since she stood no higher than my knee. To wed her would be like committing incest!' Now Hervi did rise, thoroughly upset and ruffled.

'But how should I know such a thing unless I asked?'

'Why should you want to ask?'

Le Boucher sighed. 'Why do you think? I myself feel that I have a responsibility for the girl's welfare, since it was my sword with which her father chose to end his life. Pending the state of her dowry, I am willing to offer to take her to wife. I have coin to my name and I'm a good provider, better by far than Arnaud de Cerizay ever was.'

Hervi's scalp positively seethed with horror at the notion. 'I have no intention of arranging a match for her,' he croaked. 'And the girl herself has given no indication that she desires matters to change.'

'But surely she will not challenge your authority if you make a decision?'

'I would never force her into anything she did not want.'

Le Boucher gave him a peculiar, almost pitying look. 'It is a man's right to govern his womenfolk, and their duty to obey,' he said.

'I know that, you don't have to lecture me,' Hervi snapped. 'I told you, I have no intention of seeing her wed yet.'

'But now I have spoken you will give it some thought?'

Hervi felt as if he had been pushed into a corner. Alexander would have known what to say, but Hervi's wits were not so fly. He could speak with a sword and a gesture far more easily than with words, but neither of the latter were advisable at the moment. He managed a brusque nod and a grunt of acquiescence, and made his escape.

Le Boucher remained where he was, finishing his wine, gazing out over the quiet, pastoral scene, but his eyes remained narrow, and there was no tranquillity in the harsh lines of his face.

'Like this, you mean?' Alexander pushed the silver needle into the fabric and drew out the shining yellow thread.

Monday chewed her lip at the enormous stitch. 'At least you are sewing in a straight line now,' she said kindly. Alexander had returned from his various military pursuits earlier than either of them had expected, and so she had challenged him to pick up a needle. 'If you persevere, one day you'll be able to sew as fine a seam as any dainty lady shut in her bower,' she teased.

'By which time my hands will have more holes than a sieve and my eyes will see nothing but rows and rows of tiny stitches for ever amen!' he retorted, screwing up his face.

'So you admit defeat?'

Alexander laughed. 'Part of learning how to fight is knowing when to acknowledge you are beaten and make a graceful retreat.' He handed her the yellow fabric. 'You sew. I'll cook.'

'Coward,' she accused in a bantering tone, and watched him busy himself with the evening meal. She had to admit that he had a certain flair with the cooking pot when he could be bothered. A gleam of devilry in his eyes, he fetched Hervi's wine flask and poured more than half the contents into the cauldron set on a tripod over the fire.

'He won't love you for that,' she warned laughingly.

'He can soon buy some more. Besides, he's not here. He's at the washerwomen's camp fire with Osgar and Alys and another girl, so I doubt he'll be back this side of midnight.' Drawing his knife, Alexander set about preparing the vegetables. Monday's needle flew in and out of the fabric and a companionable silence descended. This was the kind of evening she would commit to memory and cling to on the occasions when Alexander as well as Hervi chose absence over hearth.

Alexander swept the chopped ingredients into the pot of wine stock, gave it a stir, then fetched his lectern and set out his writing equipment. Monday glanced at him over her sewing and a pang surged through her, part affection, part something deeper and wilder that she had no experience to name. She only knew that it gave her pleasure to be with Alexander, and that her breath grew short and her skin hot whenever he looked at her. He was not looking now, however, for all his concentration was bent upon the exquisite forming of the letters in brown-black oak gall ink.

A delicious aroma began to waft from the cooking pot, the steam and smoke mingling in a haze on the golden evening air. We could be a contented married couple, Monday thought, and for a moment took pleasure in the dream. But even as she embellished the moment like a scribe illuminating a capital, she knew that it could not be. No couple had been more devoted than her parents, and look what had become of them. In a way they had killed each other.

Alexander had a swift, restless nature. Just now he was doing no more than taking a brief respite from hurling himself at life, and she wanted more than a canvas tent, a straw pallet and an absent husband. Her fantasies took another turn and she imagined herself dressed in finery, a great and pampered lady without a care in the world. But that too left her dissatisfied. Great ladies were born, seldom made, and for all their finery they possessed little freedom. Probably they did have cares, small and petty and corrosive.

As Monday sewed, she arrived at the conclusion that the source of freedom was to have power over her own life. The source of that power lay in the seed of the notion, and then its germination into a deed. Unless the former was actively nurtured, the latter would never grow. Monday frowned as she wrestled with the thought. Her eye fell once more on Alexander who had now finished the letter and was sanding the ink to dry it. He had turned his notions, his dreams and ideas into deeds, and was still forcing his way into the sunlight with undiminished vigour.

'Would you teach me to do that?' she asked of an impulse born of her thoughts.

'What?' He looked round.

'To read and write – like you.' She waited for him to say that it was difficult, that it was not a woman's place, or that he did not have the time.

With great care he rolled the sheet of vellum into a cylinder and tied it with a narrow strip of ribbon. 'I could if you had the determination,' he said. 'But it is not something you can learn in the course of a single evening.'

'I am willing to persevere.'

Alexander pursed his lips and rubbed his forefinger across them in a habitual gesture of puzzlement or thought. 'Why the sudden interest?'

Monday coloured. 'I want knowledge,' she said defensively. 'Nothing comes from nothing. I watch you grind up your inks, trim your quill and form those beautiful letters. I want to be able to do the same.'

He listened to her explanation thoughtfully, and a slow smile lit in the depths of his eyes. 'Very well, I will show you,' he said. 'But I hope you make a better scribe than I do a tailor!'

Over the following two weeks, between her other tasks, Monday applied herself to becoming lettered. She had made sewing look simplicity itself to Alexander, but he had discovered differently when he picked up a needle. Now, in her turn, she found that the fluid ease with which he wielded his quill was more difficult than it looked. She began with a wax tablet and a sharp wooden stylus, and when she had learned each letter of the alphabet in both its standard and capital forms, he transferred her lessons to pen and vellum.

The quill nib had to be trimmed precisely to give the correct edge and thickness to the ink, which in turn had to be ground and mixed to the right texture, neither too thick nor too runny. The vellum had to be lightly scored with guidelines for the writing, and pricked with a bradawl to give each letter its space. She had to learn how to erase her constant errors without damaging her writing surface. Although she made many mistakes, she was helped by her sempstress's eye, and Alexander was as swift with his praise as he was with his hair-clutching impatience.

He made her write out one of his compositions and then read it back to him. Then he had her pen a short letter to an imaginary friend. Her confidence grew, and she drank in the knowledge with an avid thirst that she had not even been aware of possessing until now. Alexander was amused, delighted and very proud of both her progress and her determination; so much so that he curtailed his carousing with the other knights to give her extra tuition.

Hervi, however, was against the entire exercise.

'It is not a woman's place to own such knowledge,' he remonstrated as he and Alexander groomed their horses one morning. 'I don't need those skills. Why should she?'

Alexander swept the grooming brush down Samson's sloping hindquarters and smiled ruefully to himself. Hervi, like most illiterate men of his standing, viewed the ability to read and write with deep suspicion. The skill was slowly but surely becoming essential to a man's political advancement, and those knights who clung stubbornly to the old ways were being left behind. Worse still, they were being left behind by merchants and artisans, by wealthy peasants and women.

'I see nothing wrong in teaching her,' Alexander replied mildly. 'At least she will never be at the beck and call of some scribe.'

Hervi's complexion darkened. 'Nothing but grief will come of this knowledge,' he said. 'You will fill her head with all manner of strange notions that will ruin her when she comes to marry. You are showing her a land where it will be impossible for her to dwell.'

'Oh, don't be such a stone-head, Hervi. There are many women who are literate, and their husbands don't beat them for it. Look at Duke Richard's own mother, the Duchess Eleanor. Does he not owe his freedom to her? If not for her abilities, he would still be languishing in a German prison.'

'Aye, and she herself was locked up for sixteen years by her own husband for fomenting rebellion,' Hervi retorted. 'A rebellion that would never have happened if she had known her place.'

The brothers glared at each other. 'Then you tell Monday,' Alexander said through his teeth with scorn, 'you tell her that she may not continue to learn and better herself because of your pig-ignorance.'

Hervi raised his fist to flatten Alexander.

'Yes,' said the younger man contemptuously, 'put me in my place too.'

Hervi looked at Alexander, then at his bunched fingers. Uttering a sound of disgust, he swung on his heel and stormed off. Alexander released the breath he had been holding and threw the grooming brush on the ground. It wasn't just the reading and writing, he thought. Something else was eating at Hervi. He had been sour and distracted these past few weeks, but had not seen fit to share whatever was troubling him except by way of venting his spleen. That was as maybe, but Alexander had no intention of playing the compliant scapegoat.

He was kitting Samson in the new barding of blue and yellow when Hervi reappeared, dressed for the joust in his full tourney armour – ready to do battle an hour before battle was due to be joined. Alexander studied this portent with interest, but said nothing aloud, and returned his attention to harnessing the stallion.

Hervi cleared his throat. 'He looks like a knight's horse,' he commented. 'A pity there's naught but a knave to ride him.'

Alexander flashed Hervi a look. Hervi returned it with a glower, but there was a hint of humour in the curve of his lips.

'Little difference between a knight and a knave save the clothes on their backs,' Alexander retorted with a nod at Hervi's finery.

Hervi made a disparaging sound and turned away to begin saddling up Soleil.

'What suddenly makes you such a stickler for the rule of a woman's place?' Alexander addressed his brother's spine. 'It has never concerned you before. Indeed, I remember you complaining to Arnaud that Monday had been made to wear a wimple.'

With an exasperated sigh, Hervi turned round. 'You worry at a bone until it is bald of all meat and marrow,' he growled.

'I need to understand.'

'It is very simple. I was not her guardian then; it was her

father's place to make the rules. Now it is mine.' His right hand reached to tug at his hair. 'Ah, Christ, you might as well know. I've had an offer of marriage for her from Eudo le Boucher.'

'You have what?' Alexander was horrified.

'Some weeks ago he asked me. Said he felt responsible for her.' Several strands of blond hair came away in Hervi's hand and he stared at them blankly.

'You refused him, of course.'

'I told him that she would be wed to the man I deemed most suitable when the time came.'

'Even if that man be him?' Alexander's voice was ripe with scorn.

'Of course I won't marry her to her own father's killer!' Hervi snapped indignantly. 'You can climb down off your high horse before I drag you out of the saddle. But what he said set me to thinking. She is sixteen years old, and it is time that she was wed to someone – preferably a man with a secure livelihood.'

Alexander stared at his brother in dismay. What Hervi said was pragmatic and true. But he did not want to think of Monday married and dwelling elsewhere. 'She doesn't have to marry at all. We can protect her honour, and she has the coin from Arnaud's estate as security.'

Hervi shook his head. 'I am only her guardian. Men like le Boucher realise that they have a chance to make a greater claim. She is Stafford's granddaughter, and she has a dowry of sorts. She is young, innocent and pretty. It needs little more in the company we keep to make her a shining prize.' He turned abruptly to Soleil and continued harnessing the stallion.

'Where are you going to find a man whose livelihood is secure?' Alexander asked neutrally.

'I don't know.' Hervi's tone was peevish with worry. 'But you stuffing her head with abstract notions and things not of the common world will not make my task any easier.'

'She asked me to teach her. Of her own accord she desired to be lettered. To refuse never entered my head.' On those words, Alexander mounted Samson and rode him away to warm up. He was profoundly disturbed at the thought of Monday leaving their company to take a husband. There was no one remotely suitable,

least of all Eudo le Boucher. The very notion made him recoil.
And yet Hervi was right about her being a shining prize. And
that too was a thought that until now had never entered
Alexander's mind.

Monday poured wine into two cups and handed one of them to
Alexander. Her mind was alive, fizzing with new knowledge.
There was a lightness in her movements and in her head too,
almost as if she were drunk. The tourney had gone well for the
men that afternoon and they had taken several rich ransoms from
French knights. They had celebrated around the communal fire
with dancing and singing. Hervi had gone off into the darkness
with one of the women, and Alexander had escorted Monday
back to their tent. Then, with a strange, intent glitter in his eyes,
he had taken out his inks and demonstrated to her the Arabic
system of numerals.

Monday had found the concept intriguing, the symbols so
much simpler to manipulate in calculation than the unwieldy
Roman ones. 'Did they teach you this at the monastery?' she
asked as she resumed her seat at his side.

He shook his head and drank down the wine fast, something
he always did after a tourney. It usually took him the course of a
full evening to slow the pace of his mind and body to normal.
She could sense the feverish tension in him now, and her own
emotions tingled in answering awareness.

'I taught myself,' he said. 'We had a copied manuscript by a
monk named Adelard of Bath. There was a treatise on the use of
Arabic numerals. Some of the others thought that it smacked of
devilry, but that only made me all the more determined to learn
how to use it.' He rose to collect the flagon, returned and refilled
his cup. 'Hervi believes I should not be teaching you all this. He
says that it will give you ideas beyond the scope of your daily
life.'

Monday laughed bitterly. 'What you are showing me is what
makes my daily life bearable,' she declared with a toss of her
head. 'I suppose he thinks that I should have no concerns but my
spindle and the cooking pot!'

'He thinks you will be dissatisfied with your lot if you know there is more to life.' He tilted back on his stool and moodily swung one leg.

Monday laughed again. She drained her cup and thrust its rim beneath the flagon he still held. 'He is a little too late for that. How can I not know when I see it every day in the people who come to watch the tourneys – in the lords who have the coin to hire such as us to die for them? Of course there is more. We both know it.'

'Hervi knows it too in his heart,' Alexander said.

They finished the wine. Impatient with her wimple, feeling daring and rebellious, Monday pulled out the bone fastening pin and cast the square of linen aside. Her hair cascaded down to her hips, shimmering with hints of bronze and gold. She saw Alexander's eyes widen.

'What's wrong?' The words stumbled on her tongue and she decided it had not been wise to drink with Alexander measure for measure.

'You do not often remove your wimple, even in front of me or Hervi.'

'Do you object?'

He shook his head. 'I thought it a great pity when you were made to wear one. You have lovely hair.'

Monday studied him through her lashes and wondered whether to take his words as a light-hearted compliment, or read more into them. For the moment, it was impossible to apply her mind or make a coherent judgement. 'I suppose that a wimple acts as a protection,' she said, forcing out her words with great care. 'It makes me respectable in the eyes of men. I know that there is a growing fashion among high-born women to show their hair, but the life we lead, I dare not.' She rose to her feet, intending to put her empty cup on a trestle, but the sudden motion from sitting to standing, and the potency of the wine in her blood, made her dizzy. She stumbled, then tripped over Alexander's leg. Since he had been leaning back on the stool, he lost his balance and they both ended up in a tangle on the floor of the tent, the stool overturned and the wine flagon emptying its dregs into the beaten earth.

Alexander leaned on one elbow. 'Are you all right?'

Monday stared owlishly back at him. 'Yes,' she heard herself say, although in actual fact her head was whirling. 'I mean no,' she giggled. A loud hiccup sent her hand flying to cup her mouth.

He stroked her hair away from her face. 'You look so different without that head covering.'

'Meaning?' The timbre of his voice caused an immodest melting sensation between her thighs.

'That instead of a staid matron in my arms, there is a girl who is lovelier than Iseult, Guinevere and every other woman ever immortalised by a troubadour.' The stroking hand moved down the length of her hair and came to rest with the lightest of touches on her body.

Monday giggled again and nudged his arm, which fell as if by accident on to the outer curve of her breast. She felt hot and dizzy. 'You . . . you're just saying that.'

'No, it's true, I swear it on my heart. Feel.' Taking her hand, he placed it on his breast. She felt the steady but swift beat beneath her touch. The pressure of his hand over hers was damp with sweat as he raised it from his chest to his lips and circled each fingertip with the point of his tongue. Monday shivered and gasped but she did not snatch her hand away, nor did she try to rise from the floor. Her body welcomed the pressure of his, the place between her legs was sensitive and leaden with heat. The rational part of her mind told her that here was danger, that she should make her escape while there was still time, but she discarded it with the same impatience that she had discarded her wimple. There was no harm in their playing. She could stop any time she chose.

He stroked her hair again, seemingly fascinated by its abundance. 'You've gold hidden in here,' he slurred, winding a hank around his fist, 'and bronze and amber. Wealth beyond the riches of kings. Dear God, Hervi must be mad to even think of . . .' He broke off, burying his face in the scented softness of her tresses.

'Hervi must be mad to even think of what?'

'Nothing,' he muttered. 'Nothing that matters.'

She opened her mouth to insist, but he covered her lips with his own, stealing her breath, and with it, the last of her reason.

The kiss, long and slow, was a demonstration that Alexander had learned much since that first clumsy embrace in Lavoux's stable yard. His hands caressed with deliberate, sure intent. Even more than half inebriated, he knew where to put them and how much pressure to exert. When the kiss ended, Monday tried to draw a shaken breath, feeling as if her bones had been melted from her flesh, but he gave her no time, his lips reclaiming hers, while he gently unfastened the brooch at the neck of her gown.

This was the time to cry stop, to push him away, but what her mind knew, her body rejected with a fierce will of its own and arched towards his touch. The wine was singing in her head, the world was spinning, and the sensations he was invoking were utterly delicious. When he pushed up her skirts and unfastened her loincloth, she parted her thighs eagerly and raised her hips so that he could draw the garment from beneath her.

The Monday of the wimple and the downcast eyes was a stranger who watched from a distance as a wanton, wild-haired young woman offered herself without inhibition to the man poised over her.

He stroked the place between her thighs until she moaned, and when the moan changed pitch and caught in her throat, he thrust into her, and stifled her voice with another kiss that surged and retreated in rhythm with the motion of his body. Above her, his breathing was ragged, and he was trembling with the force of caged desire. Tighter and harder, swollen and desperate.

Monday tore her mouth from his and screamed through her clenched teeth. Her nails clawed across Alexander's damp linen shirt and dug through the fabric into taut flesh as ripple upon ripple of exquisite sensation shuddered through her loins. Alexander gasped against her ear, and with a final, powerful lunge, brought himself to the bursting ecstasy of completion.

He rolled over to avoid crushing her, his breath tearing in his throat, his eyes already closing as physical release finished what drink, lust and the nervous energy engendered by jousting had begun.

Monday's head continued to swim. The place between her thighs burned and flickered. She closed her eyes, and felt better.

Tendrils of sleep unfurled and began to wrap around her, but she was uncomfortable. 'Alex . . .'

'Morning,' he mumbled. 'Talk in the morning.'

'I'm cold, hold me.'

He rolled over and gathered her in his arms. She could smell the wine on his breath. 'Warmer in bed,' he muttered.

Together they crawled beneath the coverlet of the pallet that had once belonged to her parents. Alexander smoothed her hair, stroked her arm, and began to snore. Monday burrowed against him, and within moments, she too was asleep.

In the chill of the dawn, Monday woke shivering and alone, and was immediately assaulted by several unpleasant sensations. There was a violent ache behind her eyes, a churning in her stomach, and between her thighs there was a dull, raw throb. She groaned softly and rolled over, willing consciousness to disappear.

The coverlet was gently pulled up over her shoulders, imparting warmth, and for a moment, disoriented, she thought of her mother. Her vision of a white, maternal hand was swiftly banished by the sight of one that was long-fingered and tanned, with close-clipped nails, and she tightened her lids in fear, but it was too late. Other, shocking images crowded upon her inner eye – those fingers on places far more intimate than her shoulder – stroking, playing upon her flesh like a musician upon a harp, flickering between her thighs until she knew nothing but the sharpness of the hunger and the sweetness of the pain.

'Monday?' Alexander's voice was anxious and soft. Had she opened her eyes again, she would have seen the guilt in his, but, unable to cope, she pretended that she was still dead to the world. Was he wearing his clothes, or would she see him naked if she raised her lids? Nausea flared as she remembered the surge of their bodies last night in the act of lust. Perhaps it was just a sinful dream; perhaps if she kept her eyes shut it would go away and she would not have to face the cold light of morning and things she would rather not know. She lay perfectly still, forcing herself to breathe deeply until he withdrew his hand.

There was silence, and she knew that he was standing over her, deciding whether to waken her or not. Then he sighed. 'Monday, I have to go and tend the horses. I'll come back later, and we can talk.'

She willed herself to keep up the pretence. In, out, in, out, her ribcage rising and falling with never a variation until he gave up and she was alone.

Gingerly Monday raised her head from the pillow and gazed through her snarled hair into the grey dawn light. The tent was in a state of minor chaos, indicating that she had not tidied it as was her usual habit before retiring. A sheet of vellum lay on the floor near the pallet, Arabic numerals boldly scrawled in brown ink, and her wimple was strewn half across it.

'Jesu,' she whispered and buried her head in the pillow. It was a dream, she told herself, nothing more than a fevered dream induced by too much wine. But when she turned over and sat up, her body gave her pretence the lie. Blood dabbled her inner thighs, and there was a raw throb at her core. She could smell the sourness of last night's wine and the body odours of vigorous bed sport.

Time and again she had sworn to herself that the tourney road would not be her downfall, and yet her resolve had failed her at the first temptation. Her stomach heaved and she made a sudden dive for the piss-pot, hanging over it, retching drily. Spots of lurid colour danced across her vision, accompanied by lancing pain.

When finally she was able to move, she staggered to the water jug, poured some of the contents into a wooden bowl, and washed herself thoroughly, scrubbing at her thighs with a linen washcloth until her skin was red and sore. Then she donned her clothes and bundled her hair into a working kerchief. *You've gold hidden in here* . . . She clenched her teeth on a fresh wave of nausea, and snatching the bloodied sheet from the pallet, thrust it beneath her arm and left the tent.

The brightening dawn made her wince and her headache increased until it sat like a lead ingot across her brows. How could her father have abused himself like this day upon day or did the body become so poisoned after a while that it no longer recognised the symptoms except as part of a general malaise?

Monday made her way down to the river bank and threw the sheet into the water. Then she pummelled at the cloth with a stone until the blood had diluted to the merest faded stain. She wrung out the linen and spread it over some bushes to dry. The camp sprawled before her gaze, a vast field of tents and baggage wains, soldiers and horses. Its size was swollen by the presence of Prince John, Count of Mortain. She could see his banner fluttering from a tent pole, and the surrounding area was filled with the toing and froing of squires, messengers and servants. A fresh offensive against the French was probably imminent, and with it, dangerous but steady employment for Hervi and Alexander. She shivered at the thought, some of her fear for them, some for herself. It did her no good to be too dependent on them. Trust was too easily betrayed.

That knowledge uppermost, she left her laundry and turned towards the horse lines.

Alexander was grooming Hervi's dun, his arm sweeping vigorously over the deep-golden coat. Monday paused to watch him, and fought a battle of wills with her courage. Sooner or later they would have to face each other, but what was there to say? Last night should never have happened but it had, and nothing could alter the fact. Friendship and mutual comfort had been overmatched by lust.

At the end of a long stroke, he raised his head, saw her, and immediately abandoned his grooming. 'I left you to sleep,' he said awkwardly as he approached and then halted an arm's length away.

Monday eyed him warily, her hands clenched at her sides. No words came, for she did not know how to tackle the situation. Did Alexander see her as a shameless wanton, or as an innocent who had made a terrible mistake? And should she view him as a calculating seducer, or someone who on the spur of the moment had cast his reason to the wind?

He rubbed his forehead, which was marred by two vertical frown lines. 'For what it is worth, I am sorry,' he said. 'We were both gilded to the eyeballs last night, but I admit the fault is mine. If I had been sober and in my right mind, and if Hervi hadn't . . .'

'If Hervi hadn't what?'

He shook his head. 'It doesn't matter. What we have to . . .'

'Yes, it does,' she said fiercely. 'Tell me what you were going to say.'

Alexander sighed. 'You know that Hervi rebuked me yesterday for teaching you to read and write. He says that few men will desire an educated wife, that it is pointless to give you wings when you are never going to fly, and . . .'

'Even fewer men will want a wife who is not a virgin,' she pointed out.

'You could marry me,' he said, 'then you could soar to your heart's content.'

Monday stared at him, her lips still parted from her last remark. At the back of her mind she had expected him to make just such an offer. It was the least that honour demanded, and although the code had been violated last night, she knew that Alexander had an innate sense of what was honourable. 'What will Hervi say?'

'Be damned to Hervi,' he said tersely, then shrugged. 'Hervi will be as furious as a wild boar, but in the end he'll see sense. He might even be relieved. It will stop him rejecting offers from other undesirables.'

'So he has had other offers for me?' she pounced.

Alexander's lip curled. 'Eudo le Boucher approached Hervi a while ago and he's been pursuing my brother for an answer.'

'And Hervi has not found it possible to give him an outright refusal?' Monday's voice seethed with loathing and fury. 'My father chose well when he named your brother my guardian. He might as well have left me defenceless amidst a pack of wolves! Don't touch me!' She took a swift step backwards as he held out a conciliatory hand.

His eyes darkened and he flinched at her rejection. 'Do you truly believe that Hervi would sell you to Eudo le Boucher?'

She bit her lip and felt the treachery of tears at the back of her eyes. 'I don't know what to believe any more.'

'Nothing ill of Hervi. He only has your well-being at heart.'

'Like yourself,' she scoffed.

Colour burned across his cheekbones. 'I am offering you

marriage now,' he said stiffly. 'Your honour will be restored, and so will mine. It will be for the best.'

'And you will love and cherish me all my days.'

'Your life will be mine.'

Monday swallowed the urge to hurl the offer back in his face as worthless dross, for it was not, and he was doing his best in a very awkward situation. A pity that it was not enough. If he had taken her in his arms, kissed her tenderly and said that she was his life's blood, she might have yielded. Faced by his practicality, and the bewildering surfeit of her own volatile emotions, she kept her distance.

'I need time alone to gather my wits.' She pressed her hand to her aching brow. 'My brains are still so addled that I scarce know my head from my heels.' Which was only half the truth. With each passing moment her mind was becoming clearer. 'Finish with the horses,' she said. 'I'll seek you out later when I don't feel quite so sick.' Before he could protest, she turned away towards the tents, the set of her spine brooking no interference. Nor, although she was tempted, did she glance over her shoulder. There was no point in looking back.

As she approached her own dwelling, her step grew more cautious, and when she drew aside the flap it was with a stealthy hand. The interior, however, was empty and she breathed a sigh of relief. Feeling queasy from her confrontation with Alexander, she could not have faced Hervi too.

'I cannot marry him,' she said to the stiff linen side of the tent. 'I would be chaining myself to a living hell.' She could not live the life that her parents had done, watching herself and Alexander slowly dying from its vagaries. They did not even have love to sustain them, and the emotions boiling in the air just now could as easily brew into bitterness and loathing as they could into abiding affection. She saw an image of herself in five years' time, her vitality extinguished, her body exhausted. There was a child at her feet, a baby at her breast and another in her belly. Alexander's tawny eyes were ignoring her to fix on some sparkling gossamer creature of wealth and privilege who was simpering at him among the crowd.

Monday pressed her palm against her flat stomach as the

horrifying thought crossed her mind that she might already be with child. 'No!' she denied, and tried to comfort herself with the commonly held lore that a woman never conceived the first time. Besides, done was done, and there was nothing to be gained by wringing her hands. She had to be practical, and she had to act swiftly while there was still time.

It was the work of a moment to unlock her coffer and remove the two pouches of her dowry silver from its false bottom. Ten marks in all, a hundred and thirty shillings. She stowed them in her leather travelling satchel, and crammed on top her needles, skeins of thread and sewing shears. She added a comb, a clean chemise and a spare tunic, stuffing everything down to leave room for two apples and a hunk of bread tied up in her spare wimple. Finally she looped a leather water bottle over her arm, swung her cloak around her shoulders, and was ready.

On the threshold of the tent she hesitated, and turned back to the writing instruments still littered about from the night before. She cut the quill to remove the dried ink from its tip, drew the sheet of vellum forward, and beneath the Arabic numerals wrote: *It might be for the best, but it is better this way. Do not seek me for you will not find me. Farewell and God keep you.* She bit her lip as she wrote the first letter of her name, and she had to dash a swift hand across her eyes, but her intention did not waver. Setting her pen aside, she wafted the vellum in the air to dry the ink, and then concealed the note beneath Alexander's cloak. She wanted him to find it, but not for it to be immediately visible, for she needed some space to make good her escape.

This time when she emerged from the tent, she made her way directly across the camp towards the main roadway leading to Gournai.

CHAPTER 16

Hervi bunched his fist, drew back his arm, and felled Alexander with a single, furious blow. 'You brainless whelp!' he roared. 'I ought to chop off your balls and nail them to that quintain post over there!' He hauled Alexander to his feet for the sheer purpose of knocking him down again.

Alexander spat blood where a tooth had sliced his gum, and struggled to sit up in the dust. He had known that Hervi would react in just such a manner to being told what had happened but he wondered just how far the beating would go before Hervi recovered his senses. 'I've spoken to Monday, asked her to wed me!' he cried as his tunic was seized in a bear grip and once more he was hauled upright.

'Her father entrusted her well-being to me. Sweet Christ, he will be calling out from his grave for vengeance!' Hervi shook Alexander like a terrier with a rat. 'What in God's name possessed you?'

A crowd had gathered to watch the altercation, although no one as yet knew what it was about. Osgar le Gros slouched on one hip, his arms folded. 'Ah,' he grinned, 'brotherly love.'

Hervi's eyes flickered to the growing audience. 'Piss off and bother someone else,' he snarled.

Osgar shrugged. 'More fun watching you.'

Hervi tossed Alexander back on the ground and rounded on the spectators. 'There's nothing to watch,' he said roughly, his chest heaving and his legs planted wide. 'Go on, you vultures, bugger off!' He gesticulated graphically.

With much laughter and slow sauntering, the onlookers

melted away, Osgar predictably the last to leave, with a rude gesture of his own. Alexander had silent cause to thank him, for his
intervention had deflected the worst of Hervi's fury.

'If I could undo the deed, I would,' he said from the ground.
'Since I can't, I'll make amends as best I can. There is no point in
beating me to a pulp; I won't make a very presentable bridegroom.'

Hervi bared his teeth. 'You'll make no sort of bridegroom,' he
growled, but the dusky colour had drained from his face and his
eyes no longer threatened to pop from his skull. 'How could you
be so stupid?'

'I was drunk, and if the truth were known, greatly disturbed at
the thought of Eudo le Boucher offering for her. I didn't realise
how disturbed until it was too late.'

'So you ruined her for all but yourself.'

'That wasn't my intention. I . . . I just wasn't thinking at the
time.'

'Except with your loins,' Hervi said contemptuously. 'Oh, get
up. You look like a cur waiting to be kicked.'

Which was precisely how Alexander felt. Warily he rose to his
feet and dusted himself down. His lip was throbbing and he
knew from the hot pain beneath his left eye that he was going to
have a spectacular bruise. He also knew that he had emerged
very lightly from the storm of Hervi's wrath.

'Where's Monday?' Hervi demanded.

'She said she wanted a moment alone to collect her thoughts.
I finished grooming our horses and came to find you.' He
glanced at their surroundings – the service camp of the
Angevin brothers' army, a rearguard of washerwomen, petty
servants, labourers and whores. This was the ground where
Hervi spent his leisure hours. Alexander, usually more discerning, knew that he would have given anything to have been
with his brother last night.

'I'll find a priest,' he said to Hervi, adding quickly as he saw
his brother's face, 'a proper priest to join us in marriage. Count
John or one of his commanders is bound to have a chaplain willing to witness the ceremony.'

'Oh yes,' Hervi said sarcastically, 'by all means let us observe
the proprieties.'

Alexander found his priest, a fresh-faced Benedictine, newly launched from the cloister and serving as an assistant and scribe to the Count of Mortain's senior chaplain. The young Father Ambrose had never performed a wedding before and was eager to do so to add the experience to his career.

The priest secured, Alexander went in search of Monday to bear her the glad tidings of their forthcoming nuptials. Hervi chose to work off the dregs of his anger and tension in a bout of exercise.

To while away the time beneath the walls of Vaudreuil, the besiegers were practising their arms by holding individual jousts and small tourneys. Hervi mounted Soleil and rode to join the sport. It was not so disastrous he told himself. Alexander and Monday knew and liked each other. With the yoke of a marriage vow and a gold ring, there was no reason why they could not settle to plough a straight furrow side by side. But he was still angry that it had happened the way it did. He should have seen what was beneath his nose. Dear God, he was a man himself, with a man's desires. He had been so busy fostering father-and-daughter feelings about Monday that it had never occurred to him that Alexander might view her in a different light, and he was chagrined at his own lack of vision.

From the corner of his eye, he saw a familiar red and yellow surcoat and shield, and he turned Soleil to evade the oncoming horse and rider. Hervi had no desire to keep the company of Eudo le Boucher this day. Le Boucher, however, had other ideas, and he too changed direction, spurring his battle-scarred bay to cover the ground between them so that Hervi had no choice but to turn and face him.

'You son of a whore!' le Boucher snarled as he drew level.

Hervi stared at him and tightened his fist on the lance shaft. He did not need to ask the reason for le Boucher's fury; he feared that he already knew.

Le Boucher's forefinger stabbed. 'You never had any intention of bestowing that girl outside your own family,' he attacked. 'I have just spoken to Mortain's wet-faced priest and he was only too delighted to regale me with the details. You made a fool of me, de Montroi, and no one does that!' Le Boucher's bay sidled, its eyes rolling as it was simultaneously spurred and reined back.

'You have made a fool of yourself. I gave you no commitment,' Hervi retorted, a hot wave of anger mingling with the fear in his gut. 'If you have spoken to the priest as you say, you will know that it is a matter of honour, nothing more, nothing less.'

'Then let honour be satisfied!' le Boucher spat, and drew his sword from his saddle scabbard.

Hervi swallowed. 'Christ, don't be an idiot,' he said huskily.

'Why not, I am already a fool.' The sword flashed.

Hervi touched Soleil's neck and the stallion reared, forehooves striking. Le Boucher's bay flinched sideways to escape the hooves, and the knight's blow went wide, giving Hervi time to draw his own weapon and drag his shield into position. He deliberated whether to spur for the safety of the other soldiers beneath the walls, or stay and fight it out. He parried the next blow and got in a useful counterstrike of his own that sent slivers of wood flying from le Boucher's shield.

What a stupid way to die, Hervi thought as his arm took the shock of the next assault and he found himself outmanoeuvred and forced on to the defensive. It but needed that sword edge to connect once and he was a dead man. He was only clad in his quilted gambeson, not his mail, and the weight of a sharpened edge would fillet him like a herring.

Beneath the deadly glitter of le Boucher's blade, Hervi managed to turn Soleil and dug in his spurs. The stallion burst into a hard gallop and tore towards the other soldiers on siege duty. Hervi heard the thunder of hooves in pursuit and lashed the reins down on the dun's neck. He could see the faces turned towards him, the looks of surprise and consternation; the frown of a commander. Without slackening the reins, he headed directly for their midst.

And then Soleil's leading forehoof struck the powdered earth of an old molehill and the horse pitched forward, tail over teeth. The stallion's neck struck the ground at the wrong angle and there was a sickening crack. Hervi tried to throw himself clear, but he was not swift enough and one leg was pinned beneath the dun's falling weight. He heard and felt a second crack hard upon

the first as his shin bone snapped. Agony filled the space where
the sound had been. Hervi heard himself scream, the sound thin
and high-pitched. There was nothing in the world but the white
heat of pain. Suddenly he did not care if le Boucher killed him.
Indeed, he heard himself crying out for that mercy.

Alexander had searched throughout the siege encampment for
Monday and discovered not a trace. He visited all her usual
haunts, but the closest he came to her presence was encountering
a washerwoman who told him that she had seen Monday vigorously scrubbing a linen sheet at the riverside earlier that morning.
Her information sent a guilty pang through him, for he knew
why Monday had been washing that sheet. Irritated and anxious,
he redoubled his efforts, but without success.

Finally, back at the tent, he sat down on the stripped pallet
which they had shared last night, and put his head in his hands.
He did not know where else to look and was beginning to feel
afraid. She had to be here somewhere, he told himself. Someone
must have seen her. He kicked in frustration at the side of the
coffer near his heels and the brass latch rattled at him. He saw
that it was not secured, and frowned, knowing that since the
incident with Grisel she kept it firmly locked. With a growing
apprehension, he went down on his knees and flipped back the
crudely carved lid.

Monday's effects were stored within, but they were in a state
of disarray quite alien to their usual tidiness. He rummaged
among them and saw with alarm and a sinking in his gut that her
needles and sewing threads were no longer there. Perhaps she had
gone to sit somewhere quiet to do her thinking and sew at the
same time. The thought was comforting, but it held no substance. He explored further, and his worst fears were confirmed
when he prised open the false bottom of the chest and found its
concealed space empty.

Swearing, he closed the lid and rose to his feet. His shoe
caught in the folds of his cloak and he picked up the garment to
toss it on the pallet. Then he saw the strip of vellum and the
smudged, inexperienced lettering. He stared at it with shortening
breath, then stooped to grab it and read the words in one rapid

flicker of his eyes.

. . . better this way . . . God keep you. M. Alexander crushed the writing in his fist and swore again, with virulence. Her time to think had been time to make her escape; he should have realised. Stupid, stupid. He cursed himself and he cursed Monday. Assuming that she had returned to the tent and packed straight away, she had almost half a day's start on any pursuit, and there was no inkling in her brief message as to where she was bound. She had sufficient funds to take her as far as she chose to go . . . sufficient funds to make her a victim of robbery or worse on the open roads, a young woman alone.

Perhaps she would go to her grandfather, Thomas of Stafford, as she had once contemplated. He opened his fist and smoothed out the crumpled vellum to gaze upon her handwriting. A surge of grief joined the broil of guilt and anger in his breast. She was so bright, so spirited, and he had ruined it all. He folded the note carefully this time and tucked it down inside his tunic.

He had only taken one step outside the tent when he was accosted by the young priest, Father Ambrose, who had promised to set the seal on the marriage. His earnest face was deep pink, for the heat was cooking him in his dark woollen robe, and he looked flustered.

'I am sorry, I haven't found her yet,' Alexander said, thinking it the reason for the priest's approach. 'Indeed, I believe that she has run away.'

The monk looked more worried than ever, and wrung his hands within the voluminous folds of his overlong sleeves. 'That is indeed grave news,' he murmured, 'and I am afraid that I am the bearer of no better tidings myself.'

'Why, what has happened? Have you found her?' Alexander stared at the monk in alarm. Images of Monday's corpse floating in the river filled his mind's eye. Last time she had been seen, it had been near the water.

'No, no, nothing like that,' Father Ambrose said, but his expression remained grim. 'It is your brother. There has been an accident beneath the castle walls and he has broken his leg.'

'What?' Alexander had heard the words perfectly well, but they slid over him without being absorbed.

'Come, I will bring you to him.' Ambrose made an ushering gesture. 'His horse put its hoof in a molehill and fell badly. The poor beast is dead and your brother injured. It's a difficult break, right across the shin bone.'

Alexander shook his head. 'Hervi's never been thrown in his life,' he said, and numbly followed the young Benedictine through the camp. 'Soleil's as sure-footed as a mountain goat.'

'Even a mountain goat can stumble over a molehill.'

'Hervi would have ridden around it, he was no fool,' Alexander argued, still shaking his head, still denying.

'Nevertheless, it has happened,' Ambrose said, his voice gentle but implacable.

Alexander tightened his lips. He was filled with an unjust loathing for the young priest, purely because he was the bearer of ill tidings. The clergy had never brought anything but misery into his life.

Beneath the walls of Vaudreuil, Hervi lay on the grass, a chirurgeon and his assistant bending over him, a couple of knights hovering close by. Alexander sprinted the final distance, outrunning the pink-faced monk, and flung himself down at his brother's side.

Hervi was fully conscious, his features white with pain. He was biting down on a block of wood as the chirurgeon bound the broken limb with tight bandages and ash-wood splints.

'What in God's name happened?' Alexander demanded, filled with horror at the sight of Hervi in such agony. A broken bone was always a threat to livelihood and mobility. More than that, it was a threat to life itself if the rot took hold.

The chirurgeon shrugged. 'A fall from a horse,' he said without raising his head from his handiwork. He had firm, chunky hands with clean, trimmed nails. An elaborate brown felt hat had been discarded on the grass at his side, its brim decorated with pilgrim badges from Rome, Canterbury and Compostela.

Hervi spat out the block of wood. 'I was running away from Eudo le Boucher's sword,' he groaned. 'Soleil put his hoof in a molehill and we went down . . . Ah, Christ!' His voice rose and split on a scream that sent slivers of ice down Alexander's spine.

'It is a bad break but I have set the bone as well as I can,' the chirurgeon said grimly. 'The rest is in God's hands.' He glanced up briefly at Alexander, and then beyond him to the panting Father Ambrose.

'As his fall was in God's hands too?' Alexander asked bitterly. He knew what such a wound presaged. If Hervi healed, he would have one leg shorter than the other, be less balanced and fluid on foot and even in the saddle. No one would want to employ him. 'If God had any sense of justice, he would have punished me!'

His own words struck him like a slap in the face. God was punishing him. A physical wound would have been easier to bear than the guilt assaulting him now.

'If God had any sense of justice, it would have been le Boucher's horse which foundered,' Hervi croaked, opening pain-glazed eyes. 'Never mind the wherefore and the why. Just get me to my tent. I feel like a corpse on a battlefield stretched out here with all you vultures standing around me.'

As an attempt both at bravery and a jest, it fell flat. Everyone knew that Hervi might well die of the injury. His eyes dull with worry, Alexander paid the chirurgeon and his assistant their fee, and saw his brother borne gently back to their tent.

'I have some small knowledge of leechdom,' Ambrose said as they laid Hervi down on his pallet. 'A tincture of white poppy in wine will dull the pain. I have a phial among my effects.' Without further ado, he departed to fetch it.

Hervi lay on his pallet, his injured leg held rigid in the splints, and stared around the familiarity of the tent which he had departed an hour since in perfect, robust health. 'The only reason le Boucher did not kill me,' he said, 'was that Soleil went down and he judged his death and my injury payment enough. But it is not finished. He will come after you and Monday.' He turned his head on the pillow and glanced around the tent. 'Where is the lass? Best be wed and on your way.'

Alexander swallowed. There was no point in keeping the truth from Hervi. His leg might be broken, but his wits were still about him. 'I do not know, save that she is likely more than half a day's journey from us by now.' He removed the note from his tunic and unfolding it, read it out to his brother. 'She took her dowry silver and her sewing equipment,' he said over the top of the vellum. 'I fear she does not intend returning.'

Hervi took the note in his hands and looked at the brown lettering which to him was just so much scribble. 'A fine guardian I have made,' he said with self-disgust, and raised his eyes to Alexander. 'And you have no inkling where she might have gone?'

'She did once speak of her grandfather in England, Thomas FitzParnell of Stafford. She wondered what he was like and told me that it was a secret yearning of hers to live the life of a lady of rank as her mother had once done. Perhaps she might go to him . . . It is no more than a guess.'

'You must go and find her,' Hervi said. He was grey with pain, and each word was an obvious effort to force his reason through it. 'A woman alone on the road is easy prey, and although she has the wisdom of the battle camp in her veins, she is still vulnerable.'

Alexander stared at his brother in dawning consternation as he realised the choice being set out before him. 'But I cannot leave you in this state!' he protested. 'Who will tend you?'

'I will do well enough . . . I have friends, and some silver laid by.'

'Friends like Alys and Osgar?' Alexander gazed down at Hervi, utterly horrified at the thought of leaving him in such company.

'Don't argue with me, whelp. I haven't the strength. Just go.'

Alexander frowned. 'You heard what she said in this note. I might not find her even if I go, and then I would have obeyed you for nothing. I don't want to lose you both.'

'Damn your hide Alex . . .' Hervi began, then desisted as the pain in his broken leg surged over and defeated him.

Father Ambrose returned with the phial of poppy syrup and set about administering a drugged measure of wine to the wounded man. As Hervi fell into a restless doze, the young priest sighed. 'He will need constant care over the next few days,' he said doubtfully.

Alexander gnawed his lower lip. 'He wants me to go and search for the girl. I know that I should, but I cannot leave him like this. If he is looked after at all, it will be in a rough and ready fashion that will surely lead to his death. There is no one I can trust.'

Ambrose eyed him sidelong. 'There is always the abbey at Pont l'Arche. The infirmarian there is excellent.'

'No!' A white-hot streak of fury and fear shot through Alexander.

Ambrose raised his brows in surprise and not a little consternation. 'It is less than an hour's ride – perhaps two or three by slow litter – and I promise you that they would care for him well. I served my novitiate there. The Abbot is strict, but he is just, and compassionate. '

'Not the church,' Alexander repeated, feeling as if dark walls were closing around him.

'May I ask why not?'

Alexander wanted to snarl a denial at Father Ambrose, but the monk looked so earnestly bewildered that he curbed his tongue. 'Before I joined Hervi, I served part of my novitiate at a small Benedictine priory in England. The prior there was in his dotage and the sub-prior had command of all our lives . . .' He broke off with a grimace. 'I ran away when my life became intolerable.'

Ambrose looked from Alexander to the man on the pallet, who was beginning to breathe with the heaviness of slumber. 'The abbey is not the same place as your priory, and one bad fish does not mean that every shoal in the ocean is rotten, does it?'

'No,' Alexander admitted, his shoulders stiff with rejection.

'It seems to me that you have small choice but to take your brother to Pont l'Arche,' Ambrose said quietly. 'I promise you, not a monk's promise, but a friend's, that he will be in safe hands.'

Brother Radulfus examined the wounded man with deft and gentle hands. He could see no injury other than the severely broken lower limb, although there were numerous small scars that spoke of a turbulent life. Radulfus had his own share, concealed from view by the coarse Benedictine habit that had been his since his ordination ten years ago. Now he was Brother Radulfus, infirmarian and humble monk. Then he had been Radulf de Villefranche, younger son of a minor noble and earning his bread by the sword, much as these two brothers in his presence now. The injured one was in the prime of manhood, smoothly fleshed with a taut, powerful musculature. His companion still bore the reed slenderness of youth and was both lighter of build and more refined of feature. At the moment he was studying Radulfus with wary amber-hazel eyes and more than reminded the monk of a young wolf gazing out on the world from the edge of the forest.

'Well,' said Ambrose eagerly from the background, 'can you heal him?'

Radulfus raised his greying tonsure from his drugged patient and frowned slightly at the ebullient chaplain. Ambrose's all-embracing enthusiasm had been both his downfall and his redemption during his time in the novitiate here. He was a committed supporter of lame dogs, waifs and strays. If someone did not martyr him first in order to have peace, he might become the stuff of which popular saints were made. 'That is in the hands of the Almighty,' Radulfus reproved. 'The limb is badly broken, but he is strong and otherwise healthy. With tending and prayer, he may live to walk again.' He looked at the younger man and addressed him directly. 'I make no promises, but I will do what I can.'

'Thank you.' The reply was murmured through stiff lips, the tension palpable.

'May I trouble you, Father Ambrose, to fetch some more charcoal for the brazier?' Radulfus requested gently with a lift and drop of his silver thicket eyebrows.

'Of course.' Ambrose cleared his throat, and rubbing his hands within his habit, vanished out of the door.

'I do not think that you want to thank me,' Radulfus said when he was sure they were alone. 'Indeed, I receive the impression that you are here under duress.'

'All I care is that you save his life, and if it be in your power, prevent him from being a cripple. I have silver, I can pay.'

There was more power in the voice now, the French bearing a distinct trace of an English accent to Radulfus's keen ears. 'As I said, with God's aid I will do my best. Whatever alms you give to our church are welcome, but they are not a prerequisite of your brother's place here.'

'Are they not?'

The hint of a sneer now. Someone had burned the lad and badly. 'Remind me of your name,' Radulfus said. 'Brother Ambrose told me, but I was too busy settling your brother without jolting his leg or rousing him to awareness.'

'Alexander . . . Alexander de Montroi.' The wariness did not thaw.

Radulfus folded his arms. 'I have been a monk for ten years, Alexander, and most fulfilled and content I am to live out my time in the praise and service of God, but it was not always so. I was a soldier before I took the cowl. I drank and whored and fought my way across Christendom in the pay of warring barons and gave nary a thought to the well-being of my soul.'

He saw the spark of curiosity flare in the guarded countenance. 'Then what changed your mind?'

Radulfus shrugged down his habit, and Alexander leaped backwards, his hand going to his knife and fear widening his eyes. 'No,' said the monk quickly. 'Don't worry, I have not lost my wits. I want to show you the first change in my life.' He pointed to a long silvery scar running from the base of his throat to his navel. 'Someone tried to split me like a bacon pig and almost succeeded. I was brought here to be tended – like your brother – and for the first time in my life I had the opportunity to listen to the still, small voice of God. I recovered, I stayed, and finally I took my vows. Nor have I ever regretted doing so.' He pulled his habit back over his shoulders. 'Your brother will be safe with us, I promise you, whether he has silver or not.' Radulfus eyed Alexander thoughtfully. 'You do not trust me,' he said.

Alexander breathed out and his right hand dropped from his scabbard. 'I was given to the Church when I was eleven. My father was dead and my eldest brother wanted rid of me.'

'Ah.' Radulfus nodded. 'So you did not enter the novitiate of your own free will?'

The young man shrugged. 'I would have borne with it. They taught me to read and write, and I have something of a talent with ink and quill. If they had left me in the peace of the scriptorium, I might have one day been an asset to their priory.'

'But they didn't?' Radulfus studied Alexander. So many children were vowed to the monastic life by their parents and siblings. Frequently the youngsters were miserable and homesick. Many of them were totally unsuited to a life in the cloister. Some adapted in bitter silence. Others rebelled.

'No,' Alexander said bleakly, 'they didn't. I have more scars on my body from my days as a novice than I have as a mercenary on the battlefield.' He swallowed and made a dismissive gesture. 'It is in the past. Let it be.'

'I am sorry. I can see in your face that you are not ready to forgive or forget, but I promise you that I will do everything in my power to help your brother. Once it was me lying there. What we are given in compassion, we have a sacred duty to pass on.'

Alexander was still mistrustful: his own experiences dictated caution, but Radulfus's air of placid confidence was reassuring, as was the information that he had once served as a soldier.

Father Ambrose returned, puffing beneath the weight of a wicker basket brimming with lumps of charcoal. Alexander wondered how different his own life would have been had he entered the novitiate in a place like this instead of Cranwell. Perhaps he would have been ordained by now, his hair clipped in a neat tonsure, and his hands unmarked by the grip of shield strap, sword and rein. As of now, he was adrift in the world, his anchor lying unconscious and torn up from its grounding.

Reaching to the pouch on his belt, Alexander brought forth a small draw-cord purse. 'Here,' he said. 'To help pay for his care. I will leave his packhorse too for your use to do as you see fit. When he wakes, tell him that I have gone in search of Monday. He will know what you mean.'

Brother Radulfus took the coins with dignity and inclined his head. 'I will do so,' he said. 'God go with you, and lighten your burdens.'

'God remain here, and guide your healing hands,' Alexander responded, and after a final look at Hervi, strode from the room before he was overcome by the surfeit of dammed emotion which the abbey walls were too small to hold.

By the time Alexander and Ambrose returned to Vaudreuil, it was full dark, and the camp fires of the Angevin army scattered the field before the castle like flowers in a spring meadow. An impromptu joust was taking place between the Normans and French on a flat piece of land outside the disputed castle walls, and the shouts of encouragement, the clack of lances and thunder of hooves echoed their ghosts on Alexander's mind.

Ambrose bade him farewell and returned to his official post from which he had been absent for long enough, leaving a weary Alexander to dismount alone outside his tent. All he wanted to do was stagger inside and throw himself down on his pallet, but first he had the horse to tend. With clumsy fingers he began unsaddling Samson. His mind was numb, his awareness dulled by exhaustion, both physical and mental, and when Eudo le Boucher stepped out of the shadows, he was taken entirely by surprise.

'I have been waiting for your return,' le Boucher said. 'Indeed, I was beginning to think that you had turned coward and fled.'

Alexander faced le Boucher, his heart pounding in solid, swift strokes, the numbness giving way to a potent mixture of fury and fear. 'If you have been waiting in order to atone for what you did to my brother, then I will speak to you. If not, I have nothing to say,' he answered through his teeth.

'Atone?' Le Boucher's jaw dropped. His surprise was almost comical to behold, except that there was no humour in the situation whatsoever. 'You want me to atone?' Rage thickened his voice.

'Hervi made you no promises. Any slights are all in your own mind,' Alexander said, breathing hard. 'And for your overweening self-conceit, you almost killed him!'

'Hah, so I suppose I imagine that you have deflowered the woman for whom I was negotiating in marriage?' Le Boucher's clenched fist shot out and punched Alexander to the ground. 'Then imagine this too, renegade monk!' A boot connected with Alexander's ribs and he doubled up, protecting his head with his arms and the soft parts of his body with his folded knees.

'Where is she, where have you hidden her?' le Boucher demanded between each kick and blow.

'I do not know!' Alexander choked, and straightened his legs in a sudden kick, attempting to trip le Boucher and bring him down. One shoe connected with bone and drew an involuntary yelp from the man above him. Alexander flashed over, leaped to his feet and out of le Boucher's reach. He knew that his only advantage lay in his greater speed, his ability to weave and duck until the knight tired.

Le Boucher saw it too, for after a couple of missed swipes he stopped, and looked at Alexander with hands on hips. 'You do not know, or you will not tell?' he demanded across the space between them.

'I do not know, and that is the truth,' he said through his teeth. 'Indeed, if you were not blocking my way, I would be seeking her even now.'

Le Boucher narrowed his eyes. 'We settle this with a joust,' he said decisively. 'One to one upon the slope with witnesses. Winner takes all that the loser possesses or claims to possess.'

In a distant corner of his mind, Alexander knew that he should decline, but le Boucher's sneering contempt and his own wounded fury were too potent to be rationalised. He found himself nodding his consent, derision curling his upper lip. 'Yes, let it be settled, and to the victor the profits.'

'Within a candle notch,' le Boucher said. 'Be there. If you are not, I will come after you.' And he strode away.

Alexander's hands were trembling as he reharnessed Samson and repaired to his tent to don mail and weapons. His fingers were so clumsy with shock and rage that he could scarcely buckle his sword belt or shorten his shield straps, and there was no one to ask for aid. No grey-eyed girl with nimble, efficient fingers, no brawny man with heavy-handed humour and the wisdom of experience. Their absence was his fault, and the only presence to keep him company was the accusing shade of Arnaud de Cerizay.

When he emerged from the tent and mounted up, it was to the sound of the crack of lances on the flat ground before Vaudreuil's walls. The shouts of men in effort and pleasure drifted towards him, but this time there was no answering exhilaration in his gut, only dread.

He collected a lance and rode to join their company. Le Boucher was already waiting, sitting his large bay stallion amongst a group of young knights. A cool evening wind rippled across the open land beneath the fortifications and chilled the sweat on Alexander's body. His grasp on the lance was slippery. He wondered if le Boucher's was too. It was all too easy to imagine the man as an invincible Goliath. And yet once, with no more skill at his fingertips than a peasant, Alexander had unhorsed him. Tonight he must do so again.

Le Boucher rose in his stirrups and waved his lance in the air. He filled his lungs and his huge voice bellowed forth. 'I hereby declare a joust à l'outrance between myself and Alexander de Montroi. Let all bear witness that this be a fair fight – to the yielding or to the death!'

It was not the first time that le Boucher had issued this kind of challenge. He took offence at the slightest provocation, be it real or imagined, and because he was strong and skilled in the arts of war, he usually killed or maimed his victims unless they had the good sense to run away first. Some of the onlookers sympathised with Alexander. Others could not believe his stupidity.

Alexander gripped his lance as William Marshal had taught him, and prepared for the charge. Time and again he had practised his moves at the quintain until they were a matter of instinct, not conscious thought. Time and again he had ridden victorious from the tourney ground and kept himself whole in battle. But on this occasion he had no choice of opponent, could not disengage and ride away, or rely on Hervi to deal with any difficult blows.

The torchlight against the darkness of a starless sky made vision difficult, but it would be the same for le Boucher. Alexander muttered a silent prayer to a God with whom he was on uneasy terms, and trotted Samson to the far end of the designated tilting ground. The turf was hard, but not dry, the conditions underfoot ideal. He tugged the stallion's black ears in encouragement and gathered himself. Samson snorted, small quivers of excitement rippling through his body. Against his neck, the reins rubbed a creamy line of foam.

At the other end of the tilt, le Boucher turned his bay, and without warning, drove in his spurs and hurtled across the ground at a thundering gallop. Even as Alexander responded, he knew that le Boucher had gained the first advantage, his impetus that much greater. If the lance should strike true, then Alexander would either be hurled from his saddle or skewered like a fowl on a spit.

At the last moment possible, when all that filled his vision was the oncoming horse and rider, Alexander twitched on the right rein. Le Boucher's lance head struck his shield, but on the outer edge, the full impact diminished to a glancing blow by Samson's sudden change of position. Of course, Alexander's own strike was no more than a token rap of lance on shield, a tit for tat, but at least he reached the far end of the tilt in one piece, and on the second run, le Boucher had no opportunity to steal an advantage of speed. Alexander yelled in Samson's ear and dug in his heels. The black stallion pounded towards le Boucher's bay. Yells of encouragement from the watchers filled the air and went unheeded by the combatants. Alexander had kept his lance tip low on the approach to give himself a good view of his target. Now he raised it and struck, pushing into the blow with all his strength. This time it was le Boucher who was slammed back against his cantle, a grunt of pain forced from him as his shield arm took the shock and his own strike went wide.

Alexander's lance head drove into the shield and the shaft shattered beneath the strain of impact. As he reached the end of the tilt, Osgar ran out and presented him with a fresh spear. 'Go on!' he declared, his small eyes glittering. 'For Hervi, nail the bastard!'

Alexander spun Samson, and once more thundered down the tilt towards le Boucher. The previous two passes had given him the confidence to believe that he might actually survive. At the other end of the tilt, a furious Eudo le Boucher was contemplating the fact that he might lose and thus become a laughing stock at the hands of a youth barely out of tail clouts. He clapped spurs to his destrier's flanks and howling a battle challenge, charged to meet his enemy.

The ferocious crack of lances upon shields rang across the night. Both horses were set back on their hocks by the impact,

and both men were thrown. Alexander hit the ground, the air
driving from his lungs, his shield arm totally numb. He wanted
just to lie where he had landed and let the world go away, but he
knew that he had to get up while he had the advantage. Le
Boucher, being the heavier man, would have landed with a
greater impact. Alexander crawled to his knees, and then precariously gained his feet, at the same time drawing his sword. Le
Boucher lay motionless, his body spread-eagled. Warily,
Alexander circled him, alert for any sudden moves, but the
knight remained as still as a corpse. Alexander began to think
that he had killed him. With the tip of his boot, he prodded le
Boucher, and when the man did not respond, stooped to roll him
over.

Le Boucher's limbs suddenly filled with life and he sprang
upon Alexander with the lean power of a lion and struck the
sword from his hand. Alexander doubled his knees and kicked
upwards, landing a solid blow in le Boucher's ribs, but with his
shield arm still tingling, he was no match for the mail-clad man
seated crushingly upon him.

'Yield,' le Boucher snarled at Alexander.

'Never,' Alexander panted, black stars bursting before his eyes
as he fought to breathe.

'Yield,' le Boucher repeated.

'Never!'

The pressure increased, and suddenly there was no breath left
in Alexander to deny. No air even for life itself and he felt himself slipping into darkness. He was very vaguely aware of a
burning sensation at his throat as the cord of the gold and
amethyst cross was ripped away.

'Everything,' le Boucher said. 'I claim everything.'

Alexander opened his eyes upon a patched canvas ceiling and for
a moment stared at it in total bewilderment. His left shoulder
was so stiff and painful that he could scarcely bear to move it,
and it hurt to breathe. Very gingerly he sat up, and found himself
looking at the interior of a tent not dissimilar to Hervi's in the
days before Monday had taken to caring for them. On the empty
pallet beside him lay a pair of female hose and a garish green silk

garter, together with two cups bearing the lees of what might have been hippocras.

His memory fell rather disjointedly into place. He remembered being brought here after last night's disastrous joust by a sympathetic but scolding Osgar. 'You should have known better than to fall for that old dead dog trick,' he had said scornfully. 'Christ knows, Hervi taught you better than that.'

'But I thought he *was* dead,' Alexander groaned.

'Aye, well you're the one lucky not to be.'

Alexander grimaced. He did not feel particularly lucky at the moment – possessing life, but far from alive, and without the wherewithal to live it.

Alys poked her head through the tent flap. 'Ah, you're awake,' she said, and disappeared. He heard her shouting to Osgar, and moments later the stout knight appeared, Alys hovering at his shoulder. He was wearing his mail, his sword at his hip; and outside, Alexander could hear the sounds of the camp being struck.

'We're moving position,' Osgar said, gesturing over his shoulder. 'I'll need to pack up soon.' He put his hands on his hips and studied Alexander. 'You've been a right fool, haven't you? Christ, le Boucher was yours for the taking last night if you'd only used the wits God gave you.'

'I know, there is no need to grind salt into my wounds.'

'Hah! If it weren't for my generosity, you'd have been sleeping in the open last night, you stupid whelp. Everything to that swine means everything.' Shaking his head, Osgar advanced further into the tent, and held out to Alexander the gilded leather sword belt that had been John Marshal's gift, and secure in its scabbard, the pattern-welded sword from Lavoux.

'You are in my debt to the sum of ten marks,' Osgar said gruffly. 'I took a fancy to buy them off le Boucher. God knows why, I must have been drunk.' He scrubbed his forefinger beneath his blunt nose, denying any finer feelings. 'Take it, pay me when you can. Go on, before I change my mind,' he added, his complexion reddening as Alexander stared up at him in amazement.

'I do not know what to say, thank you seems not enough.' Alexander took the sword belt and scabbard, his fingers closing around the supple leather like a drowning man clutching to the spar of a ship.

'Then say nothing,' Osgar answered brusquely. 'It is not a gift.'

Alexander nodded and eased to his feet. He buckled the sword belt over the quilted gambeson in which he had slept, and immediately felt less naked. 'You say that the camp is being struck?'

'Aye, most of the tents are down.' Osgar cast a glance around. 'And this one too, in short order. Alys has saved you some bread and gruel, but best be quick about it.'

'Where's le Boucher?'

'Gone ahead as part of the advance guard. He won't be here to see you leave, if that is your concern.'

Alexander began to feel more optimistic by the minute. He emerged into the morning, cool with a hint of autumn, and took the bowl of gruel that Alys gave him. There was a sweetening of honey and a few early blackberries stirred in, giving the dish more flavour than usual. He decided that Alys must be feeling dreadfully sorry for him.

'Where will you go?' Osgar enquired as Alexander devoured the gruel and scraped the bowl clean.

'To England, to look for Monday. There is a chance that she has gone to her grandfather at Stafford.'

Osgar sucked his teeth. 'You have neither money nor horse,' he said. 'And it's a long, long walk to the coast.'

Alexander smiled and set his bowl aside. 'I was a fool last night, but not a complete one,' he said. 'There is enough silver sewn into the lining of my cloak to see me to the coast and pay for a packhorse. And when that runs out, I can hire myself out as a foot soldier or scribe . . . And then,' he added, his smile fading, 'I'll return for Hervi.'

Osgar looked at the ground. 'A bad business,' he said, shaking his head. 'I will pray for you both . . . and I haven't said a prayer in five years.'

Alexander swallowed. 'I'll pay you back, Osgar, I swear on the bones of St Martin I will.'

Osgar clasped Alexander's arm. 'I do not doubt it, lad.'

Alexander took his leave of Osgar, and then, because it would have been churlish to leave without thanking Father Ambrose for all that he had done, he went in search of the priest.

Their meeting was brief, for the young chaplain was busy with errands for the more senior members of the household, but he found time to brush aside Alexander's gratitude with great modesty, and bid him Godspeed and better fortune than of late.

'One thing,' he added, tucking the two rolls of vellum he was holding more securely under his arm, 'Eudo le Boucher has had no joy from that horse of yours. Three times he has been thrown – and kicked in the balls to add insult to injury. I doubt they will ever become a partnership on the battlefield.' He smiled wryly as he spoke, but Alexander did not join him. While there was satisfaction in picturing Samson's antics, he knew that le Boucher was full capable of destroying the horse to wreak his revenge.

In sombre mood, he bade farewell to Father Ambrose, and, rubbing his shoulder to ease the ache, walked across the camp towards the road. French banners fluttered from the walls of Vaudreuil where King Philip and Coeur de Lion were in parlance, trying to ease their differences without giving ground. Alexander turned his back on the keep, and slung the satchel Osgar had given him over his good arm. It contained half a loaf, a chunk of sausage and a leather bottle of cider. Enough to tide him through to the evening.

A shout of warning and the thunder of hooves caused Alexander to turn swiftly and regard with astonishment the loose black stallion pounding away from the castle, mane and tail floating like banners, reins flapping on its neck and saddle empty. A soldier was sprinting in hopeless pursuit.

Alexander pursed his lips and uttered a low whistle. The horse plunged to a halt, pivoted on his hind legs and trotted over to his former master, a deep nicker of greeting rumbling from his chest. Alexander caught the bridle and stroked Samson's soft black muzzle and silky cheek. Then he looked over his shoulder at the pursuing soldier. It was one of le Boucher's henchmen, and he was wasting his breath yelling something about dog's-meat as he ran. Another soldier was struggling in a midden heap like a cast-over beetle.

Without pause for thought, Alexander clutched a handful of mane and vaulted into the saddle. He dug in his heels, and Samson took off as if the ground beneath him were hot.

Over the camp site they flew, over the road and towards the beckoning green and tawny tints of the late-summer forest, and within moments were lost to sight from the camp at Vaudreuil.

CHAPTER 17

It had been a long road and Monday's feet were sore, her gown floured with dust. She was only too glad to accept the offer of a ride in the cart of a family bound for the market in Lavoux with surplus produce to sell and barter.

The mother, plump and gregarious, shunted her five offspring along the wain towards the overflowing willow baskets of apples and pears at the back, so that Monday had room to lean against a sack of straw which acted as a cushion to the jolting of the small cart. The children, ranging in age from a tiny little girl scarce out of swaddling to a tanned, long-limbed boy on the verge of adolescence, stared at her inquisitively. Their father clicked his tongue, and the sturdy brown cob hitched between the shafts took the strain and began once more to plod along.

'Are you going to the market, mistress?' asked the woman. Her eyes were as brightly curious as those of her children. Women travelling alone were an occasional sight, but they were seldom as young as Monday, and although her dress was dusty and a mite ragged about the hem, it was still beautifully stitched and of good fabric.

'No, to the castle,' Monday replied, aware that in exchange for the ride, she owed these people a conversation, no matter that she wanted to rest her head and go to sleep. For the last week of the three that she had been on the road, she had felt unwell, sick and tired all the time. But at least her goal was in sight. 'I was once a sempstress to the lady Aline. I am hoping that she will employ me again.'

The woman eyed her. 'Why did you leave her service in the first place?' she asked forthrightly.

'My menfolk were employed by Lord Bertran. When he was killed, we had to leave.'

'And now you have no menfolk either lass?'

Monday looked down at her hands so that she would not have to meet the shrewd, sharp gaze. 'My father died in the spring,' she said, 'my mother the year before, and I have no guardians now.' Despite her best effort, her chin wobbled.

The older woman's features softened maternally. 'I'm right sorry to hear of your loss,' she said. ''Tis always hard for a woman alone, but you could do no better than to seek out lady Aline. She's in need of attendants, what with a new babe in the cradle and her husband home with a war wound. Oh aye,' she said to Monday's startled look. 'She and Hamon de Rougon were wedded and bedded within a three-month of her being widowed, and not a moment too soon. Bells were pealing on the eve of St Giles for the birth o' their son, and I've heard he's mortal lusty for a babe born only seven months after the wedding.'

Monday digested this in silence. Her own flux was almost ten days late now. She had tried to banish the terrifying suspicion that she might be with child, but each day that dawned without sign of blood made it ever more likely. Now the goodwife's words acted upon her anxiety. There would be no wedding for her, she had run away from the prospect, and she was still not sure that she had done the right thing.

'We heard last market day that the lord Hamon had taken a spear in the shoulder whilst on campaign with Duke Richard,' the woman continued as Monday said nothing. 'That will keep him home long enough to sire another one, eh?'

The youngest child clamoured to be taken into her mother's ample lap. The woman lifted her up and cuddled her. 'Nearly there now, sweetheart,' she soothed, and looked over the tousled dark head to Monday. 'Mind you, I'd like to see lady Aline cope without her servants. She'd not last more than three wags of a dog's tail with my brood.' She flicked an affectionate glance over her children.

'Lady Aline is more resourceful than you know,' Monday defended. 'She survived her first two husbands, did she not, and married the man of her choice?'

'Aye, I suppose she did that,' her companion grudgingly admitted, and then nodded at Monday's small bundle. 'So you're a sempstress, eh?'

Their conversation drifted on to the subject of sewing, and Monday gifted the woman with a brass needle and a hank of scarlet thread. The goodwife glowed with pleasure and was effusive in wishing Monday well as they parted in the marketplace.

'You look after yourself now, lass,' she said, giving Monday's arm a warm squeeze. 'I'd not like to think of a daughter of mine out in the world on her own.' She clutched the youngest child fiercely to her skirts as she spoke.

Monday smiled and thanked her, moved by the maternal concern and at the same time made bereft by its warmth, for it made her sense even more keenly the lack in her own life. Through a mist of tears, she left the family chattering around their cart as they unloaded their goods, and began walking toward the castle.

'A boy.' Aline smiled complacently down at the swaddled baby slumbering in his crib. 'But of course Hamon and I knew he would be.'

Monday gazed at the baby with his fuzz of ruddy blond hair and tiny features. The sight of him stirred her loins and churned her stomach. 'He is beautiful,' she heard herself say.

Aline looked at her sidelong, and a small frown twitched her brows, but she made no direct comment. 'We named him Giles for the saint of his birthing day. Duke Richard is to be his godfather. Hamon is so proud, he can scarcely put his head through his tunic, so much has it swelled.'

Her jest illicited no more than a slight stretch of the lips from Monday. She clasped her hands tightly across her belly and prayed silently to herself that tonight she would bleed. Then, aware that Aline was looking at her thoughtfully, she forced herself to tear her eyes from the baby, and tried to widen her smile.

'Mind you, with the wound my husband took in his shoulder, he is fortunate to have a head at all,' Aline added. 'He was sick with the battle fever when he came home, and I feared I might lose him, but by God's grace he has recovered enough to be a terrible patient.' She spoke lightly, but her gaze remained frighteningly shrewd. 'Come.' She took Monday's arm and steered her away from the cradle into the antechamber. 'You'll sleep here as before with the other maids. You can use that coffer over there for your things.'

Monday thanked her in a faltering voice. She was quite white with exhaustion, ready to drop on her feet. Aline patted her arm compassionately. 'Time enough for everything later. To look at you, I doubt you could even thread a needle at the moment. Lie down awhile and rest. The dinner horn will not sound for at least an hour, and I am not so desperate that I require you to begin sewing straight away.'

'I'm all right.' Monday raised her chin.

'Child, you are swaying where you stand, and your eyes are so dark you look as if someone has beaten you,' Aline contradicted, and steered her over to an empty pallet. 'Lie down and sleep.' She separated Monday from her bundle, and stowed it in the coffer herself, then she pushed the girl down upon the pallet and removed her shoes, clucking her tongue at the worn state of the soles. 'Sleep,' she commanded. 'Stop fighting and close your eyes.'

As if Aline's words had given her the permission she needed to yield, Monday relaxed, and although at first her eyelids flickered at the enforcement of being closed, they soon grew smooth and slack as she fell into an exhausted slumber. Aline covered her with a woollen blanket, warned her women to be silent near the newcomer and went to talk to her husband.

Hamon de Rougon was sitting over a brazier in the wall chamber that he had made his domain during the day when he tired of the noisiness of the great hall and desired a little peace. The weight of his arm was supported in a sling so that it would not drag upon his damaged shoulder, and his nose was buried in a book that Count John had lent to him, a copy of Geoffrey of Monmouth's *Historia Regum Britanniae*.

Aline was too restless, too full of quicksilver energy to settle to such a pursuit, but she understood its value to her husband who, in his quiet moments, was something of a scholar. And the gift of a valuable book tooled in gold leaf, albeit that it was only a loan, was proof of the favour in which Hamon stood with the ruling house of Anjou.

Approaching him from behind, she kissed his throat and his bearded cheek. 'Wandering in the woods again?' she teased.

'Can you suggest a better pastime?' he retorted with amusement. 'A wounded man alone and neglected, what else am I to do to make the time less tedious?'

Aline laughed and sat upon her husband's knee, forcing him to set the book aside. 'You would not value my tending so much if I let you take it for granted,' she murmured against his lips.

They kissed with enthusiasm, but Aline squealed and leaped promptly from his lap when she discovered that his injured arm was no longer in its sling. She swiped at him and rubbed the buttock he had mischievously pinched.

'I never take anything for granted,' he chuckled. 'Which is more than I can say for you.'

Aline tilted her nose in the air, but her umbrage was only feigned. She poured them both a cup of wine and sat down at his feet in front of the glowing brazier. There was silence as they each savoured the moment, the feeling perhaps keener in Aline who knew that she was fortunate not to be a widow. If the spear thrust had been a shade deeper or to one side, Hamon might not be here now, sharing this time with her.

'So,' he said after a while, 'you have taken that child-sempstress back into your employ.'

'Not so much a child,' Aline said. 'If I am not mistaken, she will bear one herself before next summer ripens. Her eyes were afraid when she looked upon our son, and her hand went to her belly.'

'She said nothing to you?' There was open curiosity in Hamon's voice. Forced to be sedentary, he took a sharp interest in trivial matters that would not usually occupy his time. He had been in the hall when Monday had arrived and had heard her petition Aline for a post in the household.

Aline shook her head. 'She was almost dead on her feet with exhaustion, so I put her to bed. She told me nothing more than she said in the hall, but I will have it out of her before too long.'

'I wonder what happened to her menfolk,' Hamon mused.

'Three of them there were to protect her honour, as I recall – her father and those two brothers; one big as a bear and the other as quiet as a deer in the forest. You were quite taken with the younger one, weren't you?'

'So was Duke Richard,' she said without expression.

'Yes, he was a handsome lad,' Hamon answered, echoing her tone. 'And accomplished too. William Marshal praised him, and he is not a man to bestow undue compliments – although to my mind, the boy acted too much on the spur of the moment without giving thought to the consequences.'

'And now Monday has arrived at our gates bereft of all three protectors and in straitened circumstances. Another week on the road and her shoes would have worn out.' Aline pursed her lips.

'You are not usually such a champion of waifs and strays, particularly pretty female ones,' Hamon prodded.

'If I thought she was a threat to your fidelity, it is your eyes I would scratch out, not hers,' Aline warned, only half laughing. 'Nay, you need not think my heart has suddenly melted. Yes, the girl is in difficulty, but it is more than just charity that moves me to take her in. She is the best sempstress I have ever encountered, and excellent company when less set down. Besides,' Aline glanced over her shoulder at Hamon, 'she is no ordinary waif and stray. Her grandfather is a powerful English baron.'

'Oh, come now, you're teasing me!'

'No, it's the truth. Monday's mother was gently born, but eloped with a household knight and they travelled the tourneys in order to live.'

'Monday told you this, I suppose?' Hamon asked neutrally.

'She wasn't romancing if that is what you mean.' Aline tossed her head.

'But she did not tell you who he was?'

'I don't think she wanted me to know. What she did reveal was in the emotion of the moment, because she was upset.' She tilted round to look at her husband. 'I vouch for her honesty. After marriage to Bertran, I am an expert at sifting lies from truth.'

Hamon rubbed his jaw. 'Then why, if her circumstances are straitened, did she not go to England, to her grandfather?'

'And arrive on his threshold with a swelling belly created out of a sordid past?' Aline rolled her eyes, and wondered at the dullness of her husband's otherwise prompt wits. Men could be so blind. 'He would as likely order her from his door as welcome her with open arms, and she too has an inordinate pride. I believe that the only way she would show herself to her high-born relatives is as a great lady in her own right . . . and I cannot see that ever coming to pass.'

Hervi stared at Brother Radulfus in horror. 'No!' he roared. 'Not my leg, you are not going to cut it off!' He tried to jerk the swollen, shiny monstrosity away from the priest's sorrowful gaze, but the pain was so intense that his voice tore into a scream and he almost lost consciousness.

'Then you will die,' Radulfus said. 'I have tried my best to save your leg, but the damage is too severe. If I do not take away the rotten flesh now, the contagion will spread throughout your body and you will be dead within two days, perhaps less.'

'Then let me die,' Hervi panted. Sweat darkened his blond hair, and bright points of fever sat on his gaunt cheekbones. 'If you save me, it will only be to life as a useless cripple. Shrive me and let me go!'

Radulfus drew back with a frown. Hervi closed his eyes and tried to draw his consciousness away from the nauseating, festering agony of the shattered limb. The abbey's infirmary was a cool, spacious room, austere but tranquil. Autumn light poured amber richness upon the tawny cream walls, and through the window arch the sky was clear blue. He imagined himself walking out in the crisp air, his two sound feet crunching through a treasure of autumn leaves. But he would never do that again. Within two days he would be nothing. They would put him in a hole in the ground and cover his rotting corpse with the darkness of soil. Once again, in a nightmare he could not escape, he relived the moment when Soleil had gone down and he had known that there was nothing he could do to outwit disaster. The crack, crack of breaking bones. Moisture his body could not spare oozed from beneath his lids in a mingling of self-pity and grief.

'You are too strong just to be shriven and released,' Radulfus said, leaning over him again. 'It may be true that you will only have one leg, but it will not make you a useless cripple. Only your mind can do that.'

Hervi swore at him then, a blasphemy that caused Radulfus's novice assistant to suck in his breath and widen his eyes. Radulfus, however, absorbed the curse without so much as a flicker. He had heard the same and worse a hundred times over and knew that they were part of a fighting man's armour, the bravado that concealed fear.

'Your brother brought you here and entrusted me with your tending,' he said. 'I will not betray that trust. When he returns, I want to see you greet each other in the flesh, not lead him to your grave.'

'Hah, what makes you think I will survive you butchering my leg off?' Hervi demanded with a mirthless baring of his teeth.

'You might not, but the alternative is certain death.'

'The only sure thing in life is that it ends in death,' Hervi retorted, and once more turned his gaze from the monk's probing stare to the cool gold of the walls, wishing he could blend into them. He had seen chirurgeons at work on the battlefield and often thought that a good, clean cut from one of his own profession would have been preferable to some of the butchery that went forth.

He had to choose between a chance of life – an altered life – or certain death. It was the decision of a cornered man with a precipice at his back. Did he trust Radulfus? He had no choice.

'Shrive me,' he said, without taking his eyes off the wall, 'and then do your worst.'

CHAPTER 18

STAFFORD,
WINTER 1195

Alexander arrived at Stafford by way of a tourney at Blyth in Nottinghamshire. It had cost him twelve marks for the two licences necessary to take part but he had made triple that amount in winnings and had gained a useful second destrier and new packhorse into the bargain.

From Blyth he travelled north, working his way from tourney to tourney, recouping his losses with a grim determination that soon saw him in possession of the full accoutrements of a successful knight. No one had yet dubbed him as such, but he was fully accomplished and bitterly experienced. He was also, at the moment, bitterly cold.

Snow clouds had been gathering on the horizon since dawn, and now, in the short mid-afternoon, had begun to release their burden. White flakes lazily twirled and settled on the land like scurf on a scalp. Alexander blinked at their frozen touch on his eyelashes and drew up the green hood of his capuchon. Stafford Castle rose through the snow veil, promising at least a bed for the night, and perhaps the end of his search. Yet it seemed to him a forbidding place and his mood scarcely lightened as he approached the hollowed-out road leading to the first of the defensive gates.

Villagers watched curiously from their doorways, but lowered their eyes when he glanced their way, or retreated into their dwellings. He had seen such looks cast before in the towns and villages of Normandy and Poitu where he and Hervi had ranged.

They were acknowledging his noble rank and cursing him behind his back.

The entrance to the lower bailey was defended by a timber palisade flanked by two wooden towers. A guard emerged from the base of one of these to challenge Alexander, his hands red with cold on the haft of his spear. 'Halt and state your business,' he declared sullenly. A large dewdrop hung from the tip of his scarlet nose.

Drawing rein, Alexander affected a pleasant but assertive manner. He knew from former experience how thankless a task guard duty could be. 'I am seeking a bed for the night, and audience with the lord of Stafford if he is in residence.'

'If it's employment you're after, he don't need no one,' the guard growled. 'Had his fill of penniless knights sniffing at his gates for midwinter lodgings.'

'Do I look penniless?' Alexander spread his arm to reveal the squirrel-fur lining of his blue cloak – an acquisition from a joust down in Salisbury. He expanded his gesture to include the horses. 'I am on my way to my brother's keep at Wooton Montroi, but it will take me until midnight to reach it, and the snow is falling faster now.'

The guard frowned, but with a loud sniff that dislodged the dewdrop reluctantly stepped aside. His reddened fist opened and closed on the haft of the spear. 'You'll get no joy out of Lord Thomas,' he warned.

'So I've been told.' Alexander rode Samson into the lower bailey which was occupied by a mass of store sheds and stables, ramshackle dwellings, animal pens and service structures.

Although Alexander's manner had exuded self-assurance to the guard, his confidence was far from solid. He had come to see Thomas FitzParnell, and see him he would, whatever the difficulty, but he was not looking forward to the encounter. What was he going to say to the old man? *I am seeking your granddaughter Monday, whom I have dishonoured?* Small wonder that Thomas of Stafford had no time for wandering knights. One had snatched away his daughter, another had debauched his grandchild. Alexander knew that he would quite likely be thrown out into the snowy night to take his chances with the cold and the wolves.

What he was going to say to Monday if she was here caused his mind to go blank and a lump of panic to tighten in his throat. And yet, if she wasn't with her grandfather, he had to face the thought that she might be lying dead in some ditch, and that he was to blame.

Leaving his horses at the stables, he paid a young groom to care for them and made his way through the inner bailey toward the lord's hall on the summit. Again he was challenged, but this time with wary respect, and in moments had exchanged the snowy January cold for the fug of the lord of Stafford's great hall.

It was not as large as the stone-built one at Lavoux, but easily outmatched his family hall at Wooton Montroi. The wooden walls were decorated with woven hangings, banners and weapons, together with a rather macabre arrangement of wolf skulls and pelts, an entire pack by the looks of things, ranging from fully grown adults to small cubs, their pelts shaded with rust and silver and sable-black.

Layers of smoke drifted on the air, finding their lazy way out through the louvres above the firepit in the centre of the room. The walls were lined with trestles which were currently occupied by the castle's servants and retainers, eating their evening meal of salt-pork stew and dark bread. The lowliest sat near the draught from the door, the last to be served, the last to leave when the meal was finished. The high table, reserved for the lord and his family, was situated on a raised wooden platform at the hall's far end, their comfort augmented by charcoal braziers. A sweeping glance showed Alexander that there was only one woman amongst the company seated there, and it wasn't Monday.

Filled with an equal mixture of relief and anxiety, he scarcely paid attention to the steward who led him down the length of the hall to a seat amid the knights and retainers immediately below the dais. Space was made for him, and a trencher of day-old bread set at his place. He exchanged the usual pleasantries with his immediate neighbours, telling them who he was and where he was bound, but not his other reason for being among them tonight.

Between polite conversation and mouthfuls of the pork stew which tasted ten times better than it looked, he glanced at the group on the dais. Its focal point was an elaborately carved high-backed chair, occupied by a robust man in late middle years. Thomas of Stafford had round, pugnacious features. His once blond hair was now the dirty yellow of encroaching age, but still abundant, tumbling over his brow like a lion's mane. Thin lips surmounted a strong jaw, which at the moment was occupied in chewing food with a thoroughness that left no room for conversation.

At his right-hand side sat his son and heir, Gervais. The young man was made in his father's image, except that his hair was still pale blond and his skin fine-grained. There were echoes of Monday's mother in his expression, although her features had been altogether gentler, and of a more harmonious blend. Alexander recognised both FitzParnells from their occasional visits to Cranwell priory.

The woman, he assumed, was Gervais's wife, a timid-looking creature with gaunt hollows beneath her cheekbones and a mannerism of constantly dabbing her mouth with her linen napkin. The rest of the places on the dais were occupied by two priests, probably chaplains, and four richly dressed men who would either be vassals or the most senior of the knights. Alexander looked around the remainder of the hall, his eyes settling on various women, none of them the one he sought. Although the pork stew was more than edible, he pushed his trencher aside less than half finished.

The meal drew to a close. Stafford lingered over a dish of nuts and raisins, and the hounds nosed between the trestles for scraps. It had been the custom at Lavoux for any petitioners to approach the lord after supper with their requests. It had been the way of Alexander's father too. He could remember sitting on his nurse's knee in the hall at Wooton Montroi, watching his father dispense favours with the tolerant lethargy that came from a bellyful of food and contentment. A sufficiency of food Thomas of Stafford might have consumed, but the lines dragging down his features were neither tolerant nor contented.

Swallowing his nervousness, Alexander rose, approached the dais, and swept Stafford a respectful bow. 'My lord, my name is Alexander de Montroi, son of Adam,' he said formally. 'My brother holds Wooton Montroi and half a dozen manors as a tenant of the King. I have lately come from the wars over the Narrow Sea, and would speak with you about certain members of your family.'

Stafford narrowed his eyes. 'I doubt that you have anything to say that will be of interest to me,' he replied coldly.

Alexander's throat was suddenly dry. He cleared it, but no offer of wine was forthcoming. Stafford just stared at him with hostile eyes. He read his own defeat in them even before he spoke another word, and yet he knew he had to try. Drawing a deep breath he said, 'For a while I travelled in the company of your daughter, Clemence, her husband, Arnaud de Cerizay, and your granddaughter, Monday. It grieves me to tell . . .'

'I have no daughter,' Stafford interrupted, his face beginning to suffuse. 'She died the day she rode out of these gates on the pillion of a faithless mercenary. I will not have her name spoken in this hall.' He gave a dismissive flip of his hand. 'Get out of my sight.'

Alexander met the older man's glower, and refused to lower his eyes as protocol demanded. He was not family and he owed no obedience to this man. 'She was a good and gentle lady,' he said, and pitched his voice so that it carried clear and true to every person seated at the high table, and beyond. 'I arrived in her presence sick and impoverished and she took it upon herself and her family to care for me. She led a decent, Christian life, and her husband, far from being a faithless mercenary, held to every code. It was her death in childbirth that broke him. You have no daughter now, my lord. I doubt your own passing will be mourned as deeply as hers.'

Horrified gasps followed his speech, and those people who were not staring at him stared at Lord Thomas to see what he would do. But Alexander was not about to give Stafford the advantage, and even as the older man drew breath, he plunged on. 'I came here out of my own sense of what was right and wrong, to tell you that your daughter and her husband are dead. I came also in search of your granddaughter – I thought that she might have approached you for succour – but when I see the kind of welcome she would have received, I am glad that she is not with you. No,' he held up his hand, 'there is no need to call your guards. I will depart of my own accord.' Turning on his heel, he left the dais and walked with rigid spine down the hall to the door. He half expected to be stopped, to be dragged back and forced to his knees before Lord Thomas, but no one called out, and no one tried to stop him.

Outside, the air was freezing and filled with a whirling dance of snowflakes, A jagged wind was blowing from the east, so sharp that it felt like a knife blade, slicing his skin and sliding along his bones. It would be impossible to travel on tonight, if not for him, then for his tired horses. He put his head down and forced his way towards the stables. Straw made a warm enough bed, and it would not be the first time in his life.

In the hall, Thomas FitzParnell jerked to his feet and without a word, stalked off to his private solar, where he closed and barred the door against all intrusion. Rage boiled like acid in his belly. He reached for the flagon, tipped himself a cupful of wine, and drank it down hard and fast. Then, with a curse, he hurled the cup at the wall and watched it shatter into a hundred fragments.

Even after all these years, the pain was too much for him to contain. His daughter, for whom he had nurtured such plans of dynasty, for whom he had cast his net far and wide to snare dazzling marriage offers, had betrayed her blood and eloped with a common, conniving tourney knight. The scandal had made him a laughing stock for months, and was still remembered with relish in several quarters.

Well, now she was dead and he was glad. No more would she drag the proud name of FitzParnell through the gutter. And the wastrel who had sullied her was dead too, and hopefully frying in hell.

A sound strangled in his throat. It was not a sob; Thomas had never cried in his life, not for a war wound not for the death of his wife, or their numerous stillborn children.

'Sir . . . Father?'

He caught his breath at the knock on the door. 'Go away!' he snarled raggedly.

The knock persisted, and finally, in irritation, Thomas lowered the bar and flung open the door. 'Can't a man find any peace?' he snapped at his son. 'I have had enough of meddling fools for one night.'

Gervais blinked rapidly, a nervous mannerism that intensely annoyed his father. It never occurred to Stafford that he might be the cause of it. 'I . . . I was thinking about what de Montroi said.' Between blinks the young man gazed into the room, taking in the wine drips on the wall and the pieces of smashed pottery.

'I am surprised that you think at all,' Stafford said snidely out of his anger. 'You've shown little enough aptitude for it before.'

Gervais compressed his lips. 'How would you know?' he said bitterly. 'Since you take no notice of anyone but yourself. I sometimes think that we should all be dead like Clemence, and then you would have no cause for complaint.'

Thomas glared at his son, but deep down he was not displeased. Gervais was almost eight and twenty, no longer a youngster and yet it was seldom he exhibited the backbone to stand up for himself. 'That would only demonstrate your inability to survive,' he retorted. 'And you full know the reason why I ignore that mewling wife of yours. Tell her to grow a belly to honour her marriage vows, and then I'll speak to her.'

'She was your choice,' Gervais said with a glitter of malice, but it was a puny attempt, blasted aside by Stafford's scornful retort.

'Yes, I selected the soil, but you are the one who ploughs the furrow night after night and sows the seed. Can you not even plant a child inside a woman?'

Gervais whitened and turned to leave. Thomas had been quite enjoying himself in a dark-tempered, perverse kind of way, but now he realised he had gone too far. 'So,' he conceded with an indifferent shrug, 'what was it that you were thinking?'

'It matters not,' Gervais said, his back turned but his motion arrested. 'As you say, you've had enough of meddling fools for one night.'

'You are here. You might as well speak as go away with it on your mind.'

Gervais sighed and turned around, his eyelids fluttering. 'Clemence is dead to you, I know, but however much you hated him, she had a husband, and de Montroi said that a daughter was born of the marriage. Surely, if her parents are dead, then you must be her guardian, and as such, you have the right to marry her to whomsoever you choose.'

Thomas narrowed his lids. 'I would have to pluck her from the gutter to do so,' he said. His voice, although gruff, had lost some of its harshness.

'Alexander de Montroi hardly looks as if he has been dwelling in the gutter. Did you see the quality of his clothes and weapons?'

'But he does not know my granddaughter's whereabouts, he said so. Where would I begin to look? I have no inclination to go searching among the mercenary camps and tourney circuits only to discover that she is either dead or a whore.'

'I could try to find her.'

'No, let the matter lie. Your duty is here, at Stafford. Go back to that wife of yours and get me a proper grandchild tonight.' Without further ado, Thomas saw his son out of the solar and once more closed and barred the door. But this time when he faced the room, his eyes were thoughtful, and when a frown did cross his features, it was in response to the sight of the smashed cup lying amidst the dregs of his wine.

Alexander approached the keep of Wooton Montroi across a wild, snow-covered land. Although it was almost noon as the keep on its hill came in sight, the day had scarcely risen out of twilight, and both he and his horses were made nervous by the howling of the wolves in the violet shadows of the woods. He knew that such cries could carry a fair distance, but that sound in midwinter was one of the most desolate and disturbing that a human could hear. Shivering, he drew his cloak tighter around his body and sunk his chin down into the rich fur lining.

This part of England was more scarcely populated than the softer lands in the south. A hundred and twenty years ago, William the Conqueror had wasted the villages in response to a rebellion against his iron rule, and even now the scars remained. Some communities had died forever; others were gradually reviving and increasing their population but it was a slow climb back from desolation. The lords of Wooton Montroi derived most of

their income from sheep, the annual wool clip being a vital source
of silver. A murrain among the flocks, or a bad year for lambs,
meant hardship and belt-tightening.

The howling of wolves was closer now, perhaps just a trick of
the dank air, but Alexander shifted his grip on the spear in his
hand and reassured himself with a glance at the honed iron point.
His packhorse tugged on the leading rein, and Samson's hide
rippled in nervous agitation.

Moments later, through the trees, Alexander's sharp eyes spotted grey movement between the trunks, and the sound of
snarling and yammering filled the air, echoing eerily like hellish
plainchant. Samson plunged and sidled, and Alexander drew the
reins between his fingers, assuring himself of control. 'Steady
lad, steady,' he murmured.

Seconds later, he rode abreast of the scene of a kill. Half a
dozen wolves were surrounding and tearing at something down
in the snow. A deer, he thought, as he saw a brown hind leg
sticking up in the air. The animals raised bloody muzzles from
their prey to watch him ride by, but with raw red meat to hand,
and a fear of man, were content to let him go on his way.

All the same, he increased his pace, and it was only by pure
chance that he heard the terrified cry for help coming from the
trees on the opposite side of the track. Drawing rein, he turned to
look, and as the cry came again, saw a monk crouched miserably
in the lower branches of a large beech tree. Alexander glanced
back at the wolves, and realised that it hadn't been a deer after all,
but a horse. He rode up to the tree.

'God bless you forever, my son,' declared the monk in a
relieved voice. His cowl was drawn up against the bitter cold, and
a heavy cloak partially covered his Benedictine habit. 'If you had
not happened along, I would have frozen on my perch, or become
another meal for those creatures back there when I was forced to
descend.'

'Is that your horse they are devouring?'

'I am afraid it is. I was leading him because he had become
lame. When he scented the wolves, he broke from me in mad-
ness, and the only thing I could do to save my own life was
shin the nearest tree with low branches.' He turned round

precariously and began to descend from his sanctuary, revealing black hair curling on white calves as he felt for footholds.

'It's not safe to linger,' Alexander said. 'You are welcome to use my packhorse, he's saddle-broken.'

'God will reward you in heaven for this,' the monk panted as he reached the ground, and took the bridle that Alexander held out to him.

'Where are you bound?'

'I was on my way to the priory at Cranwell.'

There was something in his voice that caused Alexander a greater unease than the presence of the wolves. As the monk swung astride the pack beast and extended his hand to Alexander in gesture of friendship and gratitude, his cowl slipped down to expose a tonsure of thick, greying hair, patrician features and close-set eyes the colour of blue smoke.

Alexander stared in frozen revulsion, unable to speak, unable to move.

The smile died on the monk's lips and the blue eyes narrowed in mutual recognition. 'Brother Alexander.' Sub-prior Alkmund's breath emerged in a cloud of heavy vapour.

Alexander swallowed, and the lump in his throat descended to join the icy boulder in the pit of his stomach. 'Had I known it was you, I would have ridden on,' he said with loathing.

'I am aware of it,' Alkmund responded balefully. 'You have never had any respect for your betters.'

'Betters!' Alexander gagged on the word and brandished his spear. He saw Alkmund tense. Jesu, how easy it would be just to strike. The wolves would eat the evidence, and no one would be any the wiser – except himself and God.

'Kill me, and you will be damned forever!' Alkmund hissed, his eyes darting.

Alexander's lips parted in an expression that was midway between a snarl and a grin. 'I am a mercenary, a tourney knight, and as such already damned.' He raised the spear point and felt a dark surge of pleasure at the fear in Alkmund's eyes. He had long dreamed of what he would do to the priest should their circumstances ever be reversed. In his imagination he saw the barbed head piercing the cloak and habit and sinking into soft flesh. And there the desire remained, burning in his mind's eye, but granting no motion to his tense arm.

With a gasp, he lowered the lance on to his thigh. 'Go!' he said through his teeth. 'Send the horse back to Wooton Montroi, or its value, I care not. Just go, and be thankful for your paltry life.'

Alkmund gave him a long, glittering look, and without a word turned the packhorse and dug in his heels. The animal broke into a rapid trot and within moments had disappeared down the track. The only sounds were of fading hoofbeats and the yammering of wolves.

Icy sweat clammed Alexander's armpits, and his hand was moist on the grip of his lance. He gave a shuddering swallow and willed himself not to be sick.

Silver needles of sleet stung in the bitter wind. He tugged on the reins and urged Samson back on to the track, knowing that it would take more than the heat of the hall fire at Wooton Montroi to warm the chill at his marrow. As he rode, he skirted dark memories by wondering what Brother Alkmund was doing out alone in these wild conditions instead of kneeling at his prayers in Cranwell, more than two miles away.

Reginald de Montroi was almost forty years old, a raw-boned, unsmiling man, the suspicion of a paunch bulging at his belt. He was fighting a losing battle against baldness, and the parting of his fine, brown-blond hair was now level with the top of his left ear so that he could comb the long strands over the affected area.

Entering the great hall at Wooton Montroi, Alexander was filled with confusing emotions of pleasure and depression. It had been so long since he had last been here, longer still since he had called it home. He saw his brother sitting at a trestle before the fire, dictating a letter to his scribe. A pile of tally sticks was scattered abroad, and an abacus was placed to one side. Nothing had changed, Alexander thought. Reginald had been casting his accounts again in an effort to lessen his expenditure.

Beneath his feet, the rushes were rank with age and gave off an unpleasant smell, and the smoke-stained walls were badly in need of a new coat of limewash. Reginald largely lived a bachelor existence. His wife, Adela, preferred to live in a stone manor house on her dower lands. She had given Reginald three sons in swift succession during the early years of their arranged marriage. The duty to be fruitful fulfilled, they had to all intents and purposes parted company. Alexander wished that Adela had been paying one of her rare visits to Wooton Montroi. At least then he would have been assured of a decent bed and edible food. As it was . . . Squaring his shoulders, he approached the trestle where his brother was working. Alexander had dressed for the occasion. Beneath his soldier's quilted gambeson, he wore his best blue tunic, the cuffs banded with scarlet braid. The gilded sword belt encircled his waist, and the garnet inlaid hilt of his sword rested on the lip of the polished brass scabbard mountings. The waif, the runaway monk, had returned, if not in glory, then in considerably raised circumstances.

Reginald raised his head, a look of irritation on his face. One hand smoothed the long strands of hair laid across his pate. 'What do you . . .' he started to say, and then his eyes widened. 'Holy Christ, Alexander?'

Alexander smiled. 'You look as if you've seen a spectre,' he said, and watched Reginald's hand smooth even faster. Hervi had a similar mannerism, although having more hair was wont to clutch at his. Indeed, looking at Reginald gasping and floundering, Alexander was so strongly reminded of Hervi that he was tempted to throw himself upon his eldest brother and embrace him heartily.

'Well, we never heard from you after that stupid prank at Cranwell. You might as well have been dead,' Reginald snapped, and waved the gawping scribe away. 'We hunted for you far and wide, you know.'

The temptation to embrace Reginald receded. He wasn't really like Hervi at all. They might have hunted Alexander far and wide, but not for his own good. 'I went across the Narrow Sea to Hervi,' he said, and sat down on the bench opposite Reginald.

'To Hervi?' Reginald's eyebrows shot to the top of his forehead. 'God in heaven, I did my best for you when our father died, but all you have done in return is disgrace the name of de Montroi.'

'You did your best for yourself,' Alexander said shortly. 'And

I am not the one who disgraced the name of de Montroi.' His voice was hard with contempt. Hearing it in his own ears, he compressed his lips. This visit to Reginald was not one he had been relishing, but nevertheless they were still half-brothers. 'I am sorry,' he said in a less contestant tone. 'We each see the situation differently, that much is obvious.'

Reginald gave him a look. 'I am glad for your apology,' he said. 'You always were a spoiled and troublesome brat. I suppose you are staying to dine and sleep for the night, at least?'

'If it be within my tolerance and yours.'

A rare, dry smile made creases in Reginald's cheeks. 'The only answer to that is wait and see,' he said, and ordered his squire to bring wine.

'So,' the older man took the first sip from his cup, 'what brings you home to Wooton Montroi from the glories of the tourney circuit?'

Alexander looked at his own cup. At least the squire had not filled it to the brim, which would make it less of a penance to drink. 'Wooton Montroi is your home, not mine,' he said with a shrug. 'I am naught but a stranger visiting old haunts. I had business with Thomas FitzParnell at Stafford, and Wooton Montroi is not much further. I think that perhaps I came to show you that I can make my own way in the world.'

Reginald fingered his bald spot. 'I thought you had come to claim a place at my hearth,' he admitted, 'as a household knight.'

'I would not test your good nature or mine that far,' Alexander said wryly. He took a sip of the wine and shuddered. God, it was evil. 'No, I can find gainful employment elsewhere.' Then he hesitated, his mouth twisting as if it still held wine. 'Hervi broke his leg in the autumn. His horse fell on him and his shin bone shattered. I took him to the monastery at Pont l'Arche and gave the monks silver to care for him, but I do not know if he still lives.'

'You did not stay with him?'

'There were reasons why not.' Alexander avoided Reginald's scornful stare.

'And you are not going to tell me what they are?'

'No.' Alexander gazed around the gloomy ill-kempt hall and

wished that he had not come. It had seemed obligatory at the time, but first there had been that unsettling encounter with Sub-prior Alkmund, and now this stilted, awkward conversation with a brother who had always been a stranger to him.

There was an uncomfortable silence. Reginald muttered something about having prayers said for Hervi, it being the decent thing. 'I know the prior at Cranwell will be only too pleased to undertake the duty,' he said, hunching over his cup. 'Despite the fact that you did not settle there, indeed, caused them a great deal of trouble, the relationship between us is still cordial. Indeed, I am considering having our father's tomb removed to their chapel.'

'You are what?' Alexander had taken another mouthful of wine, and now he almost gagged on it.

'The church in the village is no fitting place for the de Montrois to lie. It is too small, and it lets in rain. I have spoken to the prior and he agrees with me.'

'The prior!' Alexander half choked. 'I do not believe it! He couldn't see the nose in front of his face, let alone make plans for the future of Cranwell!'

'Not prior Guiscard!' Reginald snapped impatiently. 'He died last year of a chest ague. No, I mean Prior Alkmund. He was elected to the office at the feast of St Giles.'

This time Alexander did retch, and had to turn aside to spit into the rushes. 'How could anyone be so foolish as to elect him prior?' he demanded in a strangled voice.

Reginald frowned. 'He was judged the best man for the task, an able administrator, an eloquent speaker, a man of God . . .'

'Of the devil!' Alexander interrupted fiercely. 'Do you know why I ran away the last time?'

'You were insubordinate to the rule, and you faced serious punishment,' Reginald said coldly. 'I have no cause to doubt the word of the monks.'

Alexander shook his head and exhaled angrily. 'Of course you have no cause,' he spat. 'What is my word against theirs? Your able, eloquent man of God fondled me on the dorter stairs on the way to matins, and when I hit him in self-defence and he fell down the stairs, they bound my wrists and threw me in the cells

as if I were the one to blame.' He stared Reginald in the eyes, and
for a moment Reginald met him, but then looked away, his jaw
tightening. Alexander saw that his brother did not want to
believe. It was easier to turn aside.

'I loved our father,' Alexander said, not only sick, but sickened. 'To think of Alkmund praying over his tomb fills me with
abhorrence. It will be as if my back is laid bare for him again.'

'You are making a dunghill out of a single pile of straw,'
Reginald said harshly. 'Prior Alkmund is part of the strength of
our community. What have you ever given to Wooton Montroi?'

'What have you?' Alexander retorted, and jerked to his feet,
leaving the remainder of his wine untouched.

'Where do you think you are going?'

'To see my parents. I have a preference for their company,' he
said viciously. 'They make better listeners than you.'

The interior of the small village church of Wooton Montroi was
bitterly cold. Bird dropping stained the rafters, and a row of
sparrows perched on the arms of the olive wood cross upon the
altar, their feathers so fluffed up that their heads had almost disappeared. Breath misting in the chill air, Alexander genuflected
to the altar and the sparrows, then lit candles for the souls of his
mother and father, for Hervi and for Monday.

The tomb of Adam de Montroi lay in the chancel, the feet of
the wooden effigy resting on a lion to show that the deceased had
been on crusade. The hands, over-large in proportion to the rest
of the figure, were pressed palms together in prayer, and a sword
was girded across the pleated surcoat. The effigy's face, framed in
a mail coif, was bland and smooth, revealing nothing of the
heavy-set blond and hearty man of Alexander's memory. His
father had respected the Church, but his bones would not rest
easily in Cranwell Priory when Wooton Montroi was his true
home.

Alexander touched the cold wooden hands, and realised that
he had not thought to ask Reginald if his father's wives were to
be taken too. Either side of him they lay, the lady Ermengarde, a
hint of woodworm disturbing her wimple, for she had been there
the longest, and his mother, the lady Anna. She would not sleep

well among monks, but he doubted they would accept her into their midst.

The craftsman had carved her gown to his father's instructions, and over her tunic, she wore a slit-sided dalmatic with a wide embroidered border. As he looked at her, Alexander almost seemed to catch a drift of the exotic, rose-scented perfume she had been wont to dab on her wrists and throat. Her hair had possessed the colour and shine of pitch – black, with a sheen of gold – and she had accentuated her deep-brown eyes with cosmetics. He could remember too, the cross of gold and amethysts twinkling on her breast, and his own small fingers playing with the jewel. Without thinking, he reached for it, only to touch its plain silver replacement.

In a silent speech of thought, he vowed to regain the Byzantine cross and asked his mother and father for their forgiveness and their blessing. With a deep regret that stung the back of his eyes, he wished that he could have asked their advice too.

Leaving the church, he crossed the snow-covered village track to the alehouse, deciding to fortify himself before he returned to the keep. He was in no haste to go back. Better the village than Reginald's cold hospitality and unpalatable wine.

A new brew had recently emerged from the ale-wife's cauldron, and her customers were supping with dedication, It was not as though the stuff could be stored for more than a few days. There was silence when Alexander ducked beneath the low door and entered the tiny, smoky room, but when he held up a silver penny and asked in halting English for food and drink, the alewife herself bustled forward, wiping her hands on her apron, and guided him to a three-legged stool at the firepit. A cheap clay beaker was put in his hand and a measure of yeasty golden ale poured into it. He was furnished with a hunk of half-stale bread and some sliced smoked sausage.

Conversation resumed, but Alexander could feel the unease of the other occupants. He did not belong among them; he was a stranger, a member of the nobility with a sword at his hip. But even less did he belong with Reginald.

The alehouse door banged open again, and once more there

was a momentary silence, not so much wary this time, as disapproving. Chewing his bread and sausage, Alexander glanced at the young man who stood on the threshold, stamping snow from his shoes. Curly bronze hair tumbled to his shoulders, and his fine, almost feminine features were pinched with cold. An enormous silver brooch pinned his cloak at the shoulder, which was thrown back a little to reveal a lining of tabby catskins.

'Wine,' said the young man in broad English. 'Godfreda, give me wine.' He delved in the pouch at his belt, and as Alexander had done, held up a silver penny.

'My ale not good enough for you now?' the woman sniffed, but took the money from him.

'I need something stronger to warm my belly,' he replied with a shiver, and edged his way towards the hearth.

'Your fault for bending over to a monk,' she said, and with her nose in the air went out of the room, returning moments later with a stone jar of wine. 'You need not look at me like that, Jolin, you've not been seeing to your charcoal clamps on a night like this.'

'''Tis non o' your business what I been doing,' the young man retorted, and having gulped down the first measure, took a second, slower drink and held out his hands to the fire. His eyes, heavy-lidded with fatigue, slid to Alexander.

'Stranger in our midst,' he said, and a mocking smile curved his narrow lips. 'Have you been out in the wild wood too?'

There was a recent lover's bruise on the Saxon's throat, where someone had bitten and sucked, and the red imprint of finger-marks marred the fine line of his jaw. Alexander linked the young man's appearance with the ale-wife's comments and his own earlier meeting with Brother . . . nay, Father Alkmund. He had his answer to what the monk had been doing out alone.

'I saw the wolves,' he replied in accented English. 'You are a charcoal-burner?'

'I am.' The young man drank his wine.

'And Prior Alkmund came all the way from Cranwell alone, braving the wolves to buy charcoal?'

The delicate skin flushed with more than just the effects of wine. 'How did you know . . . Who are you?'

Alexander grimaced. 'Once I was a novice at the priory.' He finished his food and dusted his hands on his cloak. 'A word of warning to you. A wolf will bite off your hand if you come too close. Either strike first, or keep your distance. The silver in your pouch, the brooch at your shoulder. Are they worth your troubled sleep?'

'What would you know?' the young man sneered, his face bright red by now.

'More than you,' Alexander replied wearily, and draining his cup, rose to leave. 'A lifetime more than you.'

CHAPTER 19

There were buds on the trees. Hervi could see them from the infirmary window as he dressed himself. Tiny tippets of green edged the stark branches of winter, and birds had begun to court and build their nests. The sun was warmer too, deepening the monastery walls to a rich, buttery yellow.

Hervi glanced from the sight of all this bursting regeneration to his own body. Nothing was going to regenerate the limb he had lost. Below his left knee was thin air. Frequently, in his sleep, he dreamed that he could walk and run, could ride a horse, and God's life, even take a piss without finding a wall against which to lean. When he was awake, the ghost of the severed member persistently haunted him. Sometimes he could feel the illusion of solid bone and muscle so powerfully that he would reach down, and be flooded with disappointment to find nothing but a stump. How could a limb that did not exist ache so badly?

There were days when Hervi could not bear to face the world, and in a black depression, wished that he had died, but there were days too, like this one, when he thanked God that Brother Radulfus had ignored his pleas to die, and saved his life at the expense of his leg. He could easily have felt bitter at the turning of the world towards spring, but the brightening weather filled him instead with optimism. He could not help but take pleasure in the greening of the season. It was his leg that had been maimed, not his senses.

Hervi finished dressing. The left leg of his chausses had been cut short and a ribbon threaded through to secure it around his stump. In the monastery workshops, one of the brethren was fashioning a wooden peg for him, so that he would be able to walk with the aid of a stick rather than the crutch he had perforce to use at the moment. Hervi was pleased at the prospect, although he had become a master at propelling himself along on his crutch. He could keep pace with most of the monks when they took their recreation in the cloister. Stairs, of course, were a bane, and best negotiated on his buttocks, but in the months since his arrival at Pont l'Arche, he had learned to swallow his pride.

Brother Radulfus and his assistants were attending the prime service in the chapel, and apart from two other patients, the infirmary was deserted. Hervi tucked his prop beneath his arm and made his way outside in swinging strides, crutch, leg, crutch, leg, building a rhythm that led him behind the infirmary and past the latrines to the abbey gardens attached to the guest hall.

This too was empty, for the monks who tended the soil were all at prayer in the chapel, and from there, they would go to the refectory to break their fast. Hervi inhaled the moist scents of burgeoning life and made his way from bed to bed, studying what was being done, taking pleasure in the gold and purple crocus buds and the white clusters of dainty galanthus flowers. In his days as a warrior, he had been too busy living for the moment to pause and look at the world around him. Now, forced to a slower, more reflective pace, each day brought new discoveries that filled him with a sense of wonder, and a regret for time wasted.

Despite the mellowing of the sun and the budding shoots, the wind was still winter-sharp, and Hervi repaired to the gardener's tool shed. The thatched wooden hut was filled with a tidy clutter of linen sacks, trugs, axes, a mattock and a pruning saw, stacks of osiers, string, knives, wooden buckets, and a large brass cooking pot.

He noticed that a spade had been set aside for mending, and looked around until he located a hammer, pliers and a small wooden box of nails. Then he eased himself down on to a three-legged stool for which there was just room in the corner, and relinquishing his crutch, set about repairing the implement. He had always been good with his hands, had a feel for objects, a tactile intelligence. Besides, it gave him satisfaction to mend something that had gone awry and see it made whole once more.

If he could not have his old life or his leg again, at least he could restore other things that the world had broken.

Hervi whistled softly through his teeth as he worked. On the tourney circuit, the song would have been profane – 'Renard the Fox', or 'Summer is iccumen in', but here, in the abbey gardens, with six months of nothing but plainchant to fill his ears, he was happy to sing about the glories of nature as seen through spiritual eyes, and in passable Latin, composed by an abbess called Hildegard. Time flew, marked by the passage of light on the sun dial.

A shadow filled the hut entrance. 'We'll make a monk of you yet,' said Brother Radulfus, amusement in his grey eyes.

Hervi snorted, but other than that made no comment against the remark. 'Good as new,' he said instead, indicating the mended spade.

'You have a rare talent with your hands,' Radulfus said with sincerity. He had been holding a cup of milk and a piece of bread, and now passed them to Hervi. 'You missed the breaking of fast, but I knew where you would be.'

Hervi blinked in surprise. 'I only intended to sit a moment.' He accepted the food, suddenly realising how hungry he was.

'How is the leg today?'

'Aching but bearable.' Hervi tore a chunk off the bread and put it in his mouth. 'I anointed the scar with betony salve as you instructed.'

Radulfus nodded approval. 'And the dreams?'

Hervi shrugged. 'I'll survive them. I slept silent last night.' As he had done for the past month. Before that he had often woken screaming from the depths of a nightmare where Radulfus had yet to saw off his leg. He had more understanding of Alexander's night terrors now.

The monk leaned against a potting bench and produced a scroll, tied up with a length of linen cord and sealed with red wax. 'I have news,' he said. 'A letter from your brother, Alexander. Brother Markus had it given to him in Rouen by one of our brethren who was on his way from England to Rome.'

Hervi's face lit up. He grabbed the scroll out of the infirmarian's hands and breaking the seal, unrolled it, fumbling in his haste. The writing within was Alexander's. Although Hervi was not literate, he could still recognise his brother's flowing script. 'What does it say?' He passed the vellum back to Radulfus. 'Has he found the girl? Is he returning soon?'

Radulfus raised the scroll and narrowed his eyes, the better to focus on the elegantly formed letters.

'*Alexander de Montroi to his dearest brother Hervi.*' Radulfus read the salutation. '*I trust this letter finds you well recovered and in good health.*'

Hervi snorted at that and waggled his stump. 'That shows where trusting gets you,' he said, and gestured impatiently at the monk. 'Read on, read on.'

'*I wish that I had more news to impart than that which I send. Monday is not at Stafford with her grandfather. I visited him shortly after Christmastide, and although I spoke to Stafford himself, there was no news. Indeed, Lord Thomas was wrath that I should even speak the name of de Cerizay in his presence, and I stayed there not above a single night. I have made enquiries along every road I have travelled, but no one has seen or heard of a young woman answering Monday's description. It may be that I am looking in the wrong places. I pray so, and that she has found a safe haven.*'

'*I visited Wooton Montroi too, but again, I remained but a single night. Walter, Adam and Humphrey were absent on forty day service to the Crown, so there was only Reginald to endure. He remains constant to his nature, and he spoke to me of his intention of placing our father's remains with the monks at Cranwell. They have a new prior now – Alkmund.*'

'What?' Hervi's eyes flashed. 'Alkmund? You are sure it says Alkmund, not Ambrose, or Albert?'

Radulfus checked the script, but he had no need, for the writing was clear and fluent. 'Yes, I'm sure.' He frowned at Hervi. 'He is known to you?'

'I know of him,' Hervi said stiffly. 'What else does Alexander say?'

Radulfus shrugged. 'Nothing. The rest of the line has been scored out, and below it he changes the subject. *Employment evades me for the nonce, but tourneys are licensed here, and they are plentiful. I send you two marks from recent gains and hope to take ship for Normandy in the late spring. Written on the feast of St Valentine, year of Our Lord eleven hundred and ninety six.'* He looked curiously at Hervi, whose expression had lost its open good humour.

'Brother Alkmund and his perversions are the reasons that my brother fled the cloister for the tourney circuit,' Hervi said. 'Cranwell is not like this place, where a man can drink of peace. Alkmund is a wolf who preys on young boys. And now Alex writes that he has been elevated to prior. Is there no justice in the world?'

'If not, then there is always in the next,' Radulfus answered, looking uncomfortable. 'God sees all.'

'And does nothing,' Hervi said grimly, and when Radulfus chastised him, he took his crutch and left the hut. 'I am not patient enough to wait for judgement day,' he said, looking out over the garden. The letter had unsettled him, taking away the joyful simplicity of the morning and replacing it with worldly cares. He had been hoping that Alexander would discover Monday at Stafford. That had not happened and he knew that there was small chance of finding her now. Arnaud had entrusted him with Monday's welfare and he had failed. Alkmund was prior, Alexander was roaming the tourneys alone, and he was a one-legged cripple, soon to be turned out into the world with a begging bowl for company. For a moment, self-pity threatened, but it was only a fleeting sensation and quickly banished by anger, and grim resolve.

He glanced round at Brother Radulfus, who stood to one side, watchfully present, but keeping his distance, Alexander's letter still in his hand. Carefully, Hervi pivoted on his crutch. 'What was the first step you took to becoming a monk?' he asked.

Aline pirouetted before her Saracen gazing-glass and admired herself. Sea-green silk shimmered and rustled, showing off her figure to stunning effect, and highlighting the glints of green in her eyes. It was her new court gown and she was entranced.

'Monday, it's gorgeous, better than I ever imagined! You can work miracles with that eye of yours and a needle!'

Monday reddened with pleasure at the compliment. 'It suits

you well, madam.' She had worked hard on the gown, designing it to cling and flow in all the right places. It accentuated Aline's figure without being vulgar, and the colour was exactly right.

'I will be the envy of every baron's wife from here to the English coast!' Aline gloated, and swished over to her maid, Eda, to be unlaced. 'Small wonder that good sempstresses are like gold.' She stepped out of the dress, and in its place donned an ordinary gown of tawny wool. 'Here,' she said impulsively, and gave Monday her old court dress, a creation in russet-coloured silk with yellow sleeve linings. 'I want you to have this. I know it's of no use to you at the moment,' she added with a glance at Monday's obvious pregnancy, 'but when you are slim again, you can alter it to suit yourself. We are not so different in size.'

Monday took the gift and thanked Aline with delight. A silk gown was not something likely to come her way very often. 'I don't think I will ever be slim again,' she confessed, patting her swollen belly. 'I must look like a beached fat-fish.'

'Nothing of the sort, you look radiant!' Aline tilted her head to one side. 'It is because you can only see the part, not the whole.'

Monday grimaced and rearranged the folds of her gown and surcoat so that they draped more loosely about her figure. For the first five months her stomach had remained almost flat, and until the baby had begun to kick within her, she had deluded herself that the pregnancy was a figment of her imagination, that the morning queasiness, the ravenous hunger and the utter exhaustion were nothing more than symptoms of her emotional plight. Then, making up for lost time, her body had altered beyond recognition, and hiding her predicament from herself had become impossible.

'Have you decided on a name for the babe when it emerges to greet the world?' Aline enquired.

Monday shook her head. 'The nearest saint's day, I suppose,' she said, and smoothed the russet silk beneath her fingers. Within her the child kicked softly. Rising above her misgivings and her fear, a thread of protectiveness and wonder caused her hand to stop and feel the motion. New life created from a moment of drunken lust. Her gaze strayed to Aline's son, who was crawling across the floor in pursuit of a soft leather ball, his

nurse in watchful attendance. Less than a year ago he had been
curled in his mother's womb as her own baby was curled. Now
he scrabbled everywhere with frightening speed and energy, his
little character bright and fierce. Such rapid change in so short a
time.

Feeling the ripples of movement under her hand, she wondered how many of Alexander's traits her child would inherit.
She would often think of him, wonder where he was and what he
was doing. Had he searched for her after she had run away, or had
he greeted her disappearance as a welcome convenience?

'Deep thoughts?' Aline teased gently.

Monday shook her head. 'Wishful thinking,' she responded
wryly. 'Perhaps I will name my baby Jude.'

'Jude?' Aline looked perplexed. 'His celebration day is not
until October.'

'No, but he is the patron saint of lost causes, is he not?'

Panting, Alexander stood on the edge of the tourney ground and
removed his spurs with one hand, his other looped through
Samson's bridle. The horse was breathing as loudly as his master,
for they had been fighting hard, and had only come away with
the victory by sheer effort, good judgement and a liberal salting
of fortune.

On the tourney field the mêlée continued to throb and churn,
clods of soil flying high and loose to meet the shouts of men and
the joyous clang of steel on linden-wood shields. Alexander
watched, drinking in the heady sight and scent of danger and
success.

This was the largest tourney he had attended in England thus
far, a massive gathering at Salisbury to celebrate the arrival of
spring. It was early May, and men's blood was quick as the sap in
the trees. As far as the eye could see, tents stretched in bold
colours or plain canvas, depending on their owner's wealth.
There was a fairground atmosphere, for the booths and tents of
hucksters and entertainers were picketed among those of the soldiers, mercenaries and knights come to try their luck in the mock
fights and jousts.

The competition was brisk, with a steel edge, but for the

moment Alexander was riding the crest of it, his skill, his hunger that bit sharper than any who had yet come against him. But other contestants were riding in daily, and some had a lifetime of warfare behind them, and with nothing to look forward to but a cold old age, were not just hungry but ravenous.

A snub-nosed squire ran up to Alexander and gave him a money pouch containing the ransom payment that his master owed. Alexander thanked him with a grin, but bade him wait while he checked that the agreed sum was present. If offence was given, it was unfortunate, but Alexander had learned that the word of a knight was not always as honourable as the popular ballads would have folk believe. On the field, he always tried to select opponents who could afford to pay. There was no pleasure in taking away the livelihood of a man who was fighting in order to eat. Having known that road, he had too much compassion for those who still travelled down it, for he knew how easily he might join their company again.

The payment was complete, and dismissing the squire, he led Samson across the field towards the tradesmen's booths on the perimeter, and stopped outside the portable workshop of Jankin, the hafter.

Jankin had been following and servicing the soldiers of the tourney route for forty years, mostly in Flanders and Normandy, but more recently in England, where King Richard had made them legal in order to raise the funds he needed to make war on Philip of France. Jankin was approaching his sixtieth year, and a life outdoors, on the constant move, had left him with swollen, arthritic joints, and a crusty, cynical temper.

Alexander leaned against one of the ash poles supporting the old man's booth and narrowed his gaze towards the field, where a six-man mêlée was being hard fought. The sun flashed off a shield boss and dazzled his eyes, but not before he had recognised the device of Jordan de Sacqueville, one of William Marshal's retinue of knights. The Marshals' home territory was Wiltshire, and Alexander wondered if the great lord was here watching the sport.

Jankin laid down his tools and hobbled over to Alexander with a gruff enquiry as to his business.

Alexander turned to the grizzled old man and presented him with his scabbarded sword. 'Put a new grip on this for me, will you, Jan, by tomorrow if possible.'

Jankin examined the frayed, damaged binding and unravelled a length of it. 'I doubt as I can do this afore Friday,' he said curtly. 'What do you want, buckskin or cowhide?'

'Buckskin, and the best you have. I don't want my grip marred by sweat.' Alexander winced as one of the knights in the mêlée did not ward a blow properly and was sent crashing from his saddle.

'A fool's profession,' Jankin snorted.

'You make a living from it,' Alexander said drily.

'Aye, that I do. A fool and his money are soon enough parted.' He held out his snarled hand, which, despite its deformity, affected his superb skills not one whit. 'Half the payment now; half when you collect.'

Alexander laughed and shook his head, wondering how it was that despite a lifetime of heaping insults upon his clients, Jankin still remained in one piece. But then, he supposed, no one could match the old gargoyle's skill. He fished the required coins from the ransom pouch he had just been given, and handed them over. 'Tomorrow,' he said firmly.

'See what I can do.' Jankin caught the silver as deftly as a limber youth, then nodded beyond Alexander's right shoulder. 'Someone to see you.'

Alexander swung round and found himself eye to jaw with the magnificent presence of William Marshal, lord of Chepstow and Usk, Pembroke and Striguil, Orbec and Longueville in Normandy. Today he was clad not as a warrior, but as a magnate, in richly dyed silk and wool, embellished with jewellery and gold braid.

'My lord.' Alexander bowed in deference.

'I have been watching you.' Marshal's quartz-grey eyes were thoughtful but approving. 'You have learned your lessons since Lavoux; you fight well.'

'Thank you, my lord.' Alexander smiled.

'I also see that you fight alone, which is not so good. Did you not have companions last time we met?' The Marshal glanced around.

The pleasure left Alexander's expression. 'I did, my lord, but one died in a tourney, and my brother was wounded – a broken leg when his horse fell on him.'

'Your brother . . . the man my nephew John fetched out of the cells at Lavoux?'

'Yes, sir.'

'I am sorry to hear of his wound,' the Marshal said with genuine concern. 'I hope he makes a swift recovery.'

'He is in the care of the monks at Pont l'Arche abbey. After this tourney, I am bound there to see how he fares.'

William Marshal nodded and brushed his thumb back and forth across his bearded chin, his expression speculative. 'Do you fight any more today?'

'No, my lord.' He gestured over his shoulder at Jankin, who was unashamedly eavesdropping. 'My sword needs a new grip, and it will not be ready until tomorrow.'

'Friday,' Jankin contradicted, just to be awkward, and vanished into the depths of his booth.

'Well then, come to my table and join my feast. You must be hungry and thirsty after your exertion.' Marshal gave him a knowing grin. 'I know that when I was young and rash enough to fight in these hastiludes, I was capable of eating an entire pig afterwards, and of sinking a gallon of wine!'

'Reason enough for you not to want me at your board,' Alexander replied, taking his lead from Marshal's bantering tone.

Marshal laughed, displaying sound, square teeth. 'I suppose it could be, but there are other reasons equally strong why I might.' Raising his eyebrow to add emphasis to the hint, William Marshal went on his way.

'Hah, you've just looked fortune in the eye,' announced Jankin, advancing once more to his counter, a leather-worker's needle pinched between forefinger and thumb. 'I'd have charged you more if I'd known you was a friend of the lord of Chepstow.'

Alexander refused to rise to the bait. Besides, he was too stunned by what had just happened to be capable of a riposte. A vista of endless golden possibilities opened before his mind's eye.

'I'll be back for the sword tomorrow,' he said in a distracted voice, and went to picket Samson at his horse line.

'Friday!' Jankin yelled after him, and cackled.

Many young knights had been invited to sit at William Marshal's board. Alexander had fought against some of them in the course of the tourney. One or two he had defeated; with others, the encounters had been less conclusive. There was high talk and boasting, there was bragging of blood lines and much name-dropping. Each diner tried to outdo the man beside or opposite him, and the level of noise increased as the wine in the flagons was drunk down to the lees.

Alexander sat amidst this social mêlée and realised that it was just as intense as the fighting had been in the afternoon, and the techniques were no different. The man who kept his head was the one who would win. And so he bit his tongue, and remained genial without voicing any boasts of his own.

'They say the Marshal is recruiting knights to join his mesnie,' confided Alexander's neighbour, a youth called Julius, who was distantly related to the Earl of Chester.

'Who is *they*?'

Julius shrugged and tucked the last corner of a chicken and almond pasty into his mouth. 'Someone told me that he had heard it from one of the Marshal's attendants.'

'Then it is likely true,' Alexander said politely, and used his eating knife to cut his own portion of food into bite-sized slivers. He did not want to appear too finicky, but he also wanted to show that he was aware of the manners of the court as well as those of the camp.

'My father is a friend of the Marshal,' Julius declared with a slight thrust of his jaw. 'And my cousin is a knight in his service in the Forest of Dean.'

'Indeed?' Alexander's gaze wandered. Over at the high table, a musician was playing a harp and singing to the diners. He recognised the song, and also that it was about to end. Probably fortunate, for the musician's voice was high and tight, straining at the notes.

'You don't believe me, do you?' His companion's tone was belligerent as the wine took effect.

'Oh, I believe every word,' Alexander said neutrally. 'It is true that a man's connections count for much, but they are not everything.' Making his excuses, he left the trestle and approached the musician, who by now had finished his song and was gargling with a mouthful of wine.

Alexander stooped and murmured to him. At first the man shook his head, but after some further discussion and the payment of a silver penny, yielded up his harp and sat off to one side with his wine.

Alexander turned to William Marshal where he presided at the head of the table with men fortunate enough to already be members of his household. 'I ask your permission to sing for my supper, my lord,' he said with a graceful bow.

The Marshal regarded him with a twinkle in his eyes, and amusement curving beneath his moustache. 'For more than your supper, I think,' he said. 'Well then, Alexander de Montroi, show me what an accomplished courtier you are.' He gestured to the harp.

For an instant Alexander was overcome by panic as all eyes on the high table fixed upon him and were joined by stares both hostile and curious from the other trestles. A false chord twanged from the harp, setting teeth on edge and raising scornful eyebrows.

Alexander cleared his throat and his mind, and willed himself to concentrate on the harmony of the harp and the song. It had to be right. Like the tourney field and the battle ground, there was no room for error. Judging his audience, he struck up a fighting tune about the joys of tourneying, written by the troubadour Bertran de Born. At first his throat was tight and he missed the occasional note, but as the song progressed and he gained confidence, the true, golden clarity of his voice shone through, and men ceased to exchange mocking glances. Before the applause had died down, he began another piece, this time bawdy, about a tourney champion suffering from 'jouster's wilt' both on and off the field. The song was received with loud guffaws and cries that it be repeated. By the time Alexander had sung it again, twice over, his throat was aching, but he was riding on a tide of euphoria, for he knew he had carried the day.

To prove that he did have gentler sensibilities, he finished his debut on a poignant composition. The slight hoarseness of his throat gave his voice a smoky undertone, which rendered the song all the more compelling.

> Give me my steed, companion of years,
> Give me my hound, gentle in obedience,
> Give me my quill, sanity from loss.
> I will ride to foreign lands
> Saddled with songs for gold,
> Searching for the true-love to worship.
> Feel the fire of Venus illuminate my soul
> And step forth to take her hand.

He stroked the last notes from the harp and bent his head over it, while the applause beat around him. Then he looked up and smiled.

William Marshal gave him wine from his own cup, and there and then invited him to join his mesnie. 'I need men of quick wit as well as prowess on the battlefield,' he said. 'If you desire to join me, then a place is yours.'

Alexander swallowed the rich Gascony wine to soothe his throat. 'There is nothing I desire more, my lord,' he said, knowing that this man would not suffer dissimulation. The Marshal was aware of the life that Alexander lived. There was no point in pretending that a better offer was waiting around the corner. This was his ladder out of the mire, and he had no intention of letting his feet slip.

'Well then, kneel, do me fealty, and let the pact be sworn.'

And so, on a warm spring evening at Salisbury, Alexander was knighted and became William Marshal's man.

CHAPTER 20

'Come on, girl, push as hard as you can. Harder, harder, yes, that's it!' the midwife encouraged, and peered intently between Monday's widely parted thighs. Blood smeared the white flesh and the bed straw was soaked with birthing fluid. Monday sobbed between gritted teeth as the pain swelled down through her loins, became unbearable, and then retreated in a long, red scream.

'Soon be over now,' the midwife soothed. 'I can see the head.'

'I'm being split asunder!' Monday panted, and took a sip from the cup that was put to her lips. It contained a tisane of dried raspberry leaves to promote the contractions, and was sweetened with honey to keep up her strength.

'Oh, that's just the head descending the birth passage,' said the midwife cheerfully. ''Tis uncomfortable, I know, I've borne eight myself. Everything is as it should be, mark me.'

Monday grimaced. She had been in labour since dawn, and now the sun was sinking through the open casement window in the bower. Everything was open – doors, curtains, even coffer lids, and Monday's hair had been unbraided and spread over the pillow so that there should be no hindrances to the birth of the babe. Aline said it was all superstition, but she had let the midwives have their way because superstition was also tradition, and there was comfort in the rituals.

Another contraction assaulted Monday without warning, and the urge to push overwhelmed her. She groped outwards with a scream, and Aline grasped her clutching fingers. 'Push, Monday, push!' she urged.

'The head!' the midwife cried in triumph. 'The head is here!'

Monday closed her eyes. There was a terrible burning sensation between her legs, and then, on a sudden squelch and watery gush, the pressure eased and a baby's indignant wail filled the space within the bed hangings.

'A boy!' the midwife declared with satisfaction. 'You have a fine, lusty son, my dear,' and she laid the bawling infant on Monday's stomach. He was hot and slippery from the warmth of her body, bloody from her efforts to push him forth, and highly indignant at being thrust from his soft cocoon into the harshness of light and air.

Monday stared at him, experiencing shock and fear at the sight of this tiny, furious being newly emerged from her body. But there was also a sense of recognition. What had been communicated by touch alone before was now accessible to all other senses, and she was overwhelmed.

The midwife cut the cord and massaged Monday's belly to promote delivery of the afterbirth. Her assistant took the baby, wrapped him in a warmed linen towel and presented him to his mother. Monday raised tentative arms and folded them around his little body. He had a mass of black hair and tiny, perfectly formed hands, the fingers the exact shape of Alexander's in miniature. Tears brimmed in her eyes and she choked back a sob, wishing that Alexander was here to see him too.

'I cried when Giles was born,' Aline said by way of reassurance. 'I think it is something that all women do. Babes are so small and vulnerable, and they change your life forever.'

The baby had ceased to bawl, and now lay quietly in Monday's arms. His eyes were open and they met hers solemnly, as if he knew all the circumstances of her life, and how he came to be here.

Aline leaned over. 'He is going to have dark eyes as well as dark hair,' she murmured thoughtfully, but pursued her suspicions no further as the midwife interrupted with the instruction that Monday push to deliver the afterbirth.

'How is he to be named?' Aline asked instead. 'Father Vitel will want to know for the baptism.'

Monday gave her a sideways glance. 'Let him be called for his saint's day, as I said before,' she replied, and glanced towards the window where the sun had almost set, and the sky was streaked with deep bands of indigo, copper and a single strand of bright gold. 'It is the eve of St Florian. Let that be his name.'

Alexander found Hervi in the abbey stables, attending to a pack-horse with an inflamed tendon. The linen chemise and scapula of a novice monk clothed his brother's large bones, and there was a simple girdle of knotted rope at his waist from which hung a small leather pouch and a knife scabbard. Hervi was seated on a stool, his back turned, rubbing liniment into the animal's leg, and soothing the beast by murmuring to it in primitive Latin. The smell of the rub filled the air, pungent and oily.

Alexander leaned against the doorpost and cleared his throat. 'So it is Brother Hervi in more than just fraternal blood now, is it?' he asked, using humour to blanket the volatile emotions aroused in him by the sight of Hervi dressed in cloister garb.

Hervi had been totally absorbed in his task and visibly jumped as he spun on the stool to face his visitor. 'Alex!' A broad grin split his face. He wiped his hands on a rag, and reaching for his stick, levered himself upright. 'Alex, lad, I've been praying that you'd come!' He took two hobbling, uneven steps, and then no more, for Alexander crossed the space dividing them in two swift strides of his own, and threw his arms around his brother. The embrace was fervent, emotional, and then curtailed as Hervi almost lost his balance. His hands dug into Alexander's upper arms, and Alexander gripped in return to support him.

'I'm none too steady yet,' Hervi said ruefully as he righted himself and took a careful back-step so that he could examine Alexander from crown to toe. 'You look like a well-groomed young stallion perking his head over a stable door.'

'Is that a compliment?'

'No, just what my eyes see.' Hervi hobbled away to wash his hands thoroughly in a bucket of water. 'Here,' he gestured, 'empty this into the sluice for me.'

Alexander hefted the bucket with supple ease. 'And you look remarkably like a novice monk,' he retorted frostily as he tipped the water away, swilled out the pail in the nearest butt and set it to one side.

Hervi limped out into the yard and raised his face to the warm May sunshine. 'Have you spoken to Brother Radulfus yet?'

'No, The porter told me where you were, so I came straight to the stables.'

'He said nothing to you?'

'Should he have done?'

'No, I suppose not.'

Alexander eyed his brother. It had been a shock to discover him clothed as a monk. A shock, too, to see how badly his leg had been damaged by the break. Despite the seriousness of the injury, Alexander had expected Hervi to be little different from the Hervi of old. To see him clad as a novice, his face remoulded in sharp bone and gaunt hollow, was disquieting to behold. 'It is true, isn't it?' he demanded.

Hervi began to walk again, his gait a laborious seesaw, in the direction of the guest house. 'Yes, it's true,' he confirmed. 'And before you ask, the brethren here were not responsible for my decision. I made it myself, and in the months since then, I have not changed my mind.'

Alexander was stunned. 'You suddenly discovered a vocation?' he said incredulously.

'You might say that.' Hervi held up the forefinger and thumb of his free hand and brought them together. 'I was this close to death. It breathed on me, and then passed over. I reasoned that I must have been allowed to live for some purpose other than becoming a sore-ridden beggar at the gates of Rouen. Look at me, I can no longer earn a living by the sword. Look at what these garments conceal.' At the entrance to the guest house, he paused on the path and raised the scapula and robe.

Appalled, Alexander stared at the shaped wooden stump, attached by leather straps to Hervi's upper leg.

'It was either that or die,' Hervi said grimly. 'At first I chose to die, but Radulfus persuaded me otherwise. I am glad that he did . . . most days.'

'And because of this . . . this mercy, you have chosen to become a priest?' Alexander could not prevent the shudder of revulsion in his voice.

Hervi tightened his lips. 'It was one of the reasons, but not the one that made me decide. You abandoned the cloister, but that does not mean I must reject it too.' Hervi lowered his garments and entered the guest house.

Now that Alexander knew Hervi had lost his lower leg, his gaze was irresistibly drawn to the wooden stump. 'So what was your main reason?' he asked. He could not prevent the hostility in his tone.

Hervi eased himself down on to a cushioned bench in the window recess. Sunlight streaked the rushes on the floor and shone upon the tiles surrounding the central hearth, the logs laid ready but unkindled. 'You would not believe me if I told you,' he said, and laughed in self-mockery. 'Indeed, I am not even sure if I believe myself.'

'I want to hear it anyway.'

Hervi pointed to the oak sideboard, carved with a relief of dog roses and vine leaves. 'There should be wine in that flagon,' he said.

'Are you permitted to drink it?' Alexander gave him a look over his shoulder and went to pour two cups.

'For medicinal purposes, yes,' Hervi answered gravely. 'In the early days, they kept me drunker than Brother Rousseau.'

Alexander brought two cups to the recess and sat down at Hervi's side. 'Tell me,' he said.

Hervi stared at the dark surface of his wine. 'It was your letter that set me on the path – what you wrote about Brother Alkmund being elevated to the position of prior at Cranwell.'

'Why should that make you desire to take the tonsure?' Alexander said, justifiably baffled. 'It only goes to show how corrupt the clergy is.'

'They are not all corrupt,' Hervi objected. 'I have encountered nothing but kindness and encouragement here. The best way to remove the rot is from within. I can no longer fight with sword and lance, but once I was good with them, very good. Now I shall learn to fight with different weapons and then I will oust Prior Alkmund from Cranwell and see him defrocked.'

Alexander was almost tempted to laugh in his brother's face, but the determination burning there stopped him, as did the second thoughts following hard on his initial gut reaction. At first glance, Hervi was not the stuff of which a monk of rank was made. He had no learning and his nature was simple and to the point. He was also disabled, with a past life that was decidedly unsavoury, but that was only the first glance. Simple and to the point did not mean lacking in intelligence or ambition. Despite his jaundiced view of the priesthood, Alexander knew that there were moves afoot to root out the canker of worldliness that was devouring the Church's integrity. Hervi could be just the candidate to refresh jaded pallets, and in that case, his handicap might be an advantage, rather than a stumbling block.

'Have you nothing to say?' Hervi enquired as the silence drew out. 'Do you think I am mad, or a fool?'

Alexander sighed and shook his head. 'I think that you know what you are doing, but that it is a very large mouthful you have bitten off to chew.'

Hervi shrugged. 'Once, not so long ago, I watched a boy, all skin and bone, swing a sword at a straw dummy and swear that one day he was going to be a tourney champion as great as William Marshal.'

That brought a smile to Alexander's face, albeit wry. 'I am still swinging my sword at straw dummies,' he said, 'and I will never be as great as the Marshal.'

'But you have come a long way in a short time.' Hervi's glance sharpened on the smile that lingered on Alexander's face. 'Are you still following the tourneys?'

'I've attended a few, seeking news of Monday and paying my debts, but no. Speaking of William Marshal, I have been granted a place in his retinue. He saw me at a tourney in Salisbury last month, and offered me a position. From here, I ride to Longueville to join him.'

Hervi's eyes lit up and revealed how much of his warrior nature remained as he gave Alexander a hefty secular punch on the shoulder. 'The household of the Marshal himself! God's teeth, you lucky bastard!'

'Do you talk like that in front of the abbot?' Alexander asked innocently, and rubbed his abused shoulder.

'He isn't here,' Hervi dismissed with a perfunctory wave, and shook his head. 'William Marshal, I do not believe it.'

'Neither did I at first.' Alexander grinned. 'But it was more than just luck.' He told Hervi about the Salisbury tourney and the feast that had followed the fighting. He also told him about the more distant past, the disastrous joust against le Boucher, and Osgar's generosity.

'I have paid him back, but I think he was astonished to see me. It was money he thought had gone forever.' Alexander rubbed his hand over his face. 'He had no news about Monday. She is not in any camp that he has visited, and no one of the women knew anything either. It is as though she has vanished from the face of the earth. I have said prayers for her safety; time and again I have done penance, but it brings me no ease.'

Hervi grunted. 'You were a fool, a lustful, stupid fool,' he said, but without rancour. 'I was no better. If I had not been carousing with some woman of the camp, I would have been there to prevent it from ever happening.'

Alexander drank his wine. 'I believe that she is still alive,' he murmured, 'and that she does not want to be found. She wrote as much in her farewell note. Once she told me that she would be a great lady with a silk train and hordes of servants. Who knows but that she has not attained her wish.' He swished the wine in his cup and drank it down.

'The pity is that every wish carries a price,' Hervi said, rubbing the stump of his leg. 'And every price has to be paid.'

CHAPTER 21

THE WELSH MARCHES, AUTUMN 1197

The first bitter wind of autumn hurled stinging drops of rain into Alexander's face and buffeted him in the saddle. Head down, tail streaming between his hind legs, Samson ploughed into the growing storm. When they had started out from Thornbury that morning, the weather had been merely brisk – an invigorating breeze chasing patchy cloud across a pale blue sky, and chopping across the waters of the Severn estuary. Now, at dusk, all blue had been swallowed to black, and the breeze had become a wind that was now threatening to turn into a gale. It roared through the trees on either side of the road like a wild beast, tearing battalions of dying leaves from the branches and scattering them wantonly abroad.

It had crossed Alexander's mind to stop and make a shelter among the trees, but after a brief deliberation, he had decided to press on to Chepstow. Even if he arrived after dark, he would be assured a decent meal and a place to sleep by the fire. Chepstow was part of William Marshal's domain, and Alexander had messages from the earl to his castellan. Lord William had given Alexander the task of courier in the late summer, and Chepstow was only one of the places on his itinerary. There had been the rich southern manors of Caversham and Oxon, basking in the last of the harvest sunshine. From there he had ridden to the dower lands of the Marshal's mother-in-law at Weston to deliver family letters to the Countess Eve, and after a brief sojourn to rest himself and Samson, had made his way west to Bristol, and across the Severn towards Chepstow. From there he was bound for Usk and Pembroke, then back to the Marshal in Normandy.

Alexander's life in the Marshal household was varied, never dull, and filled from dawn to dusk with tasks and demands. A workhorse himself, unable to sit still, Lord William required the same of his knights. If Alexander was not performing escort duties, providing protection, or riding as a messenger, then he was occupied with quill and vellum, acting as an extra scribe in the Marshal's busy administration. Even in his supposed leisure time, Alexander was in demand to play and sing his music, or the Marshal's small sons would want to be given rides on Samson's back and attack him with their wooden swords and shields. The days were not long enough. Alexander glanced at the darkling sky and pulled a face. Not long enough at all.

And yet, even in the act of grimacing, cold, wet and hungry as he was, Alexander had never been so content in his life. He had purposes and goals, worthy ones that bore the fruit of Marshal's approval, and gave him pride in tasks well done. At two and twenty, the roads he had travelled, both physically and mentally, set him at a far distance from the frightened, defiant boy who had absconded over a monastery wall. That boy was still with him, but his features were indistinct, and the raw edge of those former emotions was felt as nothing more than an occasional twinge.

Other walls came into view now, streaked, limewashed stone against a backdrop of heavy cloud. Perched on a narrow ridge above the river Wye, the rectangular stone keep of Chepstow was almost a hundred and thirty years old. Built by a follower of the Conqueror, as part of a line of defences to keep the Welsh at bay, it had performed its function so well that it had never been seriously challenged. The steep gully on one side and the sheer drop to the river on the other ensured its impregnability. It might never rival Richard's Chateau Gaillard for magnificence and modern devices, but dour, solid Chepstow was an irrevocable part of the landscape.

Alexander clicked his tongue to Samson, encouraging the horse from a plod to a brisker trot. Behind him, the packhorse dragged for a moment and then picked up the pace. The road widened, but its surface was a hock-deep soup of mud. The smell of smoke from the castle cooking fires came and went in damp, acrid drifts, and there was an underlying scent of mutton fat and onions.

The guards on duty emerged from their shelters to challenge him as he rode through the gates and entered the lower bailey. Although he was a knight alone, he could have accomplices lurking in the darkness beyond, and since this was a border fortress, at uneasy peace with its Welsh neighbours, no chances were taken. Satisfied by the green and yellow Marshal shield he carried, and his seal of authorisation, they directed him to the stables. No grooms came forth to help him see to his horses, for they were already employed in attending half a dozen other newcomers, removing their tack and rubbing them down.

Alexander eyed the horseflesh. They were quality beasts, obviously belonging to a person of standing. There had been no one on the road in front of him, so they must have come from the opposite direction. He wondered who else was mad enough to be abroad on an evening like this, and made the enquiry of a harassed groom.

'The lord Gervais FitzParnell,' the man said, not even pausing in his stride as he brought a net of hay to a handsome dark bay stallion.

'He's a long way from Stafford,' Alexander said with surprise, and thought of the sullen young man he had encountered two years ago during his search for Monday.

The groom shrugged. 'On his father's business, so I heard – whatever that might be,' he said, and moved on to the next horse.

Alexander pondered on the matter as he saw to Samson and the pack pony, but was still no closer to a solution as he took his satchel of letters and repaired to the solid building of the hall in search of Ralph de Bloet, the seneschal. The custodian of Chepstow was not in the great hall, where diners were still picking over fruit and nuts at the end of their meal. Nor was there any sign of Gervais FitzParnell, and the high table was deserted. Children ran among the trestles, playing a boisterous game of tag, and the scraps of earlier courses were being removed to be sorted into swill for the pigs and sustenance for the poor. Alexander's stomach growled, reminding him that he had not eaten since a scant meal of bread and cheese in the saddle at noon.

He rescued a chunk of bread from a table not yet cleared, added a firm, tawny apple from the same, and devoured them both speedily, knowing that his first priority ought to be delivering the lord Marshal's letters to his seneschal.

A group of household knights were playing dice by the fire, whilst to one side their womenfolk chattered over their mending. Alexander approached them with his query, and a cheerful young man detached himself from the players to take Alexander to the second storey of the hall, where de Bloet had his private chambers.

'Now he's getting older, he doesn't sit in the hall for long after supper,' the knight said, 'and his guest was not up to lingering either. He'd taken a drenching on the road, and was complaining of the ague.'

'Gervais of Stafford?'

'You know him?'

'We have met before,' Alexander said as they climbed the torchlit stairway, and left it at that. They had not even spoken, and from what he had seen, Gervais was completely under his father's domination.

'Come!' shouted de Bloet in response to the fist that the knight banged on the door, and Alexander was admitted to a world of colour and opulence, far removed from the windswept night howling against the keep walls, a world that he had come to know well since entering the Marshal's service. The floor was covered with a thick layer of rushes upon which dried aromatic herbs had been scattered to yield their perfume every time they were crushed by a footstep. There were tapestries on the walls, embroidered hangings, and painted scenes of dancers in a garden. Two charcoal braziers gave warmth to the room, and thick beeswax candles shed pools of golden light and shadows of dark amber.

Ralph Bloet, his silver hair tonsured like a monk's by deepening middle-age, sat in a cushioned chair by one of the braziers. His nose was bony, his jowls had a decided droop, but his eyes were still hawk sharp and his voice was firm and strong as he took the packets from Alexander and asked him several pertinent questions. Lady, de Bloet, once a mistress of the old Henry, and still a beauty, with flashing dark eyes, brought Alexander a cup of sweet wine, and bade him sit in the seat opposite her husband's.

The drink flowed through Alexander's veins, invigorating him, although he knew that it would not be long before it mellowed in his bones, and with the warmth and relaxation sent him to sleep.

From the end of the room where the second brazier stood came the sound of a thick, rasping cough, and as Alexander glanced towards it, Gervais FitzParnell shuffled into the light, accompanied by a younger replica of de Bloet who had been keeping him company.

Two hot, red slashes of fever were branded across Gervais's cheekbones. His eyes were puffy and his focus glazed. 'It is you,' he wheezed at Alexander through chattering teeth. 'I was not sure . . .'

Weary though he was, Alexander rose to his feet and vacated the chair he had just taken. Without thanking him, Gervais sat down, and for a moment doubled over, shaken by cough upon cough. Alexander handed him the wine. A worried frown on her face, Lady de Bloet disappeared to consult with her women about preparing a steam inhalant to ease their guest's congestion.

Gervais took a deep drink of Alexander's wine and looked up at him through watering eyes. 'Did you find her?' he croaked.

Alexander shook his head. 'I have continued to make enquiries wherever I have travelled, but no one has any knowledge.'

'My father is looking for her too, you know.' Gervais pressed his hand across his forehead and winced in pain.

Alexander gazed at him in surprise. 'I understood that he desired nothing to do with her. Indeed, if I had not left his hall that day at Stafford, I think he would have thrown me out.'

'Girls of the family make useful alliances when you marry them off,' Gervais said huskily. 'He wants her so that he can see his line continue in grandchildren. My own wife remains barren, and putting her aside is not possible without making enemies of her family. She is kin to the earls of Chester, and it would begin a feud we could not afford.' Another paroxysm of coughing was dampened by several swallows of the sweetened wine. 'If you do find her, you will be rewarded. I have been spreading the word from town to town.'

Alexander's mouth curled slightly at the mention of a reward. Merely finding her would be a reward in itself.

'It was my suggestion that he seek her out,' Gervais continued, the fever making him loquacious. 'But he has conveniently forgotten that and made it into his own idea. Do you know what it is to have your every action found lacking, no matter how hard you try to please?'

'I think you should go to your bed and let the women tend you,' Ralph Bloet intervened firmly, and turning in his chair, beckoned to his wife.

Gervais clenched his jaw and seemed as if he was about to make a stand, but he was really too sick, and de Bloet's polite but cold tone of voice outmatched his bravado. Lady de Bloet appeared at his side, murmuring gentle words, and coaxed him to rise and go with her to a bed freshly made up with warmed linen sheets.

Alexander thought longingly of such himself, but knew that he would have to be content with a place beside the fire in the hall, with his cloak for a blanket. He was a common knight, and Gervais FitzParnell was a baron's heir.

When Gervais had gone, Ralph Bloet raised a questioning silver brow in Alexander's direction. 'The girl?'

'Stafford's granddaughter, sir, from his daughter's marriage to a landless knight.'

De Bloet pursed his lips, then he nodded. 'Ah, yes. Something of a scandal at the time if I remember. Do you know what happened to the couple?'

'They are both recently dead, God rest their souls.' Alexander thought of the simple roadside grave outside Rouen, and the other, secret one in the heart of a convent of Benedictine nuns. 'Their daughter . . . I do not know.' He lowered his gaze to the herringbone pattern on his leggings.

'There is more here than you are telling me,' de Bloet said shrewdly.

Alexander cleared his throat. 'It is true that I do not know the whereabouts of Monday de Cerizay. I wish that I did for my own peace of mind. We all have regrets in our past.'

De Bloet snorted and raised an admonishing forefinger. 'If you have regrets in your past at your tender age, you are going to sink beneath a mighty burden before you reach even half my years!'

'It was the fear of sinking that taught me to swim,' Alexander responded somewhat grimly.

In the morning, Alexander departed Chepstow for Pembroke. The wind was still howling a gale, but the rain had blown clean across the country and the sky was a race of ragged blue and grey. Gervais FitzParnell lay abed, his body racked by chills, his fever burning higher as the congestion grew in his lungs. Despite Lady de Bloet's aromatic steam inhalants, he continued to sink, until each breath he drew was tight agony. The priest was fetched, and a rider set out for Stafford to summon Lord Thomas to his son's sickbed.

On the third day following his arrival at Chepstow, and another three days before his father arrived, Gervais FitzParnell died unconscious, suffocated by the fluid in his lungs, and Monday became Thomas of Stafford's only living kin.

CHAPTER 22

LAVOUX,
SUMMER 1198

Monday was roused at first grey light by the plaintive voice of her two-year-old son demanding to be taken to the garderobe. He had recently learned to control his bladder, and using the garderobe was a novelty, much preferred over the piss-pot.

Monday sat up on her pallet and pushed her hair out of her eyes. There was an ache behind them from lack of sleep and straining to see the trail of her needle through fabric by candle glow. It had been almost three of the clock when her head had finally touched the pillow. No more than a couple of hours had passed since then, and little enough of that in sleep.

Florian tugged insistently at her sleeve. 'Want pee-wee,' he announced, his voice becoming louder, the tone imperative. Control he might have, but not the control to wait.

On the next pallet, Aline's maidservant Eda turned over and mumbled to herself, drawing the cover up around her ears. She had made it clear on past occasions what she thought of being woken from sleep by a querulous infant. 'You know where the pot is,' Monday said quietly. 'Bring it here.'

'No, want big boy's pee-wee.' He pointed towards the garderobe which lay in the thickness of the chamber's outer wall and was concealed from the main room by a heavy woollen curtain.

Monday sighed, cast her eyes heavenwards and pushed aside the bedclothes. At least he had not wet the sheets, which had been the case on several occasions. Taking his hand, she padded across the room in her chemise. Chests and coffers, the pallets of sleeping servants, were little more than dark shapes in the weak light percolating through the windows, which were protected from draughts by sheets of oiled linen.

The garderobe was cold and musty, smelling of its main function. There was a sealed pit at its base, which was intermittently broken into and emptied by two hardy individuals, a father and son. They were well-paid but not particularly popular members of the castle community – except when there was a stink to be disposed of.

A wooden board with strategically cut holes was laid across the mouth of the pit, and to one side there was a pile of soft moss and fabric scraps for wiping purposes. In a failed attempt to keep the smell from being all-pervading there was no covering across the narrow window slit behind the latrine. In the winter months, users almost froze to the seat, but today, close on the feast of St John, there was a mild, fresh breeze.

Monday lifted Florian's small shirt and raised him up so that he could perform down the dark opening. He craned his neck and demanded to know where the hole went, obviously longing to follow his stream of urine to its destination. Monday gently dissuaded him, and since she was there anyway, sat down to her own ablutions, hoping that Florian would not start asking why she had to sit when he could stand. His intellect and his thirst for knowledge were developing at a frightening rate, and just keeping pace with him was exhausting.

Florian's attention, however, had gone to the narrow window slit, and he peered out. 'Tents, Mama,' he said. 'Lots of tents.'

Monday reached for a piece of the moss. 'Yes,' she agreed, her stomach churning. 'Lots of tents.'

'Want see.' Florian turned round. The light from the aperture surrounded him, revealing a sturdy, confident child with dark hair and peat-brown eyes. He looked like his father, but he was so robust and forthright that he frequently reminded her of Hervi too.

'Later, perhaps,' she temporised as she rose from her hard wooden couch, and shook down her chemise. 'Mama has a lot to do today, and it's still too early.'

'Want see,' Florian repeated mutinously, and stamped his foot.

'Later, after mass.' She ruffled his hair, keeping her voice low and gentle.

For a moment the thing hung in the balance. Monday swept her hair off her face again and silently pleaded with her son not to throw a tantrum. She could not cope this early in the morning, not upon a sleepless night and the anxiety caused by the presence of those very tents to which Florian was so attracted.

Fortunately, he chose not to scream the roof down. He wanted to see the tents, but he was also hungry and usually when his mother said he could do something, she kept her word. He let her carry him back to her bed, and sat upon her pillow, content to play with a carved wooden figure of a horse while she dressed.

Monday donned her working gown and passed a braid belt twice around her waist before knotting it. Her hands shook slightly as she combed the night tangles from her hair, working until it was burnished with golden highlights and crackling with an energy lacking in herself.

Truces were constantly being agreed between Duke Richard and Philip of France, but sporadic war continued. There was supposed to be a truce at the moment, but men's blood still prickled with the need to fight, to stay alert, and it was this need that had drawn Hamon to organise an informal tourney on his lands. Now, in fervent response to the summons, the ghosts of Monday's former life were arraying beneath the walls of Lavoux, and she was sick with fear lest Alexander was among them. Whilst the other women had chattered together, speculating who would come and how great the gathering would be, while they took turns to preen in front of Aline's mirror and soften their hands with rosewater unguents in case someone wanted to kiss them, Monday had retreated to a corner, shielding herself with her sewing, and scarcely speaking a word.

Not that they wanted her to speak. From break of day until late into the night, she had been rushed off her hands, designing and stitching garments that were supposed to trap knights into lovesick adoration of the bodies occupying them.

Monday could have told the women all about the character of the men who fought on the tourney circuits, but it would have revealed too much of her own past, and they would only have called her a killjoy and refused to heed her warnings. Hamon's tourney was a sprinkling of spice on the mundane routine of their daily lives, and they were determined to make the most of every dangerous moment.

Monday braided her hair and concealed it beneath a wimple of cream-coloured linen. She coaxed Florian to put down his toy so that she could dress him too. Emerging from babyhood into a more independent state where he could walk, feed himself and be mostly continent, Florian now wore proper garments rather than baby smocks and caps – linen leggings and a tiny drawstring shirt topped by a smart tunic, green like her own and decorated with tawny braid. On his feet he wore soft shoes, which she had made herself from two layers of sheepskin. He looked adorable, but Monday knew to her cost how deceptive appearances could be.

She took him down to the hall, and since eating before mass was not forbidden to an infant, found him a chunk of bread and a beaker of buttermilk. The hall was slowly rousing to life. A cauldron had begun to simmer over the hearth, and a woman was stirring it with one hand and scratching her rump with the other. On the high table, the previous evening's stained cloth still covered the board, the melted-down candles were still in their sockets, and a flagon and drinking cups stood at Lord Hamon's place. A yawning woman was clearing the debris at a snail-pace. Monday noticed with a blink of surprise that Hamon had left one of his precious books on the trestle too. Obviously he had been well in his cups last night, for usually he took great and jealous care of his small collection, even to the point of keeping it under lock and key in an enamelled coffer in his private chamber.

Monday left Florian and fetched the book. It was bound in leather and embossed with gold leaf. Embedded in the front cover was a wonderful carved ivory panel. Monday's fingers traced the inlaid design with tactile delight. The servant looked at her.

'I will give the book to Lord Hamon.' She held her chin high and spoke with authority.

'Yes, mistress.' The maid twisted the melted lumps of wax off the candle spikes and dug at the more stubborn pieces with the pointed tip of a small knife, her attention studiously on her work.

Monday's place in the castle hierarchy was an ambiguous one. On the one hand she had arrived at Lavoux pregnant and alone, her previous life that of a tourney follower. The regular servants, products of a 'decent' life, regarded such a background with hauteur and scorn. On the other hand, Monday was a companion to Lady Aline, the best sempstress the keep had ever seen, and apparently of noble blood. Therefore they treated her with caution, and a cool politeness.

Monday sighed, and retreating to the lower trestle, sat down beside her son.

'What's that?' He pointed a wet, crumb-smeared finger.

'A book. No, don't touch. I'll show it to you. These are called pages, and these dark squiggles are writing – they tell a story.'

'Story.' Florian seized on the word hopefully.

Monday turned the pages with great care. It was a tale about King Arthur, written in French and full of technical details about jousting and the art of warfare. Edifying to a man perhaps, but boring to a woman, and completely out of the scope of an infant of Florian's age. And yet the flow of the words tugged at her. In her mind's eye she saw Alexander's fingers closed around a quill, the fluid motion of his hand across a sheet of vellum, and her own clumsy attempt to emulate.

'Later,' she said, guiltily aware that the word seemed to be one of the most common in her vocabulary. Later and later until it was too late.

'Tents,' said Florian firmly, appearing to think that she had postponed the story in order to take him outside. 'See tents.'

'Ah, there you are, thief,' declared Hamon in a tone that was jovial, but with a brittle edge that revealed both anger and anxiety. 'My book, if you please.'

Monday jumped and turned guiltily to face him.

His chestnut hair was damp from his early-morning ablutions, and there was a tiny cut on his chin where his barber had made a mistake. 'I'm . . . I'm sorry,' she stumbled. 'I saw you had left it on the high table and I was curious. I've never really looked at a proper book before. The church has a Bible, of course, but only the priest is allowed to read from that.' She smoothed her hand over the gorgeous cover and handed it back to him, a wistful look in her eyes.

'Oh, you can read, can you?'

She nodded, and flushed scarlet beneath the look that he gave her. The slight narrowing of his eyes, the questioning set of his lips, made her pulse quicken. Hamon was handsome, charismatic and somewhat given to playing with fire. 'Not well, my lord. I have had but small opportunity.'

'That could soon be remedied,' he said softly.

Monday kept her eyes on the trestle, not daring to meet his.

'What could soon be remedied?' Aline interrupted, joining them. Although there was a smile on her lips, it did not reach her eyes, which were full of suspicion.

'Her lack of opportunity to read,' Hamon said, holding up his book to his wife. 'I left this in the hall, and I found her looking at it. She obviously knows how to appreciate such a fine object.' His tone was slightly barbed now. 'As I keep telling you, there are people in God's world who actually read for the pleasure it brings.'

'Oh, indeed,' Aline said sweetly. 'And I keep telling you, an ass is still an ass, whether he is lettered or not.'

Utterly embarrassed by the situation, Monday rose to her feet and swung Florian up and across her hip. 'I pray your indulgence,' she said breathlessly. 'My son has been begging me to see the tents. I cannot linger.' And she made her escape, her heart hammering against her ribs and her cheeks still burning. For all that she saw Hamon's game for what it was, it did not prevent her body from responding to his attractiveness. She knew the danger, for she had responded similarly to Alexander, and it had been her downfall. Hamon might only be teasing, probing to see how far he could extend the boundaries of play before being rebuffed, but his behaviour was a danger to the stability of her life. Aline, for all her generosity, was fiercely territorial, and if she decided that Monday was a threat would think nothing of throwing her out.

Out of breath, Monday slowed to a more sedate pace as she left the inner compound and walked across the lower bailey to the castle gates. They were open to admit the dawn, and she and

Florian were by no means the first occupants to come as visitors to the tourney field. Two grooms and the kennel-keeper preceded her through the gateway, and a kitchen maid had used the excuse of gathering watercress by the stream near the ditch to spy on the array.

Monday's shoes brushed lightly over the grass, leaving a dark trail in the dew, and soon the soft leather was soaked and the hem of her gown grew heavy. The sights, sounds and smells of her early life encroached upon her senses and filled her with nostalgia. She saw women going to wash their laundry at the stream, the sound of their laughter floating on the early-morning air. She saw men grooming their horses or talking in groups, their arms folded. She saw cooking pots being stirred, and scented the unforgettable aroma of onion and wild garlic pottage. Home, this territory had once been home. A small shudder rippled down her spine. Amidst the nostalgia was the fear of suddenly happening upon a tent of patched canvas, a blue and yellow banner flying from its post, and of seeing two men mending harness at its fire, one blond and well built, the other dark, with a smile in his eyes to break her heart. Involuntarily her arms tightened around her child, and he wriggled, clamouring to be set down.

No sooner was he on the ground than he set off at a twinkling run towards the tents. For a two-year-old he was remarkably sure-footed, a source of constant pride and even more constant worry to his mother. She raised her skirts above her ankles and hurried after him.

'No, sweeting, hold my hand,' she said, grasping his chubby fingers.

'No!' Florian tried to tug away, his voice rising, and when she held on harder, he started to screech in earnest, his face becoming a dramatic, dusky red. Heads turned, and she and her son became the focus of attention ranging from disapproving through sympathetic to frankly amused.

'A good clip round the ear-'ole, that's what he needs!' declared a middle-aged woman with pursed lips and a sour face.

Monday was swept by self-defensive anger and rounded on the woman. 'I do not see that it did you much good when you were a child!' she retorted. 'Go and poke your besom elsewhere!'

The woman drew herself up to do battle, but was thrust out of the way and deflated by a large, fair-haired man with an apron-adorned paunch and a leather patch covering one eye. 'Live and let live, mistress,' he said gruffly. Turning to Monday, he lifted her in his arms, swung her round, and kissed her soundly on both cheeks. Florian, astounded by this treatment of his mother by a very odd-looking stranger, abandoned his tantrum and stared at the two of them with huge eyes and a lower lip that did not know whether to quiver with laughter or distress.

'Well, well,' Edmund One-eye declared, looking her up and down. 'Aren't you a sight for sore eyes!' He chuckled at his own weak jest. The woman who had shouted at Monday put her nose in the air and stalked off. 'Where have you been hiding yourself?'

Monday smoothed her hands over her gown. She was both delighted and afraid to have encountered Edmund. He knew everything and everyone on the tourney circuit, and although she could ask him whatever she wanted to know and be answered, others could ask him too. 'I haven't been hiding at all,' she said with a forced laugh.

'You don't expect me to believe that, do you?' Edmund sat on his haunches and appraised the little boy. 'What's your name then, young man?'

Unsure about the eye-patch, Florian covered his own eyes with his hands. 'Don't know.'

'This is Florian, my son,' Monday said.

'Fancy name.' Edmund hid his face behind his fingers and peeped through them as Florian was doing.

'He was born on St Florian's eve.'

'May, then. *When the spray begins to spring.*'

Monday gave him a wide look. The quote was the first line of a song Alexander had written. Edmund continued to play a gentle game of peep-bo with Florian, until the boy forgot to be shy, and giggled aloud.

'I have some cinnamon bread at my stall, and a cup of hot wine,' Edmund said after a few more minutes of this game.

Monday gave him a false smile and shook her head. 'It is kind of you to offer, but I . . .'

'Just for a moment. Surely you can spare the time for an old friend? Don't you want to hear the news and gossip of the camp?'

She bit her lip. 'I don't want to become a part of that gossip.'

Edmund rose from his haunches. 'You were a part of it three years ago this autumn,' he said pointedly. 'I tell you what. I promise to keep my mouth closed about this meeting, but only if you come and drink a cup with me.'

Monday looked over her shoulder. 'They will be seeking me in the castle,' she said, but remained where she was. Yes, it was true they would be looking for her, but not in earnest until after the breaking of fast, so she had time to take her own meal with Edmund . . . if she so desired. 'Just for a short while,' she capitulated, and this time her smile was a little warmer.

'There's the lass I remember,' Edmund approved, and lifting Florian in his arms, led her through the mass of tents to his booth, where a lad he introduced as Americ, his apprentice, was already busy with customers.

Edmund furnished Monday with a goblet of hot wine and a slice of his famous cinnamon bread with a generous smearing of butter. For Florian, who had already eaten, there was a small handful of raisins to nibble at, and a lump of raw dough with which to play.

'Now then.' Edmund stretched out his legs and rested his own cup on his belt buckle. 'How do you come to be living in that castle up there?'

'I thought you were going to give me your news,' Monday prevaricated, deliberately taking a huge bite of the cinnamon bread so that further speech was impossible.

Edmund narrowed his good eye at her deception. 'Depends what you want to hear, and how much you already know. You left us in the late summer, outside the walls of Vaudreuil, but was that before or after Hervi's accident?'

'Accident, what accident?' Cold sparkles ran down Monday's spine. 'I know nothing, tell me!' With a heroic effort she swallowed the cinnamon bread, and pushed the rest away untouched.

Edmund pursed his lips. 'It's not altogether clear to me,' he said. 'All I know is that Eudo le Boucher had some sort of grudge against Hervi and it came to blows. They were on horseback and Hervi's stallion threw him. Poor bastard landed badly and shattered his leg.'

Monday's hands flew to her mouth, and she stared at Edmund in horror. 'Oh no, God have mercy!'

'Oh aye, it was God indeed, or the agents of God. The lad took him to the monastery at Pont l'Arche and left him in the care of the monks. Hervi lives, so I have heard, but without the limb; they had to cut it off when the flesh rotted.'

Monday shook her head, totally overwhelmed. It was impossible to think of Hervi thus maimed when he had been so full of frank, masculine vigour. 'Poor Hervi,' she muttered. 'Poor, poor Hervi.'

'From what I have heard, he was making a good recovery, and speaking of becoming a monk himself.'

'Hervi, a priest?' Her tone was incredulous.

Edmund nodded slowly. 'I thought the same as you, but the tale came from Osgar le Gros, who had it from Alexander, so he says.'

Monday took a shaky drink of the hot wine. She had wished for Hervi not to be here among the tumult of soldiers, but not because he was maimed.

'And what of Alexander?' she said, her eyes on the cup, her voice husky as she stumbled over his name.

Edmund's single eye was piercing enough for two. 'He lives a charmed life, that one. Eudo le Boucher went after him too, and was the victor, but your lad emerged with naught more than bruised pride and a lack of funds. I have heard that he has recouped his wealth on the tourney grounds of England and that he is now a knight in the service of William Marshal himself. Again, I had this from Osgar. He saw Alexander at a tourney, oh, over a year ago, although Alexander was not competing but seeking information as to your whereabouts. Apparently he has been making efforts to find you . . . and so far his trail is cold.'

'I didn't want him to find me,' Monday said hoarsely. 'I told him as much when . . . when our ways parted.'

Edmund nodded. His gaze cut to the child, who was thoroughly absorbed in hiding the raisins in the lump of dough. 'So he does not know that he is a father?'

Monday drew a sharp breath through her teeth. 'Is it so obvious?'

'Child, I am only half blind, and that means I see more than

most men. Even if he looked nothing like the lad, I would have
harboured my suspicions.'

'I left the tourney life to make another one for myself and
Florian at Lavoux. We're settled here. I'm a sempstress and companion to the lady Aline, with a roof over my head and no worry
as to where the next meal is coming from. I could never go back
to this.' She gestured to the tumultuous world of the tourney
camp, glimpsed through the parted canvas flaps of the booth. 'I
did not want to become a soldier-of-fortune's trampled wife.'

'Nor do I blame you,' Edmund said. 'You had your share of
suffering when you followed the tourneys. But still, it is a shame
that your son will not know his father. He was a good lad at
heart, whatever happened between you, and from what I hear, he
too has made his break from this kind of life.'

'It is in the past,' she said stubbornly. 'People know me as a
diligent, respectable widow.'

'Who sits in the company of a one-eyed rogue in the midst of
a tourney ground,' Edmund retorted, making her redden. 'I can
see your need to build a shield against the world, but take care
that it does not cut you off from it. And there ends my lecture.'
He pointed at the remains she had pushed away. 'Not hungry?'

Monday shook her head. 'Do you expect me to be after what
you have told me? I have to go, I have been here too long already.
Come, sweetheart.' She took Florian in her arms.

'Well then, God be with you, child,' Edmund said gravely, and
rose to see her on her way.

'And with you.' On his threshold she hesitated, a small crease
between her brows. 'You will not tell anyone . . .'

He made the sign of the cross on his breast. 'I swear,' he said
solemnly. 'And who knows, perhaps you have chosen the right
road.'

Impulsively she kissed his cheek, and felt beneath her lips the
puckered scar that ran up to his hairline and had deprived him of
an eye. 'I won't forget,' she said.

Edmund nodded. 'Aye, keep the faith.' He waggled his moustache comically at Florian. 'He's a fine lad; may he become a
fine man.'

*

In the aftermath of a vigorous bout of lovemaking, Aline lay beside her husband. One slender white thigh twined over and between his, and her fingers tugged gently at his springy mat of chest hair. He was hers, and hers alone. No other woman was going to sink her claws into him, and he was certainly not going to sink any part of his anatomy into another woman.

Her fear at seeing Hamon and Monday together in the hall at dawn had dissipated, courtesy of the white-hot violence of the past half-hour, but the sight had left its mark on her nevertheless. Hamon had a penchant for new experiences, and Monday was obviously attracted to him, witness the way she had been blushing.

'I fear we have missed mass,' she said lazily.

'I doubt you would fear anything,' Hamon retorted with a playful tug on her hair.

Aline tasted the salt of sweat on his body with the tip of her tongue and knew he was wrong. Above all things, she feared losing him, but she was not about to say so. Hamon groaned softly with pleasure at her touch, but at the same time began to ease out from beneath her.

'We might have missed mass, but the rest of the day awaits,' he said.

'You were not so keen to leave a moment ago,' Aline said, and sat up, tossing her hair in a blatantly sexual gesture. She knew that even to a man recently satisfied, she looked desirable.

Hamon chuckled. 'And I will not be so keen again unless you stop bedevilling me and put some clothes on.'

Teasing had always spiced their volatile relationship. Aline sniffed. 'A bedmate and brood mare, that is all you want me for,' she accused.

'Oh no, that's not true!' he exclaimed, as if thoroughly hurt. 'What about all your lovely lands and their rich revenues!'

Aline knelt up on the bed, seized a pillow, and hurled it at him.

Their play was interrupted by a tentative knock on the door. Husband and wife stared at each other in surprise, for no servant would normally dare to intrude upon these moments of intimacy. A frown across his brows, Hamon secured a loincloth about his hips, and as Aline threw on her chemise, he crossed to the door and opened it a crack upon his wife's maid, Eda, and behind her his squire, Pepin.

'What is so important that it can't wait?' Hamon demanded irritably. 'Don't tell me someone's got themselves killed already?'

'No, my lord.' Pepin's voice, but recently broken, emerged as a high-pitched squeak.

'What then?'

'Lord John, the Count of Mortain, has just arrived with his household guard and a troop of soldiers.'

'What?' Hamon gaped at his squire in dismay. Not that he had anything against Count John. Indeed, they had many things in common, but Hamon hated to have his insouciance ruffled.

'The steward and seneschal are out in the bailey greeting him now. I came straight away to fetch you, sir.'

Hamon swore through clenched teeth and threw the door wide. 'Come, help me dress. Eda, to your mistress.' He jerked his thumb at the maid, then turned to Aline. 'Did you hear? Count John.'

'Yes, I heard. Eda, my court gown. What does he want, do you think?'

Hamon shrugged inside the tunic he was pulling on. 'Hospitality, soldiers . . . money, it would not surprise me. What does it matter? He is here for God knows how long, and he has to be provided for. That'll do.' He brushed Pepin's ministrations aside, and still fastening his belt, hastened out of the room and down to the great hall.

Monday returned to a keep in the throes of utter chaos, caused by the arrival of Coeur de Lion's brother. The outer bailey was a heaving mass of horses and soldiers. Florian clung tightly to her neck, his eyes enormous as she wove a precarious path through the throng.

Someone pinched her buttocks and guffawed an insult disguised as a compliment. She glared round, and a soldier grinned insolently back at her, his hand looped around his mount's neck. The pungent smell of horses and unwashed bodies was so thick that she covered her face with the end of her wimple. Suddenly, facing Aline did not seem such a daunting prospect, and she quickened her pace towards the safety of the hall.

This too was teeming with men, but of a higher rank than those outside. Their garments were of finer fabrics in richer hues, and their equipment was of a better quality. Some of them looked vaguely familiar – faces from a life she had left behind. As she made her way towards the tower stairs, she recognised Lupescar and Algais, mercenaries in the employ of John Plantagenet, Count of Mortain.

The moment Monday entered the bower, she was pounced upon by Aline, who dragged her into the antechamber. Maids were bustling to and fro with armfuls of linen, cushions, fresh candles and wall hangings. Two hefty men-at-arms were in the act of depositing a huge travelling chest against one wall. Three lean hunting dogs trotted around the room, investigating all and sundry. One of them snuffled at the rushes in the corner near the door, then cocked its leg up on the plasterwork. Monday's eyes bulged. Aline hated dogs. She only tolerated them in the hall for Hamon's sake, and before today, nothing on four paws had ever been allowed within a mile of her personal chamber.

'Jesu, I thought you had gone for the entire day!' Aline snapped. 'Come and help me now.' She pointed to a nursemaid playing a clapping game with a small child. 'Leave Florian with Giles. Eloise will look after him.'

'What do you want me to do?' Monday deposited her son on the floor beside Aline's little boy, and turned in time to receive a tunic of the most magnificent patterned silk she had ever laid eyes upon. It was a dark plum red, shiny and slippery, with a matt design of peacocks woven through it. All the hems were lavishly patterned with gold braid, and the entire garment was peppered with tiny gold beads.

'Mend this – invisibly if you want to curry royal favour. It's torn beneath the arm where he pulled it over his head.'

Suspecting that the 'he' involved was the Count of Mortain was not the same as following Aline into the main chamber and discovering him seated in a huge barrel bathtub. Steam rose from the surface in delicate fronds, and the count, his eyes closed, was luxuriating in the hot, herb-infused water that lapped around his throat.

Monday had seen the Count of Mortain once or twice from a

distance in her days on the tourney route, enough to receive the general impression of a dark-avised man, small of stature when measured against knights such as Hervi and Lupescar, but stocky and vigorous withal. The man in the tub bore her memory out and surprised her too. No one had ever spoken of Mortain as being handsome. All such accolades were reserved for his golden lion of a brother, and yet John's features were powerfully attractive. His face was not as long as Richard's, and the bones less close to the surface of the skin. The cheekbones were high, the nose short and endearingly blunt, and the mouth had a sensual curve in repose.

'Don't stand there goggling.' Aline nudged her sharply. 'Get busy with your needle.'

Monday fetched her sewing basket and retired to a corner of the room. She selected her finest silver needle and found a length of silk thread the exact same shade as the torn tunic. Then, with the utmost care and delicacy, she set about mending the garment. Now and then, to rest her eyes, she would raise her head and glance at him. His lids were still closed, and he seemed oblivious of the bustle surrounding him. She supposed that he must be accustomed to a constant stream of servants and petitioners and had learned to ignore them.

She had nearly finished her mending and was well pleased with the result, for the tear was almost invisible, when one of John's hounds trotted over to investigate her, thrusting its cold, moist muzzle into her lap. Monday was taken completely by surprise and her needle slipped stabbing deep into her forefinger. She let out a scream of shock and pain. The dog sank back on its haunches and growled at her, lips curling to reveal a dangerous array of sharp white teeth.

'Nero, here!'

The dog responded immediately to the peremptory baritone from the tub, and wagging its tail and whining, trotted over to the count.

He was sitting up now, fully awake and aware. 'Lie down,' he commanded, pointing a forceful forefinger. The dog dropped to all fours and watched him with anxious eyes, its plumed tail beating on the floor rushes.

'Damned mongrel,' John said, but with a note of lazy affection in his tone. 'Should have let the kennel-keeper drown you at birth.' He glanced across the room to Monday.

She eased the needle from her forefinger and sucked at the bright bead of blood that welled out, her own thoughts echoing John's words, but with considerably more venom.

'You are hurt?' he asked.

Monday shook her head. 'Not really. My only concern is that I do not bleed over your fine gown, my lord.'

'Well, that's very saintly if it is indeed your only concern,' he said silkily.

Monday blushed. 'It would be a pity to ruin such a fine tunic, especially since I have made the effort to mend it,' she said.

John was amused. 'It is not fear of me, then?'

She raised her head and looked at him. His eyes, now that they were open, reminded her with a pang of Alexander. They had the same thick, dark lashes, the same melting quality, although John's seemed rather to quench the light than to hold it.

'No, my lord, I do not fear you,' she replied. It was the truth. John had a vile reputation among other men. She had heard how he had taken the town of Evreux by trickery, and ordered the beheading of the French garrison. The soldiers' heads had been rammed on to spears and poles to be paraded on the city ramparts. Time and again she had heard men say that it took a very long spoon to sup with the Count of Mortain. But that was men. Women had nothing to fear from John, unless it be the danger of his devastating charm.

'Then my notoriety must be slipping. I thought all mothers threatened their naughty children with tales of what I would do to them.'

'My mother never threatened me.'

'Because you were never naughty?' One eyebrow curved, and the sensual lips parted in an irresistible smile that was both boyish and virile at one and the same time.

'Because there were fates far worse.' Her finger had ceased to bleed and Monday set the last few stitches into the red silk.

The bath water swished as John stood up, rivulets trickling

down his body. His skin was smooth and olive-tinted, unblemished by war wounds. Although stocky, he carried not an ounce of surplus flesh, and his limbs were perfectly in proportion. Whilst he lacked height, nature had been generous with other parts of his anatomy. After one swift glance, Monday lowered her eyes, her colour still high. There was a fluttering, nervous sensation in the pit of her belly. Anticipation, tension. Naked from his bath, Prince John was flirting with her, and she was aiding and abetting him.

A servant came forward with warm linen towels, and squires appeared to dress their lord. Monday gave the repaired tunic to one of them and watched the youth slip it over his lord's head. John's dark colouring took on a new glamour from the deep ruby tone of the silk. There was a rumour that the Angevin princes were descended from the devil, and looking at him, Monday could easily imagine how that rumour had come about.

As he slipped rings upon his fingers and one of the squires knelt to buckle the jewelled belt, Monday went unobtrusively into the antechamber and took a deep breath of air that was not scented by the herbal aroma of bath steam.

CHAPTER 23

John had no particular love for tourneying. The military prowess of its heroes reminded him too much of his exalted brother, Richard, who was such a genius with the strategy of the sword that he made those less gifted seem like bumbling fools. Another brother, Geoffrey, had paid his life trying to emulate Richard's prowess with sword and lance. But whatever his private thoughts, John also knew that men loved the hurly-burly of the tourneys, and they were excellent events for recruiting soldiers and garnering funds. And so, bathed and refreshed, he made an observer's sally on to the field with his host.

It did not take him long to select the men he required, but then he had not intended it to. A recruiting officer was dispatched to make offers, and John retired to a trestle set up beneath the spreading branches of two lime trees. A cloth covered the board and goblets of Italian glass cast pools of gemstone light on the bleached linen. A matching flagon sparkled, as did an aquamanile in the shape of a lion with eyes of green malachite.

John had a love of luxury and beautiful things. Whereas Richard cared little if the cup he drank from was made of cracked clay, John cared very much, and was pleased that his host and hostess had gone to the trouble. Hamon was first and foremost Richard's man, but he was also a lover of fine objects, and possessed a shrewd political eye.

Food was served in the dappled shade, the tree branches swishing gently overhead. Although John had arrived at Lavoux unannounced, Aline and her cooks had managed to produce a feast sufficient to delight the royal appetite. There were pigeons simmered in a wine and shallot sauce, small cheese pasties, bream with almonds, sweet and savoury custards, preserved fruits, spiced wafers, and as well as the best wine and mead from the stores, there was also a tawny pear cider, and sweet, strong morap, made from mulberry juice.

John settled down to enjoy the food, the soft harp music in the background, and the delightful ambience of the spring day. He had intended riding on after a brief pause for refreshment, but now he decided he would remain overnight. He did not have to be at Château Gaillard just yet, and sitting beneath these trees eating sublime food and being waited upon hand and foot was a far better pastime than indulging in skirmishes along the border with the French. Richard would have opted for the latter, but John was not his sainted brother and was sick of dwelling in his shadow. But he had learned from his earlier mistakes and knew that the only remedy was to bide his time and play the loyal hound to the hilt, grateful for any morsels that came his way.

He fed one of his dogs a sliver of pigeon meat and decided that he would not spoil the moment by thinking of Richard when there were subjects far more pleasant to occupy his mind. A little distance away, the women of the household had brought their spinning and sewing into the fresh air. John's gaze fell upon the sempstress who had mended his favourite silk robe with con-summate skill. She had an arresting face, fresh and innocent at first glance, but with something hidden that made him keep on looking. A gown of russet silk shimmered over lithe, supple curves, and her wimple was short and open, exposing her long white throat. Obviously she was married, for a small boy kept clambering in and out of her lap.

John was thirty-two years old, and it was more than half a life-time since he had taken his first woman to bed. He had been married for more than ten years to Isabella, heiress of Gloucester, but it was a match made for political purposes which had long outlived its use, and there was no love lost between him and his wife. Consummation achieved, they kept separate households. Intermittently, other women entered John's life and bed. He enjoyed their company when he had the time and the inclination, and they in their turn, enjoyed his whilst he was smiling.

Hamon was talking to him about a book he had recently acquired for his small collection. Normally John enjoyed books and reading and would have taken to the conversation with zest, but now he cut brusquely across Hamon's description. 'Yonder sempstress,' he said. 'Tell me about her.'

For a moment Hamon's mouth remained open in the surprise of aborted speech, then he rallied, his gaze falling where John's already lay. 'Ah, well, that is a story as detailed as any book,' he said, changing tack to suit his guest's mood. 'Her name is Monday de Cerizay. She is my wife's companion, and as you have seen, a sempstress of extraordinary skill.' He relaxed in his seat, thoroughly prepared to enjoy himself. 'She came to us a little over two years ago from the tourney circuit, but she is not one of the regular camp sluts.'

'No?' John prompted, without taking his eyes from her. His appetite sated, another kind of hunger was building rapidly and he shifted restlessly in his seat. Her mouth was a full, sensual cushion, and the way she pursed it as she sewed was slowly driving him mad.

'Her mother, so she says, was the daughter of an English baron. I make no claims as to the veracity of the tale, but my wife is certain that it is true, and the girl's manners are of the court, not the camp. She can even read and write.'

'Is the child hers?'

'She came to us pregnant, and the story was put about that she was a young widow in straitened circumstances.'

'But it is not true?'

Hamon shrugged. 'She has never admitted to it, but Aline suspects that the father of her child is a certain young man among the landless tourney followers. Whether he is or not, they are not part of each other now.'

John nodded and continued to study Monday with narrowed eyes, like a cat viewing its prey through the grass. He crumbled a honey cake between his fingers, but made no attempt to eat it. 'Do you want her?' he asked suddenly of Hamon.

Hamon choked on the mouthful of wine he had just drawn. 'Me, my lord?' he spluttered, as if the thought had never occurred to him. 'Aline would kill me!'

'No doubt,' John said drily, 'but that was not what I asked. Do you want her?'

Hamon drew several wheezy breaths. 'Not at the expense of a dagger in my heart should Aline find out,' he replied with a grimace.

John smiled, but said nothing, and his eyes continued to dwell on Monday with a feline, predatory intent.

That evening in Lavoux's great hall, there was more feasting, together with entertainment and dancing to honour the royal guest. Monday sat at the side table reserved for Aline's women, and unconsciously fiddled with the silver filigree brooch pinning the neck opening of the russet gown.

When she had first arrived at Lavoux, weary, pregnant, and filled with anxiety, Monday had forsworn men. It had been an easy vow to keep. Her burgeoning body was evidence enough of why it was not wise to trust them, and she could look upon even the most handsome of squires without so much as a flicker of interest, let alone lust. But gradually, the situation had changed. She had survived Florian's birth, and even if she regretted the circumstances of his begetting, she could not regret her child. He had filled her life with love when all the light had gone from it, and satisfied a yearning maternal instinct. But there were other instincts too. Submerged by pregnancy and the early days of motherhood, they were now surfacing with a vengeance. Her eyes were drawn to the young men of the household, but when they glanced her way, she would feign indifference, wanting and fearing at one and the same time. The incident with Lord Hamon in the hall this morning had led her to realise how vulnerable her position here was.

Now Prince John had arrived, and the way he looked at her made her breathing short and brought an immodest burning to her woman's parts. She kept remembering him stepping out of the bathtub, the mocking curve of his mouth as he enquired if she had ever been naughty. *Fates far worse.*

As she fiddled with the brooch, the scent of rose oil wafted from the inside of her wrist. Monday was not sure that she liked the perfume, but Aline had insisted she dab some there, and

upon the pulse at her throat. Considering that she had caught
Hamon flirting with Monday that morning, Aline seemed
remarkably magnanimous. At one time Monday might just have
credited the behaviour to Aline's mercurial nature, but now that
she knew her better, she suspected that there was a motive somewhere.

The feasting over, the dancing began – a medley of caroles and
jigs performed by musicians with bone whistles, bagpipes, lutes
and tabors. Full of high spirits, the other women dragged a
protesting Monday from her seat and into the midst of the mer-
riment. At first she hung back, feeling awkward and
self-conscious. She had not danced since her days on the tourney
field, when her mother was still alive and herself a carefree child.

But once learned, the movements belonged to the blood, and
she recalled them with increasing ease as the music took over.
Remembering the joy of meadow grass and camp fire, her feet
began to perform the steps. Neatly and surely, swift as a needle
arrowing through fabric. By the time the music ended, Monday
was flushed with exertion and gasping for breath. She was also
sparkling with the laughter of sheer enjoyment. There was just
enough time to snatch a cup of wine, and then dart back into the
ring of dancers as the next carole began. Round and round,
whirling, stepping, the music a joyous galliard of sounds.

Monday danced until her feet were sore, and her hair was
damp at her brow. She danced for her lost childhood, for all the
days of unhappiness and care, for her mother, her father, and
herself. It was both a wake and an awakening. And then, as the
tempo slowed to give folk a chance to catch their breath, Prince
John took her hand. Despite his stockiness, he was cat-light of
foot, and because they were of a similar height, they matched
well as their fingers clasped, and he turned her first to the right,
then to the left. Her spine to his chest; his hands lifting and turning. Where they touched, she burned. The dance was progressive
and he passed her down to the next man in the line, but in the
end she came back to him, and on the last, triumphant note of
pipe and tabor, he bowed over her hand and caressed the rose-
scented pulse point with the very tip of his tongue. A shudder
rippled down her spine, and sensing it, he smiled.

'So you still do not fear me?' he challenged softly.

Monday lowered her eyes. 'No, my lord, I do not,' she said unsteadily.

'Well, you should, because I want to eat you alive.'

Another dance tune struck up, livelier than the last, and couples began to move and sway. Monday used the excuse of the steps to break from John, but she performed no more than the first few turns, and instead of joining hands with the woman at her side, made a breathless excuse, and fled the hall for the safety of the floors above.

Leaning her head against the cool stone newel post on the turret stairs, she listened to the thunder of her heart in her ears. She had told him the truth. She did not fear John – she was terrified of him. She could still feel the touch of his hands on her body, and see the wolfish glint in his eyes. Her body ached with desire, but last time she had given her senses control over her reason, the aftermath had changed her life and her perceptions forever.

Monday raised her head from the stone and made her way to the small wall chamber where Florian had been put to sleep in the same bed as Aline's son, the children watched over by Giles's nurse. A cresset lamp burned on the coffer, shedding dim light on the two little heads, one reddish-fair, the other black as a raven's wing. She gazed on the rounded, innocent features of her son, the thumb touching the pursed lips, the thick black lashes seeming almost too heavy for the translucent lids. A pang knotted her belly. How easy his begetting had been, a simple, single moment, and how difficult the road since. She was the greatest fool on God's earth to be considering a repetition of the experience.

She stroked Florian's soft cheek, smiled at the nursemaid, and turned to leave, only to discover that John had followed her, and was blocking her escape. The nurse leaped to her feet with a stifled cry of surprise. John motioned her to be seated, and then ignored her.

'You did not stay to dance,' he said to Monday.

'I came to look at my son, my lord,' she answered more confidently than she felt. 'Sometimes he wakens and cries for me.'

He brushed past her into the room to look at the two sleeping children. 'I remember when my own two were this small,' he said.

Monday saw a rare expression on his face. There was gentleness there, a yielding that made the cynical mouth tender and the dark eyes less predatory. 'They are so innocent at this age,' he murmured, 'they do not put conditions on their affection, or masks on their faces in order to snatch from you what they can.'

'I did not know that you had children, my lord.' Even as she spoke, Monday knew how foolish her statement was. Unless John was barren, his reputation with women made it almost certain that he had bastards somewhere.

'A boy and a girl of different mothers,' he said. 'Richard is nine, and Joanna is seven.'

'What . . . what happened to their mothers?'

John turned his head, and the softness in his eyes was banished by hard amusement. 'You are wondering if I threw them to the wolves once my lust was sated?'

Monday held her ground. 'Should I not?'

'Is that what happened to you?' He indicated Florian. 'Did his father not want to know?'

Monday was aware of the nurse sitting on her stool. Although the woman's head was bowed, she could not help but hear what was being said. Lowering her voice, Monday turned so that she was facing away from the nurse. 'His father would have married me, but I thought it better if our ways parted.'

'So you are not the respectable widow you would have others believe?' John's voice fell to match hers, but his eyes sparkled with laughter.

'I am not a widow, no.'

'But very respectable,' he said solemnly. He too glanced towards the woman on her stool, and spoke out on a louder level now. 'I was most pleased with the miracle you worked with your needle this morning. I have another robe in need of refurbishment before I leave. Come to my chamber and I will give it to you.'

Monday stared at him. It would be like following a wolf into its lair and hoping not to be devoured.

'My squires will be there,' he said, as if he had read her mind, and made an ushering motion at the open door. 'You have naught to fear.'

Without looking at him, Monday went out. John had taken over the main bedchamber and anteroom that were the usual haunt of Aline and the women of the household. She walked past her own pallet and saw a man's saddle bags and a pair of gilt spurs standing on it. Two squires were busy in the main chamber, one polishing John's helm with an oiled cloth, the other grooming the hairiest of the dogs with a teasel brush. John dismissed them both to the outer room with a flick of his fingers.

Monday gazed around the room, which was no longer a familiar haven. Aline's personality had already been subjugated by John's. 'You do not really have a robe, do you?' she asked.

'Would I lure you here under false pretences?' A dark eyebrow rose to mock her. He went to the bed, picked up a woollen tunic and showed her a long split in the side seam.

'You might.' She took it from him and saw that it would be a simple task to mend. A squire could do it easily; there was no great degree of skill required. 'You might well indeed.'

'Don't you trust me?'

'You have not told me what happened to the women who bore your children.'

He shrugged. 'There is no mystery. Joanna's mother died soon after the birth. Richard was born of a single night's folly. His mother is well provided for.'

Monday winced at his casual mention and dismissal of a 'single night's folly', and wondered if the woman concerned had been as sanguine.

'They are in the past,' he said impatiently. 'No woman warms my bed at the moment.' A jewelled ring flashed on his index finger as he raised it. 'But if you say yes, then all that can change.'

Monday clutched the robe in her hands. The smell of sandalwood and citrus rose from its folds, speaking of the wealth and privilege that was John's to command. 'There are women aplenty in Lavoux who would share your bed, why not seek one of them?'

'Who eats plain bread when he can have honey on it?' John responded, advancing on her. 'Hamon offered me a woman as a matter of course. I could have tumbled any one of a dozen, but I didn't want them, I wanted you.'

She stared at him, a small frown between her brows.

'You really don't see, do you?' John said in a voice husky with desire and surprise. 'It's not pretence at all.' He was close enough now to touch her cheek, to feather its outline with a fingertip. Most attractive women were conscious of the power their looks wielded, but she seemed unaware of her allure, as innocent as a virgin. The thought sent an impatient flare of lust through his body. He had to have her. A fallen angel, almost, but not quite pure, and still so very young. The lures were irresistible, and John had never been a man to abstain in the name of conscience.

'I am not a whore,' she said, and her voice shook slightly, but she did not turn her face from his touch.

'I have never bedded with a whore in my life, and I am not about to begin,' he said scornfully. 'I am offering you a place in my household – as a sempstress, with, shall we say, special duties? I will pay you handsomely for your needlework.' He smiled, his tongue poking at the side of his cheek. 'Now you can either slap my face and stalk out, or put down that robe and come to bed.'

She looked through her eyelashes at the man who was tracing the line of her jaw. He had wealth and social position at his command; the riches she had dreamed about could be hers for the speaking of a single word. She wondered what he would do if she did slap his face. Probably no woman had ever dared . . . except perhaps his mother.

'Well,' he prompted, the dark eyes narrow with amusement and a hint of impatience, 'are we to stand here until dawn?'

Monday shook her head. 'I am afraid,' she confessed.

'Of me?'

'Of taking so great a step. Here at Lavoux, I have a safe home for myself and my son.'

'It is no great step from here to my bed,' he said coaxingly. His forefinger trailed down her throat into the neck opening of her gown, where further enquiry was prevented by the silver brooch. 'I will be good to you, I swear it. Besides, how safe do you think your haven really is?'

'What do you mean?'

John abandoned the brooch and instead set about removing the circlet and veil from her brow. 'Hamon de Rougon follows you with his eyes. How long before his wife's jealousy sees you out in the gutter?'

It was an overstatement, but nevertheless it contained a morsel of truth, and fed Monday's hidden anxiety.

'You will be doing yourself a great service, and giving me great pleasure,' he murmured, and stepped back, her wimple and circlet in his hand. 'A murrain on all head coverings,' he said. 'A woman's hair is meant to be admired.' He wrapped the fabric around the circlet and tossed it on the bed as if casting a quoit. Then he took the torn robe she had been clutching and disposed of that too. 'Loose it for me,' he commanded softly.

With shaking hands, Monday reached to her braid and untied the silken ribbons plaited through it. As she untwisted her hair and shook it down around her shoulders and hips in a brown-gold skein, she knew that she had taken an irrevocable step. For better or worse, she had entered the lion's den.

Monday had not known what to expect of the lord John. She had no experience by which to judge him, except the one brief incident that had led to Florian's birth. The memory of his begetting was a haze of drunken, molten lust. She had seen the whores of the tourney camp, had heard her parents behind the screen of hangings in their tent, and had observed Hamon and Aline indulge in the less intimate stages of foreplay, but it was not knowledge enough. When he laid her down on the bed and began to caress her, she was strung with tension, and this time she was as sober as a stone.

John seemed not in the least set down by her ignorance or shyness. When he saw that she was disturbed by the half-open door, he closed it on his squires, and snuffed all but one of the candles, leaving just enough light so that he could see to undress her. Monday closed her eyes so that she would not see what he was doing, but just as swiftly opened them again, feeling too vulnerable.

'I do not know what you have heard about me,' John said wryly, 'but I am no ravisher. I prefer my women willing. Here, would you like some wine?' He rolled to the side of the bed and reached out to the coffer.

'No!' Monday's throat closed on the very suggestion. 'No,'

she said in a more controlled voice, as she saw him look at her askance. 'I was . . . I was drunk the last time.'

'Ah.' He nodded knowingly. 'And that was the first time too, I suppose.'

Her face flamed. 'Yes.'

John poured wine for himself, 'Then it does seem that I have an unfair advantage, but life is never fair.' He dabbled his forefinger in the wine and anointed her left breast in a spiral of pinkish droplets leading to her nipple. Her flesh stiffened and stood proud, partly with the cold feeling of the wine, partly with the delicate pleasure of his touch. 'You can see yourself either as the victim of a predator, or the pupil of a widely travelled scholar,' he murmured as he applied more wine to her other breast, and drew a trail down over her belly, stopping as he reached the dark triangle of pubic hair.

The timbre of his voice, the slow meandering of his touch were both arousing, but what finally allayed her qualms was not his manner, but the words themselves. A victim or a pupil. He was offering her knowledge, as once she had sought the knowledge of the quill from Alexander. The more she learned, the better equipped she was to deal with life. And John would be paying her to learn.

'So, you are leaving us?' Aline eyed the folded clothes and effects packed in the small travelling chest, and then, with speculation, the young woman preparing to close and strap the lid. 'What is he like as a lover?'

Monday blushed. Since she had spent the entire night in John's bed, and he had insisted that she and Florian sit at the high table with him to break their fast, it was common knowledge throughout the castle that the Count of Mortain had taken a fancy to Lavoux's young sempstress. And it was a fancy that had outlasted the dawn, for here she was, preparing to leave with him. Curiosity, not just Aline's, was rife.

'I do not know,' Monday said as she latched the straps and nodded to the waiting servant. He toted the box on his shoulders and strode from the room, the sound of his whistling trailing jauntily in his wake.

'What do you mean, you don't know!' Aline laughed incredulously. 'You spend all night in his bed and sit in his lap this morning and you do not know!'

'Well, how should I?' Monday retorted. 'How many lovers do you think I have had to be able to make comparisons?'

Aline swiped at her, only half in play. 'Don't be facetious, tell me. After all, I directed his interest your way.'

'You did?'

'Of course. If I had not wanted him to notice you, I would never have instructed you to do your mending right beneath his nose. And if you remember, I gave you that rose oil to perfume your skin, and helped dress your hair.'

Not for the first time, Monday felt a spurt of irritation at Aline's penchant for manipulating the lives of those around her. It was also annoying that Aline should think her incapable of attracting John without assistance. 'Why should you want him to notice me?' she asked frostily.

Aline shrugged and looked at her fingernails. 'You were wearing a rut for yourself' she said, but her words carried no conviction. 'Besides, you have a royal protector now, one who enjoys reading books as much if not more than Hamon does.'

There it was, the crux of the matter, Monday thought grimly. Aline wanted her out of the way so she would not be a threat to her marriage. The knowledge hung unspoken between them. They avoided looking at each other, each aware of the resentment they would find. 'And if he tires of me when I am no longer a novelty, what then?' Monday demanded.

'Either you must make sure that he does not or if you think you can only keep him interested for a while, then you must save enough in the good times to outlast the lean. But at the back of your mind, you know that already.'

Monday fiddled with the clasp of her cloak and knew that she had more cause to be grateful to Aline than to bear a grudge. Already on her middle finger, beside her silver ring and the one that had been her mother's, there gleamed proof of John's largesse in the form of another one of faceted gold set with three garnets. She knew from her life on the tourney field that such a jewel would purchase food and lodging for at least a month. He had promised her a Spanish mare to ride upon, and her choice of the mercer's booths in Rouen to fashion herself fitting garments for the mistress of a prince. But there was more to her situation than just the garnering of wealth and knowledge. She only had to think of the wine poured out on her body to shiver with sensuous remembrance.

'I know you mean well for me,' she said, turning to Aline, 'and it is of my own free will that I am doing this now. You have been very good to me, and I will always remember your care.' Without warning, there were tears in her eyes.

Aline gave her a warm, impulsive hug. 'And you have been less of a servant than a sister to me,' she responded. 'Take care of yourself and Florian. Write to me, let me know how you are faring; I will hold you in my prayers.'

'And you in mine.'

The two women embraced again. Then Aline released Monday and slanted her a look sidelong. 'You still haven't told me what he is like as a lover,' she said mischievously.

CHAPTER 24

John's dogs roved the bedchamber, sniffing the earthy scent of new plaster on the walls and nosing the rushes which were freshly strewn and still redolent of the river meadows from which they had been cut. Everything about the great Château Gaillard was new. Two years ago, Richard's mighty fortress on the Seine at Andeli had not existed by so much as a single stone. Now it towered over the landscape, mocking King Philip of France with its saucy virility in what was supposed to be neutral territory. And the work still continued, with scaffolding embracing new sections of the wall and an army of craftsmen toiling night and day to increase Gaillard's imposing magnificence. Everything that Richard knew about castle building had gone into her construction, and so had a mass of wealth, raised by fines and taxes, by reliefs and the selling of offices.

'What's inside his braies is not so impressive,' John remarked as he followed his dogs around the chamber, sniffing like them, his nose wrinkled, and a cynical twist to his lips. 'Building his cock in stone is the only way he'll ever make it rise.' He wandered to the window embrasure and stared broodingly out.

Monday said nothing. She had not been travelling with John for long, but already she knew that he suffered from mercurial twists of mood; that a single remark could sour his temper and unloose a stream of venom upon the victim. She had also learned in this last half day, how much John admired, resented, and feared his great, golden brother Richard. She suspected that Château Gaillard was as much a thorn in John's side as it was in King Philip's.

Attendants were still carrying John's baggage into the room,

and the staff of his household, his clerks and mercenaries, chaplains and body servants, flitted in and out. Florian sat on the
floor, alternately sucking his thumb and a square of old linen to
which he had become inseparably attached. For a two-year-old,
the day's journey had been exhausting. Scooping him up in her
arms, Monday took him into a small side chamber where she
made him a bed from her cloak and sat with him, smoothing his
brow until he fell asleep.

She was rapidly discovering that the life of a prince was not so
different to that of a tourney knight. There were long days spent
in the saddle or sitting in one of the baggage wains as John's
entourage rumbled along the rutted roads of Normandy. The
only difference over the tourney circuit was that the destinations
usually had stone walls, tiled roofs, and the comforts of privilege.

When she returned to the main room, John was no longer
there. Two servants were putting together his bed which had
been unloaded in pieces from the baggage wain, and his clerks
were already at work, seated at a trestle with their writing equipment. Monday went to her small, battered travelling chest which
stood against a wall, began to unpack it, then changed her mind.
John had not said whether she would be sleeping in his chamber
or not. Perhaps he would just summon her when she was
required, and she and Florian would sleep with his other servants, such as his laundress, and the man who filled his bath. But
where they were billeted in this enormous labyrinth of a fortress,
she had no idea.

She wandered over to the clerks. 'Do you know where the
Count of Mortain has gone?'

One of them studiously ignored her, but the other raised his
head and fixed her with intelligent, bright blue eyes. He had
earnest, freckled features and his hair was an unruly brown halo
around his tonsure. 'To meet with his brother and King Philip,'
he said, adding before she could ask, 'I do not know how long he
will be gone.'

Monday nodded. What had she expected him to say? John's
preoccupations were with affairs of state. It was stupid of her to
think that he would spare a thought for her bewilderment. A
headache began to beat behind her eyes.

The clerk laid down his quill. 'We will be working long into the night,' he said, rising to his feet. 'I am going to find us food and drink. Would you like some too?'

Briefly, Monday wondered what John would do if he returned and found her eating with his clerks, but she banished the doubt with a frown of irritation at her own folly. She was tired, and creating problems where none existed. If John had wanted to house her with the rest of his servants, he would have dismissed her long before now. 'Thank you.' A smile lit up her wan features.

The clerk smiled in return and departed on his errand, returning very soon with a wicker basket crammed with enough provisions to feed a small army. There was a large stone jar of wine, two loaves, some small, savoury meatballs made of pork, herbs and breadcrumbs, hard boiled eggs, cheese wrapped in vine leaves, honey cakes, fig pastries, and sweet-sharp apples.

'You should see the kitchens, Simon,' he said to the other scribe. 'If ever hell existed on earth, it's there. All the ovens burning full blast and cooks up to their armpits in bodies – pigs and sheep mainly,' he said as an aside to reassure Monday.

'You should not jest about such matters,' the other scribe reproved and, laying down his quill, opened and closed his cramped fingers.

'I wasn't jesting,' the younger man retorted with a roll of his eyes, and beckoned Monday to help him transfer the contents of the basket to the trestle.

She sat down to eat with the scribes, and discovered, along with a ravenous appetite, that her saviour's name was Brother Ambrose of Pont l'Arche, and that he had been a scribe and chaplain in John's household for almost four years. The other one, Simon, said very little, but she gathered that he was by far the senior, and that he disapproved strongly of John's moral weakness.

'I suppose that you have seen many different women in this chamber,' Monday ventured as she devoured yet another chunk of bread. Under the onslaught of food, her headache had eased, and the friendliness of the younger scribe made her feel less vulnerable.

'A few,' Ambrose said with a shrug, 'but not as many as his

reputation suggests. There are worse sins in the world. I would not like to work in King Richard's private chamber.'

The older scribe cleared his throat warningly and Ambrose fell to eating his meal. 'It is true though,' he said between mouthfuls.

'True or not, gossip will only get you into trouble.' Simon's eyes flickered to Monday.

'It will not spread from me,' she said with dignity. 'And you are not telling secrets to the ignorant; I know of what you speak.' But Simon was right, she thought. Listening to gossip was interesting, but joining in was dangerous. With diplomacy, she excused herself to go and check upon Florian. He was still deeply asleep, and she judged that he would remain so until the early morning. She slipped off her shoes, removed her overgown, and covering herself with her cloak, lay down beside him.

She neither remembered closing her eyes, nor falling asleep, but the next thing she knew there was a hand at her shoulder, and a voice dark with wine fumes against her ear. 'Is the floor more pleasing to you than my bed?' it enquired with amusement. The words were unslurred, revealing that while John had been drinking, he was certainly not drunk.

Monday turned sleepily and received the heat of a deep kiss. His hands roved beneath her cloak, over her breasts, and lightly between her thighs until her breath caught at the pleasure. 'I thought you might want your bed to yourself,' she murmured and set her arms around his neck.

'Why should I want to sleep alone when I can sleep with you?' It was pitch-dark, the candles long since snuffed. His beard was crisp and silky against her throat, and as he lay over her, the feel of his confined erection pressed up hard against the juncture of her thighs was delicious. But not so delicious that she forgot her small son asleep beside them.

'Perhaps I should take you here on the floor like a kitchen wench,' John said, biting her neck. 'We can rut in the straw like two peasants.'

The idea was obviously appealing to him, for his breathing had grown more ragged, and he made small, grinding motions with his hips.

'Not in here, what about Florian,' she said breathlessly, 'or do you want it to be so real that a wailing child dampens your ardour mid-way?'

John swore softly with a mingling of irritation and lust. He picked her up, his fingers digging into the soft flesh of her forearm and thigh, and carried her into the main chamber, but not to the bed. They could sport there any time, and its feather softness was not appropriate to the savage tide of lust sweeping over him at the moment. Finesse had always mattered to John. His way with women, his ability as a lover, were areas where Richard was the poor relation. But now and then, to take in primeval urgency was in its own way as much a delight as lingering foreplay. He dropped her on the floor, yanked her gown up, tore her loin cloth away, and freeing his erection from his braies, entered her in a single, hard thrust.

By all the rules of decency Monday should have been shocked at what they were doing, but in the last few days as they travelled, she had begun to discover a wilder side to herself, as if agreeing to become John's mistress had freed that part of her personality. She might as well be hung for a sheep as a lamb. And having given herself permission to enjoy what had previously been forbidden territory, she was willing to play John's games.

Her legs clasped at his spine, her climax was as swift and fierce as his, and she had to stifle a scream of pure pleasure against the gilded neckband of his tunic. There was no sound in the aftermath, but the ragged counterpoint of their breathing, and the thundering of their hearts.

'Jesu!' John gasped when he could speak. 'If that had lasted any longer, I would have died!' He rolled off her and sat up on the floor. 'Not that I'd have minded,' he added breathlessly, and gave a short laugh. 'I haven't felt lust like that since I was a green youth.'

Monday sat up too, and lowered the gown he had bunched around her hips in his urgency. Her loins still trembled. She would have been happy for it to last as long as forever.

John rose and helped her to her feet. 'How old are you, Monday?' he asked, and kissed her lips gently this time, then her cheek and her eyelids.

'I am not sure, my lord. About nineteen years old, I think.'

'Nineteen,' he mused and shook his head. 'Perhaps I need your youth to remember my own.'

'My lord?'

'Ah, nothing. A man spills his seed and it reminds him of his mortality, and gives him an inordinate urge to fall asleep. Of a sudden, my bed seems more appealing than the floor.' He tugged her towards its dim outline.

'Do you want me to rub your back?' Monday asked, for already she knew that it was one of John's particular pleasures, and like a cat, he never tired of it.

'Who needs heaven in the afterlife when they can have it here on earth?' he answered with a smile in his voice.

'So, you're a fully fledged monk now,' said Father Ambrose, eyeing Hervi's neat tonsure. Strangely, the style suited him. He had shed weight since the trauma of losing his leg, and the austerity of the monastic routine had done the rest. Now his bones were more prominent, displaying a stubborn strength of character, and the hazel eyes were marked with experience, suffering, and a hidden glint of irreverent humour.

'I have taken the vows,' Hervi nodded, 'but I'm not fledged enough to spread my wings yet.' He patted the bald ring on top of his scalp somewhat self-consciously and comforted himself with the fact that sooner or later he would have lost his hair anyway if his older brothers were any indication.

'But you will.' It was a statement, not a question.

'Oh, yes,' Hervi said confidently. 'And sooner, rather than later. I am happy here, but it is not my goal.'

'Then what is?' Ambrose asked curiously.

'There is a certain priory close to my family's lands in England.'

'You want to be closer to your family?'

'Oh no!' Hervi denied with an appalled laugh. 'God forbid that myself and Reginald should see more of each other than forced. I want to go to Cranwell because the existing prior is not fit to rule; because the house is rife with lust and corruption. Replace the prior, and the monastery would be cleansed in one fell swoop.' His mouth tightened. 'Alexander was a novice there, the reason he's so wary of priests today. His back was whipped bloody to feed the man's carnal appetites. I want to put a stop to Father Alkmund's abuses, and I can best do it from within. Even given my crippled leg, I'm as active as any man. My mind may not be educated, but it is every bit as sharp as those around me.' His tone had developed vehemence, and hearing himself, he stopped, and shook his head ruefully. 'I become carried away. Patience has been one of the hardest skills to learn.' He rubbed his thigh where the leather straps of his wooden stump were chaffing. 'I need to learn more yet; I need to convince my superiors that I am full worthy and capable of responsibility.'

Ambrose eyed him. 'I think you will do that easily,' he said. 'Your will is so strong, I can almost see it.'

Hervi gave a grim smile and shook his head. 'Let us speak of different things,' he said. 'How is the life of the court these days? What news of the outside world?'

Ambrose shrugged. 'What do you want to know? The truce is straining at the seams and small pockets of warfare keep bursting the stitches. Last month there was a meeting at Château Gaillard to confirm a peace treaty, but King Philip stormed out and refused to sign. Not that my lords Richard or John were particularly put out. They have the measure of the King of France – or at least Richard does. And John makes an admirable captive, even if he cannot swing a sword with the same panache as his brother.'

'Is he trustworthy these days? I recall he was ever one for muddying the waters.'

'Oh, he's learned his lesson,' Ambrose said. 'With Richard missing, perhaps even dead on his way home from crusade, what else was John to do but make a bid for power? It was understandable. Now he knows that if he sets a foot wrong, he will be denied his inheritance in favour of Arthur of Brittany. He has to prove his value and goodwill to Richard in order to remain his heir. And Richard's lands are well within his future grasp since Richard shows no inclination to spend time with his wife.'

'Knowing Richard's 'inclinations', I would say that your lord is looking at a crown,' Hervi agreed drily.

Apart from waggling his eyebrows to show that he knew what

Hervi meant, Ambrose maintained a diplomatic silence on the subject.

'Mind you,' Hervi added, 'John spends no time with his wife either, from what I have heard. He is too busy sporting with his mistresses.'

The vices and lusts of the royal house of Anjou were not really matters to be aired in the cloisters of a dignified abbey where theology and church matters should have been the order of the day, but Ambrose could no more resist the lure than Hervi could resist asking.

'He only has the one at the moment,' Ambrose said, 'and she is not a painted courtesan, but a pleasant, fresh young woman.'

'I suppose John is thoroughly immersed in corrupting her then,' Hervi said with a grimace.

Ambrose looked thoughtful. 'I think not,' he murmured after due consideration. 'If anything she is good for him. Yes, he buys her presents and takes her to his bed at every opportunity, with little respect for what is decent, but I do believe she lightens his darker moods, and since he has only had her since the summer, the flame is still new and bright. She might appear gentle and innocent, but she is also a very resourceful young woman.'

Hervi looked into the distance, his inner vision filled with the image of a grey-eyed girl with a thick plait of bronze-brown hair. 'I knew a girl like that,' he said with pain in his voice. 'I wish I still did.'

Ambrose gave him a look sidelong. 'It is not wise for a monk to dwell on thoughts of women lest he be tempted into sin,' he warned.

'My thoughts are not carnal,' Hervi said with a sigh. 'They are of regret. Do you remember that you were asked to marry my brother Alexander to a girl he had deflowered, and that she could not be found?'

'You are thinking of her?'

Hervi nodded. 'We never discovered what had happened to her. Alex swears that she still lives, and I pray daily that he is right.'

The church bell rang through the stone arches of the cloisters, and across the abbey grounds, summoning the monks to vespers in the late gold of the autumn evening.

'Then I will pray too,' Ambrose volunteered, and rose from the stone bench on which they had been seated.

Hervi smiled, but the expression did not reach his eyes, which remained sombre.

CHAPTER 25

The bolts of fabric shimmered across the bed in waves of eye-aching colour. Silks and patterned damasks imported from Italy and the east, soft English lambswool, woven by skilled craftsmen in Flanders, finely textured linens in more muted shades, and a riot of braids and trimmings, fur tippets and coloured glass beads.

Monday could only gaze with open mouth upon such splendour. John's generosity had already clothed her in warmth and luxury beyond her imagination. Today she wore a gown of pale-blue linen topped by a tunic in darker-blue wool trimmed with thread of gold, and her shoes were of the softest leather designed in an exquisite latticework of cut-out shapes. Gifts for services rendered.

John stood beside her now, laughing at her astonishment. 'Have you nothing to say, sweetheart?'

She shook her head. 'My senses are dazzled.' She reached a tentative hand to stroke one of the cloths, a rich tawny-gold woven through with crimson peacocks. 'I have never seen such an array.'

'Well, become accustomed.' Despite the presence of the Rouen cloth merchant, he set his arm around her waist and fitted her to his side, hip suggestively against hip. 'You like that gold?'

She nodded. 'But for you, not me.'

He leaned forward to finger it too, with a connoisseur's eye. John's love of finery was as legend as his brother's military reputation, and cost the tax-payer's coffers almost as much. 'Yes,' he said, and instructed the merchant to cut enough for a long court robe. He also pointed to another, similar cloth, if anything more sumptuously worked than the first. 'As a gift for the Bishop of Rouen,' he said. 'The old goat will be delighted. And this, for my lady,' he added, and with unerring taste selected another damask the colour of a summer sea, green on blue.

Monday opened her mouth, but quickly closed it again. She had been rather taken with a soft wool in a deep, rosy pink, but knew better than to say so. She had learned that although John liked to give her gifts, they were always of his choosing. She was his pet. Pampered and indulged because it was his whim to do so. She knew that the wider she opened her eyes and the more dumbstruck she appeared, the better John liked it. He enjoyed her answering back to him in the bedchamber or in conversation only if she played the precocious child. The moment she sparred with her intellect or attempted to speak as an equal, his interest waned.

'He dislikes clever women,' she had been told by the wife of an official attached to his household. 'They remind him too much of his mother, and she has never made a secret of the fact that Richard is her favourite, and John an inconvenience, born when her body should have finished child-bearing.'

That knowledge in mind, Monday played the game of daughter and child, and knew that she was a fraud. She also knew that she could not perform either role for much longer. They were in Rouen at the moment and it was past Michaelmas. Barring mishaps, Monday was certain now of what the spring of 1199 would bring.

John selected the pink wool too, because Monday fingered it wistfully. Oh yes, she was learning all the ploys but felt cheapened by their use.

The cloth merchant departed, and as always, after one of his gift-givings, John took her eagerly to bed, lying her down across the yards of fabric he had selected.

'When we wear our new gowns, we'll remember this,' he said, and paused to laugh, his beard chafing her breasts. 'Imagine the bishop's face if he knew how the material of his new chasuble had been sanctified!'

It was just the sort of thing John would say. He had small reverence for the Church, his nature far too cynical to allow the love of God into his heart, and he was always making jibes and playing jokes at the expense of the ecclesiasts around him. Despite his mistrust of the Church, he valued his clerks and deacons and chaplains. They held high office in his household, but their role was purely administrative. John shunned spiritual advice. Within him, there was a dark core, which people saw but only John knew. And no one was ever going to be allowed close enough to probe that darkness.

Monday squirmed upon the shining, woven gold, made uncomfortable by his remark. She could imagine the bishop's face all too clearly, and unlike John, could find no recourse to humour. It was almost sacrilege. But she knew better than to say anything. John's enjoyment of their lovemaking was intensely heightened by the piquancy of coupling on fabric intended for a bishop's robe, but for once he did not bring Monday with him and she was left stranded, half aroused, half nauseous.

The moment he withdrew with a heavy sigh of satisfaction, she closed her legs, and rolled off the measure of damask. Outside, the bells of Rouen cathedral chimed the hour of nones as the grey autumn afternoon drew towards dusk.

John turned his head on the pillow. 'By God's bones,' he said throatily, 'I think I will buy another two ells of that cloth, and next time we can send it to the Pope!'

It was too much. Monday raced from the bed to the garderobe, and was violently sick, retching again and again until her stomach ached beyond bearing.

'You don't like the idea?' John asked flippantly, but his eyes were narrowed. 'Or was our sport not to your taste, sweetheart?'

Monday staggered out of the garderobe and sat down weakly on the padded bench by the window embrasure. Not for anything would she approach the bed. 'No, John,' she said in a low voice, hating herself for lying. 'Not that . . . I am with child; three fluxes I have missed so far.'

He sat up. 'With child,' he repeated a trifle blankly. 'So soon?'

She nodded. 'It seems I quicken easily.'

'Stand up.'

Her legs would scarcely support her, but she did so.

'Turn around.'

There was a long silence while John perused her rounded curves. 'Well, well, well,' he said softly. 'I discovered you, Monday. Got you with child by Tuesday.'

She could not judge by his tone or the jest whether he was pleased or not, nor did she have the courage at the moment to ask him.

'Don't look so woebegone, it is not the end of the world.' He left the bed and came to where she stood. 'I'll take care of you, you know I will.' His arm curved around her shoulders, and his fingers spread their possessive grip on her upper arm.

Monday nodded. The damp from the river Seine pervaded the room despite the hangings and the warmth of a brazier. Her flesh stood up in tiny goosebumps, and strange, hot chills ran up and down her spine. The world swam out of focus.

As her weight sagged against him, John drew her to the cushioned bench, solicitously sat her down and fetched her sweetened wine with his own hands. He smoothed her brow and kissed her temple. 'Better?'

She managed a wan smile, to which John responded with a broad one of his own. 'Good. Wear your best gown to dinner, and all your jewels. I want you to shine among all the other women of the court.' His smile became an incorrigible, irreverent grin. 'Shine,' he repeated, 'like a madonna.'

Riding through the murk of a wet December afternoon, the drizzle insinuating itself between the various layers of padding to reach his skin, Alexander did not feel that he had been particularly blessed by fortune, although his mind kept telling his protesting body that William Marshal had done him a great honour in bestowing on him the custody of a small Welsh border keep some fifteen miles north of Chepstow.

The custody of Abermon was only temporary, until the Marshal appointed a permanent tenant, but nevertheless, to be given such responsibility, if only for a brief period, was proof of the value that Lord William set on him. Abermon might be small, but it guarded the approach to Chepstow from the north, standing as it did on the Monmouth road, close to the recent Cistercian foundation at Tintern.

The previous lord of Abermon had died childless, without any close relatives to claim the inheritance. Indeed, the only claimants were the Welsh from whom the lands had been taken a hundred years ago during the reign of the first Henry. There were raids and counter-raids, sporadic fighting and squabbles, interspersed by uneasy truces.

This was what he was doing today, patching up a truce. An English settler had accused his Welsh neighbours of stealing his sheep. The Welsh had denied it vociferously, blows had been exchanged and blood spilt. If this meeting failed, yet more would stain the soil.

The meeting-place was on open ground beside a huge granite boulder with smaller rocks clustered around it. Legend said that it was a burial cairn of the old ones. Its more prosaic function was as a border marker between Welsh and Norman territory, and the traditional site for settling disputes. Oaths sworn over its rough surface were as binding as oaths sworn in a church. If not by their honour, men were induced to keep their word for fear of what the supernatural would visit on them if they broke it.

Shivering, Alexander drew rein and blew on his frozen fingers. Behind him, the men of the garrison did the same. A flask of heavily sweetened mulberry wine was passed around. The fine drizzle blew into their faces, making a dull grey and tawny haze of their surroundings. Alexander had deliberately arrived early in order to gain control of the situation, but it made for a certain amount of discomfort.

'I don't see why the Welsh could not have come to Abermon,' grumbled one of the soldiers, hunching down into his cloak. 'It's the centre for justice in these parts.'

'Not the Welsh centre,' Alexander responded, narrowing his eyes into the rain as he thought he saw something. 'They have different codes.'

'Well, they should learn to live by ours in weather like this.'

Alexander glanced round at the man, a dour serjeant of about Hervi's age. 'It is not so long ago that the Norman baron William de Braose invited seven Welsh lords to a parley in his castle at Abergavenny, and murdered them all. Then he turned on their defenceless wives and children. How can they learn to live by our codes when they encounter treachery like that? You will oblige me by holding your peace during this parley. Even if you want to wield your sword through the depths of a freezing winter, I certainly do not.'

The man's lips tightened within his full blond beard, and although he argued no further, he rolled his eyes at his companions, seeking their silent support. Alexander knew that they thought him too young for the task, that the Marshal had erred in sending a beardless boy to perform the duties of a grown man. What they had not considered was the varied experience that had fitted Alexander for such a task.

Almost simultaneously, the Welsh arrived from their side of the border on their tough, small horses, their warband of a similar size to Alexander's troop, and the English accusers appeared from the village road with an escort of neighbours sporting pitchforks and billhooks. Inwardly, Alexander groaned. Outwardly he maintained a calm façade, and dismounting, deliberately unhitched his sword belt, wrapped it around the scabbard and handed it to the blond serjeant. 'Gerald, take the men back a hundred yards.'

'Sir?'

'You heard me.'

'Yes, sir.' With obvious reluctance, Gerald pulled back. The Welsh leader, Gwyn ap Owain, stared hard at Alexander, and after a hesitation, slid down from his horse and issued a terse command to his own warband. Here too there was consternation, before they reluctantly drew away to leave their leader standing alone. Ap Owain, however, retained the sword at his hip. The villagers held their ground. Alexander sought out the man who had made the original complaint, and whose son had been wounded during the ensuing fracas between English and Welsh.

'Come forward,' he beckoned. 'The rest of you have no business here, but you might as well stay to witness the parley. Throw down your weapons and go and wait with my men. There will be peace here, not more blood-letting.'

There was some muttering, but the dissent was quickly dealt with by threat of a hefty fine at the manor court. The neighbours withdrew, leaving father and son standing together, one glowering like a gargoyle, the other looking pale and sick, his wounded arm bound in a sling.

Gwyn ap Owain regarded the proceedings with mockery in his hazel eyes. 'I see the great William Marshal has sent a diplomat this time,' he said. He was a little older than Alexander, but still under thirty, with shaggy black hair and a full moustache.

'Would you rather we test each other's mettle with weapons?'

The Welshman shrugged and gestured over his shoulder at Alexander's men. 'That was a very fine sword you handed to your serjeant. Was it given to you at your knighting?'

'I fought to earn it,' Alexander replied. The question had not been as casual as it sounded. Gwyn ap Owain was insinuating that Alexander was a young Norman of privilege who had never had to struggle for life's advantages. 'I lost it once through folly and swore never again. It has been christened with blood, but I would not spill more without good reason.'

'I can give you one,' the villager interrupted indignantly. 'The bastards stole my sheep and sliced open my son's arm!'

'We stole not so much as a hank of wool!' ap Owain retorted.

'Hah, you Welsh, you would thieve your own grandmother's last breath!'

'And you would swear a lie on her soul!'

'Peace!' Alexander said sharply, making a chopping motion with his hand. 'I did not come here for the purpose of listening to insults. They have no part in a search for the truth.'

'A naive diplomat,' ap Owain said, breathing hard.

'Rather that than a fool,' Alexander answered steadily, and beckoned the youth to come forward. 'Now, tell your tale again.'

Brandishing his bandaged arm like a trophy, the young man repeated how he had been herding his father's surplus wethers to market when he had been set upon on a lonely stretch of road by Welsh raiders. The wound to his arm had been sustained during a brawl between factions of English and Welsh in Abermon itself, and the situation had escalated from there.

Alexander studied the lad's performance, noting that he spoke out boldly with many a gesture, but his eyes slid from direct contact, and his colour was high. 'Lord Gwyn?' Alexander turned to the Welshman.

'My men were nowhere near the place on that day.' Gwyn ap Owain snapped his fingers with contempt. 'If we wanted to go raiding, think you that we would pick off such small prey like common highway robbers? Why does he think it was us?' He swept his hand towards his warband. 'Would you like to identify them now, tell me which ones were absent from my winter hearth?'

'I didn't have time for a good look at their faces. I just knew they were yours,' the youth said sullenly, his eyes continuing to slip and avoid.

'Ah,' ap Owain mocked, 'so first you know, then you don't.'

'You are confusing the boy with your trickery!' the father cried, and shook his fist.

'On the contrary, he is the one who is confusing me! If he was robbed, it was by none of mine. Where is your proof, where are your witnesses?'

Alexander saw that there was no room for negotiation. Tempers were rising and nothing was being accomplished. As the lord of Abermon he was expected to arrive at a solution, either by diplomacy or force of arms. The former seemed ready to fail, and yet his instinct told him to trust the word of the Welshman above that of the villager's lad. Something here was rotten and he needed more time to find out what.

'I am not satisfied that I am hearing . . . all the facts.' He had been about to say 'truth' but managed to change it in time. 'I want to investigate this further, garner my own information. What say that we confirm a truce and meet at this place again in two weeks' time?'

'And it will drag out and drag on?' Lord Gwyn sneered.

'No, I promise you that . . . on my own soul, not my grandmother's.'

Lord Owain narrowed his eyes. 'In two weeks,' he repeated.

'It will give you time to prepare for war, if that be the outcome.'

The Welshman's mouth curved upwards beneath the thick moustache. 'And yourself also,' he said cynically.

'I do not want war. The lord Marshal gave me care of Abermon, and I am answerable for all my actions to him. Fomenting discord with my neighbours is unlikely to win me approval.'

'It will be interesting to see if your deeds match up to your words,' ap Owain said, and with a brusque nod, mounted his horse and returned to his men.

Alexander beckoned to his own soldiers, and turned to father and son who were standing in stunned silence. The youth was green around the gills. 'I will go to war if I must,' Alexander said, with a hard glance at the young man, 'but not on a pretext. The next two weeks will sort fact from fable.'

'You're here to protect us,' the old man spluttered, his indignation making him rash. 'I haven't sweated blood for sixty years to give my flocks to devil-damned Welshmen!'

Alexander mounted Samson and stared down from the satisfying height of the destrier's back. 'You tell me two things I already know,' he said coldly. 'Now I will tell you something that you seem not to have grasped. I am not a simple hired sword to cut to pieces anyone with whom you have a difference. I am William Marshal's representative, and as such, I will observe the code of justice.' He reined Samson about. 'Go back to your home,' he said with a piercing look. 'In two weeks you will have that justice, whatever the outcome.' Then, with a curt nod, he rode away, uncaring of the curses he knew were being aimed at his back. The lord, or his justiciar, was never popular at times of judgement.

It was full dark by the time he arrived at Abermon and the drizzle had turned to fine sleet. He ordered a bathtub to be prepared, and with a sigh of relief sank into the hot, fragrant water.

A maid brought him a cup of spiced wine. She was young and pretty with a plait of white-blonde hair and eyes as blue as hyssop flowers. Alexander had seen her about the keep before now; she was the daughter of the cook, and it seemed just recently that their paths had been crossing more often. She found tasks to do in his chamber, she brought him delicacies from the kitchen, filled his bathtub, presented him with spiced wine. He watched her now through half-open lids as she put fresh towels to warm and laid out his garments, jobs that a squire would normally have performed, but of course, Alexander did not have one. He thought that perhaps it was time he found a lad to train up. The girl, her name was Annis as he recalled, was tempting but he would be a fool to take up the offer in her eyes. His custody of Abermon was temporary and although the presence of a woman in his bed would have been a great pleasure and comfort, he had to be above reproach.

It was not just the fact of being above reproach to others. Ever since that fatal night when he had abandoned moral control to wine and lust, he had kept himself on a tight rein. Looking at Annis, he saw Monday, and his desire was curbed by feelings of guilt and self-disgust. It would be so easy; it had been so easy then.

'Leave me,' he commanded, as she approached him with one of the warmed towels. There was a delicate sheen of perspiration on her brow and upper lip, and a damp splash over one breast.

'My lord?' Her blue eyes widened in question and the pink lips parted softly.

'Leave me,' he repeated. 'I can do for myself.'

She stared at him with a slightly puzzled air. 'You do not want me to help you?'

'No.'

A hurt expression entered her eyes, and goaded Alexander to snap, 'Lord damn you, girl, just get out! I want to be by myself. Is that so hard to comprehend?'

Without a word, she put the towel on the nearest coffer and fled the room, probably to cry on the stairs, he thought with a spurt of irritation, directed both at himself and at her. He drank down the spiced wine, and leaning back, closed his eyes.

A half-waking dream came to him, of Monday walking across the chamber, her arms outstretched, her brown-bronze hair cloaking her shoulders. There was a smile on her lips and for-giveness in her eyes. In her arms she carried a huge leather-bound book, and as she reached him, she opened it and he saw page after page of magnificent illuminations of all the things that might have been. He reached out to touch the pic-tures, knowing that if he could do so, everything would be made right, but before his fingertips could connect, she snapped the book shut in front of his nose and he woke up.

The bathwater was lukewarm, his skin was cold, and the room was empty – desolate and devoid of colour.

The house was situated in the merchants' quarter of Rouen, not far from the river Seine, the city's main artery of wealth and commerce. It was built of stone, with a solid wooden door, and even boasted a tiled roof. Monday gazed around the main room, with its fine central hearth and trestle benches stacked neatly against the walls. The windows were glazed, another luxury. There was a large curtained-off store room, and a sleeping loft above.

'What do you think, sweetheart?' John asked with a pleased grin. He was wearing a tunic of mulberry-coloured wool, fur-edged against the winter cold, and a Phrygian cap was set at a rakish angle on his dark curls.

'It is very fine,' Monday said, turning to study the wall hangings and an attractive set of glazed cups on the sideboard.

John beckoned to one of the servants who had accompanied them, and bade him light the kindling in the hearth. 'I am glad you like it, because it is yours,' he said.

The flames licked and crackled around the dry twigs and a delicate twirl of almost invisible smoke drifted towards the louvre. 'Mine?' Monday said in wonder. 'Am I to live here?'

'Clever girl.'

More servants busied themselves setting up one of the trestle tables and spreading it with a fine linen cloth. Baskets of delectable food appeared, and a barrel of Burgundy wine. Monday's stomach growled with queasy hunger, and hearing it, John laughed and patted her belly. 'You've a glutton in there,' he said, and filching a fig sweetmeat from one of the bowls being set out, bit one half himself, and popped the other in her mouth.

He was preparing to set out on campaign against the French. Despite the fact that a truce had been declared, it was only loosely binding, and sporadic warfare with King Philip was an inevitable part of life. Pregnant as she was, and suffering with nausea and dizziness, Monday could not follow John from camp to camp as she had done before. Nor, with him absent, could she remain in the royal residence in Rouen. This house was the ideal solution. There would be a modicum of privacy, no more hastily covering herself with the bedsheet as servants and officials entered John's chamber at the wrong moment. Fewer censorious glances. The opportunity to breathe her own air and have time for Florian.

At the moment her son was playing on the stairs to the sleeping loft, bumping down them on his bottom one by one and singing a song to himself.

As John returned to her, she threw her arms enthusiastically around his neck, and kissed him. 'It's perfect. You're so good to me!'

He nuzzled his beard against her throat. 'You can show me your gratitude after we've eaten,' he murmured. 'Jesu, if I didn't need my strength, I would say be damned to the food, and dine on you instead.' His voice was hot with lust, and Monday laughed and nuzzled his beard.

Alexander rode into Lord Gwyn's village with a single attendant at his back and an escort of two Welsh spearmen who had met and challenged him on the forested road. Slushy snow lined the track, and the black tree branches wore bolsters of white, bowed down and heavy . The sky was murky, threatening another fall, but as yet it held off, gathering over the mountains.

Gwyn's village was about two-thirds the size of Abermon, and it had no castle, only a fortified hall, lying behind a wooden stockade. People ceased their business to watch him pass, women with their drop spindles in their hands, men at their winter mending.

Hastily summoned from his hall, lord Gwyn emerged to greet his visitors, fastening his cloak as he strode across the snowy ground.

'God's greeting,' he said, one eyebrow raised in speculation. 'You come a week early and to the wrong place for our tryst.'

'I have found out what I wanted to know. It seemed foolish to wait another sevenday when the matter can be settled now.'

'And it did not seem foolish to venture into my domain so

lightly guarded?' Gwyn asked, with a gesture at Alexander's attendant, the blond serjeant.

'No more so than continuing a feud that should never have begun.'

Gwyn snorted. 'It began the day that the first Norman set foot in Wales,' he said, but diminished the sting of the comment by turning and gesturing towards his hall. 'Come, since you are here, you might as well partake of my fire and my mead.'

Gwyn's mead was strong, and not as sweet as the stuff that Abermon's steward obtained from Monmouth, and it was flavoured with herbs rather than the stronger pungence of spices. Alexander sipped appreciatively, and accepted a cask to take back with him to Abermon.

'I am glad that you have come to me,' Gwyn said, 'for I would never have come to you.'

'Yes, I know.' Alexander gazed around the hall. For a Welshman, Gwyn was wealthy, but his roof was of thatch, not tile, and by Norman standards the hall was rustic and cramped. But then the Welsh deigned not to be judged by such standards. They were warrior farmers, a rural people who set small store by towns and rigid organisation.

'So, what facts did you discover?' Gwyn asked.

Alexander took another sip of the mead and set his glazed beaker aside. 'Some of your young men were absent from your hearth on the day of the attack. I do not know their names, or their physical identity, nor do I particularly want to, but they were in Abermon for the market.' He held up a forefinger to stop Gwyn from interrupting him. 'Well, not strictly for the market, but for the other attractions of market day. Dame Sahild not only brews very fine ale, she also keeps two very amiable serving wenches. If you investigate, you will find that certain of your young men are covering up for their companions who availed themselves of the serving girls on that day.'

Gwyn darted a glance around his hall, but although there were several people going about their business, their ears obviously out on stalks, no one met his eye. 'What are you saying?'

'That you have not been told the truth by your own men, as I have not been told by the village lad.' He shook his head. 'I haven't come here to accuse your people of the deed, far from it. Indeed, their debauched behaviour exonerates them. They could not have been responsible for stealing Godric's sheep, because they were abed with Dame Sahild's girls. The sheep were stolen by the lad himself. He sold them in Monmouth and concocted the tale to cover his deceit.' Alexander pulled a wry face. 'It is a family where small love is lost. The son grew tired of waiting his turn, and decided to take part of his share during the father's lifetime.'

Lord Gwyn drew a breath through his teeth and nodded with satisfaction. 'I knew that there was something amiss.' He looked thoughtfully at Alexander. 'Your predecessor would have kept such information close to his chest and probably even gone to war rather than admit his side at fault.'

Alexander shrugged and once more reached for his mead. 'I am not my predecessor. I hold Abermon in trust for my lord Marshal, and when I return it to him, it shall be in a better state than when I received it. Only then will I profit from my duty. These last five years I have seen plenty of war, have been both the besieger and the besieged. If it came to the test, I could probably outdo my predecessor on the battlefield too.'

'Is that a threat?' Gwyn asked with a speculative smile.

'Call it a friendly warning.' Alexander finished the mead and stood up.

Gwyn rose too, and walked with him out of the hall into the frozen winter light. 'A permanent truce,' he mused. 'I do not think I can give you my word on that; there will always be reasons for dispute, but for the moment, I am willing to abide by your request for peace. After all, friendly warnings should not be ignored – from either side – should they?' He extended his hand, and after a brief pause, Alexander shook upon it, knowing that they understood each other. Whether at peace or at war, respect would remain a constant between them.

Chapter 26

Rouen,
March 1199

'My brother,' John said through his teeth. 'A murrain on my chivalrous marvel of a brother. If I told what I knew of his vices, people would still rather believe his myth than my truth.' He prowled the bedchamber, restless as a caged beast. His right fist clutched a handsome silver goblet in which there was a generous measure of spiced wine. He took a marauding gulp.

Monday turned from the coffer where she had been kneeling to remove the new tunic she had sewn for John during his sojourn in the field. There had been no warning of his arrival, just the sudden whirlwind of his presence bursting through her door, demanding comfort and attention. That was how it was with him. Long absences, when only the material wealth of her surroundings kept her believing that she had a royal lover, then abrupt visitations, frantic and intense.

'You have quarrelled with Richard?' She made her voice soothing and sympathetic.

'No,' he said shortly. 'He has quarrelled with me. It seems that the word of Philip of France holds greater weight than mine.' He was brought up short by the cradle containing his infant son and namesake. Born at the beginning of February, the baby already had a fuzz of Angevin red hair, and the fine, milky skin that accompanied such colouring.

John crouched and extended a bejewelled forefinger. The baby clenched his tiny, starfish grip around it and made a mewing sound. John's tense features softened slightly. 'I couldn't have stayed at the palace tonight,' he said, his eyes on the child. 'All those faces staring, all wondering how much is true, whether I have reneged on my oath to Richard. Do they think I am stupid?'

'Is that what you are accused of, reneging on your oath?' Monday closed the coffer lid and put the new tunic and shirt down on the bed.

'It is what I *was* accused of,' he said. 'Philip showed Richard a letter he purported to have received from me, suggesting that I was willing to change my allegiance in return for certain concessions. Do you think I would be so foolish as to write such a thing?'

Mutely Monday shook her head.

'Hah, well Richard did. Hauled me up before him in public and demanded my balls on a platter.' Freeing his finger he stood up. 'It took two days and I wore my voice hoarse before he could be persuaded that I and not Philip Augustus was telling the truth. But do you know what hurts the most? The fact that he would think me stupid enough to jeopardise everything in a letter full of crude ambition. I do not deny that I covet what Richard possesses, but in the fullness of time I know it will be mine. My sainted brother is never going to beget a child . . . not unless it becomes possible for men to have babies!' His breath emerged on a short laugh of disparagement.

'But I thought that he had a child,' Monday queried. 'I remember hearing at court that he had laid claim to a son and called him Philip.'

'Begotten on a whore who used to dress up as a young squire and would bend over backwards for him, if you take my meaning,' John said, the savage grin still on his face. 'If he begot a child on her, it was a mistake. In the heat of the moment he chose the wrong hole. What's wrong, sweetheart, have I shocked you?'

Valiantly, Monday shook her head, knowing full well that an admission would only goad him into further outrageous sallies. 'I know your brother's preferences,' she said. 'Someone of my acquaintance once took his eye.'

'If Richard's eye was all he took, then he escaped lightly,' John retorted.

Not wanting to pursue that particular course, Monday steered the subject back to its original ground. 'So are you and your brother at odds, or have you made peace?'

John shrugged. 'Peace of a sort,' he replied with a frown. 'Philip hasn't driven a large enough wedge between us to make us enemies, but I don't much fancy Richard's company at the moment.' He sucked his cheeks. 'I thought I would pay a visit to my nephew Arthur in Brittany, see how much of a man the little turd is making.'

Monday nodded. Arthur was the son of John's deceased elder brother Geoffrey, and as such, also had a claim on the Angevin inheritance, some said a better claim than John. But he was only twelve years old to John's thirty-three, and rumour had it that he displayed little of the Angevin acumen and glamour. Richard kept him as a possible successor in order to goad John and ensure his loyalty. But John could only be goaded so far. 'Is that where you are bound now?'

''Well, yes, in the morning.'

Monday did not enquire if she was to travel with him too, did not even remind him of the possibility that she was now available to do so, being well recovered from the baby's birth. If she went with John, he would expect her to give up her children, farm them out on nurses and servants so that she had no distractions from pleasing him.

He tapped the cradle with his toe. 'Summon his nurse,' he commanded. 'He's a fine boy, but it is his mother I have come to visit. Hurry,' he added, draining the wine and reaching to the ornate belt on his long tunic. 'Tonight, I haven't the patience in my bones to wait.'

The mild spring weather in Rouen had hastened the trees into leaf, tender and rustling on the branches. Fruit blossom appeared overnight in delicate tints of pink and white. The meadows to the south of the city were a riot of colour, the yellow of cowslips and coltsfoot complimented by the dusky pink of clover and the first showing of tall white dog daisies. Along the riverside, the wharfs

were hectic with cargoes being loaded on to and disgorged from
a bewildering array of vessels, ranging from the smallest two-
oared rowing boat, to the largest deep-ocean cog. And because
Rouen was a port of such size and importance, every product
conceivable was available in the markets – from a silk purse to a
sow's ear.

Monday moved through the throng with her maid Ursula in
tow, and an escort of a broad-shouldered serjeant with a quar-
terstaff. Florian clutched her hand and stared around with
delighted eyes. At three years old, he considered himself quite
grown up, and even swaggered a little, showing off the short
wooden sword thrust through his leather belt. His mood was
sunny because he had his mother to himself. A nurse was looking after his baby brother John, who was too young to join in
this visit to the booths and stalls. Florian did not mind bringing
John home a soft leather ball or a rattle on a stick, indeed, he
quite looked forward to choosing a gift. What mattered was
the fact that the baby was at home, and he was abroad in the
world.

At a confectioner's booth Monday bought gingerbread for
everyone to eat as they walked, and a box of sugared plums for
later. Florian pounced upon the gingerbread as if he had been
starved for a sennight. She smiled indulgently, and nibbled at her
own, enjoying the spicy, honeyed flavour. It was good to be out in
the sunshine among the market crowds, with the security of coins
in her pouch and the knowledge that as the mistress of the Count
of Mortain, and the mother of his child, she could purchase
whatever she wanted.

The initial heat of lust between herself and John might have
cooled, but it had still burned brightly enough to bring him to
her bed on his way to visit his nephew Arthur. In the morning
before he left, he had given her a gold ring, and a mirror in a
small, exquisite ivory case. He had kissed her softly and he had
kissed her hard, his beard chafing her tender skin, and he had
promised to return from Brittany by way of Rouen.

At the cordwainers shop, she paused to order some new shoes
for herself, and to collect a pair of small calfskin ankle boots that
the craftsman had fashioned for Florian. The little boy was

captivated when he tried them on to make sure of the fit, for they were fastened with red glass toggles, attached to drawstrings of tablet-woven green silk. He performed a little dance, and posed with his wooden sword, showing off to the passers-by.

Laughing at his antics, Monday turned to the counter to choose a style herself from the samples that the cordwainer had to offer, finally settling for a comfortable ankle shoe, the plain shape enlivened by a latticework pattern of cut-out stars.

Coins changed hands. As the cordwainer stowed the money in his pouch, he gave her a speculative glance. 'Have you heard the news going about this morning, mistress?'

She shook her head, and tucked Florian's old shoes under her arm. They were too small for him now and scuffed, but there was still enough wear left for them to be useful to a child less fortunate.

'I heard that Richard Coeur de Lion has been injured besieging a castle down in the Limousin – it's a shoulder wound, and festering.'

'Who told you?'

'I heard it from a family friend who is a servant at the tower of Rouen. He says that William Marshal has newly arrived from Vaudreuil with the Archbishop and they have personal instructions from the lord Richard to take command of the treasury. Now, I'm a simple craftsman, my lady, but I am not stupid. An order like that to such great men can only mean that the wound is a serious one.'

Monday made the sign of the cross on her breast and murmured an automatic response, while her mind flew. If what the cordwainer said was true – and rumours always had to be treated with caution – then Richard was likely dying, which meant that either John or Arthur would be the next ruler of the vast Angevin empire. 'Are you sure?'

'Only of what I have been told, mistress, not of whether it be true or not,' he replied with caution. 'I thought you might have heard something yourself.'

'No, nothing,' she said distractedly, and turned away from the booth, grabbing Florian's hand in her free one. If the news had only just reached Rouen, it was impossible that John would be aware of his brother's injury. And it could be nothing more than wild rumour.

A group of riders trotted past her, travelling from the dockside in the direction of the tower. Florian leaped up and down, imitating the pace of the horses. 'Look, Mama, a real sword,' he said, pointing to the embellished scabbard of the last man in the line, who rode a glossy black stallion. A cloak of rich, dark-blue wool was pinned at one shoulder, and a Phrygian cap decorated with braid was tilted at a jaunty angle on his dark hair. A squire followed behind, leading a laden baggage horse.

'Yes, a real sword,' Monday murmured without really noticing. There was something familiar about the rider, but she was too busy mulling over what the cordwainer had said to pay much attention.

The horsemen were swallowed up by the market crowds. 'When can I have one?' Florian demanded wistfully.

'When you're older,' Monday answered, ruffling his hair, and gave his hand to her maid. 'Ursula, let Florian choose something for John and something for himself – not a sword, unless it be of wood! I have to go to the tower and find out if what we heard is true.'

'Yes, madam.' The maid looked slightly surprised, but quickly rallied, taking the old shoes that Monday thrust at her, and the handful of silver coins.

Her manservant in tow, more for reasons of propriety than any need for protection, Monday hurried towards the tower of Rouen standing tall and solid near the banks of the Seine. If William Marshal was in residence, then at the least she would be able to see one of his representatives and have the news either confirmed or denied.

The guards on duty challenged her briefly and then passed her through. She had been a guest at the tower sufficiently often for her face to be known, her relationship with Prince John common knowledge to the soldiers.

The courtyard was crowded with knights and serjeants, many of them wearing the Marshal green and yellow on their linen surcoats. She sent her manservant to ask among them for news, and went herself to the great hall.

On the threshold, she halted and stared around. There was no sign of William Marshal, but several of his officials were present. Recognising John of Erley and Henry FitzGerold, two of his closest knights, Monday started forward, but was jerked to an abrupt halt by a sudden tug on the hem of her gown. She turned in surprise and indignation. And then her eyes widened and the colour drained from her face.

'Your pardon, my lady, I was not looking where . . . Holy Christ, Monday!'

She and Alexander stared at each other in mutual shock. The accomplished knight and the lady in her fine gown, the stuff of which dreams had once been made and lives torn apart to obtain.

'Alexander,' she said in a faint voice. Her legs were weak, and her stomach queasy. She knew that she was not physically capable of flight. The most she could do was hold her ground.

'It is you!' he said, as if he could not believe the evidence of his own eyes. They flickered over her, from the embroidered wimple held in place by a silver circlet to the dainty shoes peeping out from beneath the hem of the gown he had just trodden upon. And then they returned to her face. 'God on the cross, tell me I am not dreaming!' He touched her silk sleeve as if to make sure she was real. 'Where did you go, where have you been?'

She shook her head and averted her eyes. 'I found somewhere safe,' she murmured.

'I would have looked after you.' There was pain in his voice. 'Couldn't you have said it to my face instead of leaving that note?'

She forced herself to meet his stare. 'I could, but you would have found a way of making me stay, and we would have finished by hating each other. Don't you see?'

'I see that while Hervi and I were worrying our consciences bare, you were doing very well for yourself.'

'Oh yes, you don't know how well!' she snapped, matching him tone for tone, and was appalled to find herself on the verge of tears. 'You only had your conscience to worry about, fortunate for you!' She swallowed in a vain attempt to remove the lump that was tightening in her throat. 'I have to go,' she said, and sidestepped.

He sidestepped with her. 'No, don't run away again, at least not without an explanation.'

She looked down at her sleeve, where his touch had now become a grip. 'I can do whatever I please,' she said.

'Jesu, Monday, I . . .' She saw his own throat work and swallow. 'Then, if it please you, I ask you to stay.'

A courtier's words, but they were not a courtier's eyes that looked at her and turned her legs and her will to water. She stopped resisting him, and let him draw her to a bench at the side of the hall. People eyed their progress, and there were several raised brows, including those of John of Erley and Henry FitzGerold.

Alexander dug his hands through his hair in a gesture that was all Hervi. 'I have a report to make to Lord William, but I promise to be as swift as I can.' He searched the room and pointed towards a fair-haired young man standing with a group of retainers near the door. 'My squire, Huw, if you should have need of anything.'

'I have not said that I will stay.'

'Then, will you?'

Her first instinct was to refuse, but she checked the impulse. She was no longer a simple tourney wench to vanish without trace. She was the mother of two children, with a high position in society, albeit an ambiguous one. Alexander could discover her occupation and her dwelling-place by the simplest of enquiries. So instead, she nodded, and said huskily, 'If you are quick, before I change my mind.'

'I'll try.' He hesitated. 'You do not know how many times I have wished that night undone,' he said. 'For what it is worth, I am sorry.'

'You should know what you are responsible for before you apologise,' Monday said, and gestured him away.

He frowned at that, but obeyed her gesture, and with a sidelong step and many glances over his shoulder, headed for the tower stairs.

Monday sat on the bench, her mind numb, her hands clammy. What was she going to tell him about Florian? How would he react to discovering that he had a small son, the knowledge of whose existence had been denied to him? What would he say when she told him the source of her fine garments and the reason for the deference and speculation in men's eyes?

'Mary mother,' she whispered to herself. 'Holy mother, help me.' At one point she sprang to her feet and took several paces across the hall, before she stopped herself, her hands clenching in her fine silk gown. Whether she stayed or left, it would make no difference. She had to face up to the storm. Suddenly the reason she had come here seemed paltry and trivial. Count of Mortain, King of England, ruler of Normandy, Anjou and Aquitaine, what did it matter?

Through her agitation, she became aware of a woman pushing her way through the crowd in the hall, elbowing aside the serjeants, the squires and officials as if they were of no consequence. Then she saw that the woman was in fact her maid, and that her face was wild and distraught.

'Mistress, mistress!' Ursula cried, wringing her hands. 'Master Florian's given me the slip. I've searched and searched but I don't know where he can be!'

'What?' Monday stared at her maid in horror.

'One moment he was holding my hand as good as gold while I spoke to the haberdasher's wife, the next he had vanished into the crowd!' She burst into noisy, hysterical sobbing.

Monday grabbed her arm and shook her vigorously. 'Stop that before I slap you!' she commanded. 'Weeping the roof around your ears will not find my son. You stupid, feckless girl, I suppose you were gossiping again!'

'I wasn't, madam, I swear it, on my soul I swear it!'

Somehow Monday restrained herself from assaulting the maid beyond a shaking. Recriminations were a waste of time and small use to a lost child. 'Well, search again,' she said urgently. 'He's only three years old, he can't have gone far!' Her own words, *only three years old*, rang a knell of panic in her ears. Dragging Ursula by the arm, she hurried towards the door.

Alexander's blond squire was standing right beside it, laughing at a jest told by one of the other young men. It was only because of his proximity that Monday spared the time to speak to him, and in a manner so brusque and to the point that it left the youth quite bewildered.

In the courtyard, she found her manservant enjoying a game of dice and a cup of wine with two foot soldiers. He was none too pleased at being plucked from such diversions, but when he heard the reason, irritation turned to anxiety.

'Now,' said Monday to her weeping maid, 'show me where you lost him.'

Alexander did not see William Marshal to make his report. He was greeted by Philip, one of the Marshal's clerks. As usual there were ink stains on the man's fingers and a spare quill tucked behind his ear.

'I will tell him you are here as soon as he opens the door,' Philip said in a voice incongruously deep for his slight, boyish build. 'For the nonce he is closeted with the Archbishop, and whatever news you have for him, I doubt it will match the gravity of King Richard's illness.'

'Richard is sick?' It was news to Alexander, who had literally just ridden into Rouen, and knew nothing of the happenings in the world beyond England and Wales.

'An arrow in the shoulder on campaign in Poitu. The wound festers and Lord William has been instructed to take over the tower of Rouen. Prince John is in Brittany at the court of the lord Arthur.' The little clerk flexed his stained fingers. 'I do not know which way to turn, my lord has kept me so busy writing writs and orders. If your hands want occupation whilst you wait . . .' He gestured towards two trestle benches where scribes were industriously at work.

'Later,' Alexander said, and touched Philip's arm to show that he was not rejecting him out of hand. 'If Lord William is so busy, my report can wait, but there is someone expecting me down in the hall.'

The clerk shrugged as if to say he had expected as much. 'You young men are all the same,' he said, from his vast experience of thirty years.

Alexander descended to the hall, his mind in a whirl. There were so many things to think about that he did not know where to begin. A mortally ill Richard would put a new spin on the political thread. There were few candidates for the succession and none of them possessing Richard's charisma and military acumen. John, or Arthur. Lord William would be supporting the former, of that Alexander was certain. The Marshal's loyalty to the house of Anjou was solid, and stemmed in a great part from his respect and affection for the dowager queen Eleanor, mother to John and Richard.

He arrived in the hall, his breath short as if he had just run up the stairs instead of down them. Richard, John and Arthur would have to wait. With eager, anxious eyes he scanned the hall, but there was no sign of a slender figure clad in dark-green silk. He swore beneath his breath, for he had been gone so short a time and he had thought that she would stay. There had been no time before, everything had happened so fast, but now he began to wonder what she had been doing at the tower. She had not been dressed like a servant, and the only women of rank to be seen were the wives and daughters of the nobility. Had she married during those years of silence, and if so, was her husband among these men in the hall? Perhaps he had been trespassing on forbidden ground. Perhaps many things, all questions and no answers. Then he saw his squire shouldering towards him with the swiftness of urgency.

'Huw, what is it?' His stomach lurched, for the youngster's expression was troubled.

'I was coming to find you, sir. A lady came up to me and said to tell you that she had to leave. Her young son has gone missing in the market crowds, and she is frantic for his safety.'

'Her son?' Alexander tried to remember if there had been a gold ring of possession on her heart finger.

Huw scratched his short, freckled nose. 'Yes, sir. She's only been gone a moment.' He looked over his shoulder as if still expecting to see the hem of her gown vanishing around the door-post. 'Sir . . .?'

Alexander thrust past him and strode towards the doorway. Huw deliberated a moment, then hastened after his master.

There was no sign of Monday in the bailey, and at first Alexander thought that he had lost her. An enquiry to a gate

guard, however, assured him that she was not far in front. He saw
the curiosity and speculation in the man's eyes, but did not stay
to satisfy it, or have his own satisfied.

'Huw, keep your eyes skinned; if you see her yell out,' he said
to the following squire.

'Yes, sir . . . Who is she?'

'She was a girl I knew named Monday de Cerizay. Who she is
now, I do not know.' Alexander narrowed his eyes the better to
search the throng of people entering and leaving the tower
precincts. The news about Richard Coeur de Lion had been like
a hot stick poked in a nest of ants. Every single one of Rouen's
citizens seemed to be abroad this noontide.

The Welsh squire fastened his gaze on the crowd. In the green
silences of his native forests, he had a keen eye, sharper by far
than his master's, but in the bustle and noise of a large market
town, it was Alexander who was more attuned, and caught the
flicker of dark green, the movement of a slender figure among
dozens of others, and pushed his way towards it.

'Monday . . . Monday!' He cried her name, and on his second
shout, she turned. He caught up with her, and touched her arm.
'Can I help?'

Her eyes were wide and frightened, the clear grey ringed with
white, and her chest rose and fell with the shallow speed of her
breathing. 'My son,' she said. 'He is little more than a baby, and
he is lost somewhere in this quarter of town. He could be stolen
away or end up dead in the gutter . . . there are so many dangers,
and he doesn't know any of them.' She caught her underlip
between her teeth, and chewed on it, striving for control.

'What does he look like, what is he wearing?'

She gave him a strange, sidelong look. 'He has dark hair and
eyes,' she said shakily. 'He is three years old and he is wearing a
green tunic, the same shade as my dress, brown leggings, new
boots with green drawstrings, and he has a toy wooden sword
with him. His name is Florian.'

Alexander nodded as he absorbed the information. 'And where
shall we bring him, if either Huw or myself should find the lad?'

Her hesitation was very brief, no more than the space of an
indrawn breath. 'There are five houses close to the west side of

the cathedral, facing towards the river. Mine is the first one. The walls are limewashed, the roof is tile. You will not miss it.' She swallowed with difficulty and touched her throat.

'I will search the booths where last I saw him. If you and your squire would hunt around the perimeter of the market and down . . . down by the river.' The last word conjured up such tragic images that she could scarcely bear to speak it.

'Of course.' He took her hand and briefly squeezed it in reassurance, at the same time glancing down. There was indeed no heart ring on her manicured white fingers, but a wealth in gold and jewels on every other. It meant nothing. Not all women wore their wedding rings on that finger, and whoever her provider was, he was certainly wealthy.

She pulled away from him, and melded into the crowds with her maid and her manservant.

'Did you hear that, Huw, a small boy wearing green and brown.'

'Yes, sir. Be like hunting a single tree in a whole forest,' the squire said dubiously, glancing around at a sea of muted colours, green and brown prevalent among them.

'You had better pray that this particular sapling is found unharmed,' Alexander said. 'I don't know the boy, but his mother means a lot to me, and I owe her a debt from long in the past. Come, you take the north side and down to the river. I'll take the south.'

Herluin made leather scabbards for swords and daggers. He had been a fully fledged craftsman since the age of nineteen, and had worked on this same stall in Rouen for twenty years. He was good at his craft, and he made a living secure enough to support a wife, three daughters and two apprentices.

Today, in the spring warmth, he was working on a hunting dagger for no less a person than William Malpalu, bailiff of Rouen. The damp leather was stretched on his working board, and Herluin was carefully impressing the outline pattern, of a hare and hounds chasing each other down the front of the scabbard, when he became aware that he had an audience.

'What are you doing?' asked the small boy.

Herluin showed him. He had patience and an affinity with children. It also never did any harm to be pleasant to a youngster whose father might be a customer or a potential customer. Eyeing his clothes, taking note of the confident attitude, Herluin judged him to be well born, of wealthy merchant stock or above.

'Could you make one for my sword?' Florian produced the wooden toy from his belt.

Herluin examined it gravely. 'Perhaps I could my young master, but it would cost money. Is your mother or your nurse hereabouts?'

Florian turned and stared around. He shook his head and gave a small shrug. 'Mama had to go somewhere,' he said. 'Ursula's talking to a friend, but I can't see her now.' His voice was totally calm, no sign of panic whatsoever. 'She gets lost sometimes.'

Herluin pursed his lips, considering. 'Best stay here with me until she finds herself, then,' he said, and taking the boy into his booth, gave him a date pastry to eat and some of the less dangerous tools to look at, his thimbles and stamps for embossing the leather, a blunt engraving tool, and small pots of vegetable dye to paint the imprint of the designs.

Still there was no sign of anyone claiming the boy. 'What's your name, lad?' Herluin asked.

'Florian,' said Florian through a mouthful of a second date pastry, crumbs on his lips and on Herluin's working trestle.

'Do you know where you live?'

The boy shrugged. 'Over there,' he said, wafting a vague hand in the direction of the cathedral. 'My brother stayed at home with the nurse, but he's only a baby. I got some new shoes today, look.' He waggled his feet at the scabbard-maker, deliberately making the glass beads bounce on the end of the green drawstrings.

'Fine, very fine indeed,' Herluin admired, and at the same time felt a spark of hope. He recognised the design of the shoes as belonging to Oswald, one of the cordwainers on the far side of the market. Green drawstrings and those particular glass toggles were his trademark. If the shoes had been bought today, then Oswald would know the customer. 'Come,' said Herluin to his small visitor, and swung him up in his meaty arms. 'That maid of yours has been lost for quite long enough. Let's see if we can find her.'

Calling to another trader to keep an eye on his stall, Herluin prepared to set out in the direction of Oswald's shop. He had barely taken a step outside his booth, however, when he saw the young man standing about ten yards away, unmoving in all the movement of the crowd, his hands resting on his belt, and his gaze doing all the walking, from face to face, halting and seeking, halting and seeking. He was well dressed, in a bright-brown tunic and costly blue mantle. There was a gilded sword belt at his hip and a fine scabbard held what appeared to be an expensive weapon. What made Herluin study him more closely, however, was the physical resemblance between him and the little boy. They had the same dark hair and shape of head, the same brow and eyes. And obviously the man was intently seeking something, or someone.

Herluin strode forward. 'You looking for this sprogling, master?' he queried.

The young man turned. He looked at Herluin, then at Florian, his gaze dropping to the new shoes. Then a smile lit in his eyes, and the tension left his mouth corners. 'Yes, I do believe I am, if his name is Florian,' he said.

Herluin frowned. 'You do not know him?'

'No. I am a friend of his mother's and I was helping her to search for the lad. She told me that he was wearing new shoes with green drawstrings, brown leggings and a green tunic.' He cocked his head on one side. 'And that he had a rather fine wooden sword.' The smile in his eyes now curved his lips and made the resemblance between himself and the little boy all the more startling.

Florian wriggled in Herluin's arms, demanding to be set down. Slightly puzzled, the sheather did so. 'I thought you were his father, you look like enough,' he said to Alexander.

'No, I . . .' Alexander began with a laugh of denial, then stopped. He crouched down to the little boy, who was looking at his sword with a definite spark of lust in his eyes. Their colour was a rich sable brown, far darker than Alexander's, but an exact match for the Byzantine lady Anna de Montroi. Was it possible?

A surge of shock washed through him. Three years old, Monday had said. His name was Florian, and St Florian's eve was at the beginning of May. Alexander counted nine months back from there.

'Dear Christ,' he murmured softly beneath his breath, and looked at the little boy with wonder and shock. Florian reached out a small hand to trace the design on Alexander's scabbard and touch the brass mountings. Alexander cleared his throat. 'Come,' he said. 'Time we found your mother.' He stood up and held out his hand. Without demur, Florian took it. He would go anywhere with a knight who wore a sword so beautiful at his side.

Alexander drew a coin from his pouch and gave it to the sheather for his trouble, thanking him for taking care of Florian. 'I couldn't let him wander. I've three children myself.' The craftsman shook his head. 'You surely look like father and son.'

Alexander smiled. 'There is a resemblance, isn't there?' he said, without confirming anything.

Leaving the booth, he found Huw, and told the squire to go and look for Monday. 'Tell her I've found him safe and sound, and that I have taken him home.'

'Yes, sir.' The squire gave him a questioning look.

Alexander's face tightened. 'Some things are better said in private than on a public street,' he said. 'Go on, be quick, spare his mother the worry.'

All the way back to the house, Florian chattered fifty to the dozen. About his sword, his new shoes, a neighbour's dog which had recently had a litter of pups.

'And you have a baby brother?' Alexander picked him up on an earlier remark.

Florian nodded solemnly. 'He doesn't do anything but drink and mess himself and sleep. Mama says that when he's older he'll be able to play with me.'

'What's your brother's name?'

'John,' Florian answered promptly. It was not a common name, but neither was it rare. Children born on the eve of St John were often christened thus, and since Florian had been given the name of his birth-saint, it was likely that John had been similarly named. There was no one of that title in Monday's family, as far as Alexander knew. He still had no idea whether she was married or not, whether Florian had a step-father, and he was loath to broach the subject without knowing how the boy would react.

The house which he found by a mingling of Monday's direc-tions and Florian's pointing was a handsome dwelling, similar to the one owned by his former amour, Sara, the merchant's widow. Its patch of garden, its orchard and small stable, the whitewashed stone walls and tiled roof spoke of comfort and wealth.

The door was opened by a plump woman clutching a frac-tious, tiny baby. She wore a plain linen apron over a homespun gown, and her broad face was creased with lines of anxiety. Her gaze left Alexander and dropped to Florian, who was pushing his way confidently past her into the house. Swiftly Alexander explained what had happened, and the creases of anxiety became an expression of relief.

'You had best come inside and wait for my lady then,' she said, standing aside to let him enter in Florian's wake.

A smell of simmering stew came from the cooking pot on the hearth, and there was a bowl of freshly cooked griddle cakes standing on the tiles at the side.

The baby laid over one shoulder, the woman offered him wine, pouring a measure from a handsome glazed flagon into a match-ing cup. Alexander took the beaker with thanks and studied Florian's brother. The hair was auburn, the eyes grey-blue, and the baby features nondescript. Whole brothers or half-brothers, they could have been either.

'Is Lady Monday's husband in Rouen?' he fished.

The maid gave him a look from the corner of her eye. She sat down, drawing the baby into her ample lap. 'On the threshold, you said that you were a friend of my lady's.'

'An old friend who has not seen her for a long time.'

'Then, sir, I think you should ask *her* what you want to know. I value my position in this household; and it is dependent on my discretion.'

What she did not say gave Alexander more food for

thought. Florian showed her his new shoes, and insisted on bringing out his favourite wooden jousting toy for Alexander. Two painted knights on horses assaulted each other with lances by means of pulleys behind the destriers' flowing carved tails. A wry smile on his face, Alexander allowed Florian to unhorse his knight.

Then the door opened and Monday burst into the house, her servants and Huw hard on her heels. She went straight to Florian, picked him up, swung him round, hugged him fiercely, and then delivered him the scolding of his small life.

'But I wasn't lost,' Florian protested indignantly.

'No one knew where you were,' Monday retorted. 'If you cannot obey the rules, then you will have to stay at home with John.'

'No.' The child thrust out a mutinous lower lip.

'Then next time you stay put.' Monday turned to Alexander, who had been watching the exchange with concealed amusement. 'I cannot thank you enough for finding him. God alone knows what might have happened. Where was he?'

Alexander told her. 'It's the warrior blood in him,' he added softly, and watched her face turn pink. His wine cup was empty, but he made no effort to leave. 'We need to talk,' he said.

Monday took him into the garden behind the house. A snow of pink and white blossom clouded the apple trees, and everywhere the eye sought, it feasted on greenery. Beyond the far wall, with its trellises of honeysuckle and dog rose, Rouen Cathedral pointed towards heaven, its bells clanging out the hour of nones, and joined by the distant chime of the other churches in the city. There was birdsong and peace.

Monday drew a deep breath of tranquillity, and turned to Alexander. 'I went to Lavoux,' she said, 'to Lady Aline; I knew that she would help me.'

Alexander wondered how he could have been so blind as not to consider Lavoux. From his own perspective he had been glad to leave the place and all its dark associations, but Monday had been content there, her position in the bower secure and responsible. 'Was my offer not good enough?' He knew it was a stupid question as soon as he asked it. Of course it wasn't. He could have given her nothing like this.

Monday sighed and began to walk along a path of stepping stones that led to a small arbour with a wooden bench and an overhang of climbing roses. 'I did not want to live from hand to mouth any more,' she said, 'or to be taken for granted by you and Hervi. Yes, you would have married me in good faith, but how long would it have lasted? How long before your eyes turned elsewhere?'

'I would have done my best,' he said, tight-lipped. Her words stung him with their truth, and his own mocked him. His best? She had reason to be wary of that.

'I know you would, but it would not have been enough.' She gave him a pensive look from beneath her brows as she sat down on the bench and tucked her skirts beneath her. 'I am sorry if you are angry, but that is how I saw matters at the time.'

'I'm not angry.' He sought for equilibrium, but it was difficult. He felt as if he were walking along a narrow ledge in a storm, with a sheer drop below. 'I'm tying not to be,' he amended wood-enly. 'So you went to Lavoux?'

She nodded. 'I didn't know I was carrying Florian then – how could I? By the time I did, I had reached the conclusion that I was right to leave the tourney road. I had a safe home in which to bear my child, and then to rear him.' She plucked one of the ten-der green shoots unfurling from the trellis and brushed it beneath her nose. 'I would not be without Florian,' she murmured. 'God knows, I love him dearly, but if I had the night of his conception to live over, I would be virgin still.'

Alexander swallowed. 'I have regretted that night too,' he said. 'Even at the time I knew it was wrong, but I did not have the will to stop myself. You were so . . .' He shook his head, struggling for words. 'I still think about you,' he said, and there was a lost note in his voice.

Her complexion grew pink and she bit her lip. 'It is in the past. I'm no longer the foolish girl you took on your pallet in the throes of drunken lust.'

He winced. 'I have changed too.' He leaned against the side of the trellis, knowing that to sit down at her side was too intimate a move. 'Older and wiser,' he said ruefully. 'It is probably of no interest to you whatsoever, but I have not bedded with another woman since that night.'

She raised her head, and he saw surprise in her grey eyes, and also incredulity.

'Not one,' he reiterated, 'neither in ditch nor feather bed.'

'As a penance?'

'In a way, I suppose. What happened that night . . . it made me stop and think – with my head instead of my loins. Was the pleasure worth the consequences? I decided it wasn't.'

'So, you're celibate?'

'For the moment, although it's not a binding vow, just a matter of choice.'

The difference in their states begged the next question. Monday's colour deepened and she shredded the plucked leaf on the edge of her manicured thumb nail.

'So,' Alexander gave her a searching look, 'how came you from Lavoux to Rouen? Does Florian have a wealthy stepfather?'

'No, not a stepfather.'

'So you are not wed?'

'Why not just ask me who owns this house, and whose baby lies in the cradle? It would be simpler.'

'Then who and whose?'

She smiled at him, but without humour or warmth. 'I am the mistress of Prince John, Count of Mortain, and imminent King of England, although you will find me in his accounts as a sempstress.'

Alexander took the news without expression, although his stomach had flipped over and a part of his mind was silently mouthing John's name in disbelief. John, who was famous for his lust, debauchery and casual cruelty. And yet it explained what she had been doing at the tower of Rouen and why people had deferred to her. It explained the fine clothes, the house and jewellery. It also warned him that he was treading on the territory of a man who could destroy him with a flick of his royal little finger. 'Are you content with him?' He could not prevent a surge of jealousy.

She spread her arms, exposing the deep, hanging sleeves of her gown, the yards of valuable silk that had gone into its making.

Gold bracelets gleamed on the long bones of her wrists. 'What do you think?'

He shrugged. 'That sometimes the wishing is better than the getting.'

She lowered her arms. 'Not for me.' There was a determined jut to her jaw. 'I know what you are thinking, but you are wrong. He is good to me, and what I give in return is but a small price to pay. There are those who look down their noses and call me whore. Well, so be it. At least I am in a better case than those poor women on the tourney circuit. And John wears fine, soft clothes, bathes himself often, and I find it no burden to lie with him. I know it is not forever, but for the nonce, it suits me well.'

Alexander had no reply to the challenge in her tone. She seemed to have weighed up the advantages and pitfalls of her position, and to have few if any qualms. She appeared harder, but then those who did not build a shell to protect themselves from the world were frequently crushed by it.

'Then I am pleased for you if you have what you want,' he said, but the words sounded cold and ungenerous on his tongue.

The patter of running footfalls and the barking of a dog heralded the sudden arrival of Florian, his small face flushed with triumph. A brown and white terrier with a stumpy tail and triangular, folded-over ears scampered at his side. The dog was making frantic leaps at a leather ball filling Florian's fist, and almost knocking the child over in its exuberance.

'Teasel wanted to play,' Florian explained.

Monday and Alexander exchanged glances in which there was a mutual glimmer of amusement.

'He told you, did he?' Monday asked.

'Yes. Hilda opened the door to let him out, and I came too.' Florian threw the ball and it bounced into the middle of a clump of sage. The terrier followed with a leap that flattened the tender leaves, and caused Monday to draw her breath through her teeth in dismay. Florian's eyes strayed once more to Alexander's scabbard.

'Are you staying?' the child asked.

'Not today, I have duties at the palace.' Alexander crouched to bring himself to the boy's level. His son. The sense of wondering tenderness engulfed him again.

The dog returned, slobbering over them with the retrieved ball. Alexander grasped the slimy object, and after a brief tussle, retrieved it from the dog's jaws and hurled it across the garden. It bounced off the wall into a pile of manure waiting to be dug in.

'But you'll come back?'

Again, Alexander and Monday exchanged glances. 'I hope so,' he said. 'But a good guest waits to be invited.'

Monday frowned, her gaze flickering between man and child. 'Then if your duties do not take you elsewhere, and mine do not call me, perhaps tomorrow you could dine with us,' she said awkwardly. 'And we can finish our talk.'

He could not prevent the rush of emotion showing in his face. Even though she said 'finish', she had not slammed the door in his face. 'I would be honoured,' he said, a tawny glow in his eyes.

Stinking to high heaven, the dog returned triumphant with the ball, bits of sticky dung and wet straw adhering to the leather. At the same time, Hilda waddled from the opposite direction, prepared to take Florian back indoors. The child clung to Alexander's tunic and thrust out his lower lip to do battle – with a tantrum if necessary.

'I'm sorry, my lady,' Hilda puffed, her vast bosom heaving. 'He gave me the slip.'

Monday held up her hand. 'It's all right, let him stay.'

The terrier bounced up to the nurse, his tail awag and his paws covered in dark-brown socks of muck. Hilda screeched and scooped herself backwards in a futile attempt to avoid the dog.

Alexander's mouth twitched. 'Until tomorrow,' he said, inclining his head to Monday. 'I'll send word by my squire if I am unable to come.' He took Florian by the hand. 'Are you going to see me on my way?'

The little boy nodded. 'Where do you live?'

'Nowhere at the moment.'

'Haven't you got a home?'

'Not like yours, no.'

'You can live with us if you want.'

Alexander bit the inside of his mouth. 'I think your mother would have something to say about that.'

'She'd let you.'

They had reached the street. Turning, Alexander gave Florian back into Monday's care. Her face was almost as red as the garnets inlaying the silver brooch at her throat.

'I think, on balance, he reminds me of Hervi,' Alexander said wryly.

CHAPTER 27

Soft spring rain pattered against the closed shutters as it had been doing all day. The streets of Rouen were sticky with mud and mire, although conditions were not as bad as the soups of winter. The smell of fresh growth, the promise of warmer seasons perfumed the wet air in recompense.

Within the house the scents were of smoke and cooking, of wine and garlic, fresh bread and simmering pottage. Monday had deliberated long about what to serve Alexander when he arrived to dine. Her first impulse had been to produce a formal feast such as the royal court was accustomed to eating on important days. Gildings, disguises, rich sauces and expensive spices; perhaps even gritty sweet loaf-sugar that came from exotic eastern lands and cost the earth. That impulse had fortunately been short-lived. A courtly feast would make no impression on Alexander, who was already aware of the source of her wealth and lived in a great household himself. Besides, she seldom dined ostentatiously, even when John came visiting. It would be out of character to do so now.

The same went for her clothes. She shunned the temptation to don her aquamarine silk, all shimmering with pearls and gold embroidery, and chose instead a simple gown of lavender wool that enhanced her grey eyes with blue lights. It was full in the skirt, the panels held flat at the hem with embroidery, the sleeves tight at the wrist. She tied a girdle of woven silver and lavender thread around her waist, and donned a short cream silk wimple, securing it with a fillet of lilac braid. Beneath it, she had plaited her hair for half its length, the other half waterfalling from the end of the silk binding. Monday knew that the style flattered her.

Although not the blonde so lauded in songs and romances, her bronze-brown hair was lustrous and thick. Once Alexander had held it to his face and . . . With a hiss of self-exasperation, she cast the thought from her mind. She could not afford to think in such a fashion. All they were going to do was talk.

Downstairs, Teasel began to yap. She heard a thump on the house door, the sound of the bolt being drawn, and then Alexander's voice speaking to the maid as she bade him enter. Florian's voice chimed too, squeaky with excitement. For an instant she was assaulted by blind panic, and thought about barring her bedchamber door and refusing to come out. The self-exasperation increased. She clucked her tongue against the roof of her mouth, shook her head at herself, and descended the open wooden stairs to greet her guest.

He stood just within the doorway, his cloak sparkling with jewels of rain as he gave it to Hilda. His lean frame was enhanced by a tunic of dark-green linen. Around his neck there was a simple silver cross on a leather cord. Unbuckling his scabbard, he leaned his sword against the closed door. Florian did not so much as eye Alexander's weapon, because his attention was all given to the miniature shield he was sliding on to his own left arm. It was a replica of the full-sized thing, with leather hand grips and an enamelled face. There was no device, but the background was parti-coloured blue and gold, the de Montroi colours.

'Look, Mama, look!' Florian danced from foot to foot in excitement. 'A shield, my own shield!'

'Let me see.' Monday stooped to examine and admire it.

'I hope you don't mind,' Alexander said. 'One of the garrison soldiers makes them to eke out his pay.'

She shook her head mutely. Her son's face was aglow. It would have been mean to object, and although the shield bore the de Montroi colours, it was not marked with the family device of three spearheads. There was no significance here except to herself. What did unsettle her was the thought that the gift was a form of claim on the child.

'I brought you something too,' he said as she straightened, and held out to her a small roll of stitched leather, about a handspan long.

She stared at it, then at him, but did not take it.

'It is nothing to which your . . . landlord could object,' he said, with a wry gesture, as if he had read her mind. 'Just a gift from a guest to his hostess in appreciation for his dinner. Please.'

Still unsure that she should, Monday accepted his gift, and unrolling the leather, found herself looking not at a piece of jewellery, as she had half expected, but at a wallet of expertly trimmed quills, the goose-feather shafts dyed green and red. It was a gift harking back to the days of friendship when there had been a pleasurable spark between them, not a conflagration.

'You do not know my landlord,' she said, but did not attempt to return the wallet to him; rather, her fingers closed upon it possessively. 'But thank you. I suppose such a present is appropriate if we are about to weave tales of our past years.'

He had watched her open the wallet with eagerness and tension in his eyes, and had only relaxed when her fingers had tightened and she had drawn the package closer to her body. Now his eyelids narrowed again. 'No tales,' he said, 'just the truth.'

Her pleasure at the quills was mirrored in his face when she placed a wooden bowl before him and filled it with pottage from the cauldron, together with a chunk of dark bread – the fare of the tourney field and the battle camp. Florian wrinkled his nose, refused the pottage with a firm shake of his head, and made do with a piece of the coarse bread smeared with honey, and then a small bowl of fruit compote.

'How much does John know?' Alexander queried some time later, when Florian had been indulged, played with, and finally carried off to bed with drooping lids.

'About what?' Monday poured the last of the wine into Alexander's cup, her cheeks slightly flushed. The associations of pottage and wine, evening and firelight, evoked potent memories, bittersweet and dangerous. Perhaps she ought to have made the meal more formal. 'He knows that Florian's father is a tourney knight, but not his identity; nor has he ever sought to be better informed.' She set the flagon down on the trestle, and frowned as she searched for the words to make him understand. 'John has a suspicious nature; he thinks everyone is waiting to thrust a knife in his back. He also needs to be the centre of attention; to be the only person that matters, and if he cannot make his audience love him, then he makes them obey through fear.' She looked across the table at Alexander, her grey eyes sombre. 'He would not want to know about you unless the tale brought you low, or cast slurs on your reputation. As it is, he will hear that I have had a male visitor, and his mood will not be of the best.' Her glance flickered towards Ursula, who was quietly tidying in the background.

Alexander lifted his cup and swirled the dark wine. He too looked at Ursula. 'And you will placate him?'

'Of course I will.'

His lip curled. 'I never imagined you as some man's puppet.'

'I'm not.' Her flush deepened. 'It is of my own choosing that I yield to him. As I told you, the price is small for what I receive in exchange.'

'Then if you are happy to pay it, who am I to interfere?' he said with a gesture of dismissal, but there was sarcasm in his tone. 'Obviously my price was too high.'

She clenched her fists in her lap and felt the bite of the gold rings upon her fingers, proclaiming John's payment. With an effort she kept her temper, her words emerging stiff with control. 'I don't want to quarrel.'

He set his cup down on the board with a small thud, and breathed out with a sigh. 'Neither do I,' he said, 'and after all, I was the one who said there should be truth, not tales. When I asked if John knew, I was not entirely referring to the times we shared on the tourney field and the child we got between us.'

'Then what else?'

'I wondered if you had told him who you were – that your grandfather is Thomas of Stafford?'

'Dear God, no!' This time she did not hold back. 'That would be like giving a lighted torch to a mischievous child. I have told him nothing about my past, save that my parents travelled the tourney road.'

He nodded agreement. 'As Stafford's granddaughter, many a baron would see you as a catch for his younger son. John is not known for keeping the faith. If he tires of you, he might well sell you to the highest bidder – perhaps your own grandfather, now that you are his sole descendant.'

Monday threw him a startled look. 'My grandfather has a son, I know he does.'

'Not any more. Gervais died childless two winters ago. Your grandfather has no immediate heir, and I know that he is interested in finding you.' He told her about his visit to Stafford when she first vanished, and then his talk at Chepstow with the sick Gervais FitzParnell. 'You have become a prize, Monday,' he said gravely, 'a rare prize, the heiress you dreamed of being.'

Monday was filled with nothing but dismay at his words. She borrowed his cup and tilted the wine to her lips, but its taste, sweet and rich on her tongue, brought no comfort. 'I should have stayed at Lavoux,' she said bleakly.

There was a silence, broken only by the crackle of the logs in the hearth and the whisper of the rain against the shutters. 'I am glad you did not,' Alexander said at length. 'I might never have seen you again, or our son . . . and that would have troubled me just as much.'

'You can make no claim on him,' she said, with a surge of panic.

'Not officially, no . . . unless of course you were to marry me.'

Her stomach plummeted, taking lungs and heart with it. She stared at him, mute with shock.

'But I won't ask, because last time you ran away faster than a scalded cat.' Rising to his feet, he went to the shutters, and released the catch.

The cool April night entered in, drawing layers of hearth smoke into the open air and washing the room with the perfumes of burgeoning spring. He leaned against the wall and gazed into the night, as if he could see through it. 'Besides,' he said to the rainy darkness, 'we are strangers now, and though I may be a knight in the service of the great William Marshal, I have no home to call my own. I could still offer you no better than the open road and a few months here and there in a castle while I played the role of temporary custodian. Not to mention what John would do to me,' he added ruefully.

She studied him, trying to see beyond the self-deprecating humour. 'Then why make mention of marriage at all?'

He shrugged. 'To say that I am here if you have need of me. That I would rather you sought me out than ran away again. That was why I gave you those quills – as a symbol, if you like.'

Monday gnawed her lower lip. 'I won't run away,' she said at length.

'You promise?' He glanced round, and she saw a flash of eagerness in his eyes before he quenched the look behind lowered lids.

'I promise,' she said, wondering if she was wise, but not having the heart, or indeed, the inclination to refuse. That flash of eagerness, fierce and bright, evoked powerful feelings and memories.

He nodded. 'Then that is as far as I will dare tonight.' His hand went to the plain silver cross on his breast, and moved it back and forth on its leather cord.

'What happened to your mother's cross?' she asked, to divert the conversation into less dangerous waters.

He looked down at the one in his hand, ran his thumb over it, then let it go. 'I lost that one to Eudo le Boucher the night that Hervi was wounded. We fought about what he had done, and I lost.'

'I'm sorry, I know what it meant to you.'

'At least I came away with my life. I haven't seen le Boucher since, but I have heard that he has joined the retinue of William de Braose – like master, like servant.' He pulled an eloquent face. 'De Braose would sell his own grandmother if he thought there was profit in it. I wear a plain cross to remind me not of what I lost, but why. Do you mind if I write to Hervi at Pont l'Arche, and tell him that you are found?'

'No, I . . .'

She stopped speaking as Alexander suddenly recoiled from the window, then just as suddenly leaned forward again, his eyebrows rising to meet his hairline. 'Huw?'

His squire appeared at the opening, his damp hair curling at his brow and his features taut with excitement and anxiety. 'I was on my way to the door, sir, but I saw the open shutters and you standing there. Lord William summons you back to the tower immediately. King Richard is dead, the news has just arrived, and Lord William is in need of messengers.'

'All right, Huw, go round to the door, I'll be there directly.'

'Sir.' The squire's face disappeared, and Alexander turned from the window.

'I heard,' Monday said, forestalling his need to speak. She was already on her feet and fetching his cloak, which had been put to dry near the fire. The news was not unexpected, but still it came as a shock to hear the words actually spoken, to know that her lover was now not just the heir to the Angevin empire, but its ruler.

Alexander took the cloak from her hands, and swinging it around his shoulders, secured the clasp.

'No peace for the wicked,' he said with a heartfelt sigh. 'I won't know my head from my heels for the next few days. At least we were able to talk first. I have to go. Thank you for tonight.' He took her hands, leaned over them and kissed her, one cheek then the other, but she could tell that his mind was already racing to the tune of his squire's news.

'God speed you, take care,' she said.

'God keep you.' He squeezed her hands, released them, and was gone into the rainy April night.

Monday closed the door after him, but she left the shutters wide, and for a long time remained beside them, staring out.

CHAPTER 28

LONDON,
MAY 1199

'To me, to me!' Alexander roared.

In response to his cry, a stout leather drinking flask sailed through the air and thumped down at his feet, showering his hose with mud and spattering his linen shirt. His tunic was heaped on the ground amidst a pile of other tunics, which made up the goalposts, and his sword belt was being watched over by someone's squire, excluded from the boisterous game by a twisted ankle.

The younger men of William Marshal's household had challenged the justiciar's knights to an impromptu, not to say rough game of football on a piece of greensward within the precincts of the Tower of London. The sport usually had much broader horizons than the field on which it was currently being played – an entire village street was not unusual – but the men were making do with what they had, including someone's water bottle in lieu of a ball.

Alexander headed up the field towards the pile of tunics, kicking the bottle along the side of his foot as he ran. A huge knight on the opposing team barged him from the side. Alexander chopped the bottle frantically towards Hugh of Sandford, and went down, the air tearing from his lungs. The man who had felled him whirled in pursuit of the ball. There were no rules except that it was not to be carried, and the only enforcement of this was force itself. The game was marginally less brutal than a tourney, but certainly not as courteous.

Although winded, Alexander rolled over and scrambled to his feet. If he stayed down, someone was quite likely to trample him.

A group of spectators had gathered to watch and shout ribald comments and encouragement, their faces alight. Alexander made a rude gesture at the former, and with his hand pressed to his ribs, made off after the elusive flask. There was a tussle going on to one side, a tangle of arms and legs thrusting, kicking and punching. Alexander hovered on the periphery, but did not attempt to enter the knot and was rewarded. There came a moment when everyone had hold of each other and not the leather bottle. Alexander shot in a deft foot, tripped a knight, hooked the bottle from under, and was away down the field.

'À Montroi!' a voice howled in triumph from the crowd, as Alexander hurtled the flask and himself past the tunics, thereby earning a point for his team, and temporary immunity for himself.

'Bastard!' one of the opposing team bellowed. Alexander took no umbrage, merely grinned and blotted his brow on his forearm. The pungent smell of sweat assaulted his nostrils, reminding him that he would have to bathe before he served Lord William in any official capacity. Not that Lord William needed him at the moment. He was attending on King John in the royal rooms at the tower, with all the other great magnates of the land, discussing the first policies of the reign which had begun yesterday with John's coronation at Westminster Abbey. Alexander knew that the brief respite, if such this hurly-burly could be called, would soon be replaced by more orders that would doubtless involve chasing hither and yon with writs and requests.

Picking up the flask, he trotted back to the agreed starting point, put it down, and gave it an almighty kick towards the tunics. All hell broke loose; there was a tun of wine riding on the outcome. Once more, as the game sallied up and down the field, the Montroi battle cry rang out from amongst the spectators. Alexander glanced, and saw a cowled figure leaning heavily on a stick.

'Hervi?' he mouthed incredulously. The flask slammed into

his ribs and he staggered as one of the opposing team knocked him down, took possession, and ran off.

'Hervi?' Alexander said again, and struggled back to his feet, the game forgotten.

'If you joust like you play football, then it's a wonder you're still alive,' his brother admonished, limping forward, but not too far, a weather eye cocked on the mayhem further down the field.

'What are you doing here?' Alexander demanded.

'Hah, watching you get flattened.'

'You know what I mean.' Alexander wiped his hands down his shirt and blotted his brow again. 'Did you get my letter?'

'What letter?'

Alexander gave up. Signalling that he was leaving the game, he collected his tunic from the goal pile and left the field to join his brother.

They embraced briefly. Hugging a monk in public was not particularly good for that monk's image. 'You haven't abandoned the cloister?' Alexander asked as he led Hervi to a bench beside a stone trough. Collaring someone's page who was standing among the watchers, he sent the boy to buy wine.

Hervi's eyes gleamed with amusement. 'Not in the way you're suggesting,' he said. His face was bright with health, and he had put back some of the flesh that illness had stripped. He eased himself down on to the bench, and propped his stick between his knees.

'In what way then . . . what are you doing in England?'

'As a matter of fact, I'm with Hubert Walter's household.' Hervi tucked a satisfied smile into the corners of his cheeks.

'The Archbishop of Canterbury?' Alexander's voice rose and almost squeaked. 'You are attached to the Archbishop of Canterbury?'

'Only in a very modest way, half by chance, half by my own endeavours.'

Alexander rubbed one hand over his face and wondered if he was dreaming. Last time he had visited his brother, Hervi had been striving to learn his Latin and perfecting the art of kneeling in church with the handicap of a wooden limb. Now, here he was, free of the cloister, brimming with life, and attached to the retinue of no less a man than the great Hubert Walter himself. 'Tell me,' he said.

The page arrived with the wine, and Alexander paid him half a penny and set the pitcher down on the bench. Hervi unhooked a drinking horn from his belt. 'When Richard died, there was a regular ants' nest of coming and going across his lands. Nearly every baron and prelate known to God must have stayed in our guest house by the time they buried him.' Hervi paused to take a deep drink of the wine, grimacing as he did so. 'I've tasted nothing so foul since I was forced to dine at Reginald's table,' he declared, and passed the horn to Alexander. 'Sour as cat-piss.'

Alexander stifled a grin. A monk Hervi might be and a member of Hubert Walter's retinue, but some things could not be changed. 'English wine always is.' Closing off his nose, he took several fast gulps because he was thirsty. 'You were saying?'

'Well,' Hervi scratched his tonsure, which gleamed with mild, freckled sunburn, 'Hubert Walter was in need of a chaplain to minister to the soldiers of his entourage – not the knights, you understand; they had their own, or were confessed by someone of their own rank, but the common men required a priest to whom they could relate – one who would accept their weaknesses, who knew their way of life.'

'And you were chosen?'

'No, I made them choose me; persuaded them that I was the man most suited for the task, and that even with one leg, I was the best they would ever find. Hubert Walter was convinced. He might be getting on in years, but he is still sharp as an awl.' Hervi shook his head. 'One moment I was mending a broken pair of shears, the next I was behind a curtain listening to the tale of some serjeant's night of debauchery with a friend and three young women.'

Alexander's mouth twitched. 'What sort of penance did you mete for that?'

'The usual,' Hervi said with nonchalance. 'Bread and water for a fortnight and a lecture about such sins not pleasing the eye of God.' His eyelids crinkled at the memory. 'I also told him that his male parts would shrivel and drop off if he persisted in lying with whores. I said I had seen such cases in the days before I became a monk, and advised him to wash his member in hot vinegar so as to prevent contracting crusader's pox.'

Alexander spluttered. 'Hot vinegar!'

'A sovereign remedy,' Hervi said, straight-faced.

'A sovereign penance too.' Alexander involuntarily shielded his genitals.

Despite the vileness of the wine, Hervi reclaimed his horn and poured another measure. 'So I'm with the Archbishop's household for the nonce, but in the fullness of time . . . well you know my plans for the future, and this is but a step closer to my goal.'

'You really are determined, aren't you?'

'It was reason for living among all too many reasons to die,' Hervi said, his gaze upon the players, skidding, thrashing, hurling themselves at life on two sound legs. He rested his horn upon his entire limb. 'You said you sent me a letter, but I must have gone by the time it arrived. Was it of importance?' He answered the question himself with a shrewd nod. 'It must have been, or you would have waited until our next meeting.'

The humour engendered by the tale of the poor serjeant's penance died from Alexander's eyes. 'I've found her, Hervi, I've found Monday.'

Hervi's face lit up. 'God praise you, lad, where?'

'In Rouen.' He told his brother about the chance encounter at the tower, and what had ensued from it. 'Christ, Hervi, I have a small son I cannot even acknowledge as mine because of her situation, and I dare not press my interest for fear of losing them both.'

Hervi's first delight was quenched, but a spark of optimism remained. 'At least she's alive and you know where she is,' he said. 'Time was when I thought you a deluded fool for insisting that she still lived. I was convinced that she was dead in a ditch. And your son does not want for anything.'

'Except a father,' Alexander said bitterly. He remembered the small hand curled trustingly in his, the wistful way that Florian had looked at his sword, the giggle as the little boy threw the ball for Teasel. And further back, he remembered his own father, huge and Viking-fair, leading him around the stable yard on his first pony. 'I have done what I can for the moment. I have to bide my time, but it's hard. I want her, Hervi, and I want my son.'

Hervi frowned and rubbed his habit where wood met flesh. 'Just be careful,' he said.

'I know what is at stake.'

'Your life if you fail.'

A commotion beyond the sward caused the brothers to glance up from their conversation in time to see the new king and a group of barons and bishops emerging through an entrance protected by a heavily studded oaken door. William Marshal and Hubert Walter were among them.

'I should be about my business.' Hervi attached the horn to his belt. 'And your lord will be needing you soon.'

Some women, gaudy as butterflies, drifted over to join the King's party. John paused to speak to one of them and touched her arm in an intimate gesture. She answered him and he threw back his head and laughed.

Alexander watched the interplay. The woman's gauzy wimple fluttered in the breeze and she raised her hand to hold it in place, her long blue sleeve knotted at the base and showing a flash of yellow lining. 'I can see why he left Monday in Rouen,' he said contemptuously.

Hervi levered himself to his feet. 'If only half his reputation is true, he's had more women than I've notched up paternosters,' he commented drily. 'Besides, you should give praise to God if his interest is waning.' He pointed suddenly with his stick. 'Isn't that Thomas of Stafford lurking at the back?'

Alexander's attention swept beyond John and the women to the magnates. Aside from the Marshal, Hubert Walter of Canterbury, and William de Braose, there were also the justiciar, FitzPeter, the young Ranulf of Chester, and beside him, the dour, white-haired figure of Thomas of Stafford. He was wearing his court robes – ankle-length wool in a shade of squirrel red with fur of the same colour at cuffs and hem. A habitual scowl dragged his features down. Alexander wondered if the old man had ever smiled in his life. 'Yes, that's Stafford,' he said, and could not prevent the hostility from entering his voice.

'If only he knew,' Hervi murmured, his eyes narrowed the better to focus.

'He would make Monday a pawn to his ambition. He's like an old spider crouching in his web. Better that the Stafford lands should go to Chester or Derby in the fullness of time.'

'But she is his granddaughter. It seems a pity that they cannot be reconciled,' said Hervi. 'I know he did great harm to her parents, but they harmed him too, and he is an old man now.'

'Not so old as to be in his dotage,' Alexander retorted. 'The way he treated his son when he was alive; the way he spoke to me when I went to Stafford in search of Monday, I doubt that she would gain anything but woe from the encounter.'

'But still, they are flesh and blood.'

'Jesu, Hervi, you *are* beginning to sound like a priest. Clemence was his flesh and blood too. It was more than pride that caused him to disown her. I hazard that he could even teach John about malice.'

Hervi shrugged, accepting, but not conceding the point. 'No one can be all shadow,' he said. 'There has to be light somewhere.'

Beside him, Alexander had gone rigid, his gaze not upon the baronial gathering, but on a soldier who had been beckoned to attend William de Braose. 'Then tell me, where is the light in him?' He stabbed a forefinger.

Once more, Hervi's eyes narrowed. The soldier was tall and powerful, topping de Braose himself, which was no mean feat. There was no mistaking le Boucher's scarred face, the deep eye sockets, the swagger. 'I don't know, but there must be a glimmer somewhere,' he muttered, his conviction suddenly weightless.

Le Boucher saluted his employer and turned away to whatever task he had been commanded to perform, his path taking him directly towards Hervi and Alexander. The moment came when the black eyes settled on the brothers and widened. Le Boucher checked briefly in mid-stride, then ploughed forward with renewed ferocity. At first it appeared that he was going to march on past, but at the last moment he stopped, and dug into the pouch on his belt.

'Alms for a cripple and a lack-wit,' he said, and tossed a coin into the horn cup secured at Hervi's waist.

Alexander clenched his fists, but managed to keep them at his sides. 'And bestowed by the damned,' he retorted.

Le Boucher gave a chequered grin. 'Then I'll meet you both in hell,' he sneered, and went on his way.

'Whoreson,' Alexander muttered through his teeth.

Hervi tipped the coin from his horn. 'A clipped penny,' he said, referring to the bevelling around the edge of the silver which had all been pared off, thus making the money useless. 'False coin. I take back what I said about light and shadow.' He flipped the penny over. 'As bad one side as the other.'

CHAPTER 29

'He's not well.' Monday laid her hand across the baby's brow and felt his heat burn her palm. He had been grisly for the past two days, and despite being dosed with feverfew tisanes and having prayers said over him, had grown worse, not better.

John glanced impatiently at the crying infant, obviously seeing him as an obstacle, not his flesh-and-blood son. 'Leave him,' he said with a shrug. 'Let the nurse earn her money for once. She does little enough but sit on her fat backside.' He raised his voice so that it would carry to the store room where Hilda had retreated at John's entrance.

Monday grimaced to herself. Since his return from England at the end of May, she had sensed a change in him. The mantle of power clothed his shoulders, and he had no time for the things of the past that had kept him from boredom while he waited to succeed, herself among them. She was no longer a novelty, and rumours of other women had become solid fact. 'I am his mother, I won't leave him.' It took all her courage to defy John; she knew just how brutal the lash of his tongue could be, but she would not leave the baby when he was so sick in order to attend the court because of her lover's whim.

John prowled around the room, twitching his shoulders with irritation at the lack of space, his dark eyes fixing with disparagement on the small tunic left on a chair, the napkins airing by the fire, the pile of dyed wool in the corner with a drop spindle on top. Domesticity in which he no longer had an interest. 'It won't make any difference whether you go or stay,' he said. 'Either the brat will improve, or he won't.'

'He's your son!' she cried, appalled at his callousness.

'And Richard was my brother,' John sneered, but he came to look down at the wailing, flushed child. His expression softened slightly as he touched one burning red cheek. 'Probably no more than a tooth coming through,' he dismissed, and unfastened his cloak. 'Very well, we'll stay here. Where's the other one?'

'Ursula's taken him out.' Monday swallowed as John lowered his hands to his belt buckle.

'Don't refuse me,' he warned in a voice all the more menacing for its softness. 'Where shall it be? Here in the straw, or up the stairs?' He glanced towards the loft.

Monday wondered why he was bothering when there were so many other women he could have; perfumed and pretty, without the complication of children at their skirts. Not for love, or even the greed of lust, she thought. They had last slept together in the week before he sailed to England, and he had been full of tension, wound as taut as a crossbow string. Then it had been for comfort and release. Now, something different bristled in the air. Hostility, contempt, covetousness. It was easier tonight to see the John who had commanded the beheading of Evreux's garrison than the John who had given her smouldering looks across a picnic field at Lavoux.

'John, I . . .'

'I what, cannot wait?'

The look in his eyes was merciless. She called Hilda to attend the baby, and on weak legs climbed the stairs to the sleeping loft. Suddenly, the price that she had told Alexander was only small seemed set to beggar her.

John was not gentle; he was rough, and he took his time, leaving her sore and humiliated, her breasts bruised, her neck covered in purple marks, and a welt on her collar bone where he had torn her chemise from her body. He had been violent in his lovemaking before, but only in play, never with direct intention to hurt. She faced the wall. Below, she could hear the baby crying, and Hilda's voice crooning as she tried to shush him.

John left the bed and slowly began to don his garments. 'I

hear that you had a visitor in April, one of William Marshal's knights, no less.' His tone was chillingly casual.

A cold shiver ran down Monday's spine. She had known that John would find out, she had even said calmly to Alexander that she would placate him, but now that the time had come, she had less confidence. 'We knew each other a long time ago,' she said. 'On the tourney circuit.'

'I don't pay you to entertain other men.'

'He wasn't "other men".' She rolled over to face him. Her bruises were beginning to smart and there was a dull ache in the pit of her belly where he had surged into her. 'Florian was lost; he found him and brought him home. When I invited him to dine, it was for the sake of old times, and dine is all we did.' She spoke evenly, and held his gaze with steadfast eyes, but her body was clenched so tight that she was trembling. 'Surely who- ever told you about my visitor also told you what passed between us?'

John sat down to attach his hose to his braies, his face inscrutable. 'He is the father of your child, is he not?'

Monday swallowed. She felt sick, as much for Alexander's sake as for her own. 'It was a long time ago,' she repeated. 'I did not think our paths would ever cross again.'

'But now they have, and it seems that you desire to renew your friendship.'

She remembered John once telling her that she could either be a victim or a pupil. At the moment, she was a victim, and he was making a meal of her, bloody of tooth and claw. 'Why should you object?' she asked. 'In your exchequer I am paid as a sempstress. I have kept my body for you alone; and I have never been unfaithful. Am I forbidden to have a life outside yours?'

His face darkened as she spoke, and his movements became jerky. 'Everything you have is at my whim, sweetheart. One com- mand from me and you face ruin. Another, and your friend will find his career curtailed.'

Monday forced herself to think, to use reason above fear and loathing. 'Where would be the profit in that?' she asked, and made a conscious effort to keep her voice gentle and unchallenging. 'I know you have the power to destroy us, but it would be like taking a siege engine to a house of straw, and for no better purpose than to prove you can do it because you are the King.'

John tugged on his tunic and said nothing, but she could almost see the thoughts mulling in his mind as he deliberated between being merciful and merciless.

'Because I am the King,' he repeated, and leaned over the bed to cup her face on his palm. 'You would be surprised what people try to wheedle out of me because I am the King.'

'Not me.'

He looked into her eyes, their faces so close that she could see the first grey hair glimmering in his black beard, and the slightly enlarged pores on the fleshy part of his nose. She wanted to recoil, but knew that if she flinched, she was lost.

'Well, my little sempstress,' he murmured, 'you shouldn't go sticking your needle into tender flesh, should you?' He claimed her lips in a brief but probing kiss, and then released her. Standing up, he removed a pouch from his belt and tossed it on the bed. It fell against her shin with a heavy jink of coin. 'For services rendered,' he said, and a look of distaste crossed his face as he took in the sight of the bruises he had inflicted in his anger and his passion. 'Have you salve for those marks?'

She nodded. 'In my coffer.'

He nodded too. 'Have a care how you spend your time, and with whom,' he said, and turned on his heel. At the door, he paused and looked over his shoulder. 'I will release you when *I* am ready.'

Monday lay in her bed until she heard the door thud shut. She felt terrible, nauseous, aching, wounded. *A small price to pay.* She thought of how foolishly she had raised her chin at Alexander. The pouch of coins lay on the bed like a manacle, chaining her to John. He would keep her out of spite, she knew; was quite capable as he said of ruining lives on a whim and with a single command.

Leaving the bed, she fetched the salve from her coffer. The smell of herbs and grease increased the feeling of nausea and she almost heaved. Lips compressed, she anointed her bruises, and put her garments back on.

As she was donning her wimple, the stairs thumped, and Florian burst into the room, full of chatter about his outing, and demanding that they buy a caged finch to hang in the window. Monday put him off with noncommittal murmurs, knowing full well that she could not bear to have such a symbol of imprisonment under their roof.

Ursula followed Florian into the room, and gave Monday the squares of vellum and the ink powder she had been sent out to purchase. 'Hilda's got the little one to sleep, mistress,' she announced cheerfully. Her eyes went to the disordered bed, and without being commanded, she moved to straighten the covers.

'Leave that,' Monday said sharply. She could imagine Ursula's gaze on the stained, damp bottom sheet. 'Come here.'

Looking puzzled, but not worried, the young woman did so. There was a fine silver brooch at the throat of her gown, a new silk girdle at her slim hips, and her veil was crowned with a pretty fillet of brass and pink silk. Expensive touches, beyond the means of a serving girl. 'Mistress?' she lisped through her slightly prominent front teeth.

'How much were you paid to spy on me?'

Ursula's pale complexion burned with colour and her cow-brown eyes grew wide. 'Mistress, I know not what you mean.'

'I think you know right well. My business is mine alone, and I will answer for it personally to Lord John without you carrying tales and making trouble. If I want to speak to a friend, or buy vellum and ink to write out a recipe, it concerns no one but myself.'

'Mistress, I wouldn't tell anyone your business!' The girl wrung her hands. One of them was adorned with a silver gimmal ring, bearing the motif of two clasped hands.

'No?' Monday nodded at the jewellery. 'Either money grows on trees, or you have a fond admirer.'

It seemed impossible that Ursula could redden any further, but she did, and covered the ring with her other hand.

'Who is he?' Monday asked wearily.

'I haven't told him anything, mistress, I swear. He works with the King's hounds, breeding them. He says that when he has enough put by we can get married. There's no harm in him, mistress, I swear it. We met him today in the marketplace, and he promised Master Florian a greyhound pup!'

'And you told him that you were buying vellum and ink for your mistress?'

Ursula looked at the floor.

'And next time you see him, you will tell him that you came home to find the bed all unmade and your mistress with lover's bruises on her throat? Then he will laugh and give you another present and a promise and a kiss to keep you sweet. Oh Ursula, you goose!' Monday's mood was now tinged with more irritation than anger. 'Did you never stop to think that he was sweetening details out of you?'

'He loves me, he's not a spy!' Ursula said desperately, and her lower lip trembled, her eyes sparkling on the verge of tears.

Monday sighed and handed the girl the pouch of money that John had given to her. 'Take this,' she said, 'and go. If your swain still wants you, I will personally provide your dowry. If he suddenly seems less interested, then I will secure you a post in another household. But as from now, I do not want you in mine.'

The girl started to weep. Monday felt like a shrew, but she stood her ground. It was not as though she was casting Ursula out on her ear in nothing but the clothes she wore. Even so, it was on the tip of her tongue to relent, to fold the maid in her arms and forgive. Firmly throttling the impulse, she said, 'Collect your things and go,' and with tight lips, turned away, taking Florian in her arms instead.

Still crying, Ursula fled the room. The girl was hurt, and probably full of righteous anger that her employer could so malign her man, but Monday thought sadly that the hurt was soon going to seem as nothing compared to the raw pain of having love's dazzle stripped from her eyes. She kissed Florian's dark curls and with a sigh, set him down. A dull ache pounded at her temples, but she knew that lying down would be fruitless; sleep would never come, and her cares would only turn over and over in her mind, and grow out of all proportion until they smothered her.

With a sigh, she went downstairs to check upon the baby, saw that although restless he was at least sleeping and seemed less flushed than before. She fended off Hilda's enquiries about Ursula, and the veiled grumbles about John, and retired again to the haven of her upper chamber. The vellum and pouch of powdered ink lay on the bed. Monday took Alexander's wallet of quills from the coffer, and within a candle notch was seated by the window, the detached top of a three-legged stool for a rest, the ink mixed, and guidelines pricked out on one of the vellum sheets. She toyed with the green feathering on the quill in her hand, her eyes narrowed in thought. And finally, slowly, her tongue peeping between her teeth, she began to write.

'A letter,' said Isabelle of Pembroke, frank curiosity in her green eyes. 'Usually you are busy delivering them to other people.'

Alexander smiled at the Marshal's wife as she handed him a package. He was seated in the great hall of the Marshal keep at Orbec, taking a brief respite, having arrived with messages from Lord William to his wife and his constable late the previous evening. Now it was shortly after dawn, and the members of the Marshal household were breaking their fast on bread, cheese and buttermilk.

'A Rouen merchant brought it here three days ago,' Isabelle added. 'There is no identifying device on the seal, but I thought it might be from your brother.'

'No, Hervi's in England,' Alexander said, and turned the packet over, his hands suddenly clammy with anticipation. 'There is someone I know in Rouen. My lady, I beg you to excuse me.'

Lady Marshal raised her brows, but inclined her head and let him go. She knew full well that the someone in Rouen was one of the King's mistresses. William had told her as much one night in bed when they had been discussing plans for Alexander's future career and she had remarked that he seemed little interested in women.

'Even the quietest water has rocks beneath the surface,' William had said. 'And Alexander has been far from quiet in the past.' And he had told her about the young knight's former life, and how it meshed with that of John's mistress. 'It's not that he has no interest in women, but that he cannot have the one he wants.'

Isabelle looked thoughtfully at the young man striding out of the hall. William was probably right about the rocks beneath the surface.

Alexander took the letter to a quiet corner of the courtyard and sat down on a barrel to break the seal and unfold the contents. The writing was large, the letters inexpertly formed, and the spelling somewhat arbitrary. Here and there the vellum was very thin where mistakes had been rubbed away with a pumice stone, and elsewhere blots and spatters decorated the words. 'Oh, Monday,' he said with a shake of his head and a poignant smile on his lips.

By the time the size of the writing had been taken into account, the contents of the letter were not large, and as he pored his way through it, the smile left his face. She told him that she was well, that Florian was thriving, and that the baby had a fever but seemed to be recovering. Then added:

My lord was wrath that you had been to visit me. I told him nothing, but my maid has a loose tongue, and he knows everything. I beg you to be careful and maintain your discretion, for he gave me to know how easily he could destroy us both. For the moment he is soothed, but we dare not meet again for the nonce, even in friendship.
   I give you farewell now,
   M.

She signed the letter with a flourished initial capital, as she had done before, when she had run from him. Alexander swore between his teeth. If John had appeared in the courtyard then, king or no king, he would have taken his sword and run him through. He was tempted to rip the vellum across and across, but he forced himself to fold it up and place it in his pouch. He should have expected no less. At least she had taken the time and the risk to write to him. At least he had her letter, and although it brought no joy, there was a painful comfort in knowing that her hand had formed the words, and that she had used the quills he had given her.

From the courtyard, he went to the tilting ground and spent an hour with lance and shield, jousting at the quintain, pretending that the battered shield was John's heart until his frustration eased. For the nonce meant for the moment, not forever.

CHAPTER 30

August sweltered through Rouen like a hot sword blade. Wooden roof shingles warped and cracked, and the threat of fire was a constant anxiety. Everyone kept buckets of water to hand, dipped from the tidal river Seine, and woodwork was sluiced in an effort to limit the damage from the clear, burning air. Sickness simmered in the midden heaps and refuse ditches, and was borne on iridescent insect wings to the population. The old, the young and the vulnerable succumbed and died, as they did every year during the hottest and coldest seasons.

One of the victims was Monday's youngest son, in the first week of the severe heat.

The mild fever that had been bedevilling him over the past two months had worsened. This time there was vomiting and purging too. Within a day and night of the onset, he was dead, his small, moistureless body lying still as a doll in his cradle. Monday had small time to grieve, for the rest of the household was stricken too. So great was her fear that Florian would be taken from her as well that she had no time to fret about the baby's death, and when it was clear that Florian would survive, her own body succumbed.

By a supreme effort of will, she dragged herself from her bed to see her infant son buried in the precincts of the cathedral, but as the soil was cast down upon the tiny shrouded body, she collapsed, and had to be borne home incoherent with fever and hysteria. In the evening, the cramps started and she began to bleed.

*

In the palace of Rouen, Alexander sat over a game of merels with Walter, one of the Marshal's chamberlains, or former chamberlains as of three days past. He was almost sixty years old, and even in fine weather such as this walked with a rheumatic limp. He had chosen to retire rather than die in harness, and was on his way home to his native Wiltshire. Alexander was in Rouen, overseeing the purchase and transport of wine, linen and wool for Lady Isabelle at Orbec. Once her steward had purchased the goods to his satisfaction, they had to be brought to their destination under armed escort. The Marshal himself was in the southern provinces with the King, but before he left had hinted that he might have another duty for Alexander as a custodian. It was no use asking Walter if he knew anything. The old man was used to warding off all enquiries, no matter how cunningly phrased.

'Your move,' Alexander said.

'I know, I know.' Walter rubbed his hands together and pondered the board with watery blue eyes. '*Vincit qui patitur*, young man.' Walter had a tendency to quote Latin when he wanted to put the Marshal's knights in their place. Some but few were literate, and their grasp of Latin almost non-existent.

Alexander smiled. Walter had just told him that patience would win. '*Satis verborum*,' he retorted. '*Adduces fortuna iuvat*,' and his smile became a grin as Walter's jaw dropped 'Go on. Enough talk. Fortune favours the bold.'

The old man gave Alexander a hard look. 'And those who are too bold find themselves cut to pieces on a battlefield,' he growled, and refused to be hurried, finally making a solid, conservative move. 'Where did you learn to speak Latin?'

'In a monastery, where else?' Alexander said with a shrug, and although he spoke defensively, the familiar shudder of dread was absent. Cranwell was beginning to fade in his memory as time thickened the skin over the scars. 'I read and write it too . . . and fight with it if I must,' he added, making a bold play with one of his own pieces.

Walter eyed him suspiciously, the way he might a docile hearth hound that suddenly turned out to be part wolf.

Alexander grinned amiably. He enjoyed sparring with Walter. Besides, there was little else to do. He could have made his way to one of the dockside taverns and filled his belly with mediocre wine at an exorbitant price, and then risked being robbed on the way home, or suffering a debilitating headache the next day when he needed his wits about him. He could have strolled the streets and taken in the sights and sounds of the great port, but they were familiar to him now, and the sights and sound were also accompanied by the stinks of high summer. He could have walked to a certain house beyond the cathedral and knocked upon the door in the purple dusk. The thought gnawed away at the back of his mind. She had bade him keep his distance, but it was hard to be so close, and yet so far. He might still leave the merels board and Walter's crusty company. *Adduces fortuna iuvat*. His gaze wandered to his cloak where it lay over a stool, his saddlebag beside it. Surely, if he were to knock, she would not deny him entry?

'Your move,' Walter said, and waved a chunky hand back and forth in front of Alexander's eyes. 'Unless, of course, you want to concede the game?'

'You think me so lacking in stamina?' Alexander retorted. Tomorrow he would go, tomorrow while the steward was concluding his purchases. Broad daylight would ensure that there was no outrage to propriety. He picked up one of the bone counters, but never made his play, for just then another of the Marshal's men, Thomas of Rochford, entered the hall. He was travelling to England in Walter's company, and had gone out into the city earlier in search of a farrier for his horse. Now he strode up to them, his fair hair windblown, and news bursting on his lips.

Clapping Alexander on the shoulder, he leaned over the game. 'Guess what I just heard in the city?'

'Scandal and gossip, if business goes forth as usual,' Walter grunted. 'Go on, what?'

'You're not wrong; it is scandal and gossip,' the knight said, relishing the moment. 'No less than that King John has taken a bride. Wedded and bedded within days of their first meeting, so I heard.'

'A bride?' Alexander repeated, and set the merels piece haphazardly down.

Thomas nodded. 'The daughter and sole heiress of Aymer of Angoulême. Her name's Isobel, and she's reputedly a beauty. John's as hot for her as the fires of hell.'

'He was bound to wed sooner or later,' Walter said, his own eyes barely lighting up at the news. 'I see no scandal.'

'What about the fact that she's only twelve years old?'

'It is the age of consent, is it not?'

'Well, yes, but most men wait if they take a girl of that age to their bed. Mind you, John likes them young and innocent; the fresher the better. I . . . Where are you off?'

Alexander had surged to his feet and was reaching for his cloak. 'An errand, someone I have to see.'

Walter stared at him blankly. 'You haven't finished your game,' he said.

'Thomas will take my place.'

Thomas raised his eyebrows, but sat down on Alexander's stool. 'You owe me for this,' he said.

But Alexander scarcely heard him and gave only a distracted nod in reply, his mind already far along the road that his feet were taking.

Two strands of thought turned and tangled in his mind. The first, an instinctive reaction to Thomas's news of John's marriage, was that now he could have Monday. If John was indeed as hot as the fires of hell for his bride, then his interest in his mistress would surely wane. The second was that he ought to tell Monday the news before she heard it from some street vendor. John was her provider; she had shared his bed and borne his child. Surely not all for the sake of profit?

Uncaring now if he was seen or not, Alexander strode through the streets and alleys of Rouen. The afterlight of dusk banded the western horizon with indigo, scarlet and pale green, but over the cathedral, the sky was the luminous deep blue of night, the first stars pricking out. Candle flame and the light from rush tapers gleamed through cracks in house doors, and the smell of cooking fires was pungent on the air. Light and drunken laughter spilled from a tavern, and two drunks staggered on to the street, arms around each other. Alexander skipped to avoid them, his heart hammering against his ribs, and his mind filled with a single purpose – Monday.

Her house was silent, the shutters closed, and for no reason that he could fathom, except his nervous anticipation, a shudder of unease rippled down his spine. He raised his fist and banged on the door. A dog growled, then began to bark sharply, and was silenced with a sharp word. Then Alexander heard a slow shuffling and laboured breathing. 'Who's there?' the nurse's voice demanded, a quaver to its edge.

'It is Alexander de Montroi – I dined here in the spring, do you remember? I have to see your mistress on a matter most urgent.'

'She is sleeping, master,' the woman answered through the wood. 'Best if you come back tomorrow.'

'Sleeping at dusk? Is something the matter?' The feeling of unease increased. 'I need to see her now.'

The nurse did not reply, but he heard her stertorous breathing, and knew that she was wondering whether to let him in or keep him shut out. He could also hear the dog moving back and forth against the door and whining.

'I have to be on the road tomorrow,' he said, which was not quite the truth, but close enough. 'What else would bring me here from the palace with dark falling?'

The breathing silence lingered, and then with a rush of relief and anxiety, he heard the bar being drawn. The door opened and Hilda's face peered out at him through the crack. Her flesh hung in wasted folds on her bones, and her eyes were smudged, as if with recent weeping. Last time Alexander had set eyes on her, he had assessed her to be a little over thirty. Now she looked almost twice that age.

'You have come from the palace?' There was fear in her eyes.

'Of my own accord; no one has sent me.'

She opened the door wider and gestured for him to enter. The dog sniffed his legs, the exciting scents on his cloak, and vigorously wagged its stump of a tail. Alexander fussed the animal without paying it much attention, while the woman reset the bar across the door.

Two candles burned on a spike in the corner, illuminating a wooden image of the Virgin Mary. The fire glowed in the hearth, and a jug of wine and herbs was simmering on one of the tiles. Against the wall, Florian was sound asleep in his truckle bed. Alexander went to the boy and stooped to look at him. The black hair, slightly damp with sweat, clung to Florian's brow and his cheeks were flushed, but his breathing was slow and even. One hand was curled around a scrap of yellow woollen blanket. There was no sign of Monday or the baby, so he assumed they were sleeping upstairs.

'We have all been sick,' Hilda said before he could ask. 'Terribly sick with the flux.' She pressed her hand to her belly as if to emphasise the point. 'I never want gripes like them again, so help me Jesu. None of us is right even now. My lady, she went to bed an hour since. I made some spiced wine in case she came down, but she hasn't.' The woman shook her head and sucked on her trembling lower lip. 'We buried the little one today, you see. She ought not to be alone.' Tears filled her eyes.

'The little one?' Alexander repeated, and stared at Hilda in shock. 'The baby, you mean, the baby is dead?'

She gave a wordless nod and wiped her eyes on her sleeve. 'He was too small, not strong enough.'

Alexander crossed his breast, half turning to the statue of the Virgin as he did so. 'God rest his soul,' he muttered, appalled, and at the same time thanking Christ that Florian had been spared. He wondered if John would grieve to know. John who was occupied in Angoulême with his twelve-year-old bride, still a baby herself. Bile rose in his throat. Monday had no one to comfort her in her grief, only the nursemaid, who was obviously sick and struggling to cope.

'Has she sent word to the King?' he asked.

Hilda shook her head. 'I do not think so, sir. She did say that she would write as soon as she felt well enough.' Sniffing, blinking through her tears, she wrapped a cloth around her hand and lifted the wine jug off the hearth to pour him a cup.

He took the steaming, fragrant drink in his hand, but instead of putting it to his lips, went to the stairs. 'You're right,' he said. 'She should not be alone.'

'But, sir, it isn't prop—' Hilda began to say, then compressed her lips, wringing her hands in her gown. The dog whisked past him with a muscular thrust of its small body and clattered up the stairs, through the curtain and into the bedchamber. Steadying himself and stifling a curse, Alexander followed the animal through the heavy drape of wool across the archway.

Monday was standing in the middle of the floor, barefoot in her chemise, which reached to the middle of her shins. The fastening was unlaced, the cords hanging amidst her loosened glossy braids. But none of this fixed his attention, for he was staring at the blood that had soaked through her chemise at her crotch and thighs. The dog was snuffling there now, drawn by the odour.

'Holy Christ, Monday,' Alexander said hoarsely, and putting the cup down, started forward.

Her face was ice white, her eyes huge with fear and pain. 'Help me,' she whispered, her hand outstretched.

He caught it in his, and felt the clamminess of her skin. 'How?' he demanded with fear of his own. 'What do you want me to do?'

She gripped his sleeve and her voice was breathy and shallow with pain. 'Tell Hilda, fetch a midwife, I am losing the baby. I thought if I lay down it would stop . . . but it hasn't.'

'Losing the baby?' he repeated blankly. 'You are with child?' Even as the question left his lips, he realised how foolish it was. Ignorant though he was of women's matters, he knew that in any sort of childbirth, early or late, there was blood. Sometimes too much blood. He thought of Monday's mother, and was filled with fear.

'Almost four months,' she said, and clung to him with a little mew of pain, while more blood soaked through her chemise and sweat beaded her brow. 'I don't want to die,' she whispered, and as the contraction eased, looked up into his face. 'I keep remembering my mother . . .'

It was as if she had plucked the thought out of his mind, and it unnerved him beyond fear into anger. 'Christ, Monday, don't talk like that. Your mother died because the child was lying sideways and couldn't be born. Of course you're not going to die.' He lifted her in his arms and bore her back to the bed. The sheets

were all bloody too, but that could not be helped. For the
moment he had to find someone competent to help her.
Remembering how wounds were dealt with on the battlefield, he
seized the pillows and placed them beneath her hips, hoping that
the slight elevation would help to stem the flow. He fetched the
cup of wine and ordered her to drink it, then, with the dog scut-
tering at his heels, pelted from the room.

'Go to your mistress,' he commanded a staring Hilda. 'She is
in need of you. Where can I find a midwife at this hour?'

'A midwife?' Hilda's upper lids almost disappeared.

'She is bleeding; she needs help.' His voice was raw and urgent
with a fear that bordered on terror.

Hilda swallowed. 'Dame Hortense, on Dock Alley. She's not
the nearest, but she knows her trade.' Pale with shock, the nurse
gave him instructions, and within moments he had raised the
bar and banged out into the sultry Rouen night.

Monday awoke from a drugged sleep to sunny daylight and the
sound of the breeze swishing in the apple trees. Mild cramp
encircled her loins, but the vicious pains of earlier had ceased,
and seemed part of a recent nightmare. Perhaps they had been a
nightmare; perhaps she was still dreaming. Her mind floated on
the sunlight and she watched motes of dust dance and sparkle
with a lethargic fascination until her eyes closed. But she did not
sleep for long. Her bladder was twinging with the need to be
emptied, and her mouth was dry. Behind her lids, she saw strange
dark images, lit imperfectly by candle glow. There was a witch –
a tiny crone with a wizened face and not a tooth in her head and
she was binding something around Monday's hips. 'Will she
live?' A man spoke, husky fear in his voice, and the crone replied
in the cracked tones of the ancient. 'God and St Margaret willing,
young man. Fortunate that you sent for me when you did, else it
would have been a priest your wife would be needing.'

Wife? Monday wondered at the word. She wasn't anybody's
wife. Reaching down, she touched her waist and discovered some
sort of cord wrapped twice around it, the ends stranding down
over her belly and between her legs. So the dark images were not
just figments of her mind. The man's voice had been familiar,

and in the moment that the thought entered her head, she saw a vision of his face.

'Alexander,' she said aloud, and struggled to sit up. Aching nausea surged through her belly, and she subsided against the bolsters with a gasp.

The woman who had been seated beside a small brazier, grinding herbs in a copper vessel, ceased her work and hobbled over to Monday's side. She was the crone of the night, even more wizened in daylight, with brown blotches on blue-veined hands, and a smile like a hole in a rotten apple. Monday suppressed a shudder. 'Who are you?' she demanded. 'Where's Hilda?'

The old woman eased herself down on the coffer at the bed-side and tilted her head. The flesh had creased and slackened around her eyes, hooding them, but they were as alert and dark as a bird's, and full of salty humour. 'Hilda is below, caring for your husband and child,' she said, and clucked her tongue within her toothless mouth. 'Now I know you think I look like a hag who has flown on her besom straight from the coven, but even I have no remedy for what the years have wrought, young woman. You should thank whatever saints you favour for my experience and your life.'

Monday lowered her gaze to the sheets. They had been changed, and the smell of dried lavender drifted past her nostrils. She felt resentment at the woman's tone, was revolted by the sight of her, but also knew shame that she should recoil from the crone's outward appearance. Doubtless the old woman had indeed saved her life, and she ought to be grateful. With an effort, she raised her eyes from the fresh linen and met the piercing dark gaze. 'I do thank God, and I am grateful to you,' she said. 'But I still do not know who you are.' Her voice was hoarse and dry, and when she had spoken, her throat closed and she had to cough.

'My name, for what it matters, is Dame Hortense, and I delivered my first baby nigh on seventy years ago to a sailor's wife. There ain't nothing I don't know.' She hobbled to her feet and limped with surprising speed to the brazier, where she poured red liquid from a pitcher into a cup.

'Here, drink this down; it'll help restore you.'

Monday eyed the cup suspiciously and thought of some of the nostrums that Aline had poured down her throat at Lavoux when she was carrying Florian. And Dame Hortense's observation about having flown here on a besom had struck very close to the mark of Monday's hidden prejudice. She took a tentative sip, and was rewarded with a sharp but not unpleasant taste of wild berries, with an underlying tang of honey and herbs.

'Just because it's a nostrum doesn't mean it has to taste bad,' said the crone scornfully. 'People are too quick to judge.'

Monday reddened. 'No, I'm sorry, thank you.' She finished the liquid down to the dregs and returned the cup to the midwife.

'I suppose you'll be wanting to piss now,' Dame Hortense said in a matter-of-fact voice. 'Come, I'll help you up. You are going to feel weak in the shanks; you bled a fair mart last night.' With a surprising, wiry strength for someone so tiny and wizened, she helped Monday from the bed to the privy hole in a small antechamber beyond 'Don't bear down,' she warned. 'Bleeding's stopped, but you must be careful.'

'Why am I wearing this?' Monday indicated the girdle as she threw back the covers.

'It once belonged to the blessed St Margaret, patron of women in travail. If the bleeding holds off, you can remove it tonight.'

Dame Hortense checked the wad of linen between Monday's thighs. There was a small gush of blood commensurate with rising, but nothing that the old midwife deemed serious.

'It were a son you lost,' she said, sucking her bare gums. 'Stillborn, too young to draw breath. Your husband said as he could arrange prayers and a burial.'

Monday's lips stretched into an expression half grimace, half bleak smile. 'He is qualified,' she said. 'But he is not my husband.'

The old woman clucked her tongue again. 'Then he should be.' She guided Monday back to the bed.

Tears stung behind Monday's eyes. She felt weak and dizzy, and very tired. Drained both in mind and body. The old woman gave her a different potion to drink, one that despite the honey had a bitter undertaste that almost made her retch.

'Sleep,' said Dame Hortense. 'That is all you need, healing sleep.'

When Monday next woke, it was late in the day. The colour of the light had changed from pale to deep gold, and a somnolent warmth lay across the room. There was a weight on the bed at her right side, and a delicate smell of chicken and herbs. She slid her glance across and encountered Alexander's concerned gaze, the sunlight brightening his eyes to amber and lying along the olive planes of his face. There was stubble ringing his mouth, and his clothes were somewhat crumpled.

'Hecate says you have to drink this,' he said, and pointed to a steaming bowl of broth on the coffer.

'Who?' Monday murmured, still half asleep. She struggled to sit up against the bolsters. He helped her, plumping the cushions at her back until she was upright and comfortable.

'Dame Hortense, she of the beauteous countenance,' he said fatuously, and picked up the bowl and spoon. 'Shall I feed you, or can you manage?'

'I can manage.' A note of independence entered her voice and she took the soup from him. As her head cleared of sleep, she realised that she was hungry, and the broth not only smelled delicious, it tasted of heaven. In between spoonfuls, Monday glanced apprehensively round the room. 'Where is she?'

'Below stairs, brewing some concoction for you to swallow on the morrow. It involves beef bones, barley, and God knows what from that pouch at her belt. Smells promising though. She said that she would come up in a while to check on your progress. Hilda says that she is the best midwife in Rouen, but that she is overlooked these days. No one wants their child's first sight in the world to be that of a toothless old crone.'

'But it does not matter to women who miscarry,' Monday said, and once again tears stung hot and salty behind her eyes, filling up, brimming, then overflowing. 'I want my children back,' she said, and then began to sob.

Alexander grabbed the bowl of broth before it spilled all over the bedclothes, then he folded her in his arms and drew her tight against his body, absorbing her shudders of grief. It was useless to say that she still had Florian, she still had him, had her life before her. All that was an empty waste compared to the emotions swamping her now. The old midwife had warned him that there might be tears; that he might find himself in the path of the storm. He might lose himself too, he thought wryly as he smoothed her hair and held her close.

'As soon as you are able to move, you and Florian are coming with me,' he said. 'To the Marshal's keep at Orbec. I will not brook no for an answer, and you are in no fit state to run away, so listen, and accept.'

Amid the trembling, he thought she nodded her head, but he did not know how much she understood through her grief. But then she half raised her head. 'John,' she said in a choked voice. 'What about John?'

'I know he is jealous of you, but at the moment he has other things to occupy him. I will set matters to rights.'

She nodded again and the weeping slowed, became loud sniffs and hiccups. He presented her with a clean strip of linen swaddling on which to wipe her eyes and nose, and as her composure strengthened, gave her the broth to finish. If not as hot as before, it was still sufficiently warm to be palatable.

She looked at him, her eyes puffy and swollen, her nose pink, and saw only tenderness and concern in reply. Had she shown such a visage to John, he would have stalked out in revulsion. She wondered how he would respond to the news of his son's death, and her chin wobbled treacherously again. 'What are you doing in Rouen?' she asked, to distract her mind.

'Overseeing the purchase and escort of supplies to Orbec,' he said, then dropped his gaze to the coverlet and plucked at a loose thread on the striped wool. For a moment she thought that he was going to say something else, but he continued to tug at the thread, his lips slightly compressed.

'I am glad you came,' she said, 'but after I wrote to you, I was sure that you would not.' She toyed with the horn spoon, stirring it around the woodgrain pattern in the bottom of the bowl. 'You say that you will set matters to rights with John, but how? You will put yourself in terrible danger.'

'There is a risk, I would be foolish to deny it, but less than there was before.'

'Because my son is dead, you mean?' Her voice, apart from a slight quaver, was dangerously neutral. 'Because I am no longer as valuable – less to give up?'

He looked up and ceased his assault on the coverlet. 'I do not deny that will have a bearing on the situation,' he said awkwardly, 'but there is another, greater reason why I think he will let you go – the reason that I knocked on your door last night.' He took her hand in his, his thumb lying across her knuckles, above the gold rings that John had given her. 'I came to tell you that John has taken a wife, and that for the moment at least, he sees not beyond his wedding chamber door.' He explained what he had heard at the palace the previous evening. 'I wanted you to know before it became common coin. Not for my sake, but for yours.'

She looked down at his hand upon hers and felt the pressure. He was not telling the entire truth. He had come for his own sake as well, but she did not hold that against him. The thought of John in bed with his child bride filled her with little more than a tearful weariness. She discovered that she did not care; that losing John's children was a far greater wound than the one of losing John. Indeed, she thought it might be like plucking a thorn from her side when she was able to feel again. She drew a deep shaky breath, and looked at him through tear-spiked lashes. 'I need time to grieve and to heal. I cannot give you . . . .'

'All the time in the world,' he interrupted before she could finish the sentence. Glancing down, he softened his grip as if realising that the tension in his fingers contradicted his words. 'I promise, for what you deem a man's promise worth.'

'You should set your value higher than that,' she answered with a watery smile.

Before he could answer, Dame Hortense arrived. She was out of breath from climbing the stairs, and limping like a seesaw.

'I said take her the broth, not stay the night.' She wagged a forefinger at Alexander. 'You must leave now. Me and the mistress has women's business.'

Feeling like a child caught stealing cakes at the bakehouse door, Alexander rose to his feet, and immediately towered over

Dame Hortense. Not in the least intimidated, she fixed him with a gimlet eye.

'I've driven oxen to market bigger than you,' she said. 'Aye, and probably with more brain too.' She gave him a push. 'Go on, that son of yours keeps asking for you. Says you promised to teach him to use a sword.' Her tongue clucked, displaying what she thought of the notion. 'And don't raise your brows at me like that. I could tell he was yours the moment I laid eyes on him.'

Alexander and Monday exchanged a rueful glance. Leaning over, he kissed her damp cheek. 'Lord, what a mother-in-law she would make,' he muttered.

'What was that?' Dame Hortense poked her head forward, eyes bright with suspicion.

'I said I had best leave for Monday's sake,' Alexander replied with the most innocent of expressions. Turning, he stooped even further and kissed the old woman's leathery, withered cheek too. 'My lady,' he said, and went to the curtain. On the threshold he looked over his shoulder. 'I have to leave for Orbec tomorrow, but I'll be back to fetch you before the feast of St Michael . . . a promise.' Then he bowed and was gone.

The women listened to the sound of his footsteps on the stairs, and then his voice as he spoke to Florian. Hortense gently rubbed the side of her face.

'Last time a young man kissed me was at a festival when I was five and thirty,' she said. 'And he wasn't as handsome as yours.' She lowered her hand and hobbled over to the bedside. 'You're going to stay with him, aren't you?'

Monday gnawed her lower lip. 'I think so.'

'Shouldn't be no think about it,' Hortense opined and drew down the sheets. 'Can't see why you aren't together now, the two of ye. Now, let's have a look.'

While Hortense examined the amount of blood lost, Monday told her briefly about her life on the tourney circuit, her meeting with Alexander, and the reason they had parted.

Hortense sucked her gums. 'Aye, well, trust is easily betrayed,' she said shrewdly, 'and once betrayed, hard to mend or forgive. But you were both too young, with too many lessons still to learn.'

'He says he hasn't touched another woman since.'

'Do you believe him?'

Monday frowned, picking through the confusion of her thoughts. 'Yes,' she said after a moment. 'Alexander has never lied to me. Stretched the truth on occasion, perhaps, or held his tongue and looked innocent, but never lied.' She looked at the old woman. 'I would be a fool to think that he has been celibate because no other woman could satisfy him. It is out of guilt. Neither of us had the control to stop when the moment came, and I was the more innocent. He knew where it would lead.'

'Aye, well, it seems to me you have both paid the price,' Dame Hortense said. 'Time to let the scars thicken over old wounds. The girdle can come off now. You shouldn't bleed any more than you would at the time of your normal flux.' She reached to the knot on the tablet-woven braid and began to unfasten the complex loops and folds which had been tied in the belief that they would lessen the flow of blood.

Monday grimaced at Hortense's mention of paying a price. The words kept returning to mock her.

The midwife removed the girdle, doubled it in half, then in half again, and secured it with the ends, once more tied in a complex knot. Making the sign of the cross over it, she set the girdle to one side, and from a woven pouch slung upon her shoulder produced a variety of objects. 'You'll not be wanting to conceive again until you've healed. Now I know you have no intention of letting a man enter your bed or your body, even one as dear to you as that young man downstairs, but as you said to me yourself, you did not have the control when the moment came. And certainly no man alive can be trusted to pull out at the moment of pleasure.'

Monday was too startled at the dame's words to protest against them, and the sight of the items presented for her scrutiny completed her astonishment. There was a piece of washed raw fleece, the cut half of what she knew to be a lemon, since such fruits were occasionally used as a garnish for the finger bowls at the royal table. There was also a string of wooden beads stained in three colours following on from one another, red, yellow and blue. Staring, she wondered if they were the components of some obscure spell. Certainly Dame Hortense had the appearance of a witch.

The old woman picked up the fleece first. 'When a child is conceived, the male seed has to mix with the female seed,' she said authoritatively. 'If you do not want to quicken when you lie with a man, you must soak a piece of raw fleece in vinegar, or ass's milk, and insert it within your body as high as you can, so that your seed will not mingle with his. The lemon will perform the same task. Washing your passage in vinegar alone sometimes works, but not as well.'

Monday screwed up her face at the thought, but nodded to show that she understood. Dame Hortense eyed her narrowly. 'All for a small discomfort, it could save your life,' she said.

'Yes, I know. I'm listening,' Monday said guiltily.

'Hah, it's what you do about it,' the midwife sniffed.

Monday pointed to the string of beads, which looked similar in a way to the ones now becoming popular for the memorising of holy catechisms and rituals. 'What are they?'

Dame Hortense smacked her lips together, then gave a tooth-less smile. 'They,' she said, lifting the beads in her gnarled fingers, 'are the real power, young woman.'

'What do you do, then?' Monday frowned, for she could not imagine a use for them except in prayer.

'Look, three colours, eight and twenty beads, each represent-ing a single day in the cycle of a woman's flux. Seven red ones for the days of her monthly bleed when she is impure and no man should touch her.' Dame Hortense counted the seven along the string. 'Now there are yellow and blue ones left. The yellow rep-resent the days when it is safe to lie with a man and not conceive. Lie with him on a blue bead day and you will assuredly quicken. As long as you keep count, and your fluxes are regular each month, you can decide whether you conceive or not.' She handed Monday the string. 'It's women's magic though,' she warned. 'You have to be very sure your man will understand. Some take strong umbrage to such power.'

Monday ran the stained, polished wood through her fingers and gazed at the beads with growing comprehension. It was simple, devastatingly so, almost too simple to be true. 'How do you know it will work?'

The midwife shrugged. 'You don't reach my years without learning a trick or two.' She gave a little cackle and hugged herself. 'But I promise you it does work. I was told about it by a bishop's mistress, and she was told about it by the bishop, who did not want any bastards sullying his reputation. He came across it, so she told me, in a manuscript of the ancients.'

Monday nodded slowly. 'Like Arabic numerals,' she murmured.

'Eh?'

'Nothing,' Monday said, and moved the beads gently along their leather cord.

John had taken a brief time away from his child bride's bed to indulge in the parallel sport of hunting. A speckled silver gyrfalcon perched on his gauntlet, its fierce eyes covered by a plumed hood of purple silk. Sharp talons and cruel beak reflected the crisp light. John stroked its glossy feathers, soothing it with a bejewelled forefinger. There was a jewel in his cap too, a large amethyst securing a blue jay's feather. Complacent, well-fed satisfaction gleamed in every fold of skin, each nuance of expression. For the nonce, John was well pleased with life. He was the ruler of an empire, had stolen a march on his rivals with political cunning, and was the husband of a saucer-eyed kitten of a girl who delighted in playing all his games. The weather was superb, a fine day to fly the hawks and feel his earthbound body soar and exult with them.

Heron and crane were the intended prey of John's hawk – the most dangerous, the most difficult to bring down – and the hunting party was riding towards the river in search of their sport. From the corner of his eye John glanced at the young knight who had arrived that morning with dispatches from William Marshal, and a request for an audience of his own. John thought he knew why, and with a glint of scornful amusement had invited him along on the hunt. He was feeling indulgent, and in such a mood, his malice was tempered with humour. The young man himself seemed acutely uncomfortable, as if a thorn was sticking in his buttocks. And well he might have reason for anxiety. Even if John had not made it his business to discover the name of Monday's visitor back in the spring, the resemblance between Alexander de Montroi and the little boy was too strong to be coincidence.

John pondered whether or not to grant him audience or let him stew. He looked at the hawk perched on his leather gauntlet. It would be interesting to hear what the knight had to say, and John enjoyed piquant diversions. His lips pursed in a smile, and he crooned softly to the bird. But not yet. Draw out the thread a little longer, spin and twist it a little tighter, daring it to snap.

Alexander was finally granted his audience at the end of a long morning. The silver gyrfalcon had brought down two cranes in spectacular clashes of ferocity and desperation, and John's mood had risen from good to excellent.

The cranes were trussed together and tied across a pack pony to be borne home to the table in triumph, and the hunters sat down to break the sport with a picnic of lavish proportions. The hawks were settled in the shade and attached to bow perches by leashes, where they dozed, their hoods secured.

John popped a sliver of honey-roasted swan into his mouth and looked at Alexander with an expression so benevolent that it could have concealed even the blackest murder. 'So,' he said, 'you have your audience. What is it you want of me?' He gestured. 'You have my permission to sit.'

Alexander straightened from his bow and folded himself down on the tasselled wool blanket which was protecting the royal posterior from the prickle of the grass. He knew that John had been toying with him all morning, waiting his moment like an epicure with a poised spoon. Alexander was nervous but determined. He knew what John expected to be told, could see the smile in the other man's dark-hazel eyes as he waited with feline confidence.

'Sire, I wish I could have spoken with you the sooner, for I am the bearer of sad tidings,' he said formally, and through lowered lids saw the scowl that twitched across John's brow. Hastily he cleared his throat and continued, 'As you must know already, I am acquainted with your sempstress, Mistress Monday de Cerizay. Indeed, I think you must also be aware that I am Florian's father.'

'I am aware of many things, one of them being that you have a bold tongue,' John retorted, and washed down the meat with a swallow of wine. 'What of your tidings?'

'I was in Rouen, on business for my lord Marshal, and there was pestilence in the city. I went to make sure that Monday was safe, and . . .'

'You went to make sure,' John mocked, arching a sardonic brow. 'How thoughtful of you, especially in my absence.'

Alexander flushed beneath the barb of John's sarcasm. He fought the urge to strike the curl from the other man's lips. 'I discovered that the baby had died of the flux, and Monday herself was sick . . . sire,' he said stiffly.

John gave him a sharp look over the rim of the cup. 'Christ, she isn't dead?' A note of concern in his voice seemed to fill him with as much surprise as it did Alexander, who had marked him down for a callous, careless bastard.

'No, sire, by God's grace and that of a skilled midwife, she is recovering.'

'A midwife?' John's brows rose.

'She miscarried of another child, sire.'

John was silent. He tossed back his wine and held out his cup for a squire to refill. 'Whose?' he demanded savagely.

Alexander swallowed both his gorge and his temper. It was a cheap insult, far too cheap to be paid for with the coin of his life and Monday's misery. 'I would not be here if that answer was the wrong one, sire,' he said with dignity. 'Indeed, I would have taken Monday and my son and fled across the French border.'

John studied him through narrowed eyes and sucked his cheeks. Alexander could discern not a trace of regret or grief on his face. That one exclamation had been his only show of care. After a while John took another slice of roast swan from the platter and bit into it. He had excellent teeth, white, even and strong. 'So why are you here?' he demanded. 'Laudable as it is of you to bring me these tidings in person, any messenger would have sufficed. There must be more for you to dare this meeting.'

'Sire, I want Monday to wife.' There, it was spoken boldly in the September sunshine, with the court eavesdropping for all they were worth and John sitting on the tasselled rug, eating roast swan with a delicate precision that sat incongruously with the squat, powerful fingers. 'I want . . . I ask you to release her.'

John wiped his hands and his lips on a napkin. 'And you think that now I have a new wife and a kingdom to occupy my time, I might be amenable,' he said, and ran his tongue around the inside of his mouth.

'Yes, sire.' There was no point in denying the fact. To have done so would only have meant further wriggling on John's barbed hook.

More wine trickled into John's cup. He took a sip, then indicated that the squire should also pour for Alexander. 'As you say, you could elope across the French border and I would have small power to touch you. But am I to see your coming to me as genuine honesty and concern for my approval, or a bluff?'

Alexander took the question as rhetorical and said nothing. It was for John to decide which way the wind blew, for whatever the reply, John's mind was the final judge.

'You are bold,' John said again. 'I could have you killed, you know that, don't you?'

'Yes, sire.'

John pondered, turning his cup slowly round in his hands and staring at the darkness of the wine through the semi-transparent rock crystal. 'She is employed by me in an official capacity as a sempstress,' he said. 'And indeed, she is the best I have ever seen – not for the sewing itself, but for the design and the cut of the cloth.' He lowered the cup and looked at Alexander with narrow dark eyes in which there was no warmth. 'As to her other services,' his mouth twisted in a cruel smile, 'I've had better fucks with my own hand. You can have her body, as long as I retain the services of her needle. Tell her I want coronation gowns for myself and my wife. You can obtain the measurements from one of Isobel's ladies when we return from the hunt.'

Alexander swallowed the urge to leap upon John and throttle him out of hand for the contemptuous way he had spoken of Monday. She was inanimate to him, a means to an end, one satisfactory, one not. It was on the tip of his tongue to say that John must love his own hand best of all, because he could give to no one except himself, but he clenched his teeth on the words and smiled with false gratitude, and clung to the thought that he had the main part of his reason for baiting the wolf in his lair.

But although John had agreed, and Alexander had yielded with grateful words, neither man was satisfied with the other's response.

CHAPTER 31

LONDON,
OCTOBER 1200

Banners and green bunting edged the buildings and the water-fronts. Even the galleys and cogs moored at the wharves sported streamers and pennants to celebrate the coronation of England's new child queen. The citizens of London lined the route to Westminster Abbey, waiting for the royal procession – throngs of folk in their holiday best, rich and poor making the best of the fine, crisp weather and the excuse to make merry. The dung-collector's wife with a silk ribbon binding her best linen wimple, the apothecary in his new cloak trimmed with the belly fur of a lynx, the goldsmith's plump spouse wearing a panelled gown of Flemish cloth, a ring on every fat white finger, all were here to see and be seen – except for the cut-purses, who went about their business of freeing people of their money with unobtrusive efficiency.

Monday stood at the side of the road, a fresh wind whipping colour into her cheeks and flapping her wimple. Clouds hurtled across the sky, fresh white chasing grey between vast gaps of blue. She was flanked by Alexander and Hervi, the former wear-ing his best tunic and chausses, for although he was free at the moment, he was on duty at the Marshal household throughout the evening. Hervi too had been released from his responsibilities for half the day. Had it not been for the habit and tonsure, Monday would not have believed him a monk, he seemed so much like the Hervi she remembered. Certainly his holy vows had not imbued him with any degree of gravity. He positively doted on Florian, and Florian in his turn was absolutely fascinated by Hervi's wooden leg, and would have kept his company for that alone, if nothing else.

Smiling, Monday glanced aloft at her son. He was perched on Alexander's shoulders so that he should have a good view of the procession. In his hand was a gilded stick with a bunch of scarlet and blue ribbons twisted around its end, and tiny bells sewn on to the ends of the ribbons. Hervi had bought it for him from a passing huckster. Florian had been in ecstasy, Alexander less so at the prospect of a jingling row in his ear for the rest of the day.

'I thought monks were supposed to be impoverished,' he said with a sidelong glare.

'I am now. It was only a halfpenny from the bishop's exchequer for my dinner. I'm depending on you to be charitable now.'

At which juncture, Alexander had declared that he would fund only bread and water as a penance for the folly of giving Florian such a toy, but his eyes had been laughing.

'They're coming, I can see them!' Florian suddenly screeched, and bounced up and down on Alexander's shoulders, pointing exuberantly with the streamered stick.

Hervi's deep chuckle rumbled from the depths of his cowl. 'You will bounce your poor father into the ground before ever they arrive,' he said, then put his hand across his mouth as he realised what he had said.

Florian, however, was too busy leaning forward and peering up the road to notice Hervi's slip.

Monday folded her arms beneath her cloak in a slightly protective gesture. She was aware of Hervi's hangdog gaze, of Alexander's impassive face.

'He didn't hear me,' Hervi said.

'I know, don't worry.' She gave him a smile, but it did not reach her eyes, which were wary.

'You ought to tell him.'

'And so we will, in the fullness of time,' Alexander said, a certain sharpness in his tone. 'Let it be, Hervi. Tread your own ground, not ours.'

Hervi gave an exasperated shrug to show that he would yield even while he did not understand, and looked down the road towards the sound of trumpets, drums and fanfare. Monday did too, although her focus was not entirely on the approaching pageant, but on the path that had brought her from a sultry August evening in Rouen, her world in ruins around her, to this coronation parade in the company of Hervi and Alexander.

When she had recovered enough from her miscarriage to travel, Alexander had taken her to the Marshal's keep at Orbec to recuperate in full. Then he had gone to John. Monday did not know the details of what had been said at their meeting. Alexander had given her John's commission for coronation garments, together with the measurements of the young queen-to-be. And for the rest he had been reticent, sparing only the barest outline. 'He said nothing worth repeating,' he had replied when once she had pushed him, and the set of his lips had led her not to pursue the subject.

She had spent a month at Orbec, and been absorbed into the daily routine of the Marshal family life. Isabelle Marshal was softly spoken with a warm, maternal nature that did not stand in the way of a firm backbone. Monday took to her immediately. She was much quieter than Aline of Lavoux, less effervescent, and her enthusiasms were not whims but enduring convictions. She saw much, said little, and had a vast capacity for compassion. Although their stay at Orbec was temporary, and Monday knew it must end, it was the first time since her mother's death that she had felt not only secure, but at ease.

Florian had delighted in Orbec too. There were so many children that he was never short of playmates, and there were always activities to watch or join in. Alexander was absent for much of the month on the Marshal's business, and despite convalescing, Monday had a coronation robe to sew for the future queen. She settled to a busy routine, and discovered that she missed him, but never with enough time to brood on the feeling. When he had ridden into the bailey on his return, she happened by chance to be there, and her stomach had taken flight with a thousand tiny butterflies. But she had not flung herself into his arms, and he had not grabbed her and swung her round in his. It had still been too soon; the new growth too tender.

In October they had travelled to England for the coronation of

John's queen. Monday had rented a house in London near Watling Street, using coin she had saved during her time as John's mistress. She had visited John's bride several times to fit the coronation gown of red and gold silk. Isobel of Angoulême had given no indication of being aware that Monday was anything more to the royal household than a skilled sempstress, and Monday had maintained that pretence. John's wife was precocious for twelve – could have passed for fifteen at least. Her complexion was flawless, her hair a curtain of heavy blonde silk, and her eyes a deep, bewitching blue. A beauty, and she knew it. Kneeling at her feet to pin the hem of the crimson silk, Monday silently, if not with a little sarcasm, wished husband and wife well of each other.

Fitting John's robe had been an ordeal, a public one, for he had been busy conversing with a handful of his barons while she knelt at his feet and adjusted the hem. He had paid her scant attention, and even when their eyes had inadvertently met, his gaze had been a flat, blank wall. She had been tempted to stick a pin in him, to stamp her foot and demand not to be ignored. She had been his bedmate and the mother of his child, and deserved better. But a temptation was all it remained. She had nothing to gain and everything to lose. Nor was she even jealous, only hurt and disappointed. He made no mention of the baby and unborn child they had lost, not a single flicker of regret or grief.

An official had paid her fee in the antechamber and marked it on a tally stick. She wondered if one of the notched tallys was a record of how much John had paid her for other services, but could not bring herself to ask.

A sudden flurry of wind lifted her wimple and threw it across her face, tangling across her lips and stinging beneath an eyelid. By the time she had clawed herself free and tucked the ends of the wimple inside her cloak to prevent it from escaping again, a roan stallion was prancing abreast of them, its dour-faced rider struggling to hold it steady amidst the cacophony of the crowd. The stallion's hindquarters swung dangerously towards the onlookers and the man astride drew in the reins so tightly that the beast's head was tucked right down into its chest, emphasising the powerful crest of its neck.

'Thomas of Stafford, your grandfather,' Alexander said, without inflection.

Monday stared, and a small shiver ran down her spine. He was close enough for her to dart out and touch him. Her feet even struggled to move, but were stalled by her reason. She risked being struck either by his horse, or by the soldiers who rode escort. Looking at the mane of white hair, the rugged curves of feature, she felt no cry of blood to tell her that this was her own kin. But then she had no reason to do so. She bit her lip and followed his progress with troubled eyes.

Then someone did run out from the crowd, a child no older than Florian, attracted by a harness bell that had fallen off a horse's bridle. His mother screamed and dashed out after him. Monday screamed too as the roan horse plunged and lashed out, the shod hooves narrowly missing the woman as she scooped the infant to safety – or at least safety from death by shod hoof. Thomas of Stafford snarled at her in fury and even as the horse had lashed out, so did he, with his whip, cutting her a blow across the cheek that raised an immediate welt, and sent her and her child reeling into the crowd.

Glaring with fury, Thomas of Stafford swore at the woman and rode on. Fists shook in his wake and curses pursued him. The welt on the woman's face turned from numb white to stinging, swollen red. She howled; the child howled. People clustered around her, offering help and sympathy.

'Now do you see?' Alexander said grimly to his brother.

Hervi said nothing, but his jaw tightened and the ebullience visibly departed his large frame.

Monday shivered, and thought how close she had come to being whipped herself. Perhaps he had struck out in fear, she thought, but knew that it was a weak excuse for what she had just witnessed. Thomas of Stafford had raised his hand out of arrogance and rage – perhaps at all womankind.

Alexander squeezed her hand. 'I should not have told you,' he said.

She shook her head. 'No, you were right. I have often wondered about him, eavesdropped on tales.' And even felt sorry because none of those tales had shown her grandfather in a good light. All that could be salvaged was that he was brave and proud and a doughty warrior. 'Now I know,' she said, and returned Alexander's squeeze.

They scarcely even noticed John as he rode past on a white stallion, caparisoned in gold and jewels, his wife beside him, the yards of her crimson silk skirts billowing over her mount's flank and rump. Resembling images from an illuminated book of hours, they drifted past Monday and Alexander. The page turned, and like Stafford, they were gone.

CHAPTER 32

Monday stared at the expanse of water, frozen solid in the bitter cold spell that had turned the world to metallic shades of silver, pewter and leaden grey. The colour, the carrying screams and shrieks of laughter, came from the people sporting on the ice; young men mainly, with the shin bones of oxen lashed to the soles of their boots. Others had made long slides, the ice as bright as polished iron, and as fast as quicksilver.

Alexander turned a bright grin on her. 'All set for the sport?' he enquired.

She wrinkled her nose at him dubiously, but sat down beside Florian in the sawn-down oval bathtub that they had dragged to the great marsh outside London's northern wall. It had been Alexander's idea to adapt the bathtub. Its base had been smoothed off and liberally greased with candle wax, and a rope run through its fore end. Florian sat snug within it, covered by sheepskins, a hat and mits of the same warming his head and hands. Monday raised one leg, and Alexander braced it against his lower thigh and began to tie on the first shin-bone skate, his mits tucked beneath one arm, his fingers dextrous. For her own modesty and comfort, Monday had borrowed some of his garments — linen leggings topped by warm hose of grey wool, a tunic of checked blue and grey with a short, fur-lined cloak, a hood and cape to cover her hair, and sheepskin mits to keep her fingers from freezing. He had told her that she looked very fetching, and she had rolled her eyes at him and called him a flatterer. She had to admit that the clothes were comfortable, and movement was so much easier. Wearing a dress hampered the length of stride, and inserting extra material only made the garment drag on the ground.

Alexander finished the first skate and set about lashing the second, his breath clouding the air with each jerk of effort.

'I won't be able to stand up!' Monday laughed.

'You'll spend plenty of time on your backside,' he agreed, and finished, sat down to lash on his own skates. 'I know I did.'

'When did you learn?'

'One winter at Orbec with my lord Marshal's sons on a frozen fish pond.' He stood up and held out his hand. Very gingerly Monday took it and levered herself to her feet. It was a little like wearing wooden pattens, she thought, but with a narrower edge of balance, and a surface that was more slippery than the road to hell.

'Hold on to me,' Alexander said, amusement in his voice. 'And watch what I do. Look, you have to position your feet like this, and trust yourself to the ice. Don't think, just fly.'

He made it look effortless, but then he would, she thought, a trifle irritably. It was his athletic coordination that was one of the foundations of his jousting skill. But she could not stay irritated for long, especially after he tried to show off with an oh so casual move that went wrong, making him the first faller of the two, while she, with a frantic flailing of her arms, managed to keep her feet.

The time passed in delight, through the waist of an hourglass faster than she thought possible. Half the populace of London seemed to be out on the ice enjoying themselves. Alexander's bathtub was not the only innovation. Someone else was skidding along on a large wicker bread basket, and she also saw a piece of hurdle fencing being used. Young men played at jousting on foot, using long wooden poles, and there were several noisy clashes and bruising falls.

When her ankles began to ache, Monday retired to warm her hands at one of the chestnut-sellers' braziers on the solid land edging the ice, while Alexander pulled Florian along in the bath-tub. She watched man and child with a smile on her lips and a deep pang of affection twisting her heart, gut and loins. It was almost Christmas now, the New Year fast approaching and she could sense a change in herself, as if she were running ahead of the old season with her arms open to embrace the future. Not that anything had been settled concerning that as yet. But she thought so soon. Perhaps after Christmas. Both of them were bound for Winchester within the next few days, Alexander on the Marshal's business, she to present another gown to the young queen as a Christmas gift from John. What happened after that remained to be seen. Smiling to herself, she turned and bought a pouch of chestnuts from the seller.

Piping hot, they burned her fingers, but the heat was wonderful, and they tasted divine, slightly floury with a smoky, roasted flavour. She looked for Alexander and Florian, intending to beckon them over to share, but a hand dived at her from behind and snatched two chestnuts from the pouch.

'Well, well, who says that ghosts do not exist!' declared Eudo le Boucher, his black eyes glittering. He juggled the chestnuts from hand to hand, and then cracked one open on a broken tooth. 'Monday de Cerizay. Last I saw you was in some siege camp in Normandy in the company of the de Montroi brothers.' He spat burnt fragments of shell on to the ice and chewed on the tender white nut. 'What are you doing here?'

The cold of the day struck at Monday's core. His tone was frankly delighted, but there was nothing of friendship in it. It was like being baited by a wolf. 'I was taking pleasure in the day,' she answered, and knew that she could not even make her escape because of the skates lashed to her feet.

Le Boucher smiled, the scars on his face livid with the cold. 'You live in London?' He looked at her hands, where these days she wore no rings, save the silver one that had been with her since her tourney days, and the gold one that was her mother's.

'Not always.' She began to ease away from him and gazed around for Alexander. A couple of men and three women, obviously le Boucher's companions, were standing off to one side, watching their exchange with idle scrutiny. The women's faces were painted with cosmetics and one had a raucous laugh that reminded Monday of Grisel, the whore with whom she had fought over her mother's possessions. Not one of them was sober, and the vapour clouding from le Boucher's mouth and nostrils bore a powerful odour of ginevra.

Le Boucher cracked open the second chestnut. 'Married?' he questioned. 'Someone's goodwife?'

'It is no concern of yours.'

Le Boucher arched one eyebrow. 'Perhaps, and perhaps not.' He looked her up and down, taking pointed notice of her masculine attire. 'Do you always dress like that?'

'If it suits me.'

'Oh, it suits you, sweetheart.' He grinned, his wolfishness emphasised by his broken, discoloured teeth. 'But it's hardly the garb of bewimpled respectability, is it?'

'I doubt you would know respectability if it slapped you in the face.'

'Try me.' He extended his good cheek in mocking invitation.

Without warning, and at a tremendous pace, the oval bath-tub sliced across the ice, struck the side of le Boucher's leg and bowled him from his feet. He landed heavily on his flank, the air whooshing out of him like a punctured bladder. The woman's raucous laugh cracked out. Alexander skated up in the wake of the tub, Florian clinging to his back. He stooped to the guiding ropes and tugged the tub around, making sure that it accidentally knocked le Boucher's head in turning. He also stumbled, when before he had been so sure of his balance, and the bone blade of the skate sliced open le Boucher's hand.

Le Boucher was too winded and stunned by the force of his fall to yell or even curse. His companions started forward to help him, the loud woman still cackling and nudging the others, one of whom slipped and fell over on the ice with a howl of pain. Alexander deposited Florian in the tub, took Monday's arm, and propelled them away from the danger.

Once they were far enough removed, he swished to a halt in order to remove his skates. He was breathing hard and his eyes were battle-lit. 'Christ, if Florian had not been with us and my sword had been at my hip . . .' He shook his head and muttered beneath his breath.

Monday stooped to untie her own blades. Her hands were shaking, and it was a struggle. She looked over her shoulder, but there was no sign of any pursuit. Alexander was watching too, his eyes never still for a moment. She made herself breathe slowly and deeply, the frozen air cauterising her lungs.

'What did he say to you?'

She told him, and managed to remove her skates. 'You mentioned once that he had approached Hervi with an offer of marriage. Do you remember?'

A look of disgust flickered across his face. 'I could hardly forget, since it was the day you ran away, Hervi broke his leg and le Boucher left me for dead.'

She could sense the anger quivering in him, much of it still pent up from the incident a few moments ago. There had been a thousand changes since that day of which he had spoken, but those changes had only brought them round full circle. 'Do you think he still wants me, or was he just baiting me to see how I would respond?'

'You are Thomas of Stafford's granddaughter,' Alexander said bleakly. 'Why should he not still want you?'

'Jesu,' she whispered, and huddled inside the short cloak, her teeth chattering with anxiety and revulsion as much as with cold.

'At least he does not know where you live.' His voice sharpened. 'You didn't tell him anything, did you?'

She shook her head numbly.

Eyes narrowed, Alexander glanced around, then relaxed slightly, puffing out a deep breath. 'I doubt he will be in a fit state to set out on any kind of search for a while anyway,' he said with grim satisfaction. 'I hoped I had broken his leg as he broke Hervi's, but I don't think I hit him hard enough. Still, he'll be limping for a while. He was more than half drunk too.' He curved his arm through hers. 'Come, you're as white as the ice. I'll take you home.'

They walked back to the city, taking a circuitous route to avoid the vicinity of the chestnut-seller's brazier. Florian was too tired to do more than ask a few desultory questions about the man whom Alexander had run over with the bathtub, and an explanation that it had been an accident was accepted without more than a couple of obligatory 'whys'.

The dusk was gathering as they approached Monday's rented house, similar to but smaller than the one in Rouen, with a garden running adjacent to Cripplegate. In a world of frozen blue and silver, rime sparkling on every surface, hoary mist cloaking the distance, the bells of St Giles rang out the hour of vespers. Candle and rushlight glimmered in the dwellings and the smell of woodsmoke lay heavy on the air, the bluish layers adding to the mist.

Teasel barked behind the door and scrabbled at the wood with his paws. Monday removed the key from the hoop on her tunic belt and fitted it to the lock. As the latch gave, she turned to Alexander. 'Stay with us for tonight,' she said on a rush, as if the words had to be spoken before the door was fully open, an incantation on the threshold to protect the house from evil spirits. 'The hearth is warm, and there is mutton stew and fresh bread.'

'How could I refuse?' he said a trifle wryly. 'Food, warmth and company. What other ways are there to a man's heart?'

At which juncture Teasel flung himself through the narrow opening and leaped upon Alexander with a yelp of joy, thereby sparing Monday the need to reply.

They ate the mutton stew and talked of mundane, everyday matters in front of their son. Alexander played knucklebones with him and taught him a simple game of dice until the little boy's lids began to droop. Then he carried him up the loft stairs to the small, rope-framed bed, squeezed against the wall beside Monday's. By the time he had been tucked in, Florian was sound asleep, his dark lashes lying like fans on his cheeks, his scrap of yellow blanket touching his nose. Teasel whined, circled several times, and curled up on the little boy's feet.

Feeling a warm glow of protective tenderness, Alexander kissed his son and returned to the hearth. 'Asleep already,' he said, and picked up the knucklebones.

'He plays until he drops then wakes up ready to play again,' Monday said with a little shake of her head. She watched him toy with the knucklebones. The fluid movement, the coordinated grace had been evident even in the first days of his joining the tourney circuit as an abused, underfed stripling. She thought of the first time she had seen him, lying sallow and gaunt on his brother's pallet amid the debris of Hervi's bachelor existence. She had felt curiosity and compassion then. Friendship had grown, and become complicated by other appetites and more ambiguous emotions. They had made their dreams, lived them, and learned some difficult, painful lessons.

Up and down, toss and catch, as smooth as cream. She licked her lips and cleared her throat. 'Does your offer of marriage still stand?' There, the words were out, falling between them, but as stepping stones or a barrier she could not tell.

Alexander balanced the knucklebones on the back of his hand. 'Why do you ask?' His face was expressionless.

'Because if it does . . . I want to accept.'

'Would you have asked me tonight, if not for Eudo le Boucher?'

'Yes,' she said, her colour heightened, because the admitting made her shy and vulnerable, and his face gave nothing away. 'I would. It has been in my mind for some weeks now . . . and . . . and always in my heart. If your offer does still stand I would like Hervi to wed us before witnesses as soon as it can be arranged.'

The knucklebones curved and turned in the air, and clattered down on the hearth tiles. Alexander stared at her, his fists clenched on his knees, his breathing swift and shallow. 'If my offer still stands,' he repeated hoarsely. 'Woman, are you mad? I know I would be to deny you.'

She raised her hands to her braid, and unwinding its ribbons, shook her hair down around her shoulders in a bronze-brown skein of light, the movement symbolic, for the only man permitted to see a woman's hair spilling free was the one who shared her bed and her life. He reached across the space between them, across the stepping stones to touch the strands of its shining curtain. Then he cupped her face on his palm and kissed her.

She made a soft sound in her throat and pressed forward to meet him, their bodies locking and straining. The salute of lips became the desperate pressure of mouth on mouth, the exchange of breath, and then the ragged gasp for air. The palm of his hand smoothed over her breast and waist, his other cupped her buttocks, and pulled her into his lap. And Monday, with the knowledge of experience and the wildness of need, dug her fingers in his hair and wriggled upon the hard bulge at his groin.

He leaped beneath her touch, and groaned. She curved her lips in pleasure at the sound, and felt a gathering, sensitive heat in the bowl of her pelvis. It had been three seasons since she had lain with John and derived any satisfaction from the encounter. Now she realised just how hungry she was. And surely Alexander must be starving, if what he had said about being celibate was true. Perhaps she ought not to wriggle so much. Perhaps he would not last as far as her own release.

Alexander was entertaining similar thoughts himself, together with some conscience-probing doubts. One dilemma might solve the other, he thought hazily as she pressed down on him, creating an almost unbearable friction. He squeezed his eyes shut and forced his will through the excruciating pleasure. This was how it had been in Hervi's tent. A hasty coupling on the floor with garments bunched up out of the way, and nothing but sticky regret in the aftermath.

'Wait,' he panted, and seized her hips to make her stop. 'No, Monday, no.'

She sat up straight and looked at him, her face flushed and her grey eyes hazy with desire. Then she bit her lip, and pushed her hand through her hair in a gesture that almost maddened him out of his reason. 'It is too fast, isn't it?' she admitted with a shaken laugh. 'But sweet Jesu, I don't want to stop.'

Of their own volition his hands stroked up and down on her waist. 'I remember what happened last time. Then it was fast and sudden too, like lightning.'

'It was long ago,' she murmured, moving lightly to the cadence of his touch. 'And neither of us is drunk tonight . . . or innocent.'

'I think I am drunk on you.' He buried his face in her throat with a sound that was half laugh, half groan. 'I fear I am going to burst!'

She twisted to nip his earlobe. 'Not until I am ready, I hope.'

He grimaced. 'It is not long since you miscarried of a child. What if you should quicken tonight?'

'I won't. Dame Hortense showed me ways of protecting myself.'

Her skin was warm against his lips, a rapid pulse beating beneath it; her hair was cool and slippery against the backs of his hands. Lures that were almost impossible to resist. He clung to a very precarious control, wanting to rush headlong, but knowing that for his conscience he had to speak. 'There were old women on the tourney circuit who used to promise the camp women freedom too. But all too often they failed.'

'Dame Hortense's advice was sound, I promise you.' She laughed and brought her hands up beneath his tunic and shirt to touch the naked flesh of his ribs, her nails gently raking. 'If I did not trust her, would I be sitting in your lap doing this . . . or this?' She shifted position so that she was straddling him.

Unable to speak beyond a croak of pure, tortured pleasure, Alexander shook his head, and ceased to think at all, except with his body.

The floor rushes were prickly, and they spread his cloak over them to blanket the stalks. There was a soft feather bed in the sleeping loft, but the presence of Florian and Teasel put it out of bounds. Nor, with the molten heat of their need, could they have borne to break apart for the time it took to climb the stairs.

Alexander tugged off his tunic and shirt, and then, in the soft red glow from the fire, removed hers too. There was a brooch to unpin and a drawstring to unfasten, neither of which could be accomplished in tearing haste, and he had perforce to temper his urgency to deal with them.

Her breasts were high and round with tight pinkish-brown nipples, her belly flat with just the faintest silvery marks to show she had borne children. His instinct was to seize and engulf, but past experience had taught him that skill lay in delicacy, and his touch was feather-light, the gentlest brushing of thumbs over erect nipples, and then the suckling flicker of his tongue. She whimpered and pressed herself deeper into his lap, rocking upon him. He cupped her buttocks and rode with her, squeezing her back and forth against him, taking a dangerous step nearer to the edge of the abyss.

He moved one hand down to the exposed band of soft skin at the top of her thigh where her leggings met the loin cloth, and stroked. Again she gasped. Unfastening the ties here was tricky, but rewarding, because the motion of his fingers was a gentle pressure on sensitive flesh and each brush of knuckle or side of hand made her shudder and softly cry out.

Alexander wanted nothing more than to tear off the loincloth and thrust himself into her, but he held off, knowing that his goal would also be his rapid undoing. He tried to pace himself, slow move by slow move, concentrating on her tension to try and diminish his own, but it became increasingly difficult as she writhed against him, her mouth, her hands, the sway of her hips in constant rhythm, inviting and inciting.

He found the end of the loincloth and loosened it, managed to find a way inside, and stroked softly with the pad of his thumb. She had been kneading his spine, but now with a strangled cry, her nails were suddenly sharp half-moons gouging his skin.

'Now?' he asked raggedly.

'Oh God, sooner than now!' she sobbed.

He felt her striving on the edge, as close as himself. Their mouths joined in a driving kiss. He lifted her from his lap, tore away the loosened loincloth, and unfastened his own. She lay on his cloak, her eyes half closed, her hair spread abroad, her body open to him. There was one last, fleeting moment of control, an instant to admire and be admired, then it was gone as he covered her, and she welcomed him with arched spine, clutching arms, and tight, smooth walls that gripped and yielded with each surge of his body until there was nothing but the white-hot desperation for release. And as he broke within her, he felt her shatter with him, her cries muffled against his chest.

There was a small Welsh harp standing on the coffer. Alexander picked it up and ran his hands gently over the strings.

Wrapped in his cloak, Monday sat by the fire where they had made love and sipped from a goblet of wine. 'Beguile me a little,' she said with a languorous smile. 'Sing me a troubadour's song. Something new, something you have never sung for anyone else.'

He pursed his lips in thought, and brought the harp back to the fire. 'A troubadour's song.' He kissed her mouth with slow deliberation, and drank of her wine. 'Usually the singing is a preliminary to the bedding,' he said with humour. 'A persuasion to open heaven's gates.'

Monday arched a mischievous brow. 'You seduce women all the time, you mean?'

He smiled. 'I used to, until one of them crept up and stole my heart.'

Leaning against him, she caressed his shin and calf with her toes. 'I love to watch your fingers on the strings. I would imagine them on my body when we were on the tourney circuit, and be terrified lest anyone should read my thoughts. And then you would go off and sing to other women, and return to camp looking as if they had drained you to the marrow. Jesu, the times the palms of my hands bore the marks of my fingernails in jealousy.' She flashed him a look, half humorous, half annoyed. 'You would ruffle my hair and ask me what there was to eat. Sometimes you even kissed my cheek with the smell of another woman on your skin. You had no idea, none at all.'

'No,' he said, a note of regret in his voice. 'Not until it was too late.' He coaxed a ripple from the harp strings, and began to pick out a tune in a minor key. 'I never intended to hurt you, I swear I did not.'

Monday shrugged. 'It is in the past now.' Her eyes suddenly sparkled. 'I don't have to imagine now, because I know.' She raised her head and kissed him, breaking away before the embrace kindled out of control. 'Sing for me,' she prompted again, gesturing at the harp.

Alexander cleared his throat. 'I don't know if I can,' he said. 'You have tied my voice and my loins into a single tight knot.'

'Then your singing should indeed be persuasive.'

He laughed at that, the tension easing, and half closing his eyes, set himself to honour her.

The first song was in the manner of the troubadours as she had suggested, in the Provençal tongue, a tale of a languishing squire and unrequited love. The second was his own, composed on the spur of the moment whilst he sang the first.

> Dissolved the glory of the summer day,
> Drawn close the veil of winter night
> And now the verdure of the meadow bray
> Lies buried 'neath a shroud of white.

> Brooks are silenced by a grip of ice,

No creature moves; no songbirds call.
And love as fickle as a gambler's dice
May like the petals fade and fall.

For how long will sweet nectar last?
Drunk from the cup when skies were blue.
Now winter's come and summer's past
To test the heart if love be true

But I have filled the chalice deep
With wine as bright as stars above,
And warmly will the winter sleep,
Wrapped by the warmth of one I love.

He shrugged, declaring that it needed a deal of reworking, but Monday thought that it was perfect as it stood, straight from his mind to the harp, the tune as haunting and silvery as an icicle. Finally, he sang her another song in a language she did not understand, although once more the tune was poignant and beautiful.

'Welsh,' he said. 'I heard it in the hall of a Welsh lord when I had custody of Abermon keep for the Marshal. It's by one of their poets, Hywel ap Owain, in praise of his love.'

'It's beautiful.' There was almost a tear in her eye.

'It doesn't do you justice.' He laid the harp across his knees. 'But yes, it is a beautiful language. I know a few words. I can say my greetings and farewells; raise a cup, declare yes and no. There was little time to learn more before I had to leave.'

'Do you wish you could go back?'

Rubbing his chin, he thought for a moment. 'It was the first place that I have felt truly at home since my father died and Wooton Montroi became my brother's property,' he said slowly. 'And I know that I ruled Abermon well. I was proud of the time I spent there.' He gave a pragmatic sigh. 'But it was my first such post, and William Marshal already had an older man in mind for the permanent tenancy. Besides,' he added with a smile, 'if I had remained at Abermon, I would never have found you, would I? There will be other opportunities.' He pulled her against him, and the harp slid from his lap in a soft jangle of surprised notes. 'Now tell me,' he whispered against her lips. 'How persuaded are heaven's gates to open?'

Monday stroked his thigh, the palm of her hand massaging higher until she reached the firm heat of his renewed erection. Playfully she circled it in her hand, pulling it away from his body, then letting it spring back. 'Why don't you knock and find out?' she murmured.

CHAPTER 33

Isobel's Christmas gown was of sapphire-blue silk, the same shade as her eyes, and a perfect foil for her pale-blonde hair. Pirouetting before the mirror in her chamber, she performing dainty little steps in her vellum-thin kid slippers, admiring herself with narcissistic delight.

'Oh, you're so clever!' she cried to Monday with a clap of her hands that in an older woman would have been affected, but in Isobel was just the spontaneity of an exuberant child. Her action caused the seed pearls and silver braid hemming the sleeves to gleam and sparkle. It was in the fitted style, clinging to Isobel's figure, which was fast developing the curves of womanhood. Indeed, Monday had had to let the garment out on its first fitting that morning.

'I am glad you like it, madam,' Monday answered, and thought with no recourse to false modesty that she had indeed surpassed herself this time. The Queen's court gown was breath-taking, but then so was the Queen. 'But you could dress in sackcloth and ashes and you would still be beautiful.'

Isobel wrinkled her narrow, pert nose. 'I wouldn't want to do that,' she said, taking Monday's words literally. She danced a little more before her own reflection, then clapped her hands again. 'John will love me in this. You must have a present! Everyone has presents at Christmas!'

Monday smiled at the girl. 'I have all that I desire for this Christmas season, madam; I am to be married on the morrow,' she said, and glanced at the betrothal ring on the heart finger of her left hand. It was of plain gold, but with two clasped hands forming part of the hoop, and the inside of the band was inscribed with the words *Vouse et nul autre* – 'You and no other'. She and Alexander had bought it from a London goldsmith on the day after their sojourn by her fire, and sworn an oath of betrothal before witnesses. The betrothal in itself was as binding as marriage in a court of law, for it had been sealed by their physical union. To all intents and purposes they were man and wife.

'Even more reason for you to have a gift!' Isobel cried, and summoned one of her ladies to fetch her jewel casket.

Monday began to feel uncomfortable. It was well and good to be paid in coin for creating a gown for the young queen, but to be presented with a more personal token made it harder to keep their dealings distant. Isobel might not care that she was bestowing presents on her husband's former mistress, but Monday did, almost as much as she minded calling a child of thirteen 'madam'.

'Who is he?' Isobel took the enamelled casket from her maid and threw back the decorated lid on glints of silver and gold, the gleam of river pearls and the sultry flash of gemstones.

'A knight in the lord Marshal's employ, madam. We are to be married tomorrow by one of the King's own chaplains, Father Ambrose.' Which was what she and Alexander had decided upon. Hervi, in his capacity of her former guardian, was to give her away in lieu of family.

'Do I know the bridegroom?'

'I think not, madam, Alexander de Montroi.' The mention of his name brought a tint of pink to her cheek and a flush of warmth to her loins.

Isobel shrugged in agreement. 'No, I do not.' She rummaged among her jewels, selecting and discarding several. Monday compressed her lips and wished to be elsewhere. Having decided to give her a gift, the Queen was now obviously struggling to find something with which she could bear to part. Monday wanted to declare that it did not matter, that she desired nothing, but decorum held her rooted to the spot in silence.

'Here, a pretty brooch,' said Isobel. 'Wear it at the neck of your gown for luck, and think of me.' She held out a silver disc with a spiral plaitwork design and a red glass bead at its centre.

'Thank you, madam, you are kind.' Monday accepted it with a modest curtsey and prepared to make her escape.

'I didn't really like it anyway,' Isobel confided sidelong, with a total lack of guile.

Monday declined to say that so much was obvious. Then the door to Isobel's apartment opened, and John walked in, accompanied by his three dogs.

Her heart sinking, Monday swept a curtsey, and for her pains was surrounded by the three smelly, far too friendly hounds. As once before, John had to rescue her by whistling them to heel.

'Do you like my gown – do you?' Isobel danced before her husband as she had been dancing before the mirror.

John beckoned Monday to rise. 'It is not as beautiful as its wearer,' he complimented with an indulgent smile, 'but yes, it suits you well.'

'Guess what, Monday's getting married tomorrow, and I gave her a silver brooch.'

'Married?' John's eyebrows rose, but so at least did his mouth corners. After one swift glance, Monday kept her eyes lowered.

If Isobel had been able to read atmospheres, her hair would have stood on end. But she was innocent and ignorant, which the other two were not. As it was, she looked up at John through her lashes and clung to him like a puppy. 'You should give Monday a present too, my lord, for her wedding.'

John gazed fondly down at his wife, then flickered a lazy glance at Monday. 'Yes,' he murmured, 'why not? It behoves me to be generous in remembrance of . . . services rendered.'

Monday's face flamed. This was unbearable. 'You have been generous enough, sire.'

'You think so?' He smiled amiably. 'I am not sure that your husband-to-be would agree with you, but then he is bound to see the circumstances in a different light.' He extended one hand in a gesture of benediction; the other held Isobel to his side. 'My wife, the joy of my life, would have me give you a present. Your wedding feast on the morrow, I will provide that.'

Knowing that she could not refuse, Monday capitulated with a subdued thank you that went unremarked, for Isobel was clapping her hands again, her sapphire eyes sparkling with delight as she listed all the entertainments they would have. Glancing at her former lover, Monday saw from his indulgent expression that his generosity, for what it was worth, was quite genuine – even if it was barbed with his customary cruel humour, and motivated by indulgence toward his child wife.

It was also obvious to Monday that she and Alexander had small choice but to endure.

Since the King and Queen had taken an interest in Monday's marriage, it was inevitable that others would follow, and although Hervi and Ambrose of Pont l'Arche had been set to represent the church at the nuptials, Godfrey de Lucy, Bishop of Winchester, insisted that he be the one to sanction the couple's union. Hervi and Ambrose were to be witnesses instead, and there was nothing that Alexander and Monday could do in public but smile gracefully and agree.

It was dawn of her wedding day and Monday, still dressed in her chemise, was combing her hair and keeping a watchful eye on Florian, who was splashing noisily in the bathtub where she had earlier bathed herself in preparation for the marriage. Her wedding gown was laid out on her bed – not one of the beautiful dresses that John had given her during her time as his leman, but the russet silk bestowed on her by Aline de Lavoux. She had altered it slightly, sitting up until the small hours to add a trim of gold braid, and plaiting gold silk threads together to make a girdle. On her head she intended to wear a caul of jewelled net, secured with a brass circlet. It would be different from the wimple of tradition, but still provide the necessary head-covering that all women had to wear unless they were young virgins going to their first man. She smiled wistfully at the thought. Alexander was her first man, and she had been a young virgin.

In the tub, Florian surged back and forth, creating waves of water which sloshed over the side and drowned the floor.

'Careful!' Monday admonished.

'I'm a sea monster, a fat-fish!' Florian declared, making loud swishing noises.

Monday rolled her eyes. He had been obsessed with creatures of the deep ever since Alexander had taken him to see an enormous whale that had fetched up on the beach close to Southampton Water on the day they landed in England. 'You will be a flat-fish if you don't stop,' she punned, smiling despite herself.

There was a peremptory knock on her door, and first her heart leaped, then it sank. It was still so early, too soon to put a smile on her face for intruders to whom this wedding was nothing more than a delightful diversion, an opportunity to stand on ceremony and show off their own fine clothes. She did not even have a maid to answer the door. Hilda had been afraid of crossing the Narrow Sea, and had opted to stay in Normandy. Isobel had promised to lend one of her own maids when the woman could be spared from her duties, but not until later. If this was her now, she had a bold knock for a refined royal attendant.

Setting down her comb, Monday swept her cloak around her shoulders and padded to the door. The knock came again, harder this time.

'Monday, open up, it's me!'

She raised the latch, and Alexander pushed into the room, followed by Hervi, Huw and Father Ambrose. The latter carried a garland of evergreen and mistletoe in one hand, and was robed in a sumptuous red and gold chasuble, with a contrasting stole of dark-blue embroidered silk. Hervi wore his customary habit, although the wool showed evidence of recent sprucing. Huw bore his master's shield across his back on its long strap. Alexander's hair was damp, just beginning to curl out of recently washed sleekness; his clothes were ordinary but clean, and there was an air of urgency to his movements.

Monday clutched the cloak to her throat. 'What are you doing here?' she demanded. 'It's bad fortune for the groom to see the bride until they stand before the priest!'

'What do you think we're doing now?' Alexander responded with a grin, and went to persuade his son from the bathtub.

'I'm a fat-fish!' Florian declared with a giggle.

'No you're not, you're a minnow.' Laughing, Alexander plucked him out and into a warmed linen towel. 'Hurry up and dress, you have something special to do.'

'What?'

'Wait and see.' He pressed a forefinger to Florian's nose.

Monday set her hands to her hips and scowled at the four

grinning men. 'Will you tell me what is happening? I thought we were to be married this afternoon at the cathedral by the Bishop of Winchester?'

Alexander nodded. 'With the entire royal court in attendance.' He gestured Huw to help Florian dress, and going to Monday, took her by the shoulders. 'But that is for them. Let them have their show. This is for us . . . unless I have misjudged you and you would rather wait?'

'You mean marry here and now?' She searched his face and saw the humour in his eyes, and the determination in the set of his jaw.

'Neither prelate nor king of the realm can stop us.'

Monday took her lower lip between her teeth, but not out of consternation, rather from humour, and a mild irritation that the thing had been sprung on her.

'Barefoot in my shift,' she said. 'Is that how you intend to have me?'

He stooped closer. 'Stark naked on that bed would be even better,' he murmured against her ear, 'but I think Father Ambrose's sensibilities would be outraged.'

She reached out from beneath the cloak to pinch his thigh, and he flinched with a muffled yelp. 'You deserved it,' she said, but she was smiling.

'So what do you say?'

'What bride would not leap at the chance to be married twice in one day?' She stood on tiptoe and brushed a kiss over his lips, breaking away before the embrace could tighten.

'Do you want to dress?' he asked.

Monday shook her head. 'No. I do indeed come to you barefoot and in my shift.'

'You are worth a fortune,' he countered softly, and touched her cheek.

Hervi cleared his throat. 'Are we to have this wedding or not?' he demanded gruffly. 'Unless you make haste, you're going to have more than just myself and Huw as witnesses.'

'I am ready.' With a tender look at Alexander, Monday laid her hand upon his sleeve.

'What do I have to do, what do I have to do?' Florian

demanded, wriggling his tunic down over his small shirt, assisted by Huw.

Father Ambrose beckoned to the little boy. 'Hold this sheet for me,' he commanded, and gave Florian a folded square of bleached linen. 'It is important, very important for your part in the ceremony.'

'Why?'

Ambrose stooped to the child's level. 'Because your mother is going to be married, and part of the words I will say and the things I will do will make Alexander your papa in the eyes of the Church and the world. Do you understand?'

Florian's gaze flickered to Alexander for reassurance, and when he received a nod and a smile, he passed it on to the priest. 'Yes,' he said stoutly. Actually, he was not certain that he did, but if holding this sheet was going to turn Alexander into his father, then he was willing not only to hold it, but guard it with his life.

'Good,' Father Ambrose encouraged. 'Now then,' and turning to Monday and Alexander, he took their hands and clasped them one over the other, right over right, left over left in the ancient hand-fasting tradition, and bound his purple silk stole over and around their joined hands. 'You know the words?'

'Yes.' There was no rigid pattern to what had to be said, but Alexander knew enough of tradition and common usage to be aware of what was customary. But looking at Monday, standing at his side, her hair unbound like a virgin's, her eyes holding the colours of smoke and silver and the wide grey ocean, he could barely speak. Clearing his throat, he said hoarsely, 'Monday, here I take you as my wife, for better or worse, to have and to hold until the end of my life, and of this I give you my faith.'

Monday followed his every word, slightly moving her lips as she did so. And then it was her turn, and her hands tightened their grip on his. 'Alexander, here I take you as my husband, for better or worse, to have and to hold until the end of my life, and of this I give you my faith.'

Father Ambrose solemnly unbound the stole and beckoned the squire to bring the shield and hold it horizontally like a table. Alexander unfastened the pouch at his belt, tipped three gold bezants and a faceted gold ring on to his palm, and laid them on the shield. Ambrose blessed both the ring and the coins, making the sign of the cross, and scattering holy water upon the former. Then Alexander took the money and put it in Monday's left hand, saying, 'With this gold I thee endow,' and slid the ring on to the heart finger of her right: 'With this ring, I thee wed, in the name of the Father, Son and Holy Spirit, Amen.'

'Amen,' Monday repeated on a whisper.

Ambrose bade them both kneel. Huw leaned the shield against the wall and stood at Monday's side. Hervi positioned himself at Alexander's. 'Now, child,' the priest said to Florian, 'give the sheet to Father Hervi and go and kneel in front of Alexander and your mother.'

Florian gravely handed the embroidered bleached linen to Hervi, who winked at him, and did as Father Ambrose asked. Hervi unfolded the sheet, giving two ends to Huw, and between them they shook and spread the cloth until it covered the kneeling couple and their son. This was the act that legitimised any children born out of wedlock, giving them the same status as those born on the right side of the blanket. Ambrose spoke the appropriate words, and blessed all three of them, signing a cross in holy water upon each brow. Florian squirmed and wrinkled his nose at the cold touch, but uttered no verbal protest. The sheet was removed, and the three of them rose to their feet. Florian wiped his hand across his forehead where a drip of water was trickling down.

'What God has ordained, let no man put asunder. You may now seal this marriage by exchanging a kiss through the garland,' Ambrose said, and his solemn intonation dissolved into a beaming smile as he held up the wreath of holly and mistletoe by its grip of green ribbon binding. Holding hands, Monday and Alexander leaned forward and kissed through the hole in the garland's centre, formally to complete the ceremony, and then again for themselves, until Florian pushed his way between them.

'Are you my papa now?' he demanded of Alexander.

Stooping, Alexander lifted his son. 'Yes, I am. You belong to me.' There was triumph in his voice, and fierce joy.

'So when I grow up, I can have your sword.'

Hervi made a choking sound. 'A de Montroi to the bone,' he chuckled with a shake of his head, and embraced Monday in a warm bearhug. 'Welcome to the family, sister.'

'When you grow up, you can earn one of your own,' Alexander told Florian, his eyes brimming with amusement. 'I had to.'

'You had to earn more than your sword,' Hervi said as he released Monday. 'And you haven't finished yet. You've a wife and family to support now.'

Florian balanced in the crook of his arm, Alexander set his other around Monday's waist. She looked up at him with lambent eyes, then at Hervi. 'We will support each other,' she said.

There was blood on the snow, spots of it melting the white crust and staining the ground a trampled, rusty pink where the boar had finally been overwhelmed. The sky was dead grey with the promise of more falls to come, and the air bitter on the lungs.

Thomas of Stafford watched his huntsmen whip the dogs into line and tie the pig across a pack pony to bear it home. Three hounds had been injured, one so severely that it had had to be destroyed; but a boar was not a beast to be hunted with impunity, and Thomas had known men to be hurt too. He handed his boar spear to his squire and turned his mount in the direction of home. His feet were freezing in the stirrups; his jaw ached with cold, his bones with age, and soon it would be dusk.

Wolves howled in the forests. The peasants were paid a mark for each pelt they presented at the sheriff's door, but in bitter weather like this there was a fine dividing line between the hunter and the hunted. Last week, the body of a young man, a charcoal-burner from Wooton Montroi, had been found mauled by wolves in the woods beyond Cranwell Priory.

Thomas knew for a certainty that folk would be hugging their fires on an afternoon like this, telling tales, making and mending, preparing for the feast of Christmas and St Stephen, but three days hence. His own Christmas meal was to be wild boar, supped at a lonely table with only his knights and retainers for company. He could have travelled south to Winchester with Ranulf of Chester and Ferrars of Derby, but he could not abide the thought of John's winter court. It would mean donning formal robes and being polite to men whose teeth he would rather kick down their throats. He had endured a surfeit of false posturing at the coronation of John's queen in October. A man belonged on his lands . . . a man should have heirs to inherit those lands. If only Gervais had been virile enough to beget a son, or strong enough to fight off the ague. If only his accursed daughter had not run off with some landless wastrel and squandered her life among the Norman tourney camps.

Thomas's stomach churned with a familiar, curdled heat. Too much black bile, his physician said; what did the old turnip-wit know? Besides, at eight and fifty, his bloodline barren, he was entitled to have an excess of black bile. He discovered suddenly that the killing of the boar had depressed him. There were too many similarities between himself and the enraged pig he had seen at bay. But he had no inclination to change direction. Let others change theirs.

The hunting party emerged from the forest on to the road. The wheel patterns of wains and carts tracked the snow, mingling with the half-moon bite of horseshoes, the cloven imprint of oxen and the mark of human passing. A pile of steaming dung revealed the recent passage of at least one horse, probably two, and animals larger than carrier ponies to judge from the size of the hoofprints leading from the dung.

Thomas rode on, following those particular tracks with bored curiosity. Two sets definitely, of approximately the same size, but one biting deeper than the other, as if more weight was carried. A rider and a pack animal, he surmised, and felt a small glow of satisfaction when he rounded a turn in the track and came upon a soldier with two horses.

The man had dismounted from a chestnut ambler and was adjusting a loose girth. Attached to his saddle by a leading rein was a bay destrier with deep chest and powerful rump. Thomas admired both horses with a professional eye, and cast his gaze over the soldier in the same way that he had observed and judged his tracks.

The animals were large because the man was large. Over two yards high, with wide shoulders and narrow hips. A quilted gambeson showed a flash of blue tunic at the leg slits, denoting that the stranger was wealthy enough to afford such a colour. The hands were those of a seasoned warrior, scarred and ringless, and the face which might have been handsome once was badly disfigured. A mercenary who had lived to be successful, Thomas thought, also noting the large sword at the man's hip, the morning star strapped across his saddle roll, and the shield hanging at his mount's withers. A useful man, but probably a dangerous one. No danger now, though, with his hands occupied by a girth strap, and outnumbered by the hunting party a dozen to one.

Normally, Thomas would have ridden on by without speaking, but his curiosity had broken the mould, and drawing rein, he gave a gruff greeting.

The soldier returned it with equal but civil brevity.

'Where are you bound, stranger?'

'To Stafford, my lord, to seek audience with yourself.'

'You know me?' Thomas's heavy lids widened. He wiped a drip from his nose on a horizontal forefinger and felt slightly discomforted.

'I saw you in London, my lord, at the young queen's coronation.'

'What were you doing there?' Thomas hated the thought that he had been observed without being aware. It smacked too much of his earlier thoughts about the hunter becoming the hunted.

'I was in the service of William de Braose, my lord.'

'And now you are not?'

'That depends on you, my lord.' He set his foot in the stirrup and regained the saddle, thereby towering over Lord Thomas. The chestnut snorted and pawed the ground.

'Why should it depend on me? De Braose has twice as much land and influence. He can afford to pay you.'

'I was thinking more in the way of a reward, my lord.'

'A reward? For what?' Thomas's voice developed a belligerent note. He was accustomed to controlling the lie of the land, and was beginning to wish that he had not followed the rash impulse to stop and speak to this stranger.

'Information.' The soldier drew the reins through his fingers

and kicked his mount into motion, so that Thomas had perforce
to follow.

'What sort of information?'

'About your granddaughter, Monday de Cerizay. I might be
able to help you find her.'

Cold fingers walked down Thomas's spine. He wondered what
this soldier knew that he did not. Then he thought of the young
man who had upbraided him in his own keep several years ago
about the missing girl, and inevitably of Gervais, his son, three
winters dead. 'If your best is might, then you need not bother
riding on to Stafford,' he replied, showing that there was no soft
underbelly in which to pin a spear. 'Either you can and we will
talk, or you cannot and you are wasting my time.'

The scars seemed to writhe on the soldier's face as his jaw
tightened. 'I can, my lord, that I promise you. Only last week I
saw and spoke to her.'

'Last week?' Thomas stared at him with narrowed eyes. 'Then
she is here, in England?'

'I will tell you what I know when we have negotiated the
reward.'

Grudgingly Thomas agreed. 'But before that, I would know
who you are, and what your interest is,' he said. 'Otherwise, I will
pay you nothing.'

Equally grudging, his companion shrugged. 'My name is
Eudo le Boucher, and I have served in the wars in Normandy
beneath King Richard and King John. I was negotiating to wed
with your granddaughter, but the agreement was reneged by her
guardian, and then she vanished.'

Thomas stared at the man. No ancestors had been invoked,
thereby revealing that le Boucher was of common stock. Most
men threw in a couple of 'son ofs' to emphasise the glory of
their bloodline. 'You say "negotiating". Do I understand that no
contract was made?'

'Unfortunately not, except by word of mouth, and that I
cannot prove.'

'You surely do not expect me to agree to your claim?'
Thomas's voice was husky with unconcealed revulsion. His
daughter had run off with a tourney knight, but at least the man

had possessed some breeding, being the youngest son of a noble Norman house. It was the first good thought he had ever harboured about Arnaud de Cerizay.

'No, my lord. But I thought that the amount of the reward might reflect my loss. I know that you will wish to betroth her elsewhere.'

They had reached the sunken, rutted road that led to the castle's great wooden gates. Thomas stared at the towers and walls that dominated the landscape, symbol of his power. 'Your loss,' he said with a curled lip. 'You want money for what was never yours.'

'I need only hold my silence, and it will never be yours either . . . my lord.' Le Boucher inclined his head in mocking deference. 'But that would be of benefit to neither of us.'

'You forget your place,' Thomas said coldly, but made no move to dismiss the man. He needed him, and they were both aware of the fact.

Le Boucher gave a cold half-smile. 'Oh no, that I have always known.'

Chapter 34

PEMBROKE, FEBRUARY 1201

The salt wind that had blown *The Argos* across the Irish Sea from Wexford to Pembroke howled through the scaffolding and beat against the new stone walls of curtain and keep that were being built to replace the old timber fortifications. Now *The Argos* rolled at anchor in the Pembroke river, battered but intact. The Irish Sea had been kind by its lights and mauled her but slightly. On the outward journey, the vessel had almost foundered in high seas and lashing rain. Only the intervention of God had brought her and the Marshal household safely to Wexford, and Lord William had made the vow to found a religious house in Leinster in gratitude for his life.

'I really thought we were going to die,' Alexander said to Monday, and closed his eyes, his body embalmed by the hot luxury of bath water for the first time in almost two months. 'I've never seen waves so big – higher than that stone wall out there, and our ship as tiny as a beetle crawling up its side. I've never been so sick either . . . or so terrified.'

Monday shivered and wished that Alexander did not have such a descriptive turn of phrase. She could imagine it all too clearly. How close she had come to being a widow, within eight weeks of being married. Although from the amount of time they had spent together thus far, she could scarcely believe that they were husband and wife at all. 'To have and to hold' had been in very short evidence. 'But you're home now,' she said, and knelt by the hearth to prepare him a cup of hot wine.

There were several wooden houses in the bailey, and Monday and Florian had been given one to occupy during Alexander's absence. The Countess had followed her husband to Ireland with a very limited entourage. There was no room on the ship for the knight's wives and their children, and Ireland was neither a tame nor a safe land. William Marshal had gone to visit his vassals and take their oaths of allegiance. Isabelle had travelled with him because it was through her that Marshal held the Irish lands, but it was very much a military visit, not one that required a sempstress. The Argos had sailed in the New Year, just two weeks after Monday and Alexander were married. For the last six, Monday had been living an industrious nun's life at Pembroke in a stark white winter landscape. Her needle had never been so busy.

The spices steeped in the wine gave the steam an aromatic fragrance. She brought it to him, and touched the back of his neck, where his hair was curling in the hot vapour from the tub. A sweet-sharp pang arrowed through her loins, and the touch became a caress.

He took a drink, his free hand rising to cover hers. 'Home,' he sighed with pleasurable agreement. 'You do not know how much I have missed you.'

'I can guess,' she said mischievously, her eyes on the bath water at the juncture of his thighs.

He followed the direction of her gaze and laughed. 'That's only the half of it.'

Her eyes widened as she feigned maidenly shock. Then with a giggle, she stooped over and kissed him on the mouth, her hands roving lower over his chest, a molten heat at her core.

Monday propped herself upon one elbow and trailed the fingers of her other hand over Alexander's ribs and abdomen in a light caress. He lay with eyes closed, the thunder of his heartbeat slowing in the aftermath of their urgent lovemaking.

She was glad that The Argos had docked at compline. It meant that they had all the night together without intrusion. Florian was sound asleep in his small bench bed against the wall. Although a hellion during the day, he slept like an angel at night. There would be no stopping his exuberance in the morning, she thought, when he discovered his father had returned.

'We won't be staying at Pembroke much above a week,' Alexander murmured, as she toyed with the sprinkling of wiry hairs on his breastbone. 'Lord Marshal is set to meet with the King and spend Easter with him at court.'

Monday grimaced. She would lief as not spend any more time in proximity to John. He had provided her wedding feast and the entertainments, had been at his most charming, but she had only been able to enjoy the second ceremony and the celebrations because of Alexander's thoughtfulness and foresight in providing the first. John had also claimed the right of kissing the bride beneath a sprig of mistletoe for luck, and his salute had gone beyond all bounds of propriety. She could still recall the feel of his tongue in her mouth, the taste of him, the grip of his fingers on her spine, and the taunting look he had cast at Alexander.

'You do not have to come. I will understand if you do not,' Alexander said neutrally.

'And not see you again for weeks, perhaps months on end? I can endure John if I must, but not the parting.'

'I do not believe you will have to endure him for long. My lord has hinted about giving me custody of one of his keeps or a feudal tenancy in the near future. "Now that you have a family," he told me, "a son to provide for." '

'Countess Isabelle said as much to me before you sailed,' Monday murmured. 'And I agreed with her that you were not only ripe for promotion, but eager to settle down to the yoke of government.'

'You did, did you?'

'Of course I did. Men might think that they move the wheels of progress but frequently it is their womenfolk who grease them for ease. Now Isabelle will speak to William in the leisure of their own chamber, as I am speaking to you. And he will be in a good mood and agree with her that yes, Alexander de Montroi should have a tenancy of his own as soon as possible. Her thoughts enforce his own and make him all the more likely to set the wheels in motion.'

He raised one eyebrow, but there was a half-smile on his lips. 'God preserve all men from the manipulations of women!' he laughed.

'I thought that was what brought you to the bed in the first place . . . my manipulations,' she said throatily, and ran her fingers down his chest, over the line of his lower ribs and into the hollow of his diaphragm. He gave a sudden flinch and a hiss of pain was forced through his teeth. Monday snatched her hand away, her expression filled with consternation. 'What is it, what's wrong?'

'Nothing . . . or at least nothing now. We were jousting for sport at Waterford and I took a shield rim in the side, probably cracked a bone. It's only sore if touched in the wrong place. In truth, I had forgotten about it.' He felt the injury himself with tentative fingers. 'Still, I won the bout. There's a pouch of silver in my coffer for you.'

'I would rather have you whole than any amount of silver,' she said, and smoothed her hand down over the stripe of hair below his navel.

'That is why I practise.' He cupped his hand in her hair and pulled her down to kiss him, and beneath her hand, his flesh stirred with renewed vigour. 'Rather a false move on the tourney field than that of battle.'

Monday shivered. 'I know that they are both a part of you,' she said, 'but I would rather have Alexander the scribe and poet than Alexander the warrior.'

'What about Alexander the lover?' he cajoled.

Monday shivered again, this time in response to what he was doing with his hands. 'Oh, him most of all,' she sighed.

The luxury of lying abed in a loved one's arms, of leisure and pleasure, did not last beyond a day. Lord William declared his intention of visiting his castles within the earldom of Pembroke, and summoned his escort to be ready to ride at dawn on the second morning for his keep at Haverford.

'I'm sorry, love,' Alexander whispered as he dressed in the

freezing dark by the light of a single candle. 'After Haverford it's
Cardigan, then Cilgerran. We'll be a week at least.'

Monday sighed inwardly, but kept too much disappointment
from showing on her face. 'But I'll have you for the journey to
court,' she said. Wearing her chemise, and wrapped in her cloak
for warmth, she tightened the laces in Alexander's quilted
gambeson, acting as his squire. Huw was out in the stables,
preparing the horses, and this was a last moment of intimacy.
'And that too will be at least a week.' Finished with the laces, she
fetched his mail hauberk, staggering slightly beneath its weight,
which lay in excess of thirty pounds. Alexander stooped into it,
carefully sliding his arms into the sleeves and easing his head
through the neck hole so that none of the rivets or a sharp edge
on a ring joint should tear his flesh. Then he stood straight and
jumped up and down. Jingling musically, the hauberk swished
down into place over his body, reaching below the knee and slit
front and back to the groin to allow for horse-riding. He had not
donned his mail leggings, but sported plain chausses and hose.
Full armour was only worn to war. The mail shirt was a symbol
of his knighthood today, rather than a protection against enemy
weapons. Monday supposed that she ought to be glad for small
mercies.

He reached to his sword belt, which lay on the coffer, and as he
picked it up, the strap end knocked Monday's prayer beads on to
the floor with a clatter. Alexander picked them up. They were a
fashion that returning crusaders had brought home from the
east. He remembered that his mother had possessed a set in
brown and cream agate. Monday's were positively garish to look
upon, and quite out of character – large wooden beads stained
red, yellow and blue, something that a child might own. He
resolved to buy her a more attractive set when they arrived at
court, and put the matter from his mind. Monday took the beads
from him and stowed them within the coffer, her complexion
slightly pink, as though she too were embarrassed by the sight of
them.

The sound of the falling beads, added to the stealthy noises
that had preceded it, had woken Florian. Sleepy still, knuckling
his eyes, he stumbled from his bed.

Unable to take the boy in his arms, which were clad in cold steel mesh, Alexander quickly buckled the belt and crouched to be on a level with him. 'Florian, I have to ride out with Lord William, but I promise to be home again soon.' He gripped his son's small hands in his own. 'Be a good boy for your mother; look after her.'

Florian yawned hugely. 'Don't want to. I want to come with you.' A mutinous lip jutted.

'It is too dark and cold, and you should still be abed.'

'Shouldn't!' Florian stamped his foot on the beaten earth floor.

'You want to be a knight one day, do you not?'

'Yes, but . . .'

'A knight must do as his liege lord commands. Today, although it would give me more pleasure to stay here with you and your mother, I have to ride at Lord William's side to protect him. And although it would give you more pleasure to ride with me, your duty is here with your mother. Next week, when I return, we are all to travel back to England. You can ride by my side then.'

'As your squire?' The mutinous lip disappeared.

'If you can behave in the meantime.'

Florian's dark eyes lit up. 'You promise?'

'On my honour. Now, the hour advances. Bring me my sword. And then, if you are swift to get dressed, you can see me out on the road.'

With alacrity, Florian went to lift his father's scabbarded sword from where it leaned against the wall, and with a frown of concentration on his face, brought it to him. It was almost as long as he was, the incised pommel on a level with his eyes. Alexander accepted the weapon gravely, treating the act as a ceremony, and attached the scabbard to his belt with great care, aware that Florian was watching his every move with wide, dark eyes, filled with a vision of knighthood. And why not? Alexander thought. Most men made do with reality, but to strive for the vision was no mean ambition.

The sword in place, he gently ruffled Florian's hair and reminded him about donning his clothes, then he turned to Monday. 'You as well, if you would see me on my way,' he murmured, and drew her lightly against him so that the hauberk rings would not bruise her flesh through the linen chemise.

'What's your bribe to stop me from tears and temper?' she teased.

He wound his fingers in her hair, drew her face up to his and whispered in her ear. Monday listened, then laughed and shook her head. 'You promise?' she said, echoing her son's earlier words.

'On my honour.'

'I'll hold you to it.' She set her arms around his neck, and for a moment the world went away. But it was no more than a moment. The taste of the kiss was still warm on her lips as he opened the door and stepped out into the dank February morning.

William Marshal and his troop rode out on the heels of the dawn, by which time Monday and Florian, warmly dressed, were there among the other members of the household to wave them on their way. Alexander smiled and blew her an echo of that earlier kiss. Monday returned it, watched until the last horse had disappeared under the portcullis, then, with a sigh, turned to her duties.

Florian went off to play at knights with several of the Marshal children. Lord William's marriage had been a prolific one, and in twelve years, Isabelle had produced eight children, four girls and four boys. And there was about to be a ninth addition.

Later that morning, the Countess summoned Monday to her chamber. 'I would like you to make me a gown,' she requested. 'One that will be flattering enough for the court, but comfortable should I start to swell.' She pressed her hand over the slight mound of her belly. Even when she was not pregnant the toll of carrying and bearing had left those muscles slack. Otherwise, the Countess Isabelle was tall and slender, with a sheaf of blonde hair and clear sea-green eyes. She was also less than two and thirty and had grown from girl to woman in a permanent state of pregnancy.

'Not that I am quite sure yet; I have only missed one flux,' she added, 'but it is as well to be prepared.'

'Indeed, madam,' Monday replied, and thought about the

string of beads in her coffer. Perhaps she should explain their efficacy to the Countess. Perhaps she ought to explain the beads to Alexander too, she thought wryly, before it became a secret by dint of not being divulged sooner.

Together, the two women began sorting through a coffer of fabric for something splendid enough for court, and plenteous enough to cover the bulge of pregnancy. The current fashion was for fitted dresses that clung tightly to the body, the trimness of the waist emphasised by girdles of double-looped braid. Obviously such an outfit was quite out of the question for a breeding woman. Even with the cleverest of stitching, a swelling belly was difficult to conceal, especially on someone who had borne eight children already. The cut had to be loose, and therefore the looseness had to be made into a feature.

It soon became obvious that there was not enough fabric in a single length to make such a gown, and no time before they left to purchase any new bolts of material. Isabelle shook her head with disappointment. 'The old green samite and a prayer that I do not grow too swiftly will have to do,' she sighed.

But Monday was not to be so easily defeated. An idea was beginning to form in her mind, and she set out a length of pale-blue linen, and another of darker-blue Flemish wool. Then she borrowed a wax tablet and stylus from Isabelle's chaplain and sketched what she had in mind. 'The blue linen for an under-gown with tight sleeves, and the fabric left from cutting the sleeves made into side panels to give you space to walk. It will be loose over the stomach. Then a sleeveless dress from the blue wool, rather like a man's surcoat, but worn without a belt, deeper sleeve holes, and heavily embroidered.'

Countess Isabelle was utterly enchanted by the idea. 'Aren't you clever!' she praised, and her green eyes gleamed. 'I'm glad that your husband is in William's employ. It means that I can now boast the services of the best sempstress in the land!' She cocked her head on one side. 'I think I will make it a condition of your husband's tenancy – that his wife should provide me with two new gowns each year. One at midsummer, one at Christmas.'

Monday paused in the act of folding the blue wool. 'His

tenancy?' she repeated slowly, and looked over her shoulder at Isabelle.

The Countess gave her a conspiratorial smile. 'William has decided to settle a fief on him before midsummer. I do not suppose I should have told you, but I have never been very good at keeping news to myself. And before you ask, I do not know where. William has not decided as yet.'

Monday began to stumble out words of gratitude, but the Countess waved them away. 'My husband only repays loyalty that has been earned by hard work and diligence,' she said.

In a daze, Monday gathered up the fabric and rose to her feet. When she and Alexander had spoken about the likelihood of being given a place to settle, she had never dreamed that it would come so soon. The near future had meant the next couple of years, not months.

The chamber door burst open and a tangle of children jostled into the room, chief among them Isabelle's eldest son, Will, a leather ball tucked under his arm. At eleven years old, tall for his age, with his father's sturdy bone structure and a genial, confident mien, he was preparing to depart boyhood for adolescence. Standing near him with two of the younger boys, Florian looked as dark and fey as an elfin child.

'Madam my mother, we have visitors,' Will said, his formal tone sitting quite at odds with the exuberance of his entry and the mud smearing the knees of his chausses and bedaubing his tunic.

'We seed 'em from the meadow,' announced Walter Marshal, closest in age to Florian, his mop of fair curls making him look larger than he actually was. 'Lots of them with banners.' He jumped up and down, encouraging Florian to do the same. 'On big horses.'

The Countess stared at the children. Monday could see that she was torn between wanting more information and delivering them a sound scolding about their manners. 'Visitors,' she repeated, pursing her lips. 'Does anyone know who?'

'I tried to enquire,' said Will in an aggrieved tone, 'but they thought we were peasant children. One of the knights drew his sword at us. So we came to tell you.'

'I know the knight with the sword,' Florian announced.

'Do not!' Walter gave him a shove.

'I do. I saw him in . . . in London.' Florian returned the shove with enough determination to knock Walter down.

'Enough!' the Countess commanded, her pale complexion suddenly flushed. 'It is small wonder they thought you peasants. William, go and change your clothes. Berenice, Olwen, take charge of the younger ones.' She snapped her fingers at two of her women.

'But I did see him in London!' Florian protested, his voice piping high with the determination to be heard. 'My papa knocked him down with a bathtub!'

Isabelle stared at him. 'With a bathtub?' she repeated, her own voice rising. Her gaze flickered to Monday for an explanation, and then filled with consternation. 'What's wrong?'

Monday groped behind her, found the solid comfort of the coffer, and sat down on it, for her legs were suddenly weak with shock. Over the past two months, dwelling in the distant safety of Pembroke keep, she had given small thought to Eudo le Boucher. Surely he could not have traced her here . . . unless he had traced Alexander.

'If Florian is right,' she said in a voice as pale as her face, 'the man is not a knight, but a mercenary such as Richard's Mercadier, or the King's Lupescar. I knew him a long time ago . . . in a different life. I don't want to see him again.'

The Countess frowned, and Monday could see that her curiosity was thoroughly whetted.

She swallowed. 'His name is Eudo le Boucher, and he was responsible for my father's death and my brother-in-law's maiming on the tourney field.' And quite probably he had not finished being responsible for other things.

'Then small wonder you do not want to see him,' said Isabelle. 'You had best stay here whilst I go down and discover precisely who has come to claim my hospitality.'

'Le Boucher was last in the employ of William de Braose.'

'De Braose? Oh, Jesu, I hope not!'

Monday was not surprised that Isabelle looked horrified. He was one of the most important barons along the Welsh march, but something of a swaggering bully, not renowned for his manners. De Braose and Marshal rubbed along reasonably well together; they had interests in common, but Isabelle found him a demanding boor, and would far rather her husband be the one to deal with him.

'If le Boucher seeks me, will you tell him that I am not here?'

Isabelle pursed her lips. 'You want me to lie for you?'

Monday shivered. 'He killed my father,' she repeated.

Isabelle considered for a moment. 'I will do my best,' she said dubiously. 'When I return, you can tell me about the bathtub!' Her expression troubled, she summoned a maid to attend her, and swept out of the room.

Monday closed her eyes. Her armpits were icy and she knew as she took the fabric for the Countess's new gown to the sewing trestle that she dared do no cutting out, for she was trembling like a leaf.

'It was him, Mama,' Florian said, as the Marshal children were ushered away by the two nurses to be spruced up for what might be an important visitor.

'Yes, sweetheart, I believe you.' Monday bit her lip. To keep herself busy she set about finding some thread to match the fabric.

'Does he really kill people?'

The need for reassurance in Florian's voice, the edge of fear in a child usually brimming with confidence, made Monday check her flyaway emotions. 'Not children,' she said, folding him in her arms for reassurance. 'He won't harm anyone here, I promise you.'

'I wish my papa was here.'

Monday thought it rather a blessing that he wasn't. 'He'll be back soon,' she soothed. 'Now, do you want to help me look for some thread in this colour?'

She settled Florian beside her and told him a story about a coat of many colours. They found the thread, and Florian discovered some glass beads in his mother's workbox and lined them up, creating different patterns. Finally, bored with that, his aplomb restored, he wandered across the chamber to join the Marshal children in a game of hoodman blind.

Monday too had been calmed by the interlude, and although she was still perturbed, she felt sound enough to apply herself to the laying out and cutting of the blue linen. She had just picked up her shears and was giving the fabric a final smooth when Isabelle returned, accompanied by a man in late middle-age, with thick white hair, a bulbous nose and weathered complexion. Monday had seen him once before, when she had stood one of many at the coronation parade, and watched him almost ride down a woman and child.

The other women in the chamber were staring too. Men not of the household were very seldom permitted into Isabelle's private bower.

Monday's scalp crawled. She pressed her hand against the blunt outer edge of the shears, concentrating on the bite of the iron against her flesh.

Isabelle came forward, preparing to play the gracious, if somewhat caught-by-surprise, hostess. 'Monday, I know you wished to be left in peace, but you have an important visitor. This is Thomas FitzParnell, lord of Stafford. Lord Thomas, this is Monday de Montroi, with whom you requested to speak.'

Monday squeezed the shears until her hand ached, and the blades crossed over. There was nowhere to run, the doorway blocked off by her grandfather's imposing figure. Besides, his men would be in the hall, and she relished a confrontation with Eudo le Boucher even less.

Thomas of Stafford rested his fists on his belt. 'I can see that you know me, even if I have never laid eyes upon you,' he said in a harsh voice. His chest rose and fell rapidly and compounded the aggression in his stance.

Monday just stared. This was the man whose rule her mother had fled, choosing love over obedience, and of whom she had so seldom spoken, and only then in a neutral tone that revealed nothing except by absence.

'Well, girl, aren't you going to speak? You do have a tongue in your head?'

Monday swallowed, her throat so dry that she thought she was going to choke. 'What is there to say?' she replied. 'Yes, I saw you at the Queen's coronation when you rode past me. Yes, I know my connection to your blood line, and how you severed it before I was born.'

Isabelle glanced between the two of them. 'I will bring wine,' she murmured, and gestured to a padded bench against the wall. 'If it please you, be seated, my lord.'

'Thank you, I will stand,' Stafford said, without even looking at her. 'My arse has been in a saddle the day long.'

Isabelle's face flamed. Her head high, she went to fetch the wine, and dismissed the goggling women to another chamber, leaving only the crone who kept the fire going, for propriety's sake. Not that propriety was much in evidence.

'Of course I severed it,' Thomas said in a tone that suggested Monday was a half-wit for even bringing up the subject. 'What else could I have done? Your mother was as good as betrothed to a man of my choosing, and against all respect and honour for her family, she despoiled herself with a common tourney knight. She was sixteen years old, with a head full of feathers from listening to too many troubadour tales. I went after her, you know, ordered her to return or be cut off. She thrust her wedding ring under my nose and told me she was never coming back.'

Monday leaned against the sewing trestle. The backs of her legs were trembling again, and she felt sick and cold. 'Then what do you want now?' She raised her voice in challenge, trying to find a refuge from her fear. 'Why seek me, when I have such common tourney blood in my veins? I have lived my life amongst whores and hucksters – have been a whore and a huckster myself.' She threw the last words down in challenge.

Thomas's mouth curled with distaste. 'I know all about your past,' he said.

'From whom, Eudo le Boucher?'

That surprised him. She saw the rise and twitch of his eyebrows, the annoyed firming of his thin, bloodless lips. 'My sources matter not. Suffice to say that while your mother lived you were cared for and held to a moral path whatever the squalor of your habitation. But after your father killed her, and then himself, you were led astray by undesirables.'

Although Monday laughed, her emotion was raw anger at his sanctimonious bigotry. Instead of squeezing the shears, she opened and closed them. 'Undesirables,' she repeated, nodding her head. 'Is that what you think? I must admit to you that I have never found my husband in the least undesirable. I could not say the same of le Boucher, and yet you see fit to employ him in your retinue.'

'He is nothing,' Thomas said impatiently, with a throwing gesture. 'I can dismiss him as easily as he was hired. He has served his purpose now.'

'As we all exist to serve your purpose and then be discarded? What is it you want of me?' She jutted her chin.

He crossed the room until he stood a sword's length from her, and then he perused her slowly from head to toe, as if assessing the points of a beast in a marketplace. 'You've better bones than your mother,' he acknowledged grudgingly. 'Good child-bearing hips, and height to pass on to your sons.'

'It must be the common blood in me,' she retorted.

Thomas ignored the sally. 'I have heard, too, that you have had no difficulty in conceiving.'

'I will not be a brood mare to your ambitions,' Monday said icily. 'If your son and heir were still alive, would you be here today?'

Thomas flushed. 'I have come in all good faith to offer to take you back to Stafford, to your rightful family place. To bury the shame of the past. You are my granddaughter, my heir, and your sons will be lords of Stafford when I am dead.'

'Whose shame?' Monday said in a quavering voice. 'My mother's, or your own?'

Thomas's flush deepened. His eyes watered, and he drew breath in laboured gasps. Despite her fury and disgust, Monday began to fear that he would have an apoplexy in front of her.

The Countess reappeared with a large basket tray bearing a flagon and cups. 'Some wine to quench your thirst,' she said, declaring the obvious into the terrible silence pervading the room.

The very trivia of her words, speaking of hospitality and domestic routine, broke the spell. Thomas flung round and strode over to the flagon. 'I offer her a barony and all she does is cast insults at me,' he snarled.

'I only return what was thrown in the first place,' Monday retorted. Remaining backed against the coffer for support, she watched him slosh wine into a cup and drink it down hard and fast. A second measure followed the first.

Isabelle looked nonplussed. There was no precedent for dealing with a situation like this.

Thomas paced the length of the chamber. 'You have spirit,' he allowed, hurling a glance at Monday. 'And you know how to hold your own. It's a pity you were not born male.'

She wondered if his words were supposed to be an apology of sorts. Certainly his tone had calmed, and there was almost a twinkle in the gimlet eyes. But his hide was so tough, his perceptions so distorted that he did not realise he had just piled another insult on top of all the others. 'Yes, what a pity,' she repeated with sarcasm, but saw that it was lost on him. 'If you make me your heir, that means that you accept my husband as your successor too. A common tourney knight like my father.'

Thomas drained his second cup of wine, filtering the dregs through his teeth. 'I had thought about that,' he said. 'Long and hard on the way here.' Returning to the flagon, he poured himself a third measure of wine, and swirled it around in the goblet. 'An annulment is for the best, I think.'

'An annulment!'

'It will be costly, I know, but I can recoup the amount on your next marriage.'

'You will find no grounds,' Monday choked out, so furious that she could scarcely speak. 'There is no consanguinity, no lack of consummation, nor was I forced against my will. Your spy will also no doubt have told you that my vows to Alexander were witnessed by no less than the Bishop of Winchester and the entire royal court!'

'Grounds can always be found,' he dismissed with a wave of his hand.

Swallowing, Monday opened and closed the shears again, then set them gently down on the coffer, not daring to keep them in her hand. 'Let the family ties remain severed,' she said huskily. 'I renounce the blood knot that you would rebind for your own selfish need.' Unable even to bear the sight of him, she turned her back, her spine rigid with the effort of control.

'Perhaps it would be for the best if you left, my lord,' Isabelle said quietly, looking between the two of them.

Stafford's jaw worked, and Isabelle took an involuntary back-step from the red glare he gave her. She inhaled to scream for help, but he tipped the remainder of his wine on the rushes, and without a word, jaw clamped, strode from the room.

A stunned silence filled the space where rage had been. The Countess started to follow him, but stopped after three paces and turned back to Monday.

In a voice that was flat, devoid of emotion, Monday said, 'He was offering me a treasure wrapped in poison. I had to fight; I could not let him win . . . Sweet Virgin, I feel sick.' She put her face in her hands, retreating, trying to shut herself away. But it was no use; the door would not close.

Isabelle poured wine into one of the other cups on the tray and brought it to Monday. 'Here, drink this, it's Gascon, our best, and strongest.'

Monday felt the cold pottery rim against her knuckles. She wrapped a trembling hand around the cup and took a swallow. Her gorge rose, and she clenched her teeth until the spasm passed.

Isabelle placed a supportive arm around her shoulders. 'Do I understand from what I heard that you are Stafford's heiress?'

Monday forced herself to breathe slowly. If she could master the sense of panic, the cold sweat, she would not be sick. 'My mother was his only daughter,' she said in a constricted voice. 'She eloped with a household knight rather than agree to the marriage my grandfather had arranged for her. He declared her dead from that moment forth. Now, because it suits him, because I am the sole surviving member of his blood line, he wants to put the past aside as if it never happened, and use me as a substitute for my mother . . . arrange a match for me, annul my marriage because it suits not his purpose.' She swallowed, and looked at Isabelle with glistening eyes. 'If my grandfather had given me one kind word, shown one mark of care or respect, I would have taken his hand and built a bridge.' She sniffed. 'I . . . I know that men often conceal their feelings by being bluff and brusque, but his were not feelings for me, but for himself. I wish he was different. I wish I hadn't said those words.' The first tears of reaction rolled down her face. 'If wishes were horses, then beggars would ride. Isn't that what they say?'

To which Isabelle had no answer.

CHAPTER 35

On the borders of February and March, the onslaught of spring had been curtailed by a heavy fall of snow. The cold gnawed at Hervi's stump and penetrated his marrow as he rode through the woods toward the forbidding grey arches of Cranwell Priory.

He was accompanied by his brother, Reginald, and an escort of two knights. There were wolves in the vicinity – a pack from the higher peaks and wastes to the north had strayed south in search of food. In these woods, too, there had been deaths and disappearances. Three young men in the last six years, and a pair of sweethearts who had entered the trees to make love and emerged two years later as whitened bones dug from a shallow grave by rooting pigs.

The sheriff's men had been unable to find a trail. Poachers were mooted as the most likely culprits, and a salutary warning was issued to the villagers not to tolerate them in their midst. But still the disappearances continued, and the woods and wastes between Wooton Montroi and Cranwell were rarely trammelled by lone travellers.

'Although God alone knows what business takes you to the Priory,' Reginald said on a burst of irritation.

Hervi smiled wryly. 'God's business,' he said with a sidelong glance at his eldest brother. The years had not been kind to Reginald. His hair was receding with tide-like rapidity, and the flesh drooped on his solid bones, making him look like one of the slot hounds panting through the snow beside them. Hervi had not seen Reginald in more than ten years, and having spent two nights in his company at Wooton Montroi was prepared to forgo the experience for at least another decade. He could have ridden directly to Cranwell, but conscience had nagged him into paying at least a cursory visit to his former abode.

'I do not believe you are a priest,' Reginald muttered for the hundredth time. 'And a crippled one at that.' He gazed, as he had been gazing for the last two days, at the rigid shape beneath Hervi's habit.

'I don't see myself as a cripple,' Hervi retorted. 'A man's mind is what matters, and I count myself less disadvantaged than you on that score.'

'That's a matter of opinion,' Reginald growled.

'Oh, indeed it is.'

They rode in silence for a while, Reginald hunched into his cloak, a scowl on his face, Hervi facing the bitter wind with a complexion inured to the weather by constant exposure. The bay beneath him had been particularly chosen by Hervi for its smooth, even pace. He had even trained the animal to come at a whistle and stand perfectly still to be caught and mounted. A one-legged man needed every advantage he could get. He did not think he would ever be as fond of the horse as he had been of Soleil, but there was a growing bond between them.

'You still haven't told me why you're going to Cranwell,' Reginald said at length.

Hervi faced straight ahead. 'Letters from the Bishop of Stafford and the Archbishop of Canterbury to deliver to the prior, if you must know.'

'What, they chose you as a messenger?' Reginald looked incredulous. The word 'cripple' hung unspoken in the air.

'No, I snatched the letters out of their hands and rode off with them!' Hervi snapped. Then he shook his head and drew a deep breath. Reginald would never be any different. 'I thought also that I would visit the place where you intend to transfer our parents' tombs. Alexander told me some time ago that you had an insane notion to move them from Wooton Montroi to Cranwell. I note they remain in their own church as yet, but I am curious to see what Cranwell has to offer that their home does not.'

Reginald's scoured red cheeks grew redder still. 'Prior Alkmund wanted me to pay a huge endowment to lodge them in his chapel. When I said it was too much, he suggested that I give the priory grazing rights on some of my land instead. I told him that I would think on it.'

And in his usual, procrastinating way, was still thinking, in the hope that the matter would resolve itself, Hervi thought. 'You could always graze more sheep, open the forest and use the revenues to build a new church at Wooton,' he suggested.

'Yes, I suppose I could.' Reginald looked doubtful.

Hervi suppressed the urge to throttle his eldest brother. What Reginald really needed was to be seated on a barrel of pitch at the moment it exploded. 'Tell me about Prior Alkmund,' he said, aiming for the core of what he wanted to know.

'He's a monk,' Reginald said with a shrug, as if it explained everything.

'So am I, but if that makes him and me similar in any way then I'll eat my saddle.'

'Jesu, I don't know.' Reginald knotted his brow as if in pain at being forced to think. 'He's courteous enough, I suppose, but aloof with it. You can't tell what's in his mind, and that is strange, for his eyes are so light a blue that you would think to see straight through them.'

'Appearances are often deceptive.'

Reginald rubbed at a smudge of mud on his mount's thick winter coat. 'He has a compassionate side, though, because he often distributes alms to the poor roundabout, instead of leaving such a task to his almoner.' Reginald shook his head at Hervi's snort of disbelief. 'No, it is true. I myself have seen him riding out with baskets of bread. And he must have courage too, for he ventures across these woodland wastes without escort.'

'Does he now?' Hervi digested the information with cynical eyes and pursed lips. 'And nothing ill has ever befallen him?'

'Only once, when he was nearly eaten by wolves, so I heard, but no, for the rest he has remained unharmed. Why, what's the matter?'

Hervi shook his head. 'Nothing.'

'Why do you want to know about him?' Reginald persisted.

'Are you aware that he has a carnal weakness for young men and whips?'

'Oh, not that old tale again,' Reginald scoffed. 'I heard some such nonsense from Alexander, but the lad was romancing. He's always held a grudge about being given to the Church. If he was beaten, then doubtless it was justified. Would they have made a prior of Alkmund if he had a stain like that on his character?'

Hervi drew rein. Overhead the sky was a bitter, bleached grey. The wind rattled through the naked black branches of oak and chestnut, and his breath was white on the air as he faced Reginald. 'You have escorted me far enough,' he said in a voice that although not raised, was ragged at the seams as he strove to contain his fury. 'The priory is not much further, and you have told me all that I need to know – about you, if not that accursed prior. I will keep my own company for the last two furlongs.'

Reginald stared, his face a mixture of bewilderment and indignation.

'A blind man could find the path with more ease than you,' Hervi said, and slapped the reins down on his mount's neck.

Reginald watched his brother ride on and dithered, both spurring his mount and reining it back so that the poor beast became thoroughly confused and turned round in circles. Finally, he decided to lay the blame of thick-wittedness at Hervi's door and turned for the familiarity of home.

Ignoring the bite of the chainmail, the smell of a man who had travelled hard and far that day, Monday flung herself into Alexander's arms the moment he entered the hall, and clung to him. They kissed, and she tasted the salt of sweat on his upper lip, and her skin was chafed by his stubble. She had never encountered such welcome sensations in all her life.

He laughed, breaking the embrace, to hold her away by the waist and look at her. 'I have only been gone a single week,' he jested, 'not a whole year!'

'It seemed like a whole year,' she said, and there was no jest in her own voice. Ever since her grandfather had ridden out, she had been waiting in a fever of anxiety for Alexander's return, each minute dragging out to the length of a day. She wanted to blurt it all out to him now, but she also knew it was not fair to

pounce on him the moment he set foot in the keep. Nor was it
news to be imparted in the midst of a throng.

'Well, for your sins, you are going to have me underfoot from
Whitsun onwards.' He grinned.

She gave him a questioning look. Whatever had happened, he
was obviously mightily pleased with himself. She had not seen
him so buoyant since their tourney days, when carrying off the
prize had been like fire to him. 'Meaning?'

'Meaning that my lord has asked me to take custody of
Abermon once more, as from May. He's sending the current
castellan to tend estates in Ireland. I have it for us, a castle and a
home.' He swung her round in his embrace. 'What do you say to
that?'

She tightened her arms around him. 'That I could not want for
anything more.' Her tone was fierce rather than joyous, and
Alexander, for all his delight, was no fool. He held her gently
away.

'Love, what is it?'

Monday shook her head. 'Wait until you have eaten and
bathed,' she said. 'It is nothing that cannot wait.' She tried to
sound eager. 'The Countess told me that the Marshal was to give
you a keep before midsummer, but not that it was Abermon.'

He frowned, and would have pursued his query, but Florian
appeared out of nowhere, and like a missile from a sling hurled
himself upon Alexander with delighted shrieks of 'Papa, Papa!',
thus putting an end to any serious conversation.

But the moment was only put off. Alexander remained in the
hall with his family to consume the food that was served up to the
returned soldiers, Florian seated upon his knee and chattering
nine to the dozen. As soon as he had finished, however, he
repaired with his family to their dwelling across the bailey.

Monday had been silent throughout the meal, merely toying
with the meat stew on her trencher, but drinking more wine than
was her wont. Now there was a high colour to her cheeks, but her
movements were still neat and steady as she poured hot water
from the cauldron into a large pottery bowl, and laid a cloth and
a jar of herb-scented soap beside it.

She helped Alexander to remove his hauberk, as she had

helped him to put it on a week since. Flecks of rust dappled her fingers, and made freckles on Alexander's face.

'Needs scouring,' he said. 'I'll set Huw to work on the morrow. We have two days before we leave for the court.'

Monday nodded, and without speaking, aided him to take off the padded gambeson, the linen streaked black by the steel. Florian sat down in a corner with his father's helmet, and industriously, if not very skilfully, began cleaning it with an oily rag.

Alexander straightened and eyed his wife. She had retreated within herself. He could almost see the barrier she was building to shut herself away. He had spoken to her of Abermon, of how much it meant to him, and would to her, and she had given the appearance of being raptly attentive, when all the time he knew that her mind was elsewhere. 'Tell me,' he said, catching her arm, turning her round as she started away with the folded gambeson. 'It will make no difference to my comfort whether you unburden yourself now or when I have washed.' Taking the garment from her, he threw it across the coffer so that there was no barrier between them.

Monday sighed. 'My grandfather came to Pembroke on the morning you left.'

'Your grandfather?' Alexander stared at her. 'How did he know you were here?' he demanded.

'Eudo le Boucher.'

She did not have to say any more. Alexander cursed and dug his fingers through his hair. 'What happened, what did he say?'

'He offered me his barony,' Monday said with a bitter laugh, and told him of her interview with her grandfather. 'Then he said that there were always grounds for an annulment and stormed out.' She caught her underlip in her teeth and looked at him anxiously. 'He won't be able to find any, will he?'

Alexander's expression had been tightening and darkening all the time that she spoke. 'Not so much as a single clause,' he said contemptuously. 'Not even the Pope himself could put us asunder.' He grasped her round the waist and pulled her into his arms. 'I promise you, sweetheart, he is going to find procuring an annulment as impossible as moving a mountain.'

There was anger in his kiss, and love, and a heavy seasoning of lust. Monday responded with a soft gasp and pressed into the embrace; hip to hip, straining and rubbing. Then, mindful of Florian, quietly occupied in his corner, they broke apart, looking at each other.

'There is nothing he can do,' Alexander repeated forcefully.

'I know. It's just that . . .' She grimaced and touched her wedding ring, pressing her forefinger into the incised design so that it left its imprint on her skin. 'He made me feel vulnerable and afraid.'

'Small wonder,' Alexander said grimly as he began to wash. 'I only wish that I had been there to receive him.'

Monday thought it a blessing that he had been absent, for such an encounter would have gone beyond words, of a certainty. Turning away, she fetched a linen towel from its warming place by the central hearth. 'I did not know my own tongue could be so sharp,' she said. 'I think I cut him as much as he cut me.'

'But you were using it in self-defence. He was the one who attacked first.'

'So you think I am justified?' she said neutrally.

'You would have been less justified not to speak out.' He threw down the cloth and took the towel from her hands. 'It is in the past. Any guilt is not yours, but his.'

She gave him a dubious look. 'You would have made a very comforting priest.'

'God forbid. That is in the past too!' He snorted. 'The family priesthood is safe in my brother's hands now, God shine on him wherever he is.' Donning the clean tunic and shirt she handed him, he kissed her. 'The memory will fade with time; I promise.'

'Yes, I know.' Monday returned his kiss, and rubbed her forehead against his shoulder, seeking comfort.

Attempting to lighten her mood, he fetched his belt and attached purse from the coffer. 'I brought you a present from my wandering,' he said. 'An Irish priest was selling these in Haverford.' He placed a drawstring pouch of soft kidskin in her hand.

Monday hesitated, her underlip caught in her teeth.

'Go on, open it,' he urged.

A smile in her eyes, she pulled the woven drawcords apart. 'I think I can guess,' she said, and tipped the string of prayer beads out into her palm. Striated, glorious colours slid between her fingers – cream and cinnamon, salmon pink, gold, and soft fern-green. Polished and sensual. 'Alexander, they're beautiful!'

'You like them?'

'Why, yes!' She ran them from hand to hand, and he saw the genuine pleasure sparkling in her eyes.

'I thought they were an improvement on those old prayer beads of yours.'

'But I haven't got any . . .' she began, and then her colour heightened. Leaving him, she went to her coffer and fished out the string of beads that Dame Hortense had given her. 'These, you mean?'

He nodded and pulled a face. 'Small wonder you never bring them down to mass, they're hideous.'

Her cheeks flushed. 'They're not for prayer, or not in the sense that you mean.'

'Then for what?'

She gave him an assessing look, then indicated the bed bench at the side of the room. 'Sit down and I will tell you.'

A large iron brazier filled with glowing lumps of charcoal cast out waves of heat to warm the prior's private quarters. The best charcoal, Hervi noted, no brown ends, and profligately used. But then, although it did not show on his thin, ascetic frame, Prior Alkmund was a man of appetites.

'It is not often that we receive visitors from beyond the county's borders,' Alkmund said pleasantly, and gestured Hervi to be seated on a cushioned box chair near the roasting wooden coals. 'Let alone one intrepid enough to travel through bad weather and danger with the burden of ill health.'

Hervi rubbed his leg and made a deliberate effort to remain civil and calm. The man looked like the icon of a holy martyr, with his patrician bones and narrow Romanesque brows, but he made Hervi's hackles rise beyond their very roots. 'I thank you for your concern, but there is nothing wrong with my health. I can do most things that any other able-bodied man can do. The weather is not pleasant, I grant you, but I have endured worse. And I encountered no danger. Should I have done?'

'The woods are always dangerous for those who are not familiar with their ways, Father Hervi,' Alkmund replied smoothly, as he poured dark wine from a pitcher into two cups.

'I am told that you often venture abroad on errands of mercy without an escort.'

Alkmund smiled, but his eyes were watchful as he gave Hervi the wine. 'May I ask who told you?'

'One of your neighbours, Reginald de Montroi,' Hervi said. He had no intention of telling Alkmund that he too was a Montroi. 'He provided me with an escort as far as your gates. He told me that wolves of both the four- and two-legged kind abound in these parts. Are you not afraid?'

'Not with God at my side.'

Hervi took a drink of the wine. It was sweet and heavy, dark as blood, and made him want to retch. 'I have brought letters,' he said. 'From the Archbishop, summoning you to an assembly concerning the initiation of oblates and novices.' Leaning to the leather satchel at his side, he withdrew a sealed packet and held it out to Alkmund.

'The Archbishop sends a one-legged monk as his messenger?' The long, thin fingers avoided contact with Hervi's as they took the package.

'Appearances are not everything,' Hervi said softly, and folded his hands within his habit sleeves. It was at times like these that he missed the comforting weight of the sword at his left hip.

Alkmund slit the seal on the package. 'Indeed not. You must be a man of rare talents to triumph despite your disability. How came you to have but one leg?'

'An accident with a scythe,' Hervi answered with a shrug, making it obvious from his tone that he did not want to discuss the subject. 'Do you have many novices here?'

'We receive our share,' Alkmund said, and frowned as he scanned the lines of writing. As well he might, Hervi thought, watching him from beneath lowered lids. There were moves afoot within the Church to discourage the donation of small children to religious houses. A monastic life should be born of a true vocation, and initiates should be in late adolescence at least. But it wasn't just that Cranwell's supply of younger oblates was likely to be curtailed. Hervi knew that the Bishop of Stafford said in his own particular letter that he had heard disquieting tales about the kind of training Cranwell's novices were receiving, and that a full inspection was to be conducted after Easter.

Alkmund glanced at Hervi. 'Do you know what is contained in these letters?'

'The gist only.'

'There have never been any complaints about this priory,' Alkmund said, tight-lipped. 'The local families send their sons here to receive a decent education. We are praised for our standards and our piety. Whoever has been spreading this slander deserves to be whipped.'

Hervi's face suffused with dusky colour, and his eyes watered with the effort of controlling his rage. He could not speak, knew that if he moved, it would be to snap Prior Alkmund's elegant throat.

Alkmund appeared not to notice Hervi's immobility, his attention all centred upon the unpalatable tidings in the two letters. 'Let them come,' he said through his teeth. 'They will find nothing untoward at this priory.'

'That remains to be seen,' Hervi said, and rose stiffly to his feet, knowing that he had to breathe clean air. Outside a bell was tolling, calling the brothers to the service of lauds. 'You will excuse me. I need to wash before prayers.'

Alkmund inclined his head. 'Whatever we have is yours,' he said in a tone that declared the opposite.

Hervi banged out of the room. The raw February air hit the cold sweat on his body and turned it to ice. There was rage in his veins, and because he had to control it, it made him sick. Clamping his jaw, ignoring the nausea in his stomach, he limped back to the priory guest house, washed his face and hands in the ewer provided, and went to join the monks in prayer. And when prayer was finished, he started asking questions, and he began to look around.

It was late afternoon, the sky fading to dusk, when, a cresset lamp in his hand, Hervi followed the dark, evil-smelling stairway

down past the latrine shaft and came to the cells which had fea-
tured so vividly in Alexander's dreams. A heavy oak door faced
him, its surface pitted with black iron studs. Hervi slid aside the
grille and peered into the depths. There was a rustling of straw,
a scurry and a squeak, but no larger movement. He set his hand
to the latch and pushed. At first nothing happened. He used the
weight of his good side, and the door moved a few inches, prevented from widening further by a clump of straw wedged
behind. Holding the lamp on high, he eased into the room, and
gazed around in the gigantic flares of light and shadow. Rank
straw carpeted the floor of beaten earth, and as Hervi walked,
blue mould puffed upwards from each footstep. He coughed on
the smell and buried his nose and mouth in his habit. Somewhere
water was dripping, and the place possessed a bone-deep chill. As
he trod forward, he encountered a soft lump in the straw, and he
recoiled with a hiss of disgust, thinking that he had set his foot
upon a dead rat. The cresset lamp flared wildly and almost blew
out. Drip, drip, went the water, the sound echoing until he could
almost fancy he heard voices in the walls.

The dead rat proved to be a hunk of bread, stale but not as yet
tainted with the mould. Hervi picked it up and turned it over in
his hands, noting the marks of teeth other than rodent.

'You will not find anyone in here.'

His heart thumping, Hervi whirled round, and found himself
facing not Father Alkmund, as he had expected, but a smaller
monk, with a dapper silver tonsure and sharp, neat features. A
hoop of large iron keys hung on the rope belt at his waist. 'Who
are you?' Hervi's demand was brusque with the tension that was
crawling over his flesh.

'I am Brother Willelm, the preceptor.' He cocked his head
slightly to one side like a bird. 'Are you lost?'

It would have been face-saving and diplomatic to say that he
was, but Hervi had heard of Brother Willelm before. 'You are the
one who let the novice, Alexander de Montroi, escape, aren't
you?' he said.

The monk stiffened and drew back a little. His glance flickered towards the musty draught fingering through the wedged
door. 'What do you know about that?'

'Everything.' Hervi turned the hunk of bread over in his hand. 'You say that I will not find anyone here, but I seem to have found his breakfast.' He tossed the piece of loaf, and Brother Willelm instinctively put out his hand to catch it.

'Are you here to investigate us?' he demanded.

'No, just to make a preliminary report to my superiors about the way matters stand at Cranwell.' Hervi stirred his toe in the mouldy straw. 'What do you think of the rule here?'

'It is not for me to say.' Once again the preceptor looked over his shoulder.

'Then who am I to ask . . . the novices?'

He saw the slight twitch of flesh along Brother Willelm's cheekbone and knew that he had struck a telling blow. 'Where is the last occupant of this cell?'

'Prior Alkmund is strict about discipline,' Willelm said reluctantly. 'He will tolerate no deviation from the rule, and is swift to punish those who stray.'

'I had heard that he was a saint who ventures out alone in the teeth of danger to bring comfort to the poor and the sick,' Hervi said without inflection.

Brother Willelm winced again.

'Is it true?'

'Indeed he does go abroad as you say.' The monk looked down at the bread in his hand and then back at Hervi. 'How do you know about Alexander de Montroi?'

Hervi shrugged. 'I have not always led the life of a monk,' he said, choosing his words carefully, knowing that they might well be reported back to the prior. 'Alexander lodged with me for some time, and told me what had happened at Cranwell.'

'He was a troublemaker,' Willelm said.

'Yes, I saw the stripes across his back. He still bears the scars almost ten years on.' Hervi turned to pace the dank and loathsome cell. 'Night after night he would awaken screaming about skeletons appearing out of the walls. If he so much as saw a priest he would flinch in fear.' Coming full circle, he stopped again before the agitated preceptor. 'You saved his life when you "forgot" to lock this door, even if your reasons were selfish.'

The preceptor rose in Hervi's estimation when he did not

attempt to deny the truth of the statement, and proved his troubled conscience by asking, 'What . . . what became of him?'

'He is a hearth knight of William the Marshal, Earl of Pembroke, and is wed to a lady who has connections with the King himself. They have a young son and great hopes of future prosperity.' There was deep satisfaction in Hervi's voice, and it kindled a spark of relief in Brother Willelm's expression.

'I was worried for his person as well as his soul,' he admitted. 'And I did pray that God would bring him to a safe harbour.'

Hervi's mouth curved wryly. He would hardly call the tourney route a safe harbour.

'There was a novice in here,' Brother Willelm volunteered in a voice filled with shame and not a little distaste. 'He was moved two hours since to the infirmary. Prior Alkmund decided that he had learned his lesson.'

'What was his crime?'

'Running down the dorter stairs and being late for offices.'

'And for that he was locked up in here?'

'As I said, Father Alkmund's regime is strict.' The preceptor avoided Hervi's gaze.

'In the infirmary, you say?' Hervi turned towards the door.

'Yes, but I don't think that you should . . .' Willelm began, then broke off with a distressed, helpless gesture of his hands.

'Even more reason to do so, then,' Hervi said grimly, and stumped up the stairs.

There were four monks in the infirmary, and three of them were elderly. The fourth lay on his stomach at the far end, a youngster of fourteen or fifteen with blond, untonsured hair and fine, regular features. He had not been tied, there were no marks on his wrists, but from the way he was lying, he had obviously been whipped. His face was pale and bleached of expression. Reminded of Alexander, Hervi was filled with tender rage.

'Let me see your injuries,' Hervi said, and drawing down the sheet, gently eased the linen alb off the novice's shoulders. Deep pink welts crisscrossed the white skin, the blows skilfully laid so as not to draw blood. Hervi's lips tightened. He swore a soldier's oath beneath his breath.

The youth turned his head and gazed at Hervi out of

wounded dark-blue eyes. 'I was running when I should have walked,' he said, and his throat bobbled up and down. 'And I was late for vespers.'

'Those are not causes for this kind of punishment,' Hervi said. 'Has this ever happened before?'

'Only once, in the autumn, when I dropped a basket of apples during the harvest and they were all ruined.'

'Son, I swear to you it will not happen again, whatever the cause,' Hervi said grimly, and gently covered the youth again. 'There are going to be changes here, and very, very soon.'

Hervi attended early-evening prayers with the other monks in the chapel, stiffly declined Alkmund's offer of supper in his private chamber, and opted to dine in the refectory with everyone else and then sleep on a spare pallet in the dorter. Hervi was not by nature fanciful, but a feeling of oppression crept over him. Alexander's skeletons were too close for comfort. He dozed, but his body was as alert as it had been in his soldiering days, ready for the slightest move to be made upon him.

But nothing happened. The monks descended to their evening prayers. Routine was smoothly observed, and no sinister dark shadows attempted to part Hervi from his life. He rose at dawn, prayed with the others, then went to saddle his horse.

'God speed you on your way and grant you a safe journey,' said Prior Alkmund, his manner icy. Their first interview, coupled with Hervi's snub of the previous evening, had shown which way the wind was blowing.

'I am sure God will,' Hervi responded as he eased his position in the saddle to make his damaged leg more comfortable. 'I will pray for your soul.' With a curt nod and a click of his tongue, he urged the horse into a trot.

Alkmund watched him ride out of the priory gates, but did not delay beyond the last sight of bay rump and black tail. Fetching his cloak, he saddled up his own grey cob, told the almoner and gatekeeper he was going out on one of his visits, and took the same path as Hervi.

Hervi breathed deeply of the sharp winter air. It cleansed his lungs of the miasma of Cranwell, and his soul stretched itself like a tree towards the light. The priory should be torn down stone by stone, he thought, and each stone piled on top of Alkmund to make his grave. When Hubert Walter of Canterbury heard what was happening at Cranwell, Alkmund would be disgraced and defrocked. Hervi hung on to the thought, knowing that for two pins he would have spared the Church the necessity of investigation by dealing with Alkmund himself.

There had been a fresh sifting of snow overnight, and his horse moved silently along the forest path. Spring was on the horizon, but it was impossible to imagine this wood filled with bluebells and thrusting, budding greenery. Yet there was beauty in the starkness too, Hervi thought, and glanced around, appreciating nature in order to soothe his mind.

Something flickered in the corner of his eye – as if the woods had moved, for the colours were the same. But when he looked round, he saw nothing. All that rose in the air was the vapour of his own breath. He was alone . . . completely. Prickles of apprehension ran down his spine. Thoughts of wolves came to mind, but his horse seemed equable enough; calm gelding though it was, it would have taken to its heels with a vengeance at the first scent of danger. All the same, Hervi felt for the security of the eating knife thrust through his rope girdle, and put down his cowl so that he had a wider range of vision

There it was again. Hervi whipped round, and saw the grey horse moving between the trees, its hoofbeats muffled to silence by the snow, the prior on its back. Realising that Hervi had seen him, Alkmund urged the grey on to the road, waving for him to wait.

Hervi had a strong impulse to kick the bay into a canter and ignore the gesture, but against his better judgement, he drew rein. Forcing a horse to speed on this kind of terrain was dangerous, and he still had nightmares of Soleil going down, and the awful crack of shattering bone.

Alkmund caught up, and Hervi saw that his chest was heaving and his eyes fever-bright, but their blueness was of ice, not incandescence.

'I must talk to you,' Alkmund said. 'I very much fear you have received the wrong impression of Cranwell.'

'Oh, not in the least. It is everything I expected,' Hervi replied. 'You need not waste your breath in persuasion.' He clicked his tongue to the horse and kicked its flanks. Then, as the gelding moved off, Hervi decided to tell Alkmund that he would owe his downfall to the de Montrois. He knew that it was being unnecessarily vindictive, but he could not prevent himself. The glance over his shoulder as he drew breath to speak saved his life. The club which Alkmund had swung at his skull caught him a grazing blow down the side of the face, bruising flesh instead of crushing bone.

Hervi cried out at the suddenness of the assault. It was on his bad side, and it unbalanced him. The gelding circled and plunged, eyes showing a rim of white. Hervi struggled to maintain control of the horse as Alkmund swung at him again. He had to raise his arm to block the blow and the club smashed down. There was heat and pain, and a flowering numbness. He is going to kill me, Hervi thought. If I do not stop him, he is going to kill me, and who will know?

The thought of his corpse being left in the forest to be devoured by wolves, or to rot unsought in a shallow grave until the village pigs dug him up, sent a surge of panic through him, swiftly followed by one of rage and indignation. Christ, he had been a soldier before he became a monk. He wasn't going to let a creature like this murder him.

Dragging hard on the rein, he curved the gelding to one side to avoid the next strike of the club, ducked in under the swing, and seizing Alkmund's wrist in his good hand, twisted with all his might. Alkmund screamed and dropped the club. Hervi's move fetched both men off their horses and they crashed to the ground in a tangle of limbs.

Sobbing through his teeth, Alkmund threshed to his feet and tugged his eating knife from its sheath on his belt. Snow crystals gleamed on his scalp, melting to water on his tonsured skin. Lips writhed back from his teeth, he hung over the winded Hervi.

'They will come looking for me,' Hervi said. His bowels were loose with fear, but on the edge of death, his mind was sharp.

'And find nothing. These woods are notorious for the danger they hold.'

'The Archbishop will not let matters rest, let alone my body. And even if you should cover your tracks, there are still those who will testify against you, those whom you can no longer reach with your whip.' Beneath the cover of his habit, Hervi fumbled with the fastening of his wooden limb. The stump was doubled beneath him, one strap broken in the fall.

'You are lying,' Alkmund dismissed, but there was a glimmer of consternation in his eyes.

'You know that I am not. Why else should Canterbury decide to meddle in Cranwell's affairs?'

'Who then?' The knife menaced closer, bleak light gleaming along the blade.

Hervi gently freed the second strap and curled his fingers around the shaped crown of the stump. All the time he looked at Alkmund, willing him not to see the motion of his fingers, willing him not to strike. 'Do you remember Alexander de Montroi?'

The consternation sharpened, turning almost to fear. 'Of course I remember him,' Alkmund snarled. 'A half-infidel brat with the stink of hell about him. If he is your witness, you are a fool.'

'He is now one of William Marshal's knights and stepping high on fortune's ladder,' Hervi said softly, watching his moment, his fingers tightening. 'And I can vouch for his character with Hubert Walter of Canterbury, since I know everything about him. You see, I am Hervi de Montroi, his brother.'

Alkmund's eyes widened. The dagger flashed, and Hervi surged. Steel met wood as the knife stuck in the oak of Hervi's peg leg. Hervi wrenched the limb away, the weapon still embedded, and returned it back-handed against the side of Alkmund's head, with all the force that had once made him so powerful a swordsman. A look of utter shock on his face, Alkmund collapsed. Despite the strength of the blow, the knife remained embedded in the wood, testament to Alkmund's own fury.

The makeshift weapon poised, Hervi crawled on one knee to the prior. Alkmund stared at him. Blood ran from his nostrils and one ear, and there was a soft dent in the side of his head like a giant thumbprint.

'Dear Christ,' Hervi whispered, feeling both relief and nausea.

He had long thought about killing Alkmund of Cranwell, but it had been a suppressed desire, something that he kept caged in the darkest part of his mind. His goal had been to depose the man, rob him of his power. Now he had done both, and no blame to his soul, for he had only been defending himself against certain death.

Crossing himself, making the same sign over the body in the snow, he muttered the appropriate words and closed the staring blue eyes. Then, turning aside, he retched until his stomach ached as fiercely as the rest of his bruised body.

When he had recovered, he worked the knife from his wooden limb, noting that he would require a replacement as soon as he could find a carpenter to shape one. With tremors of cold and shock in his hands, he managed to fasten it back on after a fashion. It was not sound enough to enable him to drag a body any distance. A whistle brought his bay gelding trotting out of the trees, its ears pricked.

Now he unfastened his rope girdle, removed the corpse's too, and tied them both together. Then he joined Alkmund's wrists and knotted the rope firmly around them, and lashed the other end to the saddle. With soothing words as much for himself as the gelding, he set his good leg in the stirrup and mounted up. Then he turned into the trees, Alkmund's body dragging and bumping behind.

He drew rein in a thicket about two miles from the main track, and here he cut the rope with Alkmund's knife. Dismounting, he rolled the body into the deepest, darkest covering of trees and low bushes until there was nothing to see.

The forest had claimed another victim, and in so doing was now a safer place.

His thoughts sombre, but the weight lifting from his heart with each step the gelding took, Hervi rode towards the light leading out of the trees.

CHAPTER 36

'Your granddaughter?' John's look was one of utter astonishment. Then he laughed and waved his hand as if shooing a fly. 'I do not believe it!' He glanced round at his close circle of officials and barons, sharing the jest with them.

Thomas of Stafford reddened beneath their amusement, but with more anger than chagrin. 'Sire, it is true. I have at least one witness to swear, and others can be found. The girl herself admits to being of my blood.' Thomas had followed the court to Canterbury for the Easter festival, hoping for an audience with the King, and his dogged persistence in refusing to move from the royal antechamber had paid off. John had agreed to see him. That it was only the better to be rid of him did not bother Thomas. What he had to say would give him the attention he required.

John rubbed his jaw, his beard badgered with silver. 'Then what is your complaint?' he demanded. 'Why seek audience of me for what is a matter of your own family?'

'Sire, I want her marriage annulled, and I know that you have influence with her.'

John laughed, then ceased abruptly. 'Had you come to me earlier, I would have been able to help,' he said, 'but it is too late now. She is wedded and bedded, the proceedings overseen by the Bishop of Winchester himself. I myself bestowed the bride upon her husband, and paid for their wedding feast. There is nothing to be done.'

Stafford tightened his fists against the prickly embroidered wool of his blue court robe. 'Nothing?' he repeated angrily, and looked at the handsome, dark-eyed man slouched in the carved chair, the crown of England dangling from an indolent forefinger. Green and red stones winked in the candlelight. Gold shimmered. It was all dross. 'I gave no consent to the match, and I am her only living kin. I have been seeking her for more than five years, but that infidel she married kept her whereabouts from me until he had her safely at the church door. He has denied me my granddaughter!'

John sucked his teeth. 'I think you overstate your case, my lord. Is it not true that you disowned the girl's mother for running away with a tourney knight?'

'That was while I still had a son and the hope of grandchildren of his loins,' Thomas replied, breathing heavily. 'Now I have only the girl, and Alexander de Montroi is no suitable husband for her.'

'A tourney knight,' John mused, rubbing salt into the wound, his eyes shrewd. 'One generation begets another, eh?'

Behind tight lips and lowered brows, Thomas fumed. 'I want the wench to marry the man of my choice; to be in my wardship, and under my control. And I am prepared to pay for it.'

John swung the crown gently on his finger, and swung his leg too, echoing the rhythm. 'I repeat, there is nothing I can do,' he murmured, gazing at the crown. 'Your granddaughter and Alexander de Montroi are married . . . until death do them part.' The dark eyes flashed from beneath the saturnine brows, then returned to admiring the gold.

Thomas sucked a sharp breath through his teeth and wondered if he had understood aright. Was John suggesting that de Montroi should die? Was he giving implicit permission? Or was it just an unfortunate turn of phrase?

'William Marshal is here in Canterbury with his entourage,' John continued smoothly. 'I am going to ask him to hold a tourney for the younger knights, and give a fine warhorse and all its trappings as the prize. I have no interest myself, but I know that it will amuse the Queen, and other men are fond of the sport.' He rubbed the side of his nose. 'It might be worth staying to watch.'

Given a normal audience, Thomas would have snarled that tourneys were for fortune-seekers and gutter-sweepings, but the fact that this was the King, and his statement highly open to interpretation, held him silent.

'If your granddaughter should ever become a widow, we could come to some arrangement,' John added nonchalantly. 'Although I could never wish more for Alexander de Montroi than a long and prosperous life.' And he exposed his beautiful white teeth in a smile that was just a shade too lupine.

A glimmer of understanding shed a bleak light in Thomas's mind. It was about control, about having and losing, resentment and jealousy . . . and perhaps even revenge. He met the King's eyes briefly with his own. Both men guarded the deeper thoughts, but the exchange was enough, and a kindred intent recognised.

'Perhaps, sire, I will take your advice and remain for the tourney,' murmured Thomas, inclining his head.

John shrugged. 'It is your decision,' he said, and turned to speak to one of his clerks, indicating that the audience was at an end.

Deep in thought, Thomas of Stafford left the palace and returned to his lodgings.

Jankin the hafter sucked his few remaining chipped teeth, and folding his arms against the pole of his booth, considered Alexander with his customary jaundiced eye.

'I'd credited you with more sense than returning to the tourney life,' he scoffed. 'Mashed in the wits like the rest of them, you are.'

Alexander smothered a grin inside his mouth. Many things changed in the world, but Jankin's crusty demeanour was a constant. 'It's only for three days,' he said. 'My lord, William Marshal, is taking part, and I am fighting behind his banner. Besides, it will be more show than genuine battle.' He looked out across the tourney field, where carpenters were busy erecting tiered stands for the spectators to sit upon. Such comfort was an innovation. Usually competitors fought to please themselves, not their audience.

'If you think that, then you truly do have mashed turnip where your brains should be,' Jankin said scathingly. 'There'll be more grudge fights than a few out there on that field. No one's going to draw their blows just because the Queen and her ladies are watching.'

Alexander shook his head. 'I don't know why I talk to you,' he said with disgust.

'Because I tell you the truth, no matter that it sticks in your craw, and because I'm the best hafter and sword-mender this side of Jerusalem.'

Alexander could argue with neither statement. In point of fact, he was rather fond of the old rogue. 'Do you have employment come the winter season?' he asked.

'Might have.' Jankin shrugged. 'Why do you want to know?'

'I thought you could make yourself useful for once. I've been given custody of a Welsh border keep as from Pentecost, and I could use a man of your unmatched skills.'

'Have to think about it,' Jankin growled. 'If I had a castle waiting my attention, I'd not risk my neck in a tourney. I'd ride away from here while I still had two arms, two legs and a head on my shoulders.'

'Do you know something that I do not?'

Jankin shrugged. 'I've got ears,' he said. 'I hear rumours.'

'Such as?' With difficulty, Alexander controlled the urge to pick up Jankin by those very ears and shake the information out of him.

The hafter eyed him, drawing the moment out, and Alexander could have sworn that there was relish in the rheumy old eyes. 'Such as that you are a married man with a wife related to Thomas of Stafford.'

'Indeed I am, and proudly so. What of it?'

'I also heard that Thomas of Stafford is not so proud. In fact, he even approached the King about the possibility of getting the match annulled.'

Alexander gaped at the ancient little weasel of a man in front of him. Bad-tempered, smelly, ugly. It was beyond comprehension. 'How in the name of hell do you acquire such information?' he demanded incredulously.

'Told you, I use me lugs.' He poked his finger in his ear and waggled it around. 'Overheard one of John's clerks talking to a friend when they was standing outside me workshop. They never think that an old husk like me can hear every word they says.' He removed his finger, examined it, then wiped it down his tunic.

'Even if you're only going to play at tourneys these next three days, you guard your back, lad. Wouldn't surprise me to see treachery afoot.'

'What did the King say?' A feeling of cold surged in the pit of Alexander's belly. His own code was to treat men honourably and hope they would deal honourably with him in return. In William Marshal, that hope was fulfilled, but other men had different values.

'I don't know the exact words, but he said that an annulment was out of the question – that marriage was a commitment unto death, and that there was nothing to be done. But Stafford hasn't ridden out in high dudgeon. He's still here, and intends visiting the tourney. Strange, would you not say, for a man who has cause to hate the very sight of jousting knights.' Jankin investigated the other ear. 'So, if I were you, I'd watch my back until I could rest it against my keep wall.'

'You think Stafford would plot my death?'

'Certainly less difficult than arranging an annulment.' Jankin eyed him shrewdly. 'Course, I could be wrong, but I've spent too many years seeing the worst in people, and eleven times out o' a dozen, I'm right. If you've the smallest lick o' sense, you'll find reason not to take part.'

Alexander shook his head. 'I cannot do that.'

'It's your hide. Is this your wife now?' Licking his palm, he slicked it across his hair. 'Doesn't bear much resemblance to Thomas of Stafford, do she?'

Alexander turned and saw Monday approaching him, one hand occupied by Florian's, the other by a long basket. Bright-gold fabric peeped over the top. She moved with a lissom sway, and she was smiling at life.

'If you say a single word to her, I swear I will kill you with my own hands,' Alexander growled.

'No need to be jealous of me, I'm just an old man.'

'You know what I mean.' Alexander fixed him with a warning stare.

Jankin shrugged. 'Aye, reckon as I do,' he capitulated, and held up the knife that Alexander had given him. 'Be ready by noon tomorrow. Does the offer of employment still stand?'

'I never go back on my word, no matter how rashly given,' Alexander said wryly, and braced himself as Florian pounced upon him.

'Papa, Papa, guess what, I've just seen a man who can swallow swords!'

'Have you now? Well, there's a useful trick.'

'I have warned him about trying the same himself,' Monday laughed, and folded her arm around her husband's. She glanced briefly at the hafter, who nodded and bowed, before resuming the mining of his ears.

Alexander led his small family away from Jankin's unsettling proximity, and across the burgeoning tourney field. The old sights, sounds and scents, the anticipation, were joined now by apprehension.

'What was that about giving your word?' Monday asked.

'Oh, nothing. I know him from the English tourney circuit. He's not the most endearing of characters, but there is no one to better his work. I have invited him to spend the winter months at Abermon.'

'Then why are you frowning?'

'I'm not. The sun's in my eyes.'

She gave him a look which said that she was not convinced.

Alexander did not even attempt to persuade her otherwise. He had learned from experience that a change of direction was by far the wiser ploy. 'What's that for?' He pointed to the folds of gold linen in the basket.

'We'll be needing a banner to fly from Abermon's battlements beside the Marshal lion,' she said. 'If I begin sewing now, it will be ready for Whitsuntide.'

That deserved a kiss. And hearing her speak so practically of the future made him believe above Jankin's caution that he had one. Florian pushed between his parents, demanding attention, demanding that Alexander come and see the man who could swallow swords. Alexander ruffled the unruly feather-layers of his son's hair. 'Come on then, sprogling,' he said with a smile, and pushed the warning to the back of his mind, determined to enjoy the day.

*

Eudo le Boucher was enjoying the day too. News of the tourney had spread like wildfire, and as a seasoned jouster, his services had been widely courted, enabling him to name his price. William Marshal was to lead one team. His counterpart was William of Salisbury, the King's own bastard-born half-brother, and both men were the best of friends. The tourney was for display only, an amusement for the Queen and a chance for fighting men to vent a little pent-up energy in feats of arms. The thought amused le Boucher, who did not know how to play gently. Strike and be damned. He intended to take as many ransoms as he could on the morrow. And the richer his victims' blood, the better.

'So whose side do I choose?' he enquired of the tawny-haired young woman sprawled naked across his body in the aftermath of lust. She had been expensive, but the price was warranted by her skills and her looks. And it was not as if he was lacking for funds. 'Pembroke, or Salisbury?'

'Toss a coin,' she murmured, and wove her fingers through his thick chest hair. 'Is not Pembroke reputed to be the greatest jouster who has ever lived?'

'In his youth, perhaps. He is past fifty years old now.'

'Who will pay you the most?' She shifted along his body, arching her silken thigh over his genitals.

Le Boucher thrust against her flesh. The smell of attar of roses filled his nostrils. Her mouth and her nipples were reddened with cosmetics, and she had plucked her cunny hair, leaving her slit exposed.

'That remains to be seen.' His voice thickened with lust, even as his manhood was thickening with new arousal. He lifted her hips, positioned her, and impaled himself. She gasped, and tightened around his flesh, her muscles playing up and down his length like a musician on a bone flute. His jaw clenched, he began to ram.

The second coupling, hot and hard on the heels of the first, left him almost senseless, and he drifted into a semi-conscious dream state, sweat beading his body, and his heart thundering against his scarred ribs. He could hear the slosh of water and giggle of women from the bathhouse below; the moan of another client in a room beyond. The sounds drifted and became woven into the fabric of his waking dream. The water turned to a sunlit river bank, and he rode along the water's edge on a destrier and saw a young couple seated in the shade of a willow tree. The girl had a tumble of bronze-brown hair and lucent grey eyes. Her companion was limber and dark, and as he turned, Eudo's eyes were drawn to the gold cross glinting in the opening of his unlaced tunic. Not a scar in sight, taut and slender with youth, Alexander de Montroi filled Eudo with bitter envy. Swinging down from the horse, he drew his sword and struck a mighty blow, only to have the weapon recoil off the sun's rays flashing through the purple stones in the cross. The youth stared at him with contempt, and Eudo was powerless to prevent de Montroi from taking the sword and laying its edge against his throat. He felt the pressure against his skin, and on a ragged sob of breath, his eyes burst open.

The girl was holding the gold and amethyst cross on her palm. In her other hand was a tiny pair of sewing clippers, the kind that women carried in their belt pouches, and she was just about to sever the leather cord that fastened the jewel around his neck.

'Thieving bitch!' he roared, and seizing her by the hair, threw her across the chamber. Her head cracked against the wall. She screamed and tried to scramble away from him, blood running into one eye from a cut on her eyebrow.

'I'll mark you for life!' he swore. Frightened because of the dream, because he had let down his guard, he reached across the disordered bedclothes and tugged his long knife from its sheath on his belt.

She screamed all the louder and cowered, covering her face with her hands. 'It was pretty!' she sobbed through her fingers. 'I meant no harm!'

'Lying whore!' He seized a fistful of her amber hair and jerked her head back. 'So pretty that you wanted to have it for yourself!' He laid the knife slantwise against her cheek.

Footsteps stamped up the stairs, with deliberation rather than the haste of someone haring to the rescue. Le Boucher kept tight hold of the woman, but raised the knife, and stared at the door. 'Quiet,' he growled.

The latch rattled. 'Le Boucher, open up. I want a word, and I haven't got all day, even if you have.' The voice was gravelly and ill-at-ease, and le Boucher recognised it immediately.

'Go swive a sheep!' the soldier snarled as a matter of habit, but his dark eyes were narrow with calculation. What in the name of Christ's ten toes did Thomas of Stafford want with him so badly that he was willing to seek him in a brothel? After Pembroke, they had not parted on the best of terms. Stafford had been looking to foist his rage on a scapegoat and le Boucher had refused to be it.

Stafford rattled the latch again. 'I have employment for you. Open up, I'll make it worth your while.'

The woman whimpered. Winding her dull-gold hair more firmly around his fist, he used the knife to slice it short to her skull in a single swipe of the blade, and kicked her away from him. Then, still naked except for the cross around his neck and the knife in his hand, he raised the bar and yanked open the door.

Thomas of Stafford walked past him into the room. He wore a dark, shin-length cloak with a deep hood pulled up around his face. In its shadows, his eyes glittered and his nose was a bony stripe of light. 'Put some clothes on and throw the woman out,' he commanded with a glance at the weeping, scalped whore. Without noticing, he stood upon the thick hank of hair that le Boucher had chopped off.

'I am not your servant to command,' le Boucher said, and shoving past Stafford, sat down on the rumpled bed. A heavy scowl drew his brows together. 'How much is worth my while?'

'Open to negotiation. Get rid of the girl.' The older man glanced around with distaste, and his look did not change as he fixed it on le Boucher's nakedness.

'No,' le Boucher said, 'we'll go elsewhere.' He leaned across the bed and picked up his shirt, the armpits stained yellow and the laces grubby. 'Have you come alone?'

'I have two squires waiting in the street outside.'

Rising from the bed, le Boucher went to the shutters and threw them wide. Leaning out, his penis in his hand, he took a long, luxurious piss. Beneath him, there were shouts of outrage. Grinning, he shook off the drops and turned back into the room.

'The Cock Inn is just round the corner,' he said. 'It's as appropriate as any, wouldn't you say?'

'Just get dressed,' Stafford said. 'I'll meet you below.'

'Not scared that I might take a shit out of the window too?'

'Do it and you are dead.' The old man stalked from the room, kicking up the whore's hair in a shower of spun silk.

First le Boucher grinned, then he looked thoughtful. Stafford must want him badly indeed to tolerate such foul behaviour. 'I'm going to be rich,' he said to the cowering girl. 'What a pity you couldn't keep your hands to yourself.'

The Cock Inn was not one of Canterbury's most salubrious alehouses, but it was one of its busiest. By and large its clientele were of the kind that thought nothing of pissing out of windows on passers-by. There were cut-purses, whores and pimps, beggars with their day's takings to swill down their throats or gamble away, and there were members of the general population who dwelt in the vicinity of the inn. Everyone came here for the cock-fights that gave the inn its name and which took place twice a week in the back yard with prize birds from miles around.

The crowing of the birds, and the raucous conversation of the men who had come to gamble, made the Cock seem even fuller than it was, but le Boucher's bulk, his ugly, scarred face and the war sword at his hip, ensured that he and Stafford were granted a space at a trestle table squeezed into the back of the main room. Stafford himself made no attempt to exert his authority, and kept the hood of his cloak pulled around his ears.

'You move in exalted company, my lord,' le Boucher mocked, as a jug of ale was slopped down in front of them, together with two leather tankards. No one in the Cock drank wine. That was for the élite establishments near the bishop's palace.

'Not for long. I'm returning to Stafford as soon as the court leaves Canterbury.'

'Then what do you want of me that is so urgent it brings you to seek me in a brothel?' Le Boucher poured ale into his tankard and was not surprised when Stafford grimaced and covered his own empty cup with the palm of his hand.

'I want to hire you to compete in the court tourney tomorrow.'

'Hah, you and half a dozen others. William de Braose has offered me a new horse and armour to return to him, and a payment of half a mark for every ransom I take.' He drank down the ale, which was quite reasonable all things considered, and wiped the froth from his moustache. 'Why the sudden interest in the tourney? I thought you hated them on principle?'

Stafford clenched his fist on the stained board, and looked down at the gold seal ring on his curled-under thumb. 'Men die in tourneys,' he said.

'Is that why you hate them?'

'No, of course not. The more that are killed, the better,' Stafford snapped. 'I wish the damned lot of you to perdition. De Braose you say. Whose side is he on – the Marshal's, or Salisbury's?'

'The Marshal's. They both have lands in Wales.' Le Boucher wondered if Thomas of Stafford was turning senile. A wrinkled face and a wrinkled brain. He poured another cup of ale.

Stafford pursed his lips, then, coming to a decision, inhaled deeply. 'I will pay you your sword's weight in silver if there is a fatal accident involving Alexander de Montroi.'

'You want me to kill Alexander de Montroi?' Le Boucher stared at the old man. There was no senility in the flint-coloured eyes. They were hard and shrewd and ruthless.

'Yes.'

'For a sword's weight in silver?'

'Will you do it?'

Le Boucher raised the cup to his lips and drank deeply. Christ, the old bugger was actually going to pay him to fulfil his dearest wish. On a sword's weight of silver he could retire, need never fight again unless he wished. 'It is a reasonable price for a man's life,' he said slowly, 'but it is not enough.'

'Then name your fee.'

The sound of a cock-fight surged from the yard beyond; the excited yelling of men, the squawk and crow of the birds.

'The weight of my sword and shield in silver,' he said after a pause for deliberation. 'And paid into my hands by tomorrow noon.'

The flinty eyes narrowed. 'No. Half then, half when de Montroi is dead.'

'Then find someone else. I work for coin, not promises.' He pushed away from the trestle and stood up.

Stafford watched him. 'Sit down,' he said scornfully. 'No man walks out on a fortune.'

'One that he might never receive,' le Boucher grunted, and remained standing, but made no attempt to leave. 'I want it all.'

'And so you shall, but not before he is dead.' Stafford gestured once more at the trestle. 'I pay for results, not promises.'

They stared at each other. Le Boucher knew that Stafford was right. He could not walk away, and Alexander de Montroi had long been a thorn in his side. But although he was willing to be employed, he would let no man be his master. Slowly he stepped over the bench, and reseating himself, rested his elbows on the trestle.

Outside there was a crescendo of shouts, followed by a ragged silence. Into it, a single cockerel crowed victory.

'You asked me to name my fee,' le Boucher said. 'Now we negotiate.'

Alexander too was drinking with company that afternoon, but in the open around a crackling fire; the smell of onion pottage wafting from the cauldron set over the flames. Strolling the tourney camp with Monday and Florian, he had come across a familiar patched red and green tent, although the red had faded to a dull orangey-pink. Osgar had been sitting outside it, mending a piece of harness, his appearance more portly and ruddy than ever. His hair had receded, and what remained was cropped close to his skull, so that he resembled an apple dumpling. There were effusive greetings to be made, past years to be brought into the present, old times to reminisce. The first jug of wine vanished in short order – most of it into Osgar's belly. He had always had a prodigious thirst.

'Alys wouldn't come with me,' Osgar mourned, pinching wine out of his moustaches, which had grown in length as the hair on his head diminished. 'Stupid wench refused to get on the boat. I've had horses do it to me before, but never a woman. I gave her a bag of silver and my spare pack pony – left her at a tavern in le Havre. I miss her, though.'

'Why come to England?' Monday asked, and dissuaded Florian from poking a kindling twig into the fire.

'Tourneys are licensed here. John used to be my paymaster in Normandy. Thought I'd have a look at somewhere new, and hire myself out.' He touched the soft blue wool of Alexander's tunic sleeve. 'You've done well enough here.' He spoke with pride rather than envy, as though at the progress of a protégé. 'I remember the first day you came to Hervi, sick with starvation, clad in rags. Who would have thought that within ten years you'd be one of the lord Marshal's knights?'

'Only myself,' Alexander said with self-mockery.

Osgar snorted and took another drink. 'I must admit, I never expected you to amount to anything, especially after le Boucher almost killed you and Hervi.'

'It was sink or swim,' Alexander said, and smiled across the fire at Monday. 'In a way, I suppose I should thank Eudo le Boucher for casting me into the deepest, blackest water of my life. It took a long, long time to reach the shore, but I'm content with the land I've found.'

Monday returned his smile, then leaned forward to reprimand Florian again. 'He's restless,' she said to the men. 'I'll take him round the booths for a while.'

'Can I see the sword-swallower again?' Florian leaped to his feet, dusting his hands on his tunic.

'Isn't there someone who swallows noisy small boys?' Alexander asked with a wooden expression. Florian pummelled him on the arm, and Alexander yelped and pretended to cower. 'Save me!' he implored of Monday.

Laughing, she prised Florian off his father. 'We'll bring you some gingerbread,' she promised, and departed.

Alexander smoothed his rumpled tunic. 'He's an imp,' he chuckled.

'Like father like son,' Osgar observed, and setting down his empty cup, hunched towards the heat of the flames. 'Did you know that Eudo le Boucher is here for the tourney too?' he asked once Monday and Florian were out of earshot.

Alexander sighed. 'I had thought it a possibility, but I haven't seen him as yet. We are not on friendly terms, to say the least. Last I knew of him, he was in the pay of Staff—' The realisation hit him like a fist, and he muttered an obscene curse.

Osgar stared at him. 'What is it?'

Alexander shook his head, his mind's eye filled with the image of the ugly little hafter. 'Nothing. I was warned earlier that I might have enemies here interested in attending my funeral.' He looked at Osgar's broad, corpulent form. For a man so large, he was fairly light on his feet, and if not the most skilled and deft of fighters, he was certainly experienced, and had managed to keep himself in one piece to the age of forty. That had to count for much.

'Do you want a patron?' he asked.

'Why, do you know of one?' A rueful smile curled Osgar's lips. 'The Marshal would take one look at me and throw me on the midden heap by the ear.' He tugged at one swollen, mis-shapen lobe, the result of constant buffeting and injury down the years.

'It's not the Marshal who is seeking,' Alexander replied gently, 'it is me. Huw, my squire, is swift and light, I have no complaints, but I would feel better protected with a man of more substance at my back on the morrow. And if you want, if you can stave your wanderlust, there is a place at my hearth should I survive this tourney.'

Osgar blinked in bemusement. 'I do not know what to say.' He looked down at his beefy red hands and laughed. 'Hearth knight to Hervi's little brother, Jesu!'

'Christ, I'm not offering out of charity or obligation, you dolt!' Alexander snapped. 'I need you to protect my hide from holes! If you refuse, then I'll have to find someone else and in short order . . .'

Osgar wiped his hands on his tunic. 'All right,' he said. 'Be buggered to my esteem, I will do it, and in my heart, gladly. To be your man, I do so swear, let God be my witness.' Clasping his palms he held them out to be pressed between Alexander's in the ritual of fealty. They exchanged the kiss of peace, and once more settled by the fire.

'What I do not understand,' Osgar said, scratching his bald forehead, 'is why you are competing at all. If I were you, I'd make myself scarce elsewhere.'

'Lord William expects my presence on the field.'

'Even if you tell him Eudo le Boucher is likely to come at you?'

'If I avoid le Boucher on the tourney field, I will only be saving the confrontation until later. In the middle of a mock battle, strange though it may seem, I have more chance of emerging alive.'

'So you actually want to meet him on the field?'

'I don't want to meet him anywhere,' Alexander said wryly. 'But if I have no choice but to do so, then better here than on a lonely road in the middle of nowhere, or down a blind city alley.'

Osgar nodded and puffed out his cheeks, making his face look as though it was about to burst. 'I'll see to it he doesn't put in any foul blows,' he said. 'I owe it to Hervi too, after what that bastard did to him.'

Alexander fed another log to the fire beneath the cooking pot and mused that in a perverse way, Eudo le Boucher had changed Hervi's and his own lives for the better. Without that fall from Soleil, Hervi would still be riding the tourney circuits, wenching and drinking more than he should in dubious company. Instead, he was an ordained priest in the household of Hubert of Canterbury, a soldier's chaplain with fulfilment and purpose. And without le Boucher bringing him to nothing in the dust, Alexander knew that he too would have continued much as before. Whoring and drinking on the tourney route, his triumphs reaching a zenith with his physical strength, and then waning to leave him in the gutter. He spoke none of this to Osgar, however. In part it would have been cruel, for Osgar still travelled the tourney road like a plodding ox, and besides, he knew that the older knight would not even begin to comprehend the irony.

'Have you seen Hervi since his fall?'

Osgar shook his head. 'I thought about going to Pont l'Arche, to enquire after him, but I knew they would turn me away – a common mercenary.'

Alexander forbore to point out that the monks at Pont l'Arche had taken Hervi, a common mercenary. He understood Osgar's reluctance. His own aversion to monks and monasteries had been hard to overcome, indeed still lurked in the background.

'I didn't want to see him lying there broken,' Osgar added. 'It would have been like looking at myself. There but for the grace of God who shuns all men like me . . .' He knuckled his forehead as though it was literally hurting him to think.

'He has made a life for himself out of the ruins of the old,' Alexander said reassuringly. 'If anything, a better life. The old Hervi is still there, but tempered by the new.' He gave Osgar a light punch on the arm. 'Just think, you know a priest now who will gladly listen to your confession and not give you a penance beyond your fulfilling.'

Osgar laughed, and his expression lightened. 'Do you know his whereabouts?'

'Not of this moment. I had half expected to see him here, but a wooden leg hasn't confined him to one place. Hubert Walter often uses him as a messenger. You'll meet him soon enough if you join my retinue. I . . . Jesu, is that Edmund One-eye?'

It was a question that did not require answering. Her arm linked through his, Monday was leading a familiar stocky figure towards their fire, and Florian appeared to be chewing a large slab of spiced bread.

Osgar swivelled on his stool, and followed Alexander's gaze across the tourney ground. 'The past always catches up with you in the end,' he chuckled.

Alexander laughed with him, but there was an underlying irony to the curve of his lips.

CHAPTER 37

Monday watched her husband run his hands over Samson, checking him for soundness. Florian sat on the destrier's back, his legs scarcely straddling the high war saddle, and his small hands gripping the raised pommel.

In his full prime, the black stallion was magnificent, compact and powerful, but nimble as a wraith. He and Alexander had been partners for such a long time, the understanding between them so attuned, that there was scarce need for bridle or saddle, and Alexander rode with the lightest of hands.

The horse butted Alexander, seeking treats. With a laugh and a protest, the man dodged, and produced a stale end of bread from his pouch. Samson lipped it off him and gave a whicker of pleasure and triumph. 'That's your lot,' he said. 'Else you'll be too stuffed to do your duty.'

Monday was not deceived by Alexander's jesting. Something about the day's sport was worrying him. They had been late to bed after an evening of reminiscence with Osgar and Edmund, and once there, they had made love with an intensity on Alexander's part that surpassed even that time after they had been skating, and when it was finished, he held her, reluctant even at three of the clock to let her go. Less than four hours later he had been up with the dawn and tensely prowling. It was as if the coming tourney was not a piece of show for John's queen, but a battle in truth. And yet she had caught no whiff of atmosphere from Countess Isabelle or the other women, who were all looking forward to the afternoon's sport and the feast which was to follow it.

'Do you think there will be any serious fighting?' she probed.

He turned his back to run his hands down Samson's forelegs.

'Unlikely,' he said. 'Marshal and Salisbury are friends. It will be to prove valour and nought else.'

His tone was casual, but that meant nothing. It was his face she needed to see. 'Something is gnawing at you,' she said.

He checked hind leg, tapping Samson's fetlock to make him lift his hoof for inspection. 'It's a long time since I fought in a proper tourney – those in Wales were mere games.'

'I thought this one was a mere game too.'

There was a brief hesitation before he replied. 'Well, yes, it is, but the setting is different. Instead of a wet meadow in the middle of nowhere with a handful of folk looking on, this will be before the entire court, and Lord Marshal will expect the best performance from all of his men. As you know, there is no one to match him. To do him justice, we'll have to shine like stars.' He set the stallion's hind hoof down and dusted his hands. 'Since he has bestowed a keep on me, I need to show myself worthy in the eyes of the world.'

Monday was more than half convinced. His words had the ring of truth. If only his expression were not so blank. 'You look the very image of worthiness,' she said with pride, and reached a possessive hand to smooth his linen surcoat. He wore the Marshal colours, and the Marshal rampant red lion appliquéd in silk on the breast of the surcoat. Beneath it his mail glittered, fresh from a burnishing with sand and vinegar.

'God grant it goes deeper than looks,' he said, and taking her hand, drew her against him.

His body was as taut as a wound bow, and their kiss seemed to wind his tension even further. It was as if he was going to war. On that disquieting thought, their embrace broke as Osgar arrived in his usual noisy fashion, demanding to know if Alexander was ready.

'As ready as I'll ever be.' Alexander lifted Florian down from the saddle and gave him a hug. 'Be a good boy for your mother. Don't go straying off. There will be danger today with all those warhorses and soldiers.'

'I'm not scared,' Florian said with a thrust of his small chin.

'No, and that is why I am.' Alexander ruffled his son's hair, kissed Monday again, and mounted up.

'Good fortune.' Of an impulse, she untied the plaited ribbons binding her wimple to her brow, and presented them to him in token of her wish.

He tucked them in his sword belt, saluted her, and touched Samson lightly with his heels.

'Doesn't your papa look magnificent?' she said to Florian, as they waved him on his way, Osgar lumbering at his side.

Florian nodded. 'I'm going to be a great knight when I grow up,' he said. 'And join in tourneys too.'

Monday's smile was somewhat poignant. Silently she thanked God that such a time was more than ten years away. Proud though she was of her husband, it did not stop her feeling a pang of apprehension whenever he went out to fight, and today's concern was exacerbated by Alexander's behaviour.

Anxiety was put to the back of her mind, however, when she joined Countess Isabelle and the other members of the Marshal retinue on the trestle lodges that had been set up for the noble spectators. Isabelle was wearing her new blue dress with the full surcoat and looked radiant. Pregnancy had given a bloom to her skin and her green eyes were bright and clear. Her older sons, William and Gilbert, were helping to squire for their father, and only the younger ones sat in the lodges with her. Florian immediately joined Walter, the nearest to him in age, and they were soon engrossed in conversation, punctuated by a game of heads and tails using a clipped penny.

Monday sat among Isabelle's women and gazed out over the tourney field. It was obvious that even from the favourable and raised position of the lodges, not all the sport would be seen, for the field was large and bordered by trees, but even so, the area was much smaller than the size usual for Normandy.

The knights were beginning to arrive and warm up. Small knots of them swirled and challenged each other, loosening stiff muscles, practising strokes. Others stood in groups talking, their squires holding their horses. A quintain post had been set up, and a party of the Marshal's men were practising their skills by lifting a woman's wire circlet off the peg with a lance. Alexander and Samson were among them, and Monday watched with a fresh surge of pride as her husband neatly lifted the circlet from its mounting without even checking Samson's speed. Threaded through his belt were her plaited wimple ribbons. As if sensing her scrutiny, he raised his head towards the stands, and dipped her a salute with his lance. She waved in return. So did Florian, announcing to everyone within earshot that his papa was the best knight on the field. Walter took exception, and a minor brawl ensued, swiftly quelled by a nursemaid.

The King and Queen arrived and everyone rose. Isobel looked exquisite in her sapphire Christmas gown, a coronet of seed pearls securing a wimple of floaty cream silk, and a girdle of silver braid decorated with more pearls and amethysts encircling her tiny waist.

'To think that I was once as slender as that,' the Countess remarked with a wistful little sigh. 'When I married William, he could span my waist with his two hands.' She smoothed her own loose but still fetching garments. 'Now he has to use both arms.'

'But you have his faith,' Monday murmured. 'You know that he does not so much as look at another woman. If you were wed to the King, could you say the same?'

Isabelle gave her a sidelong look. 'I do not suppose that I could,' she replied. 'And I would not have you think for one moment that I am not content with my life. I know how fortunate I am to have William for a husband, for all that he was chosen for me. The Queen probably counts herself fortunate too, though,' she said judiciously. 'John indulges her every whim. If he has mistresses, he does not flaunt them in front of her, and she is not a grown woman like you or me to need more than clothes and games to keep her content.'

Monday gave a rueful smile, thinking of the time that she had spent with John. 'The King does not want a grown woman by his side,' she said. 'As long as she remains with her clothes and games, he will be as faithful as he knows how.'

'You sound bitter.'

She shook her head. 'I don't mean to. Perhaps it is the fact that he never once came to me or showed his sorrow when our baby died and I miscarried of another. My novelty to him had worn off by then. It was Alexander who grieved with me.' Her gaze went once more to the field, where more and more knights were arriving. There was going to be small room to swing a sword. The green and yellow Marshal colours blazed in a concentrated knot of spring brightness as the warriors assembled. It was harder to discern Alexander among the mass now. Only William Marshal stood out, for he was easily the largest man among his knights. His horse was a Spanish cross-breed, dappled grey in colour, with a pure silver mane and tail. He rode between his soldiers, talking, laughing, discussing the fight to come.

The King sat down and the rest of the spectators followed. The lodges were almost full now, an air of anticipation breathing excitement and high spirits among the finely robed spectators.

Isabelle gave Monday a gentle nudge, 'There's de Braose now,' she said with just a touch of asperity to her humour. 'I thought he would be late. He came to us last night and stayed drinking until the early hours. He'll have a sore head even before he starts today.'

Monday had no liking for William de Braose. He was one of John's closest friends, as he had been Richard's. A powerful marcher lord, he wore his nobility with a heavy hand, was arrogant and brutal to those he saw as beneath him, or those he could not use for his own ends. He was also as shrewd and intelligent as a wild boar. No one crossed de Braose. Today he and William Marshal were fighting as a team. She watched de Braose's knights join the field. His device too was that of a rampant lion, although many of his warriors bore their own shields and blazons.

The Earl of Salisbury and his nephew, Guillaume de Warenne, took to the field as captains of the opposing side, and joined Marshal and de Braose for a friendly exchange of banter. A huge bay stallion paraded past the stands. The man astride wore a surcoat of parti-coloured orange and gold. His face was covered by an old-fashioned nasal-bar helm, his lower jaw protected by an aventail of chain mail stitched on to a leather flap. A morning star dangled nonchalantly from his bunched right fist.

Monday pressed her fingers to her mouth and swore through them.

Isabelle turned an astonished stare on her. 'Whatever's wrong?'

'There's a soldier down there . . . he's Alexander's sworn

enemy. There will be bloodshed, I know there will!'

Isabelle seized her sleeve as she began to rise from her seat. 'Which one?'

'There, on the bay, with the nasal helm.'

Isabelle narrowed her eyes, the better to focus. 'He's one of Will de Braose's men, escorted him home last night,' she said, and shook her head. 'Don't worry, he'll be fighting on the same side as your husband, today at least.' Then she looked at Monday's white face and her eyes narrowed. 'How sworn an enemy?' she asked.

'He was at Pembroke, with my grandfather. He was the one who threatened your sons and mine with a sword. I told you about him then . . . do you not remember?'

'Well, yes, I . . .'

'I have to warn Alexander.' She tried to shake off Isabelle's hand, but as she began to rise, the Countess forced her back down with surprising strength in her smooth white hand.

'Alexander has eyes to see,' she said. 'Look, they are almost ready to begin. You will only be a danger to them and yourself!'

Even as the Countess spoke, the officials charged with seeing fair play in the tourney moved into position at the sides of the field. The four battle captains saluted them to show that they were ready, and rode back to their ranks.

Biting her lip, Monday sat down on the bench. Her heart was in her throat, and she felt sick. If Alexander and le Boucher were to come face to face on the field, being on the same side would make no difference whatsoever to the outcome, she was sure of it.

'Your husband is no fool,' Isabelle murmured in her ear. 'He knows how to take care of himself on the field of battle, else William would not have put such trust in him.'

Her words had been intended to reassure. To a certain extent they did indeed take the edge off Monday's terror, reducing it to mere fear, but they also set her to thinking of Alexander's earlier behaviour. He had known, she realised with a surge of anger; had known and kept it to himself. To stop her from worrying, she knew he would answer if she challenged him. But she was not made of glass to be wrapped in soft padding against the world. Then, because she was angry with him when he was in such imminent danger, she felt guilty too, and clucked her tongue in anxiety and self-irritation.

Further along the stands, Queen Isobel rose from her carved seat of honour, and dropped a large embroidered kerchief, to signal the opening of the tourney. Her expression was radiant with delight and her voice rang out, clear and young as a high-pitched bell. 'Let the tourney commence!' A fanfare sounded – three notes from a huge decorated hunting horn – and the battle was joined. Armour flashed, and weapons glittered in the spring sunshine as the two assembled lines charged towards each other. The drumming of hooves carried through the soil and up into the wooden stands, making the benches vibrate.

The Marshal's grey was the first to clash, striking at Salisbury's centre. Other knights rapidly engaged, and the lines broke up into individual clumps of fighting.

Eyes wide with apprehension, Monday sought among the press for Alexander. The Marshal's grey was easy to pick out, as was the Marshal himself in the forefront of the mock battle. By prearrangement, he and Salisbury exchanged huge blows before the King and Queen, but for dramatic effect. Neither had any intention of hurting or defeating the other. Monday sought beyond them. John of Erley confused her for a moment, for he too rode a black horse; then she saw Alexander, Osgar and Huw, warming up against three knights from the opposing side. None of them were in difficulty, Alexander's movements smooth and coordinated. Eudo le Boucher was on the far side of the field and busy with an opponent.

Monday made a conscious effort to unclench her fists. The tips of her nails had left half-moon imprints in the flesh of her palms. Perhaps she was jumping at shadows. They had the power to frighten, but not to hurt. And this was a display for the Queen, nothing as serious as the tourneys which had taken place on Norman soil. She glanced round at the other spectators and saw that they were all enjoying themselves immensely. Try as she might, she could not force a smile on to her own face.

On the tourney field, Alexander's wariness was pushed to the back of his mind by the sheer joy of indulging in the mock battle.

Although content with his life as it was now, there was still a glorious pleasure in controlling sword, shield and horse so that they became one fluid extension of his will. He knew where each blow and stroke would land, and with how much force. It was a beautiful, brutal, deadly dance, and it made his blood sing.

At first, as the Marshal had instructed, he played to the lodges, exaggerating his performance for the young Queen. A glance at the stands through the eye slits in his helm showed him Monday sitting bolt upright beside Isabelle of Pembroke, but from this distance he could only see the blur of her face, not her expression. Florian was the single bobbing dark head amongst all the blonds and light browns of the Marshal children. Perhaps he should have told Monday outright of the danger, but it was only a suspicion, and there was no point in burdening her without cause. Let her enjoy the day. From what he could tell, Eudo le Boucher was keeping his distance on the far side of the field, each of them pretending that the other was not there. On that thought, he touched Samson lightly with his heel, altered the grip on his sword, and set about earning himself a reputation.

For the next hour, Alexander, Osgar and Huw fought as a skilled and successful team. They took two ransoms, and forced another team of knights to turn tail and flee before they too became victims. A few grumbles were heard about Alexander and Osgar being professional jousters, but these were just from men trying to excuse their own paltry talents, and Alexander dismissed them with a contemptuous laugh, and several well-placed sword strokes. That first hour winnowed the wheat from the chaff. By the end of it, only the professional men were left, those with the stamina, ability and intelligence to survive. Eudo le Boucher was among them, but unobtrusively so. He made no grand gestures for the Queen, nor flaunted his talents but fought a rearguard action from the periphery of the field.

Alexander was beginning to think about taking a respite off the field at one of the gaily coloured refuge tents set up on the perimeter when Osgar's stallion overreached itself on a turn and went lame. Huw, to his credit, fought off Osgar's opponent, but the squire was panting with exertion and in no fit state to take on another assault should it materialise. Alexander signalled to quit the field, and the three of them began to move as quickly as Osgar's lame destrier would allow towards the nearest boundary.

Before they could reach safety, three knights from the opposing team descended on them with raucous halloos of delight. They were just returning from a refuge, had been fortified by sweetened wine, and were riding fresh horses.

Alexander swore through his teeth and looked around, but there was no one to come to their aid; everyone else was engaged. 'Go,' he snapped to Huw, 'make a run for the refuge. You'll only be forced to yield if you stay!'

The squire would have protested, but Alexander smacked the flat of his sword down on the rump of the young man's mount, and with a squeal of protest it broke into a canter. 'Go!' he bellowed. 'That's an order!'

Then he turned to deal with the three who had come upon him and Osgar. Keeping his shield tight into his body to protect against incoming sword blows, he turned Samson hard to the right, and struck at the man on the left end. His horse plunged sideways and fouled the mounts of the other two, causing a moment's chaos. It was enough for Alexander to strike again, twisting his sword beneath the shield of his opponent, so that the edge touched the man's throat. 'Yield!' he commanded.

'Call it even!' one of the others snarled as he pressed his own blade at Osgar's windpipe. The portly knight wheezed an apology to Alexander through the grille slits in his helm.

'Even then,' said Alexander, breathing hard, and lifted away his blade. The other released Osgar, but with a heavy push that sent him reeling against his cantle.

The battle renewed, Alexander cutting a blow here, another there, dodging and manoeuvring to engage all three, whilst Osgar doggedly tried to defend himself on his lame horse. It quickly became obvious, however, that reaching the side, for Osgar at least, was an impossibility. If his horse had been sound, he could have won past, but it was too lame even to raise a trot.

'Marshal!' came the joyful rallying cry, and a green and gold surcoat joined the fray, a flanged mace swinging in the clenched fist of John of Erley. He had dinted no more than two blows into the middle warrior's shield when two more of Salisbury's team thundered up to bolster their colleagues. What had been a small knot of fighting men was rapidly becoming an entangled snarl.

'*Marshal!*' came another enormous bellow, and a morning star caught the light, glittering as it was swung and smashed down. Only it struck a green and yellow shield instead of landing on one of the opposing team's. '*Marshal!*' roared Eudo le Boucher again, and once more slammed his flail into Alexander's shield. The limewood split like a cracked nut, and the shock of the blow numbed Alexander's left arm from wrist to shoulder. This was it, he thought; the assault that he had been expecting. Le Boucher had been biding his time, waiting for a vulnerable moment. That flail would batter, crush and ultimately kill, without drawing a drop of blood.

Alexander pressed Samson with his knees, turning the stallion to avoid the next assault, but Osgar's lame horse blundered across their path and the two animals collided. Osgar's mount lost its footing and fell, bringing Samson down too. Le Boucher spurred forward, driving his own destrier straight at the fallen tangle of men and horses.

The first hour of battle, with all its dramatic gestures and colourful display had lulled Monday into relaxing a little. Lady Marshal had brought a skin of sweetened wine with her, and she shared a cup with Monday. It had been spiced with pepper and nutmeg, and had warmed and soothed as it slipped down. A second cup had made Monday feel quite mellow, and although she was unable to enjoy the sport, she was at least able to watch it without perching on the edge of the bench. Still, it was with relief that she saw Alexander, Osgar and Huw begin making their way towards one of the refuge tents. Telling Isabelle that she intended going down to speak to them, she rose from her place and eased along the benches until she came to her son. An hour was a long time for a small child to sit still, and she knew that Florian would be more than ready for a diversion.

'Do you want to speak to your papa for a moment?'

Florian nodded with alacrity, and leaping to his feet, took her hand.

She swung him down on to the grass at the perimeter of the field, and turned to look at the tourney again. Where Alexander had been a moment since was now a scene of utter mayhem – a floundering pack of knights and horses. Weapons glittered on high, and the blows exchanged were in deadly earnest. She saw a morning star flail whip up and out, then descend.

'*Marshal, à moi!*' someone yelled at the top of their lungs, the sound cut off in a sharp grunt as if whoever it was had been struck in the gut.

Monday stared into the mass of fighting men, and pressed Florian to her side. Others were galloping to join the fight, the Marshal rallying cry joined by those of Salisbury and de Warenne. She strained her eyes, seeking Alexander. A green and gold shield flashed. A dark horse reared, and its rider was thrown, the mêlée closing over him as he fell. She covered Florian's eyes with the palm of her hand, her own silent scream ringing in her head. Dear God, Alexander, no!

'Mama, stop it, I can't see!' Florian pushed at her hand.

While she was still staring at the mêlée in horror, the arm not holding her son was seized, and the tip of a dagger pressed against her spine above the line of her embroidered belt.

'Quietly, or you die,' a voice growled against her ear. She tried to twist and see her attacker, but the pain in her arm was too great, and her resistance was met by the pricking of the knife against skin. 'You and the boy, both.'

An arm was thrown across hers, her assailant's cloak concealing the coercion as he thrust her forward. 'Move.'

'What are you doing, where are you taking us?'

'You'll soon find out.'

Monday stamped on his foot with all the force in her body. She was wearing wooden pattens over her soft leather shoes, and she hurt him, because he swore; but he did not relinquish his grip and the dagger broke skin and entered flesh in retaliation. She felt the hot burn of the blade's entry, and gasped.

'I mean it, I will kill you.' He shoved her forward again, towards a waiting covered litter, and bundled her into it, face down across the padded travelling cushions. Florian was flung in after her, kicking and shrieking. He bounced off his mother and sat up. Eyes wide with terror, he stared at the man rising from the cushions opposite.

The soldier with the knife darkened the rear entrance of the litter. Acting by pure instinct, the boy ducked under the man's armpit and threw himself out. He landed on his knees, tearing his hose, but immediately scrambled to his feet and ran into the crowd, screaming for all that he was worth that someone was trying to kill him and his mama.

'Leave him,' Thomas of Stafford said sharply to the soldier, his eyes on Monday, lying face down before him. 'We have my granddaughter, and that is enough. Quickly, before they raise the hue and cry.'

The soldier shouted to an accomplice at the front of the litter and pulled himself inside. Monday heard the sound of reins smacking down and the click of a tongue. The cart lurched into motion. With swift and brutal efficiency, her assailant bound her hands behind her back, and tied one of the ends through a stave in the litter's side, so that she could not jump out after Florian.

She struggled up and glared across the cushions at her grandfather. After a single, futile tug at her bonds, she was still. 'I despise you,' she said with revulsion.

Stafford shrugged. 'Do what you will; it makes no difference to me. Perhaps the feeling is mutual. I look at you and I cannot help but see Arnaud de Cerizay in the bones of your face and the cut of your wanton nature.'

'Then why do you want me?'

'You are strong and fecund. Your blood is mine beneath, and I can have the choosing of your husband.'

'I already have a husband,' Monday spat.

Stafford sighed. 'Not any more. You are in mourning for one, and it is best if you are comforted in the bosom of your family.'

Monday thought of the scene she had witnessed in the moment she was grabbed. The pile of men, the flash of weapons, the screams. Eudo le Boucher. She began to shake. 'You murdering, whoreson bastard,' she hissed, and fought against her bonds in earnest, but they were securely tied. The soldier crouched at the rear of the litter, one eye cocked on her struggles, the other on the road behind to watch for pursuit.

'Rail all you want,' Stafford said impassively. 'It makes no difference to me. I should have done this to your mother when she defied me, then there would have been none of this now. I blame myself for being too lenient a father.'

'You are mad!' Tears filled Monday's eyes, half rage, half wild grief. 'You think that William Marshal will let matters rest?'

'Possession is nine-tenths of the law, and the other tenth is the King. I know for a fact that if I pay him a suitable sum to look the other way, he will do so. As to the child . . . he can always be reared in a monastery. I am a patron of Cranwell Priory, and they welcome oblates.'

Monday went wild, tugging at her bonds, kicking and screaming. In the end, Thomas leaned over and struck her a hard backhand blow across the cheek, and she slumped against the side of the litter, panting and crying.

'Do not force me to beat you,' he said. 'A woman with a marked body is a shame unto herself and her household, for it shows that she has transgressed the tolerance of her menfolk.'

'You bastard,' Monday wept again, more softly, and turned her head to the wooden side of the litter so that she would not have to look at him.

He grunted, and watched her for a moment with narrowed eyes. 'You'll learn,' he said, and went to look out of the front of the wain at the countryside opening out before them.

Monday bit her lip and stifled her tears, concentrating instead on the strength of her rage. Her grandfather might have control of her physical body, but not of her mind. And he could not keep her tied up all of the time. Just one moment was all she needed. Her breathing calmed. The ropes hurt her wrists. At least Florian had escaped. The image of her child running in panic through the tourney crowd brought an involuntary twitch to her bound wrists. She balanced her maternal outrage by telling herself that he would find the Marshals, and that pursuit of her grandfather would be organised in very short order.

'Please, oh God, please,' she whispered.

Over and over again, she saw flashes of the mêlée behind her eyes; the plunging horses, the glitter of steel, a morning star horizontal to the sky and Alexander falling. He couldn't be dead. She would have known. Or perhaps the visions were haunting her mind because she did know.

Bowing her head, Monday fought off a fresh wave of hysteria. It would exhaust her to no good purpose. She felt drained already, and she needed all her strength for further fights to come. Again she prayed, her lips scarcely moving, but her plea to God more vehement than a full-fledged scream.

Through the eye slits in his helm, Alexander saw the flash of iron-shod hooves as Osgar's horse strove valiantly to rise, and failed. There was a weight across his body that was making breathing almost impossible. His lungs burned, stars burst before his eyes. Pressing his palms flat on the damp soil, he pushed upward. The weight did not ease, but it groaned loudly and he realised that Osgar was lying on top of him. His ears buzzed; he drew a morsel of air, not nearly enough for his starving lungs.

'Marshal!' The cry echoed round his head, hollow and distorted. 'Marshal! Braose!'

Then, blessedly, the weight was lifted from him, and he gulped air frantically into his lungs. There could never be enough.

'Easy now, lad, steady,' said the voice of William Marshal. 'Can you move?'

For answer, Alexander sat up, his movements ginger as pain coursed through his ribs. 'From what I can tell, nothing's broken, but everything hurts,' he wheezed.

William Marshal had dismounted and was bending over him with concern. 'The wonder is neither of you are dead, the fall you both took.'

'Dead.' Alexander repeated the word and choked back a laugh. The Marshal looked at him askance. 'Look at my shield,' Alexander panted.

Marshal glanced around, then picked one up from the ground close by. There was an enormous hole punched through its centre, totally obliterating the scarlet lion.

'Eudo le Boucher wanted me dead.'

'Who?'

'Braose's knight, on the bay.' Alexander eased very carefully to his feet. 'He supposedly came to my aid, bellowing "Marshal!" at the top of his voice, and then set about me with his flail. But it was no less than I was expecting.'

'Are you saying it was deliberate treachery?' Marshal's look of incredulity began to turn to one of anger. He jerked his head up and sought around the field, with obvious intent.

Alexander nodded. 'Not that my lord de Braose would know,' he said hastily, aware of how quickly the tourney might escalate into a full-blown feud. 'I had been warned by other people on the circuit to watch my back. Le Boucher and I have long been enemies. There's nothing I can prove.' He gave a shrug, and stooped to Osgar, who was sitting on the ground, groaning and clutching his side. 'Mind you, if I had known you were going to crush me to death, I'd have kept away from you also.'

'You have me to thank for your life,' Osgar growled. 'I was your shield for a couple of his blows while you were down. 'God, I think he's broken every rib in my body.'

'I'll see you reimbursed, I promise.' Alexander squeezed Osgar's shoulder, and received a howl in reply.

'There is no sign of this le Boucher now,' Marshal said, returning his gaze to Alexander.

'I would expect no less, sir.' Alexander went to Samson, who was being held by one of Marshal's squires. He ran his hands swiftly over the horse to check that he had sustained no injury from the fall. 'A murderer does not linger beside the corpse of his victim.'

The Marshal shook his head and looked perplexed. 'He must have a deep grudge against you indeed.'

'Fuelled by coin from Stafford.' Alexander swung stiffly into the saddle and gathered the reins. 'He would rather I was not his grandson-by-marriage.'

'You are saying that Thomas of Stafford hired that knight to kill you?' The Marshal was horrified, but not incredulous.

'I have no proof,' Alexander said. 'I would like to think not, but it is hard not to draw damning conclusions. The only qualm Eudo le Boucher has about taking life is how much he is going to be paid for doing it. This time, of course, it is spiced by a personal grudge.'

Marshal's jaw tightened. 'You should have come to me,' he

said. 'If I had known any of this, you would never have taken part in the joust. I would have sent you to Abermon a full month early.'

'There are still long knives in dark corners. I wanted to bring the crisis out into the open.'

'You mean you wanted to die before a crowd, the King and Queen included?' William Marshal folded his hands around his sword belt and stared at Alexander as if he thought him mad.

'I knew this way I had a chance.'

'And you think it will prevent the long knives in dark corners?'

'I think it will lessen the number of opportunities. Do I have your permission to leave the field?' Alexander did not want to dwell on the matter, and his tone was slightly brusque. What he did want was a drink of the strongest wine he could lay hands upon and a fresh shield so that he could rejoin the fighting. It would return a modicum of normality to the day, and if he did retire, it would only be to brood.

Marshal rubbed his beard and made a gesture of assent. 'I'll escort you, and your companion,' he said, and remounted his grey.

Osgar's horse hobbled on three legs. Osgar shuffled like a troll, and clutched his abused ribs. The Marshal saw them to the refuge, although no one rode up to challenge them in the short distance they travelled.

Huw was waiting at the refuge, a cup of wine already held out to Alexander. 'I should have stayed, my lord,' he said, full of self-recrimination.

'It would have made no difference.' Alexander took the wine, drank half, and gave the remainder to Osgar. 'You would have been able to do nothing.'

'Aye, look what happened to me, and I'm twice your meat,' Osgar said, and sat down on a vacant stool to nurse his ribs.

Alexander took Huw's shield and threaded the straps round his left arm. 'Did you see where le Boucher went?'

'He left the field the moment that Lord William came to your aid – rode back towards the town, I think . . . Are you going back to fight, sir?' The squire looked at his lord wide-eyed.

'Why not? It's safe enough now, and I've sustained no lasting damage. Do you get the spare shield and join me. Another cup of wine first, though.' He grabbed the now empty goblet from Osgar and handed it to the squire.

'Papa, Papa!' Like a bolt from a crossbow, his son struck him foursquare, almost knocking him to the ground. Small arms gripped around his thighs and clung grimly.

Alexander shook off the shield, disengaged the desperate clutch and lifted Florian in his arms.

'What are you doing here alone, sprogling? Shouldn't you be with a nurse or your mother?' He gazed round for evidence of either while Florian burrowed against his neck, shudders rippling through his small frame.

'He says that someone has taken her away.' Edmund One-eye pushed past Huw and stood before Alexander. 'I found him not five minutes ago, running through the crowds in a high old state. I brought him straight to you.'

'What do you mean, taken her away?' Alexander flashed a look at the stands. He could see the Countess Isabelle, but the place beside her was empty. His blood ran cold.

'I couldn't get much out of the lad,' said One-eye. 'But from what I gather, they were coming to see you, here, and they were snatched at dagger-point. He managed to escape, but his mother was forced into a travelling litter. Jankin the hafter was with me when we found him. He's taken his mule and gone to see if he can pick up a trail, or make any sense of it.'

'I know the sense,' Alexander said grimly, and kissing his son, smoothing his hair, said, 'Did you see any of them who tried to take you away?'

Hiccuping, sobbing, Florian lifted a tear-streaked face from the security of his father's neck. 'An old man. He came to see Mama before, when we were . . . when we were . . .' He struggled for words.

'At Pembroke?'

Florian nodded and buried his head again. 'There was a man with a knife too . . . He said he would kill Mama.'

'You know who it is?' asked One-eye.

'Stafford.' Alexander ground the word out through clenched

teeth. 'And I am not surprised. More fool me for not seeing beyond the threat to my own life. You say that Jankin has gone in pursuit?'

'Only armed with as much information as the boy could tell us. He may be following the wrong litter for all we know.' Edmund's expression filled with pity and rage. 'We could not stand by and do nothing.'

'No, and for that I thank you. Will you take Florian to the Countess Isabelle, and ask her to care for him until I return?' Alexander tugged his seal ring off his finger and placed it in Edmund's meaty fist. 'She will know your good faith not only by Florian, but by this ring.' Alexander was desperate to be on the road in pursuit of his wife's abductors, but he made himself be patient. 'Florian, look at me, come on, it's all right. That's it, good boy. Your mama's going to be all right. The old man who took her won't do her any harm. He wants her to go and live with him, that's all.'

'But she doesn't want to. She lives with us!'

'Yes, I know. And that's why I have to go and get her back. You go with Edmund to the lady Isabelle, and I promise that I'll return with your mother as soon as I can.'

Florian looked doubtful, but made no protest as he was handed from Alexander's arms to Edmund's. His thumb went in his mouth and he hid his face once more, this time in the abundance of Edmund's salt-grey beard.

Alexander gestured Huw to mount up, and bidding Osgar remain where he was, tied a square of white linen bandaging to a spear and rode on to the tourney field in search of the Marshal.

CHAPTER 38

Once beyond Canterbury, Stafford directed the litter to leave the road and draw aside into a copse of hazel and birch trees, their branches clothed in the new and tender green of spring. Here, the two cobs were removed from the shafts and saddled up. Stafford took one, forcing Monday to ride pillion behind him, her wrists lashed to the cantle. The knight and the driver took the other, and leaving the road, set off across country.

Monday sat in silence behind her grandfather. The cords chafed her wrists. A tight knot of misery and rage rotated at her core. Time and again she almost opened her mouth to tell Stafford what she thought of him, but checked the words unspoken. The more she rebelled, the closer he would bind her. If she appeared submissive, her spirit broken, then he might not be so vigilant. It was all she had, and she clung to it grimly whilst trying to avoid the slightest contact with him. Each stride of the horse almost brushed his cloak against her. She was close enough to see a louse wandering through his hair.

'Where are we going?' she asked.

'There's a village on the other side of those woods. I told my men to meet me there.'

Her heart sank. 'Your men?'

'Just a small escort for the journey home.' His shoulders twitched as if with impatience.

'To Stafford?'

'Don't ask so many questions,' he said irritably. 'A woman should speak only when spoken to.'

Monday bit her tongue and stared at the woods through which they were riding. There was spring birdsong, sun-dapple and shade.

Christ had risen, the world had turned its face to the sun. It was a day for trysting and joy, but her grandfather had sown it with death. Her eyes filled with scalding moisture, and tears spilled unchecked down her face. Her hands were tied; she could not wipe them away.

'You'll learn not to weep in my household,' Stafford said without looking round. 'Backbone, that's what you'll be given.'

Monday almost choked on her stifled outrage. Backbone meant standing up for yourself, not taking in silence whatever some man chose to mete out from the depths of his own inadequacy.

'Women,' Stafford snorted as they emerged from the woods and followed a track down the side of freshly ploughed village strips. 'Some young man casts a look and they lose all sense and reason. Like bitches on heat. They run away into the forest to copulate with the first wolf that howls.' His tone was sour and contemptuous.

Monday was sickened, but through her revulsion there ran a treacherous thread of pity for his utter blindness. Perhaps he had never once been happy in his life, and because joy was alien to him, it was an enemy to be slaughtered.

The village consisted of no more than a handful of houses and a small straw-thatched church. There was not a single cottar to be seen, not even so much as a hen or a goose. Clustered around the pond in the centre of the village, however, were a dozen mounted men, and some spare horses.

Thomas of Stafford swung down from the dun's saddle, untied Monday from the cob, and sat her down on the ground. A knight on a bay stallion rode over, leading a large, strong chestnut horse. 'Your remount, my lord,' said Eudo le Boucher, presenting the reins to Stafford.

Stafford took them with a grunt. Monday glared at the knight with revulsion. Clenching her teeth, pressing her tongue against the roof of her mouth, she made herself silent, knowing that she would ruin her own chances by unleashing her fury and grief.

He smiled at her in reply, the scar on his face twisting away into the shadows of his helm.

'You owe me the rest of the payment, my lord,' he said to Stafford.

'Not until my granddaughter is safely away,' Thomas said through his stained teeth.

'And is she not now?'

'Not far enough. You'll have your silver when we cross the Thames.'

'That wasn't the bargain.'

Stafford met le Boucher's anger squarely. 'As I recall, the bargain was that you received the rest of the payment when the task was finished – which it isn't until I'm satisfied.' Setting his foot in the chestnut's stirrup, he mounted up and snapped his fingers at Monday. 'Up, granddaughter,' he said.

Monday knew that to refuse would just be cutting off her nose to spite her face. If she did not come willingly, they would force her, and probably hurt her into the bargain. There was already a minor knife wound in the small of her back. With eyes downcast, she went to the horse, set her foot on Stafford's and allowed him to pull her up behind him.

'There is no need to tie my wrists to the saddle,' she said in a small voice. 'I will not try and escape again.'

Stafford hesitated, then dropped the end he had been about to wrap around the cantle. 'I don't suppose you could get further than five yards if you did,' he admitted grudgingly, then looked at le Boucher. 'He is dead, I trust?'

The knight shrugged. 'I did not wait to listen for the beat of life in his breast, but yes, he is dead.'

'You are sure?'

'God's arse, he went down beneath my flail with another man and ended up at the bottom of the pile. Of course he's dead! If you had desired his head on a pole or his heart as proof, you should have said.'

The two men glared at each other. 'Ready the escort,' Thomas dismissed brusquely. 'We are wasting time.'

Le Boucher turned away with a curl of his lip. Monday looked down at her lap, fixing her gaze on the fine woollen weave of her dress so that neither man should see the blaze in her eyes. Le Boucher had trusted to fate to finish Alexander. And that left a shining chink of hope.

*

Jankin the hafter was waiting for Alexander on the Faversham road. His mule was creamed with sweat, its flanks heaving, and Jankin himself was red in the face and looked more alive than he had probably done in his entire life.

'They're not using the litter any more,' he announced, his own breath whistling in his throat. 'Found it in the trees about a mile further on. They've taken to horseback and cut across the fields.'

Alexander swore.

'I couldn't keep pace with them. Harold's done for as it is.' Jankin patted the mule's steaming hide.

'A trail's not too difficult to follow this time of year,' said John Marshal. 'We'll find them.'

Alexander glowered at the Marshal's nephew and swallowed a sarcasm about him being ever the optimist. His rage had to be controlled and directed at Thomas of Stafford, not the men that William Marshal had given him. He leaned over the saddle to slap Jankin on the shoulder. 'I'll pay for your retirement too if you come to Abermon.'

Jankin rolled his eyes. 'Promises,' he said. 'Just go and get your lass, and leave me and the mule in peace.'

Alexander turned Samson and pricked him with the spur, but after a hundred yards of bouncing canter, he drew on the rein and slowed to a trot. If there was distance to be covered, then endurance was required, not a headlong dash.

They came to the place where the litter had been concealed in the copse, and as John Marshal had predicted, there was indeed an easy trail leading off across the fields towards some woods. As they circled to follow it, Alexander gazed skywards. It was well after noon, with about four hours of daylight left. Four hours to find her before night cast its cloak, and covered up the tracks.

Dusk had swallowed the sun and cast blue shadows over the land when Stafford's band came to another village. Being on the pilgrim road to the shrine of the blessed St Thomas at Canterbury, the settlement was accustomed to hosting benighted pilgrims, and the priest said that providing the men left their weapons at the church door, they were welcome to spend the night in the nave. He even provided a charcoal brazier for warmth, and pointed out a house where one of the families was willing to provide the soldiers with food, for a consideration.

When he looked askance at Monday's bound wrists, Thomas gave him a glare that told him to mind his own business, but deigned to reply loftily, 'She is out of her wits. We have been to Canterbury to pray for her.' His voice echoed in the vastness of the nave, its harshness emphasised.

'But it was not successful?'

'She is much improved from her original condition.'

Monday chewed the inside of her mouth as the priest walked away. There had been no point in crying out to him that she was a prisoner against her will. What could he do against a dozen soldiers? What could she do?

'These cords are rubbing my wrists raw,' she complained, showing Thomas the red weals half hidden by the leather. 'Could you not for simple charity take them off for a while?'

'No,' he said curtly, and taking her arm, steered her across to the wall. 'Sit.' He pushed her down. Even through her shift, undergown and tunic, she felt the coldness of the flagstones. Across the nave, the narrow stained windows leached very little light.

'Stay there,' her grandfather commanded, as if talking to a dog. He ordered one of the soldiers to stand guard over her, and disappeared out of the door.

Monday contemplated leaping to her feet and making a run for safety, but dismissed the notion as impractical. Her dress was one of her best ones, worn in honour of the tourney, and as such had panels of material in the side, to make it sweeping and full. If she tried to run without her hands free to lift its heavy folds away from her feet, she would fall flat on her face.

It was almost a full half-candle notch before her grandfather returned, bringing with him a wooden bowl of broth and a piece of dark bread. He had already eaten. So much was obvious from the soup stains on his tunic and the underside of his moustache. He set the bowl down beside her, and drawing his knife, cut the knot on her cords. 'Eat your soup,' he said gruffly.

She flexed her fingers and gently rubbed the tender chafed skin. Only now was she beginning to comprehend what

Alexander must have felt as a novice monk, trussed up for three days. She found it difficult to grip the bowl, but somehow she managed. Nor did she feel much like drinking the fatty, luke-warm contents, but knew that to remain strong she had to eat. The taste was not unpleasant, she had known worse on the tour-ney circuit, but the bread had to be softened in the soup to make it anywhere near edible.

As she struggled with her meal, Eudo le Boucher sauntered over. He was wearing his sword in defiance of the priest's rule, and the hood of his cloak was pulled up over his head.

'My payment,' he said to her grandfather, and held out his large, scarred palm. 'Do not tell me to wait until morning. No more excuses. I am leaving now.'

Stafford turned. The light from the window painted him in shades of blue and grey. 'How will you see in the dark?'

'The moon's rising. There'll be enough light. My payment.' His fingers waggled impatiently.

'All right, all right. It's in my saddle roll.' Stafford started to walk away, then turned, and commanded the same young soldier as before to keep an eye on Monday. Another knight was ordered to accompany Stafford and le Boucher outside.

Monday watched them leave, then looked at her guard. Pockmarks scarred his face, making him appear older than he was. She judged him to be younger than Alexander's squire. Of course, his youth did not necessarily mean he was untried. To be a member of this troop, he must have ability. But then, she was not without experience herself.

'I need to relieve myself,' she said.

'Lady?' He looked at her askance, and she saw a flicker of panic in his eyes. The tone of his address told her that the men had been warned to treat her with courtesy. It was one matter for her grandfather to abuse her, quite another for the soldiers.

'I need to piss,' she said more forthrightly. 'We've been riding all day, and never a thought to my needs. If you do not take me outside, I shall have to squat here in the church and be shamed.'

He cleared his throat and looked acutely embarrassed. Monday eyed him steadily, compounding his discomfort. Men were so strange, she thought. Jests about bodily functions were loud and uproarious between themselves, but introduce a woman into their midst and their tongues tied up in knots.

'All right,' he said, 'but I will have to bind your wrists.'

Monday rose to her feet, and made a fair imitation of someone desperately controlling a full bladder. 'Are you going to hold up my skirts for me then?' she enquired.

The young soldier visibly swallowed. Obviously his experiences of life thus far had not prepared him for this one. 'Go on, then,' he said, tight-lipped. 'But do not think to pull the wool over my eyes. I'll be guarding you close.'

Monday gave him a withering look, and with her head carried high, walked down the nave and out of the elaborately carved church doorway. The young guard walked so close behind that he almost trod on the hem of her gown.

At their horse line, her grandfather was still arguing with Eudo le Boucher even in the act of counting out the silver. The mercenary was insisting on checking the contents of every single pouch, and the money flashed in the moonlight as each bag was examined.

Monday moved in the opposite direction, towards three gnarled apple trees, their branches gleaming as the moon rose.

'I'll go behind these,' she whispered to the soldier.

He followed her.

'At least turn your back,' she hissed as if in outrage. 'How far do you think I'm going to get if I run?'

He shook his head, rubbed the back of his neck in perplexity, but reluctantly did as she requested.

Immediately Monday removed her cloak, unfastened her belt, and with feverish speed tore off her tunic and underdress, leaving only her thin linen chemise. It had a drawstring neck and sleeves, was pleated and full in the body, but the hem finished just below her knees. Now her legs were unhampered.

The guard started to turn his head.

'Don't look!' Monday gasped. He continued to turn. She seized her cloak off the ground and threw it over his head, at the same time hooking her leg behind his ankle. He went down hard, his shout muffled by the good, thick wool of the cloak. Monday tugged the dagger out of his belt. Unable to bring herself to stab him, but desiring to render him *hors de combat*, she stamped as hard as she could on his genitals.

He doubled up, writhing, the cloak still engulfing his head, and she took to her heels.

She sped through the priest's orchard and across his glebe land. There was light enough to see, but only just, and given a strange bluish cast by the moon. At first she ran blindly, her only goal to put distance between herself and her captors, but as her breath began to scrape in her lungs, she realised that she would soon and easily be caught. They had horses, and the light that enabled her to run would guide them too.

To the right of the glebe land, she could see the small glimmers of rush dips and candles from the village houses, and the occasional glow of an outdoor firepit. To the left were more open fields, stretching away to woodland more than two miles distant. Briefly she dithered before deciding on the village, where at least there would be witnesses to her capture should she fail to escape. She did not for one moment expect the villagers to put up any resistance on her behalf to armed men.

At first as she ran, her hand pressed to her side, there was only the sound of her own breath tearing in her throat, and the light thud of her footfalls. But then her straining ears caught the sound of pursuit, and she could not prevent the whimper that rose in her throat. If they captured her, they would tie more than her wrists this time.

She snatched a look over her shoulder, and saw the lights of torches bobbing up and down to the motion of cantering horses. Their closeness terrified her and she redoubled her efforts, with the result that she measured her length on the grass of the common grazing land. As she fell, she saw that the lights of the village were closer too, perhaps even reachable. She scrambled to her feet, and ran on. Three tethered goats loomed out of the dusk. Monday screamed at their sudden appearance, and they scattered, bleating, in mutual shock. The darker line of a stream obstructed her path on the village boundary. Behind her, she heard a shout. The drum of hoofbeats was much closer now. She dared not turn around to look, but kept on running, one foot in front of the other, her legs tight with pain and her chest on fire.

The shout was repeated and mingled with the drum of hoof-beats.

'Run, Monday, Christ, run!'

She splashed into the water, which was icy cold, and although only shin-deep, sprayed up around her thighs as she plunged through it and scrambled up the far bank. 'Alexander?' she shrieked, and turned in time to see the flame-lit figure of Eudo le Boucher slew his horse round on the edge of the stream and fling his lighted torch at another horseman coming up hard behind.

'Alexander!' Monday screamed.

'Get into the village, stay there!' he bellowed at her. Light flashed off a shield boss and along the edge of a drawn sword. She heard le Boucher's weapon rasp from the scabbard.

'Go!' Alexander roared.

Her legs almost buckled but she did as he bade her. There was nothing she could do if she stayed but hamper him, but she could return with witnesses.

The shriek of sword meeting sword split the night. Sparks flashed and splinters of metal flew off the blades. No knight ever fought sword to sword unless he was forced, for the damage done to the steel was terrible. But Eudo le Boucher had no shield, and Alexander was determined to win past the guard of that slender bar of iron and destroy the man behind it.

He and his troop had reached the village as dusk darkened into night, and discovered chaos and consternation among the abductors, who were spread out in search of their escaped captive. Alexander had left half his troop to deal with Stafford's men still in the vicinity of the church and with the other half had set off in pursuit of the flaming torches, across the glebe and grazing land.

'I should have killed you in France, Montroi,' le Boucher panted as their horses circled on the edge of the stream.

Alexander did not waste his breath. There was nothing to be said that would encompass the weight of his emotions. Actions spoke the louder, so Hervi was always saying, with a pious look on his face. The blows he was swinging were for Hervi, for Arnaud de Cerizay, for Monday, and for himself.

The dark made it difficult to see. The gleam of metal just before it struck, the shimmer of hauberk rings were the only warning. Alexander was swift, but le Boucher was heavier, and although Alexander had won past le Boucher's guard a couple of times, the triple-linked hauberk beneath had turned the blows.

Both men drew back to gain their breath. Alexander listened to le Boucher's lungs between the roaring of his own, and decided that the older man was more spent than he was. Taking a gamble, he touched Samson with the spur. The horse lunged towards le Boucher's bay. Alexander struck rapidly, aiming low, and slashed a stirrup leather. Le Boucher uttered a bellow of fury, and threw off Alexander's sword with his own, but his balance had been seriously affected and he wavered in the saddle. Alexander attacked again. Le Boucher kicked his other foot out of the stirrup, clung tightly with his thighs, and smacked his horse on the rump with the flat of his sword.

The bay hurled forward against Samson, rearing and striking. Samson went back on his haunches, almost lost his footing in the soft soil, and had to plunge and skitter sideways to stay upright. This led him straight into the stream. Icy water showered up around man and horse. Samson floundered to gain purchase on the gravel bottom with his hind hooves. His mane was in Alexander's mouth, and the stallion's lurching made it impossible for him to do anything but grip in the saddle and keep his shield high.

He felt le Boucher's sword slam down on the painted limewood, felt the surge of the stallion as he cleared the bank, and then the shock as the two animals clashed again. He prodded Samson with the spur and the destrier reared and struck with his forehooves, cutting open the bay's shoulder. The bay shied away and was reined around by le Boucher. Once more the destriers pounded together and sword met sword in a diagonal cross of blue light, smaller sparks shivering off as the steel was damaged. Alexander's wrist bent over and his tendons strained. He did not have the brute strength to match le Boucher, and there was nothing he could do to prevent the sword from being torn from his hand to fall in the trampled mud.

On the offensive now, with the scent of victory tantalising, le Boucher went at Alexander full hammer. Alexander braced his shielded left arm to withstand the onslaught and tried to reach the dagger at his right hip. Le Boucher rose in the saddle and brought an almighty blow down on Alexander's shield. The blade caught on the iron boss. Alexander struggled to heave him off, and for a moment the two men strained. There was an abrupt snapping sound and the pressure on Alexander was suddenly released, jerking him backwards and bruising his spine against the cantle.

Le Boucher roared out in terror and anguish. Twice, three times, the sound split the night, and ended on a breathless crow. He lost control of the horse and toppled from the saddle, hit the ground, and lay weakly writhing.

Alexander stared in blank surprise. He dismounted, but remembering their joust beneath the walls of Vaudreuil, drew his dagger and circled him, well out of assault distance. There was blood, more blood than Alexander had ever seen, as black and shiny as a river of pitch in the moonlight. The broken, jagged hilt of the mercenary's sword protruded from a deep wound on his upper thigh near his crotch, the hilt still quivering. Even as Alexander looked on in wincing horror, le Boucher's shaking hand reached to the hilt, grasped it as if to pull it out, then went into spasm, made a claw, and fell away.

Still, even knowing that he was dead, Alexander circled a moment longer before approaching le Boucher, and kept the dagger to hand as he stooped over the body and unlaced the neck opening of the mail coif. There was no pulse beat in the powerful corded throat, and only the glimmer of darkness in the eyes.

Alexander eased his fingers inside the tunic, and against the hot skin found a greasy leather cord. He tugged it up and out, and the gold and amethyst cross sparkled into his vision. The tip of the dagger sliced it free, and Alexander closed his palm over the warm metal.

'Now you have nothing,' he said to le Boucher. '*Requiescat in pace.*' He made the sign of the cross, and turning his back on the corpse, remounted Samson, who was patiently standing. Le Boucher's bay circled nervously at a distance. Alexander left him for the others of his troop to find, and urged the black across the stream towards the village, intent on finding Monday.

The alehouse was the second most visited dwelling in the village, the first being the church, and that was only because of the priest's perseverance. The brewster, Widow Aggie, was renowned for her skills, and the news of a fresh batch of ale brought customers from miles around. This particular fine, moonlit evening, a bush of green willow leaves had been hung on the pole thrusting out from her eaves, informing her clients that there was another brew of ale to be consumed, the sooner the better to preserve its quality.

In consequence of this, and the fact that folk wanted to gossip about the presence of soldiers in the village, there was a sizeable crowd gathered at Dame Aggie's when Monday staggered into their enclave, and stood panting and dripping in the middle of the alehouse floor. Her shift clung to her body, leaving very little to the imagination, her hair was loose to her hips and her eyes were wild.

Several of the more superstitious folk crossed themselves and muttered charms against spirits and fairy folk.

The priest, however, immediately disabused them of the notion. ''Tis the young woman who was with the soldiers,' he said, rising from his place near the fire, a thin line of foam gracing his upper lip. 'They said she was out of her wits. They'd taken her to Canterbury to the shrine o' St Thomas to pray for a cure.' He spoke in English, of which Monday understood very little.

She looked from one to the other of the gathered villagers. Their stares were frankly curious, but none would meet her eyes. 'You have to help me,' she implored the priest, knowing that he spoke French. 'I have been abducted against my will. Come with me, quickly, can't you hear the fighting?' She gestured towards the door, where the faint sounds of a brawl could indeed be heard now that the alehouse was silent.

The priest opened his mouth. 'Daughter . . .' he began, then fell silent, his eyes on the entrance.

Thomas of Stafford strode into the alehouse, a drawn sword in his hand. His face was a grim mask, the effort of control obvious in the bunched muscles of his jaw. 'Pay her no attention, priest,' he growled. 'She is wood-wild, as I told you.'

'But she says that . . .'

'I know what she says, but is there not a full moon outside? Look at her; would any sane person cast off their clothes and run amok in the night?'

Monday backed, until the heat of the central hearth scorched her spine. She sidestepped. 'Keep away from me,' she spat. 'It is you who is suffering from moon-madness. If there was a single sane bone in your body, you would ride away now, before it is too late.'

'Come here, girl.'

'I will not,' Monday hissed.

Stafford advanced. The look in his eyes was terrifying, but it had little effect on Monday. If Alexander was killed out there then she did not care to live either, and if he survived, she was determined to survive with him. Either way, she faced her grandfather with blazing eyes and a complete lack of fear.

The customers watched the entertainment in bemused astonishment. No one tried to intervene, not even the priest, for it was beyond them.

Stafford loomed. He was close now, almost close enough to strike with his sword if he chose. Monday had a premonition that he would do so, out of sheer vindictiveness. Her eyes flickered, seeking a way out.

Then, beyond him, in the doorway, she saw Alexander. There were splashes of blood on his surcoat, and a swipe of it on his cheek. His shoulders were rising and falling rapidly with exertion. He began to raise his sword, and she saw the effort involved.

Stafford took another step.

Monday darted to one side, seized someone's precious mug of ale and flung it at her grandfather. He recoiled, spluttering, and she ducked under his sword arm, giving him a hefty push as she did so. He tottered on one heel, overbalanced, and sat down heavily on the fire, the sword flying out of his hand. Smoke gushed and sparks flew. The stink of burning wool filled the air. Coughing and choking, two of the customers intervened to pull

Stafford off the fire before he asphyxiated everyone.

When the smoke cleared, the strange girl, the soldier in the doorway, and Stafford's sword were gone.

When Stafford limped outside, it was to utter silence. Not a single one of his men remained, except as corpses. All the horses had gone, including the packhorse bearing le Boucher's silver. One by one the alehouse customers trooped out after him, their cups in their hands.

High above their heads, a bright silver moon cast its magical light over a tranquil, silent land.

Once again, Monday rode pillion on a horse, but this time, her arms encircled the rider's waist, and her cheek was laid against the softness of his cloak. A blanket covered her chemise, and another soldier had lent her his hood and shoulder cape, so she was reasonably warm, if somewhat outlandishly dressed. But nothing mattered a whit except that she and Alexander were safe and together. Under the April moon, the road to Canterbury shone like a fairing ribbon.

'I am glad you did not fight him,' she said.

'So am I,' he said wearily. 'I might not have carried the victory.' She felt him draw a deep breath. 'I have what I want, and I suspect that in itself will break him.'

'But he must have thought he could succeed.' Monday shivered. 'And to do that, he must have known that . . . that John would turn a blind eye.'

Alexander said nothing.

'Mustn't he?' she persisted.

'People, lands are bought and sold every day.' He twisted in the saddle to look at her, and she sat up. 'Yes, John probably did know, and while the expense and the risk were not his, was prepared to gaze in the opposite direction.' He sighed. 'I think that the King and your grandfather have certain similar traits – an unwillingness to share being the major one. And both of them bear me a grudge for taking you.'

Monday shivered. 'Then what are we going to do?'

'Nothing. Go and take up residence in Abermon. It's far enough removed from John's politics, and nowhere near Stafford.

And if I receive promotion, it will like as not be across the Irish sea. After this episode, no one will dare lay a finger on us for fear of the cry of treachery.'

'Yes, I suppose so.' Suddenly she felt very tired.

'I know so. Here.' Reaching round, he pressed the Byzantine cross into her hand. 'I lost it the day I lost you at Vaudreüil,' he said. 'Now, tonight, I have it back. That surely is proof of our future. Hold it for me.'

He turned to the front again, intent on guiding the horse. Monday rubbed her finger over the facets of the cross, and feeling comforted, closed her eyes and leaned against his cloak once more.

CHAPTER 39

A stiff March wind whipped white clouds across the sky and ruffled the heads of the first flowers carpeting the woods. In the solar at Abermon, young Clemence de Montroi drowsed replete in her cradle, her blue eyes closed and a fluff of blonde hair peeking from beneath her bonnet.

'She looks like you,' Alexander remarked to the monk who was stooping over the foot of the cradle, a wondering look in his eyes. 'And certainly she has your appetite and your bellow.'

'You begot her,' Hervi retorted with a smile.

'What does that mean?' Florian piped up.

'It means that I'm her father,' Alexander said with a look at his brother.

'You couldn't have arrived at a better time.' Monday linked her arm through Hervi's and kissed his cheek. 'It's my churching ceremony on the morrow, and there'll be a feast and celebration.'

'Excellent timing then,' said Hervi, and placed his finger against the baby's hand. She yawned, and without opening her eyes, clutched him fiercely with her tiny fingers. 'The first girl in how many generations of Montrois?'

'At least five,' Alexander said smugly.

'Aye, well, you've broken the mould in more ways than one.'

'So have you.'

Hervi made a sound in his throat and gently removed his finger from the baby's grasp. 'I suppose that's true enough,' he said, 'but it was your doing in the first place . . . and before you protest or get that guilty look on your face, I'm not apportioning blame. Far from it. I have a far greater contentment now than I ever did on the tourney field.' Taking his stick, he limped over to the bench against the wall, where Monday had just finished plumping some embroidered cushions. She went to bring wine. Florian wriggled on to the seat beside his uncle, changed his mind, and ran off to fetch his pouch of marbles.

'Quicksilver, just like you,' Hervi said with a smile. 'Are you content at Abermon?'

'If you mean do I miss the hurly-burly of life at court and on the tourney field, then no to the first, and only a little to the second. There is enough to do here, keeping peace with the Welsh and skirmishing them to treaty point when all else fails. After last year, I'm glad to be no more than a common border knight for nine-twelfths of the year. And for the other three, I see enough variety in the lord Marshal's service to stop me from yearning. Besides,' he glanced at his wife as she returned with two cups of sweetened mulberry wine, the kind that was Hervi's favourite, 'why should I yearn when I have all I want here?'

'No reason.' Hervi shrugged, took a generous mouthful from his cup, and gave a small shudder of pleasure.

Monday narrowed her eyes at her brother-in-law. 'No reason?' she repeated suspiciously. 'What have you heard?'

'Oh, nothing, just a rumour on my travels.' He took another drink of the wine, and then sighed. 'Well, actually, it's more than a rumour. I heard for a fact three days ago from the Bishop of Stafford that your grandfather has died, and that his estates have several claimants. Aside from my desire to see you, it is one of the reasons I'm here. I wondered if . . .'

'No!' Alexander snarled.

Hervi's gaze widened.

Monday caught her husband's eye, and made a calming motion with the flat of her hand. Hervi had no inkling of what had happened last year; very few people had beyond those directly involved, and any rumours of scandal and foul play had been firmly smothered. 'No,' she repeated calmly. 'I have no desire to wrangle with lawyers over my inheritance. I would have to prove my blood line, I would have to face down men far greater than myself, and for something that I do not even want.'

Hervi drew breath.

'I have not told you this, but my grandfather offered his estates to me once, with certain conditions. I refused then, and I refuse now. I cannot mourn his passing; in a way I am pleased, because perhaps now he will find peace. He knew only bitterness and anger in this world.' She crossed herself. 'I will say a prayer for his soul at mass.'

Hervi looked at Alexander and Monday, his brows raised in question. 'Is there more I should know?'

Florian returned with his pouch of marbles and spilled them out on the floor at the adults' feet, brightly coloured beads of glass and wood. Blue and red and yellow.

Alexander shook his head. 'I don't think so,' he said quietly. 'Some matters are not for sharing.'

There was a peculiar silence. Hervi stared at Alexander, then gave a shrug. 'Perhaps you are right,' he said, and after another pause, added, 'Did you know that Cranwell Priory has been abandoned?'

'What?' Alexander lowered his cup.

'It is true. Last spring. Prior Alkmund went missing in the winter – never returned from one of his outings. Investigations revealed all that you told me and more. The remaining monks were transferred to Tutbury.' As Hervi spoke, his colour heightened, and by the time he had finished, the flesh across his cheekbones was a dusky red.

'Hervi . . . ?'

'Matters not for sharing,' he said gruffly, and stooped to admire his nephew's marbles.

'These have got holes in the middle,' Florian declared, showing Hervi a handful of the more luridly coloured wooden ones. 'I found them on a string in one of the coffers.'

Monday sat cross-legged on the bed, patiently rethreading the twenty-eight wooden beads in their correct order as Alexander closed and barred their chamber door.

'Hervi's abed . . . at last,' he said, and made a pretence of wiping his brow. 'Jesu, I thought Osgar and I were never going to get him there. He seemed to have six legs, not one. Still, he's snoring like a bear now.'

She raised her head from her task and smiled at him. In the

privacy of their chamber, her hair was bound in a loose bronze-brown plait, her wimple discarded on the coffer. This morning's churching ceremony, forty days after Clemence's birth, had given them sanction to lie together again as man and wife. With a feast to oversee, guests both English and Welsh to entertain, and finally her drunk one-legged brother-in-law to escort to his small wall chamber, such an opportunity had only just arisen.

Alexander sat down beside her on the bed, almost but not quite touching. Monday slanted him a glance through her lashes, and resumed her threading. She intended taking no chances. After their narrow and traumatic escape of last spring, the first bed they had come to had seen a vigorous confirmation of the life in each other, and Clemence had been the result. Loved though their daughter was, Monday had no intention of producing another infant nine months from this night.

'Do you remember when you wanted to be a great lady with a silk train a mile long?' he asked, watching her string the beads.

'Silk trains become mired in the dirt,' she said softly. 'Silk trains trip you up and make you walk slowly through life, when you could be running barefoot through the fields. Besides, that was the dream of someone else. I knew her once, and even travelled for a time with her, but we parted company in Rouen when I met the someone else that you had become.' She tilted her head to one side and regarded him with a half-smile. 'What about your own dreams of glory?'

'Like strong wine.' Lying back, he pillowed his head on his arms. 'Heady at the time, but vile the next day. I started my life as a younger son with nothing. A single castle will content me well enough.' He reached one hand to tug at her plait. 'Do you want to know what my dreams are at the moment?'

She turned round, the completed string of beads dangling from her fingertips, her gaze provocative. 'I think I can guess,' she murmured, and went into his arms.

AUTHOR'S NOTE

Many strands of research go to make up the writing of a historical novel, and are woven into a whole so that (hopefully) no loose threads show. But sometimes I cannot resist explaining how a particular thread came to be woven, and the author's note is my opportunity to do so!

Medieval contraception was a haphazard affair. Frowned on by the Church, it was nevertheless practised with varying degrees of success. The most widely used form was *coitus interruptus*. To a certain extent also, a breast-feeding woman was protected from conceiving. Wealthy women who hired wet nurses were therefore more at risk of becoming pregnant than their less well-off sisters. The safeguards mentioned in *The Champion* were also known to a small section of society. To those in the know, contraceptive lore was available in Greek and Arabic texts, and although not foolproof, tampons of sheep's wool and douches of vinegar lessened the likelihood of pregnancy. I admit to a touch of author's licence with the wooden beads, but it could have happened. The second-century Greek gynaecologist Soranus recommended that a woman should avoid intercourse during fertile times of the month, and a system of counting the days would have been essential.

Although many of the personalities in *The Champion* are people who actually lived, Monday, Alexander, their families and acquaintances are imaginary. I have, however, striven to take their characters and circumstances from twelfth- and thirteenth-century life. Couples did flout the rules if they had sufficient courage. In the *Histoire de Guillaume le Mareschal*, there is an incident where William Marshal comes across a run-away monk and a noblewoman eloping together. To many knights and soldiers, the tourney circuit was a way of life. It was a training ground and employment market, a place where fortunes and reputations were made and broken. Despite the Church's condemnation of tourneying, it continued to flourish, and developed through the following two centuries into a vastly popular spectator sport with ever more elaborate rules and equipment. William Marshal rose from the ranks of the common tourney knights to become, on John's death, the regent of England.

King John is known to have had at least five mistresses, and probably more. History has left us the traces of Susannah and Clemence, and probably Alina, but the others are unnamed. In the circumstances, I felt justified in making Monday one of them.

THE CONQUEST

Elizabeth Chadwick

A tale of love, betrayal, conflict and loss across two generations, set during the Norman Conquest.

When a comet appears in the sky over England in 1066, Ailith, a young Saxon wife, feels sure that it can only bode well, in spite of her husband's fears. With a child on its way, the couple are prosperous and content. Yet, within a year, Ailith's joy turns to heartache as her husband and her child are taken from her and the conquering Normans advance.

Ailith's grief turns to love for a brief period with Rolf de Brize, a handsome and womanising Norman invader. She bears him one daughter, but in the aftermath of the Battle of Hastings she discovers a betrayal she cannot forgive . . .

Years later, the spirited and strong-willed Julitta is determined to find happiness, and yet her life has been filled with pain: from surviving life in a brothel in Southwark to suffering the pain of a forbidden love and a bitter, loveless marriage. Her quest takes her on a Pilgrimage to Compostella to a colourful horse fair in Bordeaux, to the terrors of piracy on the open sea.

'The best writer of mediaeval fiction currently around'
Historical Novel Review

THE LOVE KNOT

Elizabeth Chadwick

In the summer of 1140, Oliver Pascal returns home from a long
pilgrimage to discover England ravaged by civil war. Among the
survivors he finds is Richard, an illegitimate royal son, and the
boy's young nurse, Catrin. Widowed, stubborn and proud, she has
much in common with Oliver, a man still grieving for a wife lost in
childbirth, but the endurance of the love that grows between them
is threatened by the deepening seriousness of the conflict. When
Oliver is taken prisoner, Catrin returns to the husband she
mistakenly thought had died in battle.

But when Oliver is seriously wounded in his efforts to regain his
lands, Catrin hastens to his side, her marriage a disaster. Beyond
the perils of injury in battle lies the danger of childbirth, the
upheaval of continuing war and the risk of loving in exchange for
nothing but heartbreak. Then Catrin's husband makes his final
demand on her loyalty . . .

'One of Elizabeth Chadwick's strengths is her stunning grasp of
historical detail . . . her characters are beguiling, and the story
intriguing and very enjoyable'
Barbara Erskine

THE MARSH KING'S DAUGHTER

Elizabeth Chadwick

England 1216: dissatisfaction with King John has bred a civil war that threatens the social order.

Unwanted and unloved, rebellious Miriel Weaver is forced to a convent by her violent stepfather. Her plan to escape from the harsh life of a novice nun crystallises with the arrival of a recuperating soldier of fortune Nicholas de Caen. Miriel sees in his pride and self-sufficiency a kindred spirit and, once he is well enough to leave, a way out.

The two part on bad terms that are to ultimately blight both their lives. When they meet again by chance, they agree to call a truce – but the truce becomes friendship, the friendship a dangerous passion . . .

'Elizabeth Chadwick knows exactly how to write convincing and compelling historical fiction'
Marina Oliver